THE EYE OF
THE TIGER

&

GOLDEN FOX

Also by Wilbur Smith

THE COURTNEYS

Birds of Prey
When the Lion Feeds
The Sound of Thunder
A Sparrow Falls
Monsoon

THE COURTNEYS OF AFRICA

The Burning Shore
Power of the Sword
Rage
A Time to Die

THE BALLANTYNE NOVELS

A Falcon Flies
Men of Men
The Angles Weep
The Leopard Hunts in Darkness

also

The Dark of the Sun
Shout at the Devil
Gold Mine
The Diamond Hunters
The Sunbird
Eagle in the Sky
Cry Wolf
Hungry as the Sea
Wild Justice
Elephant Song
River God
The Seventh Scroll
Warlock

Wilbur Smith was born in Central Africa in 1933. He was educated at Michaelhouse and Rhodes University.

He became a full-time writer in 1964 after the successful publication of *When the Lion Feeds*, and has since written twenty-eight novels, all meticulously researched on his numerous expeditions worldwide. His books are now translated into twenty-six languages.

He owns a farm and game reserve and has an abiding concern for the peoples and wildlife of his native continent, an interest strongly reflected in his novels.

WILBUR SMITH

THE EYE OF
THE TIGER

&

GOLDEN FOX

PAN BOOKS

WILBUR SMITH

THE EYE OF THE TIGER

&

GOLDEN FOX

PAN BOOKS

The Eye of the Tiger first published 1975 by William Heinemann Ltd.
First published by Pan Books 1998
Golden Fox first published 1990 by Macmillan.
First published by Pan Books 1990

This omnibus edition published 2004 by Pan Books
an imprint of Pan Macmillan Ltd
Pan Macmillan, 20 New Wharf Road, London N1 9RR
Basingstoke and Oxford
Associated companies throughout the world
www.panmacmillan.com

ISBN 0 330 43921 9

Copyright © Wilbur Smith 1975, 1990

The right of Wilbur Smith to be identified as the
author of this work has been asserted by him in accordance
with the Copyright, Designs and Patents Act 1988.

1 3 5 7 9 8 6 4 2

A CIP catalogue record for this book is available from
the British Library.

Printed and bound in Great Britain by
Mackays of Chatham plc, Chatham, Kent

THE EYE OF THE TIGER

For my wife, Danielle,
with love

'TIGER! TIGER! burning bright
In the forests of the night . . .
In what distant deeps or skies
Burnt the fire of thine eyes?'

William Blake

I was once Harry Fletcher's name was, I worked mid-morning each day at the... during the tournament each day, running the outriggers around fathom deep. Just past high noon was November the 6th when one picked on the first of the fish as they drove down on the purple swell of the Mozambique current.

By this time I was desperate for a fish. My charter was a party of ocean adventure wheel from New York named Chuck McGeorge, one of thy regulars who made the annual six-thousand-mile pilgrimage to St Mary's Island at the big marlin. He was a short, wiry little man, bald as an ostrich egg and gnome at the temples, with a wizened brown monkey face but the good hard legs that are necessary to take on the big fish.

When at last we saw the fish, he was riding high in the water, showing the full length of his fin, longer than a man's arm and with the curious curve that denotes... it from shark or porpoise. ...as the instant that I felt, and he came out on the foredeck daft and yelled with excitement, his grey curls dancing on his dark cheeks and his teeth flashing in the brilliant tropical sunlight.

The fish tensed and wallowed, the water opening about him so that he looked like a toast log, black and heavy and massive, his tail fin echoing the graceful curve of the dorsal before he slid down into the next trough and the water closed over his broad glistening back.

I turned and glanced down into the cockpit. Chubby was already helping Chuck into the big fighting chair, clinching

I t was one of those seasons when the fish came late. I worked my boat and crew hard, running far northwards each day, coming back into Grand Harbour long after dark each night, but it was November the 6th when we picked up the first of the big ones riding down on the wine purple swells of the Mozambique current.

By this time I was desperate for a fish. My charter was a party of one, an advertising wheel from New York named Chuck McGeorge, one of my regulars who made the annual six-thousand-mile pilgrimage to St Mary's island for the big marlin. He was a short wiry little man, bald as an ostrich egg and grey at the temples, with a wizened brown monkey face but the good hard legs that are necessary to take on the big fish.

When at last we saw the fish, he was riding high in the water, showing the full length of his fin, longer than a man's arm and with the scimitar curve that distinguishes it from shark or porpoise. Angelo spotted him at the instant that I did, and he hung out on the foredeck stay and yelled with excitement, his gipsy curls dangling on his dark cheeks and his teeth flashing in the brilliant tropical sunlight.

The fish crested and wallowed, the water opening about him so that he looked like a forest log, black and heavy and massive, his tail fin echoing the graceful curve of the dorsal, before he slid down into the next trough and the water closed over his broad glistening back.

I turned and glared down into the cockpit. Chubby was already helping Chuck into the big fighting chair, clinching

1

the heavy harness and gloving him up, but he looked up and caught my eye.

Chubby scowled heavily and spat over the side, in complete contrast to the excitement that gripped the rest of us. Chubby is a huge man, as tall as I am but a lot heavier in the shoulder and gut. He is also one of the most staunch and consistent pessimists in the business.

'Shy fish!' grunted Chubby, and spat again. I grinned at him.

'Don't mind him, Chuck,' I called, 'old Harry is going to set you into that fish.'

'I've got a thousand bucks that says you don't,' Chuck shouted back, his face screwed up against the dazzle of the sun-flecked sea, but his eyes twinkling with excitement.

'You're on!' I accepted a bet I couldn't afford and turned my attention to the fish.

Chubby was right, of course. After me, he is the best billfish man in the entire world. The fish was big and shy and scary.

Five times I had the baits to him, working him with all the skill and cunning I could muster. Each time he turned away and sounded as I brought *Wave Dancer* in on a converging course to cross his beak.

'Chubby, there is a fresh dolphin bait in the ice box: haul in the teasers, and we'll run him with a single bait,' I shouted despairingly.

I put the dolphin to him. I had rigged the bait myself and it swam with a fine natural action in the water. I recognized the instant in which the marlin accepted the bait. He seemed to hunch his great shoulders and I caught the flash of his belly, like a mirror below the surface, as he turned.

'Follow!' screamed Angelo. 'He follows!'

I set Chuck into the fish at a little after ten o'clock in the morning, and I fought him close. Superfluous line in

2

the water would place additional strain on the man at the rod. My job required infinitely more skill than gritting the teeth and hanging on to the heavy fibreglass rod. I kept *Wave Dancer* running hard on the fish through the first frenzied charges and frantic flashing leaps until Chuck could settle down in the fighting chair and lean on the marlin, using those fine fighting legs of his.

A few minutes after noon, Chuck had the fish beaten. He was on the surface, in the first of the wide circles which Chuck would narrow with each turn until we had him at the gaff.

'Hey, Harry!' Angelo called suddenly, breaking my concentration. 'We got a visitor, man!'

'What is it, Angelo?'

'Big Johnny coming up current.' He pointed. 'Fish is bleeding, he's smelt it.'

I looked and saw the shark coming. The blunt fin moving up steadily, drawn by the struggle and smell of blood. He was a big hammerhead, and I called to Angelo.

'Bridge, Angelo,' and I gave him the wheel.

'Harry, you let that bastard chew my fish and you can kiss your thousand bucks goodbye,' Chuck grunted sweatily at me from the fighting chair, and I dived into the main cabin.

Dropping to my knees I knocked open the toggles that held down the engine hatch and I slid it open.

Lying on my belly, I reached up under the decking and grasped the stock of the FN carbine hanging in its special concealed slings of inner tubing.

As I came out on to the deck I checked the loading of the rifle, and pushed the selector on to automatic fire.

'Angelo, lay me alongside that old Johnny.'

Hanging over the rail in *Wave Dancer*'s bows, I looked down on to the shark as Angelo ran over him. He was a hammerhead all right, a big one, twelve feet from tip to tail, coppery bronze through the clear water.

3

I aimed carefully between the monstrous eyestalks which flattened and deformed the shark's head, and I fired a short burst.

The FN roared, the empty brass cases spewed from the weapon and the water erupted in quick stabbing splashes.

The shark shuddered convulsively as the bullets smashed into his head, shattering the gristly bone and bursting his tiny brain. He rolled over and began to sink.

'Thanks, Harry,' Chuck gasped, sweating and red-faced in the chair.

'All part of the service,' I grinned at him, and went to take the wheel from Angelo.

At ten minutes to one, Chuck brought the marlin up to the gaff, punishing him until the great fish came over on his side, the sickle tail beating feebly, and the long beak opening and shutting spasmodically. The glazed single eye was as big as a ripe apple, and the long body pulsed and shone with a thousand flowing shades of silver and gold and royal purple.

'Cleanly now, Chubby,' I shouted, as I got a gloved hand on the steel trace and drew the fish gently towards where Chubby waited with the stainless-steel hook at the gaff held ready.

Chubby withered me with a glance that told me clearly that he had been pulling the steel into billfish when I was still a gutter kid in a London slum.

'Wait for the roll,' I cautioned him again, just to plague him a little, and Chubby's lip curled at the unsolicited advice.

The swell rolled the fish up to us, opening the wide chest that glowed silver between the spread wings of the pectoral fins.

'Now!' I said, and Chubby sank the steel in deep. In a burst of bright crimson heart blood, the fish went into its death frenzy, beating the surface to flashing white and drenching us all under fifty gallons of thrown sea water.

I hung the fish on Admiralty Wharf from the derrick of the crane. Benjamin, the harbour-master, signed a certificate for a total weight of eight hundred and seventeen pounds. Although the vivid fluorescent colours had faded in death to flat sooty black, yet it was impressive for its sheer bulk – fourteen feet six inches from the point of its bill to the tip of its flaring swallow tail.

'Mister Harry done hung a Moses on Admiralty,' the word was carried through the streets by running bare-footed urchins, and the islanders joyously snatched at the excuse to cease work and crowd the wharf in fiesta array.

The word travelled as far as old Government House on the bluff, and the presidential Land-Rover came buzzing down the twisting road with the gay little flag fluttering on the bonnet. It butted its way through the crowd and deposited the great man on the wharf. Before independence, Godfrey Biddle had been St Mary's only solicitor, island-born and London-trained.

'Mister Harry, what a magnificent specimen,' he cried delightedly. A fish like this would give impetus to St Mary's budding tourist trade, and he came to clasp my hand. As State Presidents go in this part of the world, he was top of the class.

'Thank you, Mr President, sir.' Even with the black homburg on his head, he reached to my armpit. He was a symphony in black, black wool suit, and patent leather shoes, skin the colour of polished anthracite and only a fringe of startlingly white fluffy hair curling around his ears.

'You really are to be congratulated.' President Biddle was dancing with excitement, and I knew I'd be eating at Government House on guest nights again this season. It had taken a year or two – but the President had finally accepted me as though I was island-born. I was one of his children, with all the special privilege that this position carried with it.

Fred Coker arrived in his hearse, but armed with his photographic equipment, and while he set up his tripod and disappeared under the black cloth to focus the ancient camera, we posed for him beside the colossal carcass. Chuck in the middle holding the rod, with the rest of us grouped around him, arms folded like a football team. Angelo and I were grinning and Chubby was scowling horrifically into the lens. The picture would look good in my new advertising brochure – loyal crew and intrepid skipper, hair curling out from under his cap and from the vee of his shirt, all muscle and smiles – it would really pack them in next season.

I arranged for the fish to go into the cold room down at the pineapple export sheds. I would consign it out to Rowland Wards of London for mounting on the next refrigerated shipment. Then I left Angelo and Chubby to scrub down *Dancer*'s decks, refuel her across the harbour at the Shell basin and take her out to moorings.

As Chuck and I climbed into the cab of my battered old Ford pick-up, Chubby sidled across like a racecourse tipster, speaking out of the corner of his mouth.

'Harry, about my billfish bonus—' I knew exactly what he was going to ask, we went through this every time.

'Mrs Chubby doesn't have to know about it, right?' I finished for him.

'That's right,' he agreed lugubriously, and pushed his filthy deep-sea cap to the back of his head.

6

I put Chuck on the plane at nine the next morning and I sang the whole way down from the plateau, honking the horn of my battered old Ford pick-up at the island girls working in the pineapple fields. They straightened up with big flashing smiles under the brims of the wide straw hats and waved.

At Coker's Travel Agency I changed Chuck's American Express traveller's cheques, haggling the rate of exchange with Fred Coker. He was in full fig, tailcoat and black tie. He had a funeral at noon. The camera and tripod laid up for the present, photographer became undertaker.

Coker's Funeral Parlour was in the back of the Travel Agency opening into the alley, and Fred used the hearse to pick up tourists at the airport, first discreetly changing his advertising board on the vehicle and putting the seats in over the rail for the coffins.

I booked all my charters through him, and he clouted his ten per cent off my traveller's cheques. He had the insurance agency as well, and he deducted the annual premium for *Dancer* before carefully counting out the balance. I recounted just as carefully, for although Fred looks like a schoolmaster, tall and thin and prim, with just enough island blood to give him a healthy all-over tan, he knows every trick in the book and a few which have not been written down yet.

He waited patiently while I checked, taking no offence, and when I stuffed the roll into my back pocket, his gold pince-nez sparkled and he told me like a loving father, 'Don't forget you have a charter party coming in tomorrow, Mister Harry.'

'That's all right, Mr Coker – don't you worry, my crew will be just fine.'

'They are down at the Lord Nelson already,' he told me delicately. Fred keeps his finger firmly on the island's pulse.

'Mr Coker, I'm running a charter boat, not a temperance

7

society. Don't worry,' I repeated, and stood up. 'Nobody ever died of a hangover.'

I crossed Drake Street to Edward's Store and a hero's welcome. Ma Eddy herself came out from behind the counter and folded me into her warm pneumatic bosom.

'Mister Harry,' she cooed and fussed me, 'I went down to the wharf to see the fish you hung yesterday.' Then she turned still holding me and shouted at one of her counter girls, 'Shirley, you get Mister Harry a nice cold beer now, hear?'

I hauled out my roll. The pretty little island girls chittered like sparrows when they saw it, and Ma Eddy rolled her eyes and hugged me closer.

'What do I owe you, Missus Eddy?' From June to November is a long off-season, when the fish do not run, and Ma Eddy carries me through that lean time.

I propped myself against the counter with a can of beer in my hand, picking the goods I needed from the shelves and watching their legs as the girls in their mini-skirts clambered up the ladders to fetch them down – old Harry feeling pretty good and cocky with that hard lump of green stuff in his back pocket.

Then I went down to the Shell Company basin and the manager met me at the door of his office between the big silver fuel storage tanks.

'God, Harry, I've been waiting for you all morning. Head Office has been screaming at me about your bill.'

'Your waiting is over, brother,' I told him. But *Wave Dancer*, like most beautiful women, is an expensive mistress, and when I climbed back into the pick-up, the lump in my pocket was severely depleted.

They were waiting for me in the beer garden of the Lord Nelson. The island is very proud of its associations with the Royal Navy, despite the fact that it is no longer a British possession but revels in an independence of six years'

8

standing; yet for two hundred years previously it had been a station of the British fleet. Old prints by long-dead artists decorated the public bar, depicting the great ships beating up the channel or lying in grand harbour alongside Admiralty Wharf – men-of-war and merchantmen of John Company victualled and refitted here before the long run south to the Cape of Good Hope and the Atlantic.

St Mary's has never forgotten her place in history, nor the admirals and mighty ships that made their landfall here. The Lord Nelson is a parody of its former grandeur, but I enjoy its decayed and seedy elegance and its associations with the past more than the tower of glass and concrete that Hilton has erected on the headland above the harbour.

Chubby and his wife sat side by side on the bench against the far wall, both of them in their Sunday clothes. This was the easiest way to tell them apart, the fact that Chubby wore the three-piece suit which he had bought for his wedding – the buttons straining and gaping, and the deep-sea cap stained with salt crystals and fish blood on his head – while his wife wore a full-length black dress of heavy wool, faded greenish with age, and black button-up boots beneath. Otherwise their dark mahogany faces were almost identical, though Chubby was freshly shaven and she did have a light moustache.

'Hello, Missus Chubby, how are you?' I asked.

'Thank you, Mister Harry.'

'Will you take a little something, then?'

'Perhaps just a little orange gin, Mister Harry, with a small bitter to chase it down.'

While she sipped the sweet liquor, I counted Chubby's wages into her hand, and her lips moved as she counted silently in chorus. Chubby watched anxiously, and I wondered once again how he had managed all these years to fool her on the billfish bonus.

Missus Chubby drained the beer and the froth emphasized her moustache.

'I'll be off then, Mister Harry.' She rose majestically, and sailed from the courtyard. I waited until she turned into Frobisher Street before I slipped Chubby the little sheath of notes under the table and we went into the private bar together.

Angelo had a girl on each side of him and one on his lap. His black silk shirt was open to the belt buckle, exposing gleaming chest muscles. His denim pants fitted skin-tight, leaving no doubt as to his gender, and his boots were hand-tooled and polished westerns. He had greased his hair and sleeked it back in the style of the young Presley. He flashed his grin like a stage lamp across the room and when I paid him he tucked a banknote into the front of each girl's blouse.

'Hey, Eleanor, you go sit on Harry's lap, but careful now. Harry's a virgin – you treat him right, hear?' He roared with delighted laughter and turned to Chubby.

'Hey, Chubby, you quit giggling like that all the time, man! That's stupid – all that giggling and grinning.' Chubby's frown deepened, his whole face crumbling into folds and wrinkles like that of a bulldog. 'Hey, Mister barman, you give old Chubby a drink now. Perhaps that will stop him cutting up stupid, giggling like that.'

At four that afternoon Angelo had driven his girls off, and he sat with his glass on the table top before him. Beside it lay his bait knife honed to a razor edge and glinting evilly in the overhead lights. He muttered darkly to himself, deep in alcoholic melancholy. Every few minutes he would test the edge of the knife with his thumb and scowl around the room. Nobody took any notice of him.

Chubby sat on the other side of me, grinning like a great brown toad – exposing a set of huge startlingly white teeth with pink plastic gums.

'Harry,' he told me expansively, one thick muscled arm around my neck. 'You are a good boy, Harry. You know what, Harry, I'm going to tell you now what I never told you before.' He nodded wisely as he gathered himself for the declaration he made every pay day. 'Harry, I love you man. I love you better than my own brother.'

I lifted the stained cap and lightly caressed the bald brown dome of his head. 'And you are my favourite eggshell blond,' I told him.

He held me at arm's length for a moment, studying my face, then burst into a lion's roar of laughter. It was completely infectious and we were both still laughing when Fred Coker walked in and sat down at the table. He adjusted his pince-nez and said primly, 'Mister Harry, I have just received a special delivery from London. Your charter cancelled.' I stopped laughing.

'What the hell!' I said. Two weeks without a charter in the middle of high season and only a lousy two-hundred-dollar reservation fee.

'Mr Coker, you have got to get me a party.' I had three hundred dollars left in my pocket from Chuck's charter.

'You got to get me a party,' I repeated, and Angelo picked up his knife and with a crash drove the point deeply into the table top. Nobody took any notice of him, and he scowled angrily around the room.

'I'll try,' said Fred Coker, 'but it's a bit late now.'

'Cable the parties we had to turn down.'

'Who will pay for the cables?' Fred asked delicately.

'The hell with it, I'll pay.' And he nodded and went out. I heard the hearse start up outside.

'Don't worry, Harry,' said Chubby. 'I still love you, man.'

Suddenly beside me Angelo went to sleep. He fell forward and his forehead hit the table top with a resounding crack. I rolled his head so that he would not drown in the puddle of spilled liquor, returned the knife to its sheath, and took charge of his bank roll to protect him from the girls who were hovering close.

Chubby ordered another round and began to sing a rambling, mumbling shanty in island patois, while I sat and worried.

Once again I was stretched out neatly on the financial rack. God how I hate money – or rather the lack of it. Those two weeks would make all the difference as to whether or not *Dancer* and I could survive the off-season, and still keep our good resolutions. I knew we couldn't. I knew we would have to go on the night run again.

The hell with it, if we had to do it, we might as well do it now. I would pass the word that Harry was ready to do a deal. Having made the decision, I felt again that pleasurable tightening of the nerves, the gut thing that goes with danger. The two weeks of cancelled time might not be wasted after all.

I joined Chubby in song, not entirely certain that we were singing the same number, for I seemed to reach the end of each chorus a long time before Chubby.

It was probably this musical feast that called up the law. On St Mary's this takes the form of an Inspector and four troopers, which is more than adequate for the island. Apart from a great deal of 'carnal knowledge under the age of consent' and a little wife-beating, there is no crime worthy of the name.

Inspector Peter Daly was a young man with a blond moustache, a high English colour on smooth cheeks and pale blue eyes set close together like those of a sewer rat. He wore the uniform of the British colonial police, the cap with the silver badge and shiny patent leather peak, the khaki drill starched and ironed until it crackled softly as he walked, the polished leather belt and Sam Browne cross-straps. He carried a malacca cane swagger stick which was also covered with polished leather. Except for the green

12

and yellow St Mary's shoulder flashes, he looked like the Empire's pride, but like the Empire the men who wore the uniform had also crumbled.

'Mr Fletcher,' he said, standing over our table and slapping the swagger stick lightly against his palm. 'I hope we are not going to have any trouble tonight.'

'Sir,' I prompted him. Inspector Daly and I were never friends – I don't like bullies, or persons who in positions of trust supplement a perfectly adequate salary with bribes and kick-backs. He had taken a lot of my hard-won gold from me in the past, which was his most unforgivable sin.

His mouth hardened under the blond moustache and his colour came up quickly. 'Sir,' he repeated reluctantly.

Now it is true that once or twice in the remote past Chubby and I had given way to an excess of boyish high spirits when we had just hung a Moses fish – however, this did not give Inspector Daly any excuse for talking like that. He was after all a mere expatriate out on the island for a three-year contract – which I knew from the President himself would not be renewed.

'Inspector, am I correct in my belief that this is a public place – and that neither my friends nor I are committing a trespass?'

'That is so.'

'Am I also correct in thinking that singing of tuneful and decent songs in a public place does not constitute a criminal act?'

'Well, that is true, but—'

'Inspector, piss off,' I told him pleasantly. He hesitated, looking at Chubby and me. Between the two of us we make up a lot of muscle, and he could see the unholy battle gleam in our eyes. You could see he wished he had his troopers with him.

'I'll be keeping an eye on you,' he said and, clutching at his dignity like a beggar's rags, he left us.

'Chubby, you sing like an angel,' I said and he beamed at me.

'Harry, I'm going to buy you a drink.' And Fred Coker arrived in time to be included in the round. He drank lager and lime juice which turned my stomach a little, but his tidings were an effective antidote.

'Mister Harry, I got you a party.'

'Mister Coker, I love you.'

'I love you too,' said Chubby, but deep down I felt a twinge of disappointment. I had been looking forward to another night run.

'When are they arriving?' I asked.

'They are here already – they were waiting for me at my office when I got back.'

'No kidding.'

'They knew that your first party had cancelled, and they asked for you by name. They must have come in on the same plane as the special delivery.'

My thinking was a little muzzy right then or I might have pondered a moment how neatly one party had withdrawn and another had stepped in.

'They are staying up at the Hilton.'

'Do they want me to pick them up?'

'No, they'll meet you at Admiralty Wharf ten o'clock tomorrow morning.'

I was grateful that the party had asked for such a late starting time. That morning *Dancer* was crewed by zombies. Angelo groaned and turned a light chocolate colour every time he bent over to coil a rope or rig the rods and Chubby sweated neat alcohol and his expression was truly terrifying. He had not spoken a word all morning.

I wasn't feeling all that cheerful myself. *Dancer* was

snugged up alongside the wharf and I leaned on the rail of the flying bridge with my darkest pair of Polaroids over my eyes and although my scalp itched I was afraid to take off my cap in case the top of my skull came with it.

The island's single taxi, a '62 Citroën, came down Drake Street and stopped at the top end of the wharf to deposit my party. There were two of them, and I had expected three, Coker had definitely said a party of three.

They started down the long stone-paved wharf, walking side by side, and I straightened up slowly as I watched them. I felt my physical distress fade into the realms of the inconsequential, to be replaced by that gut thing again, the slow coiling and clenching within, and the little tickling feeling along the back of my arms and in the nape of the neck.

One was tall and walked with that loose easy gait of a professional athlete. He was bare-headed and his hair was pale gingery and combed carefully across a prematurely balding pate so the pink scalp showed through. However, he was lean around the belly and hips, and he was aware. It was the only word to describe the charged sense of readiness that emanated from him.

It takes one to recognize one. This was a man trained to live with and by violence. He was muscle, a *soldier*, in the jargon. It mattered not for which side of the law he exercised his skills – law enforcement or its frustration – he was very bad news. I had hoped never to see this kind of barracuda cruising St Mary's placid waters. It gave me a sick little slide in the guts to know that it had found me out again. Quickly I glanced at the other man, it wasn't so obvious in him, the edge was blunted a little, the outline blurred by time and flesh, but it was there also – more bad news.

'Nice going, Harry,' I told myself bitterly. 'All this, and a hangover thrown in.'

15

Clearly now I recognized that the older man was the leader. He walked half a pace ahead, the younger taller man paying him that respect. He was a few years my senior also, probably late thirties. There was the beginnings of a paunch over the crocodile skin belt, and pouches of flesh along the line of his jawbone, but his hair had been styled in Bond Street and he wore his Sulka silk shirt and Gucci loafers like badges of rank. As he came on down the wharf he dabbed at his chin and upper lip with a white handkerchief and I guessed the diamond on his little finger at two carats. It was set in a plain gold ring and the wrist watch was gold also, probably by Lanvin or Piaget.

'Fletcher?' he asked, stopping below me on the jetty. His eyes were black and beady, like those of a ferret. A predator's eyes, bright without warmth. I saw he was older than I had guessed, for his hair was certainly tinted to conceal the grey. The skin of his cheeks was unnaturally tight and I could see the scars of plastic surgery in the hair line. He'd had a facelift, a vain man then, and I stored the knowledge.

He was an old soldier, risen from the ranks to a position of command. He was the brain, and the man that followed him was the muscle. Somebody had sent out their first team and, with a clairvoyant flash, I realized why my original party had cancelled.

A phone call followed by a visit from this pair would put the average citizen off marlin-fishing for life. They had probably done themselves a serious injury in their rush to cancel.

'Mr Materson? Come aboard—' One thing was certain, they had not come for the fishing, and I decided on a low and humble profile until I had figured out the percentages, so I threw in a belated ' – sir.'

The muscle man jumped down to the deck, landing soft-

16

footed like a cat and I saw the way that the folded coat over his arm swung heavily, there was something weighty in the pocket. He confronted my crew, thrusting out his jaw and running his eyes over them swiftly.

Angelo flashed a watered-down version of the celebrated smile and touched the brim of his cap. 'Welcome, sir.' And Chubby's scowl lightened momentarily and he muttered something that sounded like a curse, but was probably a warm greeting. The man ignored them and turned to hand Materson down to the deck where he waited while his bodyguard checked out *Dancer*'s main saloon. Then he went in and I followed him.

Our accommodation is luxurious, at a hundred and twenty-five thousand nicker it should be. The air-conditioning had taken the bite out of the morning heat and Materson sighed with relief and dabbed again with his handkerchief as he sank into one of the padded seats.

'This is Mike Guthrie.' He indicated the muscle who was moving about the cabin checking at the ports, opening doors and generally over-playing his hand, coming on very tough and hard.

'My pleasure, Mr Guthrie.' I grinned with all my boyish charm, and he waved airily without glancing at me.

'A drink, gentlemen?' I asked, as I opened the liquor cabinet. They took a Coke each, but I needed something medicinal for the shock and the hangover. The first swallow of cold beer from the can revitalized me.

'Well, gentlemen, I think I shall be able to offer you some sport. Only yesterday I hung a very good fish, and all the signs are for a big run—'

Mike Guthrie stepped in front of me and stared into my face. His eyes were flecked with brown and pale green, like a hand-loomed tweed.

'Don't I know you?' he asked.

17

'I don't think I've ever had the pleasure.'

'You are a London boy, aren't you?' He had picked up the accent.

'I left Blighty a long time ago, mate,' I grinned, letting it come out broad. He did not smile, and dropped into the seat opposite me, placing his hands on the table top between us, spreading his fingers palm downwards. He continued to stare at me. A very tough baby, very hard.

'I'm afraid that it is too late for today,' I babbled on cheerfully. 'If we are going to fish the Mozambique, we have to clear harbour by six o'clock. However, we can make an early start tomorrow—'

Materson interrupted my chatter. 'Check that list out, Fletcher, and let us know what you are short.' He passed me a folded sheet of foolscap, and I glanced down the handwritten column. It was all scuba diving gear and salvage equipment.

'You gentlemen aren't interested in big game fishing then?' Old Harry showing surprise and amazement at such an unlikely eventuality.

'We have come out to do a little exploring – that's all.'

I shrugged. 'You're paying, we do what you want to do.'

'Have you got all that stuff?'

'Most of it.' In the off-season I run a cut-rate package deal for scuba buffs which helps pay expenses. I had a full range of diving sets and there was an air compressor built in to *Dancer*'s engine room for recharging. 'I don't have the air bags or all that rope—'

'Can you get them?'

'Sure.' Ma Eddy had a pretty good selection of ship's stores, and Angelo's old man was a sail-maker. He could run up the air bags in a couple of hours.

'Right then, get it.'

I nodded. 'When do you want to start?'

'Tomorrow morning. There will be one other person with us.'

'Did Mr Coker tell you it's five hundred dollars a day – and I'll have to charge you for this extra equipment?'

Materson inclined his head and made as if to rise.

'Would it be okay to see a little of that out front?' I asked softly, and they froze. I grinned ingratiatingly.

'It's been a long lean winter, Mr Materson, and I've got to buy this stuff and fill my fuel tanks.'

Materson took out his wallet and counted out three hundred pounds in fivers. As he was doing so he said in his soft purry voice, 'We won't need your crew, Fletcher. The three of us will help you handle the boat.'

I was taken aback. I had not expected that. 'They'll have to draw full wages, if you lay them off. I can't reduce my rate.'

Mike Guthrie was still sitting opposite me, and now he leaned forward. 'You heard the man, Fletcher, just get your niggers off the boat,' he said softly.

Carefully I folded the bundle of five-pound notes and buttoned them into my breast pocket, then I looked at him. He was very quick, I could see him tense up ready for me and for the first time he showed expression in those cold speckled eyes. It was anticipation. He knew he had reached me, and he thought I was going to try him. He wanted that, he wanted to take me apart. He left his hands on the table, palms downwards, fingers spread. I thought how I might take the little finger of each hand and snap them at the middle joint like a pair of cheese sticks. I knew I could do it before he had a chance to move, and the knowledge gave me a great deal of pleasure, for I was very angry. I haven't many friends, but I value the few I have.

'Did you hear me speak, boy?' Guthrie hissed at me, and I dredged up the boyish grin again and let it hang at a ridiculous angle on my face.

19

'Yes, sir, Mr Guthrie,' I said. 'You're paying the money, whatever you say.'

I nearly choked on the words. He leaned back in his seat, and I saw that he was disappointed. He was muscle, and he enjoyed his work. I think I knew then that I was going to kill him, and I took enough comfort from the thought to enable me to hold the grin.

Materson was watching us with those bright little eyes. His interest was detached and clinical, like a scientist studying a pair of laboratory specimens. He saw that the confrontation had been resolved for the present, and his voice was soft and purry again.

'Very well, Fletcher.' He moved towards the deck. 'Get that equipment together and be ready for us at eight tomorrow morning.'

I let them go, and I sat and finished the beer. It may have been just my hangover, but I was beginning to have a very ugly feeling about this whole charter and I realized that after all it might be best to leave Chubby and Angelo ashore. I went out to tell them.

'We've got a pair of freaks, I'm sorry but they have got some big secret and they are dealing you out.' I put the aqualung bottles on the compressor to top up, and we left *Dancer* at the wharf while I went up to Ma Eddy's and Angelo and Chubby took my drawing of the air bags across to his father's workshop.

The bags were ready by four o'clock and I picked them up in the Ford and stowed them in the sail locker under the cockpit seats. Then I spent an hour stripping and reassembling the demand valves of the scubas and checking out all the other diving equipment.

At sundown I ran *Dancer* out to her moorings on my own, and was about to leave her and row ashore in the dinghy when I had a good thought. I went back into the cabin and knocked back the toggles on the engine-room hatch.

I took the FN carbine from its hiding-place, pumped a cartridge into the breech, set her for automatic fire and clicked on the safety catch before hanging her in the slings again.

B efore it was dark, I took my old cast net and waded out across the lagoon towards the main reef. I saw the swirl and run beneath the surface of the water which the setting sun had burnished to the colour of copper and flame, and I sent the net spinning high with a swing of shoulders and arms. It ballooned like a parachute, and fell in a wide circle over the shoal of striped mullet. When I pulled the drag line and closed the net over them, there were five of the big silvery fish as long as my forearm kicking and thumping in the coarse wet folds.

I grilled two of them and ate them on the veranda of my shack. They tasted better than trout from a mountain stream, and afterwards I poured a second whisky and sat on into the dark.

Usually this is the time of day when the island enfolds me in a great sense of peace and I seem to understand what the whole business of living is all about. However, that night was not like that. I was angry that these people had come out to the island and brought with them their special brand of poison to contaminate us. Five years ago I had run from that, believing I had found a place that was safe. Yet beneath the anger, when I was honest with myself, I recognized also an excitement, a pleasurable excitement. That gut thing again, knowing that I was at risk once more. I was not sure yet what the stakes were, but I knew they were high and that I was sitting in the game with the big boys once again.

I was on the left-hand path again. The path I had chosen at seventeen, when I had deliberately decided against the university bursary which I had been awarded and instead I bunked from St Stephen's orphanage in north London and lied about my age to join a whaling factory ship bound for the Antarctic. Down there on the edge of the great ice I lost my last vestige of appetite for the academic life. When the money I had made in the south ran out I enlisted in a special service battalion where I learned how violence and sudden death could be practised as an art. I practised that art in Malaya and Vietnam, then later in the Congo and Biafra – until suddenly one day in a remote jungle village while the thatched huts burned sending columns of tarry black smoke into an empty brazen sky and the flies came to the dead in humming blue clouds, I was sickened to the depths of my soul. I wanted out.

In the South Atlantic I had come to love the sea, and now I wanted a place beside it, with a boat and peace in the long quiet evenings.

First I needed money to buy those things – a great deal of money – so much that the only way I could earn it was in the practice of my art.

One last time, I thought, and I planned it with utmost care. I needed an assistant and I chose a man I had known in the Congo. Between us we lifted the complete collection of gold coins from the British Museum of Numismatology in Belgrave Square. Three thousand rare gold coins that fitted easily into a medium-sized briefcase, coins of the Roman Caesars and the Emperors of Byzantium, coins of the early states of America and of the English Kings – florins and leopards of Edward III, nobles of the Henrys and angels of Edward IV, treble sovereigns and unites, crowns of the rose from the reign of Henry VIII and five-pound pieces of George III and Victoria – three thousand coins, worth, even on a forced sale, not less than two million dollars.

Then I made my first mistake as a professional criminal. I trusted another criminal. When I caught up with my assistant in an Arab hotel in Beirut I reasoned with him in fairly strong terms, and when finally I put the question to him of just what he had done with the briefcase of coins, he snatched a .38 Beretta from under his mattress. In the ensuing scuffle he had his neck broken. It had been a mistake. I didn't mean to kill the man – but even more I didn't mean him to kill me. I hung a 'DON'T DISTURB' sign on his door and I caught the next plane out. Ten days later the police found the briefcase with the coins in the left-luggage department at Paddington Station. It made the front page of all the national newspapers.

I tried again at an exhibition of cut diamonds in Amsterdam, but I had done faulty research on the electronic alarm system and I tripped a beam that I had overlooked.

The plain clothes security guards who had been hired by the organizers of the exhibition rushed headlong into the uniformed police coming in through the main entrance and a spectacular shoot-out ensued, while a completely unarmed Harry Fletcher slunk away into the night to the sound of loud cries and gunfire.

I was half-way to Schiphol airport by the time a ceasefire was called between the opposing forces of the law – but not before a sergeant of the Dutch police received a critical chest wound.

I sat anxiously chewing my nails and drinking innumerable beers in my room in the Holiday Inn near Zürich Airport, as I followed the gallant sergeant's fight for life on the TV set. I would have hated like all hell to have another fatality on my conscience, and I made a solemn vow that if

23

the policeman died I would forget for ever about my place in the sun.

However, the Dutch sergeant rallied strongly and I felt an immense proprietary pride in him when he was finally declared out of danger. And when he was promoted to assistant inspector and awarded a bonus of five thousand crowns I persuaded myself that I was his fairy godfather and that the man owed me eternal gratitude.

Still, I had been shaken by two failures and I took a job as an instructor at an Outward Bound School for six months while I considered my future. At the end of six months, I decided for one more try.

This time I laid the groundwork with meticulous care. I emigrated to South Africa, where I was able with my qualifications to obtain a post as an operator with the security firm responsible for bullion shipments from the South African Reserve Bank in Pretoria to overseas destinations. For a year I worked with the transportation of hundreds of millions of dollars' worth of gold bars, and I studied the system in every minute detail. The weak spot, when I found it, was at Rome – but again I needed help.

This time I went to the professionals, but I set my price at a level that made it easier for them to pay me out than put me down and I covered myself a hundred times against treachery.

It went as smoothly as I had planned it, and this time there were no victims. Nobody came out with a bullet or a cracked skull. We merely switched part of a cargo and substituted leaded cases. Then we moved two and a half tons of gold bars across the Swiss border in a furniture removals van.

In Basle, sitting in a banker's private rooms furnished with priceless antiques, above the wide swift waters of the Rhine on which the stately white swans rode in majesty, they paid me out. Manny Resnick signed the transfer into my numbered account of one hundred and fifty thousand pounds sterling and he laughed a fat hungry little laugh.

'You'll be back, Harry – you've tasted blood now and you'll be back. Have a nice holiday, then come to me again when you've thought up another deal like this one.'

He was wrong, I never went back. I rode up to Zürich in a hire car and flew to Paris Orly. In the men's room there, I shaved off the beard and picked up the briefcase from the pay locker that contained the passport in the name of Harold Delville Fletcher. Then I flew out PanAm for Sydney, Australia.

Wave Dancer cost me one hundred and twenty-five thousand pounds sterling and I took her under a deck load of fuel drums across to St Mary's, two thousand miles, a voyage on which we learned to love each other.

On St Mary's I purchased twenty-five acres of peace, and built the shack with my own hands – four rooms, a thatched roof and a wide veranda, set amongst the palms above the white beach. Except for the occasions when a night run had been forced upon me, I had walked the right-hand path since then.

It was late when I had done my reminiscences and the tide was pushing high up the beach in the moonlight before I went into the shack, but then I slept like an innocent.

They were on time the following morning. Charly Materson ran a tight outfit. The taxi deposited them at the head of the wharf while I had *Dancer* singled up at stem and stern and both engines burbling sweetly.

I watched them come, concentrating on the third member of the group. He was not what I had expected. He was tall and lean with a wide friendly face and dark soft

25

hair. Unlike the others, his face and arms were darkly suntanned, and his teeth were large and very white. He wore denim shorts and a white sweatshirt and he had a swimmer's wide rangy shoulders and powerful arms. I knew instantly who was to use the diving equipment.

He carried a big green canvas kitbag over one shoulder. He carried it easily, though I could see that it was weighty, and he chatted gaily with his two companions who answered him in monosyllables. They flanked him like a pair of guards.

He looked up at me as they came level and I saw that he was young and eager. There was an excitement, an anticipation, about him, that reminded me sharply of myself ten years previously.

'Hi,' he grinned at me, an easy friendly grin, and I realized that he was an extremely good-looking youngster.

'Greetings,' I replied, liking him from the first and intrigued as to how he had found a place with the wolf pack. Under my direction they took in the mooring lines and, from this brief exercise, I learned that the youngster was the only one of them familiar with small boats.

As we cleared the harbour, he and Materson came up on to the flying bridge. Materson had coloured slightly and his breathing was raggedy from the mild exertion. He introduced the newcomer.

'This is Jimmy,' he told me, when he had caught his breath. We shook hands and I put his age at not much over twenty. Close up I had no cause to revise my first impressions. He had a level and innocent gaze from sea-grey eyes, and his grip was firm and dry.

'She's a darling boat, skipper,' he told me, which was rather like telling a mother that her baby is beautiful.

'She's not a bad old girl.'

'What is she, forty-four, forty-five feet?'

'Forty-five,' I said, liking him a little more.

26

'Jimmy will give you your directions,' Materson told me. 'You will follow his orders.'

'Fine,' I said, and Jimmy coloured a little under his tan.

'Not orders, Mr Fletcher, I'll just tell you where we want to go.'

'Fine, Jim, I'll take you there.'

'Once we are clear of the island, will you turn due west.'

'Just how far in that direction do you intend going?' I asked.

'We want to cruise along the coast of the African mainland,' Materson cut in.

'Lovely,' I said, 'that's great. Did anybody tell you that they don't hang out the welcome mat for strangers there?'

'We will stay well offshore.'

I thought a moment, hesitating before turning back to Admiralty Wharf and packing the whole bunch ashore.

'Where do you want to go – north or south of the river-mouth?'

'North,' said Jimmy, and that altered the proposition for the good. South of the river they patrolled with helicopters and were very touchy about their territorial waters. I would not go in there during daylight.

In the north there was little coastal activity. There was a single crash boat at Zinballa, but when its engines were in running order, which was a few days a week, then its crew were mostly blown out of their minds with the virulent palm liquor brewed locally along the coast. When crew and engines were functioning simultaneously, they could raise fifteen knots, and *Dancer* could turn on twenty-two any time I asked her.

The final trick in my favour was that I could run *Dancer* through the maze of off-shore reefs and islands on a dark night in a roaring monsoon, while it was my experience that the crash boat commander avoided this sort of extravagance. Even on a bright sunny day and in a flat calm, he preferred the quiet and peace of Zinballa Bay. I had heard that he suffered acutely from sea sickness, and held his present appointment only because it was far away from the capital, where as a minister of the government the commander had been involved in a little unpleasantness regarding the disappearance of large amounts of foreign aid.

From my point of view he was the ideal man for the job.

'All right,' I agreed, turning to Materson. 'But I'm afraid what you're asking is going to cost you another two-fifty dollars a day – danger money.'

'I was afraid it might,' he said softly.

I brought the *Dancer* around, close to the light on Oyster Point.

It was a bright morning with a high clear sky into which the stationary clouds that marked the position of each group of islands towered in great soft columns of blinding white.

The solemn progress of the trade winds across the ocean was interrupted by the bulwark of the African continent on which they broke. We were getting the backlash here in the inshore channel, and random squalls and gusts of it spread darkly across the pale green waters and flecked the surface chop with white. *Dancer* loved it, it gave her an excuse to flounce and swish her bottom.

'You looking for anything special – or just looking?' I asked casually, and Jimmy turned to tell me all about it. He was itchy with excitement, and the grey eyes sparkled as he opened his mouth.

'Just looking,' Materson interrupted with a ring in his voice and a sharp warning in his expression, and Jimmy's mouth closed.

'I know these waters. I know every island, every reef. I might be able to save you a lot of time – and a bit of money.'

28

'That's very kind of you,' Materson thanked me with heavy irony. 'However, I believe we can manage.'

'You are paying,' I shrugged, and Materson glanced at Jimmy, inclined his head in a command to follow and led him down into the cockpit. They stood together beside the stern rail and Materson spoke to him quietly but earnestly for two minutes. I saw Jimmy flush darkly, his expression changing from dismay to boyish sulks and I guessed that he was having his ear chewed to ribbons on the subject of secrecy and security.

When he came back on to the flying bridge he was seething with anger, and for the first time I noticed the strong hard line of his jaw. He wasn't just a pretty boy, I decided.

Evidently on Materson's orders, Guthrie, the muscle, came out of the cabin and swung the big padded fighting chair to face the bridge. He lounged in it, even in his relaxation charged with the promise of violence like a resting leopard, and he watched us, one leg draped over the arm rest and the linen jacket with the heavy weight in its pocket folded in his lap.

A happy ship, I chuckled, and ran *Dancer* out through the islands, threading a fine course through the clear green waters where the reefs lurked darkly below the surface like malevolent monsters and the islands were fringed with coral sand as dazzling white as a snowdrift, and crowned with dark thick vegetation over which the palm stems curved gracefully, their tops shaking in the feeble remnants of the trade.

It was a long day as we cruised at random and I tried to get some hint of the object of the expedition. However, still smarting from Materson's reprimand, Jimmy was tight mouthed and grim. He asked for changes of course at intervals, after I had pointed out our position on the large-scale admiralty chart which he produced from his bag.

Although there were no extraneous markings on his chart, when I examined it surreptitiously I was able to figure that we were interested in an area fifteen to thirty miles north of the multiple mouths of the Rovuma River, and up to sixteen miles offshore. An area containing perhaps three hundred islands varying in size from a few acres to many square miles – a very big haystack in which to find his needle.

I was content enough to perch up on *Dancer*'s bridge and run quietly along the seaways, enjoying the feel of my darling under me and watching the activity of the sea animals, and birds.

In the fighting chair Mike Guthrie's scalp started to show through the thin cover of hair like strips of scarlet neon lighting.

'Cook, you bastard,' I thought happily, and neglected to warn him about the tropical sun until we were running home in the dusk. The next day he was in agony with white goo smeared over his bloated and incarnadined features and a wide cloth hat covering his head, but his face flashed like the port light of an ocean-goer.

By noon on the second day I was bored. Jimmy was poor company for although he had recovered a little of his good humour he was so conscious of security that he even thought for thirty seconds before accepting an offer of coffee.

It was more for something to do than because I wanted fish for my dinner that when I saw a squadron of small kingfish charging a big shoal of sardine ahead of us, I gave the wheel to Jimmy.

'Just keep her on that heading,' I told him and dropped down into the cockpit. Guthrie watched me warily from his swollen crimson face as I glanced into the cabin and saw that Materson had my bar open and was mixing himself a gin and tonic. At seven hundred and fifty a day I didn't grudge it to him. He hadn't emerged from the cabin in two days.

I went back to the small tackle locker and selected a pair of feather jigs and tossed them out. As we crossed the track of the shoal I hit a kingfish and brought him out kicking, flashing golden in the sun.

Then I recoiled the lines and stowed them, wiped the blade of my heavy bait-knife across the oil stone to brighten up the edge and split the kingfish's belly from anal vent to gills and pulled out a handful of bloody gut to throw it into the wake.

Immediately a pair of gulls that had been weaving and hovering over us screeched with greed and plunged for the scraps. Their excitement summoned others and within minutes there was a shrieking, flapping host of them astern of us.

Their din was not so loud that it covered the metallic snicker close behind me, the unmistakable sound of the slide on an automatic pistol being drawn back and released to load and cock. I moved entirely from instinct. Without thought, the big bait-knife spun in my right hand as I changed smoothly to a throwing grip and I turned and dropped to the deck in a single movement, breaking fall with heels and left arm as the knife went back over my right shoulder and I began the throw at the instant that I lined up the target.

Mike Guthrie had a big automatic in his right hand. An old-fashioned naval .45, a killer's weapon, one which would blow a hole in a man's chest through which you could drive a London cab.

Two things saved Guthrie from being pinned to the back of the fighting chair by the long heavy blade of the bait-knife. Firstly, the fact that the .45 was not pointed at me and, secondly, the expression of comical amazement on the man's scarlet face.

I prevented myself from throwing the knife, breaking the instinctive action by a major effort of will, and we stared at each other. He knew then how close he had come, and the grin he forced to his swollen sunburned lips was shaky and unconvincing. I stood up and pegged the knife into the bait chopping board.

'Do yourself a favour,' I told him quietly. 'Don't play with that thing behind my back.'

He laughed then, blustering and tough again. He swivelled the seat and aimed out over the stern. He fired twice, the shots crashing out loudly above the run of *Dancer's* engines and the brief smell of cordite was whipped away on the wind.

Two of the milling gulls exploded into grotesque bursts of blood and feathers blown to shreds by the heavy bullets, and the rest of the flock scattered with shrieks of panic. The manner in which the birds were torn up told me that Guthrie had loaded with explosive bullets, a more savage weapon than a sawn-off shotgun.

He swivelled the chair back to face me and blew into the muzzle of the pistol like John Wayne. It was fancy shooting with that heavy calibre weapon.

'Tough cooky,' I applauded him, and turned to the bridge ladder, but Materson was standing in the doorway of the cabin with the gin in his hand and as I stepped past him he spoke quietly.

'Now I know who you are,' he said, in that soft purry voice. 'It's been worrying us, we thought we knew you.'

I stared at him, and he called past me to Guthrie.

'You know who he is now, don't you?' and Guthrie shook his head. I don't think he could trust his voice. 'He had a beard then, think about it – a mug shot photograph.'

'Jesus,' said Guthrie. 'Harry Bruce!' I felt a little shock at hearing the name spoken out loud again after all these years. I had hoped it was forgotten for ever.

32

'Rome,' said Materson. 'The gold heist.'

'He set it up.' Guthrie snapped his fingers. 'I was sure I knew him. It was the beard that fooled me.'

'I think you gentlemen have the wrong address,' I said with a desperate attempt at a cool tone, but was thinking quickly, trying to weigh this fresh knowledge. They had seen a mugshot – where? When? Were they law men or from the other side of the fence? I needed time to think – and I clambered up to the bridge.

'Sorry,' muttered Jimmy, as I took the wheel from him. 'I should have told you he had a gun.'

'Yeah,' I said. 'It might have helped.' My mind was racing, and the first turning it took was along the left-hand path. They would have to go. They had blown my elaborate cover, they had sniffed me out and there was only one sure way. I looked back into the cockpit but both Materson and Guthrie had gone below.

An accident, take them both out at one stroke, aboard a small boat there were plenty of ways a greenhorn could get hurt in the worst possible way. They had to go.

Then I looked at Jimmy, and he grinned at me.

'You move fast,' he said. 'Mike nearly wet himself, he thought he was going to get that knife through his gizzard.'

The kid also? I asked myself – if I took out the other two, he would have to go as well. Then suddenly I felt the same physical nausea that I had first known long ago in the Biafran village.

'You okay, skipper?' Jimmy asked quickly, it had shown on my face.

'I'm okay, Jim,' I said. 'Why don't you go fetch us a can of beer.'

While he was below I reached my decision. I would do a deal. I was certain that they didn't want their business shouted in the streets. I'd trade secrecy for secrecy. Probably they were coming to the same conclusion in the cabin below.

I locked the wheel and crossed quietly to the corner of the bridge, making sure my footsteps were not picked up in the cabin below.

The ventilator there funnels fresh air into the inlet above the saloon table. I had found that the ventilator made a reasonably effective voice tube, that sound was carried through it to the bridge.

However, the effectiveness of this listening device depends on a number of factors, chief of these being the direction and strength of the wind and the precise position of the speaker in the cabin below.

The wind was on our beam, gusting into the opening of the ventilator and blotting out patches of the conversation in the cabin. However, Jimmy must have been standing directly below the vent for his voice came through strongly when the wind roar did not smother it.

'Why don't you ask him now?' and the reply was confused, then the wind gusted and when it cleared, Jimmy was speaking again.

'If you do it tonight, where will you—' and the wind roared, ' – to get the dawn light then we will have to—' Then entire discussion seemed to be on times and places, and as I wondered briefly what they hoped to gain by leaving harbour at dawn, he said it again. 'If the dawn light is where—' I strained for the next words but the wind killed them for ten seconds, then ' – I don't see why we can't—' Jimmy was protesting and suddenly Mike Guthrie's voice came through sharp and hard. He must have gone to stand close beside Jimmy, probably in a threatening attitude.

'Listen, Jimmy boy, you let us handle that side of it. Your job is to find the bloody thing, and you aren't doing so good this far.'

They must have moved again for their voices became

34

indistinct and I heard the sliding door into the cockpit opening and I turned quickly to the wheel and freed the retaining handle just as Jimmy's head appeared over the edge of the deck as he came up the ladder.

He handed me the beer and he seemed to be more relaxed now. The reserve was gone from his manner. He smiled at me, friendly and trusting.

'Mr Materson says that's enough for today. We are to head for home.'

I swung *Dancer* across the current and we came in from the west, past the mouth of Turtle Bay and I could see my shack standing amongst the palms. I felt a sudden chilling premonition of loss. The fates had called for a new deck of cards, and the game was bigger, the stakes were too rich for my blood but there was no way I could pull out now.

However, I suppressed the chill of despair, and turned to Jimmy. I would take advantage of his new attitude of trust and try for what information I could glean.

We chatted lightly on the run down the channel into Grand Harbour. They had obviously told him that I was off the leper list. Strangely the fact that I had a criminal past made me more acceptable to the wolf pack. They could reckon the angles now. They had found a lever, so now they could handle me – though I was pretty sure they had not explained the whole proposition to young James.

It was obviously a relief for him to act naturally with me. He was a friendly and open person, completely lacking in guile. An example of this was the way that his surname had been guarded like a military secret from me, and yet around his neck he wore a silver chain and a Medic-alert tag that warned that J. A. NORTH, the wearer, was allergic to penicillin.

Now he forgot all his former reserve, and gently I drew small snippets of information from him that I might have use for in the future. In my experience it's what you don't know that can really hurt you.

I chose the subject that I guessed would open him up completely.

'See that reef across the channel, there where she's breaking now? That's Devil Fish Reef and there is twenty fathoms sheer under the sea side of her. It's a hangout of some real big old bull grouper. I shot one there last year that weighed in at over two hundred kilos.'

'Two hundred—' he exclaimed. 'My God, that's almost four hundred and fifty pounds.'

'Right, you could put your head and shoulders in his mouth.'

The last of his reserves disappeared. He had been reading history and philosophy at Cambridge but spent too much time in the sea, and had to drop out. Now he ran a small diving equipment supply company and underwater salvage outfit, that gave him a living and allowed him to dive most days of the week. He did private work and had contracted to the Government and the Navy on some jobs.

More than once he mentioned the name 'Sherry' and I probed carefully.

'Girl friend or wife?' and he grinned.

'Sister, big sister, but she's a doll – she does the books and minds the shop, all that stuff,' in a tone that left no doubt as to what James thought about book-keeping and counter-jumping. 'She's a red-hot conchologist and she makes two thousand a year out of her sea shells.' But he didn't explain how he had got into the dubious company he was now keeping, nor what he was doing halfway around the world from his sports shop. I left them on Admiralty Wharf, and took *Dancer* over to the Shell Basin for refuelling before dark.

That evening I grilled the kingfish over the coals, roasted a couple of big sweet yams in their jackets and was washing it down with a cold beer sitting on the veranda of the shack and listening to the surf when I saw the headlights coming down through the palm trees.

The taxi parked beside my pick-up, and the driver stayed at the wheel while his passengers came up the steps on to the stoep. They had left James at the Hilton, and there were just the two of them now – Materson and Guthrie.

'Drink?' I indicated the bottles and ice on the side table. Guthrie poured gin for both of them and Materson sat opposite me and watched me finish the last of the fish.

'I made a few phone calls,' he said when I pushed my plate away. 'And they tell me that Harry Bruce disappeared in June five years ago and hasn't been heard of since. I asked around and found out that Harry Fletcher sailed into Grand Harbour here three months later – inward bound from Sydney, Australia.'

'Is that the truth?' I picked a little fish bone out of my tooth, and lit a long black island cheroot.

'One other thing, someone who knew him well tells me Harry Bruce had a knife scar across his left arm,' he purred, and I involuntarily glanced at the thin line of scar tissue that laced the muscle of my forearm. It had shrunk and flattened with the years, but was still very white against the dark sun-browned skin.

'Now that's a hell of a coincidence,' I said, and drew on the cheroot. It was strong and aromatic, tasting of sea and sun and spices. I wasn't worried now – they were going to make a deal.

'Yeah, isn't it,' Materson agreed, and he looked around him elaborately. 'You got a nice set-up here, Fletcher. Cosy, isn't it, really nice and cosy.'

'It beats hell out of working for a living,' I admitted.

' – Or out of breaking rocks, or sewing mail bags.'

'I should imagine it does.'

'The kid is going to ask you some questions tomorrow. Be nice to him, Fletcher. When we go you can forget you ever saw us, and we'll forget to tell anybody about that funny coincidence.'

'Mr Materson, sir, I've got a terrible memory,' I assured him.

After the conversation I had overhead in *Dancer*'s cabin, I expected them to ask for an early start time the following morning, for the dawn light seemed important to their plans. However, neither of them mentioned it, and when they had gone I knew I wouldn't sleep so I walked out along the sand around the curve of the bay to Mutton Point to watch the moon come up through the palm trees. I sat there until after midnight.

The dinghy was gone from the jetty but Hambone, the ferry man, rowed me out to *Dancer*'s moorings before sun-up the following morning and as we came alongside I saw the familiar shape shambling around the cockpit, and the dinghy tied alongside.

'Hey, Chubby.' I jumped aboard. 'Your Missus kick you out of bed, then?'

Dancer's deck was gleaming white even in the bad light, and all the metal work was brightly burnished. He must have been at it for a couple of hours; Chubby loves *Dancer* almost as much as I do.

'She looked like a public shit-house, Harry,' he grumbled. 'That's a sloppy bunch you got aboard,' and he spat noisily over the side. 'No respect for a boat, that's what.'

He had coffee ready for me, as strong and as pungent as only he can make it, and we drank it sitting in the saloon.

Chubby frowned heavily into his mug and blew on the steaming black liquid. He wanted to tell me something.

'How's Angelo?'

'Pleasuring the Rawano widows,' he growled. The island does not provide sufficient employment for all its able-bodied young men – so most of them ship out on three-year labour contracts to the American satellite tracking station and airforce base on Rawano island. They leave their young wives behind, the Rawano widows, and the island girls are justly celebrated for the high temperature of their blood and their friendly dispositions.

'That Angelo's going to shag his brain loose, he's been at it night and day since Monday.'

I detected more than a trace of envy in his growl. Missus Chubby kept him on a pretty tight lead – he sipped noisily at the coffee.

'How's your party, Harry?'

'Their money is good.'

'You not fishing, Harry.' He looked at me. 'I watch you from Coolie Peak, man, you don't go near the channel – you are working inshore.'

'That's right, Chubby.' He returned his attention to his coffee.

'Hey, Harry. You watch them. You be good and careful, hear. They bad men, those two. I don't know the young one – but the others they are bad.'

'I'll be careful, Chubby.'

'You know the new girl at the hotel, Marion? The one over for the season?' I nodded, she was a pretty slim little wisp of a girl with lovely long legs, about nineteen with glossy black hair, freckled skin, bold eyes and an impish smile. 'Well, last night she went with the blond one, the one with the red face.' I knew that Marion sometimes combined business with pleasure and provided for selected

39

hotel guests services beyond the call of duty. On the island this sort of activity drew no social stigma.

'Yes,' I encouraged Chubby.

'He hurt her, Harry. Hurt her bad.' Chubby took another mouthful of coffee. 'Then he paid her so much money she couldn't go to the police.'

I liked Mike Guthrie a little less now. Only an animal would take advantage of a girl like Marion. I knew her well. She had an innocence, a child-like acceptance of life that made her promiscuity strangely appealing. I remembered how I had thought I might have to kill Guthrie one day – and tried not to let the thought perish.

'They are bad men, Harry. I thought it best you know that.'

'Thanks, Chubby.'

'And don't you let them dirty up *Dancer* like that,' he added accusingly. 'The saloon and deck – they were like a pigsty, man.'

He helped me run *Dancer* across to Admiralty Wharf and then he set off homewards, grumbling and muttering blackly. He passed Jimmy coming in the opposite direction and shot him a single malevolent glance that should have shrivelled him in his tracks.

Jimmy was on his own, fresh-faced and jaunty.

'Hi, skipper,' he called, as he jumped down on to *Dancer*'s deck, and I went into the saloon with him and poured coffee for us.

'Mr Materson says you have some questions for me, is that right?'

'Look, Mr Fletcher, I want you to know that I didn't mean offence by not talking to you before. It wasn't me – but the others.'

'Sure,' I said. 'That's fine, Jimmy.'

'It would have been the sensible thing to ask your help long ago, instead of blundering around the way we have

40

been. Anyway, now the others have suddenly decided it's okay.'

He had just told me much more than he imagined, and I adjusted my opinion of Master James. It was clear that he possessed information, and he had not shared it with the others. It was his insurance, and he had probably insisted on seeing me alone to keep his insurance policy intact.

'Skipper, we are looking for an island, a specific island. I can't tell you why, I'm sorry.'

'Forget it, Jimmy. That's all right.' What will there be for you, James North, I wondered suddenly. What will the wolf pack have for you once you have led them to this special island of yours? Will it be something a lot less pleasant than penicillin allergy?

I looked at that handsome young face, and felt an unaccustomed flood of affection for him – perhaps it was his youth and innocence, the sense of excitement with which he viewed this tired and wicked old world. I envied and liked him for that, and I did not relish seeing him pulled down and rolled in the dirt.

'Jim, how well do you know your friends?' I asked him quietly, and he was taken by surprise, then almost immediately he was wary.

'Well enough,' he replied carefully. 'Why?'

'You have known them less than a month,' I said as though I knew, and saw the confirmation in his expression. 'And I have known men like that all my life.'

'I don't see what this has to do with it, Mr Fletcher.' He was stiffening up now, I was treating him like a child and he didn't like that.

'Listen, Jim. Forget this business, whatever it is. Drop it, and go back to your shop and your salvage company.'

'That's crazy,' he said. 'You don't understand.'

'I understand, Jim. I really do. I travelled the same road, and I know it well.'

41

'I can look after myself. Don't worry about me.' He had flushed up under his tan, and the grey eyes snapped with defiance. We stared at each other for a few moments, and I knew I was wasting time and emotion. If anyone had spoken like this to me at the same age I would have thought him senile.

'All right, Jim,' I said. 'I'll drop it, but you know the score. Just play it cool and loose, that's all.'

'Okay, Mr Fletcher.' He relaxed slowly, and then grinned a charming and engaging grin. 'Thanks anyway.'

'Let's hear about this island,' I suggested and he glanced about the cabin.

'Let's go up on the bridge,' he suggested, and out in the open air he took a stub of pencil and a scrap pad from the map bin above the chart table.

'I reckon it lies off the African shore about six to ten miles, and ten to thirty miles north of the mouth of the Rovuma River—'

'That covers a hell of a lot of ground, Jim – as you may have noticed during the last few days. What else do you know about it?'

He hesitated a little longer, before grudgingly doling out a few more coins from his hoard. He took the pencil and drew a horizontal line across the pad.

'Sea level—' he said, and then above the line he raised an irregular profile that started low, and then climbed steeply into three distinct peaks before ending abruptly, ' – and that's the silhouette that it shows from the sea. The three hills are volcanic basalt, sheer rock with little vegetation.'

'The Old Men—' I recognized it immediately, '—but you are a long way out in your other calculations, it's more like twenty miles offshore—'

'But within sight of the mainland?' he asked quickly. 'It has to be within sight.'

'Sure, you could see a long way from the tops of the hills,' I pointed out as he tore the sheet from the pad and carefully ripped it to shreds, and dropped them into the harbour.

'How far north of the river?' He turned back to face me.

'Offhand I'd say sixty or seventy miles,' and he looked thoughtful.

'Yes, it could be that far north. It could fit, it depends on how long it would take—' He did not finish, he was taking my advice about playing it cool. 'Can you take us there, skip?'

I nodded. 'But it's a long run and best come prepared to sleep on the boat overnight.'

'I'll fetch the others,' he said, eager and excited once more. But on the wharf he looked back at the bridge.

'About the island, what it looks like and all that, don't discuss it with the others, okay?'

'Okay, Jim,' I smiled back at him. 'Off you go.' I went down to have a look at the admiralty chart. The Old Men were the highest point on a ridge of basalt, a long hard reef that ran parallel to the mainland for two hundred miles. It disappeared below the water, but reappeared at intervals, forming a regular feature amongst the haphazard sprinkling of coral and sand islands and shoals.

It was marked as uninhabited and waterless, and the soundings showed a number of deep channels through the reefs around it. Although it was far north of my regular grounds, yet I had visited the area the previous year as host to a marine biology expedition from UCLA who were studying the breeding habits of the green turtles that abounded there.

We had camped for three days on another island across the tide channel from the Old Men, where there was an all-weather anchorage in an enclosed lagoon, and brackish

43

but just drinkable water in a fisherman's well amongst the palms. Looking across from the anchorage, the Old Men showed exactly the outline that Jimmy had sketched for me, that was how I had recognized it so readily.

Half an hour later, the whole party arrived; strapped on the roof of the taxi was a bulky piece of equipment covered with a green canvas dust sheet. They hired a couple of lounging islanders to carry this, and the overnight bags they had with them, down the wharf to where I was waiting.

They stowed the canvas package on the foredeck without unwrapping it and I asked no questions. Guthrie's face was starting to fall off in layers of sun-scorched skin, leaving wet red flesh exposed. He had smeared white cream over it. I thought of him slapping little Marion around his suite at the Hilton, and I smiled at him.

'You look so good, have you ever thought of running for Miss Universe?' and he glowered at me from beneath the brim of his hat as he took his seat in the fighting chair. During the run northwards he drank beer straight from the can and used the empties as targets. Firing the big pistol at them as they tumbled and bobbed in *Dancer*'s wake.

A little before noon, I gave Jimmy the wheel and went down to use the heads below deck. I found that Materson had the bar open and the gin bottle out.

'How much longer?' he asked, sweaty and flushed despite the air-conditioning.

'Another hour or so,' I told him, and thought that Materson was going to find himself with a drinking problem the way he handled spirits at midday. However, the gin had mellowed him a little and – always the opportunist – I loosened another three hundred pounds from his wallet as an advance against my fees before going up to take *Dancer* in on the last leg through the northern tide channel that led to the Old Men.

The triple peaks came up through the heat haze, ghostly

44

grey and ominous, seeming to hang disembodied above the channel.

Jimmy was examining the peaks through his binoculars, and then he lowered them and turned delightedly to me.

'That looks like it, skipper,' and he clambered down into the cockpit. The three of them went up on to the foredeck, passed the canvas-wrapped deck cargo, and stood shoulder to shoulder at the rail staring through the sea fret at the island as I crept cautiously up the channel.

We had a rising tide pushing us up the channel, and I agreed to use it to approach the eastern tip of the Old Men, and make a landing on the beach below the nearest peak. This coast has a tidal fall of seventeen feet at full springs, and it is unwise to go into shallow water on the ebb. It is easy to find yourself stranded high and dry as the water falls away beneath your keel.

Jimmy borrowed my hand-bearing compass and packed it with his chart, a Thermos of iced water and a bottle of salt tablets from the medicine chest into his haversack. While I crept cautiously in towards the beach, Jimmy and Materson stripped off their footwear and trousers.

When *Dancer* bumped her keel softly on the hard white sand of the beach I shouted to them.

'Okay – over you go,' and with Jimmy leading, they went down the ladder I had rigged from *Dancer*'s side. The water came to their armpits, and James held the haversack above his head as they waded towards the beach.

'Two hours!' I called after them. 'If you're longer than that you can sleep ashore. I'm not coming in to pick you up on the ebb.'

Jimmy waved and grinned. I put *Dancer* into reverse and backed off cautiously, while the two of them reached the beach and hopped around awkwardly as they donned their trousers and shoes and then set off into the palm groves and disappeared from view.

After circling for ten minutes and peering down through the water that was clear as a trout stream, I picked up the dark shadow across the bottom that I was seeking and dropped a light head anchor.

While Guthrie watched with interest I put on a faceplate and gloves and went over the side with a small oyster net and a heavy tyre lever. There was forty feet of water under us, and I was pleased to find my wind was still sufficient to allow me to go down and prise loose a netful of the big double-shelled sun clams in one dive. I shucked them on the foredeck, and then, mindful of Chubby's admonitions, I threw the empty shells overboard and swabbed the deck carefully before taking a pailful of the sweet flesh down to the galley. They went into a casserole pot with wine and garlic, salt and ground pepper and just a bite of chilli. I set the gas-plate to simmer and put the lid on the pot.

When I went back on deck, Guthrie was still in the fighting chair.

'What's wrong, big shot, are you bored?' I asked solicitously. 'No little girls to kick around?' His eyes narrowed thoughtfully. I could see him checking out my source of information.

'You've got a big mouth, Bruce. Somebody is going to close it for you one day.' We exchanged a few more pleasantries, none of them much above this level, but it served to pass the time until the two distant figures appeared on the beach and waved and hallooed. I pulled up the hook, and went in to pick them up.

Immediately they were aboard, they called Guthrie to them and assembled on the foredeck for one of their group sessions. They were all excited, Jimmy the most so, and he gesticulated and pointed out into the channel, talking quietly but vehemently. For once they seemed all to be in agreement, but by the time they had finished talking there was an hour of sunlight left and I refused to agree to Materson's demands that I should continue our explorations that evening. I had no wish to creep around in the darkness on an ebb tide.

Firmly I took *Dancer* across to the safe anchorage in the lagoon across the channel, and by the time the sun went down below a blazing horizon I had *Dancer* riding peacefully on two heavy anchors, and I was sitting up on the bridge enjoying the last of the day and the first Scotch of the evening. In the saloon below me there was the interminable murmur of discussion and speculation. I ignored it, not even bothering to use the ventilator, until the first mosquitoes found their way across the lagoon and began whining around my ears. I went below and the conversation dried up at my entry.

I thickened the juice and served my clam casserole with baked yams and pineapple salad and they ate in dedicated silence.

'My God, that is even better than my sister's cooking,' Jimmy gasped finally. I grinned at him. I am rather vain about my culinary skills and young James was clearly a gourmet.

I woke after midnight and went up on deck to check *Dancer*'s moorings. She was all secure and I paused to enjoy the moonlight.

A great stillness lay upon the night, disturbed only by the soft chuckle of the tide against *Dancer*'s side – and far off the boom of the surf on the outer reef. It was coming in big and tall from the open ocean, and breaking in thunder and white upon the coral of Gunfire Reef. The name was well chosen, and the deep belly-shaking thump of it sounded exactly like the regular salute of a minute gun.

The moonlight washed the channel with shimmering silver and highlighted the bald domes of the peaks of the

Old Men so they shone like ivory. Below them the night mists rising from the lagoon writhed and twisted like tormented souls.

Suddenly I caught the whisper of movement behind me and I whirled to face it. Guthrie had followed me as silently as a hunting leopard. He wore only a pair of jockey shorts and his body was white and muscled and lean in the moonlight. He carried the big black .45, dangling at arm's length by his right thigh. We stared at each other for a moment before I relaxed.

'You know, luv, you've just got to give up now. You really aren't my type at all,' I told him, but there was adrenalin in my blood and my voice rasped.

'When the time comes to rim you, Fletcher, I'll be using this,' he said, and lifted the automatic, 'all the way up, boy,' and he grinned.

We ate breakfast before sun-up and I took my mug of coffee to the bridge to drink as we ran up the channel towards the open sea. Materson was below, and Guthrie lolled in the fighting chair. Jimmy stood beside me and explained his requirements for this day.

He was tense with excitement, seeming to quiver with it like a young gundog with the first scent of the bird in his nostrils.

'I want to get some shots off the peaks of the Old Men,' he explained. 'I want to use your hand-bearing compass, and I'll call you in.'

'Give me your bearings, Jim, and I'll plot it and put you on the spot,' I suggested.

'Let's do it my way, skipper,' he replied awkwardly, and I could not prevent a flare of irritation in my reply.

48

'All right, then, eagle scout.' He flushed and went to the port rail to sight the peaks through the lens of the compass. It was ten minutes or so before he spoke again.

'Can we turn about two points to port now, skipper?'

'Sure we can,' I grinned at him, 'but, of course, that would pile us on to the end of Gunfire Reef – and we'd tear her belly out.'

It took another two hours of groping about through the maze of reefs before I had worked *Dancer* out through the channel into the open sea and circled back to approach Gunfire Reef from the east.

It was like the child's game of hunt the thimble; Jimmy called 'hotter' and 'colder' without supplying me with the two references that would enable me to place *Dancer* on the precise spot he was seeking.

Out here the swells marched in majestic procession towards the land, growing taller and more powerful as they felt the shelving bottom. *Dancer* rolled and swung to them as we edged in towards the outer reef.

Where the swells met the barrier of coral their dignity turned to sudden fury, and they boiled up and burst in leviathan spouts of spray, pouring wildly over the coral with the explosive shock of impact. Then they sucked back, exposing the evil black fangs, white water cascading and creaming from the barrier, while the next swell moved up, humping its great slick back for the next assault.

Jimmy was directing me steadily southwards in a gradual converging course with the reef, and I could tell we were very close to his marks. Through the compass he squinted eagerly, first at one and then the other peak of the Old Men.

'Steady as you go, skipper,' he called. 'Just ease her down on that heading.'

I looked ahead, tearing my eyes away from the menacing coral for a few seconds, and I watched the next swell charge

49

in and break – except at a narrow point five hundred yards ahead. Here the swell kept its shape and ran on uninterrupted towards the land. On each side, the swell broke on coral, but just at that one point it was open.

Suddenly I remembered Chubby's boast.

'I was just nineteen when I pulled my first jewfish out of the hole at Gunfire Break. Weren't no other would fish with me – don't say as I blame them. Wouldn't go into the Break again – got a little more brains now.'

Gunfire Break, suddenly I knew that was where we were heading. I tried to remember exactly what Chubby had told me about it.

'If you come in from the sea about two hours before high water, steer for the centre of the gap until you come up level with a big old head of brain coral on your starboard side, you'll know it when you see it, pass it close as you can and then come round hard to starboard and you'll be sitting in a big hole tucked in neatly behind the main reef. Closer you are on the back of the reef the better, man—' I remembered it clearly then, Chubby in his talkative phase in the public bar of the Lord Nelson, boastful as one of the very few men who had been through the Gunfire Break. 'No anchor going to hold you there, you got to lean on the oars to hold station in the gap – the hole at Gunfire Break is deep, man, deep, but the jewfish in there are big, man, big. One day I took four fish, and the smallest was three hundred pounds. Could have took more – but time was up. You can't stay in Gunfire Break more than an hour after high water – she sucks out through the Break like they pulled the chain on the whole damned sea. You come out the same way you went in, only you pray just a little harder on the way out – 'cos you got a ton of fish on board, and ten feet less water under your keel. There is another way out through a channel in the back of the reef. But I don't even like to talk about that one. Only tried it once.'

Now we were bearing down directly on the Break, Jimmy was going to run us right into the eye of it.

'Okay, Jim,' I called. 'That's as far as we go.' I opened the throttle and sheered off, making a good offing before turning back to face Jimmy's wrath.

'We were almost there, damn you,' he blustered. 'We could have gone in a little closer.'

'You having trouble up there, boy?' Guthrie shouted up from the cockpit.

'No, it's all right,' Jimmy called back, and then turned furiously to me. 'You are under contract, Mr Fletcher—'

'I want to show you something, James—' and I took him to the chart table. The Break was marked on the admiralty chart by a single laconic sounding of thirty fathoms, there was no name or sailing instruction for it. Quickly I pencilled in the bearings of the two extreme peaks of the Old Men from the break, and then used the protractor to measure the angle they subtended.

'That right?' I asked him, and he stared at my figures.

'It's right, isn't it?' I insisted and then reluctantly he nodded.

'Yes, that's the spot,' he agreed, and I went on to tell him about Gunfire Break in every detail.

'But we have to get in there,' he said at the end of my speech, as though he had not heard a word of it.

'No way,' I told him. 'The only place I'm interested in now is Grand Harbour, St Mary's Island,' and I laid *Dancer* on that course. As far as I was concerned the charter was over.

Jimmy disappeared down the ladder, and returned within minutes with reinforcements – Materson and Guthrie, both of them looking angry and outraged.

'Say the word, and I'll tear the bastard's arm off and beat him to death with the wet end,' Mike Guthrie said with relish.

'The kid says you pulling out?' Materson wanted to know. 'Now that's not right – is it?'

I explained once more about the hazards of Gunfire Break and they sobered immediately.

'Take me close as you can – I'll swim in the rest of the way,' Jimmy asked me, but I replied directly to Materson.

'You'd lose him, for certain sure. Do you want to risk that?'

He didn't answer, but I could see that Jimmy was much too valuable for them to take the chance.

'Let me try,' Jimmy insisted, but Materson shook his head irritably.

'If we can't get into the Break, at least let me take a run along the reef with the sledge,' Jimmy went on, and I knew then what we were carrying under the canvas wrapping on the foredeck.

'Just a couple of passes along the front edge of the reef, past the entrance to the break.' He was pleading now, and Materson looked questioningly at me. You don't often have opportunities like this offered you on a silver tray. I knew I could run *Dancer* within spitting distance of the coral without risk, but I frowned worriedly.

'I'd be taking a hell of a chance – but if we could agree on a bit of old danger money—'

I had Materson over the arm of the chair and I caned him for an extra day's hire – five hundred dollars, payable in advance.

While we did the business, Guthrie helped Jimmy unwrap the sledge and carry it back to the cockpit.

I tucked the sheath of bank notes away and went back to rig the tow lines. The sledge was a beautifully constructed toboggan of stainless steel and plastic. In place of snow runners, it had stubby fin controls, rudder and hydrofoils, operated by a short joystick below the Perspex pilot's shield.

There was a ring bolt in the nose to take the tow line by

which I would drag the sledge in *Dancer's* wake. Jimmy would lie on his belly behind the transparent shield, breathing compressed air from the twin tanks that were built into the chassis of the sledge. On the dashboard were depth and pressure gauges, directional compass and time elapse clock. With the joystick Jimmy could control the depth of the sledge's dive, and yaw left or right across *Dancer's* stern.

'Lovely piece of work,' I remarked, and he flushed with pleasure.

'Thanks, skipper, built it myself.' He was pulling on the wet suit of thick black Neoprene rubber and while his head was in the clinging hood I stooped and examined the maker's plate that was riveted to the sledge's chassis, memorizing the legend.

Built by North's Underwater World.
5, Pavilion Arcade.
BRIGHTON. SUSSEX.

I straightened up as his face appeared in the opening of the hood.

'Five knots is a good tow speed, skipper. If you keep a hundred yards off the reef, I'll be able to deflect outwards and follow the contour of the coral.'

'Fine, Jim.'

'If I put up a yellow marker, ignore it, it's only a find, and we will go back to it later – but if I send up a red, it's trouble, try and get me off the reef and haul me in.'

I nodded. 'You have three hours,' I warned him. 'Then she will begin the ebb up through the break and we'll have to haul off.'

'That should be long enough,' he agreed.

Guthrie and I lifted the sledge over the side, and it wallowed low in the water. Jimmy clambered down to it and settled himself behind the screen, testing the controls, adjusting his face-plate and cramming the mouthpiece of the breathing device into his mouth. He breathed noisily and then gave me the thumbs up.

I climbed quickly to the bridge and opened the throttles. *Dancer* picked up speed and Guthrie paid out the thick nylon rope over the stern as the sledge fell away behind us. One hundred and fifty yards of rope went over, before the sledge jerked up and began to tow.

Jimmy waved, and I pushed *Dancer* up to a steady five knots. I circled wide, then edged in towards the reef, taking the big swells on *Dancer*'s beam so she rolled appallingly.

Again Jimmy waved, and I saw him push the control column of the sledge forwards. There was a turmoil of white water along her control fins and then suddenly she put her nose down and ducked below the surface. The angle of the nylon rope altered rapidly as the sledge went down, and then swung away towards the reef.

The strain on the rope made it quiver like an arrow as it strikes, and the water squirted from the fibres.

Slowly we ran parallel to the reef, closing the break. I watched the coral respectfully, taking no chances, and I imagined Jimmy far below the surface flying silently along the bottom, cutting in to skim the tall wall of underwater coral. It must have been an exhilarating sensation, and I envied him, deciding to hitch a ride on the sledge when I got the opportunity.

We came opposite the Break, passed it and just then I heard Guthrie shout. I glanced quickly over the stern and saw the big yellow balloon bobbing in our wake.

'He found something,' Guthrie shouted.

Jimmy had dropped a light leaded line, and a sparklet bulb had automatically inflated the yellow balloon with carbon dioxide gas to mark the spot.

I kept going steadily along the reef, and a quarter of a

mile farther the angle of the tow line flattened and the sledge popped to the surface in a welter of water.

I swung away from the reef to a safe distance, and then went down to help Guthrie recover the sledge.

Jimmy clambered into the cockpit, and when he pulled off his face-plate his lips were trembling and his grey eyes blazed. He took Materson's arm and dragged him into the cabin, splashing sea water all over Chubby's beloved deck.

Guthrie and I coiled the rope then lifted the sledge into the cockpit. I went back to the bridge, and took *Dancer* on a slow return to the entrance of Gunfire Break.

Materson and Jimmy came up on to the bridge before we reached it. Materson was affected by Jimmy's excitement.

'The kid wants to try for a pick up.' I knew better than to ask what it was.

'What size?' I asked instead, and glanced at my wrist-watch. We had an hour and a half before the rip tide began to run out through the break.

'Not very big—' Jimmy assured me. 'Fifty pounds maximum.'

'You sure, James? Not bigger?' I didn't trust his enthusiasm not to minimize the effort involved.

'I swear it.'

'You want to put an airbag on it?'

'Yes, I'll lift it with an airbag and then tow it away from the reef.'

I reversed *Dancer* in gingerly towards the yellow balloon that played lightly in the angry coral jaws of the Break.

'That's as close as I'll go,' I shouted down into the cockpit, and Jimmy acknowledged with a wave.

He waddled duck-footed to the stern and adjusted his equipment. He had taken two airbags as well as the canvas cover from the sledge, and was roped up to the coil of nylon rope.

I saw him take a bearing on the yellow marker with the

55

compass on his wrist, then once again he glanced up at me on the bridge before he flipped backwards over the stern and disappeared.

His regular breathing burst in a white rash below the stern, then began to move off towards the reef. Guthrie paid out the bodyline after him.

I kept *Dancer* on station by using bursts of forward and reverse, holding her a hundred yards from the southern tip of the Break.

Slowly Jimmy's bubbles approached the yellow marker, and then broke steadily beside it. He was working below it, and I imagined him fixing the empty airbags to the object with the nylon slings. It would be hard work with the suck and drag of the current worrying the bulky bags. Once he had fitted the slings he could begin to fill the bags with compressed air from his scuba bottles.

If Jimmy's estimate of size was correct it would need very little inflation to pull the mysterious object off the bottom, and once it dangled free we could tow it into a safer area before bringing it aboard.

For forty minutes I held *Dancer* steady, then quite suddenly two swollen green shiny mounds broke the surface astern. The airbags were up – Jimmy had lifted his prize.

Immediately his hooded head surfaced beside the filled bags, and he held his right arm straight up. The signal to begin the tow.

'Ready?' I shouted at Guthrie in the cockpit.

'Ready!' He had secured the line, and I crept away from the reef, slowly and carefully to avoid up-ending the bags and spilling out the air that gave them lift.

Five hundred yards off the reef, I kicked *Dancer* into neutral and went to help haul in the swimmer and his fat green airbags.

'Stay where you are,' Materson snarled at me as I

56

approached the ladder and I shrugged and went back to the wheel.

'The hell with them all,' I thought, and lit a cheroot – but I couldn't prevent the tickle of excitement as they worked the bags alongside, and then walked them forward to the bows.

They helped Jimmy aboard, and he shrugged off the heavy compressed air bottles, dropping them to the deck while he pushed his face-plate on to his forehead.

His voice, ragged and high-pitched, carried clearly to me as I leaned on the bridge rail.

'Jackpot!' he cried. 'It's the—'

'Watch it!' Materson cautioned him, and James cut himself off and they all looked at me, lifting their faces to the bridge.

'Don't mind me, boys,' I grinned and waved the cheroot cheerily. They turned away and huddled. Jimmy whispered, and Guthrie said, 'Jesus Christ!' loudly and slapped Materson's back, and then they were all exclaiming and laughing as they crowded to the rail and began to lift the airbags and their burden aboard. They were clumsy with it, *Dancer* was rolling heavily, and I leaned forward with curiosity eating a hole in my belly.

My disappointment and chagrin were intense when I realized that Jimmy had taken the precaution of wrapping his prize in the canvas sledge cover. It came aboard as a sodden, untidy bundle of canvas, swathed in coils of nylon rope.

It was heavy, I could see by the manner in which they handled it – but it was not bulky, the size of a small suitcase.

They laid it on the deck and stood around it happily. Materson smiled up at me.

'Okay, Fletcher. Come take a look.'

It was beautifully done, he played like a concert pianist

57

on my curiosity. Suddenly I wanted very badly to know what they had pulled from the sea. I clamped the cheroot in my teeth as I swarmed down the ladder, and hurried towards the group in the bows. I was halfway across the foredeck, right out in the open, and Materson was still smiling as he said softly. 'Now!'

Only then did I know it was a set-up, and my mind began to move so fast that it all seemed to go by in extreme slow motion.

I saw the evil black bulk of the .45 in Guthrie's fist, and it came up slowly to aim into my belly. Mike Guthrie was in the marksman's crouch, right arm fully extended, and he was grinning as he screwed up those speckled eyes and sighted along the thick-jacketed barrel.

I saw Jimmy North's handsome young face contort with horror, saw him reach out to grip the pistol arm but Materson, still grinning, shoved him roughly aside and he staggered away with *Dancer*'s next roll.

I was thinking quite clearly and rapidly, it was not a procession of thought but a set of simultaneous images. I thought how neatly they had dropped the boom on me, a really professional hit.

I thought how presumptuous I had been in trying to make a deal with the wolf pack. For them it was easier to hit than to negotiate.

I thought that they would take out Jimmy now that he had watched this. That must have been their intention from the start. I was sorry for that. I had come to like the kid.

I thought about the heavy soft explosive lead slug that the .45 threw, about how it would tear up the target, hitting with the shock of two thousand foot pounds.

Guthrie's forefinger curled on the trigger and I began to throw myself at the rail beside me with the cheroot still in my mouth, but I knew it was too late.

The pistol in Guthrie's hand kicked up head high, and I saw the muzzle flash palely in the sunlight. The cannon roar of the blast and the heavy lead bullet hit me together. The din deafened me and snapped my head back and the cheroot flipped up high in the air leaving a trail of sparks. Then the impact of the bullet doubled me over, driving the air from my lungs, and lifted me off my feet, hurling me backwards until the deck rail caught me in the small of the back.

There was no pain, just that huge numbing shock. It was in the chest, I was sure of that, and I knew that it must have blown me open. It was a mortal wound, I was sure of that also and I expected my mind to go now. I expected to fade, going out into blackness.

Instead the rail caught me in the back and I somer-saulted, going over the side head-first and the quick cold embrace of the sea covered me. It steadied me, and I opened my eyes to the silver clouds of bubbles and the soft green of sunlight through the surface.

My lungs were empty, the air driven out by the impact of the bullet, and my instinct told me to claw to the surface for air, but surprisingly my mind was still clear and I knew that Mike Guthrie would blow the top off my skull the moment I surfaced. I rolled and dived, kicking clumsily, and went down under *Dancer*'s hull.

On empty lungs it was a long journey, *Dancer*'s smooth white belly passed slowly above me, and I drove on desperately, amazed that there was strength in my legs still.

Suddenly darkness engulfed me, a soft dark red cloud, and I nearly panicked, thinking my vision had gone – until suddenly I realized it was my own blood. Huge billowing clouds of my own blood staining the water. Tiny zebra-striped fish darted wildly through the cloud, gulping greedily at it.

I struck out, but my left arm would not respond. It trailed limply at my side, and blood blew like smoke about me.

There was strength in my right arm and I forged on under *Dancer*, passed under her keel and rose thankfully towards her far waterline.

As I came up I saw the nylon tow rope trailing over her stern, a bight of it hanging down below the surface and I snatched at it thankfully.

I broke the surface under *Dancer*'s stern, and I sucked painfully for air, my lungs felt bruised and numb, the air tasted like old copper in my mouth but I gulped it down.

My mind was still clear. I was under the stern, the wolf pack was in the bows, the carbine was under the engine hatch in the main cabin.

I reached up as high as I could and took a twist of the nylon rope around my right wrist, lifted my knees and got my toes on to the rubbing strake along *Dancer*'s waterline.

I knew I had enough strength for one attempt, no more. It would have to be good. I heard their voices from up in the bows, raised angrily, shouting at each other, but I ignored them and gathered all my reserve.

I heaved upwards, with both legs and the one good arm. My vision starred with the effort, and my chest was a numbed mass, but I came clear of the water and fell half across the stern rail, hanging there like an empty sack on a barbed-wire fence.

For seconds I lay there, while my vision cleared and I felt the slick warm outpouring of blood along my flank and belly. The flow of blood galvanized me. I realized how little time I had before the loss of it sent me plunging into blackness. I kicked wildly and tumbled headlong on to the cockpit floor, striking my head on the edge of the fighting chair, and grunting with the new pain of it.

I lay on my side and glanced down at my body. What I

saw terrified me, I was streaming great gouts of thick blood, it was forming a puddle under me.

I clawed at the deck, dragging myself towards the cabin, and reached the combing beside the entrance. With another wild effort I pulled myself upright, hanging on one arm, supported by legs already weak and rubbery.

I glanced quickly around the angle of the cabin, down along the foredeck to where the three men were still grouped in the bows.

Jimmy North was struggling to strap his compressed air bottles on to his back again, his face was a mask of horror and outrage and his voice was strident as he screamed at Materson.

'You filthy bloody murderers. I'm going down to find him. I'm going to get his body – and, so help me Christ, I'll see you both hanged—'

Even in my own distress I felt a sudden flare of admiration for the kid's courage. I don't think it ever occurred to him that he was also on the list.

'It was murder, cold-blooded murder,' he shouted, and turned to the rail, settling the face-plate over his eyes and nose.

Materson looked across at Guthrie, the kid's back was turned to them, and Materson nodded.

I tried to shout a warning, but it croaked hollowly in my throat, and Guthrie stepped up behind Jimmy. This time he made no mistake. He touched the muzzle of the big .45 to the base of Jimmy's skull, and the shot was muffled by the neoprene rubber hood of the diving-suit.

Jimmy's skull collapsed, shattered by the passage of the heavy bullet. It came out through the glass plate of the diving mask in a cloud of glass fragments. The force of it clubbed him over the side, and his body splashed alongside. Then there was silence in which the memory of gunfire seemed to echo with the sound of wind and water.

'He'll sink,' said Materson calmly. 'He had on a weight belt – but we had better try and find Fletcher. We don't want him washed up with that bullet hole in his chest.'

'He ducked – the bastard ducked – I didn't hit him squarely—' Guthrie protested, and I heard no more. My legs collapsed and I sprawled on the deck of the cockpit. I was sick with shock and horror and the quick flooding flow of my blood.

I have seen violent death in many guises, but Jimmy's had moved me as never before. Suddenly there was only one thing I wanted to do before my own violent death overwhelmed me.

I began to crawl towards the engine-room hatch. The white deck seemed to stretch before me like the Sahara desert, and I was beginning to feel the leaden hand of a great weariness upon my shoulder.

I heard their footsteps on the deck above me, and the murmur of their voices. They were coming back to the cockpit.

'Ten seconds, please God,' I whispered. 'That's all I need,' but I knew it was futile. They would be into the cabin long before I reached the hatch – but I dragged myself desperately towards it.

'Then suddenly their footsteps paused, but the voices continued. They had stopped to talk out on the deck, and I felt a lift of relief for I had reached the engine hatch.

Now I struggled with the toggles. They seemed to have jammed immovably, and I realized how weak I was, but I felt the revitalizing stir of anger through the weariness.

I wriggled around and kicked at the toggles and they flew back. I fought my weakness aside and got on to my knees. As I leaned over the hatch a fresh splattering of bright blood fell on the white deck.

'Eat your liver, Chubby,' I thought irrelevantly, and prised up the hatch. It came up achingly slowly, heavy as all the earth, and now I felt the first lances of pain in my chest as bruised tissue tore.

The hatch fell back with a heavy thump, and instantly the voices on deck were silent, and I could imagine them listening.

I fell on my belly and groped desperately under the decking and my right hand closed on the stock of the carbine.

'Come on!' There was a loud exclamation, and I recognized Materson's voice, and immediately the pounding of running footsteps along the deck towards the cockpit.

I tugged wearily at the carbine, but it seemed to be caught in the slings and resisted my efforts.

'Christ! There's blood all over the deck,' Materson shouted.

'It's Fletcher,' Guthrie yelled. 'He came in over the stern.'

Just then the carbine came free and I almost dropped it down into the engine-room, but managed to hold it long enough to roll clear.

I sat up with the carbine in my lap, and pushed the safety catch across with my thumb, sweat and salt water streamed into my eyes blurring my vision as I peered up at the entrance to the cabin.

Materson ran into the cabin three paces before he saw me, then he stopped and gaped at me. His face was red with effort and agitation and he lifted his hands, spreading them in a protective gesture before him as I brought up the carbine. The diamond on his little finger winked merrily at me.

I lifted the carbine one-handed from my lap, and its immense weight appalled me. When the muzzle was pointed at Materson's knees I pressed the trigger.

With a continuous shattering roar the carbine spewed out a solid blast of bullets, and the recoil flung the barrel upwards, riding the stream of fire from Materson's crotch up across his belly and chest. It flung him backwards against the cabin bulkhead, and split him like the knife-stroke that guts a fish while he danced a grotesque and jerky little death jig.

I knew that I should not empty the carbine, there was still Mike Guthrie to deal with, but somehow I seemed unable to release my grip on the trigger and the bullets tore through Materson's body, smashing and splintering the woodwork of the bulkhead.

Then suddenly I lifted my finger. The torrent of bullets ceased and Materson fell heavily forward.

The cabin stank with burned cordite and the sweet heavy smell of blood.

Guthrie ducked into the companionway of the cabin, crouching with right arm outflung and he snapped off a single shot at me as I sat in the centre of the cabin.

He had all the time he needed for a clean shot at me, but he hurried it, panicky and off-balance. The blast slapped against my ear drums, and the heavy bullet disrupted the air against my cheek as it flew wide. The recoil kicked the pistol high, and as it dropped for his next shot I fell sideways and pulled up the carbine.

There must have been a single round left in the breech, but it was a lucky one. I did not aim it, but merely jerked at the trigger as the barrel came up.

It hit Guthrie in the crook of his right elbow, shattering the joint and the pistol flew backwards over his shoulder, skidded across the deck and thudded into the stern scuppers.

Guthrie spun aside, the arm twisting grotesquely and hanging from the broken joint and at the same instant the firing pin of the carbine fell on an empty chamber.

We stared at each other, both of us badly hit, but the old antagonism was still there between us. It gave me strength to come up on my knees and start towards him, the empty carbine falling from my hand.

Guthrie grunted and turned away, gripping the shattered arm with his good hand. He staggered towards the .45 lying in the scuppers.

I saw there was no way I could stop him. He was not mortally hit, and I knew he could shoot probably as well with his good left hand. Still I made my last try and dragged myself over Materson's body and out into the cockpit, reaching it just as Guthrie stooped to pick the pistol out of the scuppers.

Then *Dancer* came to my aid, and she reared like a wild horse as a freak swell hit her. She threw Guthrie off balance, and the pistol went skidding away across the deck. He turned to chase it, his feet slipped in the blood which I had splashed across the cockpit and he went down.

He fell heavily, pinning his shattered arm under him. He cried out, and rolled on to his knees and began crawling swiftly after the glistening black pistol.

Against the outer bulkhead of the cockpit the long flying gaffs stood in their rack like a set of billiard cues. Ten feet long, with the great stainless-steel hooks uppermost.

Chubby had filed the points as cruelly as stilettos. They were designed to be buried deep into a game fish's body, and the shock of the blow would detach the head from the stock. The fish could then be dragged on board with the length of heavy nylon rope that was spliced on to the hook.

Guthrie had almost reached the pistol as I knocked open the clamp on the rack and lifted down one of the gaffs.

Guthrie scooped up the pistol left-handed, juggling it to get a grip on it, concentrating his whole attention on the weapon and while he was busy I came up on my knees again and lifted the gaff with one hand, throwing it up high and reaching out over Guthrie's bowed back. As the hook flashed down over him I hit the steel in hard, driving it full length through his ribs, burying the gleaming steel to the curve. The shock of it pulled him down on to the deck and once again the pistol dropped from his hand and the roll of the boat pushed it away from him.

Now he was screaming, a high-pitched wail of agony with the steel deep in him. I tugged harder, single-handed, trying to work it into heart or lung and the hook broke from the stock. Guthrie rolled across the deck towards the pistol. He groped frantically for it, and I dropped the gaff stock and groped just as frantically for the rope to restrain him.

I have seen two women wrestlers fighting in a bath of black mud, in a nightclub in the St Pauli district of Hamburg – and now Guthrie and I performed the same act, only in place of mud we fought in a bath of our own blood. We slithered and rolled about the deck, thrown about mercilessly by *Dancer*'s action in the swell.

Guthrie was weakening at last, clawing with his good hand at the great hook buried in his body, and with the next roll of the sea I was able to throw a coil of the rope around his neck and get a firm purchase against the base of the fighting chair with one foot. Then I pulled with all the remains of my strength and resolve.

Suddenly, with a single explosive expulsion of breath, his tongue fell out of his mouth and he relaxed, his limbs stretched out limply and his head lolled loosely back and forth with *Dancer*'s roll.

I was tired beyond caring now. My hand opened of its own accord and the rope fell from it. I lay back and closed my eyes. Darkness fell over me like a shroud.

When I regained consciousness my face felt as though it had been scalded with acid, my lips were swollen and my thirst raged like a forest fire. I had lain face up under a tropical sun for six hours, and it had burned me mercilessly.

Slowly I rolled on to my side, and cried out weakly at the immensity of pain that was my chest. I lay still for a while to let it subside and then I began to explore the wound.

The bullet had angled in through the bicep of my left arm, missing bone, and come out through the tricep, tearing a big exit hole. Immediately it had ploughed into the side of my chest.

Sobbing with the effort I traced and probed the wound with my finger. It had glanced over a rib, I could feel the exposed bone was cracked and rough-ended where the slug had struck and been deflected and left slivers of lead and bone chips in the churned flesh. It had gone through the thick muscle of my back – and torn out below the shoulder blade, leaving a hole the size of a *demi tasse* coffee cup.

I fell back on to the deck, panting and fighting back waves of giddy nausea. My exploration had induced fresh bleeding, but I knew at least that the bullet had not entered the chest cavity. I still had some sort of a chance.

While I rested I looked blearily about me. My hair and clothing were stiff with dried blood, blood was coated over the cockpit, dried black and shiny or congealed.

Guthrie lay on his back with the gaff hook still in him and the rope around his neck. The gases in his belly had already blown, giving him a pregnant swollen look.

I got up on to my knees and began to crawl. Materson's body half-blocked the entrance to the cabin, shredded by gunfire as though he had been mauled by a savage predator.

I crawled over him, and found I was whimpering aloud as I saw the icebox behind the bar.

67

I drank three cans of Coca-Cola, gasping and choking in my eagerness, spilling the icy liquid down my chest, and moaning and snuffling through each mouthful. Then I lay and rested again. I closed my eyes and just wanted to sleep for ever.

'Where the hell are we?' The question hit me with a shock of awareness. *Dancer* was adrift on a treacherous coast, strewn with reefs and shoals.

I dragged myself to my feet and reached the blood-caked cockpit.

Beneath us flowed the deep purple blue of the Mozambique, and a clear horizon circled us, above which the massive cloud ranges climbed to a tall blue sky. The ebb and the wind had pushed us far out to the east, we had plenty of sea room.

My legs collapsed under me, and I may have slept for a while. When I woke my head felt clearer, but the wound had stiffened horribly. Each movement was agony. On my hand and knees I reached the shower room where the medicine chest was kept. I ripped away my shirt and poured undiluted acriflavine solution into the cavernous wounds. Then I plugged them roughly with surgical dressing and strapped the whole as best I could, but the effort was too much.

The dizziness overwhelmed me again and I crashed down on to the linoleum floor unconscious.

I awoke light-headed, and feeble as a new-born infant.

It was a major effort to fashion a sling for the wounded arm, and the journey to the bridge was an endless procession of dizziness and pain and nausea.

Dancer's engines started with the first kick, sweet as ever she was.

'Take me home, me darling,' I whispered, and set the automatic pilot. I gave her an approximate heading. *Dancer* settled on course, and the darkness caught me again. I went down sprawling on the deck, welcoming oblivion as it washed over me.

It may have been the altered action of *Dancer*'s passage that roused me. She no longer swooped and rolled with the big swell of the Mozambique, but ambled quietly along over a sheltered sea. Dusk was falling swiftly.

Stiffly I dragged myself up to the wheel. I was only just in time, for dead ahead lay the loom of land in the fading light. I slammed *Dancer*'s throttle closed, and kicked her into neutral. She came up and rocked gently in a low sea. I recognized the shape of the land – it was Big Gull Island.

We had missed the channel of Grand Harbour, my heading had been a little southerly and we had run into the southern-most straggle of tiny atolls that made up the St Mary's group.

Hanging on to the wheel for support I craned forward. The canvas-wrapped bundle still lay on the foredeck – and suddenly I knew that I must get rid of it. My reasons were not clear then. Dimly I realized that it was a high card in the game into which I had been drawn. I knew I dare not ferry it back into Grand Harbour in broad daylight. Three men had been killed for it already – and I'd had half my chest shot away. There was some strong medicine wrapped up in that sheet of canvas.

It took me fifteen minutes to reach the foredeck, and I blacked out twice on the way. When I crawled to the bundle of canvas I was sobbing aloud with each movement.

For another half-hour I tried feebly to unwrap the stiff canvas and untie the thick nylon knots. With only one hand and my fingers so numb and weak that they could not close properly it was a hopeless task, and the blackness kept filling my head. I was afraid I would go out with the bundle still aboard.

Lying on my side I used the last rays of the setting sun to take a bearing off the point of the island, lining up a clump of palms and the point of the high ground – marking the spot with care.

Then I opened the swinging section of the foredeck railing through which we usually pulled big fish aboard, and I wriggled around the canvas bundle – got both feet on to it and shoved it over the side. It fell with a heavy splash and droplets splattered in my face.

My exertions had re-opened the wounds and fresh blood was soaking my clumsy dressing. I started back across the deck but I did not make it. I went out for the last time as I reached the break of the cockpit.

The morning sun and a raucous barnyard squawking woke me, but when I opened my eyes the sun seemed shaded, darkened as though in eclipse. My vision was fading, and when I tried to move there was no strength for it. I lay crushed beneath the weight of weakness and pain. *Dancer* was canted at an absurd angle, probably stranded high and dry on the beach.

I stared up into the rigging above me. There were three black-backed gulls as big as turkeys sitting in a row on the cross stay. They twisted their heads sideways to look down at me, and their beaks were clear yellow and powerful. The upper part of the beak ended in a curved point that was a bright cherry red. They watched me with glistening black eyes, and fluffed out their feathers impatiently.

I tried to shout at them, to drive them away but my lips would not move. I was completely helpless, and I knew that soon they would begin on my eyes. They always went for the eyes.

One of the gulls above me grew bold and spreading his wings, planed down to the deck near me. He folded his wings and waddled a few steps closer, and we stared at each other. Again I tried to scream, but no sound came and the gull waddled forward again, then stretched out his neck, opened that wicked beak and let out a hoarse screech of menace. I felt the whole of my dreadfully abused body cringing away from the bird.

Suddenly the tone of the screeching gulls altered, and the air was filled with their wing beats. The bird that I was watching screeched again, but this time in disappointment and it launched itself into flight, the draught from its wings striking my face as it rose.

There was a long silence then, as I lay on the heavily listing deck, fighting off the waves of darkness that tried to overwhelm me. Then suddenly there was a scrabbling sound alongside.

I rolled my head again to face it, and at that moment a dark chocolate face rose above deck level and stared at me from a range of two feet.

'Lordy!' said a familiar voice. 'Is that you, Mister Harry?'

I learned later that Henry Wallace, one of St Mary's turtle hunters, had been camped out on the atolls and had risen from his bed of straw to find *Wave Dancer* stranded by the ebb on the sand bar of the lagoon with a cloud of gulls squabbling over her. He had waded out across the bar, and climbed the side to peer into the slaughterhouse that was *Dancer*'s cockpit.

I wanted to tell him how thankful I was to see him, I wanted to promise him free beer for the rest of his life – but instead I started to weep, just a slow welling up of tears from deep down. I didn't even have the strength to sob.

'Little scratch like that,' marvelled MacNab. 'What's all the fussing about?' and he probed determinedly.

I gasped as he did something else to my back; if I had had the strength I would have got up off the hospital bed and pushed that probe up the most convenient opening of his body. Instead I moaned weakly.

'Come on, Doc. Didn't they teach you about morphine and that stuff back in the time when you should have failed your degree?'

MacNab came around to look in my face. He was plump and scarlet-faced, fiftyish and greying in hair and moustache. His breath should have anaesthetized me.

'Harry, my boy, that stuff costs money – what are you, anyway, National Health or a private patient?'

'I just changed my status – I'm private.'

'Quite right, too,' MacNab agreed. 'Man of your standing in the community,' and he nodded to the sister. 'Very well then, my dear, give Mister Harry a grain of morphine before we proceed,' and while he waited for her to prepare the shot he went on to cheer me up. 'We put six pints of whole blood into you last night, you were just about dry. Soaked it up like a sponge.'

Well, you wouldn't expect one of the giants of the medical profession to be practising on St Mary's. I could almost believe the island rumour that he was in partnership with Fred Coker's mortician parlour.

'How long you going to keep me in here anyway, Doc?'

'Not more than a month.'

'A month!' I struggled to sit up and two nurses pounced on me to restrain me, which required no great effort. I could still hardly raise my head. 'I can't afford a month. My God, it's right in the middle of the season. I've got a new party coming next week—'

The sister hurried across with the syringe.

' – You trying to break me? I can't afford to miss a single party—'

The sister hit me with the needle.

'Harry old boy, you can forget about this season. You won't be fishing again,' and he began picking bits of bone and flakes of lead out of me while he hummed cheerily to himself. The morphine dulled the pain – but not my despair.

72

If *Dancer* and I missed half a season we just couldn't keep going. Once again they had me stretched out on the financial rack. God, how I hated money.

MacNab strapped me up in clean white bandages, and spread a little more sunshine.

'You going to lose some function in your left arm there, Harry boy. Probably always be a little stiff and weak, and you going to have some pretty scars to show the girls.' He finished winding the bandage and turned to the sister. 'Change the dressings every six hours, swab out with Eusol and give him his usual dose of Aureo Mycytin every four hours. Three Mogadon tonight and I'll see him on my rounds tomorrow.' He turned back to grin at me with bad teeth under the untidy grey moustache. 'The entire police force is waiting outside this very room. I'll have to let them in now.' He started towards the door, then paused to chuckle again. 'You did a hell of a job on those two guys, spread them over the scenery with a spade. Nice shooting, Harry boy.'

Inspector Daly was dressed in impeccable khaki drill, starched and pristine, and his leather belts and straps glowed with a high polish.

'Good afternoon, Mr Fletcher. I have come to take a statement from you. I hope you feel strong enough.'

'I feel wonderful, Inspector. Nothing like a bullet through the chest to set you up.'

Daly turned to the constable who followed him and motioned him to take the chair beside the bed, and as he sat and prepared his shorthand pad the constable told me softly, 'Sorry you got hurt, Mister Harry.'

'Thanks, Wally, but you should have seen the other guys.'

Wally was one of Chubby's nephews, and his mother did my laundry. He was a big, strong, darkly good-looking youngster.

73

'I saw them,' he grinned. 'Wow!'

'If you are ready, Mr Fletcher,' Daly cut in primly, annoyed by the exchange. 'We can get on.'

'Shoot,' I said, and I had my story well prepared. Like all good stories, it was the exact and literal truth, with omissions. I made no mention of the prize that James North had lifted, and which I had dumped again off Big Gull Island – nor did I tell Daly in which area we had conducted our search. He wanted to know, of course. He kept coming back to that.

'What were they searching for?'

'I have no idea. They were very careful not to let me know.'

'Where did all this happen?' he persisted.

'In the area beyond Herring Bone Reef, south of Rastafa Point.' This was fifty miles from the break at Gunfire Reef.

'Could you recognize the exact point where they dived?'

'I don't think so, not within a few miles. I was merely following instructions.'

Daly chewed his silky moustache in frustration.

'All right, you say they attacked you without warning,' and I nodded. 'Why did they do that – why would they try to kill you?'

'We never really discussed it. I didn't have a chance to ask them.' I was beginning to feel very tired and feeble again, I didn't want to go on talking in case I made a mistake. 'When Guthrie started shooting at me with that cannon of his I didn't think he wanted to chat.'

'This isn't a joke, Fletcher,' he told me stiffly, and I rang the bell beside me. The sister must have been waiting just outside the door.

'Sister, I'm feeling pretty bad.'

'You'll have to go now, Inspector.' She turned on the two policemen like a mother hen, and drove them from the ward. Then she came back to rearrange my pillows.

She was a pretty little thing with huge dark eyes, and her tiny waist was belted in firmly to accentuate her big nicely shaped bosom on which she wore her badges and medals. Lustrous chestnut curls peeped from under the saucy little uniform cap.

'What is your name, then?' I whispered hoarsely.

'May.'

'Sister May, how come I haven't seen you around before?' I asked, as she leaned across me to tuck in my sheet.

'Guess you just weren't looking, Mister Harry.'

'Well, I'm looking now.' The front of her crisp white uniform blouse was only a few inches from my nose. She stood up quickly.

'They say here you're a devil man,' she said. 'I know now they didn't tell me lies.' But she was smiling. 'Now you go to sleep. You've got to get strong again.'

'Yeah, we'll talk again then,' I said, and she laughed out loud.

The next three days I had a lot of time to think for I was allowed no visitors until the official inquest had been conducted. Daly had a constable on guard outside my room, and I was left in no doubt that I stood accused of murder most vile.

My room was cool and airy with a good view down across the lawns to the tall dark-leafed banyan trees, and beyond them the massive stone walls of the fort with the cannon upon the battlements. The food was good, plenty of fish and fruit, and Sister May and I were becoming good, if not intimate, friends. She even smuggled in a bottle of Chivas Regal which we kept in the bedpan. From her I heard how the whole island was agog with the cargo that *Wave Dancer* had brought into Grand Harbour. She told me they buried Materson and Guthrie on the second day in the old cemetery. A corpse doesn't keep so well in those latitudes.

In those three days I decided that the bundle I had

dropped off Big Gull Island would stay there. I guessed that from now on there would be a lot of eyes watching me, and I was at a complete disadvantage. I didn't know who the watchers were and I didn't know why. I would keep down off the sky-line until I worked out where the next bullet was likely to come from. I didn't like the game. They could deal me out and I would stick to the action I could call and handle.

I thought a lot about Jimmy North also, and every time I felt myself grieving unnecessarily I tried to tell myself that he was a stranger, that he had meant nothing to me, but it didn't work. This is a weakness of mine which I must always guard against. I become too readily emotionally bound up with other people. I try to walk alone, avoiding involvement, and after years of practice I have achieved some success. It is seldom these days that anyone can penetrate my armour the way Jimmy North did.

By the third day I was feeling much stronger. I could lift myself into a sitting position without assistance and with only a moderate degree of pain.

They held the official inquest in my hospital room. It was a closed session, attended only by the heads of the legislative, judicial and executive branches of St Mary's government.

The President himself, dressed as always in black with a crisp white shirt and a halo of snowy wool around his bald pate, chaired the meeting. Judge Harkness, tall and thin and sunburned to dark brown, assisted him – while Inspector Daly represented the executive.

The President's first concern was for my comfort and well-being. I was one of his boys.

'You be sure you don't tire yourself now, Mister Harry. Anything you want you just ask, hear? We have only come here to hear your version, but I want to tell you now not to worry. There is nothing going to happen to you.'

76

Inspector Daly looked pained, seeing his prisoner declared innocent before his trial began.

So I told my story again, with the President making helpful or admiring comments whenever I paused for breath, and when I finished he shook his head with wonder.

'All I can say, Mister Harry, is there are not many men would have had the strength and courage to do what you did against those gangsters, is that right, gentlemen?'

Judge Harkness agreed heartily, but Inspector Daly said nothing.

'And they were gangsters too,' he went on. 'We sent their fingerprints to London and we heard today that those men came here under false names, and that both of them have got police records at Scotland Yard. Gangsters, both of them.' The President looked at Judge Harkness. 'Any questions, Judge?'

'I don't think so, Mr President.'

'Good.' The President nodded happily. 'What about you, Inspector?' And Daly produced a typewritten list. The President made no effort to hide his irritation.

'Mister Fletcher is still a very sick man, Inspector. I hope your questions are really important.'

Inspector Daly hesitated and the President went on brusquely, 'Good, well then we are all agreed. The verdict is death by misadventure. Mister Fletcher acted in self-defence, and is hereby discharged from any guilt. No criminal charges will be brought against him.' He turned to the shorthand recorder in the corner. 'Have you got that? Type it out and send a copy to my office for signature.' He stood up and came to my bedside. 'Now you get better soon, Mister Harry. I expect you for dinner at Government House soon as you are well enough. My secretary will send you a formal invitation. I want to hear the whole story again.'

Next time I appear before a judicial body, as I surely

shall, I hope for the same consideration. Having been officially declared innocent I was allowed visitors.

Chubby and Mrs Chubby came together dressed in their standard number one rig. Mrs Chubby had baked one of her splendid banana cakes, knowing my weakness for them.

Chubby was torn by relief at seeing me still alive and outrage at what I had done to *Wave Dancer*. He scowled at me fiercely as he started giving me a large slice of his mind.

'Ain't never going to get that deck clean again. It soaked right in, man. That damned old carbine of yours really chewed up the cabin bulkhead. Me and Angelo been working three days at it now, and it still needs a few more days.'

'Sorry, Chubby, next time I shoot somebody I'm going to make them stand by the rail first.' I knew that when Chubby had finished repairing the woodwork the damage would not be detectable.

'When you coming out anyway? Plenty of big fish working out there on the stream, Harry.'

'I be out pretty soon, Chubby. One week tops.'

Chubby sniffed. 'Did hear that Fred Coker wired all your parties for rest of the season – told them you were hurt bad and switched their bookings to Mister Coleman.'

I lost my temper then. 'You tell Fred Coker to get his black arse up here soonest,' I shouted.

Dick Coleman had a deal with the Hilton Hotel. They had financed the purchase of two big game fishing boats, which Coleman crewed with a pair of imported skippers. Neither of his boats caught much fish, they didn't have the feel of it. He had a lot of difficulty getting charters, and I guessed Fred Coker had been handsomely compensated to switch my bookings to him. Coker arrived the following morning.

'Mister Harry, Doctor MacNab told me you wouldn't be

78

able to fish again this season. I couldn't let my parties down, they fly six thousand miles to find you in a hospital bed. I couldn't do that – I got my reputation to think of.'

'Mr Coker, your reputation smells like one of those stiffs you got tucked away in the back room,' I told him, and he smiled at me blandly from behind his gold-rimmed spectacles, but he was right of course, it would be a long time still before I could take *Dancer* out after the big billfish.

'Now don't you fuss yourself, Mister Harry. Soon as you better I will arrange a few lucrative charters for you.'

He was talking about the night run again, his commission on a single run could go as high as seven hundred and fifty dollars. I could handle that even in my present beaten-up condition, it involved merely conning *Dancer* in and out again – just as long as we didn't run into trouble.

'Forget it, Mr Coker. I told you from now on I fish, that's all,' and he nodded and smiled and went on as though I had not spoken.

'Had persistent inquiries from one of your old clients.'

'Body? Box?' I demanded. Body was the illegal carrying to or from the African mainland of human beings, fleeing politicians with the goon squad after them – or on the other hand aspiring politicians trying for radical change in the regime. Boxes usually contained lethal hardware and it was a one-way traffic. In the old days they called it gun-running.

Coker shook his head and said, 'Five, six,' – from the old nursery rhyme: 'Five, six. Pick up sticks.' In this context sticks were tusks of ivory. A massive, highly organized poaching operation was systematically wiping out the African elephant from the game reserves and tribal lands of East Africa. The Orient was an insatiable and high-priced market for the ivory. A fast boat and a good skipper were needed to get the valuable cargo out of an estuary mouth, through the dangerous inshore waters, out to where one of the big ocean-going dhows waited on the stream of the Mozambique.

'Mr Coker,' I told him wearily. 'I'm sure your mother never even knew your father's name.'

'It was Edward, Mister Harry,' he smiled carefully. 'I told the client that the going rate was up. What with inflation and the price of diesel fuel.'

'How much?'

'Seven thousand dollars a trip,' which was not as much as it sounds after Coker had clouted fifteen per cent, then Inspector Peter Daly had to be slipped the same again to dim his eyesight and cloud his hearing. On top of that Chubby and Angelo always earned a danger money bonus of five hundred each for a night run.

'Forget it, Mr Coker,' I said unconvincingly. 'You just fix a couple of fishing parties.' But he knew I couldn't fight it.

'Just as soon as you fit enough to fish, we'll fix that. Meantime, when do you want to do the first night run? Shall I tell them ten days from today? That will be high spring tide and a good moon.'

'All right,' I agreed with resignation. 'Ten days' time.'

With a positive decision made, it seemed that my recovery from the wounds was hastened. I had been in peak physical condition which contributed, and the gaping holes in my arm and back began to shrink miraculously.

I reached a milestone in my convalescence on the sixth day. Sister May was giving me a bed bath, with a basin of suds and a face cloth, when there was a monumental demonstration of my physical well-being. Even I, who was no stranger to the phenomenon, was impressed, while Sister May was so overcome that her voice became a husky little whisper.

'Lord!' she said. 'You've sure got your strength back.'

'Sister May, do you think we should waste that?' I asked, and she shook her head vehemently.

From then onwards I began to take a more cheerful view of my circumstances, and not surprisingly the canvas-wrapped secret off Big Gull Island began to nag me. I felt my good resolutions weakening.

'I'll just take a look,' I told myself. 'When I am sure the dust has really settled.'

They were allowing me up for a few hours at a time now, and I felt restless and anxious to get on with it. Not even Sister May's devoted efforts could blunt the edge of my awakening energy. MacNab was impressed.

'You heal well, Harry old chap. Closing up nicely – another week.'

'A week, hell!' I told him determinedly. Seven days from now I was making the night run. Coker had set it up without trouble – and I was just about stony broke. I needed that run pretty badly.

My crew came up to visit me every evening, and to report progress on the repairs to *Dancer*. One evening Angelo arrived earlier than usual, he was dressed in his courting gear – rodeo boots and all – but he was strangely subdued and not alone.

The lass with him was the young nursery grade teacher from the government school down near the fort. I knew her well enough to exchange smiles on the street. Missus Eddy had summed up her character for me once.

'She's a good girl, that Judith. Not all flighty and flirty like some others. Going to make some lucky fellow a good wife.'

She was also good-looking with a tall willowy figure, neatly and conservatively dressed, and she greeted me shyly.

81

'How do, Mister Harry.'

'Hello, Judith. Good of you to come,' and I looked at Angelo, unable to hide my grin. He couldn't meet my eye, colouring up as he hunted for words.

'Me and Judith planning to marry up,' he blurted at last. 'Wanted you to know that, boss.'

'Think you can keep him under control, Judith?' I laughed delightedly.

'You just watch me,' she said with a flash of dark eyes that made the question superfluous.

'That's great – I'll make a speech at your wedding,' I assured them. 'You going to let Angelo go on crewing for me?'

'Wouldn't ever try to stop him,' she assured me. 'It's good work he's got with you.'

They stayed for another hour and when they left I felt a small prickle of envy. It must be a good feeling to have someone – apart from yourself. I thought some day if I ever found the right person I might try it. Then I dismissed the thought, raising my guard again. There were a hell of a lot of women – and no guarantee you will pick right.

MacNab discharged me with two days to spare. My clothes hung on my bony frame, I had lost nearly two stone in weight and my tan had faded to a dirty yellow brown, there were big blue smears under my eyes and I still felt weak as a baby. The arm was in a sling and the wounds were still open, but I could change the dressing myself.

Angelo brought the pick-up to the hospital and waited while I said goodbye to Sister May on the steps.

'Nice getting to know you, Mister Harry.'

'Come out to the shack some time soon. I'll grill you a mess of crayfish, and we'll drink a little wine.'

'My contract ends next week. I'll be going home to England then.'

'You be happy, hear,' I told her.

Angelo drove me down to Admiralty, and with Chubby we spent an hour going over *Dancer*'s repairs.

Her decks were snowy white, and they had replaced all the woodwork in the saloon bulkhead, a beautiful piece of joinery with which even I could find no fault.

We took her down the channel as far as Mutton Point and it was good to feel her riding lightly under my feet and hear the sweet burble of her engines. We came home in the dusk to tie up at moorings and sit out on the bridge in the dark, drinking beer out of the can and talking.

I told them that we had a run set for the following night, and they asked where to and what the cargo was. That was all – it was set, there was no argument.

'Time to go,' Angelo said at last. 'Going to pick Judith up from night school,' and we rowed ashore in the dinghy.

There was a police Land-Rover parked beside my old pick-up at the back of the pineapple sheds and Wally, the young constable, climbed out as we approached. He greeted his uncle, and then turned to me.

'Sorry to worry you, Mister Harry, but Inspector Daly wants to see you up at the fort. He says it's urgent.'

'God,' I growled. 'It can wait until tomorrow.'

'He says it can't, Mister Harry.' Wally was apologetic, and for his sake I went along.

'Okay, I'll follow you in the pick-up – but we got to drop Chubby and Angelo off first.'

I thought it was probably that Daly wanted to haggle about his pay off. Usually Fred Coker fixed that, but I guessed that Daly was raising the price of his honour.

Driving one-handed and holding the steering wheel with a knee while I shifted gear with my good hand, I followed the red tail lights of Wally's Land-Rover rattling over the drawbridge and parked beside it in the courtyard of the fort.

The massive stone walls had been built by slave labour in the mid-eighteenth century and from the wide ramparts

83

the long thirty-six-pounder cannon ranged the channel and the entrance to Grand Harbour.

One wing was used as the island police headquarters, jail and armoury – the rest of it was government offices and the Presidential and State apartments.

We climbed the front steps to the charge office and Wally led me through a side door, and along a corridor, down steps, another corridor, more stone steps.

I had never been down here before and I was intrigued. The stone walls here must have been twenty feet thick, the old powder store probably. I half expected the Frankenstein monster to be lurking behind the thick oak door, iron studded and weathered, at the end of the last passage. We went through.

It wasn't Frankenstein, but next best. Inspector Daly waited for us with another of his constables. I noticed immediately they both wore sidearms. The room was empty except for a wooden table and four P.W.D. type chairs. The walls were unpainted stonework and the floor was paved.

At the back of the room an arched doorway led to a row of cells. The lights were bare hundred-watt bulbs hanging on black electrical cable that ran exposed across the beamed roof. They cast hard black shadows in the angles of the irregularly shaped room.

On the table lay my FN carbine. I stared at it uncomprehendingly.

Behind me Wally closed the oak door.

'Mr Fletcher, is this your firearm?'

'You know damn well it is,' I said angrily. 'Just what the hell are you playing at, Daly?'

'Harold Delville Fletcher, I am placing you under arrest for the unlawful possession of Category A firearms. To wit, one unlicensed automatic rifle type Fabrique Nationale Serial No. 4163215.'

'You're off your head,' I said, and laughed. He didn't like

that laugh. The weak little lips below his moustache puckered up like those of a sulky child and he nodded at his constables. They had been briefed, and they went out through the oak door.

I heard the bolts shoot home, and Daly and I were alone. He was standing well away from me across the room – and the flap of his holster was unbuttoned.

'Does his excellency know about this, Daly?' I asked, still smiling.

'His excellency left St Mary's at four o'clock this afternoon to attend the conference of Commonwealth heads in London. He won't be back for two weeks.'

I stopped smiling. I knew it was true. 'In the meantime I have reason to believe the security of the State is endangered.'

He smiled now, thinly and with the mouth only. 'Before we go any further I want you to be sure I am serious.'

'I believe you,' I said.

'I have two weeks with you alone, here, Fletcher. These walls are pretty thick, you can make as much noise as you like.'

'You are a monstrous little turd, you really are.'

'There is only one of two ways you are going to leave here. Either you and I come to an arrangement – or I'll get Fred Coker to come and fetch you in a box.'

'Let's hear your deal, little man.'

'I want to know exactly – and I mean exactly – where your charter carried out their diving operations before the shoot out.'

'I told you – somewhere off Rastafa Point. I couldn't give you the exact spot.'

'Fletcher, you know the spot to within inches. I'm willing to stake *your* life on that. You wouldn't miss a chance like that. You know it. I know it – and they knew it. That's why they tried to sign you off.'

'Inspector, go screw,' I said.

'What is more it was nowhere near Rastafa Point. You were working north of here, towards the mainland. I was interested – I had some reports of your movements.'

'It was somewhere off Rastafa Point,' I repeated doggedly.

'Very well,' he nodded. 'I hope you aren't as tough as you put out, Fletcher, otherwise this is going to be a long messy business. Before we start though, don't waste our time with false data. I'm going to keep you here while I check it out – I've got two weeks.'

We stared at each other, and my flesh began to crawl. Peter Daly was going to enjoy this, I realized. There was a gloating expression on those thin lips and a smoky glaze to his eyes.

'I had a great deal of experience in interrogation in Malaya, you know. Fascinating subject. So many aspects to it. So often it's the tough, strong ones that pop first – and the little runts that hang on for ever—'

This was for kicks, I saw clearly that he was aroused by the prospect of inflicting pain. His breathing had changed, faster and deeper, there was fresh colour in his cheeks.

'—of course, you are at a physical low ebb right now, Fletcher. Probably your threshold of pain is much lowered after your recent misadventures. I don't think it will take long—'

He seemed to regret that. I gathered myself, tightening up for an attempt.

'No,' he snapped. 'Don't do it, Fletcher.' He placed his hand on the butt of the pistol. He was fifteen feet away. I was one-armed, weak, there was a locked door behind me, two armed constables – my shoulders sagged as I relaxed.

'That's better.' He smiled again. 'Now I think we will handcuff you to the bars of a cell, and we can get to work. When you have had enough you have merely to say so. I think you will find my little electrical set-up simple but effective. It's merely a twelve-volt car battery – and I clip the terminals on to interesting parts of the body—'

He reached behind him – and for the first time I noticed the button of an electric bell set on the wall. He pressed it and I heard the bell ring faintly beyond the oaken door.

The bolts shot back and the two constables came back in.

'Take him through to the cells,' Daly ordered, and the constables hesitated. I guessed they were strangers to this type of operation.

'Come on,' snapped Daly, and they stepped up on either side of me. Wally laid a hand lightly on my injured arm, and I allowed myself to be led forward towards the cells – and Daly.

I wanted to have a chance at him, just one chance.

'How's your mom, Wally?' I asked casually.

'She's all right, Mister Harry,' he muttered embarrassedly.

'She get the present I sent up for her birthday?'

'Yeah, she got it.' He was distracted as I intended.

We had come level with Daly, he was standing by the doorway to the cells, waiting for us to go through, slapping the malacca swagger stick against his thigh.

The constables were holding me respectfully, loosely, unsure of themselves, and I stepped to one side pushing Wally slightly off balance – then I spun back, breaking free.

Not one of them was ready for it, and I covered the three paces to Daly before they had realized what I was doing – and I put my right knee into him with my full body weight behind it. It thumped into the crotch of his legs, a marvellously solid blow. Whatever the price I was going to have to pay for the pleasure, it was cheap.

Daly was lifted off his feet, a full eighteen inches in the air, and he flew backwards to crash against the bars. Then he doubled up, both hands pressed into his lower body, screaming thinly – a sound like steam from a boiling kettle. As he went over I lined up for another shot at his face, I wanted to take his teeth out with a kick in the mouth – but the constables recovered their wits and leaped forward to drag me away. They were rough now, twisting the arm.

'You didn't ought to do that, Mister Harry,' Wally shouted angrily. His fingers bit into my bicep and I gritted my teeth.

'The President himself cleared me, Wally. You know that,' I shouted back at him, and Daly straightened up, his face twisted with agony, still holding himself.

'This is a frame up.' I knew I had only a few seconds to talk, Daly was reeling towards me, brandishing the swagger stick, his mouth wide open as he tried to find his voice.

'If he gets me in that cell he's going to kill me, Wally—'

'Shut up!' screeched Daly.

'He wouldn't dare try this if the President—'

'Shut up! Shut up!' He swung the swagger stick, a side-arm cut, that hissed like a cobra. He had gone for my wounds deliberately, and the supple cane snapped around me like a pistol shot.

The pain of it was beyond belief, and I convulsed, bucking involuntarily in their grip. They held me.

'Shut up!' Daly was hysterical with pain and rage. He swung again, and the cane cut deeply into half-healed flesh. This time I screamed.

'I'll kill you, you bastard.' Daly staggered back, still hunched with pain, and he fumbled with his holstered pistol.

What I had hoped for now happened. Wally released me and jumped forward.

'No,' he shouted. 'Not that.'

He towered over Daly's slim crouching form and with one massive brown hand he blocked Daly's draw.

'Get out of my way. That's an order,' shouted Daly, but Wally unclipped the lanyard from the pistol's butt and disarmed him, stepping back with the pistol in his hand.

'I'll break you for this,' snarled Daly. 'It's your duty—'

'I know my duty, Inspector,' Wally spoke with a simple dignity, 'and it's not to murder prisoners.' Then he turned to me. 'Mister Harry, you'd best get out of here.'

'You're freeing a prisoner—' Daly gasped. 'Man, I'm going to break you.'

'Didn't see no warrant,' Wally cut in. 'Soon as the President signs a warrant, we'll fetch Mister Harry right back in again.'

'You black bastard,' Daly panted at him, and Wally turned to me.

'Get!' he said. 'Quickly.'

It was a long ride out to the shack, every bump in the track hit me in the chest. One thing I had learned from the evening's jollifications was that my original thoughts were correct – whatever that bundle off Big Gull Island contained, it could get a peace-loving gentleman like myself into plenty of trouble.

I was not so trusting as to believe that Inspector Daly had made his last attempt at interrogating me. Just as soon as he recovered from the kick in his multiplication machinery which I had given him, he was going to make another attempt to connect me up to the lighting system. I wondered if Daly was acting on his own, or if he had partners – and I guessed he was alone, taking opportunity as it presented itself.

I parked the pick-up in the yard and went through on to the veranda of my shack. Missus Chubby had been out to

89

sweep and tidy while I was away. There were fresh flowers in a jam-jar on the dining-room table – but more important there were eggs and bacon, bread and butter in the icebox.

I stripped off my blood-stained shirt and dressing. There were thick raised welts around my chest that the cane had left, and the wounds were a mess.

I showered and strapped on a fresh dressing, then, standing naked over the stove, I scrambled a pan full of eggs with bacon and while it cooked, I poured a very dark whisky and took it like medicine.

I was too tired to climb between the sheets, and as I fell across the bed I wondered if I would be fit enough to work the night run on schedule. It was my last thought before sun-up.

And after I had showered again and swallowed two Doloxene painkillers with a glass of cold pineapple juice and eaten another panful of eggs for breakfast I thought the answer was yes. I was stiff and sore, but I could work. At noon I drove into town, stopped off at Missus Eddy's store for supplies and then went on down to Admiralty.

Chubby and Angelo were on board already, and *Dancer* lay against the wharf.

'I filled the auxiliary tanks, Harry,' Chubby told me. 'She's good for a thousand miles.'

'Did you break out the cargo nets?' I asked, and he nodded.

'They are stowed in the main sail locker.' We would use the nets to deck load the bulky ivory cargo.

'Don't forget to bring a coat – it will be cold out on the stream with this wind blowing.'

'Don't worry, Harry. You the one should watch it. Man, you look bad as you were ten days ago. You look real sick.'

'I feel beautiful, Chubby.'

'Yeah,' he grunted, 'like my mother-in-law,' then he

changed the subject. 'What happened to your carbine, man?'

'The police are holding it.'

'You mean we going out there without a piece on board?'

'We never needed it yet.'

'There is always a first time,' he grunted. 'I'm going to feel mighty naked without it.'

Chubby's obsession with armaments always amused me.

Despite all the evidence that I presented to the contrary, Chubby could never quite shake off the belief that the velocity and range of a bullet depended upon how hard one pulled the trigger – and Chubby intended that his bullets go very fast and very far indeed.

The savage strength with which he sent them on their way would have buckled a less robust weapon than the FN. He also suffered from a complete inability to keep his eyes open at the moment of firing.

I have seen him miss a fifteen-foot tiger shark at a range of ten feet with a full magazine of twenty rounds. Chubby Andrews was never going to make it to Bisley, but he just naturally loved firearms and things that went bang.

'It will be a milk run, a ruddy pleasure cruise, Chubby, you'll see,' and he crossed his fingers to avert the hex, and shuffled off to work on *Dancer*'s already brilliant brasswork, while I went ashore.

The front office of Fred Coker's travel agency was deserted and I rang the bell on the desk. He stuck his head through from the back room.

'Welcome, Mister Harry.' He had removed his coat and tie and had rolled up his shirt sleeves, about his waist he wore a red rubber apron. 'Lock the front door, please, and come through.'

The back room was in contrast to the front office with its gaudy wallpaper and bright travel posters. It was a long,

91

gloomy barn. Along one wall were piled cheap pine coffins. The hearse was parked inside the double doors at the far end. Behind a grimy canvas screen in one corner was a marble slab table with guttering around the edges and a spout to direct fluid from the guttering into a bucket on the floor.

'Come in, sit down. There is a chair. Excuse me if I carry on working while we talk. I have to have this ready for four o'clock this afternoon.'

I took one look at the frail naked corpse on the slab. It was a little girl of about six years of age with long dark hair. One look was enough and I moved the chair behind the screen so I could see only Fred Coker's bald head, and I lit a cheroot. There was a heavy smell of embalming fluid in the room, and it caught in my throat.

'You get used to it, Mister Harry.' Fred Coker had noticed my distaste.

'Did you set it up?' I didn't want to discuss his gruesome trade.

'It's fixed,' he assured me.

'Did you square our friend at the fort?'

'It's all fixed.'

'When did you see him?' I persisted, I wanted to know about Daly. I was very interested in how Daly felt.

'I saw him this morning, Mister Harry.'

'How was he?'

'He seemed all right.' Coker paused in his grisly task and looked at me questioningly.

'Was he standing up, walking around, dancing a jig, singing, tying the dog loose?'

'No. He was sitting down, and he was not in a very good mood.'

'It figures.' I laughed and my own injuries felt better. 'But he took the pay off?'

'Yes, he took it.'

'Good, then we have still got a deal.'

'Like I told you, it's all fixed.'

'Lay it on me, Mr Coker.'

'The pick up is at the mouth of the Salsa stream where it enters the south channel of the main Duza estuary.' I nodded, that was acceptable. There was a good channel and the holding ground off the Salsa was satisfactory.

'The recognition signal will be two lanterns – one over the other, placed on the bank nearest the mouth. You will flash twice, repeated at thirty-second intervals and when the lower lantern is extinguished you can anchor. Got that?'

'Good.' It was all satisfactory.

'They will provide labour to load from the lighters.'

I nodded, then asked. 'They know that slack water is three o'clock – and I must be out of the channel before that?'

'Yes, Mister Harry. I told them they must finish loading before two hundred hours.'

'All right then – what about the drop off?'

'Your drop off will be twenty-five miles due east of Rastafa Point.'

'Fine.' I could check my bearings off the lighthouse at Rastafa. It was good and simple.

'You will drop off to a dhow-rigged schooner, a big one. Your recognition signal will be the same. Two lanterns on the mast, you will flash twice at thirty seconds, and the lower lamp will extinguish. You can then off load. They will provide labour and will put down an oil slick for you to ride in. I think that is all.'

'Except for the money.'

'Except for the money, of course.' He produced an envelope from the front pocket of his apron. I took it gingerly between thumb and forefinger and glanced at his calculations scribbled in ballpoint on the envelope.

'Half up front, as usual, the rest on delivery,' he pointed out.

That was thirty-five hundred, less twenty-one hundred for Coker's commission and Daly's pay-off. It left fourteen hundred, out of which I had to find the bonus for Chubby and Angelo – a thousand dollars – not much over.

I grimaced. 'I'll be waiting outside your office at nine o'clock tomorrow morning, Mr Coker.'

'I'll have a cup of coffee ready for you, Mister Harry.'

'That had better not be all,' I told him, and he laughed and stooped once more over the marble slab.

We cleared Grand Harbour in the late afternoon, and I made a fake run down the channel towards Mutton Point for the benefit of a possible watcher with binoculars on Coolie Peak. As darkness fell, I came around on to my true heading, and we went in through the inshore channel and the islands towards the wide tidal mouth of the Duza River.

There was no moon but the stars were big and the break of surf flared with phosphorescence, ghostly green in the afterglow of the setting sun.

I ran *Dancer* in fast, picking up my marks successively – the loom of an atoll in the starlight, the break of a reef, the very run and chop of the water guided me through the channels and warned of shoals and shallows.

Angelo and Chubby huddled beside me at the bridge rail. Occasionally one of them would go below to brew more of the powerful black coffee, and we sipped at the steaming mugs, staring out into the night watching for a flash of paleness that was not breaking water but the hull of a patrol boat.

Once Chubby broke the silence. 'Hear from Wally you had some trouble up at the fort last night.'

'Some,' I agreed.

'Wally had to take him up to the hospital afterwards.'

'Wally still got his job?' I asked.

'Only just. The man wanted to lock him up but Wally was too big.'

Angelo joined in. 'Judith was up at the airport at lunch time. Went up to fetch a crate of school books, and she saw him going out on the plane to the mainland.'

'Who?' I asked.

'Inspector Daly, he went across on the noon plane.'

'Why didn't you tell me before?'

'Didn't think it was important, Harry.'

'No,' I agreed. 'Perhaps it isn't.'

There were a dozen reasons why Daly might go out to the mainland, none of them remotely connected with my business. Yet it made me feel uneasy – I didn't like that kind of animal prowling around in the undergrowth when I was taking a risk.

'Wish you'd brought that piece of yours, Harry,' Chubby repeated mournfully, and I said nothing but wished the same.

The flow of the tide had smoothed the usual turmoil at the entrance to the southern channel of the Duza and I groped blindly for it in the dark. The mud banks on each side were latticed with standing fish traps laid by the tribal fishermen, and they helped to define the channel at last.

When I was sure we were in the correct entrance, I killed both engines and we drifted silently on the incoming tide. All of us listened with complete concentration for the engine beat of a patrol boat, but there was only the cry of a night heron and the splash of mullet leaping in the shallows.

Ghost silent, we were swept up the channel; on each side the dark masses of mangrove trees hedged us in and the smell of the mud swamps was rank and fetid on the moisture-laden air.

The starlight danced in spots of light on the dark agitated surface of the channel, and once a long narrow dugout canoe slid past us like a crocodile, the phosphorescence gleaming on the paddles of the two fishermen returning from the mouth. They paused to watch us for a moment and then drove on without calling a greeting, disappearing swiftly into the gloom.

'That was bad,' said Angelo.

'We will be drinking a lager in the Lord Nelson before they could tell anyone who matters.' I knew that most of the fishermen on this coast kept their own secrets, close with words like most of their kind. I was not perturbed by the sighting.

Looking ahead I saw the first bend coming up, and the current began to push *Dancer* out towards the far bank. I hit the starter buttons, the engines murmured into life, and I edged back into the deep water.

We worked our way up the snaking channel, coming out at last into the broad placid reach where the mangrove ended and firm ground rose gently on each side.

A mile ahead I saw the tributary mouth of the Salsa as a dark break in the bank, screened by tall stands of fluffy headed reeds. Beyond it the twin signal lanterns glowed yellow and soft, one upon the other.

'What did I tell you, Chubby, a milk run.'

'We aren't home yet.' Chubby the eternal optimist.

'Okay, Angelo. Get up on the bows. I'll tell you when to drop the hook.'

We crept on down the channel and I found the words of the nursery rhyme running through my mind as I locked

96

the wheel and took the hand spotlight from the locker below the rail.

'Three, Four, knock at the door, Five, Six, pick up sticks.'

I thought briefly of the hundreds of great grey beasts that had died for the sake of their teeth – and I felt a draught of guilt blow coldly along my spine at my complicity in the slaughter. But I turned my mind away from it by lifting the spotlight and aiming the agreed signal upstream at the burning lanterns.

Three times I flashed the recognition code but I was level with the signal lanterns before the bottom one was abruptly extinguished.

'Okay, Angelo. Let her go,' I called softly as I killed the engines. The anchor splashed over and the chain ran noisily in the silence. *Dancer* snubbed up, and swung around at the restraint of the anchor, facing back down the channel.

Chubby went to break out the cargo nets for loading, but I paused by the rail, peering across at the signal lantern. The silence was complete, except for the clink and croak of the swamp frogs in the reed banks of the Salsa.

In that silence I felt more than heard the beat like that of a giant's heart. It came in through the soles of my feet rather than my ears.

There is no mistaking the beat of an Allison marine diesel. I knew that the old Second World War Rolls-Royce marines had been stripped out of the Zinballa crash boats and replaced by Allisons, and right now the sound I was feeling was the idling note of an Allison marine.

'Angelo,' I tried to keep my voice low, but at the same time transmit my urgency. 'Slip the anchor. For Christ's sake! Quick as you can.'

For just such an emergency I had a shackle pin in the chain, and I thanked the Lord for that as I dived for the controls.

As I started engines, I heard the thump of the four-pound hammer as Angelo drove out the pin. Three times he struck, and then I heard the end of the chain splash overboard.

'She's gone, Harry,' Angelo called, and I threw *Dancer* in to drive and pushed open the throttles. She bellowed angrily and the wash of her propellers spewed whitely from below her counter as she sprang forward.

Although we were facing downstream, *Dancer* had a five-knot current running into her teeth and she did not jump away handily enough.

Even above our own engines I heard the Allisons give tongue, and from out of the reed-screened mouth of the Salsa tore a long deadly shape.

Even by starlight, I recognized her immediately, the widely flared bows, and the lovely thrusting lines, grey-hound waisted and the square chopped-off stern – one of the Royal Navy crash boats who had spent her best days in the Channel and now was mouldering into senility on this fever coast.

The darkness was kind to her, covering the rust stains and the streaky paintwork, but she was an old woman now. Stripped of her marvellous Rolls marines – and underpowered with the more economical Allisons. In a fair run *Dancer* would toy with her – but this was no fair run and she had all the speed and power she needed as she charged into the channel to cut us off, and when she switched on her battle lights they hit us like something solid. Two glaring white beams, blinding in their intensity so I had to throw up my hand to protect my eyes.

She was dead ahead now, blocking the channel, and on her foredeck I could see the shadowy figures of the gun crew crouching around the three-pounder on its wide traversing plate. The muzzle seemed to be looking directly into my left nostril – and I felt a wild and desperate despair.

98

It was a meticulously planned and executed ambush. I thought of ramming her, she had a marine ply wooden hull, probably badly rotted, and *Dancer's* fibreglass bows might stand the shock – but with the current against her *Dancer* was not making sufficient speed through the water.

Then suddenly a bull-horn bellowed electronically from the dark behind the dazzling battle lights.

'Heave to, Mr Fletcher. Or I shall be forced to fire upon you.'

One shell from the three-pounder would chop us down, and she was a quick firer. At this range they would smash us into a blazing wreck within ten seconds.

I closed down the throttles.

'A wise decision, Mr Fletcher – now kindly anchor where you are,' the bull-horn squawked.

'Okay, Angelo,' I called wearily, and waited while he rigged and dropped the spare anchor. Suddenly my arm was very painful again – for the last few hours I had forgotten about it.

'I said we should have brought that piece,' Chubby muttered beside me.

'Yeah, I'd love to see you shooting it out with that dirty great cannon, Chubby. That would be a lot of laughs.'

The crash boat manoeuvred alongside inexpertly, with gun and lights still trained on us. We stood helplessly in the blinding illumination of the battle lights and waited. I didn't want to think, I tried to feel nothing – but a spiteful inner voice sneered at me.

'Say good-bye to *Dancer*, Harry old sport, this is where the two of you part company.'

There was more than a good chance that I would be facing a firing squad in the near future – but that didn't worry me as much as the thought of losing my boat. With *Dancer* I was Mister Harry, the damnedest fellow on St Mary's and one of the top billfish men in the whole cock-eyed world. Without her, I was just another punk trying to scratch his next meal together. I'd prefer to be dead.

The crash boat careered into our side, bending the rail and scraping off a yard of our paint before they could hook on to us.

'Motherless bastards,' growled Chubby, as half a dozen armed and uniformed figures poured over our side, in a chattering undisciplined rabble. They wore navy blue bell bottoms and bum-freezers with white flaps down the back of the neck, white and blue striped vests, and white berets with red pom-poms on the top – but the cut of the uniform was Chinese and they brandished long AK.47 automatic assault rifles with forward-curved magazines and wooden butts.

Fighting amongst themselves for a chance to get in a kick or a shove with a gun butt, they drove the three of us down into the saloon, and knocked us into the bench seat against the for'ard bulkhead. We sat there shoulder to shoulder while two guards stood over us with machine-guns a few inches from our noses, and fingers curved hopefully around the triggers.

'Now I know why you paid me that five hundred dollars, boss,' Angelo tried to make a joke of it, and a guard screamed at him and hit him in the face with the gun butt. He wiped his mouth, smearing blood across his chin, and none of us joked again.

The other armed seamen began to tear *Dancer* to pieces. I suppose it was meant to be a search, but they raged through her accommodation wantonly smashing open lockers or shattering the panelling.

One of them discovered the liquor cabinet, and although there were only one or two bottles, there was a roar of approval. They squabbled noisily as seagulls over a scrap of offal, then went on to loot the galley stores with appropriate hilarity and abandon. Even when their commanding officer was assisted by four of his crew to make the hazardous journey across the six inches of open space that separated the crash boat from *Dancer*, there was no diminution in the volume of shouting and laughter and the crash of shattering woodwork and breaking glass.

The commander wheezed heavily across the cockpit and stooped to enter the saloon. He paused there to regain his breath.

He was one of the biggest men I had ever seen, not less than six foot six tall and enormously gross – a huge swollen body with a belly like a barrage balloon beneath the white uniform jacket. The jacket strained at its brass buttons and sweat had soaked through at the armpits. Across his breast he wore a glittering burst of stars and medals, and amongst them I recognized the American Naval Cross and the 1918 Victory Star.

His head was the shape and colour of a polished black iron pot, the type they traditionally use for cooking missionaries, and a naval cap, thick with gold braid, rode at a jaunty angle upon it. His face ran with rivers of glistening sweat, as he struggled noisily with his breathing and mopped at the sweat, staring at me with bulging eyes.

Slowly his body began to inflate, swelling even larger, like a great bullfrog, until I grew alarmed – expecting him to burst.

The purple-black lips, thick as tractor tyres, parted and an unbelievable volume of sound issued from the pink cavern of his mouth.

'Shut up!' he roared. Instantly his crew of wreckers froze into silence, one of them with his gun butt still raised to attack the panelling behind the bar.

The huge officer trundled forward, seeming to fill the entire saloon with his bulk. Slowly he sank into the padded leather seat. Once more he mopped at his face, then he looked at me again and slowly his whole face lit up into the most wonderfully friendly smile, like an enormous chubby and lovable baby; his teeth were big and flawlessly white and his eyes nearly disappeared in the rolls of smiling black flesh.

'Mr Fletcher, I can't tell you what a great pleasure this is for me.' His voice was deep and soft and friendly, the accent was British upper class – almost certainly acquired at some higher seat of learning. His English was better than mine.

'I have looked forward to meeting you for a number of years.'

'That's very decent of you to say so, Admiral.' With that uniform he could not rank less.

'Admiral,' he repeated with delight, 'I like that,' and he laughed. It began with a vast shaking of belly and ended with a gasping and straining for breath. 'Alas, Mr Fletcher, you are deceived by appearances,' and he preened a little, touching the medals and adjusting the peak of his cap. 'I am only a humble Lieutenant Commander.'

'That's really tough, Commander.'

'No. No, Mr Fletcher – do not waste your sympathy on me. I wield all the authority I could wish for.' He paused for deep breathing exercises and to wipe away the fresh ooze of sweat. 'I hold the powers of life and death, believe me.'

'I believe you, sir,' I told him earnestly. 'Please don't feel you have to prove your point.'

He shouted with laughter again, nearly choked, coughed up something large and yellow, spat it on to the floor and then told me, 'I like you, Mr Fletcher, I really do. I think a sense of humour is very important. I think you and I could become very close friends.' I doubted it, but I smiled encouragingly.

'As a mark of my esteem you may use the familiar form when addressing me – Suleiman Dada.'

102

'I appreciate that – I really do, Suleiman Dada, and you may call me Harry.'

'Harry,' he said. 'Let's have a dram of whisky together.' At that moment another man entered the saloon. A slim boyish figure, dressed not in his usual colonial police uniform but in a lightweight silk suit and lemon-coloured silk shirt and matching tie, with alligator-skin shoes on his feet.

The light blond hair was carefully combed forward into a cow's lick, and the fluffy moustache was trim as ever, but he walked carefully, seeming to favour an injury. I grinned at him.

'So, how does the old ball-bag feel now, Daly?' I asked kindly, but he did not answer and went to sit across from Lieutenant Commander Suleiman Dada.

Dada reached out a huge black paw and relieved one of his men of the Scotch whisky bottle he carried, part of my previous stock, and he gestured to another to bring glasses from the shattered liquor cabinet.

When we all had half a tumbler of Scotch in our hands, Dada gave us the toast.

'To lasting friendship, and mutual prosperity.' We drank, Daly and I cautiously, Dada deeply and with evident pleasure. While his head was tilted back and his eyes closed, the crew man attempted to retrieve the bottle of Scotch from the table in front of him.

Without lowering the glass Dada hit him a mighty open-handed clout across the side of the head, a blow that snapped his head back and hurled him across the saloon to crash into the shattered liquor cabinet. He slid down the bulkhead and sat stunned on the deck, shaking his head dazedly. Suleiman Dada, despite his bulk, was a quick and fearsomely powerful man, I realized.

He emptied the glass, set it down, and refilled it. He looked at me now, and his expression changed. The clown

103

had disappeared, despite the ballooning rolls of flesh, I was confronting a shrewd, dangerous and utterly ruthless opponent.

'Harry, I understand that you and Inspector Daly were interrupted in the course of a recent discussion,' and I shrugged.

'All of us here are reasonable men, Harry, of that I am certain.' I said nothing, but studied the whisky in my glass with deep attention. 'This is very fortunate – for let us consider what might happen to an unreasonable man in your position.' He paused, gargled a little with a sip of whisky. Sweat had formed like a rash of little white blisters on his nose and chin. He wiped it away. 'First of all, an unreasonable man might watch while his crew were taken out one at a time and executed. We use pickaxe handles here. It is a gruelling business, and Inspector Daly assures me that you have a special relationship with these two men.' Beside me Chubby and Angelo shifted uneasily in their seats. 'Then an unreasonable man would have his boat taken in to Zinballa Bay. Once that happened there would be no way in which it would ever be returned to him. It would be officially confiscated, out of my humble hands.' He paused, and showed me the humble hands, stretching them towards me. They would have fitted a bull gorilla. We both stared at them for a moment. 'Then the unreasonable man might find himself in Zinballa jail – which, as you are probably aware, is a maximum security political prison.'

I had heard of Zinballa prison, as had everyone on the coast. Those who came out of it were either dead or broken in body and spirit. They called it the 'Lion Cage'.

'Suleiman Dada, I want you to know that I am one of nature's original reasonable men,' I assured him, and he laughed again.

'I was certain of it,' he said. 'I can tell one a mile off,' then again he was serious. 'If we leave here immediately,

104

before the turn of the tide we can be out of the inshore channel before midnight.'

'Yes,' I agreed, 'that we could.'

'Then you could lead us to this place of interest, wait while we satisfy ourselves as to your good faith – which I for one do not doubt one moment – you and your crew will then be free to sail away in your magnificent boat and you could sleep tomorrow night in your own bed.'

'Suleiman Dada – you are a generous and cultivated man. I also have no reason to doubt your good faith,' – no more than that of Materson and Guthrie, I silently qualified the statement – 'and I have a peculiarly intense desire to sleep tomorrow night in my own bed.'

Daly spoke for the first time, snarling quietly under his little moustache. 'I think you should know that a turtle fisherman saw your boat anchored in the lagoon across the channel from the Old Men and Gunfire Reef on the night before the shooting incident – we will expect to be taken that way.'

'I have nothing against a man who takes a bribe, Daly – God knows I have done so myself – but then where is the honour among thieves that the poet sings of?' I was very disappointed in Daly, but he ignored my recriminations.

'Don't try any more of your tricks,' he warned me.

'You really are a champion turd, Daly. I could win prizes with you.'

'Please, gentlemen.' Dada held up his hands to halt my flow of rhetoric. 'Let us all be friends. Another small glass of whisky – and then Harry will take us all on a tour of interest.' Dada topped up our glasses, and paused before drinking again. 'I think I should warn you, Harry – I do not like rough water. It does not agree with me. If you take me into rough water I shall be very very angry. Do we understand each other?'

'Just for you I shall command the waters to stand still,

Suleiman Dada,' I assured him, and he nodded solemnly, as though it was the very least he expected.

The dawn was like a lovely woman rising from the couch of the sea, soft flesh tones and pearly light, the cloud strands like her hair tresses flowing and tousled, gilded blonde by the early sunlight.

We ran northwards, hugging the quieter waters of the inshore channel. Our order of sailing placed *Wave Dancer* in the van, she ambled along like a blood filly mouthing the snaffle, while half a mile astern the crash boat waddled and wallowed, as the Allisons tried to push her up on to the plane. We were headed for the Old Men and Gunfire Reef.

On board *Dancer* I had the con, standing alone at the wheel upon the open bridge. Behind me stood Peter Daly, and an armed seaman from the crash boat.

In the saloon below us, Chubby and Angelo still sat on the bench seat and three more seamen, armed with assault rifles, kept them there.

Dancer had been looted of all her galley stores, so none of us had breakfasted, not even a cup of coffee.

The first paralysing despair of capture had passed – and I was now thinking frenetically, trying to plot my way out of the maze in which I was trapped.

I knew that if I showed Daly and Dada the break at Gunfire Reef they would either explore it and find nothing – which was the most likely for whatever had been there was now packaged and deposited at Big Gull Island – or they would find some other evidence at the break. In both cases I was in for unpleasantness – if they found nothing Daly would have the very great pleasure of connecting me up to the electrical system in an attempt to make me talk.

If they found something definite my presence would become superfluous – and a dozen eager seamen would vie for the job of executioner. I didn't like the sound of pick-handles – it promised to be a messy business.

Yet the chances of escape seemed remote. Although she was half a mile astern the three-pounder of the foredeck of Dada's crash boat kept us on an effective leash, and we had aboard Daly and four members of the goon squad.

I lit my first cheroot of the day and its effect was miraculous, almost immediately I seemed to see a pinprick of light at the end of the long dark tunnel. I thought about it a little longer, puffing quietly on the black tobacco, and it seemed worth a try – but first I had to talk to Chubby.

'Daly,' I turned to speak over my shoulder. 'You had better get Chubby up here to take the wheel, I have got to go below.'

'Why?' he demanded suspiciously. 'What are you going to do?'

'Let's just say that whatever it is happens every morning at this time, and nobody else can do it for me. If you make me say more, I shall blush.'

'You should have been on the stage, Fletcher. You really slay me.'

'Funny you should mention that. It had crossed my mind.'

He sent the guard to fetch Chubby from the saloon, and I handed the con to him.

'Stick around, I want to talk to you later,' I muttered out of the side of my mouth and clambered down into the cockpit. Angelo brightened a little when I entered the saloon, and flashed a good imitation of the old bright grin, but the three guards, clearly bored, turned their weapons on me enthusiastically and I raised my hands hurriedly.

'Easy, boys, easy,' I soothed them and sidled past them

down the companionway. However, two of them followed me. When I reached the heads they would have entered with me and kept me company. 'Gentlemen,' I protested, 'if you continue to point those things at me during the next few critical moments you will probably pioneer the sovereign cure for constipation.' They scowled at me uncertainly and as I closed the door firmly upon them I added, 'But you really don't want a Nobel prize – do you?'

When I opened it again they were waiting in exactly the same attitudes, as though they had not moved. With a conspiratory gesture I beckoned them to follow. Immediately they showed interest, and I led them to the master cabin. Below the big double bunk I had spent many hours building in a concealed locker. It was about the size of a coffin, and was ventilated. It would accommodate a man lying prone. During the time when I was running human cargo it had been a hidey hole in case of a search – but now I used it as a store for valuables and illicit or dangerous cargo. It contained at the present time five hundred rounds of ammunition for the FN, a wooden crate of hand grenades, and two cases of Chivas Regal Scotch whisky.

With exclamations of delight the two guards slung their machine-guns on their shoulder straps and dragged out the whisky cases. They had forgotten about me and I slipped away and returned to the bridge. I stood next to Chubby, delaying the moment of take-over.

'You took your time,' growled Daly.

'Never rush a good thing,' I explained, and he lost interest and strolled back to stare across our wake at the following gunboat.

'Chubby,' I whispered. 'Gunfire Break. You told me once there was a passage through the reef from the landward side.'

'At high springs, for a whaleboat and a good man with a steady nerve,' he agreed. 'I did it when I was a crazy kid.'

'It's high spring in three hours. Could I run *Dancer* through?' I asked.

Chubby's expression changed. 'Jesus!' he whispered, and turned to stare at me in disbelief.

'Could I do it?' I insisted quietly, and he sucked his teeth noisily, looking away at the sunrise, scratching the bristles of his chin.

Then suddenly he reached an opinion, and spat over the side. 'You might, Harry – but nobody else I know could.'

'Give me the bearings, Chubby, quickly.'

'It was a long time ago, but,' sketchily he described the approach, and the passage of the break, 'there are three turns in the passage, left right then left again, then there is a narrow neck, brain coral on each hand – *Dancer* might just get through but she'll leave some paint behind. Then you are into the big pool at the back of the main reef. There is room to circle there and wait for the right sea before you shoot the gap out into the open water.'

'Thanks, Chubby,' I whispered. 'Now go below. I let the guards have the spare whisky. By the time I start my run for the break they will be blasted right out through the top of their skulls. I will signal three stamps on the deck, then it will be up to you and Angelo to get those pieces away from them and wrap them up tightly.'

The sun was well up, and the triple-peaked silhouette of the Old Men was rising only a few miles dead ahead when I heard the first raucous shout of laughter and crash of breaking furniture below. Daly ignored it and we ran on over the quiet inshore waters towards the reverse side of Gunfire Reef. Already I could see the jagged line of the Reef, like the black teeth of an ancient shark. Beyond it the tall oceanic surf flashed whitely as it burst, and beyond that lay the open sea.

I edged in towards the reef, and eased open the throttles a fraction. *Dancer*'s engine beat changed, but not enough to alert Daly. He lounged against the rail, bored and unshaven and probably missing his breakfast. I could distinctly hear the boom of the surf on coral now, and from below, the sounds of revelry became continuous. Daly noticed at last, frowned and told the other guard to go below and investigate. The guard, also bored, disappeared below with alacrity and never returned.

I glanced astern. My increase in speed was slowly opening the gap between *Dancer* and the crash boat, and steadily we edged in closer to the reef.

I was looking ahead anxiously, trying to pick up the marks and bearings that Chubby had described to me. Gently I touched the throttles, opening them another notch. The crash boat fell a little farther astern.

Suddenly I saw the entrance to Gunfire Break a thousand yards ahead. Two pinnacles of old weathered coral marked it, and I could see the colour difference of clear sea water pouring through the gap in the coral barrier.

Below there was another screech of wild laughter, and one of the guards reeled drunkenly into the cockpit. He reached the rail only just in time and vomited copiously into the wake. Then his legs gave way and he collapsed on to the deck and lay in an abandoned huddle.

Daly let out an angry exclamation and raced down the ladder. I took the opportunity to push the throttles open another two notches.

I stared ahead, gathering myself for the effort. I must try and open the gap between *Dancer* and her escort a little more, every inch would help to confound her gunners.

I planned to come up level with the channel, and then commit *Dancer* to it under full power, risking the submerged coral fangs rather than test the aim of the gunners aboard the crash boat. It was half a mile of narrow, tortuous channel through the coral before we reached the open sea. For most of it, *Dancer* would be partially screened by coral outcrops, and the weaving of the channel would help to confuse the range of the three-pounder. I was hoping also that the surf working through the gap would give *Dancer* plenty of up-and-down movement, so that she would heave and weave unpredictably like one of those little ducks in a shooting gallery.

One thing was certain: that intrepid mariner, Lieutenant Commander Suleiman Dada, would not risk pursuit through the channel, so I could give his gun layer a rapidly increasing range to contend with.

I ignored the alcoholic din from below, and I watched the mouth of the channel approach rapidly. I found myself hoping that the seamanship of the crash boat's crew and commander was a faithful indication of their marksmanship.

Suddenly Peter Daly flew up the ladder to confront me. His face was pink with anger and his moustache tried to bristle its silky hairs. His mouth worked for a moment before he could speak.

'You gave them the liquor, Fletcher. Oh, you crafty bastard.'

'Me?' I asked indignantly. 'I wouldn't do a thing like that.'

'They're drunk as pigs – all of them,' he shouted, then he turned and looked over the stern. The crash boat was a mile behind us, and the distance was increasing.

'You are up to something,' he shrilled at me, and groped in the side pocket of his silk jacket. At that moment we came level with the entrance to the channel.

I hit both throttles wide open, and *Dancer* bellowed and hurled herself forward.

Still groping in his pocket, Daly was thrown off balance. He staggered backwards, still shouting.

I spun the wheel to full right lock, and *Dancer* whirled like a ballet dancer. Daly changed the direction of his stagger, thrown wildly across the deck he came up hard

111

against the side rail as *Dancer* leaned over steeply in her turn. At that moment Daly dragged a small nickelled-silver automatic from his side pocket. It looked like a .25, the type ladies carry in their handbags.

I left *Dancer*'s wheel for an instant. Stooping, I got my hand on Daly's ankles and lifted sharply. 'Leave us now, comrade,' I said as he went backwards over the rail, falling twelve feet, striking the lower deck rail a glancing blow and then splashing untidily into the water alongside.

I darted back to the wheel, catching *Dancer*'s head before she could pay off, and at the same time stamping three times on the deck.

As I lined *Dancer* up for the entrance I heard the shouts of conflict in the saloon below, and winced as a machine-gun fired with a sound like ripping cloth – Barrapp – and bullets exploded out through the deck behind me, leaving a jagged hole edged with white splinters. At least they were fired at the roof, and were unlikely to have hit either Angelo or Chubby.

Just before I entered the coral portals, I glanced back once more. The crash boat still lumbered along a mile behind, while Daly's head bobbed in the churning white wake. I wondered if they would reach him before the sharks did.

Then there was no more time for idle speculation. As *Dancer* dashed headlong into the channel I was appalled by the task I had set her.

I could have leant over and touched coral outcrops on each hand, and I could see the sinister shape of more coral lurking below the shallow turbulent waters ahead. The waters had expended most of their savagery on the long twisting run through the channel, but the farther in we went the wilder they would become, making *Dancer*'s response to the helm just that much more unpredictable.

The first bend in the channel showed ahead, and I put

112

Dancer to it. She came around willingly, swishing her bottom, and with only a trifling yaw that pushed her outwards towards the menacing coral.

As I straightened her into the next stretch, Chubby came swarming up the ladder. He was grinning hugely. Only two things put him into that sort of mood – and one of them was a good punch up. He had skinned his right knuckle.

'All quiet below, Harry. Angelo's looking after them.' He glanced around. 'Where's the policeman?'

'He went for a swim.' I did not take my attention from the channel. 'Where is the crash boat? What are they doing?'

Chubby peered across at her. 'No change. It doesn't seem to have sunk in yet – hold on, though—' his voice changed, ' – yes, there they go. They are manning the deck gun.'

We drove on swiftly down the channel, and I risked a quick glance backwards. At that instant I saw the long streak of white cordite smoke blow like a feather from the three-pounder, and an instant later there was the sharp crack of shot passing high overhead, followed immediately by the flat report of the shot.

'Ready for it now, Harry. Left-hander coming up.'

We swept into the next turn, and the next round fell short, bursting in a shower of fragment and blue smoke on one of the coral heads fifty yards off our beam.

I coaxed *Dancer* smoothly into the turn, and as we went into it another shell fell in our wake, lifting a tall and graceful column of white water high above the bridge. The following wind blew the spray over us.

We were halfway through now, and the waves that rushed to meet us were six feet high and angry with the restraint enforced upon them by the walls of coral.

The guncrew of the crash boat were making alarmingly

erratic practice. A round burst five hundred yards astern, then the next went between Chubby and me, a stunning blaze of passing shot that sent me reeling in the backwash of disrupted air.

'Here's the neck now,' Chubby called anxiously and my spirit quailed as I saw how the channel narrowed and how bridge-high buttresses of coral guarded it.

It seemed impossible that *Dancer* would pass through so narrow an opening.

'Here we go, Chubby, cross your fingers,' and, still under full throttle, I put *Dancer* at the neck. I could see him grasping the rail with both hands, and I expected the stainless steel to bend with the strength of his grip.

We were halfway through when we hit, with a jarring rending crash. *Dancer* lurched and hesitated.

At the same moment another shell burst alongside. It showered the bridge with coral chips and humming steel fragments, but I hardly noticed it as I tried to ease *Dancer* through the gap.

I sheered off the wall, and the tearing scraping sound ran along our starboard side. For a moment we jammed solidly, then another big green wave raced down on us, lifting us free of the coral teeth and we were through the neck. *Dancer* lunged ahead.

'Go below, Chubby,' I shouted. 'Check if we holed the hull.' Blood was dripping from a fragment scratch on his chin, but he dived down the ladder.

With another stretch of open water ahead, I could glance back at the crash boat. She was almost obscured by an intervening block of coral, but she was still firing rapidly and wildly. She seemed to have heaved to at the entrance to the channel, probably to pick up Daly – but I knew she would not attempt to follow us now. It would take her four hours to work her way round to the main channel beyond the Old Men.

The last turn in the channel came up ahead, and again *Dancer*'s hull touched coral; the sound of it seemed to tear into my own soul. Then at last we burst out into the deep pool in the back of the main reef, a circular arena of deep water three hundred yards across, fenced in by coral walls and open only through the Gunfire Break to the wild surf of the Indian Ocean.

Chubby appeard at my shoulder once more. 'Tight as a mouse's ear, Harry. Not taking on a drop.' Silently I applauded my darling.

Now for the first time we were in full view of the gun crew half a mile away across the reef, and my turn into the pool presented *Dancer* to them broadside. As though they sensed that this was their last chance they poured shot after shot at us.

It fell about us in great leaping spouts, too close to allow me any latitude of decision. I swung *Dancer* again, aimed her at the narrow break, and let her race for the gap in Gunfire Reef.

I committed her and when we had passed the point of no return, I felt my belly cramp up with horror as I looked ahead through the gap to the open sea. It seemed as though the whole ocean was rearing up ahead of me, gathering itself to hurl down upon the frail little vessel like some rampaging monster.

'Chubby,' I called hollowly. 'Will you look at that.'

'Harry,' he whispered, 'this a good time to pray.'

And *Dancer* ran out bravely to meet this freak Goliath of the sea.

It came up, humping monstrous shoulders as it charged, higher and higher still it rose, a glassy green wall and I could hear it rustling – like wildfire in dry grass.

Another shot passed close overhead but I hardly noticed it, as *Dancer* threw up her head and began to climb that mountainous wave.

115

It was turning pale green along the crest high above, beginning to curl, and *Dancer* went up as though she were on an elevator.

The deck canted steeply, and we clung helplessly to the rail.

'She's going over backwards,' Chubby shouted, as she began to stand on her tail. 'She's turtling, man!'

'Go through her,' I called to *Dancer*. 'Cut through the green!' and as though she heard me she lunged with her sharp prow into the curl of the wave an instant before it could fall upon us and crush the hull.

It came aboard us in a roaring green horror, solid sheets of it swept *Dancer* from bows to stern, six feet deep, and she lurched as though to a mortal blow.

Then suddenly we burst out through the back of the wave, and below us was a gaping valley, a yawning abyss into which *Dancer* hurled herself, falling free, a gut-swooping drop down into the trough.

We hit with a sickening crash that seemed to stun her, and which threw Chubby and me to the deck. But as I dragged myself up again, *Dancer* shook herself free of the tons of water that had come aboard, and she ran on to meet the next wave.

It was smaller, and *Dancer* beat the curl and porpoised over her.

'That's my darling,' I shouted to her and she picked up speed, taking the third wave like a steeplechaser.

Somewhere close another three-pound shell cracked the sky, but then we were out and running for the long horizon of the ocean and I never heard another shot.

The guard who had passed out in the cockpit from an excess of Scotch whisky must have been washed overboard by the giant wave, for we never saw him again. The other three we left on a small island thirty miles north of St

Mary's where I knew there was water in a brackish well, and which would certainly be visited by fishermen from the mainland.

They had sobered by that time, and were all inflicted with nasty hangovers. They made three forlorn figures on the beach as we ran southwards into the dusk. It was dark when we crept into Grand Harbour. I picked up moorings, not tying up to the wharf at Admiralty. I did not want *Dancer*'s glaring injuries to become a subject of speculation around the island.

Chubby and Angelo went ashore in the dinghy – but I was too exhausted to make the effort, and dinnerless I collapsed across the double bunk in the master cabin and slept without moving until Judith woke me after nine in the morning. Angelo had sent her down with a dinner pail of fish cakes and bacon.

'Chubby and Angelo gone up to Missus Eddy's to buy some stores they need to repair the boat,' she told me. 'They'll be down soon now.'

I wolfed the breakfast and went to shave and shower. When I returned she was still there, sitting on the edge of the bunk. She clearly had something to discuss.

She brushed away my clumsy efforts at dressing my wound, and had me sit while she worked on it.

'Mister Harry, you aren't going to get my Angelo killed or jailed, are you?' she demanded. 'If you go on like this, I'm going to make him come ashore.'

'That's great, Judith.' I laughed at her concern. 'Why don't you send him across to Rawano for three years, while you sit here.'

'That's not kind, Mister Harry.'

'Life is not very kind, Judith,' I told her more gently. 'Angelo and I are both doing the best we can. Just to keep my boat afloat, I've got to take a few chances. Same with

117

Angelo. He told me that he's saved enough to buy you a nice little house up near the church. He got the money by running with me.'

She was silent while she finished the dressing, and when she would have turned to go I took her hand and drew her back. She would not look at me, until I took her chin and lifted her face. She was a lovely child, with great smoky eyes and a smoothly silken skin.

'Don't fuss yourself, Judith. Angelo is like a kid brother to me. I'll look after him.'

She studied my face a long moment. 'You really mean that, don't you?' she asked.

'I really do.'

'I believe you,' she said at last, and she smiled. Her teeth were very white against the golden amber skin. 'I trust you.'

Women are always saying that to me. 'I trust you.' So much for feminine intuition.

'You name one of your kids for me, hear?'

'The first one, Mister Harry.' Her smile blazed and her dark eyes flashed. 'That's a promise.'

'They do say that when you fall from a horse you should immediately ride him again – so as not to lose your nerve, Mister Harry.' Fred Coker sat at his desk in the travel agency, behind him a poster of a beefeater and Big Ben – 'England Swings', it said. We had just discussed at great length our mutual concern at Inspector Peter Daly's perfidious conduct, though I suspected that Fred Coker's concern was considerably less than mine. He had collected his commission in advance and nobody had put his head in a noose, nor had they almost wrecked his boat. We were now discussing the subject of whether or not our business arrangement should continue.

118

'They also say, Mr Coker, that a man with his buttocks hanging out of the holes in his trousers should not be too fussy,' I said, and Coker's spectacles glittered with satisfaction. He nodded his head.

'And that, Mister Harry, is probably the wiser of the two sayings,' he agreed.

'I'll take anything, Mr Coker. Body, box or sticks. Just one thing, the cost of dying has gone up to ten thousand dollars a run – all in advance.'

'Even at that price, we'll find work for you,' he promised, and I realized I had been working cheaply before.

'Soon,' I insisted.

'Very soon,' he agreed. 'You are fortunate. I do not think that Inspector Daly will be returning to St Mary's now. You will save the commission usually payable there.'

'He owes me that at least,' I agreed.

I made three night runs in the next six weeks. Two body carries, and a box job – all below the river into Portuguese waters. The bodies were both singles, silent black men dressed in jungle fatigues, and I took them far south, deep penetrations. They waded ashore on remote beaches and I wondered briefly upon what unholy missions they travelled – how much pain and death would arise from those secret landings.

The box job involved eighteen long wooden crates with Chinese markings. We picked up from a submarine out in the channel, and dropped off in a river-mouth, unloading into pairs of dugout canoes lashed together for stability. We spoke to no one and nobody challenged us.

They were milk runs and I cleared eighteen thousand dollars – enough to carry me and my crew through the off-season in the style to which we were accustomed. More important, the intervals of quiet and rest were sufficient to heal my wounds and give me back my strength. At first I lay for hours in the hammock under the palms, reading or

119

sleeping. Then as it came back to me, I swam and fished and sun-baked, went for oysters and crayfish – until I was hard and lean and sunbrowned again.

The wound healed into a thickened and irregular cicatrice, tribute to MacNab's surgical skills, it curled around my chest and on to my back like an angry purple dragon. In one thing he had been correct, the massive damage to my upper left arm left it stiff and weakened. I could not lift my elbow above shoulder-level, and I lost my title in Indian wrestling to Chubby in the bar of the Lord Nelson. However, I hoped that swimming and regular exercise would strengthen it.

As my strength returned so did my curiosity and sense of adventure. I began dreaming about the canvas-wrapped package off Big Gull Island. In one dream I swam down and opened the package – it contained a tiny feminine figure, the size of a Dresden doll, a golden mermaid with Sister May's lovely face and a truly startling bosom, the tail was the graceful sickle shape of a marlin's. The little mermaid smiled shyly and held out her hand to me. On her palm lay a shiny silver shilling.

'Sex, money and billfish—' I thought when I woke, '—good old uncomplicated Harry, real Freud food.' I knew then that pretty soon I would be going for Big Gull Island.

It was very late in the season before I could prevail on Fred Coker to arrange a straight fishing charter for me, and it turned sour as cheap wine. The party consisted of two overweight, flabby German industrialists with fat bejewelled wives. I worked hard for them, and put both men into fish.

The first was a good black marlin, but the party screwed down on his stardrag, freezing the reel while the fish was still green and crazy to run. It lifted the German's huge backside out of the seat, and before I could release the stardrag for him, it had my three hundred dollar rod down on the gunwale. The fibre-glass rod snapped like a matchstick.

The other member of the party, after losing two decent fish, panted and sweated three hours over a baby blue marlin. When he finally brought it to the gaff, I could hardly bring myself to put the steel in, and I was too ashamed to hang it on Admiralty. We took the photographs on board *Dancer* and I smuggled it ashore wrapped in a tarpaulin. Like Fred Coker I also have a reputation to preserve. The German industrialist, however, was so delighted by his prowess that he slipped an extra five hundred dollars into my avaricious little paw. I told him it was a truly magnificent fish which was a thousand-dollar lie. I always give good value. Then the wind backed into the south, the temperature of the water in the channel dropped four degrees and the fish were gone. For ten days we hunted far north but it was over, another season was past.

We stripped and cleaned all the billfish equipment and laid it away in thick yellow grease. I pulled *Dancer* up on to the slip at the fuelling basin and we went over her hull, cleaning it down, re-working the temporary patches I had put on the injuries she had received at Gunfire Reef.

Then we painted her until she glistened, sleek and lovely, before we refloated her and took her out to moorings. There we worked lackadaisically on her upper works, stripping varnish, sandpapering, re-varnishing, checking out the electrical system, re-soldering a connection here, replacing wiring there.

I was in no hurry. It would be three weeks before my next charter arrived – an expedition of marine biologists from a Canadian university.

In the meantime the days were cooler, and I was feeling the old glow of good health and bodily well-being again. I dined at Government House, sometimes as often as once a week, and each time I had to tell the full story of the shoot-out with Guthrie and Materson. President Biddle knew the story by heart and corrected me if I omitted a single detail. It always ended with the President crying excitedly, 'Show them your scar, Mister Harry,' and I had to open the starched front of my dress shirt at the dinner table.

They were good lazy days. The island life drifted placidly by. Peter Daly never returned to St Mary's – and at the end of six weeks, Wally Andrews was promoted to acting Inspector and commanding officer of the police force. One of his first acts was to return to me my FN carbine.

This quiet time was spiced by the secret tingle of anticipation which I felt. I knew that one day soon I was going back to Big Gull Island and the piece of unfinished business that lay there in the shallow limpid waters – and I teased myself with the knowledge.

Then one Friday evening I was rounding out the week with my crew in the bar of the Lord Nelson. Judith was with us, having replaced the flock that had previously gathered around Angelo on Friday nights. She was good for him, he no longer drank to the morbid stage.

Chubby and I had just begun the first duet of the evening and were keeping within a few beats of each other when Marion slipped into the seat beside me.

I put one arm around her shoulders and held my tankard to her lips while she drank thirstily, but the distraction caused me to forge even further ahead of Chubby in the song.

Marion worked on the switchboard at the Hilton Hotel. She was a pretty little thing with a sexy pugface and long straight black hair. It was she whom Mike Guthrie had used for a punch-bag so long ago.

When Chubby and I straggled to the end of the chorus,

Marion told me, 'There is a lady asking for you, Mister Harry.'

'What lady?'

'At the hotel, one of the guests, she came in on this morning's plane. She knew your name and everything. She wants to see you. I told her I would see you tonight and give you the message.'

'What is she like?' I asked Marion with interest.

'She's beautiful, Mister Harry. Such a lady too.'

'Sounds like my type,' I agreed, and ordered a pint for Marion.

'Aren't you going to see her now?'

'With you beside me, Marion, all the beautiful ladies of the world can wait until tomorrow.'

'Oh, Mister Harry, you are a real devil man,' she giggled, and snuggled a little closer.

'Harry,' said Chubby on my other side, 'I'm going to tell you now what I never told you before.' He took a long swallow from his tankard, then went on with sentimental tears swimming in his eyes. 'Harry, I love you, man. I love you better than my own brother.'

I went up to the Hilton a few minutes before midday. Marion came through from her cubicle behind the reception desk. She still had her earphones around her neck.

'She's waiting for you on the terrace.' She pointed across the vast reception area with its *ersatz* Hawaiian décor. 'The blonde lady in the yellow bikini.'

She was reading a magazine, lying on her belly on one of the reclining sun couches, and she had her back to me so my first impression was of masses of blonde hair, thick and shiny, teased up like the mane of a lion, then falling in a slick golden cascade.

She heard my footsteps on the paving. She glanced around, pushed her sunglasses up on top of her head, then she stood up to face me, and I realized that she was tiny, seeming to reach not much higher than my chest. The bikini also was tiny and showed a flat smooth belly with a deep navel, firm shoulders lightly tanned, small breasts, and a trim waist. Her legs had lovely lines and her neat little feet were thrust into open sandals, the nails painted clear red to match her long fingernails. Her hands as she pushed at her hair were small and shapely.

She wore heavy make-up, but wore it with rare skill, so that her skin had a soft pearly lustre and colour glowed subtly on her cheeks and lips. Her eyes had long dark artificial lashes, and the eyelids were touched with colour and line to give them an exotic oriental cast.

'Duck, Harry!' Something deep inside me shouted a warning, and I almost obeyed. I knew this type well, there had been others like her – small and purringly feline – I had scars to prove it, scars both physical and spiritual. However, one thing nobody can say about old Harry is that he runs for cover when the knickers are down.

Courageously I stepped forward, crinkling my eyes and twisting my mouth into the naughty small boy grin that usually dynamites them.

'Hello,' I said, 'I'm Harry Fletcher.'

She looked at me, starting at my feet and going up six feet four to the top where her gaze lingered speculatively and she pouted her lower lip.

'Hello,' she answered, her voice was husky, breathless-sounding – and carefully rehearsed. 'I'm Sherry North, Jimmy North's sister.'

We were on the veranda of the shack in the evening. It was cool and the sunset was a spectacular display of pyrotechnics that flamed and faded above the palms.

She was drinking a Pimms No. I filled with fruit and ice – one of my seduction specials – and she wore a kaftan of light floating stuff through which her body showed in shadowy outline as she stood against the rail backlit by the sunset. I could not be certain as to whether or not she wore anything beneath the kaftan – this and the tinkle of ice in her glass distracted me from the letter I was reading. She had showed it to me as part of her credentials. It was a letter from Jimmy North written a few days before his death. I recognized the handwriting and the turn of phrase was typical of that bright and eager lad. As I read on, I forgot the sister's presence in the memory of the past. It was a long bubbling letter, written as though to a loving friend, with veiled references to the mission and its successful outcome, the promise of a future in which there would be wealth and laughter and all good things.

I felt a pang of regret and personal loss for the boy in his lonely sea grave, for the lost dreams that drifted with him like rotting seaweed.

Then suddenly my own name leapt from that page at me, ' – you can't help liking him, Sherry. He's big and tough-looking, all scarred and beat up like an old tom cat that's been out alley-fighting every night. But under it, I swear he is really a softy. He seems to have taken a shine to me. Even gives me fatherly advice!—'

There was more in the same vein that embarrassed me so that my throat closed up and I took a swallow of whisky, which made my eyes water and the words swim, while I finished the letter and refolded it.

I handed it to Sherry, and walked away to the end of the veranda. I stood there for a while looking out over the bay.

The sun slid below the horizon and suddenly it was dark and chill.

I went back and lit the lamp, setting it up high so the glare did not fall in our eyes. She watched me in silence until I had poured another Scotch and settled in my cane-backed chair.

'Okay,' I said, 'you're Jimmy's sister. You've come to St Mary's to see me. Why?'

'You liked him, didn't you?' she asked, as she left the rail and came to sit beside me.

'I like a lot of people. It's a weakness of mine.'

'Did he die — I mean, was it like they said in the newspapers?'

'Yes,' I said. 'It was like that.'

'Did he ever tell you what they were doing out here?'

I shook my head. 'They were very cagey — and I don't ask questions.'

She was silent then, dipping long tapered fingers into her glass to pick out a slice of pineapple, nibbling at the fruit with small white teeth, dabbing at her lips with a pink pointed tongue like that of a cat.

'Because Jimmy liked and trusted you, and because I think you know more than you've told anyone, also because I need your help, I am going to tell you a story — okay?'

'I love stories,' I said.

'Have you heard of the "pogo stick"?' she asked.

'Sure, it's a child's toy.'

'It's also the code name for an American naval experimental vertical take-off all-weather strike aircraft.'

'Oh yes, I remember, I saw an article in *Time Magazine*. Questions in the Senate. I forget the details.'

'There was opposition to the fifty million development allocation.'

'Yes, I remember.'

'Two years ago, on the 16th August to be precise, a

prototype "pogo stick" took off from Rawano airforce base in the Indian Ocean. It was armed with four air-to-surface "killer whale" missiles, each of them equipped with tactical nuclear warheads—'

'That must have been a fairly lethal package.'

She nodded. 'The "killer whale" is designed as an entirely new concept in missiles. It is an anti-submarine device which will seek and track surfaced or submerged naval craft. It can kill an aircraft carrier or it can change its element – air for water – and go down a thousand fathoms to destroy enemy submarines.'

'Wow,' I said, and took a little more whisky. We were talking heady stuff now.

'Do you recall the 16th August that year – were you here?'

'I was here, but that's a long time ago. Refresh my memory.'

'Cyclone Cynthia,' she said.

'God, of course.' It had come roaring across the island, winds of 150 miles an hour, taking away the roof of the shack and almost swamping *Dancer* at her moorings in Grand Harbour. These cyclones were not uncommon in this area.

'The "pogo stick" took off from Rawano a few minutes before the typhoon struck. Twelve minutes later the pilot ejected and the aircraft went into the sea with her four nuclear missiles and her flight recorder still aboard. Rawano radar was blanked out by the typhoon. They were not tracking.'

It was starting to make some sort of sense at last.

'How does Jimmy fit into this?'

She made an impatient gesture. 'Wait,' she said, then went on. 'Do you have any idea what the value of that cargo might be in the open market?'

'I should imagine you could write your own cheque –

give or take a couple of million dollars.' And old bad Harry came to attention, he had been getting exercise lately and growing stronger.

Sherry nodded. 'The test pilot of the "pogo stick" was a Commander in the US Navy named William Bryce. The aircraft developed a fault at fifty thousand feet, just before he came out through the top of the weather. He fought her all the way down, he was a conscientious officer, but at five hundred feet he knew he wasn't going to make it. He ejected and watched the aircraft go in.'

She was speaking carefully, and her choice of words was odd, too technical for a woman. She had learned all this, I was certain – from Jimmy? Or from somebody else?

Listen and learn, Harry, I told myself.

'Billy Bryce was three days on a rubber raft on the ocean in a typhoon before the rescue helicopter from Rawano found him. He had time to do some thinking. One of the things he thought about was the value of that cargo – and he compared it to the salary of a Commander. His evidence at the court of inquiry omitted the fact that the "pogo stick" had gone down within sight of land, and that Bryce had been able to take a fix on a recognizable land feature before he was blown out to sea by the typhoon.'

I could not see any weakness in her story – it looked all right – and very interesting.

'The court of inquiry gave a verdict of "pilot error" and Bryce resigned his commission. His career was destroyed by that verdict. He decided to earn his own retirement annuity and also to clear his reputation. He was going to force the US Navy to buy back its "killer whale" missiles and to accept the evidence of the flight recorder.'

I was going to ask a question, but again Sherry stopped me with a gesture. She did not want her recital interrupted.

'Jimmy had done some work for the US Navy – a hull inspection of one of their carriers – and he had met Bryce at that time. They had become friends, and so Billy Bryce naturally came to Jimmy. Between them they had not sufficient capital for the expedition they needed to mount, so they planned to find financial backers. It isn't the kind of thing you can advertise in *The Times*, and they were working on it when Billy Bryce was killed in his Thunderbird on the M4 near the Heathrow turn-off.'

'There seems to be some sort of curse on this thing,' I said.

'Are you superstitious, Harry?' she asked, looking at me through those slanted tiger eyes.

'I don't knock it,' I admitted, and she nodded, seeming to file the information away before she went on.

'After Billy was dead, Jimmy went on with the project. He found backers. He wouldn't tell me who, but I guessed they were unsavoury. He came out here with them – and you know the rest.'

'I know the rest,' I agreed, and instinctively massaged the thickened scar tissue through the silk of my shirt. 'Except of course the site of the crash.'

We stared at each other.

'Did he tell you?' I asked, and she shook her head.

'Well, it was an interesting story.' I grinned at her. 'It's a pity we can't check out the truth of it.'

She stood up abruptly and went to the veranda rail. She hugged her arms and she was so angry that if she'd had a tail she would have switched it like a lioness.

I waited for her to recover, and the moment came when she shrugged her shoulders and turned back to me. Her smile was light.

'Well, that's that! I thought I was entitled to some of the rewards. Jimmy was my brother – and I came a long way to find you because he liked and trusted you. I thought we could work together – but I guess if you want it all, there's not much I can do about it.'

She shook out her hair, and it rippled and shone in the lamplight. I stood up.

'I'll take you home now,' I said, and touched her arm. She reached up with both arms, and her fingers locked in the thick curly hair at the back of my neck.

'It's a long way home,' she whispered, and pulled my head down, standing on her tiptoes.

Her lips were very soft and moist, and her tongue was thrusting and restless. After a while she drew back and smiled up at me, her eyes were unfocused and her breath was short and fast.

'Perhaps it wasn't a wasted journey, after all?'

I picked her up, and she was light as a child, hugging my neck, pressing her cheek to mine as I carried her into the shack. I learned long ago to eat hearty whenever there was food, because you never know when the famine is going to hit.

Even the soft light of dawn was cruel to her as she lay sprawled in sleep beneath the mosquito net on the big double bed. Her make-up had smeared and caked, and she slept with her mouth open. The mane of blonde hair was a tangled bush and it did not match the triangle of thick dark curls at the base of her belly. I felt repelled by her this morning, for I had learned during the night that Miss Sherry was a raving sadist.

I slipped out of the bed and stood over her a few moments, searching her sleeping face in vain for a resemblance to Jimmy North. I left her, and, still naked, walked out of the shack and down to the beach.

The tide was in and I plunged into the cool clear water and swam out to the entrance to the bay. I swam fast, driving hard in an Australian crawl, and the salt water stung the deep scratches in my back.

It was one of my lucky mornings, old friends were

waiting for me beyond the reef, a school of big bottle-nosed porpoise, who came flashing to meet me, their tall fins cutting the dark surface as they steeplechased over the swells. They circled me, whistling and snorting, the blow-holes in the tops of their heads gulping like tiny mouths and their own huge mouths fixed in idiotic grins of pleasure.

They teased me for ten minutes before one of the big old bulls allowed me to get a grip on his dorsal fin and gave me a tow. It was a thrilling sleigh ride that had the water creaming wildly about my chest and head. He took me half a mile offshore before the force of water tore me from his back.

It was a long swim back, with the bull dolphin circling me and giving me an occasional friendly prod in the backside, inviting me aboard for another ride. At the reef they whistled farewell and slid gracefully away, and I was happy when I waded ashore. The arm ached a little, but it was the healthy ache of healing and growing strength.

The bed was empty, and the bathroom door was locked. She was probably shaving her armpits with my razor, I thought. I felt a flare of annoyance, an old dog like me doesn't like his routine disturbed. I used the guest shower to sluice off the salt and my annoyance receded under the rush of hot water. Then fresh but unshaven and hungry as a python, I went through to the kitchen. I was frying gammon with pineapple and buttering thick cuts of toast when Sherry came into the kitchen.

She was once more immaculate. She must have carried a complete cosmetic counter in the Gucci handbag, and her hair was dressed and lacquered into its mane and fall.

Her smile was brilliant. 'Good morning, lover,' she said and came to kiss me lingeringly. I was now well disposed towards the world and all its creatures. I no longer felt repelled by this glittering woman. The fine mood of the

131

dolphins had returned and my gaiety must have been infectious. We laughed a lot over the meal and afterwards I took the coffee pot out on to the veranda.

'When are we going to find the pogo stick?' she asked suddenly, and I poured another mug of strong black coffee without answering. Sherry North had evidently decided that a night of her company had made me her slave for life. Now I may not be a connoisseur of women, but on the other hand I have had some little experience – I mean I'm not exactly a virgin – and I didn't rate Sherry North's charms as worth four killer whale missiles and the flight recorder of a secret strike aircraft.

'Just as soon as you show me the way,' I answered carefully. It is an old-fashioned feminine conceit that if a man pleasures them with skill and aplomb, then he must be made to pay for it. I have long believed that it should be the other way around.

She reached across and held my wrist, the tiger's eyes were suddenly big and soulful.

'After last night,' she whispered huskily, 'I know that there is a lot ahead of us, Harry. You and I, together.'

I had lain awake for hours during the night and reached my decision. Whatever lay in the package was not an entire aircraft, but probably some small part of it – something that identified it clearly. It was almost certainly not either the flight recorder or one of the missiles. Jimmy North would not have had sufficient time to remove the recorder from the fuselage, even if he had known where it was situated and had the proper tools. On the other hand the package was the wrong shape and size for a missile, it was a squat round object, not aerodynamically designed.

It was almost certainly some fairly innocuous object. If I took Sherry North with me to recover it, I would be playing only a minor card from my hand – although it would look like a major trump.

132

I would be giving nothing away, not the site of the crash at Gunfire Reef, nor any of the valuable objects associated with it.

On the other hand, I would be beating the tall grass for tigers. It would be very instructive to see exactly how Mademoiselle North reacted, once she thought she knew the site of the crash.

'Harry,' she whispered again. 'Please,' and she leaned closer. 'You must believe me. I have never felt like this before. From the first moment I saw you – I just knew—'

I roused myself from my calculations and leaned towards her, assuming an expression of simple-minded passion and lust.

'Darling—' I began but my voice choked up, and I enfolded her in a bear hug, feeling her stiffen irritably as I smeared her lipstick and ruffled the meticulously dressed hairstyle. I could sense the effort it required for her to respond with equal passion.

'Do you feel the same way?' she asked from the depths of my embrace, smothered against my chest, and for the fun of watching her play the role she had assigned herself, I picked her up again and carried her through to the frowsy rumpled bed.

'I will show you how I feel for you,' I muttered hoarsely.

'Darling,' she protested desperately, 'not now.'

'Why not?'

'We have so much to do. There will be time later – all the time in the world.' With a show of reluctance I set her down, although truthfully I was thankful for I knew that on top of a huge breakfast of gammon and three cups of coffee, it would have given me heartburn.

It was a few minutes after noon when I cleared Grand Harbour, and swung away south and east. I had told my crew to take a day ashore, I would not be fishing.

Chubby looked down at Sherry North, sprawled bikini-clad on the cockpit deck, and scowled noncommittally, but Angelo rolled his eyes expressively and asked, 'Pleasure cruise?' with a certain inflection.

'You've got a filthy mind,' I scolded him and he laughed delightedly, as though I had paid him the nicest compliment, and the two of them walked away up the wharf.

Dancer romped down the necklace of atolls and islands until, a little after three o'clock, I ran the deep-water passage between Little Gull Island and Big Gull Island, and rounded into the shallow open water between the east shore of Big Gull and the blue water of the Mozambique.

There was enough breeze to make the day pleasantly cool, and to kick up a white flecky chop off the surface.

I manoeuvred carefully, squinting over at Big Gull as I put *Dancer* in position. When I hit the marks I pushed a little upwind to allow for *Dancer's* fall-back. Then I cut the engines and hurried down to the foredeck to drop the hook.

Dancer came around and settled down like a well-behaved lady.

'Is this the place?' Sherry had watched everything I did with her disconcerting feline stare.

'This is it,' and I risked overplaying my part as the besotted lover by pointing out the marks to her.

'I lined up those two palms, the ones leaning over, with that single palm right up on the skyline, see it?'

She nodded silently, again I caught that look as though the information was being carefully filed and remembered.

'Now what do we do?' she asked.

'This is where Jimmy dived,' I explained. 'When he came back on board he was very excited. He spoke secretly

134

with the others – Materson and Guthrie – and they seemed to catch his excitement. Jimmy went down again with rope and a tarpaulin. He was down a long time – and when he came up again, it started, the shooting.'

'Yes,' she nodded eagerly, the reference to her brother's death seemed to leave her unmoved. 'We should go now, before someone else sees us here.'

'Go?' I asked, looking at her. 'I thought we were going to have a look?'

She recognized her mistake. 'We should organize it properly, come back when we are prepared, when we have made arrangements to pick up and transport—'

'Lover,' I grinned, 'I didn't come all this way not to take at least one quick look.'

'I don't think you should, Harry,' she called after me, but already I was opening the engine-room hatch.

'Let's come back another time,' she persisted, but I went down the ladder to the rack which held the air bottles and took down a Draeger twin set. I fitted the breathing valve and tested the seal, sucking air out of the rubber mouthpiece.

Glancing quickly up at the hatch to make sure she was not watching me, I reached across and threw the concealed cut-out switch on the electrical system. Now nobody could start *Dancer*'s engines while I was overboard.

I swung the diving ladder over the stern and then dressed in the cockpit – short-sleeved Neoprene wet suit and hood, weight belt and knife, Nemrod wrap-around face-plate and fins.

I slung the scuba set on my back and picked up a coil of light nylon rope and hooked it on to my belt.

'What happens if you don't come back?' Sherry asked, showing apprehension for the first time. 'I mean what happens to me?'

'You'll pine to death,' I told her, and went over the side, not in a showy back flip but a simple use of the steps, more in keeping with my age and dignity.

The water was transparent as mountain air, and as I went head down I could see every detail of the bottom fifty feet below.

It was a coral landscape, lit with dappled light and wondrous colour. I drifted down to it, and the sculptured shapes of the coral were softened and blurred with sea growth and restless with the sparkling jewels of myriad tropical fish. There were deep gullies and standing towers of coral, fields of eel grass between, and open stretches of blinding white coral sand.

My marks had been remarkably accurate, considering the fact that I had been only just conscious from blood loss. I had dropped the anchor almost directly on top of the canvas package. It lay on one of the open spaces of coral sand, looking like some horrible sea monster, green and squat with the loose ropes floating about it like tentacles.

I crouched beside it, and shoals of tiny fish, zebra-striped in gold and black, gathered around me in such numbers that I had to blow bubbles at them and shoo them off, before I could get on with the job.

I unclipped the nylon rope from my belt, and lashed one end securely to the package with a series of half-hitches. Then I rose to the surface slowly paying out the line. I surfaced thirty feet astern of *Dancer*, swam to the ladder, and clambered into the cockpit. I made the end of the line fast to the arm of the fighting chair.

'What did you find?' Sherry demanded anxiously.

'I don't know yet,' I told her. I had resisted the temptation to open the package on the bottom. I hoped it might be worth the sacrifice to watch her expression as I opened the canvas.

I stripped my diving gear and washed it off with fresh

water before stowing it all carefully away. I wanted the tension to eat into her a little longer.

'Damn you, Harry. Let's get it up,' she burst out at last.

I remembered the package as being as heavy as all creation, but then my strength had been almost gone. Now I braced myself against the gunwale and began recovering line. It was heavy, but not impossibly so, and I coiled the wet line as it came in with the old tunny fisherman's wrist action.

The green canvas broke the surface alongside, sodden and gushing water. I reached over and got a purchase on the knotted rope, with a single heave I lifted it over the side and it clunked weightily on to the deck of the cockpit – metal against wood.

'Open it,' ordered Sherry impatiently.

'Right away, madam,' I said, and drew the bait-knife from the sheath on my belt. It was razor sharp, and I cut the ropes with a single stroke for each.

Sherry was leaning forward eagerly as I drew the stiff wet folds of canvas aside, and I was watching her face.

The greedy, anticipatory expression flared suddenly into triumph as she recognized the object. She recognized it before I did, and then instantly she dropped a curtain of uncertainty over her eyes and face.

It was nicely done, she was an actress of skill. Had I not been watching carefully for it, I would have missed the quick play of emotion.

I looked down at the humble object for which already so many men had been killed or mutilated, and I was torn with surprise and puzzlement – and disappointment. It was not what I had expected.

Half of it was badly eaten away as though by a sand-blasting machine, the bronze was raw and shiny and deeply etched. The upper half of it was intact, but tarnished heavily with a thick skin of greenish verdigris, but the lug

137

for the shackle was intact and the ornamentation was still clear through the corrosion – a heraldic crest – or part of it – and lettering in a flowery antique style. The lettering was fragmentary, most of it had been etched away in an irregular flowing line, leaving the bright worn metal.

It was a ship's bell, cast in massive bronze, it must have weighed close to a hundred pounds, with a domed and lugged top and a wide flared mouth.

Curiously I rolled it over. The clapper had corroded solidly, and barnacle and other shellfish had encrusted the interior. I was intrigued by the pattern of wear and corrosion on the outside, until suddenly the solution occurred to me. I had seen other metal objects marked like this after long submersion. The bell had been half buried on the sandy bottom, the exposed portion had been subjected to the tidal rush of Gunfire Break, and the fine grains of coral sand had abrased away a quarter of an inch of the outer skin of the metal.

However, the portion that had been buried was protected, and now I examined the remaining lettering more closely.

VV N L

There was an extended 'V' or a broken 'W' followed immediately by a perfect 'N' – then a gap and a whole 'L'; beyond that the lettering had been obliterated again.

The coat of arms worked into the metal on the opposite side of the barrel was an intricate design with two rampant beasts – probably lions – supporting a shield and a mailed head. It seemed vaguely familiar, and I wondered where I had seen it before.

I rocked back on my heels and looked at Sherry North. She was unable to meet my gaze.

'Funny thing,' I mused. 'A jet aircraft with a bloody great brass bell hanging on its nose.'

'I don't understand it,' she said.

'No more do I.' I stood up and went to get a cheroot from the saloon. I lit it and sat back in the fighting chair.

'Okay. Let's hear your theory.'

'I don't know, Harry. Truly I don't.'

'Let's try some guesses,' I suggested. 'I'll begin.'

She turned away to the rail.

'The jet aircraft turned into a pumpkin,' I hazarded. 'How about that one?'

She turned back to me. 'Harry, I don't feel well. I think I'm going to be sick.'

'So, what must I do?'

'Let's go back now.'

'I was thinking of another dive – look around a bit more.'

'No,' she said quickly. 'Please, not now. I don't feel up to it. Let's go. We can come back if we have to.'

I studied her face for evidence of her sickness: she looked like an advert for health food.

'All right,' I agreed; there was not really much point in another dive, but only I knew that. 'Let's go home and try and work it out.'

I stood up and began rewrapping the brass bell.

'What are you going to do with that?' she asked anxiously.

'Redeposit it,' I told her. 'I am certainly not going to take it back to St Mary's and display it in the market place. Like you said, we can always come back.'

'Yes,' she agreed immediately. 'You are right, of course.'

I dropped the package over the side once more and went to haul the hook.

On the homeward run I found Sherry North's presence

139

on the bridge irritated me. There was a lot of hard thinking
I had to do. I sent her down to make coffee.

'Strong,' I told her, 'and with four spoons of sugar. It will
be good for your seasickness.'

She reappeared on the bridge within two minutes.

'The stove won't light,' she complained.

'You have to open the main gas cylinders first.' I
explained where to find the taps. 'And don't forget to close
them when you finish, or you'll turn the boat into a bomb.'

She made lousy coffee.

It was late evening when I picked up moorings in Grand
Harbour, and dark by the time I dropped Sherry at the
entrance of the hotel. She didn't even invite me in for
a drink, but kissed me on the cheek and said, 'Darling, let
me be alone tonight. I am exhausted. I am going to bed
now. Let me think about all this, and when I feel better we
can plan more clearly.'

'I'll pick you up here – what time?'

'No,' she said. 'I'll meet you at the boat. Early. Eight
o'clock. Wait for me there – we can talk in private. Just the
two of us, no one else – all right?'

'I'll bring *Dancer* to the wharf at eight,' I promised her.

It had been a thirsty day, and on the way home I stopped
off at the Lord Nelson.

Angelo and Judith were with a noisy party of their own
age in one of the booths. They called me over and made
room for me between two of the girls.

I brought them each a pint, and Angelo leaned over
confidentially. 'Hey, skipper, are you using the pick-up
tonight?'

'Yes,' I said. 'To get me home.' I knew what was coming,

of course. Angelo acted as though he had shares in the vehicle.

'There's a big party down at South Point tonight, boss,' suddenly he was very free with the 'boss' and 'skipper', 'I thought if I run you out to Turtle Bay, then you'd let us have the truck. I'd pick you up early tomorrow, promise.'

I took a swallow at my tankard and they were all watching me with eager hopeful faces.

'It's a big party, Mister Harry,' said Judith. 'Please.'

'You pick me up seven o'clock sharp, Angelo, hear?' and there was a spontaneous burst of relieved laughter. They clubbed in to buy me another pint.

I had a disturbed night, with restless sleep interspersed with periods of wakefulness. I had the dream again, when I dived to the canvas package. Once more it contained a tiny Dresden mermaid, but this time she had Sherry North's face and she offered me the model of a jet fighter aircraft that changed into a golden pumpkin as I reached for it. The pumpkin was etched with the letters:

VVNL

It rained after midnight, solid sheets of water, that poured off the eaves, and the lightning silhouetted the palm fronds against the night sky.

It was still raining when I went down to the beach, and the heavy drops exploded in minute bomb bursts of spray upon my naked body. The sea was black in the bad light, and the rain squalls reached to the horizon. I swam alone, far out beyond the reef, but when I came back to the beach the excursion had not provided the usual lift to my spirits.

141

My body was blue and shivering with the cold, and a vague but pervading sense of trouble and depression pressed heavily upon me.

I had finished breakfast when the pick-up came down the track through the palm plantation, splashing through the puddles, splattered with mud and with headlights still burning.

In the yard Angelo hooted and shouted, 'You ready, Harry?' and I ran out with a sou'-wester held over my head.

Angelo smelled of beer and he was garrulous and slightly bleary of eye.

'I'll drive,' I told him, and as we crossed the island he gave me a blow-by-blow description of the great party – from what he told me it seemed there might be an epidemic of births on St Mary's in nine months' time.

I was only half listening to him, for as we approached the town so my sense of disquiet mounted.

'Hey, Harry, the kids said to thank you for the loan of the pick-up.'

'That's okay, Angelo.'

'I sent Judith out to the boat – she's going to tidy up, Harry, and get the coffee going for you.'

'She shouldn't have worried,' I said.

'She wanted to do that specially – sort of thank you, you know.'

'She's a good girl.'

'Sure is, Harry. I love that girl,' and Angelo burst into song, 'Devil Woman' in the style of Mick Jagger.

When we crossed the ridge and started down into the valley I had a sudden impulse. Instead of continuing straight down Frobisher Street to the harbour, I swung left on to the circular drive above the fort and hospital and went up the avenue of banyan trees to the Hilton Hotel. I parked the pick-up under the canopy and went through to the reception lobby.

142

There was nobody behind the desk this early in the morning, but I leaned across the counter and peered into Marion's cubicle. She was at her switchboard and when she saw me her face lit up in a wide grin and she lifted off her earphones.

'Hello, Mister Harry.'

'Hello, Marion, love,' I returned the grin. 'Is Miss North in her room?'

Her expression changed. 'Oh no,' she said, 'she left over an hour ago.'

'Left?' I stared at her.

'Yes. She went out to the airport with the hotel bus. She was catching the seven-thirty plane.' Marion glanced at the cheap Japanese watch on her wrist. 'They would have taken off ten minutes ago.'

I was taken completely off-balance, of all things I had least expected this. It didn't make sense for many seconds – and then suddenly and sickeningly it did.

'Oh Jesus Christ,' I said. 'Judith!' and I ran for the pick-up. Angelo saw my face as I came and he sat up straight in the seat and stopped singing.

I jumped into the driver's seat and started the engine, thrusting the pedal down hard and swinging in a roaring two-wheeled turn.

'What is it, Harry?' Angelo demanded.

'Judith?' I asked grimly. 'You sent her down to the boat, when?'

'When I left to fetch you.'

'Did she go right away?'

'No, she'd have to bath and dress first.' He was telling it straight, not hiding the fact they had slept together. He sensed the urgency of the situation. 'Then she'd have to walk down the valley from the farm.' Angelo had lodgings with a peasant family up near the spring, it was a three-mile walk.

143

'God, let us be in time,' I whispered. The truck was bellowing down the avenue, and I hit the gears in a racing change as we went out through the gates in a screaming broadside, and I slammed down hard again on the accelerator, pulling her out of the skid by main strength.

'What the hell is it, Harry?' he demanded once again.

'We've got to stop her going aboard *Dancer*,' I told him grimly as we roared down the circular drive above the town. Past the fort a vista of Grand Harbour opened beneath us. He did not waste time with inane questions. We had worked together too long for that and if I said so then he accepted it as so.

Dancer was still at her moorings amongst the other island craft, and halfway out to her from the wharf Judith was rowing the dinghy. Even at this distance I could make out the tiny feminine figure on the thwart, and recognize the short business-like oar-strokes. She was an island girl, and rowed like a man.

'We aren't going to make it,' said Angelo. 'She'll get there before we reach Admiralty.'

At the top of Frobisher Street I put the heel of my left hand on the horn ring, and blowing a continuous blast I tried to clear the road. But it was a Saturday morning, market day, and already the streets were filling. The country folk had come to town in their bullocks, carts and ancient jalopies. Cursing with a terrible frustration, I hooted and forced my way through them.

It took us three minutes to cover the half mile from the top of the street down to Admiralty Wharf.

'Oh God,' I said, leaning forward in the seat as I shot through the mesh gates, and crossed the railway tracks.

The dinghy was tied up alongside *Wave Dancer*, and Judith was climbing over the side. She wore an emerald green shirt and short denim pants. Her hair was in a long braid down her back.

I skidded the truck to a halt beside the pineapple sheds, and both Angelo and I hit the wharf at a run.

'Judith!' I yelled, but my voice did not carry out across the harbour.

Without looking back, Judith disappeared into the saloon. Angelo and I raced down to the end of the jetty. Both of us were screaming wildly, but the wind was in our faces and *Dancer* was five hundred yards out across the water.

'There's a dinghy!' Angelo caught my arm. It was an ancient clinker-built mackerel boat, but it was chained to a ring in the stone wharf.

We jumped into it, leaping the eight foot drop and falling in a heap together over the thwart. I scrambled to the mooring chain. It had quarter-inch galvanized steel links, and a heavy brass padlock secured it to the ring.

I took two twists of chain around my wrist, braced one foot against the wharf and heaved. The padlock exploded, and I fell backwards into the bottom of the dinghy.

Angelo already had the oars in the rowlocks.

'Row,' I shouted at him. 'Row like a mad bastard.'

I was in the bows cupping my hands to my mouth as I hailed Judith, trying to make my voice carry above the wind.

Angelo was rowing in a dedicated frenzy, swinging the oar blades flat and low on the back reach and then throwing his weight upon them when they bit. His breathing exploded in a harsh grunt at each stroke.

Halfway out to *Dancer* another rain squall enveloped us, shrouding the whole of Grand Harbour in eddying sheets of grey water. It stung my face, so I had to screw up my eyes.

Dancer's outline was blurred by grey rain, but we were coming close now. I was beginning to hope that Judith would sweep and tidy the cabins before she struck a match to the gas ring in the galley. I was also beginning to hope that I was wrong – that Sherry North had not left a farewell present for me.

Yet still I could hear my own voice speaking to Sherry North the previous day. 'You have to open the main gas cylinders first – and don't forget to close them when you finish, or you'll turn the boat into a bomb.'

Closer still we came to *Dancer* and she seemed to hang on tendrils of rain, ghostly white and insubstantial in the swirling mist.

'Judith,' I shouted, she must hear me now – we were that close. There were two fifty-pound cylinders of Butane gas on board, enough to destroy a large brick-built house. The gas was heavier than air, once it escaped it would slump down, filling *Dancer's* hull with a murderously explosive mixture of gas and air. It needed just one spark from battery or match.

I prayed that I was wrong and yelled again. Then suddenly *Dancer* blew.

It was flash explosion, a fearsome blue light that shot through her. It split her hull with a mighty hammer stroke, and blew her superstructure open, lifting it like a lid.

Dancer reared to the mortal blow, and the blast hit us like a storm wind. Immediately I smelled the electric stench of the blast, acrid as an air-sizzling strike of lightning against iron-stone.

Dancer died as I watched, a terrible violent death, and then her torn and lifeless hull fell back and the cold grey waters rushed into her. The heavy engines pulled her swiftly down, and she was gone into the grey waters of Grand Harbour.

Angelo and I were frozen with horror, crouching in the violently rocking dinghy, staring at the agitated water that was strewn with loose wreckage – all that remained of a beautiful boat and a lovely young girl. I felt a vast desolation descend upon me, I wanted to cry aloud in my anguish, but I was paralysed.

Angelo moved first. He leapt upright with a sound in his throat like a wounded beast. He tried to throw himself over the side, but I caught and held him.

'Leave me,' he screamed. 'I must go to her.'

'No.' I fought with him in the crazily rocking dinghy. 'It's no good, Angelo.'

Even if he could get down through the forty feet of water in which *Dancer's* torn hull now lay, what he would find might drive him mad. Judith had stood at the centre of that blast, and she would have been subjected to all the terrible trauma of massive flash explosion at close range.

'Leave me, damn you.' Angelo got one arm free and hit me in the face, but I saw it coming and rolled my head. It grazed the skin from my cheek, and I knew I had to get him quieted down.

The dinghy was on the point of capsizing. Though he was forty pounds lighter than me, Angelo fought with maniac strength. He was calling her name now.

'Judith, Judith,' on an hysterical rising inflection. I released my grip on his shoulder with my right hand, and swung him slightly away from me, lining him up carefully. I hit him with a right chop, my fist moving not more than four inches. I hit him cleanly on the point below his left ear, and he dropped instantly, gone cold. I lowered him to the floorboards and laid him out comfortably. I rowed back to the wharf without looking back. I felt completely numbed and drained.

I carried Angelo down the wharf and I hardly felt his weight in my arms. I drove him up to the hospital and MacNab was on duty.

'Give him something to keep him muzzy and in bed for the next twenty-four hours,' I told MacNab, and he began to argue.

'Listen, you broken-down old whisky vat,' I told him quietly, 'I'd love an excuse to beat your head in.'

He paled until the broken veins in his nose and cheeks stood out boldly.

'Now listen – Harry old man,' he began. I took a step towards him, and he sent the duty sister to the drug cupboard.

I found Chubby at breakfast and it took only a minute to explain what had happened. We went up to the fort in the pick-up, and Wally Andrews responded quickly. He waived the filing of statements and other police procedure and instead we piled the police diving equipment into the truck and by the time we reached the harbour, half of St Mary's had formed a silent worried crowd along the wharf. Some had seen it and all of them had heard the explosion.

An occasional voice called condolences to me as we carried the diving equipment to the mackerel boat.

'Somebody find Fred Coker,' I told them. 'Tell him to get down here with a bag and basket,' and there was a buzz of comment.

'Hey, Mister Harry, was there somebody aboard?'

'Just get Fred Coker,' I told them, and we rowed out to *Dancer*'s moorings.

While Wally kept the dinghy on station above us, Chubby and I went down through the murky harbour water.

Dancer lay on her back in forty-five feet, she must have rolled as she sank – but there was no need to worry about access to her interior, for her hull had been torn open along the keel. She was far past any hope of refloating.

Chubby waited at the hole in the hull while I went in.

What remained of the galley was filled with swirling excited shoals of fish. They were in a feeding frenzy and I choked and gagged into the mouthpiece of my scuba when I saw what they were feeding upon.

The only way I knew it was Judith was the tatters of

148

green cloth clinging to the fragments of flesh. We got her out in three main pieces, and placed her in the canvas bag that Fred Coker provided.

I dived again immediately, and worked my way through the shattered hull to the compartment below the galley where the two long iron gas cylinders were still bolted to their beds. Both taps were wide open, and somebody had disconnected the hoses to allow the gas to escape freely.

I have never experienced anger so intense as I felt then. It was that strong for it fed upon my loss. *Dancer* was gone – and *Dancer* had been half my life. I closed the taps and reconnected the gas hose. It was a private thing – I would deal with it personally.

When I walked back along the wharf to the pick-up, all that gave me comfort was the knowledge that *Dancer* had been insured. There would be another boat – not as beautiful or as well beloved as *Dancer* – but a boat nevertheless.

In the crowd I noticed the shiny black face of Hambone Williams – the harbour ferryman. For forty years he had plied his old dinghy back and forth at threepence a hire.

'Hambone,' I called him over. 'Did you take anybody out to *Dancer* last night?'

'No, sir, Mister Harry.'

'Nobody at all?'

'Only your party. She left her watch in the cabin. I took her out to fetch it.'

'The lady?'

'Yes, the lady with the yellow hair.'

'What time, Hambone?'

'About nine o'clock – did I do wrong, Mister Harry?'

'No, it's all right. Just forget it.'

We buried Judith next day before noon. I managed to get the plot beside her mother and father for her. Angelo liked that. He said he did not want her to be lonely up

149

there on the hill. Angelo was still half doped, and he was quiet and dreamy eyed at the graveside.

The next morning the three of us began salvage work on *Dancer*. We worked hard for ten days and we stripped her completely of anything that had a possible value – from the big-game fishing reels and the FN carbine to the twin bronze propellers. The hull and superstructure were so badly broken up as to be of no value.

At the end of that time *Wave Dancer* had become a memory only. I have had many women, and now they are just a pleasant thought when I hear a certain song or smell a particular perfume. Like them, already *Dancer* was beginning to recede into the past.

On the tenth day I went up to see Fred Coker – and the moment I entered his office I knew there was something very wrong. He was shiny with nervous sweat, his eyes moved shiftily behind the glittering spectacles and his hands scampered about like frightened mice – running over his blotter or leaping up to adjust the knot of his necktie or smooth down the thin strands of hair on his polished cranium. He knew I'd come to talk insurance.

'Now don't get excited please, Mister Harry,' he advised me. Whenever people tell me that, I become very excited indeed.

'What is it, Coker? Come on! Come on!' I slammed one fist on the desk top, and he leapt in his chair so the gold-rimmed spectacles slid down his nose.

'Mister Harry, please—'

'Come on! You miserable little grave worm—'

'Mister Harry – it's about the premiums on *Dancer*.' I stared at him.

'You see – you have never made a claim before – it seemed such a waste to—'

I found words. 'You pocketed the premiums,' I whispered, my voice failing me suddenly. 'You didn't pay them over to the company.'

'You understand,' Fred Coker nodded. 'I knew you'd understand.'

I tried to go over the desk to save time, but I tripped and fell. Fred Coker leapt from his chair, slipping through my outstretched groping fingers. He ran through the back door, slamming it behind him.

I ran straight through the door, tearing off the lock, and leaving it hanging on broken hinges.

Fred Coker ran as though all the dark angels pursued him, which would have been better for him. I caught him at the big doors into the alley and lifted him by the throat, holding him with one hand, pressing his back against a pile of cheap pine coffins.

He had lost his spectacles, and he was weeping with fright, big slow tears welling out of the helpless short-sighted eyes.

'You know I'm going to kill you,' I whispered, and he moaned, his feet dancing six inches above the floor.

I pulled back my right fist and braced myself solidly on the balls of my feet. It would have taken his head off. I couldn't do it – but I had to hit something. I drove my fist into the coffin beside his right ear. The panelling shattered, stove in along its full length. Fred Coker shrieked like an hysterical girl at a pop festival, and I let him drop. His legs could not hold him and he sank to the concrete floor.

I left him lying there moaning and blubbering with terror – and I walked out into the street as near to bankrupt as I'd been in the last ten years.

Mister Harry transformed in a single stroke into Fletcher,

wharf rat and land-bound bum. It was a classic case of reversion to type – before I reached the Lord Nelson I was thinking the same way I had ten years before. Already I was calculating the percentages, seeking the main chance once more.

Chubby and Angelo were the only customers in the public bar so early in the afternoon. I told them, and they were quiet. There wasn't anything to say.

We drank the first one in silence, then I asked Chubby, 'What will you do now?' and he shrugged.

'I've still got the old whaleboat—' It was a twenty-footer, admiralty design, open-decked, but sea-kindly. 'I'll go for stump again, I reckon.' Stump were the big reef crayfish. There was good money in the frozen tails.

It was how Chubby had earned his bread before *Dancer* and I came to St Mary's.

'You'll need new engines, those old Sea Gulls of yours are shot.' We drank another pint, while I worked out my finances – what the hell, a couple of thousand dollars was not going to make much difference to me. 'I'll buy two new twenty horse Evinrudes for the boat, Chubby,' I volunteered.

'Won't let you do it, Harry.' He frowned indignantly, and shook his head. 'I got enough saved up working for you,' and he was adamant.

'What about you, Angelo?' I asked.

'Guess I'll go sell my soul on a Rawano contract.'

'No,' Chubby scowled at the thought. 'I'll need crew for the stump-boat.'

They were all settled then. I was relieved, for I felt responsible for them both. I was particularly glad that Chubby would be there to care for Angelo. The boy had taken Judith's death very badly. He was quiet and withdrawn, no longer the flashing Romeo. I had kept him working hard on the salvage of *Dancer*, that alone seemed

152

to have given him the time he needed to recover from the wound.

Nevertheless he began drinking hard now, chasing tots of cheap brandy with pints of bitter. This is the most destroying way to take in alcohol, short of drinking meths, that I know of.

Chubby and I took it nice and slow, lingering over our tankards, yet under our jocularity was a knowledge that we had reached a crossroads and from tomorrow we would no longer be travelling together. It gave the evening the fine poignancy of impending loss.

There was a South African trawler in harbour that night that had come in for bunkers and repairs. When at last Angelo passed out cold, Chubby and I began our singing. Six of the trawler's beefy crew members voiced their disapproval in the most slanderous terms. Chubby and I could not allow insults of that nature to pass unchallenged. We all went out to discuss it in the backyard.

It was a glorious discussion, and when Wally Andrews arrived with the riot squad he arrested all of us, even those who had fallen in the fray.

'My own flesh and blood—' Chubby kept repeating as he and I staggered arm and arm into the cells. 'He turned on me. My own sister's son—'

Wally was human enough to send one of his constables down to the Lord Nelson for something to make our durance less vile. Chubby and I became very friendly with the trawlermen in the next cell, passing the bottle back and forth between the bars.

When we were released next morning, Wally Andrews declining to press charges, I drove out to Turtle Bay to begin closing up the shack. I made sure the crockery was clean, threw a few handfuls of mothballs in the cupboards and did not bother to lock the doors. There is no such thing as burglary on St Mary's.

153

For the last time I swam out beyond the reef, and for half an hour hoped that the dolphins might come. They did not and I swam back, showered and changed, picked up my old canvas and leather campaign bag from the bed and went out to where the pick-up was parked in the yard. I didn't look back as I drove up through the palm plantation, but I made myself a promise that I'd be coming this way again.

I parked in the front lot of the hotel and lit a cheroot. When Marion finished her shift at noon she came out the front entrance and set off down the drive with her cheeky little bottom swinging under the mini skirt.

I whistled and she saw me. She slipped into the passenger's seat beside me.

'Mister Harry, I'm so sorry about your boat—' We talked for a few minutes until I could ask the question.

'Miss North, while she was staying at the hotel, did she make any phone calls or send a cable?'

'I don't remember, Mister Harry, but I could check for you.'

'Now?'

'Sure,' she agreed.

'One other thing, could you also check with Dicky if he got a shot of her?' Dicky was the roving hotel photographer, it was a good chance that he had a print of Sherry North in his file.

Marion was gone for nearly three-quarters of an hour, but she returned with a triumphant smile.

'She sent a cable on the night before she left.' Marion handed me a flimsy copy. 'You can keep this copy,' she told me as I read the message.

It was addressed to: 'MANSON FLAT 5 CURZON STREET 97 LONDON W.1.' and the message read: 'CONTRACT SIGNED RETURNING HEATHROW BOAC FLIGHT 316 SATURDAY.' There was no signature.

'Dicky had to go through all his files – but he found one.' She handed me a six-by-four glossy print. It was of Sherry North reclining on a sun couch on the hotel terrace. She wore her bikini and sunglasses, but it was a good likeness.

'Thanks, Marion.' I gave her a five-pound note.

'Gee, Mister Harry,' she grinned at me as she tucked it into the front of her bra. 'For that price you can take what you fancy.'

'I've got a plane to catch, love.' I kissed her on the little snub nose, and slapped her bottom as she climbed out of the cab.

Chubby and Angelo came out to the airport. Chubby was to take care of the pick-up for me. We were all subdued, and shook hands awkwardly at the departure gate. There wasn't much to say, we had said it all the night before.

As the piston-engined aircraft took off for the mainland, I glimpsed the two of them standing together at the perimeter fence.

I stopped over three hours at Nairobi before catching the BOAC flight on to London. I did not sleep during the long night flight. It was many years since I had returned to my native land – and I was coming back now on a grim mission of vengeance. I wanted very much to talk to Sherry North.

When you are flat broke, that is the time to buy a new car and a hundred-guinea suit. Look brave and prosperous, and people will believe you are.

I shaved and changed at the airport and instead of a Hillman I hired a Chrysler from the Hertz Depot at Heathrow, slung my bag in the boot and drove to the nearest Courage pub.

155

I had a double portion of ham and egg pie, washed down with a pint of Courage while I studied the road map. It was all so long ago that I was unsure of my directions.

The lush and cultivated English countryside was too tame and green after Malaya and Africa, and the autumn sunshine was pale gold when I was used to a brighter fiercer sun – but it was a pleasant drive over the downs and into Brighton.

I parked the Chrysler on the promenade opposite the Grand Hotel and dived into the warren of The Lanes. They were filled with tourists even this late in the season.

Pavilion Arcade was the address I had read so long ago on Jimmy North's underwater sledge, and it took me nearly an hour to find it. It was tucked away at the back of a cobbled yard, and most of the windows and doors were shuttered and closed.

'North's Underwater World' had a ten-foot frontage on to the lane. It was also closed, and a blind was drawn across the single window. I tried without success to peer round the edge of the blind, but the interior was darkened, so I hammered on the door. There was no sound from within, and I was about to turn away when I noticed a square piece of cardboard that had once been stuck on to the bottom of the window but had fallen to the floor inside. By twisting my head acrobatically, I could read the handwritten message which had fortunately fallen face up: Enquiries to Seaview, Downers Lane, Falmer, Sussex. I went back to the car and took the road map out of the glove compartment.

It began to rain as I pushed the Chrysler through narrow lanes. The windscreen wipers flogged sullenly at the spattering drops and I peered into the premature gloom of early evening.

Twice I lost my way but finally I pulled up outside a gate in a thick hedge. The sign nailed to the gate read: NORTH SEAVIEW, and I believed that it might be possible to look southwards on a clear day and see the Atlantic.

I drove down between hedges, and came into the paved yard of an old double-storeyed red-brick farmhouse, with oak beams set into the walls and green moss growing on the wood-shingle roof. There was a light burning downstairs.

I parked the Chrysler and crossed the yard to the kitchen door, turning up my collar against the wind and rain. I beat on the door, and heard somebody moving around inside. The bolts were shot back and the top half of the stable door opened on a chain. A girl looked out at me.

I was not immediately impressed by her for she wore a baggy blue fisherman's jersey and she was a tall girl with a swimmer's shoulders. I thought her plain – in a striking manner.

Her brow was pale and broad, her nose was large but not bony or beaked, and below it her mouth was wide and friendly. She wore no make-up at all, so her lips were pale pink and there was a peppering of fine freckles on her nose and cheeks.

Her hair was drawn back severely from her face into a thick braid behind her neck. Her hair was black, shimmering iridescent black in the lamplight, and her eyebrows were black also, black and boldly arched over eyes that seemed also to be black until the light caught them and I realized they were the same dark haunted blue as the Mozambique current when the noon sun strikes directly into it.

Despite the pallor of her skin, there was an aura of good

157

and glowing health about her. The pale skin had a lustre and plasticity to it, a quality that was somehow luminous so that when you studied her closely – as I was now doing – it seemed that you could see down through the surface to the flush of clean blood rising warmly to her cheeks and neck. She touched the tendril of silky dark hair that escaped the braid and floated lightly on her temple. It was an appealing gesture, that betrayed her nervousness and belied the serene expression in the dark blue eyes.

Suddenly I realized that she was an unusually handsome woman, for, although she was only in her mid-twenties, I knew she was no longer girl – but full woman. There was a strength and maturity about her, a deep sense of calm that I found intriguing.

Usually the women I choose are more obvious, I do not like to tie up too much of my energy in the pursuit. This was something beyond my experience and for the first time in years I felt unsure of myself.

We had been staring at each other for many seconds, neither of us speaking or moving.

'You're Harry Fletcher,' she said at last, and her voice was low and gently modulated, a cultivated and educated voice. I gaped at her.

'How the hell did you know that?' I demanded.

'Come in.' She slipped the chain and opened the bottom of the stable door, and I obeyed. The kitchen was warm and welcoming and filled with the smell of good food cooking.

'How did you know my name?' I asked again.

'Your picture was in the newspaper – with Jimmy's,' she explained. We were silent again, once more studying each other.

She was taller even than I had thought at first, reaching to my shoulder, with long legs clad in dark blue pants and the tops thrust into black leather boots. Now I could see the narrow waist and the promise of good breasts beneath the thick jersey.

At first I had thought her plain, ten seconds later I had reckoned her handsome, now I doubted I had ever seen a more beautiful woman. It took time for the full effect to sink in.

'You have me at a disadvantage,' I said at last. 'I don't know your name.'

'I'm Sherry North,' she answered, and I stared at her for a moment before I recovered from the shock. She was a very different person from the other Sherry North I had known.

'Did you know that there is a whole tribe of you?' I asked at last.

'I don't understand.' She frowned at me. Her eyes were enchantingly blue under the lowered lashes.

'It's a long story.'

'I'm sorry.' For the first time she seemed to become aware that we were standing facing each other in the centre of the kitchen. 'Won't you sit down. Can I get you a beer?'

Sherry took a couple of cans of Carlsberg lager from the cupboard and sat opposite me across the kitchen table.

'You were going to tell me a long story.' She popped the tabs on the cans, and slid one across to me, then looked at me expectantly.

I began to tell her the carefully edited version of my experiences since Jimmy North arrived at St Mary's. She was very easy to talk to, like being with an old and interested friend. Suddenly I wanted to tell her everything, the entire unblemished truth. It was important that from the very beginning it should be right, with no reservations.

She was a complete stranger, and yet I was placing trust in her beyond any person I had ever known. I told her everything exactly as it had happened.

She fed me after dark had fallen, a savoury casserole out

159

of an earthenware pot which we ate with home-made bread and farm butter. I was still talking but no longer about the recent events on St Mary's, and she listened quietly. At last I had found another human being with whom I could talk without reserve.

I went back in my life, in a complete catharsis I told her of the early days, even of the dubious manner in which I had earned the money to buy *Wave Dancer*, and how my good resolutions since then had wavered.

It was after midnight when at last she said: 'I can hardly believe all you've told me. You don't look like that – you look so,' she seemed to search for the word, 'wholesome.' But you could see it was not the word she wanted.

'I work hard at being that. But sometimes my halo falls over my eyes. You see, appearances are deceptive,' I said, and she nodded.

'Yes, they are,' and there was a significance in the way she said it, a warning perhaps. 'Why have you told me all this? It is not really very wise, you know.'

'It was just time that somebody knew about me, I suppose. Sorry, you were elected.'

She smiled. 'You can sleep in Jimmy's room tonight,' she said. 'I can't risk you rushing out and telling anybody else.'

I hadn't slept the night before and suddenly I was exhausted. I felt as though I did not have the strength to climb the stairs to the bedroom – but I had one question still to ask.

'Why did Jimmy come to St Mary's? What was he looking for?' I asked. 'Do you know who he was working with, who they were?'

'I don't know.' She shook her head, and I knew it was the truth. She wouldn't lie to me now, not after I had placed such trust in her.

'Will you help me find out? Will you help me find them?'

'Yes, I'll help you,' she said, and stood up from the table. 'We'll talk again in the morning.'

Jimmy's room was under the eaves, the pitch of the roof giving it an irregular shape. The walls were lined with photographs and packed bookshelves, silver sporting trophies and the treasured bric-à-brac of boyhood.

The bed was high and the mattress soft.

I went to fetch my bag from the Chrysler while Sherry put clean sheets upon the bed. Then she showed me the bathroom and left me.

I lay and listened to the rain on the roof for only a few minutes before I slept. I woke in the night and heard the soft whisper of her voice somewhere in the quiet house.

Barefooted and in my underpants I opened the bedroom door and crept silently down the passage to the stairs. I looked down into the hall. There was a light burning and Sherry North stood at the wall-hung telephone. She was speaking so quietly into the receiver, cupping her hands to her mouth, that I could not catch the words. The light was behind her. She wore a flimsy nightdress, and her body showed through the thin stuff as though she was naked.

I found myself staring like a peeping Tom. The lamp-light glowed on the ivory sheen of her skin, and there were intriguing secret hollows and shadows beneath the transparent cloth.

With an effort I pulled my eyes off her and went back to my bed. I thought about Sherry's telephone call and felt a vague disquiet, but soon sleep overtook me once more.

I n the morning the rain had stopped but the ground was slushy and the grass heavy and wet when I went out for a breath of cold morning air.

I expected to feel awkward with Sherry after the previous night's outpourings of the soul, but it was not so. We talked easily at breakfast, and afterwards she said, 'I promised I'd help you; what can I do?'

'Answer a few questions.'

'All right, ask me.'

Jimmy North had been very secretive, she did not know he was going to St Mary's. He had told her he had a contract to install some electronic underwater equipment at the Cabora-Bassa Dam in Portuguese Mozambique. She had taken him up to the airport with all his equipment. As far as she knew he was travelling alone. The police had come to the shop in Brighton to tell her of his murder. She had read the newspaper reports, and that was all.

'No letters from Jimmy?'

'No, nothing.' I nodded, the wolf pack must have intercepted his mail. The letter I had been shown by Sherry's impostor was certainly genuine.

'I don't understand anything about this. Am I being stupid?'

'No.' I took out a cheroot, and almost lit it before I stopped myself. 'Okay if I smoke one of these?'

'It doesn't bother me,' she said, and I was glad, for it would have been hell giving them up. I lit it and drew in the fragrant smoke.

'It looks as though Jimmy stumbled on something big. He needed backing and he went to the wrong people. As soon as they thought they knew where it was, they killed him and tried to kill me. When that didn't work they sent out someone impersonating you. When she thought she knew the location of this object, she set a trap for me and went home. Their next move will be a return to the area off Big Gull Island, where they are due for another disappointment.'

She refilled the coffee cups, and I noticed that she had applied make-up this morning – but so lightly that the freckles still showed. I reconsidered the previous night's judgement – and confirmed that she was one of the most beautiful women I had ever met, even in the early morning.

She was frowning thoughtfully, staring into her coffee cup and I wanted to touch one of her slim strong-looking hands that lay on the tablecloth near my own.

'What were they after, Harry? And who are these people who killed him?' she asked at last.

'Two excellent questions. I have leads to both – but we will tackle the questions in the order you asked them. Firstly, what was Jimmy after? When we know that we can go after his murderers.'

'I have no idea at all what it could be.' She looked up at me. The blue of her eyes was lighter than it had been last night, it was the colour of a good sapphire. 'What clues have you?'

'The ship's bell. The design upon it.'

'What does it signify?'

'I don't know, but it shouldn't be too hard to find out.' I could no longer resist the temptation. I placed my hand over hers. It felt as firm and strong as it looked and her flesh was warm. 'But first I should like to check the shop in Brighton and Jimmy's room here. There might be something we can use.'

She had not withdrawn her hand. 'All right, shall we go to the shop first? The police have already been through it all, but they might have overlooked something.'

'Fine. I'll buy you lunch.' I squeezed her hand, and she turned it in my grasp and squeezed back.

'I'll take you up on that,' she said, and I was too

astonished by my own reaction to her grip to find a light reply. My throat was dry and my pulse beat as though I'd run a mile. Gently she removed her hand and stood up.

'Let's do the breakfast dishes.'

If the girls of St Mary's could only have seen Mister Harry drying dishes, my reputation would have shattered into a thousand pieces.

She let us into the shop the back way, through a tiny enclosed yard which was almost filled with unusual objects, all of them associated with diving and the under-water world – discarded air bottles and a portable compressor, brass portholes and other salvage from wrecked ships, even the jawbone of a killer whale with all its teeth intact.

'I haven't been in for a long time,' Sherry apologized as she unlocked the back door of the shop. 'Without Jimmy—' she shrugged and then went on, ' – I must really get down to selling up all this junk and closing the shop down. I could re-sell the lease, I suppose.'

'I'm going to look round, okay?'

'Fine, I'll get the kettle going.'

I started in the yard, searching quickly but thoroughly through the piles of junk. There was nothing that had significance as far as I could see. I went into the shop and poked around amongst the seashells and sharks' teeth on the shelves and in the display case. Finally I saw a desk in the corner and began going through the drawers.

Sherry brought me a cup of tea and perched on the corner of the desk while I piled old invoices, rubber bands and paper clips on the top. I read every scrap of paper and even rifled through the ready reckoner.

'Nothing?' Sherry asked.

'Nothing,' I agreed and glanced at my watch. 'Lunch-time,' I told her.

She locked up the shop and by good fortune we stumbled

on English's restaurant. They gave us a secluded table in the back room and I ordered a bottle of Pouilly Fuissé to go with the lobster. Once I recovered from the shock of the price, we laughed a lot during the meal, and it wasn't just the wine. The feeling between us was good and growing stronger.

After lunch we drove back to Seaview and we went up to Jimmy's room.

'This is our best bet,' I guessed. 'If he was keeping secrets, this is where they would be.' But I knew I had a long job ahead of me. There were hundreds of books and piles of magazines – mostly *American Argosy*, *Trident*, *The Diver* and other diving publications. There was also a complete shelf of springback files at the foot of the bed.

'I'll leave you to it,' Sherry said, and went.

I took down the contents of a shelf, sat at the reading table and began to skim through the publications. Immediately I saw it was an even bigger task than I had thought. Jimmy had been one of those people who read with a pencil in one hand. There were notes pencilled in the margin, comments, queries and exclamation marks, and anything that interested him was underlined.

I read doggedly, looking for something that could remotely be linked to St Mary's.

Around eight o'clock I began on the shelf that held the springback files. The first two were filled with newspaper clippings on shipwrecks or other marine phenomena. The third of them had an unlabelled, black imitation leather cover. It held a thin sheaf of papers, and I saw immediately that they were out of the ordinary.

They were a series of letters filed with their envelopes and stamps still attached. There were sixteen of them in all, addressed to Messrs Parker and Wilton in Fenchurch Street.

Every letter was in a different hand, but all were executed in the elegant penmanship of the last century.

The envelopes were sent from different parts of the old Empire – Canada, South Africa, India – and the nineteenth-century postage stamps alone must have been of considerable value.

After I had read the first two letters, it was clear that Messrs Parker and Wilton were agents and factors, and they had acted for a number of distinguished clients in the service of Queen Victoria. The letters were instructions to deal with estates, moneys and securities.

All the letters were dated during the period from August 1857 to July 1858 and must have been offered by a dealer or an antique auctioneer as a lot.

I glanced through them quickly, but the contents were really very dull. However, something on the single page of the tenth letter caught my eye and I felt my nerves jump.

Two words had been underlined in pencil and in the margin was a notation in Jimmy North's handwriting.

'B. Mus. E.6914(8).'

However, it was the words themselves that held me.

'Dawn Light.'

I had heard those words before. I wasn't sure when, but they were significant.

Quickly I began at the top of the page. The sender's address was a laconic 'Bombay', and it was dated 16th Sept. 1857.

My Dear Wilton,

I charge you most strictly with the proper care and safe storage of five pieces of luggage consigned in my name to your London address aboard the Hon. Company's ship *Dawn Light*. Due out of this port before the 25th instant and bound for the Company's wharf in the Port of London.

Please acknowledge safe receipt of same with all despatch.

I remain yours faithfully,

Colonel Sir Roger Goodchild.

Officer Commanding 101st Regiment

Queens Own India Rifles.

Delivery by kind favour of Captain commanding Her Majesty's Frigate *Panther*.

The paper rustled and I realized that my hand was shaking with excitement. I knew I was on to it now. This was the key. I laid the letter carefully on the reading table and placed a silver paper-knife upon it to weight it down.

I began to read it again slowly, but there was a distraction. I heard the engine noise of an automobile coming down the lane from the gate. Headlights flashed across the window and then rounded the corner of the house.

I sat up straight, listening. The engine noise died, and car doors slammed shut.

There was a long silence then before I heard the murmur and growl of voices – men's voices. I began to stand up from the table.

Then Sherry screamed. It rang clearly through the old house, and cut into my brain like a lance. It aroused in me a protective instinct so fierce that I was down the stairs and into the hall before I realized I had moved.

The door to the kitchen was open and I paused in the doorway. There were two men with Sherry. The heavier and elder of the two wore a beige camelhair topcoat and a tweed cap. He had a greyish, heavy lined face and deep-sunk eyes. His lips were thin and colourless.

He had Sherry's left hand twisted up between her shoulder-blades, and was holding her jammed against the wall beside the gas stove.

The other man was younger, and he was slim and pale,

bare-headed with long straw-yellow hair falling to the shoulders of his leather jacket. He was grinning gleefully as he held Sherry's other hand over the blue flames of the gas ring, bringing it down slowly.

She was struggling desperately, but they held her and her hair had come loose as she fought.

'Slowly, lad,' the man in the cap spoke in a thick strangled voice. 'Give her time to think about it.'

Sherry screamed again as her fingers were forced down remorselessly towards the hissing blue flames.

'Go ahead, luv, shout your head off,' laughed the blond. 'There isn't anybody to hear you.'

'Only me,' I said, and they spun to face me, with expressions of comical amazement.

'Who—' asked the blond, releasing Sherry's arm and reaching quickly for his back pocket.

I hit him twice, left in the body and right in the head, and although neither shot pleased me particularly – there was not the right solidness at impact – the man went down, falling heavily over a chair and crashing into the cupboard. I had no more time for him, and I went for the one in the cloth cap.

He was still holding Sherry in front of him, and as I started forward he hurled her at me. It took me off-balance and I was forced to grab her, to save both of us from falling.

The man turned and darted out of the door behind him. It took me a few seconds to disentangle myself from Sherry and cross the kitchen. As I barged out into the yard he was halfway to an elderly Triumph sports car, and he glanced over his shoulder.

I could almost see him make the calculation. He wasn't going to be able to get into the car and turn it to face the lane before I caught him. He swerved to the left and sprinted into the dark mouth of the lane with the skirts of the camel-hair coat billowing behind him. I raced after him.

The surface was greasy with wet clay, and he was making heavy going of it. He slid and almost fell, and I was right behind him, coming up swiftly when he turned and I heard the snap of the knife and saw the flash of the blade as it jumped out. He dropped into a crouch with the knife extended and I ran straight in without a check.

He didn't expect that, the glint of steel will stop most men dead. He went for my belly, a low underhand stroke, but he was shaky and breathless and it lacked fire. I blocked on the wrist and at the same time hit the pressure point in his forearm. The knife dropped out of his hand and I threw him over my hip. He fell heavily on his back, and although the mud softened the impact I dropped on one knee into his belly. It had two hundred and ten pounds of body weight behind it and it drove the air out of his lungs in a loud whoosh. He doubled up like a foetus in the womb, wheezing for breath, and I flipped him over on to his face. The cloth cap fell off his head and I found that he had a thick shock of dark hair shot through with strands of silver. I took a good handful of it, sat on his shoulders and pushed his face deep into the yellow mud.

'I don't like little boys who bully girls,' I told him conversationally, and behind me the engine of the Triumph roared into life. The headlights blazed out and then swung in a wide arc until they burned directly up the narrow lane.

I knew I hadn't taken the blond out properly, it had been a hurried botchy job. I left the man in the mud and ran back down the lane. The wheels of the Triumph spun on the paving of the barnyard and, with its headlights blazing dazzlingly into my eyes, it jumped forward, slewing and skidding as it left the paving and entered the muddy lane. The driver met the skid and came straight at me.

I fell flat and rolled into the cold ooze of a narrow open drain that carried run-off water through the tall hedge.

The Triumph hit the side a glancing blow and the hedge

pushed it slightly off its line. The nearside wheels spun viciously on the edge of the stone coping of the drain inches from my face, and mud and a shower of twigs fell on me. Then it was past.

It checked as it came level with the man in the muddy camel-hair coat. He was kneeling on the verge of the road and now he dragged himself into the passenger seat of the Triumph. Just as I crawled out of the drain and ran up behind the sports car it pulled away again, mud spraying from the spinning rear wheels. In vain I raced after it, but it gathered speed and tore away up the slope.

I gave up, turned and ran back down the lane, groping for the keys of the Chrysler in my sodden trouser pockets, and realized I had left them on the table in Jimmy's room.

Sherry was leaning in the open doorway of the kitchen. She held her burned hand to her chest and her hair was in tangled disarray. The sleeve of her jersey was torn loose from the shoulder.

'I couldn't stop him, Harry,' she gasped. 'I tried.'

'How bad is it?' I asked her, abandoning all thought of chasing the sports car when I saw her distress.

'Slightly singed.'

'I'll take you to a doctor.'

'No. It doesn't need it,' but her smile was lopsided with pain. I went up to Jimmy's room and from my travelling medicine kit I took a Doloxene for the pain and Mogadon to let her sleep.

'I don't need it,' she protested.

'Do I have to hold your nose and force them down?' I asked, and she grinned, shook her head and swallowed them.

'You'd better take a bath,' she said, 'you are soaked,' and suddenly I realized I was sodden and cold. When I came back to the kitchen, glowing from the bath, she was already whoozy with the pills, but she had made coffee for us and

170

strengthened it with a tot of whisky. We drank it sitting opposite each other.

'What did they want?' I asked. 'What did they say?'

'They thought I knew why Jimmy had gone to St Mary's. They wanted to know.'

I thought about that. Something didn't make sense, it worried me.

'I think—' Sherry's voice was unsteady and she staggered slightly as she tried to stand. 'Wow! What did you give me?'

I picked her up and she protested weakly, but I carried her up to her room. It was chintzy and girlish, with rose-patterned wallpaper. I laid her on the bed, pulled off her shoes and covered her with the quilt.

She sighed and closed her eyes. 'I think I'll keep you around,' she whispered. 'You're very useful.'

Thus encouraged, I sat on the edge of the bed and gentled her to sleep, smoothing her hair off her temples and stroking the broad forehead; her skin felt like warm velvet. She was asleep within a minute. I switched off the light, and was about to leave when I thought better of it.

I slipped off my own shoes and crept in under the quilt. In her sleep she rolled quite naturally into my arms, and I held her close.

It was a good feeling and soon I slept also. I woke in the dawn. Her face was pressed into my neck, one leg and arm were thrown over me and her hair was soft and tickling against my cheek.

Without waking her, I gently disengaged myself, kissed her forehead, picked up my shoes and went back to my own room. It was the first time I had spent an entire night with a beautiful woman in my arms, and done nothing but sleep. I felt puffed up with virtue.

The letter lay upon the reading table in Jimmy's room where I had left it and I read it through again before I went to the bathroom. The pencilled note in the margin 'B. Mus. E. 6914(8)' puzzled me and I fretted over it while I shaved.

The rain had stopped and the clouds were breaking up when I went down into the yard to examine the scene of the previous night's encounter. The knife lay in the mud and I picked it up and tossed it over the hedge. I went into the kitchen, stamping my feet and rubbing my hands in the cold.

Sherry had started breakfast.

'How's the hand?'

'Sore,' she admitted.

'We'll find a doctor on the way up to London.'

'What makes you think I'm going to London?' she asked carefully, as she buttered toast.

'Two things. You can't stay here. The wolf pack will be back.' She looked up at me quickly but was silent. 'The other is that you promised to help me – and the trail leads to London.'

She was unconvinced, so while we ate I showed her the letter I had found in Jimmy's file.

'I don't see the connection,' she said at last, and I admitted frankly, 'It's not clear to me even.' I lit my first cheroot of the day as I spoke, and the effect was almost magical. 'But as soon as I saw the words *Dawn Light* something went click—' I stopped. 'My God!' I breathed. 'That's it. The *Dawn Light!*' I remembered the scraps of conversation carried to the bridge of *Wave Dancer* through the ventilator from the cabin below.

'To get the dawn light then we will have to—' Jimmy's voice, clear and tight with anticipation. 'If the dawn light is where—' Again the words repeated had puzzled me at the time. They had stuck like burrs in my memory.

I began to explain to Sherry, but I was so excited that it came tumbling out in a rush of words. She laughed, catching my excitement but not understanding the explanations.

'Hey!' she protested. 'You are not making sense.'

I began again, but halfway through I stopped and stared at her silently.

'Now what is it?' She was half amused, half exasperated. 'This is driving me crazy, also.'

I snatched up my fork. 'The bell. You remember the bell I told you about. The one Jimmy pulled up at Gunfire Reef?'

'Yes, of course.'

'I told you it had lettering on it, half eaten away by sand.'

'Yes, go on.'

With the fork I scratched on the butter, using it as a slate.

' – VV N L—'

I drew in the lettering that had been chased into the bronze.

'That was it,' I said. 'It didn't mean anything then – but now—' Quickly I completed the letters, 'DAWN LIGHT'.

And she stared at it, nodding slowly as it fitted together.

'We have to find out about this ship, the *Dawn Light*.'

'How?'

'It should be easy. We know she was an East Indiaman – there must be records – Lloyd's – the Board of Trade?'

She took the letter from my hand and read it again. 'The gallant colonel's luggage probably contained dirty socks and old shirts.' She pulled a face and handed it back to me.

'I'm short of socks,' I said.

173

Sherry packed a case, and I was relieved to see that she had the rare virtue of being able to travel light. She went down to speak to the tenant farmer while I packed the bags into the Chrysler. He would keep an eye on the cottage during her absence, and when she came back she merely locked the kitchen door and climbed into the Chrysler beside me.

'Funny,' she said. 'This feels like the beginning of a long journey.'

'I have my plans,' I warned and leered at her.

'Once I thought you looked wholesome,' she said sorrowfully, 'but when you do that—'

'Sexy, isn't it?' I agreed, and took the Chrysler up the lane.

I found a doctor in Haywards Heath. Sherry's hand had now blistered badly, fat white bags of fluid hung from her fingers like sickly grapes. He drained them, and rebandaged the hand.

'Feels worse now,' she murmured as we drove on northwards, and she was pale and silent with the pain of it. I respected her silence, until we were into the suburbs of the city.

'We had better find some place to stay,' I suggested. 'Something comfortable and central.'

She looked across at me quizzically.

'It would probably be a lot more comfortable and cheaper if we got a double room somewhere, wouldn't it?'

I felt something turn over in my belly, something warm and exciting. 'Funny you should say that, I was just about to suggest the same.'

'I know you were,' she laughed for the first time in two hours. 'I saved you the trouble.' She shook her head, still laughing. 'I'll stay with my uncle. He's got a spare room in his apartment in Pimlico, and there is a little pub around the corner. It's friendly and clean – you could do worse.'

174

'I am crazy about your sense of humour,' I muttered.

She phoned the uncle from a call box, while I waited in the car.

'It's fixed up,' she told me, as she climbed into the passenger seat. 'He's at home.'

It was a ground-floor apartment in a quiet street near the river. I carried Sherry's bag for her as she led the way, and rang the doorbell.

The man that opened the door was small and lightly built. He was sixtyish and he wore a grey cardigan, darned at the elbows. His feet were thrust into carpet slippers. The homely attire was somehow incongruous, for his iron-grey hair was neatly cropped as was the short stiff moustache. His skin was clear and ruddy, but it was the fierce predatory glint of the eye and the military set of the shoulders that warned me. This man was aware.

'My uncle, Dan Wheeler.' Sherry stood aside to introduce us. 'Uncle Dan this is Harry Fletcher.'

'The young man you were telling me about,' he nodded abruptly. His hand was bony and dry and his gaze stung like nettles. 'Come in. Come in, both of you.'

'I won't bother you, sir—' it was quite natural to call him that, an echo of my military training from so long ago, 'I want to find digs myself.'

Uncle Dan and Sherry exchanged glances and I thought she shook her head almost imperceptibly, but I was looking beyond them into the apartment. It was monastic, completely masculine in the severity and economy of furniture and ornaments. Somehow that room seemed to confirm my first impressions of the man. I wanted as little to do with him as I could arrange while seeing as much of Sherry as I possibly could.

'I'll pick you up in an hour for lunch, Sherry,' and when she agreed I left them and returned to the Chrysler. The pub that Sherry recommended was the Windsor Arms, and

175

when I mentioned the uncle's name as she suggested, they put me in a quiet back room with a fine view of sky and television aerials. I lay on the bed fully clothed, and considered the North family and its relatives while I waited for the hour to run by. Of one thing only was I certain – that Sherry North the Second was not going to pass me silently in the night. I was going to keep pretty close station upon her, and yet there was much about her that still puzzled me. I suspected that she was a more complicated person than her serene and lovely face suggested. It was going to be interesting finding out. I put the thought aside, sat up and reached for the telephone. I made three phone calls in the next twenty minutes. One to Lloyd's Register of Shipping in Fenchurch Street, another to the National Maritime Museum at Greenwich and the last to the India Office Library in Blackfriars Road. I left the Chrysler in the private parking lot behind the pub, a car is more trouble than it is worth in London, and I walked back to the uncle's apartment. Sherry answered the door herself, and she was ready to leave. I liked that about her, she was punctual.

'You didn't like Uncle Dan, did you?' she challenged me over the lunch table and I ducked.

'I made some phone calls. The place that we are looking for is in Blackfriars Road. It's in Westminster. The India Office Library. We will go down there after we've eaten.'

'He really is very sweet when you get to know him.'

'Look, darling girl, he's your uncle. You keep him.'

'But why, Harry? It interests me.'

'What does he do for a living – army, navy?'

She stared at me. 'How did you know that?'

'I can pick them out of a crowd.'

'He's army, but retired – why should that make a difference?'

'What are you going to try?' I waved the menu at her. 'If

176

you take the roast beef, I'll go for the duck,' and she accepted the decoy, and concentrated on the food.

The India Office Archives were housed in one of those square modern blocks of greenish glass and airforce-blue steel panels.

Sherry and I armed ourselves with visitor's passes and signed the book. We made our way first to the Catalogue Room and thence to the marine section of the archives. These were presided over by a neatly dressed but stern-faced lady with greying hair and steel-rimmed spectacles.

I handed her a requisition slip for the dossier which would include material on the Honourable Company's ship *Dawn Light* and she disappeared amongst the laden ceiling-high tiers of steel shelving.

It was twenty minutes before she returned and placed a bulky dossier on the counter top before me.

'You'll have to sign here,' she told me, indicating a column on the stiff cardboard folder. 'Funny!' she remarked. 'You are the second one who has asked for this file in less than a year.'

I started at the signature J. A. North in the last space. We were following closely in Jimmy's footsteps, I thought, as I signed 'RICHARD SMITH' below his name.

'You can use the desks over there, dear.' She pointed across the room. 'Please try and keep the file tidy, won't you, then.'

Sherry and I sat down at the desk shoulder to shoulder, and I untied the tape that secured the file.

The *Dawn Light* was of the type known as the Blackwall frigate, characteristically built at the Blackwall yards in the early nineteenth century. The type was very similar to the naval frigates of that period.

She had been built at Sunderland for the Honourable English East India Company, and she was of 1330 net register tons. At the waterline her dimensions were 226 feet with a beam of twenty-six feet. Such a narrow beam would have made her very fast but uncomfortable in a stiff blow.

She had been launched in 1832, just the year before the Company lost its China monopoly, and this stroke of ill-fortune seemed to have dogged her whole career.

Also in the file were a whole series of reports of the proceedings of various courts of inquiry. Her first master gloried in the name of Hogge and on her maiden voyage he piled the *Dawn Light* on to the bank at Diamond Harbour in Hooghly River. He was found by the court of inquiry to be under the influence of strong drink at the time and stripped of his command.

'Made a pig of himself,' I observed to Sherry, and she groaned softly and rolled her eyes at my wit.

The trail of misfortune continued. In 1840 while making passage in the South Atlantic the elderly mate who had the dog watch let her come up, and away went her masts. Wallowing helpless with her top hamper dragging along-side, she was found by a Dutchman. They cut away the wreckage and she was dragged into Table Bay. The Salvage Court made an award of £12,000.

In 1846 while half her crew were ashore on the wild coast of New Guinea they were set upon by the canni-bals and slaughtered to a man. Sixty-three of her crew died.

Then on the 23rd September, 1857, she sailed from Bombay, outward bound for St Mary's the Cape of Good Hope, St Helena and the Pool of London.

'The date.' I placed my finger on the line. 'This is the voyage that Goodchild talks of in the letter.'

Sherry nodded without reply, I had learned in the last few minutes that she read faster than I did. I had to restrain her from turning each page when I was only three-quarters finished. Now her eyes darted across each line, her colour was up, a soft flush upon her pale cheeks, and she was biting her underlip.

'Come on,' she urged me. 'Hurry up!' and I had to hold her wrist.

The *Dawn Light* never reached St Mary's – she disappeared. Three months later, she was considered lost at sea with all hands and the underwriters were ordered by Lloyd's to make good their assurances to the owners and shippers.

The manifest of her cargo was impressive for such a small ship for she had loaded out of China and India a cargo that consisted of:

364 chests of tea	72 tons on behalf of Messrs
494 half-chests of tea	Dunbar and Green.
101 chests of tea	65 tons on behalf of Messrs
618 half-chests of tea	Simpson, Wyllie & Livingstone.
577 bales of silk	82 tons on behalf of Messrs Elder and Company.
5 cases goods	4 tons on behalf of Col. Sir Roger Goodchild.
16 cases goods	6 tons on behalf of Major John Cotton.
10 cases goods	2 tons on behalf of Lord Elton.
26 boxes various spices	2 tons on behalf of Messrs Paulson and Company.

Wordlessly I laid my finger on the fourth item of the manifest, and again Sherry nodded, with her eyes shining like sapphires. The claim had been settled and the matter appeared closed until, four months later in April, 1858 the East Indiaman *Walmer Castle* arrived in England, carrying aboard the survivors from the *Dawn Light*.

There were six of them. The first mate, Andrew Barlow, a boatswain's mate, and three topmast men. There was also a young woman of twenty-two years, a Miss Charlotte Cotton, who had been a passenger making the homeward passage with her father, a Major in the 40th Foot.

The mate, Andrew Barlow, gave his evidence to the Court of Inquiry, and beneath the dry narrative and the ponderous questions and guarded replies lay an exciting and romantic story of the sea, an epic of shipwreck and survival.

As we read I saw the meagre scraps of knowledge I had scraped together fit neatly into the story.

Fourteen days out from Bombay, the *Dawn Light* was set upon by a furious storm out of the south-east. For seven days the savagery of the storm raged unabated, driving the ship before her. I could imagine it clearly, one of those great cyclones that had torn the roof from my own shack at Turtle Bay.

Once again *Dawn Light* was dismasted, no spars were left standing except the fore lower mast, mizzen lower mast, and bowsprit. The rest had carried away on the tempest and there was no opportunity to set up a jury mainmast or send yards aloft in the mountainous seas.

Thus when land was sighted to leeward, there was no chance that the ship might avoid her fate. A conspiracy of wind and current hurled her down into the throat of a funnel-shaped reef upon which the storm surf burst like the thunder of the heavens.

The ship struck and held, and Andrew Barlow was able with the help of twelve members of his crew to launch one of the boats. Four passengers including Miss Charlotte Cotton left the stricken ship with them, and Barlow, with an unlikely combination of good fortune and seamanship, was able to find a passage through the wild sea and murderous reefs into the quieter waters of the inshore channel.

Finally they ran the boat ashore on the spindrift-smothered beach of an island. Here the survivors huddled for four days while the cyclone blew itself out.

Barlow alone climbed to the summit of the southernmost of the treble peaks of the island. The description was completely clear. It was the Old Men and Gunfire Reef. There was no doubt of it. This then was how Jimmy North had known what he was looking for – the island with three peaks and a barrier of coral reef.

Barlow took bearings off the sea-battered hull of the *Dawn Light* as she lay in the jaws of the reef, swept by each successive wave. On the second day the ship's hull began to break up, and while Barlow watched from the peak, the front half of her was carried up over the reef to disappear into a dark gaping hole in the coral. The stern fell back into the sea and was smashed to matchwood.

When at last the skies cleared and the wind dropped, Andrew Barlow discovered that his small party were all that survived from a ship's company of 149 souls. The others had perished in the wild sea.

To the west, low against the horizon, he descried a low land mass which he hoped was the African mainland. He embarked his party in the ship's boat once more and they made the crossing of the inshore channel. His hopes were fulfilled, it was Africa – but as always she was hostile and cruel.

The seventeen lost beings began a long and dangerous journey southwards, and three months later only Barlow, four seamen and Miss Charlotte Cotton reached the island port of Zanzibar. Fever, wild animals, wild men and misfortune had whittled away their numbers – and even those who survived were starved to gaunt living skeletons, yellowed with fever and riddled with dysentery from foul water.

The court of inquiry had highly commended Andrew Barlow, and the Hon. Company had made him an award of £500 for meritorious service.

When I finished reading, I looked up at Sherry. She was watching me.

'Wow!' she said, and I also felt drained by the magnitude of the old drama.

'It all fits, Sherry,' I said. 'It's all there.'

'Yes,' she said.

'We must see if they have the drawings here.'

The Prints and Drawings Room was on the third floor and a quick search by an earnest assistant soon revealed the *Dawn Light* in all her splendour.

She was a graceful three-masted ship with a long low profile. She had no crossjack or mizzen course. Instead she carried a large spanker and a full set of studding sails. The long poop gave space for several passenger cabins, and she carried her boats on top of her deckhouse aft.

She was heavily armed, with thirteen black-painted gunports a side, from which she could run out her long eighteen-pounder cannon to defend herself, in those hostile seas east of the Cape of Good Hope across which she plied to China and India.

'I need a drink,' I said, and picked up the drawings of the *Dawn Light*. 'I'll get them to make copies of these for us.'

'What for?' Sherry wanted to know.

The assistant emerged from her lair amongst the piled trays of old prints and sucked in her cheeks at my request for copies.

'I'll have to charge you seventy-five pence,' she tried to discourage me.

'That's reasonable,' I said.

'And we won't have them ready until next week,' she added inexorably.

'Oh dear,' said I, and gave her the smile. 'I did need them tomorrow afternoon.'

The smile crushed her, she lost the air of purpose and tried to tuck her straying wisps of hair into the side frames of her glasses.

'Well, I'll see what I can do then,' she relented.

'That's very sweet of you, really it is,' and we left her looking confused, but pleased.

M y sense of direction was returning and I found my way to El Vino's without trouble. The evening flood of journalists from Fleet Street had not yet swamped it and we found a table at the back. I ordered two Vermouths and we saluted each other over the glasses.

'You know, Harry, Jimmy had a hundred schemes. His whole life was one great treasure hunt. Every week he had found, almost found, the location of a treasure ship from the Armada or a sunken Aztec city, a buccaneer wreck—' she shrugged. 'I have a built-in resistance to believing any of it. But this one—' She sipped the wine.

'Let's go over what we have,' I suggested. 'We know that Goodchild was very concerned that his agent receive five cases of luggage and put it into safe keeping. We know that he was going to ship it aboard *Dawn Light* and he sent advance notice, probably through a personal friend, the captain of the naval frigate *Panther*.'

'Good,' she agreed.

'We know that those cases were listed on the ship's

manifest. That the ship was lost, presumably with them still on board. We know the exact location of the wreck. We have had it confirmed by the ship's bell.'

'Still good.'

'We only do not know what those cases contained.'

'Dirty socks,' she said.

'Four tons of dirty socks?' I asked, and her expression changed. The weight of the cargo had not meant anything to her.

'Ah,' I grinned at her, 'it went over your head. I thought so. You read so fast you only take in half of it.'

She pulled a face at me.

'Four tons, my darling girl, is a great deal of something – whatever it is.'

'All right,' she agreed. 'Figures don't mean much to me, I admit. But it sounds a lot.'

'Say the same weight as a new Rolls-Royce – to put it in terms you might understand,' and her eyes widened and turned a darker blue.

'That *is* a lot.'

'Jimmy obviously knew what it was, and had proof sufficient to convince some very hard-headed backers. They took it seriously.'

'Seriously enough to—' and she stopped herself. For an instant I saw the old grief for Jimmy's death in her eyes. I was embarrassed by it, and I looked away, making a show of taking the letter out of my inner pocket.

Carefully I spread it on the table top between us. When I looked at her, she had recovered her composure once more.

The pencilled note in the margin engaged my attention again.

'B.Mus. E.6914(8).' I read it aloud. 'Any ideas?'

'Bachelor of Music.'

'Oh, that's great,' I applauded.

'You do better,' she challenged, and I folded the letter away with dignity and ordered two more drinks.

'Well, that was a good run on that scent,' I said when I had paid the waiter. 'We have an idea what it was all about. Now, we can go on my other lead.'

She sat forward and encouraged me silently.

'I told you about your impostor, the blonde Sherry North?' and she nodded. 'On the night before she left the island she sent a cable to London.' I produced the flimsy from my wallet and handed it to Sherry. While she read it, I went on: 'This was clearly an okay to her principal, Manson. He must be the big man behind this. I am going to start moving in on him now.' I finished my Vermouth. 'I'll drop you back with your martial uncle, and contact you again tomorrow.'

Her lips set in a line of stubbornness which I had not seen before and there was a glint in her eyes like the blue of gun-metal.

'Harry Fletcher, if you think you are going to ditch me just when things start livening up, you must be off your tiny head.'

The cab dropped us in Berkeley Square and I led her into Curzon Street.

'Take my arm quickly,' I muttered, glancing over my shoulder in a secretive manner. Instantly she obeyed, and we had gone fifty yards before she whispered, 'Why?'

'Because I like the feel of it,' I grinned at her and spoke in a natural voice.

'Oh, you!' She made as if to pull away, but I held her and she capitulated. We sauntered up the street towards Shepherd Market, stopping now and then to window-shop like a pair of tourists.

No. 97 Curzon Street was one of those astronomically expensive apartment blocks, six storeys of brick facing, and an ornate street door of bronze and glass beyond which was a marbled foyer guarded by a uniformed doorman. We went on past it, up as far as the White Elephant Club and there we crossed the street and wandered back on the opposite pavement.

'I could go and ask the doorman if Mr Manson occupied Flat No. 5,' Sherry volunteered.

'Great,' I said. 'Then he says "yes", what do you do then? Tell him Harry Fletcher says hello?'

'You are really very droll,' she said, and once more she tried to take her hand away.

'There is a restaurant diagonally opposite No. 97.' I prevented her withdrawal. 'Let's get a table in the front window, drink some coffee and watch for a while.'

It was a little past three o'clock when we settled at the window seat with a good view across the street, and the next hour passed pleasantly. I found it not a difficult task to keep Sherry amused, we shared a similar sense of humour and I liked to hear her laugh.

I was in the middle of a long, complicated story when I was interrupted by the arrival outside No. 97 of a Silver Wraith Rolls-Royce. It pulled to the kerb and a chauffeur in a smart dove-grey uniform left the car and entered the foyer. He and the doorman fell into conversation, and I resumed my story.

Ten minutes later, there was sudden activity opposite. The elevator began a series of rapid ascents and descents, each time discharging a load of matching crocodile-skin luggage. This was carried out by the doorman and chauffeur and packed into the Rolls. It seemed endless, and Sherry remarked, 'Somebody is off on a long holiday.' She sighed wistfully.

'How do you fancy a tropical island with blue water and white sands, a thatched shack amongst the palms—'

'Stop it,' she said. 'On an autumn day in old London, I just can't bear the thought.'

I was about to move into a stronger position when the footman and chauffeur stood to attention and once more the glass doors of the lift opened and a man and woman stepped out of it.

The woman wore a full-length honey mink and her blonde hair was piled high on her head in an elaborate lacquered Grecian style. Anger struck me like a fist in the guts as I recognized her.

It was Sherry North, the First. The nice lady who had blown Judith and *Wave Dancer* to the bottom of Grand Harbour.

With her was a man of medium height with soft brown hair fashionably long and curly over his ears. He had a light tan, probably from a sun lamp, and he was dressed too well. Very expensively, but as flamboyantly as an entertainment personality.

He had a heavy jaw and a long fleshy nose with soft gazelle eyes, but his mouth was pinched and hungry. A greedy mouth that I remembered so well.

'Manson!' I said. 'Jesus! Manson Resnick – Manny Resnick.' He would be just the one Jimmy North would find his way to with his outrageous proposition. In exactly the same way that so long ago I had gone to him with my plans for the gold heist at Rome Airport. Manny was an underworld entrepreneur, and he had clearly climbed a long way up the ladder since our last meeting.

He was keeping great style now, I thought, as he crossed the pavement and entered the back seat of the Rolls, settling down next to the mink-clad blonde.

'Wait here,' I told Sherry urgently, as the Rolls pulled away towards Park Lane.

I ran out on to the pavement and searched wildly for a cab to follow them. There were none and I ran after the Rolls praying desperately for the sight of a big black cab with its top light burning, but ahead of me the Rolls swung

187

right into South Audley Street and accelerated smoothly away.

I stopped at the corner and it was already far ahead, infiltrating the traffic towards Grosvenor Square.

I turned and ambled disappointedly back to where Sherry waited. I knew that Sherry had been correct. Manny and the blonde were off on a long journey. There was no point in hanging around No. 97 Curzon Street any longer.

Sherry was waiting for me outside the restaurant.

'What was that all about?' she demanded and I took her arm. As we walked back towards Berkeley Square, I told her.

'That man is probably the one who ordered Jimmy murdered, who was responsible for having half my chest shot away, who had them to roast your lovely pinkies – in short, the big man.'

'You know him?'

'I did business with him a long time ago.'

'Nice friends you have.'

'I'm trying for a better class lately,' I said, and squeezed her arm. She ignored my gallantry.

'And the woman. Is she the one from St Mary's, the one who blew up your boat and the young girl?'

I experienced a violent return of the anger which had gripped me a few minutes earlier when I had seen that sleek, meticulously polished predator dressed in mink.

Beside me Sherry gasped, 'Harry, you are hurting me!'

'Sorry.' I relaxed my grip on her arm.

'I guess that answers my question,' she muttered ruefully, and massaged her upper arm.

The private bar of the Windsor Arms was all dark oak panels and antique mirrors. It was crowded by the time Sherry and I returned. Outside darkness had fallen and there was an icy wind stirring the fallen leaves in the gutters.

The warmth of the pub was welcome. We found seats in a corner, but the crowd pushed us together, forcing me to place an arm around Sherry's shoulders, and our heads were close so we could hold a very private conversation in this public place.

'I can guess where Manny Resnick and his friend are headed,' I said.

'Big Gull Island?' Sherry asked, and when I nodded she went on, 'He'll need a boat and divers.'

'Don't worry, Manny will get them.'

'And what will we do?'

'We?' I asked.

'A form of speech,' she corrected herself primly. 'What will you do?'

'I have a choice. I can forget about it all – or I can go back to Gunfire Reef and try to find out what the hell was in Colonel Goodchild's five cases.'

'You'll need equipment.'

'It might not be as elaborate as Manny Resnick's will be, but I could get enough together.'

'How are you for money, or is that a rude question?'

'The answer is the same. I could get enough together.'

'Blue water and white sand,' she murmured dreamily.

' – and the palm fronds clattering in the trade winds.'

'Stop it, Harry.'

'Fat crayfish grilling on the coals, and me beside you singing in the wilderness,' I went on remorselessly.

'Pig,' she said.

'If you stay here, you'll never know if it was dirty socks,' I pressed her.

'You'd write and tell me,' she pleaded.

'No, I wouldn't.'

'I'll have to come with you,' she said at last.

'Good girl.' I squeezed her shoulder.

'But I insist on paying my own way, I refuse to become a

189

kept woman.' She had guessed how hard pressed I was financially.

'I should hate to erode your principles,' I told her happily, and my wallet sighed with relief. It was going to be a near-run thing to mount an expedition to Gunfire Reef on what I had left.

There was much we had to discuss now that the decision had been made. It seemed only minutes later that the landlord was calling, 'Time, gentlemen.'

'The streets are dangerous at night,' I warned Sherry. 'I don't think we should chance it. Upstairs I have a very comfortable room with a fine view—'

'Come on, Fletcher.' Sherry stood up. 'You had better walk me home, or I shall set my uncle on to you.'

As we walked the half block to her uncle's apartment, we agreed to meet for lunch next day. I had a list of errands to perform in the morning including making the airline reservations, while Sherry had to have her passport renewed and pick up the photostat drawings of the *Dawn Light*.

At the door of the apartment we faced each other, suddenly both of us were shy. It was so terribly corny that I almost laughed. We were like a pair of old-fashioned teenagers at the end of our first date – but sometimes corny feels good.

'Good night, Harry,' she said, and with the age-old artistry of womankind she showed me in some indefinable manner that she was ready for kissing.

Her lips were soft and warm, and the kiss went on for a long time.

'My goodness,' she whispered throatily, and drew away at last.

'Are you sure you won't change your mind – it is a beautiful room, hot and cold water, carpets on the floor, TV—'

She laughed shakily and pushed me gently backwards. 'Goodnight, dear Harry,' she repeated, and left me.

I went out into the street and strolled back towards my pub. The wind had dropped but I could smell the damp emanating from the river close by. The street was deserted but the kerb was lined with parked vehicles, bumper to bumper they reached to the corner.

I sauntered along the pavement, in no hurry for bed, even toying with the idea of a stroll down the Embankment first. My hands were thrust deep into the pockets of my car coat, and I was feeling relaxed and happy as I thought about this woman.

There was a lot to think about Sherry North, much that was unclear or not yet explained, but mainly I cherished the thought that perhaps here at last was something that might last longer than a night, a week, or a month – something that was already strong and that would not be like the others, diminishing with the passage of time, but instead would grow ever stronger.

Suddenly a voice beside me said, 'Harry!' It was a man's voice, a strange voice, and I turned instinctively towards it. As I did so I knew that it was a mistake.

The speaker was sitting in the back seat of one of the parked cars. It was a black Rover. The window was open and his face was merely a pale blob in the darkness of the interior.

Desperately I tried to pull my hands out of my pockets and turn to face the direction from which I knew the attack would come. As I turned I ducked and twisted, and something whirred past my ear and struck my shoulder a numbing blow.

I struck backwards with both elbows, connecting solidly and hearing the gasp of pain. Then my hands were clear and I was around, moving fast, weaving, for I knew they would use the cosh again.

They were just midnight shapes, menacing and huge, dressed in dark clothing. It seemed there were a legion of them, but there were only four – and one in the car. They were all big men, and the one had the cosh up to strike again. I hit him under the chin with the palm of my hand, snapping his head backwards and I thought I might have broken his neck, for he went down hard on the pavement.

A knee drove for my groin, but I turned and caught it on the thigh, using the impetus of the turn to counter-punch. It was a good one, jolting me to the shoulder, and the man took it in the chest, and was thrown backwards, but immediately one of them was hugging the arm, smothering it and a fist caught me in the cheek under the eye. I felt the skin tear open.

Another one was on my back, an arm around my throat throttling me, but I heaved and pushed. In a tight knot, locked together, we surged around the pavement.

'Hold him still,' another voice called, low and urgent. 'Let me get a shot at him.'

'What the bloody hell do you think we are trying to do?' panted another, and we fell against the side of the Rover. I was pinned there, and I saw the one with the cosh was on his feet. He swung again, and I tried to roll my head, but it caught me in the temple. It did not put me out completely, but it knocked all the fight out of me. I was instantly weak as a child, hardly able to support my own weight.

'That's it, get him into the back.' They hustled me into the centre seat of the back of the Rover and one of them crowded in on each side of me. The doors slammed, the engine whirred and caught and we pulled away swiftly.

My brain cleared, but the side of my head was numb and felt like a balloon. There were three of them in the front seat, one on each side of me in the back. All of them were breathing heavily, and the one next to the driver was massaging his neck and jaw tenderly. The one on my right had been eating garlic, and he panted heavily as he searched me for weapons.

'I think you should know that something died in your mouth a long time ago, and it's still there,' I told him, with a thickened tongue and an ache in my head, but the effort was not worth it. He showed no sign of having heard, but continued doggedly with this task. At last he was satisfied and I readjusted my clothing.

We drove in silence for five minutes, following the river towards Hammersmith, before they had all recovered their breath and tended their wounds, then the driver spoke.

'Listen, Manny wants to talk to you, but he said it's no big thing. He was merely curious. He said also that if you gave us a hard time, not to go to no trouble, just to sign you off and toss you in the river.'

'Charming chap, Manny,' I said.

'Shut up!' said the driver. 'So you see, it's up to you. Behave yourself and you get to live a little longer. I heard you used to be a sharp operator, Harry. We been expecting you to show up, ever since Lorna missed you on the island – but sure as hell we didn't expect you to parade up and down Curzon Street like a brass band. Manny couldn't believe it. He said, "That can't be Harry. He must have gone soft." It made him sad. "How are the mighty fallen. Tell it not in the streets of Ashkelon," he said.'

'That's Shakespeare,' said the one with the garlic breath.

'Shut up,' said the driver and then went on. 'Manny was sad but not that sad that he cried or anything, you understand.'

'I understand,' I mumbled.

'Shut up,' said the driver. 'Manny said, "Don't do it here. Just follow him to a nice quiet place and pick him up. If he comes quietly you bring him to talk to me – if he cuts up rough then toss him in the river."'

'That sounds like my boy, Manny. He always was a soft-hearted little devil.'

'Shut up,' said the driver.

'I look forward to seeing him again.'

'You just stay good and quiet and you might get lucky.'

I stayed that way through the night as we picked up the M4 and rushed westwards. It was two in the morning when we entered Bristol, skirting the city centre as we followed the A4 down to Avonmouth.

Amongst the other craft in the yacht basin was a big motor yacht. She was moored to the wharf and she had her gangplank down. Her name painted on the stern and bows was *Mandrake*. She was an ocean-goer, steel-hulled painted blue and white, with pleasing lines. I judged her fast and sea-kindly, probably with sufficient range to take her anywhere in the world. A rich man's toy. There were figures on her bridge, lights burning in most of her portholes, and she seemed ready for sea.

They crowded me as we crossed the narrow space to the gangplank. The Rover backed and turned and drove away as we climbed to the *Mandrake's* deck.

The saloon was too tastefully fitted out for Manny Resnick's style, it had either been done by the previous owners or a professional decorator. There were forest-green wall-to-wall carpets and matching velvet curtains, the furniture was dark teak and polished leather and the pictures were choice oils toned to the general décor.

This was half a million pounds worth of vessel, and I guessed it was a charter. Manny had probably taken her for six months and put in his own crew – for Manny Resnick had never struck me as a blue-water man.

As we waited in the centre of the wall-to-wall carpeting, a grimly silent group, I heard the unmistakable sounds of the gangplank being taken in, and the moorings cast off. The tremble of her engines become a steady beat, and the harbour lights slid past the saloon portholes as we left the entrance and thrust out into the tidal waters of the River Severn.

I recognized the lighthouses at Portishead Point and Red Cliff Bay as *Mandrake* came around for the run down-river past Weston-super-Mare and Berry for the open sea.

Manny came at last, he wore a blue silk gown and his face was still crumpled from sleep, but his curls were neatly combed and his smile was white and hungry.

'Harry,' he said, 'I told you that you would be back.'

'Hello, Manny. I can't say it's any great pleasure.'

He laughed lightly and turned to the woman as she followed him into the saloon. She was carefully made up and every hair of the elaborate hairstyle was in its place. She wore a long white house-gown with lace at throat and cuffs.

'You have met Lorna, I believe, Lorna Page.'

'Next time you send somebody to hustle me, Manny, try for a little better class. I'm getting fussy in my old age.'

Her eyes slanted wickedly, but she smiled.

'How's your boat, Harry? Your lovely boat?'

'It makes a lousy coffin.' I turned back to Manny. 'What's it going to be, Manny, can we work out a deal?'

He shook his head sorrowfully. 'I don't think so, Harry. I would like to – truly I would, if just for old times' sake. But I can't see it. Firstly, you haven't anything to trade – and that makes for a lousy deal. Secondly, I know you are too sentimental. You'd louse up any deal we did make for purely emotional reasons. I couldn't trust you, Harry, all the time you'd be thinking about Jimmy North and your boat, you'd be thinking about the little island girl that got in the way, and about Jimmy North's sister who we had to get rid of—' I took a mild pleasure in the fact that Manny had obviously not heard what had happened to the goon squad he had sent to take care of Sherry North, and that she was still very much alive. I tried to make my voice sincere and my manner convincing.

'Listen, Manny, I'm a survivor. I can forget anything, if I have to.'

He laughed again. 'If I didn't know you better, I'd believe you, Harry.' He shook his head again. 'Sorry, Harry, no deal.'

'Why did you go to all the trouble to bring me down here, then?'

'I sent others to do the job twice before, Harry. Both times they missed you. This time I want to make sure. We will be cruising over some deep water on the way to Cape Town, and I'm going to hang some really heavy weights on to you.'

'Cape Town?' I asked. 'So you are going after the *Dawn Light* in person. What is so fascinating about that old wreck?'

'Come on, Harry. If you didn't know, you wouldn't be giving me such a hard time.' He laughed, and I thought it best not to let them know my ignorance.

'You think you can find your way back?' I asked the blonde. 'It's a big sea and a lot of islands look the same. I think you should keep me as insurance,' I insisted.

'Sorry, Harry.' Manny crossed to the teak and brass bar. 'Drink?' he asked.

'Scotch,' I said, and he half filled a glass with the liquor and brought it to me.

'To be entirely truthful with you, part of this is for Lorna's benefit. You made the girl bitter, Harry, I don't know why – but she wanted especially to be there when we say goodbye. She enjoys that sort of thing, don't you, darling, it turns her on.'

I drained the glass. 'She needs turning on – as you and I both know, she's a lousy lay without it,' I observed, and

Manny hit me in the mouth, crushing my lips and the whisky stung the raw flesh.

'Lock him up,' he said softly. As they hustled me out of the saloon, and along the deck towards the bows, I took pleasure in knowing that Lorna would have painful questions to answer. On either hand the shore lights moved steadily past us in the night, and the river was black and wide.

F orward of the bridge there was a low deckhouse above the forecastle, and a louvred companionway opened on to a deck ladder that descended to a small lobby. This was obviously the crew's quarters, doors opened off the lobby into cabins and a communal mess.

In the bows was a steel door and a stencilled sign upon it read 'FORECASTLE STORE'. They shoved me through the doorway and slammed the heavy door. The lock turned and I was alone in a steel cubicle probably six by four. Both bulkheads were lined with storage lockers, and the air was damp and musty.

My first concern was to find some sort of weapon. The cupboards were all of them locked and I saw that the planking was inch-thick oak. I would need an axe to hack them open, nevertheless I tried. I attempted to break in the doors using my shoulder as a ram, but the space was too confined and I could not work up sufficient momentum.

However, the noise attracted attention. The door swung open and one of the crew stood well back with a big ugly .41 Rueger Magnum in his hand.

'Cut it out,' he said. 'There ain't anything in there,' and he gestured to the pile of old life-jackets against the far wall. 'You just sit there nice and quiet or I'll call some of

197

the boys to help me work you over.' He slammed the door and I sank down on to the life-jackets.

There was clearly a guard posted at the door full-time. The others would be within easy call. I hadn't expected him to open the door and I had been off-balance. I had to get him to do it again – but this time I would have a go. It was a poor chance, I realized. All he had to do was point that cannon into the storeroom and pull the trigger. He could hardly miss.

I looked down at the pile of life-jackets, and stood again to pull them aside. Beneath them was a small wooden fruit box, it contained discarded cleaning materials. A nylon floorbrush, cleaning rags, a tin of Brasso, half a cake of yellow soap, and a brandy bottle half filled with clear fluid. I unscrewed the cap and sniffed it. It was benzine.

I sat down again and reassessed my position, trying to find a percentage in it without much success.

The light switch was outside the doorway and the light overhead was in a thick glass cover. I stood up and climbed halfway up the lockers, wedging myself there while I unscrewed the light cover and examined the bulb. It gave me a little hope.

I climbed down again and selected one of the heavy canvas life-jackets. The clasp of the steel strap on my wristwatch made a blunt blade and I sawed and hacked at the canvas, tearing a hole large enough to get my forefinger in. I ripped the canvas open and pulled out handfuls of the white kapok stuffing. I piled it on the floor, tearing open more life-jackets until I had a considerable heap.

I soaked the cotton waste with benzine from the bottle and took a handful of it with me when I climbed again to the light fitting. I removed the bulb and was plunged instantly into darkness. Working by sense of touch alone, I pressed the benzine-soaked stuffing close to the electricity terminals. I had nothing to use as insulation so I held the steel strap of my wristwatch in my bare hands and used it to dead-short the terminals.

There was a sizzling blue flash, the benzine ignited instantly and 180 volts hit me like a charge of buckshot, knocking me off my perch. I fell in a heap on to the deck with a ball of flaming kapok in my hands.

Outside I heard faint shouts of annoyance and anger. I had succeeded in shorting the entire lighting system of the forecastle. Quickly I tossed the burning kapok on to the prepared pile, and it burned up fiercely. I brushed the sparks from my hands, wrapped the handkerchief around my mouth and nose, snatched up one of the undamaged life-belts and went to stand against the steel door.

In seconds the benzine burned away and the cotton began to smoulder, fiercely pouring out thick black smoke that smelled vile. It filled the store, and my eyes began to stream with tears. I tried to breathe shallowly but the smoke tore my lungs and I coughed violently.

There was another shout beyond the door.

'Something is burning.' And it was answered, 'For Chrissake, get those lights on.'

It was my cue, I began beating on the steel door and screaming at the top of my voice. 'Fire! The ship is on fire!' It was not all acting. The smoke in my prison was thick and solid, and more boiled off the burning cotton kapok. I realized that if nobody opened that door within the next sixty seconds I would suffocate and my screams must have carried conviction. The guard swung the door open, he carried the big Rueger revolver and shone a flashlight into the storeroom.

I had time only to notice those details and to see that the ship's lights were still dead, shadowy figures milled about in the gloom, some with flashlights – then a solid black cloud of smoke boiled out of the storeroom.

I came out with the smoke like a fighting bull from its

pen, desperate for clean air and terrified at how close I had come to suffocating. It gave strength to my efforts.

The guard went sprawling under my rush and the Rueger fired as he went down. The muzzle flame was bright as a flashbulb, lighting the whole area and allowing me to get my bearings on the companion ladder to the deck.

The blast of the shot was so deafening in the confined space that it seemed to paralyse the other shadowy figures. I was halfway to the ladder before one of them leaped to intercept me. I drove my shoulder into his chest and heard the wind go out of him like a punctured football.

There were shouts of concern now, and another big dark figure blocked the foot of the ladder. I had gathered speed across the lobby and I put that and all my weight into a kick that slogged into his belly, doubling him over and dropping him to his knees. As he went over a flashlight lit his face and I saw it was my friend with the garlicky breath. It gave me a lift of pleasure to light me on my way, and I put one foot on his shoulder and used it as a springboard to leap halfway up the ladder.

Hands clutched at my ankle but I kicked them away, and dragged myself to the deck level. I had only one foot on the rungs, and I was clinging with one hand to the life-jacket and with the other to the brass handrail. In that helpless moment, the doorway to the deck was blocked by yet another dark figure – and the lights went on. A sudden blinding blaze of light.

The man above me was the lad with the cosh, and I saw his savage delight as he raised it over my helpless head. The only way to avoid it was to let go the handrail and drop back into the forecastle, which was filled with surging angry goons.

I looked back and was actually opening my grip when behind me, the gunman with the Rueger Magnum sat up groggily, lifted the weapon, tried to brace himself against the ship's movement and fired at me. The heavy bullet cracked past my ear, almost splitting my ear drum and it hit the coshman in the centre of his chest. It picked him up and hurled him backwards across the deck. He hung in the rigging of the foremast with his arms spread like those of a derelict scarecrow, and with a desperate lunge I followed him out on to the deck and rolled to my feet still clutching the life-jacket.

Behind me the Rueger roared again and I heard the bullet splinter the coping of the hatch. Three running strides carried me to the rail and I dived over the side in a gut-swooping drop until I hit the black water flat, but I was dragged deep as the boil of the propellers caught me and swirled me under.

The water was shockingly cold, it seemed to drive in the walls of my lungs and probe with icy lances into the marrow of my bones.

The life-jacket helped pull me to the surface at last and I looked wildly about me. The lights of the coast seemed clear and very bright, twinkling whitely across the black water. Out here in the seaway there was a chop and swell to the surface, alternately lifting and dropping me.

Mandrake slid steadily onwards towards the black void of the open sea. With all her lights blazing she looked as festive as a cruise ship as she sailed away from me.

Awkwardly I rid myself of my shoes and jacket, then I managed to get my arms into the sleeves of the life-jacket. When I looked again *Mandrake* was a mile away, but suddenly she began to turn and from her bridge the long white beam of a spotlight leaped out and began to probe lightly and dance across the surface of the dark sea.

Quickly I looked again towards the land, seeking and finding the riding lights of the buoy at English Ground and relating it to the lighthouse on Flatholm. Within seconds the relative bearing of the two lights had altered slightly,

201

the tide was ebbing and the current was setting westerly. I turned with it and began to swim.

The *Mandrake* had slowed and was creeping back towards me. The spotlight turned and flared, swept and searched, and steadily it came down towards me.

I pushed with the current, using a long side stroke so as not to break the surface and show white water, restraining myself from going into an overarm stroke as the brightly lit ship crept closer. The beam of the spotlight was searching the open water on the far side of *Mandrake* as she drew level with me.

The current had pushed me out of her track, and the *Mandrake* was as close as she would come on this leg – about one hundred and fifty yards off – but I could see the men on her bridge. Manny Resnick's blue silk gown glowed like a butterfly's wing in the bridge lights and I could hear his voice raised angrily, but could not make out the words.

The beam reached towards me like the long cold white finger of an accuser. It quartered the sea in a tight search pattern, back and across, back and across, the next pass must catch me. It reached the end of its traverse, swung out and came back. I lay full in the path of the swinging beam, but at the instant it swept over me, a chance push of the sea lifted a swell of dark water and I dropped into the trough. The light washed over me, diffused by the crest of the swell, and it did not check. It swept onwards in the relentless search pattern.

They had missed me. They were going on, back towards the mouth of the Severn. I lay in the harsh embrace of the canvas life-jacket and watched them bear away and I felt sick and nauseated with relief and the reaction from violence. But I was free. All I had to worry about now was how long it would take to freeze to death.

I began swimming again, watching *Mandrake*'s lights dwindle and lose themselves against the spangled back-drop of the shore.

I had left my wristwatch in the forecastle so I did not know how long it was before I lost all sense of feeling in my arms and legs. I tried to keep swimming but I was not sure if my limbs were responding.

I began to feel a wonderful floating sense of release. The lights of the land faded out, and I seemed to be wrapped in warmth and soft white clouds. I thought that if this was dying it wasn't as bad as its propaganda, and I giggled, lying sodden and helpless in the life-jacket.

I wondered with interest why my vision had gone, it wasn't the way I had heard it told. Then suddenly I realized that the sea fog had come down in the dawn, and it was this that had blinded me. However, the morning light was growing in strength, I could see clearly twenty feet into the eddying fog banks.

I closed my eyes and fell asleep; my last thought was that this was probably my last thought. It made me giggle again as darkness swept over me.

Voices woke me, voices very clear and close in the fog, the rich and lovely Welsh accents roused me. I tried to shout, and with a sense of great achievement it came out like the squawk of a gull.

Out of the fog loomed the dark ungainly shape of an ancient lobster boat. It was on the drift, setting pots, and two men hung over the side, intent on their labours.

I squawked again and one of the men looked up. I had an impression of pale blue eyes in a weathered and heavily lined ruddy face, cloth cap and an old briar pipe gripped in broken yellow teeth.

'Good morning,' I croaked.

'Jesus!' said the lobster man around the stem of his pipe.

I sat in the tiny wheelhouse wrapped in a filthy old

blanket, and drank steaming unsweetened tea from a chipped enamel mug – shivering so violently that the mug leaped and twitched in my cupped hands.

My whole body was a lovely shade of blue, and returning circulation was excruciating agony in my joints. My two rescuers were taciturn men, with a marvellous sense of other people's privacy, probably bred into them by a long line of buccaneers and smugglers.

By the time they had set their pots and cleared for the homeward run it was after noon and I had thawed out. My clothes had dried over the stove in the miniature galley and I had a belly full of brown bread and smoked mackerel sandwiches.

We went into Port Talbot, and when I tried to pay them with my rumpled fivers for their help, the older of the two lobster men turned a blue and frosty eye upon me.

'Any time I win a man back from the sea, I'm paid in full, mister. Keep your money.'

The journey back to London was a nightmare of country buses and night trains. When I stumbled out of Paddington Station at ten o'clock the next morning I understood why a pair of bobbies paused in their majestic pacing to study my face. I must have looked like an escaped convict.

The cabby ran a world-weary eye over my two days' growth of dark stiff beard, the swollen lip and the bruised eye. 'Did her husband come home early, mate?' he asked, and I groaned weakly.

Sherry North opened the door to her uncle's apartment and stared at me with huge startled blue eyes.

'Oh my God, Harry! What on earth happened to you? You look terrible.'

'Thanks,' I said. 'That really cheers me up.'

She caught my arm and drew me into the apartment. 'I've been going out of my mind. Two days. I've even called the police, the hospitals – everywhere I could think of.'

The uncle was hovering in the background and his presence set my nerves on edge. I refused the offer of a bath and clean clothes – and instead I took Sherry back with me to the Windsor Arms.

I left the door to the bathroom open while I shaved and bathed so that we could talk, and although she kept out of direct line of sight while I was in the tub, I thought it was developing a useful sense of intimacy between us.

I told her in detail of my abduction by Manny Resnick's trained gorillas, and of my escape – making no attempt to play down my own heroic role – and she listened in a silence that I could only believe was fascinated admiration.

I emerged from the bath with a towel wound round my waist and sat on the bed to finish the tale while Sherry doctored my cuts and abrasions.

'You'll have to go to the police now, Harry,' she said at last. 'They tried to murder you.'

'Sherry, my darling girl, please don't keep talking about the police. You make me nervous.'

'But, Harry—'

'Forget about the police, and order some food for us. I haven't eaten since I can remember.'

The hotel kitchen sent up a fine grilling of bacon and tomatoes, fried eggs, toast and tea. While I ate, I tried to relate the recent rapid turn of events to our previous knowledge, and alter our plans to fit in.

'By the way, you were on the list of expendables. They didn't intend merely holding a barbecue with your fingers. Manny Resnick was convinced that his boys had killed you—' and a queasy expression passed over her lovely face.

'They were apparently getting rid of anyone who knew anything at all about the *Dawn Light*.'

I took another mouthful of egg and bacon and chewed in silence.

'At least we have a timetable now. Manny's charter – which is incidentally called *Mandrake* – looks very fast and powerful, but it's still going to take him three or four weeks to get out to the islands. It gives us time.'

She poured tea for me, milk last the way I like it.

'Thanks, Sherry, you are an angel of mercy.' She stuck out her tongue at me, and I went on. 'Whatever it is we are looking for, it just has to be something extraordinary. That motor yacht Manny has hired himself looks like the Royal Yacht. He must be laying out close to a hundred thousand pounds on this little lark. God, I wish we knew what those five cases contain. I tried to sound Manny out – but he laughed at me. Told me I knew or I wouldn't be taking so much trouble—'

'Oh, Harry.' Sherry's face lit up. 'You've given us the bad news – now stand by for the good.'

'I could stand a little.'

'You know Jimmy's note on the letter – B. Mus?'

I nodded. 'Bachelor of Music?'

'No, idiot – British Museum.'

'I'm afraid you just lost me.'

'I was discussing it with Uncle Dan. He recognized it immediately. It's reference to a work in the library of the British Museum. He holds a reader's card. He's researching a book, and works there often.'

'Could we get in there?'

'We'll give it a college try.'

I waited almost two hours beneath the vast golden and blue dome of the Reading Room at the British Museum, and the craving for a cheroot was like a vice around my chest.

I did not know what to expect – I had simply filled in the withdrawals form with Jimmy North's reference number – so when at last the attendant laid a thick volume before me, I seized it eagerly.

It was a Secker and Warburg edition, first published in 1963. The author was a Doctor P. A. Ready and the title was printed in gold on the spine: LEGENDARY AND LOST TREASURES OF THE WORLD.

I lingered over the closed book, teasing myself a little, and I wondered what chain of coincidence and luck had allowed Jimmy North to follow this paperchase of ancient clues. Had he read this book first in his burning obsession with wrecks and sea treasure and had he then stumbled on the batch of old letters? I would never know.

There were forty-nine chapters, each listing a separate item. I read carefully down the list.

There were Aztec treasures of gold, the plate and bullion of Panama, buccaneer hoards, a lost goldmine in the Rockies of North America, a valley of diamonds in South Africa, treasure ships of the Armada, the *Lutine* bullion ship from which the famous *Lutine* Bell at Lloyd's had been recovered, Alexandra the Great's chariot of gold, more treasure ships – both ancient and modern – from the Second World War to the sack of Troy, treasures of Mussolini, Prester John, Darius, Roman generals, privateers and pirates of Barbary and Coromandel. It was a vast profusion of fact and fancy, history and conjecture. The treasures of lost cities and forgotten civilizations, from Atlantis to the fabulous golden city of the Kalahari Desert – there was so much of it, and I did not know where to look.

With a sigh I turned to the first page, ducking the introduction and preface. I began to read.

By five o'clock I had skimmed through sixteen chapters which could not possibly relate to the *Dawn Light* and had read five others in depth and by this time I understood how Jimmy North could have been bitten by the romance and excitement of the treasure hunter. It was making me itchy also – these stories of great riches, abandoned, waiting merely to be gathered up by someone with the luck and fortitude to ferret them out.

I glanced at the new Japanese watch with which I'd replaced my Omega, and hurried out of the massive stone portals of the museum and crossed Great Russell Street to my rendezvous with Sherry. She was waiting in the crowded saloon bar of the Running Stag.

'Sorry,' I said, 'I forgot the time.'

'Come on.' She grabbed my arm. 'I'm dying of thirst and curiosity.'

I gave her a pint of bitter for her thirst, but could only inflame her curiosity with the title of the book. She wanted to send me back to the library, before I had finished my supper of ham and turkey from the carvery behind the bar, but I held out and managed to smoke half a cheroot before she drove me out into the cold.

I gave her the key to my room at the Windsor Arms, placed her in a cab and told her to wait for me there. Then I hurried back to the Reading Room.

The next chapter of the book was entitled 'THE GREAT MOGUL AND THE TIGER THRONE OF INDIA.'

It began with a brief historical introduction describing how Babur, descendant of Timur and Genghis Khan, the two infamous scourges of the ancient world, crossed the mountains into northern India and established the Mogul Empire. I recognized immediately that this fell within the area of my interest, the *Dawn Light* had been outward bound from that ancient continent.

The history covered the period of Babur's illustrious successors, Muslim rulers who rose to great power and influence, who built mighty cities and left behind such monuments to man's sense of beauty as the Taj Mahal. Finally it described the decline of the dynasty, and its destruction in the first year of the Indian mutiny when the avenging British forces stormed and sacked the ancient citadel and fortress of Delhi – shooting the Mogul princes out of hand and throwing the old emperor Bahadur Shah into captivity.

Then abruptly the author switched his attention from the vast sweep of history.

In 1665 Jean Baptiste Tavernier, a French traveller and jeweller, visited the court of the Mogul Emperor Aurangzeb. Five years later he published in Paris his celebrated *Travels in the Orient*. He seems to have won special favour from the Muslim Emperor, for he was allowed to enter the fabled treasure chambers of the citadel and to catalogue various items of special interest. Amongst these was a diamond which he named the 'Great Mogul'. Tavernier weighed this stone and listed its bulk at 280 carats. He described this paragon as possessing extraordinary fire and a colour as clear and white 'as the great North Star of the heavens'.

Tavernier's host informed him that the stone had been recovered from the famed Golconda Mines in about 1650 and that the rough stone had been a monstrous 787 carats.

The cut of the stone was a distinctive rounded rose, but was not symmetrical – being proud on the one side. The stone has been unrecorded since that time and many believe that Tavernier actually saw the Koh-i-noor or the Orloff. However, it is highly improbable that such a trained observer and craftsman as Tavernier could have erred so widely in his weights and descriptions. The Koh-i-noor before it was recut in London weighed a mere 191 carats, and was certainly not a rose cut. The Orloff, although rose cut, was and is a symmetrical gem stone and weighs 199 carats. The descriptions simply cannot be mated with that of Tavernier, and all the evidence points to the existence of a huge white diamond that has dropped out of the known world.

In 1739 when Nadir Shah of Persia entered India and captured Delhi, he made no attempt to hold his conquest, but contented himself with vast booty, which included the Koh-i-noor diamond and the peacock throne of Shah Jehan. It seems probable that the Great Mogul diamond was overlooked by the rapacious Persian and that after his withdrawal, Mohammed Shah the incumbent Mogul Emperor, deprived of his traditional throne, ordered the construction of a substitute. However, the existence of this new treasure was veiled in secrecy and although there are references to its existence in the native accounts, only one European reference can be cited.

The journal of the English Ambassador to the Court of Delhi during the year of 1747, Sir Thomas Jenning, describes an audience granted by the Mogul Emperor at which he was 'clad in precious silks and bedecked with flowers and jewels, seated upon a great throne of gold. The shape of the throne was as of a fierce tiger, with gaping jaws and a single glittering cyclopean eye. The body of the tiger was amazingly worked with all manner of precious stones. His majesty was gracious enough to allow me to approach the throne closely and to examine the eye of the tiger which he assured me was a great diamond descended from the reign of his ancestor Aurangzeb'.

Was this Tavernier's 'Great Mogul' now incorporated into the 'Tiger Throne of India'? If it was, then credence is given to a strange set of circumstances which must end our study of this lost treasure.

In 1857 on the 16th September, desperate street fighting filled the streets of Delhi with heaps of dead and wounded, and the outcome of the struggle hung in the balance as the British forces and loyal native troops fought to clear the city of the mutinous sepoys and seize the ancient fortress that dominated the city.

While the fighting raged within, a force of loyal native troops from 101st regiment under two European officers was ordered to cross the river and encircle the walls to seize the road to the north. This was in order to prevent members of the Mogul royal family or rebel leaders from escaping the doomed city.

The two European officers were Captain Matthew Long and Colonel Sir Roger Goodchild—

The name leapt out of the page at me not only because someone had underlined it in pencil. In the margin, also in pencil, was one of Jimmy North's characteristic exclamation marks. Master James's disrespect for books included those belonging to such a venerable institution as the British Museum. I found I was shaking again, and my cheeks felt hot with excitement. This was the last fragment missing from the puzzle. It was all here now and my eyes raced on across the page.

No one will ever know what happened on that night on a lonely road through the Indian jungle – but six

211

months later, Captain Long and the Indian Subahdar, Ram Panat, gave evidence at the court martial of Colonel Goodchild.

They described how they had intercepted a party of Indian nobles fleeing the burning city. The party included three Muslim priests and two princes of the royal blood. In the presence of Captain Long one of the princes attempted to buy their freedom by offering to lead the British officers to a great treasure, a golden throne shaped like a tiger and with a single diamond eye.

The officers agreed, and the princes led them into the forest to a jungle mosque. In the courtyard of the mosque were six bullock carts. The drivers had deserted, and when the British officers dismounted and examined the contents of these vehicles they proved indeed to contain a golden throne statue of a tiger. The throne had been broken down into four separate parts to facilitate trans-portation – hindquarters, trunk, forequarters and head. In the light of the lanterns these fragments nestled in beds of straw, blazing with gold and encrusted with precious and semi-precious stones.

Colonel Roger Goodchild then ordered that the princes and priests should be executed out of hand. They were lined up against the outer wall of the mosque and despatched with a volley of musketry. The Colonel himself walked amongst the fallen noblemen administer-ing the *coup-de-grâce* with his service revolver. The corpses were afterwards thrown into a well outside the walls of the mosque.

The two officers now separated, Captain Long with most of the native troops returning to the patrol of the city walls, while the Colonel, Subahdar Ram Panat and fifteen sepoys rode off with the bullock carts.

The Indian Subahdar's evidence at the court martial

described how they had taken the precious cargo west-wards passing through the British lines by the Colonel's authority. They camped three days at a small native village. Here the local carpenter and his two sons laboured under the Colonel's direction to manufacture four sturdy wooden crates to hold the four parts of the throne. The Colonel in the meantime set about remov-ing from the statue the stones and jewels that were set into the metal. The position of each was carefully noted on a diagram prepared by Goodchild and the stones were numbered and packed into an iron chest of the type used by army paymasters for the safekeeping of coin and specie in the field.

Once the throne and the stones had been packed into the four crates and iron chest, they were loaded once more on to the bullock carts and the journey towards the railhead at Allahabad was continued.

The luckless carpenter and his sons were obliged to join the convoy. The Subahdar recalled that when the road entered an area of dense forest, the Colonel dismounted and led the three craftsmen amongst the trees. Six pistol shots rang out and the Colonel returned alone.

I broke off my reading for a few moments to reflect on the character of the gallant Colonel. I should have liked to introduce him to Manny Resnick, they would have had much in common. I grinned at the thought and read on.

The convoy reached Allahabad on the sixth day and the Colonel claimed military priority to place his five crates upon a troop train returning to Bombay. Having done this he and his small command rejoined the regiment at Delhi.

Six months later, Captain Long supported by the

Indian Petty Officer, Ram Panat, brought charges against the commanding officer. We can believe that thieves had fallen out, Colonel Goodchild had perhaps decided that one share was better than three. Be that as it may, nothing has since given a clue to the whereabouts of the treasure.

The trial conducted in Bombay was a *cause célèbre* and was widely reported in India and at home. However, the weakness of the prosecution's case was that there was no booty to show, and dead men tell no tales.

The Colonel was found not guilty. However, the pressure of the scandal left him no choice but to resign his commission and return to London. If he managed somehow to take with him the Great Mogul diamond and the golden tiger throne, his subsequent career gave no evidence of his possessing great wealth. In partnership with a notorious lady of the town he opened a gaming house in the Bayswater Road which soon acquired an unsavoury reputation. Colonel Sir Roger Goodchild died in 1871, probably from tertiary syphilis contracted during his remarkable career in India. His death revived stories of the fabulous throne, but these soon subsided for lack of hard facts and the secret passed on with that sporting gentleman.

Perhaps we should have headed this chapter – 'The Treasure That Never Was'.

'Not on, cock,' I thought happily. 'It was – and is.' And I began once more at the beginning of the story, but this time I made careful notes for Sherry's benefit.

S he was waiting for me when I returned, sitting wakefully in the armchair by the window, and she flew at me when I entered.

'Where have you been?' she demanded, 'I've been sitting here all evening eating my heart out with curiosity.'

'You are not going to believe it,' I told her, and I thought she might do me a violence.

'Harry Fletcher, you've got ten seconds to cut out the introductory speeches and give me the goodies – after that I scratch your eyes out.'

We talked until long after midnight, and by then we had the floor strewn with papers over which we pored on knees and elbows. There was an Admiralty Chart of the St Mary's Archipelago, the copies of the drawings of the *Dawn Light*, the notes I had made of the mate's description of the wreck, and those I had made in the Reading Room of the British Museum.

I had out my silver travelling flask and we drank Chivas Regal from the plastic tooth mug as we argued and schemed – trying to guess in what section of the *Dawn Light*'s hull the five crates had been stowed, guessing also how she had broken up on the reef, what part of her had been washed into the break and what part had fallen to the seaward side.

I had made sketches of a dozen eventualities, and I had opened a running list of my minimum equipment requirements for an expedition, to which I added, as various items came to mind, or as Sherry made intelligent suggestions.

I had forgotten that she must be a first rate scuba diver, but I was reminded of this as we talked. I was aware now that she would not be a passenger on this expedition, my feelings towards her were becoming tinged with professional respect, and the mood of exhilaration mixed with camaraderie was building to a crescendo of physical tension.

Sherry's pale smooth cheeks were flushed with excitement, and we were shoulder to shoulder as we knelt on the carpeted floor. She turned to say something, she was chuckling and the blue lights in her eyes were teasing and inviting, only inches from mine.

Suddenly all the golden thrones and legendary diamonds in this world must wait their turn. We both recognized the moment, and we turned to each other with unashamed eagerness. We were in a consuming fever of urgency, and we became lovers without rising from the floor, right on top of the drawings of the *Dawn Light* – which was probably the happiest thing that had ever happened to that ill-starred vessel.

When at last I lifted her to the bed and we twined our bodies together beneath the quilt, I knew that all the brief amorous acrobatics that had preceded my meeting with this woman were meaningless. What I had just experienced transcended the flesh and became a thing of the spirit – and if it was not loving, then it was the nearest thing to it that I would ever know.

My voice was husky and unsteady with wonder as I tried to explain it to her. She lay quietly against my chest, listening to the words I had never spoken to another woman, and she squeezed me when I stopped talking – which was clearly a command to continue. I think I was still talking when we both fell asleep.

From the air, St Mary's has the shape of one of those strange fish from the ocean's abysmal depths, a squat mis-shapen body with stubby body fins and tailfins in unusual places, and a huge mouth many sizes too big for the rest of it.

The mouth was Grand Harbour and the town nestled in the hinge of the jaws. The iron roofs flash like signal mirrors from the dark green cloak of vegetation. The aircraft circled the island, treating the passengers to a vista of snowy white beaches and water so clear that each detail of the reefs and deeps were whorled and smeared below the surface like some vast surrealistic painting.

Sherry pressed her face to the round Perspex window and exclaimed with delight as the Fokker Friendship sank down over the pineapple fields where the women paused in their labours to look up at us. We touched down and taxied to the single tiny airport building on which a billboard announced 'St Mary's Island – Pearl of the Indian Ocean' and below the sign stood two other pearls of great price.

I had cabled Chubby and he had brought Angelo with him to welcome us. Angelo rushed to the barrier to embrace me and grab my bag, and I introduced him to Sherry.

Angelo's whole manner underwent a profound change. On the island there is one mark of beauty that is esteemed above all else. A girl might have buck teeth and a squint, but if she possessed a 'clear' complexion she would have suitors forming squadrons around her. A clear complexion did not mean that she was free of acne, it was rather a gauge of the colour of the skin – and Sherry must have had one of the clearest complexions ever to land on the island.

Angelo stared at her in a semi-catatonic state as she shook his hand. Then he roused himself, handed me back my bag and instead took hers from her hand. He then fell in a few paces behind her, like a faithful hound, staring at her solemnly and only breaking into his flashing smile whenever she glanced in his direction. He was her slave from the first moment.

Chubby trundled forward to meet us with more dignity, as big and timeless as a cliff of dark granite, and his face was contorted in a frown of even greater ferocity than usual as he took my hand in a huge horny fist and muttered something to the effect that it was good to see me back.

He stared at Sherry and she quailed a little beneath the

217

ferocity of his gaze, but then something happened that I had never seen before. Chubby lifted his battered old sea cap from his head, exposing the gleaming polished brown dome of his pate in an unheard-of display of gallantry, and he smiled so widely that we could see the pink plastic gums of his artificial teeth. He pushed Angelo aside when Sherry's bags were brought out of the hold, picked up one in each hand and led her to the pick-up. Angelo followed her devotedly and I struggled along in the rear under the weight of my own luggage. It was fairly obvious that my crew approved of my choice, for once.

We sat in the kitchen of Chubby's house and Mrs Chubby fed us on banana cake and coffee while Chubby and I worked out a business deal. For a hard-bargained fee, he would charter his stump boat with its two spanking new Evinrude motors for an indefinite period. He and Angelo would crew it at the old wages, and there would be a large 'billfish bonus' at the end of the charter, if it were successful. I went into no detail as to the object of the expedition, but merely let them know that we would be camping on the outer islands of the group and that Sherry and I would be working underwater.

By the time we had agreed and slapped hands on the bargain, the traditional island rite of agreement, it was mid-afternoon and the island fever had already started to reassert its hold on my constitution. Island fever prevents the sufferer from doing today what can reasonably be put off until the morrow, so we left Chubby and Angelo to begin their preparations while Sherry and I stopped only briefly at Missus Eddy's for provisions before pushing the pick-up over the ridge and down through the palms to Turtle Bay.

'It's a story book,' murmured Sherry, as she stood under the thatch on the wide veranda of the shack. 'It's make-believe.' She shook her head at the sway-boled palm trees and the aching white sands beyond.

218

I went to stand behind her, placing my arms around her middle and drawing her to me. She leaned back against me, crossing her own arms over mine and squeezing my hands.

'Oh, Harry, I didn't think it would be like this.' There was a change taking place within her, I could sense it clearly. She was like a winter plant, too long denied the sun, but there were reserves in her that I could not fathom and they troubled me. She was not a simple person, nor easily understood. There were barriers, conflicts within her that showed only as dark shadows in the depths of her ocean-blue eyes, shadows like those of killer sharks swimming deep. More than once when she believed herself unobserved I had caught her looking at me in a manner which seemed at once calculating and hostile – as though she hated me.

That had been before we came to the island, and now it seemed that, like the winter plant, she was blooming in the sun; as though here she could cast aside some restraint of the soul which had curbed her spirit before.

She kicked off her shoes, and barefooted turned within my encircling arms to stand upon tiptoe to kiss me.

'Thank you, Harry. Thank you for bringing me here.'

Mrs Chubby had swept the floors and aired the linen, placed flowers in the jars and charged the refrigerator. We walked through the shack hand in hand – and though Sherry murmured admiration for the utilitarian décor and solid masculine furnishings, yet I thought I detected that gleam in her eye which a woman gets just before she starts pushing the furniture around and throwing out the lovingly accumulated but humble treasures of a man's lifetime.

As she paused to rearrange the bowl of flowers that Mrs Chubby had placed upon the broad camphor-wood refectory table, I knew we were going to see some changes at Turtle Bay – but strangely the thought did not perturb me. I realized suddenly that I was sick to death of being my own cook and housekeeper.

We changed into swimsuits in the main bedroom – for I had found in the very few hours since we had become lovers that Sherry had an overdeveloped sense of personal modesty, and I knew it would take time before I could wean her to the standard casual Turtle Bay swimming attire. However, it was some compensation for my temporary overdress to see Sherry North in a bikini.

It was the first time I had really had an opportunity to look at her openly. The most striking single thing about her was the texture and lustre of her skin. She was tall, and if her shoulders were too wide and her hips a little too narrow, her waist was tiny and her belly was flat with a small delicately chiselled navel. I have always thought that the Turks were right in considering the navel as a highly erotic portion of a woman's anatomy – Sherry's would have launched a thousand ships.

She didn't like me staring at it. 'Oh, Grandma – what big eyes you've got,' she said, and wrapped a towel around her waist like a sarong. But she walked bare-footed through the sand with an unconscious push and sway of buttock and breast that I watched with uninhibited pleasure.

We left our towels above the high water mark and ran down over the hard wet sand to the edge of the clear warm sea. She swam with a deceptively slow and easy stroke, that drove her through the water so swiftly that I had to reach out myself and drive hard to catch and hold her.

Beyond the reef we trod water and she was puffing a little. 'Out of training,' she panted.

While we rested I looked out to sea and at that moment a line of black fins broke the surface together in line abreast, bearing down on us swiftly and I could not restrain my delight.

'You are an honoured guest,' I told her. 'This is a special

welcome.' The dolphins circled us, like a pack of excited puppies, gambolling and squeaking while they looked Sherry over carefully. I have known them sheer away from most strangers, and it was a rarity for them to allow themselves to be touched on a first meeting and then only after assiduous wooing. However, with Sherry it was love at first sight, almost of the calibre that Chubby and Angelo had demonstrated.

Within fifteen minutes they were dragging her on the Nantucket sleigh ride while she squealed with glee. The instant she fell off the back of one, there was another prodding her with his snout, competing fiercely for her attention.

When at last they had exhausted us both and we swam in wearily to the beach, one of the big bull dolphins followed Sherry into water so shallow it reached to her waist. There he rolled on his back while she scratched his belly with handfuls of coarse white sand and he grinned that fixed idiotic dolphin grin.

After dark, while we sat on the veranda and drank whisky together, we could still hear the old bull whistling and slapping the water with his tail, in an attempt to seduce her into the sea again.

The next morning I gamely fought off a fresh onslaught of island fever, and the temptation to linger in bed, especially as Sherry awoke beside me with the pink glossy look of a little girl, and her eyes were clear, her breath sweet and her lips languorous.

We had to check through the equipment we had salvaged from *Wave Dancer*, and we needed an engine to drive the compressor. Chubby was sent off with a fistful of banknotes and returned with a motor that required much loving attention. As that occupied me for the rest of the day, Sherry was sent off to Missus Eddy's for camping equipment and provisions. We had set a three-day deadline for our departure and our schedule was tight.

It was still dark when we took our places in the boat, Chubby and Angelo at the motors in the stern and Sherry and I perched like sparrows on top of the load.

The dawn was a flaming glory of gold and hot red, promise of another fiery day, as Chubby took us northwards on a course possible only for a small boat and a good skipper. We ran close in on island and reef, sometimes with only eighteen inches of water between our keel and the fierce coral fangs.

All of us were in a mood of anticipation. I truly do not believe it was the prospect of vast wealth that excited me then – all I really needed in my life was another good boat like *Wave Dancer* – rather it was the thought of rare and exquisite treasure, and the chance to win it back from the sea. If what we sought had been merely bullion in bars or coins I do not think it would have intrigued me half as much. The sea was the adversary and once more we were pitted against each other.

The blazing colours of the dawn faded into the hard hot blue of the sky as the sun rose out of the sea, and Sherry North stood up in the bows to strip off her denim jacket and jeans. Under them she wore her bikini and now she folded the clothes away into her canvas duffle bag and produced a tube of sun lotion with which she began to anoint her fine pale body.

Chubby and Angelo reacted with undisguised horror. They held a hurried and scandalized consulation after which Angelo was sent forward with a sheet of canvas to rig a sun shelter for Sherry. There followed a heated exchange between Angelo and Sherry.

'You will damage your skin, Miss Sherry,' Angelo protested, but she drove him in defeat back to the stern.

There the two of them sat like mourners at a wake, Chubby's whole face creased into a huge brown scowl and Angelo openly wringing his hands in anxiety. Finally, they could stand it no longer and after another whispered discussion Angelo was elected as emissary once more and he crawled forward over the cargo to enlist my support.

'You can't let her do it, Mister Harry,' Angelo pleaded. 'She will go *dark*.'

'I think that's the idea, Angelo,' I told him. However, I did warn Sherry to take care of the sun at noon. Obediently she covered herself when we ran ashore on a sandy beach to eat our midday meal.

It was the middle of the afternoon when we raised the triple peaks of the Old Men and Sherry exclaimed, 'Just as the old mate described them.'

We approached the island from the sea side, through the narrow stretch of calm water between the island and the reef. When we passed the entrance to the channel through which I had taken *Wave Dancer* to escape from the Zinballa crash boat, Chubby and I grinned at each other in fond recollection, then I turned to Sherry and pointed it out to her.

'I plan to set up our base camp on the island, and we will use the gap to reach the area of the wreck.'

'It looks a little risky.' She eyed the narrow channel with reserve.

'It will save us a round journey of nearly twenty miles each day – and it isn't as bad as it looks. Once I took my big fifty-foot cruiser through there at full throttle.'

'You must be crazy.' She pushed her dark glasses up on top of her head to look at me.

'By now you should be a good judge of that.' I grinned at her, and she grinned back.

'I am an expert already,' she boasted. The sun had darkened the freckles on her nose and cheeks and given her skin a glow. She had one of those rare skins that do not redden and become angry when exposed to sunlight. Instead it was the kind that quickly turned a golden honey brown.

It was high tide when we rounded the northern tip of the island into a protected cove and Chubby ran the whaleboat on to the sand only twenty yards from the first line of palm trees.

We off-loaded the cargo, carrying it up amongst the palms well above the high-water mark and once again covered it with tarpaulins to protect it from the ubiquitous sea salt.

It was late by the time we had finished. The heat had gone out of the sun, and the long shadows of the palms barred the earth as we trudged inland, carrying only our personal gear and a five-gallon container of fresh water. In the back of the most northerly peak, generations of visiting fishermen had scratched out a series of shallow caves in the steep slope.

I selected a large cave to act as our equipment store, and a smaller one as living quarters for Sherry and me. Chubby and Angelo chose another for themselves, about a hundred yards along the slope and screened from us by a patch of scrub.

I left Sherry to sweep out our new quarters with a brush improvised from a palm frond, and to lay out our sleeping bags on the inflatable mattress while I took my cast net and went back to the cove.

It was dark when I returned with a string of a dozen big striped mullet. Angelo had the fire burning and the kettle bubbling. We ate in contented silence, and afterwards Sherry and I lay together in our cave and listened to the big fiddler crabs clicking and scratching amongst the palms.

'It's primeval,' Sherry whispered, 'as though we are the first man and woman in the world.'

'Me Tarzan, you Jane,' I agreed, and she chuckled and drew closer to me.

I n the dawn Chubby set off alone in the whaleboat on the long return journey to St Mary's. He would return next day with a full load of petrol and fresh water in jerry-cans. Sufficient to last us for two weeks or so.

While we waited for him to return, Angelo and I took on the wearying task of carrying all the equipment and stores up to the caves. I set up the compressor, charged the empty air bottles and checked the diving gear, and Sherry arranged hanging space for our clothes and generally made our quarters comfortable.

The next day, she and I roamed the island, climbing the peaks and exploring the valleys and beaches between. I had hoped to find water, a spring or well overlooked by the other visitors – but naturally there was none. Those canny old fishermen overlooked nothing.

The south end of the island, farthest from our camp, was impenetrable with salt marsh between the peak and the sea. We skirted the acres of evil-smelling mud and thick swamp grass. The air was rank and heavy with rotted vegetation and dead fish.

Colonies of red and purple crabs had covered the mudflats with their holes from which they peered stalk-eyed as we passed. In the mangroves, the herons were breeding, perched long-legged upon their huge shaggy nests, and once I heard a splash and saw the swirl of something in one of the swamp pools that could only have been a crocodile. We left the fever swamps and we climbed to the higher ground, then we picked our way through the thickets of shrub growth towards the southernmost peak.

Sherry decided we must climb this one also. I tried to

dissuade her for it was the tallest and steepest. My protests went completely unnoticed, and even after we had made our way on to a narrow ledge below the southern cliff of the peak, she pressed on determinedly.

'If the mate of the *Dawn Light* found a way to the top – then I'm going up there too,' she announced.

'You'll get the same view from there as from the other peaks,' I pointed out.

'That's not the point.'

'What is the point, then?' I asked, and she gave me the pitying look usually reserved for small children and half-wits, refused to dignify the question with an answer, and continued her cautious sideways shuffle along the edge.

There was a drop of at least two hundred feet below us, and if there is one deficiency in my formidable arsenal of talent and courage, it is that I have no head for heights. However, I would rather have balanced on one leg atop St Paul's Cathedral than admit this to Miss North, and so with great reluctance I followed her.

Fortunately it was only a few paces farther that she uttered a cry of triumph and turned off the ledge into a narrow vertical crack that split the cliff-face. The fracturing of the rock had formed a stepped and readily climbable chimney to the summit, into which I followed her with relief. Almost immediately Sherry cried out again.

'Oh dear God, Harry, look!' and she pointed to a protected area of the wall, in the back of the dark recess. Somebody long ago had patiently chipped an inscription into the flat stone surface.

A. BARLOW.
WRECKED ON THIS PLACE
14th OCT. 1858.

As we stared at it, I felt her hand grope for mine and squeeze for comfort. No longer the intrepid mountaineer, her expression was half fearful as she studied the writing.

'It's creepy,' she whispered. 'It looks as though it was written yesterday – not all those years ago.'

Indeed, the letters had been protected from weathering so that they seemed fresh cut and I glanced around almost as though I expected to see the old seaman watching us.

When at last we climbed the steep chimney to the summit we were still subdued by that message from the remote past. We sat there for almost two hours watching the surf break in long white lines upon Gunfire Reef. The gap in the reef and the great dark pool of the Break showed very clearly from our vantage point, while it was just possible to make out the course of the narrow channel through the coral. From here Andrew Barlow had watched the *Dawn Light* in her death throes, watched her broken up by the high surf.

'Time is running against us now, Sherry,' I told her, as the holiday mood of the last few days evaporated. 'It's fourteen days since Manny Resnick sailed in the *Mandrake*. He will not be far from Cape Town by now. We will know when he reaches there.'

'How?'

'I have an old friend who lives there. He is a member of the Yacht Club – and he will watch the traffic and cable me the moment *Mandrake* docks.'

I looked down the back slope of the peak, and for the first time noticed the blue haze of smoke spreading through the tops of the palms from Angelo's cooking fire.

'I have been a little half-arsed on this trip,' I muttered, 'we have been behaving like a group of school kids on a picnic. From now on we will have to tighten up the security – just across the channel there is my old friend Suleiman

227

Dada, and *Mandrake* will be in these waters sooner than I'd like. We will have to keep a nice low silhouette from now on.'

'How long will we need, do you think?' Sherry asked.

'I don't know, my sweeting – but be sure that it will be longer than we think possible. We are shackled by the need to ferry all our water and petrol from St Mary's – we will only be able to work in the pool during a few hours of each tide when the condition and the height of the water will let us. Who knows what we are going to find in there once we start, and finally we may discover that the Colonel's parcels were stowed in the rear hold of the *Dawn Light* – that part of the ship that was carried out into the open water. If it was, then you can kiss it all goodbye.'

'We've been over that part of it before, you dreadful old pessimist,' Sherry rebuked me. 'Think happy thoughts.'

So we thought happy thoughts and did happy things until at last I made out the tiny dark speck, like a water beetle on the brazen surface of the sea, as Chubby returned from St Mary's in the whaleboat.

We climbed down the peak and hurried back through the palm groves to meet him. He was just rounding the point and entering the cove as we came out on the beach. The whaleboat was low in the water under her heavy cargo of fuel and drinking water. And Chubby stood in the stern as big and solid and as eternal as a great rock. When we waved and shouted he inclined his head gravely in acknowledgement.

Mrs Chubby had sent a banana cake for me and for Sherry a large sunhat of woven palm fronds. Chubby had obviously reported Sherry's behaviour, and his expression was more than normally lugubrious when he saw that the damage was already being done. Sherry was toasted to an edible medium rare.

It was after dark by the time we had carried fifty jerry-cans up to the cave. Then we gathered about the fire where Angelo was cooking an island chowder of clams that he had gathered from the lagoon that afternoon. It was time to tell my crew the true reason for our expedition. Chubby I could trust to say nothing, even under torture – but I had waited to get Angelo into the isolation of the island before telling him. He has been known to commit the most monstrous indiscretions – usually in an attempt to impress one of his young ladies.

They listened in silence to my explanation, and remained silent after I had finished. Angelo was waiting for a lead from Chubby – and that gentleman was not one to charge his fences. He sat scowling into the fire, and his face looked like one of those copper masks from an Aztec temple. When he had created the correct atmosphere of theatrical suspense he reached into his back pocket and produced a purse, so old and well handled that the leather was almost worn through.

'When I was a boy and fished the pool at Gunfire Break, I took a big old Daddy grouper fish. When I open his belly pouch I found this in him.' From the purse he took out a round disc. 'I kept it since then, like a good luck charm, even though I was offered ten pounds for it by an officer on one of my ships.'

He handed me the disc and I examined it in the firelight. It was a gold coin, the size of a shilling. The reverse side was covered with oriental characters which I could not read – but the obverse face bore a crest of two rampant lions supporting a shield and an armoured head. The same design as I had last seen on the bronze ship's bell at Big Gull Island. The legend below the shield read: 'AUS: REGIS & SENAT: ANGLIA'. while the rim was struck with the bold title 'ENGLISH EAST INDIA COMPANY'.

'I always promised me that I would go back to Gunfire

Break – looks like this is the time,' Chubby went on, as I examined the coin minutely. There was no date on it, but I had no doubt that it was a gold mohur of the company. I had read of the coin but never seen one before.

'You got this out of a fish's gut, Chubby?' I asked, and he nodded.

'Guess that old grouper seen it shine and took a snap at it. Must have stuck in his belly until I pulled him out.'

I handed the coin back to him. 'Well then, Chubby, that goes to show there is some truth in my story.'

'Guess it does, Harry,' he admitted, and I went to the cave to fetch the drawings of the *Dawn Light* and a gas lantern. We pored over the drawings. Chubby's grandfather had sailed as a topmastman in an East Indiaman, which made Chubby something of an expert. He was of the opinion that all passengers' luggage and other small pieces would be stowed in the forehold beside the forecastle – I wasn't going to argue with him. Never hex yourself, as Chubby had warned me so often.

When I produced my tide tables and began calculating the time differences for our latitude, Chubby actually smiled, although it was hard to recognize it as such. It looked much more like a sneer, for Chubby had no faith in rows of printed figures in pamphlets. He preferred to judge the tides by the sea clock in his own head. I have known him to call the tides accurately for a week ahead without reference to any other source.

'I reckon we will have a high tide at one-forty tomorrow,' I announced.

'Man, you got it right for once,' Chubby agreed.

W ithout the enormous loads that had been forced on her recently, the whaleboat seemed to run with a new lightness and eagerness. The two Evinrudes put her up on the plane, and she flew at the narrow channel through the reef like a ferret into a rabbit-hole.

Angelo stood in the bows, using hand signals to indicate underwater snags to Chubby in the stern. We had picked good water to come in on, and Chubby met the dying surf with confidence. The little whaleboat tossed up her head and kicked her heels over the swells, splattering us with spray.

The passage was more exhilarating than dangerous, and Sherry whooped and laughed with the thrill of it.

Chubby shot us through the narrow neck between the coral cliffs with feet to spare on either side, for the whaleboat had half of *Wave Dancer's* beam, then we zigzagged through the twisted gut of the channel beyond and at last burst out into the pool.

'No good trying to anchor,' Chubby growled, 'it's deep here. The reef goes down sheer. We got twenty fathoms under us here and the bottom is foul.'

'How you going to hold?' I asked.

'Somebody got to sit at the motor and keep her there with power.'

'That's going to chew fuel, Chubby.'

'Don't I know it,' he growled.

With a tide only half made, the occasional wave was coming in over the reef. Not yet with much force, just a frothing spill that cascaded into the pool, turning the surface to ginger beer with bubbles. However, as the tide mounted so the surf would come over stronger. Soon it would be unsafe in the pool and we would have to run for it. We had about two hours in which to work, depending on the stage of neap and spring tides. It was a cycle of too little or too much. At low tide there was insufficient water to negotiate the entrance channel – and at high tide the surf breaking over the reef might overwhelm the open whaleboat. Each of our moves had to be finely judged.

Now every minute was precious. Sherry and I were already dressed in our wet suits with face-plates on our foreheads, and it was necessary only for Angelo to lift the heavy scuba sets on to our backs and to clinch the webbing harness.

'Ready, Sherry?' I asked, and she nodded, the ungainly mouthpiece already stuffed into her pretty mouth.

'Let's go.'

We dropped over the side, and sank down together beneath the cigar-shaped hull of the whaleboat. The surface was a moving sheet of quicksilver above us, and the spill over the reef charged the upper layer of water with a rash of champagne bubbles.

I checked with Sherry. She was comfortable, and breathing in the slow rhythm of the experienced diver that conserves air and ventilates the body effectively. She grinned at me, her lips distorted by the mouthpiece and her eyes enormously enlarged by the glass faceplate, and she gave me the high sign with both thumbs.

I pointed my head straight for the bottom and began pedalling with my swimming fins, going down fast, reluctant to waste air on a slow descent.

The pool was a dark hole below us. The surrounding walls of coral shut out much of the light, and gave it an ominous appearance. The water was cold and gloomy, I felt a prickle of almost superstitious awe. There was something sinister about this place, as though some evil and malignant force lurked in the sombre depths.

I crossed my fingers at my sides, and went on down, following the sheer coral cliff. The coral was riddled with dark caves and ledges that overhung the lower walls. Coral of a hundred different sorts, outcropped in weird and lovely shapes, tinted with the complete spectrum of colour. Weeds and marine growth waved and tossed in the movement of the water, like the hands of supplicating beggars, or the dark manes of wild horses.

I looked back at Sherry. She was close behind me and she smiled again. Clearly she felt nothing of my own sense of awe. We went on down.

From secret ledges protruded the long yellow antennae of giant crayfish, gently they moved, sensing our presence in the disturbed water. Clouds of multi-coloured coral fish floated along the cliff-face; they sparkled like gemstones in the fading blue light that penetrated into the depths of the pool.

Sherry tapped my shoulder and we paused to peer into a deep black cave. Two great owl eyes peered back at us, and as my eyes became accustomed to the light I made out the gargantuan head of a grouper. It was speckled like a plover's egg, splotches of brown and black on a beige-grey ground and the mouth was a wide slash between thick rubbery lips. As we watched, the huge fish assumed a defensive attitude. It blew itself out, increasing its already impressive girth, spread the gill covers, enlarged the head and finally it opened its mouth in a gape that could have swallowed a man whole – a cavernous maw, lined with spiked teeth. Sherry seized my hand. We drew away from the cave, and the fish closed its mouth and subsided. Any time I wanted to claim a world record grouper I knew where to come looking. Even allowing for the magnifying effect of water I judged that he was close to a thousand pounds in weight.

We went on down the coral wall, and all around us was the wondrous marine world seething with life and beauty, death and danger. Lovely little damsel fish nestled in the venomous arms of giant sea anemone, immune to the deadly darts; a moray eel slid like a long black battle pennant along the coral wall, reached its lair and turned to threaten us with dreadful ragged teeth and glittering snake-like eyes.

Down we went, pedalling with our fins, and now at last I saw the bottom. It was a dark jungle of sea growth, dense stands of sea bamboo and petrified coral trees thrust out of the smothering marine foliage, while mounds and hillocks of coral were worked and riven into shapes that teased the imagination and covered I knew not what.

We hung above this impenetrable jungle and I checked my time-elapse wristwatch and depth gauge. I had one hundred and twenty-eight feet, and time elapsed was five minutes forty seconds.

I gave Sherry the hand signal to remain where she was and I sank down to the tops of the marine jungle and gingerly parted the cold slimy foliage. I worked my way down through it and emerged into a relatively open area below. It was a twilight area roofed in by the bamboo and peopled with strange new tribes of fish and marine animals.

I knew at once that it would not be a simple task to search the floor of the pool. Visibility here was ten feet or less, and the total area we must cover was two or three acres in extent.

I decided to bring Sherry down with me and for a start we would make a sweep along the base of the cliff, keeping in line abreast and within sight of each other.

I inflated my lungs and used the buoyancy to rise from the bottom, out through the thick belt of foliage into the clear.

I did not see Sherry at first, and I felt a quick dart of concern stab me. Then I saw the silver stream of her bubbles rising against the black wall of coral. She had moved away, ignoring my instruction, and I was annoyed. I finned towards her and was twenty feet from her when

I saw what she was doing. My annoyance gave way instantly to shock and horror.

The long series of accidents and mishaps that were to haunt us in Gunfire Break had begun.

Growing out of the coral cliff was a lovely fernlike structure, graceful sweeps, branching and rebranching, pale pink shading to crimson.

Sherry had broken off a large branch of it. She held it in her bare hands and even as I raced towards her I saw her legs brush lightly against the red arms of the dreaded fire coral.

I seized her wrists and dragged her off the cruel and beautiful plant. I dug my thumbs into her flesh, shaking her hands viciously, forcing her to drop her fearsome burden. I was frantic in the knowledge that from their cells in the coral branches tens of thousands of minute polyps were firing their barbed poison darts into her flesh.

She was staring at me with great stricken eyes, aware that something bad had happened, but not yet sure what it was. I held her and began the ascent immediately. Even in my anxiety I was careful to obey the elementary rules of ascent, never overtaking my own bubbles but rising steadily with them.

I checked my watch – eight minutes thirty seconds elapsed. That was three minutes at one hundred and thirty feet. Quickly I calculated my decompression stops, but I was caught between the devil of diver's bends and the deep blue sea of Sherry's coming agony.

It hit her before we were halfway to the surface, her face contorted and her breathing went into the shallow ragged panting of deep distress until I feared she might beat the mechanical efficiency of her demand valve, jamming it so that it could no longer feed her with air.

She began to writhe in my grip and the palms of her hands blushed angrily, the livid red weals rose like whip-

235

lashes across her thighs – and I thanked God for the protection her suit had given to her torso.

When I held her at a decompression stop fifteen feet below the surface she fought me wildly, kicking and twisting in my grip. I cut the stop fine as I dared, and took her to the surface.

The instant our heads broke clear I spat out my mouthpiece and yelled: 'Chubby! Quick!'

The whaleboat was fifty yards away, but the motor was ticking over steadily and Chubby spun her on her own tail. The instant she was pointed at us, he gave the con to Angelo and scrambled up into the bows. Coming down on us like a great brown colossus.

'It's fire coral, Chubby,' I shouted. 'She's hit hard. Get her out!'

Chubby leaned out and took hold of the webbing harness at the back of her neck and he lifted her bodily from the water; she dangled from his big brown fists like a drowning kitten.

I ditched my scuba set in the water for Angelo to recover, shrugging out of the harness, and when I scrambled over the side, Chubby had laid her on the floorboards and he was leaning over her, folding her in his arms to quieten her struggles and still her moans and sobs of agony.

I found my medical kit under a pile of loose equipment in the bows, and my fingers were clumsy with haste as I heard Sherry's sobs behind me. I snapped the head of an ampoule of morphine and filled a disposable syringe with the clear fluid. Now I was angry as well as concerned.

'You stupid broad,' I snarled at her. 'What made you do a crazy, half-witted thing like that?'

She could not answer me, her lips were shaking and blue, flecked with spittle. I took a pinch of skin on her thigh and thrust the needle into it as I expelled the fluid into her flesh. I went on angrily.

236

'Fire coral – my God, you aren't an effing conchologist's backside. Isn't a kid on the island that stupid.'

'I didn't think, Harry,' she panted wildly.

'Didn't think—' I repeated, her pain was goading me to new excesses of anger. 'I don't think you've got anything in your head to think with, you stupid little birdbrain.'

I withdrew the needle, and ransacked the medicine box for the anti-histamine spray.

'I should put you over my knee, you—'

Chubby looked up at me. 'Harry, you talk to Miss Sherry just one more word like that and, man – I'm going to have to break your head, hear?'

With only mild surprise I realized that he meant it. I had seen him break heads before, and knew it was some-thing to avoid, so I told him, 'Instead of making speeches – how about you get us the hell out of here and back to the island.'

'You just treat her gentle, man, otherwise I'm going to roast your arse so you wish you'd been the one that sat on a bunch of fire coral instead of her, hear?'

I ignored this mutinous outburst and sprayed the ugly scarlet weals, coating them with a protective and soothing skin, and then I lifted her into my arms and held her like that while the morphine smoothed out the fearful burning agony of the stings and Chubby ran us back to the island.

When I carried Sherry up to the cave she was already half comatose from the drug. All that night I stayed by her side, helping her through the shivering and sweating fever produced by the virulent poison. Once she moaned and whispered half in delirium, 'I'm sorry, Harry. I didn't know. It's the first time I've dived in coral water. I didn't recognize it.'

Chubby and Angelo did not sleep either. I heard the murmur of their voices from the fireside and every hour one of them would cough outside the cave entrance and then inquire anxiously:

237

'How's she doing, Harry?'

By the morning Sherry had fought off the worst effects of the poisoning, and the stings had subsided into an ugly rash of blisters. However, it was another thirty-six hours before any of us could raise the enthusiasm to tackle the pool again, then the tides were wrong. We had to wait another day.

The precious hours were slipping away. I could imagine the *Mandrake* making fair passage, she had looked a fast and powerful vessel and each day wasted whittled away the lead I had counted upon.

On the third day, we ran out again to the pool. It was mid-afternoon and we took a chance with the water in the channel, scraping through early in the flood with inches to spare over the sharp coral snags.

Sherry was still in mild disgrace and, with her hands wrapped in acriflavine bandages, she was left in the whaleboat to keep Angelo company. Chubby and I dived together, going down fast and pausing above the swaying bamboo tops only long enough to drop the first marker buoy. I had decided it was necessary to search the pool bottom systematically. I was marking off the whole area into squares, anchoring inflatable buoys above the marine forest on thin nylon line.

We worked for an hour and found nothing that was obviously wreckage, although there were masses of coral covered with marine growth that would bear closer investigation. I marked these on the underwater slate attached to my thigh.

At the end of that hour, our air reserves in the double ninety-cubic-foot bottles were uncomfortably low. Chubby used more air than I did, for he was a much bigger man and his technique lacked finesse, so I regularly checked his pressure gauge.

I took him up and was especially careful on the

decompression periods, although Chubby showed his usual impatience. He had never seen as I had, a diver come up too fast so the blood in his veins starts fizzing like champagne. The resultant agonies can cripple a man and an air bubble lodged in the brain can do permanent damage.

'Any luck?' Sherry called as soon as we surfaced, and I gave her the thumbs down as we swam to the whaleboat. We drank a cup of coffee from the thermos and I smoked an island cheroot while we rested and chatted. I think we were all mildly disappointed that success had not been immediate, but I kept their spirits up by anticipating the first find.

Chubby and I changed our demand valves on to freshly charged bottles and down we went again. This time I would only allow forty-five minutes working at 130 feet, for the effects of gas absorption into the blood are cumulative, and repeated deep diving greatly increases the danger.

We worked carefully through the forests of bamboo stems and over the tumbled coral blocks, exploring the gullies and cracks between them, pausing every few minutes to map the locations of interesting features, then going on, back and forth on the legs of a search pattern between my marker buoys.

Time elapse was forty-three minutes, and I glanced across at Chubby. None of our wet suits would fit him, so he dived naked except for an ancient black wollen bathing costume. He looked like one of my friendly dolphins – only not as graceful – as he forced his way through the thickets. I grinned at the thought and was about to turn away when a chance ray of light pierced the canopy above us and glinted upon something white on the floor below Chubby. I finned in quickly, and examined the white object. At first I thought it was a piece of clam shell, but then I noticed that it was too thick and regular in shape. I sank down closer to it and saw that it was embedded in a decaying sheet of coelentrate coral. I groped for the small jemmy bar on my webbing belt, drew it from its sheath and prised off the lump of coral containing the white object. The lump weighed about five pounds and I slipped it into my netting carrybag.

Chubby was watching me and I gave him the signal for the ascent.

'Anything?' Sherry called immediately we surfaced. Her confinement to the whaleboat was obviously playing the devil with her nerves. She was irritable and impatient – but I was not letting her dive until the ugly, suppurating lesions on her hands and thighs had healed. I knew how easily secondary infection could attack those open sores under these conditions, and I was feeding her antibiotics and trying to keep her quiet.

'I don't know,' I answered, as we swam to the boat and I handed the net bag up to her. She took it eagerly, and while we climbed aboard and stripped our equipment she was examining it closely, turning it over in her hands.

Already the surf was breaking heavily on the reef, boiling into the pool and the whaleboat was swinging and bobbing in the disturbance. Angelo was having difficulty holding her on station – and it was time to go. We had spent as much time underwater as I considered safe for one day, and soon now the heavy oceanic surf would begin leaping the coral barrier and sweeping the pool.

'Take us home, Chubby,' I called and he went to the motors. All our attention was focused on the wild ride back through the channel. With the flood of the tide the swells came up under our stern, surfing us, coming through under our hull so fast that our relative speed was reversed and the whaleboat's steering was inverted so we threatened to broach to and tumble broadside on to the coral walls of the channel. However, Chubby's seamanship never faltered, and at last we shot out into the protected waters behind the reef and turned for the island.

Now I could give my attention to the object I had recovered from the pool. With Sherry giving me a great deal of advice that I did not really need, and cautioning me to exercise care, I placed the lump of dead coral on the thwart and gave it a smart crack with the jemmy bar. It split into three pieces and revealed a number of articles that had been ingested and protected by the living coral polyps.

There were three round grey objects the size of marbles and I picked one out of the coral bed and weighed it in my hand. It was heavy. I handed it to Sherry.

'Guesses?' I asked.

'Musket balls,' she said without hesitation.

'Of course,' I agreed. I should have recognized it and I made amends by identifying the next object.

'A small brass key.'

'Genius!' she said with irony, and I ignored her as I worked delicately to free the white object which had first caught my attention. It came away at last and I turned it over to examine the blue design worked on one side.

It was a segment of white glazed porcelain, a chip from the rim of a plate which had been ornamented by a coat of arms. Half of the design was missing but I recognized the rampant lion immediately, and the words, 'Senat. ANGLIA'. It was the device of John Company again, part of a set of ship's plate.

I passed it to Sherry and suddenly I saw how it must have been. I told her my vision and she listened quietly, fondling the chip of porcelain. 'When at last the surf broke her back and the coral tore her in half, she would have gone down by the middle, and all her heavy cargo and gear would have shifted – tearing out her inner bulkhead. It would all have poured out of her, cannon and shot, plate and silver, flask and cup, coin and pistol – it would have littered the floor of the pool, a rich sowing of man-made articles and the coral has sucked it up and absorbed it.'

'The treasure crates?' Sherry demanded. 'Would they have fallen out of the hull?'

'I don't know,' I admitted, and Chubby, who had been listening intently, spat over the side and growled.

'The forehold was always double-skinned, three-inch oak planks, to hold the cargo from shifting in a storm. Anything was in there then, is still in there now.'

'And that opinion would have cost you ten guineas in Harley Street,' I told Sherry, and winked at her. She laughed and turned to Chubby.

'I don't know what we would do without you, Chubby dear,' and Chubby scowled murderously and suddenly found something of engrossing interest out on the distant horizon.

It was only later, after Sherry and I had taken our swim on one of the secluded beaches and had changed into fresh clothes and were sitting around the fire drinking Chivas Regal and eating fresh prawns netted in the lagoon, that the elation of our first minor finds wore off – and I began soberly to consider the implications of the *Dawn Light* broken up and scattered across the marine hothouse of the pool.

If Chubby were wrong and the treasure crates, with their enormous weight of gold, had smashed through the sides of the hold and fallen free, then it would be an endless task searching for them. I had seen two hundred blocks and mounds of coral that day – any one of which could have concealed a part of the tiger throne of India.

If he were correct and the hold had retained its cargo, then the coral polyps would have spread over the entire front section of the vessel as it lay on the bottom, covering the woodwork with layer upon layer of calcified stone, until it had become an armoured repository for the treasure, disguised with a growth of marine plants.

We discussed it in detail, all of us beginning to appreciate the magnitude of the task we had set ourselves, and we agreed that it fell into two separate parts.

First we had to locate and identify the treasure cases, and then we had to wrest them from the stubborn embrace of the coral.

'You know what we are going to need, don't you, Chubby?' I asked, and he nodded.

'You still got those two cases?' I felt ashamed to mention the word gelignite in front of Sherry. It reminded me too vividly of the project for which Chubby and I had found it necessary to lay in large stocks of high explosive. That had been three years ago, during a lean season when I had been desperate for ready cash to keep myself and *Wave Dancer* aloft. Not even by stretching the letter of the law could our project have been considered legal, and I would rather have closed that chapter and forgotten it – but we needed gelignite now.

Chubby shook his head. 'Man, that stuff began sweating like a stevedore in a heatwave. If you belched within fifty feet of it – it would have blown the top off the island.'

'What did you do with it?'

'Angelo and I took it out into the Mozambique Channel and gave it a deep six.'

'We will need at least a couple of cases. It will take a full shot to break up those big chunks down there.'

'I'll speak to Mister Coker again – he should be able to fix it.'

'Do that, Chubby. Next time you go back to St Mary's you tell Fred Coker to get us three cases.'

'What about the pineapples we saved from *Wave Dancer?*' Chubby asked.

'No good,' I told him, I did not want my obituary to read, 'The man who tried to fuse MK VII hand-grenades in 130 feet of water.'

I was wakened the next morning by the unnatural hush, and the static charged heat of the air. I lay awake listening, but even the fiddler crabs were silent and the perpetual rattle of the palm fronds was stilled. The only sound was the low and gentle breathing of the woman beside me. I kissed her lightly on the cheek and managed to withdraw my bad arm from under her head without waking her. Sherry boasted that she never used a pillow, it was bad for the spine she told me with an air of rectitude, but this didn't prevent her from using any convenient portion of my anatomy as a substitute.

I ambled out of the cave trying to restore the circulation to my limb by massage, and while I made a libation to my favourite palm tree I studied the sky.

It was a sickly dawn, smeared with a dark haze that dimmed the stars. The heated air lay heavy and languorous against the earth, with no breeze to stir it, and my skin prickled in the charged atmosphere.

Chubby was feeding twigs to the fire and blowing life into it, when I returned. He looked up at me and confirmed my diagnosis.

'Weather going to break.'

'What is coming, Chubby?' and he shrugged. 'Glass is down to 28.2, but we'll know by noon,' and he went back to huffing and puffing over the fire.

The weather had affected Sherry also. The hair at her temples was damp with perspiration and she snapped at me peevishly as I changed her dressings, but minutes later she came up behind me as I dressed, and laid her cheek against my naked back.

'Sorry, Harry, it's just so sticky and close this morning,' and she ran her lips across my back, touching the thick raised cicatrice of the bullet scar with her tongue.

'Forgive?' she asked.

Chubby and I dived into the pool at eleven o'clock that morning. We had been down thirty-eight minutes without making any further significant discovery when I heard the tinny clink! clink! clink! – transmitted through the water. I paused and listened, noticing that Chubby had stopped also. It came again, thrice repeated.

On the surface, Angelo had immersed half of a three-foot length of iron rail into the water and was beating out the recall signal upon it with a hammer from the tool kit.

I gave Chubby the open-handed 'wash out' sign and we began the ascent at once.

As we climbed into the boat I asked impatiently, 'What is it, Angelo?' and in reply he pointed out to seaward over the jagged and irregular back of the reef.

I pulled off my mask and blinked my eyes, refocusing after the limited horizons of the marine world.

It lay low and black against the sea, a thin dark smear as though some playful god had drawn a charcoal line across the horizon – but even as I watched, it seemed to grow – spreading wider into the paler blue of the sky, darker and still darker it rose out of the sea. Chubby whistled softly and shook his head.

'Here comes Lady C. and, man, she is in a big hurry.'

The speed of that low dark front was uncanny. It lifted up, drawing a funereal curtain across the sky and as Chubby gunned the motors and ran for the channel the first racing streamers of cloud spread across the sun.

Sherry came to sit beside me on the thwart and help me strip the clinging wet rubber suit.

'What is it, Harry?' she asked.

'Lady C,' I told her. 'It's the cyclone, the same one that killed the *Dawn Light*. She's out hunting again,' and Angelo fetched the lifebelts from the forepeak and handed one to each of us. We tied them on and sat close together and watched it come on in awesome grandeur, overwhelming the sun, changing the sky from a high pure blue dome into a low grey roof of filthy scudding cloud.

We were running hard before her, leaving the channel and flying across the inner waters to the shelter of the cove. All our faces were turned to watch it, all our hearts quailed at the sense of our own frailty before such force and power.

The cloud front passed over our heads as we ran into the bay, and immediately we were plunged into a twilight world, fraught with the fury to come. The cloud dragged a skirt of cold damp air beneath it. It passed over us, and we shivered in the sudden drop in temperature. With a shriek, the wind was upon us, turning the air into a mixture of sand and driven spray.

'The motors,' Chubby bellowed at me, as the whaleboat touched the beach. Those two new Evinrudes represented half the savings of a lifetime and I understood his concern.

'We'll take them with us.'

'And the boat?' Chubby persisted.

'Sink it. There's a firm bottom of sand for it to lie on.'

As Chubby and I freed the motors, Angelo and Sherry lashed the folds of the tarpaulin over the open deck to secure the equipment, and then used the nylon diving lines to tie down the irreplaceable scuba sets and the waterproof cases that contained my medical kit and tools.

Then, while Chubby and I hefted the two heavy Evinrudes, Angelo allowed the wind to push the whaleboat out into the bay where he pulled the drainplugs and she filled

246

immediately with water. The steep wind-maddened sea poured in over the side, and she went down swiftly in twenty feet of water.

Angelo returned to the beach using a dogged side-stroke with the waves breaking over his head. By this time, Sherry and I had almost reached the line of palm trees.

Doubled under my load, I glanced back. Chubby was lumbering after us. He was similarly burdened by the second motor, doubled also under the dead weight of metal and wading through the waist-high torrent of blown white sand. Angelo emerged from the water and followed him.

They were close behind us as we ran into the trees. If I had hoped to find shelter here, then I was a fool, for we found ourselves transferred from an exposed position of acute discomfort into one of real and deadly danger.

The great winds of the cyclone had thrashed the palms into a lunatic frenzy. The sound of it was a deafening clattering roar that was stunning in its intensity. The long graceful stems of the palms whipped about wildly, and the wind clawed loose the fronds and sent them flying off into the haze of sand and spray like huge misshapen birds.

We ran in single file along one of the ill-defined footpaths, Sherry leading us, covering her head with both hands, while I was for the first time grateful for the scanty cover given me by the big white motor on my shoulder for all of us were exposed to the double threat of danger.

The whipping of the tall palms flung from the fifty-foot-high heads their cluster of iron-hard nuts. Big as a cannon-ball and almost as dangerous, these projectiles bombarded us as we ran. One of them struck the motor I carried, a blow that made me stagger, another fell beside the path and on the second bounce hit Sherry on the lower leg. Even though most of its power was spent, still it knocked her down and rolled her in the sand like a running springbok hit by a high-powered rifle. When she regained her feet she was limping heavily – but she ran on through the lethal hail of coconuts.

We had almost reached the saddle of the hills when the wind increased the power of its assault. I heard its shrieking overhead on a higher angrier note, and coming in across the tree-tops roaring like a wild beast.

It hurled a new curtain of sand at us, and as I glanced ahead I saw the first palm tree begin to go.

I saw it lean out wearily, exhausted by its efforts to resist the wind, the earth around its base heaved upwards as the root system was torn from the sandy soil. As it came down so it gathered speed; swinging in a terrible arc, like the axe of the headsman, it fell towards us. Sherry was fifteen paces ahead of me, just beginning the ascent of the saddle and she had her face turned downwards, watching her own feet, her hands still held to her head.

She was running into the path of the falling tree, and she seemed so small and fragile beneath that solid bole of descending timber. It would crush her with a single gargantuan blow.

I screamed at her, but although she was so close she could not hear me. The roaring of the wind seemed to swamp all our senses. Down swung the long limber stem of the palm tree, and Sherry ran on into its path. I dropped the motor, shrugging it from my shoulder and I ran forward. Even then I saw I could not reach her in time, and I dived belly down, reaching out to the full stretch of my right arm and I hit Sherry's back foot, slapping it across the other as she swung it forward. The ankle tap of the football field, and it tripped her. She fell flat on her face in the sand. As the two of us lay outstretched the palm tree descended. The fury of its stroke rushed through the air even above the sound of the wind and it struck with a blow that was transmitted through the earth into my body, jarring me and rattling the teeth in my skull.

Instantly I was up and dragging Sherry to her feet. The palm tree had missed her by eighteen inches and she was stunned and terrified. I hugged her for a few moments, trying to give her comfort and strength. Then I lifted her over the palm stem that blocked the path, pointed her at the saddle and gave her a shove.

'Run!' I shouted and she staggered onwards. Angelo helped me lift the motor on to my shoulder once more. We clambered over the tree and toiled on up the slope after Sherry's running figure.

All around us in the palm groves I could hear the thud and crash of other trees falling and I tried to run with my face upturned to catch the next threat before it developed, but another flying coconut hit me a glancing blow on the temple, dimming my vision for a moment and I staggered on blindly, taking my chances amongst the monstrous guillotines of the falling palms.

I reached the crest of the saddle without realizing it, and I was unprepared for the full unbroken force of the wind in my back. It hurled me forward, the ground fell away from under my feet as I was thrown over the saddle, my knees gave way and the motor and I rolled headlong down the reverse slope. On the way down we caught up with Sherry North, taking her in the back of the legs. She collapsed on top of me and joined the motor and me on our hurried descent.

One moment I was on top and the next Miss North was seated between my shoulder blades then the motor was on top of both of us.

When we reached the bottom of the steepest pitch and lay together in a battered and weary heap, we were protected by the saddle from the direct fury of the wind so it was possible to hear what Sherry was saying. It was immediately obvious that she bitterly resented what she considered to be an unprovoked assault, and she was loudly casting doubt on my parentage, character and breeding. Even in my own desperate straits her anger was suddenly terribly comical, and I began to laugh. I saw that she was trying to find sufficient strength to hit me so I decided to distract her.

> '—Jack and Jill went up the hill
> They each had a dollar and a quarter—'

I croaked at her,

> '—Jill came down with half a crown
> They didn't go up for water.'

She stared at me for a moment as though I had started frothing at the mouth, then she started to laugh also, but the laughter had a wild hysterical note to it.

'Oh you swine!' she sobbed with laughter, tears streaming down her cheeks and her sodden sand-caked hair dangling in thick dark snakes about her face.

Angelo thought she was weeping when he reached us and he drew her tenderly to her feet and helped her down the last few hundred yards to the caves, leaving me to hoist the motor once more to my bruised shoulder and follow them.

Our cave was well placed to weather the cyclone winds, probably chosen by the old fishermen with that in mind. I retrieved the canvas fly leaf from where it was wrapped around the bole of a palm tree and used it to screen the entrance, piling stones upon the trailing end to hold it down and we had a dimly lit haven into which we crept like two wounded animals.

I had left my motor with Chubby in his cave. I felt at that moment that if I never saw it again it would be too soon, but I knew Chubby would treat it with all the loving care of a mother for her sickly infant and that when the cyclone passed on, it would once more be ready for sea.

Once I had rigged the tarpaulin to screen the cave and keep out the wind, Sherry and I could strip and clean ourselves of the salt and sand. We used a basinful of the precious fresh water for this purpose, each of us taking it in turn to stand in the basin and be sponged down by the other.

I was a mass of scratches and bruises from my long battle with the motor, and although my medical kit was still in the boat at the bottom of the bay, I found a large bottle of mercurochrome in my bag. Sherry began a convincing imitation of Florence Nightingale, with the antiseptic and a roll of cotton wool she anointed my wounds, murmuring condolences and sympathetic sounds.

I rather enjoy being fussed over, and I stood there in a semi-hypnotic state lifting an arm or moving a leg as I was bidden. The first hint that I received that Miss North was not treating my crippling injuries with the true gravity they deserved was when she suddenly emitted a hoot of glee and daubed my most delicate extremity with a scarlet splash of mercurochrome.

'Rudolph the red-nosed reindeer,' she chortled, and I roused myself to protest bitterly.

'Hey! That stuff doesn't wash off.'

'Good!' she cried. 'I'll be able to find you now if you ever get lost in a crowd.' I was shocked by such unseemly levity. I gathered about me my dignity and went to find a pair of dry pants.

Sherry reclined on the mattress and watched me scratching in my bag.

'How long is this going to last?' she asked.

'Five days,' I told her, as I paused to listen to the unabated roar of the wind.

'How do you know?'

'It always lasts five days,' I explained, as I stepped into my shorts and hoisted them.

'That's going to give us a little time to get to know each other.'

W e were caged by the cyclone, locked together in the confined few square feet of the cave, and it was a strange experience.

Any venture out into the open forced upon us by nature, or to check how Chubby and Angelo were faring, was fraught with discomfort and danger. Although the trees were stripped of most of their fruit during the first twelve hours and the weaker trees fell during that period also – yet there was still the occasional tree that came crashing down, and the loose trash and fronds flew like arrows on the wind with sufficient force to blind a person or inflict other injury.

Chubby and Angelo worked away quietly on the motors, stripping them down and cleaning them of salt water. They had something to keep them busy.

In our cave, once the initial novelty had passed there developed some crisis of will and decision which I did not properly understand, but which I sensed was critical.

I had never pretended to understand Sherry North in any depth, there were too many unanswered questions, too many areas of reserve, barriers of privacy beyond which I was not allowed to pass. She had not to this time made any declaration of her feelings, there was never any discussion of the future. This was strange, for any other woman I had ever known expected – nay demanded – declarations of love and passion. I sensed also that this indecision was causing her as much distress as it was me. She was caught up in something against which she struggled, and in the process her emotions were being badly mauled.

However, with Sherry there was nothing spoken of – for I had accepted the tacit agreement and we did not discuss any of our feelings for each other. I found this restricting, for I am a lover with a florid turn of speech. If I have not yet succeeded in talking a bird down out of a tree – it is probably because I have never seriously made the attempt. I could make this adjustment without too much pain, however, it was the lack of a future that chafed at me.

It seemed that Sherry did not look for our relationship to last longer than the setting of the sun, yet I knew that she could not feel this way, for in the moments of warmth that interspersed those of gloom, there could be no doubts.

Once when I started to speak of my plans for when we had raised the treasure – how I would have another boat built to my design, a boat that incorporated all the best features of the beloved *Wave Dancer* – how I would build a new dwelling at Turtle Bay that would not deserve the title of shack – how I would furnish it and people it – she took no part in the discussion. When I ran out of words, she turned away from me on the mattress and pretended to sleep although I could feel the tension in her body without touching her.

At another time I found her watching me with that hostile, hating look. While an hour later she was in a frenzy of physical passion which was in diametric contrast.

She sorted and mended my clothing from the bag, sitting cross-legged on the mattress and working with neat business-like stitches. When I thanked her, she became caustic and derisive, and we ended up in a blazing row until she flung herself out of the cave and ran through the raging wind to Chubby's cave. She did not return until after dark, with Chubby escorting her and holding a lantern to light her way.

253

Chubby regarded me with an expression that would have melted a lesser man and frostily refused my invitation to drink whisky, which meant that he was either very sick or very disapproving, then he disappeared again into the storm muttering darkly.

By the fourth day my nerves were in a jangling mess, but I had considered the problem of Sherry's strange behaviour from every angle and I reached my conclusions.

Cooped up with me in that tiny cave she was being forced at last to consider her feelings for me. She was falling in love, probably for the first time in her life, and her fiercely independent spirit was hating the experience. I cannot say in truthfulness that I was enjoying it very much either – or rather I enjoyed the short periods of repentance and loving between each new tantrum – but I looked forward fervently to the moment when she accepted the inevitable and succumbed completely.

I was still awaiting that happy moment when I awoke in the dawn of the fifth day. The island was in a grip of a stillness that was almost numbing after the uproar of the cyclone. I lay and listened to the silence without opening my eyes, but when I felt movement beside me I rolled my head and looked into her face.

'The storm is over,' she said softly, and rose from the bed.

We walked out side by side into the early morning sunlight, blinking around us at the devastation which the storm had created. The island looked like the photographs of a World War I battlefield. The palms were stripped of their foliage, the bare masts pointed pathetically at the sky and the earth below was littered thickly with palm fronds and coconuts. The stillness hung over it all, no breath of wind, and the sky was pale milky blue, still filled with a haze of sand and sea.

From their cave Chubby and Angelo emerged, like big

bear and little bear, at the end of winter. They too stood and looked about them uncertainly.

Suddenly Angelo let out a Comanche whoop and leaped four feet in the air. After five days of forced confinement his animal spirits could no longer be suppressed. He took off through the palm trees like a greyhound.

'Last one in the water is a fascist,' he shouted, and Sherry was the first to accept the challenge. She was ten paces behind him when they hit the beach but they dived simultaneously into the lagoon, fully clad, and began immediately pelting each other with handfuls of wet sand. Chubby and I followed at a sedate pace more in keeping with our years. Still wearing his vividly striped pyjamas, Chubby lowered his massive hams into the sea.

'I got to tell you, man, that feels good,' he admitted gravely. I drew deeply on my cheroot as I sat beside him waist deep, then I handed him the butt.

'We lost five days, Chubby,' I said, and immediately he scowled.

'Let's get busy,' he growled, sitting in the lagoon in yellow and purple striped pyjamas, cheroot in his mouth, like a big brown bullfrog.

From the peak we looked down into the shallow waters of the lagoon and although they were still a little murky with spindrift and churned sand, yet the whaleboat was clearly visible. She had drifted sideways in the bay and was lying on the bottom in twenty feet of water with the yellow tarpaulin still covering her deck.

We raised the whaleboat with air bags and once her gunwales broke the surface we were able to bale her out and row her into the beach. The rest of that day was needed to unload the waterlogged cargo, clean and dry it, pump the air bottles, get the motors aboard and prepare for the next visit to Gunfire Reef.

I was beginning to become seriously concerned by the delays which had left us sitting on the island, day after day, while Manny Resnick and his merry men cut away the lead we had started with.

That evening we discussed it around the campfire, and agreed that we had made also no progress in ten days other than to confirm that part of the *Dawn Light's* wreckage had fallen into the pool.

However, the tides were set fair for an early start in the morning and Chubby ran us through the channel with hardly sufficient light to recognize the coral snags, and when we took up our station in the back of the reef the sun was only just showing its blazing upper rim above the horizon.

During the five days we had lain ashore, Sherry's hands had almost entirely healed, and although I suggested tactfully that she should allow Chubby to accompany me for the next few days, my tact and concern were wasted. Sherry North was suited and finned and Chubby sat in the stern beside the motors holding us on station.

Sherry and I went down fast, and entered the forest of sea bamboo, picking up position from the markers that Chubby and I had left on our last dive.

We were working in close to the base of the coral cliff and I placed Sherry on the inside berth where it would be easier to hold position in the search pattern while she orientated herself.

We had hardly begun the first leg and had swum fifty feet from the last marker when Sherry tapped urgently on her bottles to attract my attention and I pushed my way through the bamboo to her.

She was hanging against the side of the coral cliff upside down like a bat, closely examining a fall of coral and debris that had slid down to the floor of the pool. She was in deep shade under the loom of dark coral so I was at her side before I saw what had attracted her.

Propped against the cliff, its bottom end lying in the mound of debris and weed, was a long cylindrical object which itself was heavily infested with marine growth and had already been partially ingested by the living coral.

Yet its size and regular shape indicated that it was man-made – for it was nine feet long and twenty inches thick, perfectly rounded and slightly tapered.

Sherry was studying it with interest and when I came up she turned to meet me and made signs of incomprehension.

I had recognized what it was immediately and the skin of my forearms and at the nape of my neck felt prickly with excitement. I made a pistol of my thumb and forefinger and mimed the act of firing it, but she did not understand and shook her head so I scribbled quickly on the underwater slate and showed it to her.

'Cannon.'

She nodded vigorously, rolled her eyes and blew bubbles to register triumph before turning back to the cannon.

It was about the correct size to be one of the long nine-pounders that had formed part of the *Dawn Light*'s armament but there was no chance that I should be able to read any inscription upon it, for the surface was crocodile-skinned with growth and corrosion. Unlike the bronze bell that Jimmy North had recovered, it had not been buried in the sand to protect it.

I floated down along the massive barrel examining it closely and almost immediately found another cannon in the deeper gloom nearer the cliff. However, three-quarters of this weapon had been incorporated into the cliff, built into it by the living coral polyps.

I swam in closer, ducking under the first barrel and went into the jumble of debris and fallen coral blocks. I was

257

within two feet of this amorphous mass when with a shock which constricted my breathing and flushed warmly through my blood I recognized what I was looking at.

Quickly and excitedly I finned over the mound of debris, finding where it ended and the unbroken coral began, forcing my way up through the sea bamboo to estimate its size, and pausing to examine any opening or irregularity in it.

The total mass of debris was the size of a couple of railway Pullman coaches, but it was only when I pushed aside a larger floating clump of weed and peered into the squared opening of a gun port, from which the muzzle of a cannon still protruded and which had not been completely altered in shape by the encroaching coral, that I was certain that what we had discovered was the entire forward section of the frigate *Dawn Light*, broken off just behind the main mast.

I looked around wildly for Sherry and saw her finned feet protruding from another portion of the wreckage. I pulled her out, removed her mouthpiece and kissed her lustily before replacing it. She was laughing with excitement and when I signalled her that we were ascending, she shook her head vehemently and shot away from me to continue her explorations. It was fully fifteen minutes later that I was able to drag her away and take her up to the whaleboat.

We both began talking at once the moment we had the rubber mouthpieces out of the way. My voice is louder than hers, but she is more persistent. It took me some minutes to assert my rights as expedition leader and I could begin to describe it to Chubby.

'It's the *Dawn Light* sure enough. The weight of her armament and cargo must have pulled her down the instant she was clear of the reef. She went down like a stone, and she is lying against the foot of the cliff. Some of her cannons have fallen out of the hull, and they're lying jumbled around it—'

'We didn't recognize it at first,' Sherry chimed in again, just when I had her quietened down. 'It's like a rubbish dump. Just an enormous heap.'

'From what I could judge she must have broken her back abaft the main mast, but she's been smashed up badly for most of her length. The cannon must have torn up her gundeck and it's only the two ports nearest the bows that are intact—'

'How does she lie?' Chubby demanded, coming immediately to the pith of the matter.

'She's bottom up,' I admitted. 'She must have rolled as she went down.'

'That makes it a real problem, unless you can get in at a gun port or under the waist,' Chubby growled.

'I had a good look,' I told him, 'but I couldn't find a point at which we could penetrate the hull. Even the gunports are solid with growth.'

Chubby shook his head mournfully. 'Man, looks like this place is badly hexed,' and immediately all three of us made the cross-fingered sign against it.

Angelo told him primly, 'You talking up a storm. Shouldn't say that, hear?' but Chubby shook his head again, and his face collapsed into pessimistic folds.

I slapped him on his back and asked him, 'Is it true that you pass iced water – even in hot weather?' and my attempt at humour made him look as cheerful as an unemployed undertaker.

'Oh, leave Chubby alone,' Sherry came to his rescue. 'Let's go down again and try and find a break in the hull.'

'We'll take half an hour's rest,' I said, 'a smoke and a mug of coffee – then we'll go take another look.'

We stayed down so long on the second dive that Chubby

259

had to sound the triple recall signal – and when we surfaced the pool was boiling. The cyclone had left a legacy of high surf, and on the rising tide it was coming in heavily across the reef and pounding in through the gap, higher in the channel than we had ever known it.

We clung to the thwarts in silence as Chubby took us home on a wild ride, and it was only when we entered the quieter waters of the lagoon that we could continue the discussion.

'She's as tight as the Chatwood lock on the national safe deposit,' I told them. 'The one gun port is blocked by the cannon, and I got into the other about four feet before I ran into part of the bulkhead which must have collapsed. It's the den of a big old Moray eel that looks like a python – he's got teeth on him like a bulldog and he and I aren't friends.'

'What about the waist?' Chubby demanded.

'No,' I said, 'she's settled down heavily, and the coral has closed her up.'

Chubby put on an expression which meant that he had told us so. I could have beaten him over the head with a spanner, he was so smug – but I ignored him and showed them the piece of woodwork that I had prised off the hull with a crowbar.

'The coral has closed everything up solid. It's like those old forests that have been petrified into stone. The *Dawn Light* is a ship of stone, armour-plated with coral. There is only one way we will get into her – and that is to pop her open.'

Chubby nodded, 'That's the way to do it,' and Sherry wanted to know:

'But if you use explosive, won't it just blow everything to bits?'

'We won't use an atomic bomb,' I told her. 'We'll start with half a stick in the forward gunport. Just enough to kick out a chunk of that coral plating,' and I turned back to Chubby. 'We need that gelignite right away, every hour is precious now, Chubby. We've got a good moon. Can you take us back to St Mary's tonight?' and Chubby did not bother to answer such a superfluous question. It was an indirect slur on his seamanship.

There was a horned moon, with a pale halo around it. The atmosphere was still full of dust from the big winds. The stars also were misty and very far away, but the cyclone had blown great masses of oceanic plankton into the channel so that the sea was a glowing phosphorescent mass wherever it was disturbed.

Our wake glowed green and long, spread behind us like a peacock's tail, and the movement of fish beneath the surface shone like meteors. Sherry dipped her hand over the side and brought it out burning with a weird and liquid flame, and she cooed with wonder.

Later when she was sleepy she lay against my chest under the tarpaulin I had spread to keep off the damp and we listened to the booming of the giant manta rays out in the open water as they leaped high and fell to smack the surface of the sea with their flat bellies and tons of dead weight.

It was long after midnight when we raised the lights of St Mary's like a diamond necklace around the throat of the island.

The streets were utterly deserted as we left the whaleboat at her moorings and walked up to Chubby's house. Missus Chubby opened to us in a dressing-gown that made Chubby's pyjamas look conservative. She had her hair in large pink plastic curlers. I had never seen her without a hat before and I was surprised that she was not as bald as her spouse. They looked so alike in every other way.

She gave us coffee before Sherry and I climbed into the pick-up and drove to Turtle Bay. The bedclothes were damp and needed airing but neither of us complained.

I stopped at the Post Office in the early morning and my box was half filled, mostly with fishing equipment catalogues and junk mail, but there were a few letters from old clients inquiring for charter – that gave me a pang – and one of the buff cable envelopes which I opened last. Cables have always borne bad news for me. Whenever I see one of those envelopes with my name peering out of the window like a long-term prisoner I have this queasy feeling in my stomach.

The message read: 'MANDRAKE SAILED CAPETOWN OUTWARD BOUND ZANZIBAR 12.00 HOURS FRIDAY 16TH. STEVE.'

My premonitions of evil were confirmed. *Mandrake* had left Cape Town six days ago. She had made a faster passage than I would have believed possible. I felt like rushing to the top of Coolie Peak to search the horizon. Instead I passed the cable to Sherry and drove down to Frobisher Street.

Fred Coker was just opening the street door of his travel agency as I parked outside Missus Eddy's store and sent Sherry in with a shopping list while I walked on down the street to the Agency.

Fred Coker had not seen me since I had dropped him moaning on the floor of his own morgue, and now he was sitting at his desk in a white shark-skin suit and wearing a necktie which depicted a Hula girl on a palm-lined beach and the legend 'Welcome to St Mary's! Pearl of the Indian Ocean.'

He looked up with a smile that went well with the tie, but the moment he recognized me his expression changed to utter dismay. He let out a bleat like an orphan lamb and shot out of his chair, heading for the back room.

I blocked his escape and he backed away before me, his gold-rimmed glasses glittering like the sheen of nervous sweat that covered his face until the chair caught him in the back of his knees and he collapsed into it. Only then did I give him my big friendly grin – and I thought he would faint with relief.

'How are you, Mister Coker?' He tried to answer but his voice failed him. Instead he nodded his head so rapidly that I understood he was very well.

'I want you to do me a favour.'

'Anything,' he gabbled, suddenly recovering the power of speech. 'Anything, Mister Harry, you have only to ask.'

Despite his protestations it took him only a few minutes to recover his courage and wits. He listened to my very reasonable request for three cases of high explosive, and went into a pantomime to impress me with the utter impossibility of compliance. He rolled his eyes, sucked in his cheeks and made clucking noises with his tongue.

'I want it by noon tomorrow – latest,' and he clasped his forehead as if in agony.

'And if it's not here by twelve o'clock precisely, you and I will continue our discussion on the insurance premiums—'

He dropped his hand and sat upright, his expression once more willing and intelligent.

'That's not necessary, Mister Harry. I can get what you ask – but it will cost a great deal of money. Three hundred dollars a case.'

'Put it on the slate,' I told him.

'Mister Harry!' he cried, 'you know I cannot extend credit.'

I was silent, but I slitted my eyes, clenched my jaws and began to breathe deeply.

'Very well,' he said hurriedly. 'Until the end of the month, then.'

'That's very decent of you, Mister Coker.'

'It's a pleasure, Mister Harry,' he assured me. 'A very great pleasure.'

'There is just one other thing, Mr Coker,' and I could see him mentally quail at my next request, but he braced himself like a hero.

'In the near future I expect to be exporting a small consignment to Zürich in Switzerland.' He sat a little forward in his seat. 'I do not wish to be bothered with customs formalities – you understand?'

'I understand, Mister Harry.'

'Do you ever have requests to send the body of one of your customers back to the near and dear?'

'I beg your pardon?' He looked confused.

'If a tourist were to pass away on the island – say of a heart attack – you would be called on to embalm his corpse for posterity and to ship it out in a casket. Am I correct?'

'It has happened before,' he agreed. 'On three occasions.'

'Good, so you are familiar with the procedure?'

'I am, Mister Harry.'

'Mister Coker, lay in a casket and get yourself a pile of the correct forms. I'll be shipping soon.'

'May I ask what you intend to export – in lieu of a cadaver?' He phrased the question delicately.

'You may well ask, Mister Coker.'

I drove down to the fort and spoke to the President's secretary. He was in a meeting, but he would see me at one o'clock if I would care to lunch with him in his office. I accepted the invitation and, to pass the hours until then, I drove up the track to Coolie Peak as far as the pick-up would take me. There I parked it and walked on to the ruins of the old look-out and signal station. I sat on the parapet looking out across a vista of sea and green islands while I smoked a cheroot and did my last bit of careful planning and decision-making, glad of this opportunity to make certain of my plans before committing myself to them.

I thought of what I wanted from life, and decided it was

three things – Turtle Bay, *Wave Dancer II* and Sherry North, not necessarily in that order of preference.

To stay on at Turtle Bay, I had to keep a clean pair of hands in St Mary's, to have *Wave Dancer II* I needed cash and plenty of it, and Sherry North – well, that took plenty of hard thought, and at the end of it my cheroot had burned to a stub and I ground it out on the stone parapet. I took a deep breath and squared my shoulders.

'Courage, Harry me lad,' I said and drove down to the fort.

The President was delighted to see me, coming out into the reception room to welcome me and rising on tiptoe to place an arm around my shoulders and lead me into his office.

It was a room like a baronial hall with a beamed ceiling, panelled walls and English landscapes in massive ornate frames and dark smoky-looking oils. The diamond-paned window rose from the floor to the ceiling and looked out over the harbour, and the floor was lush with oriental carpets.

Luncheon was spread on the oaken conference table below the windows – smoked fish, cheese and fruit with a bottle of Château Lafite '62 from which the cork had been drawn.

The President poured two crystal glasses of the deep red wine, offered one to me and then plopped two cubes of ice into his own glass. He grinned impishly as he saw my startled expression. 'Sacrilege, isn't it?' He raised the glass of rare wine and ice cubes to me. 'But, Harry, I know what I like. What is suitable on the Rue Royale isn't necessarily suitable on St Mary's.'

'Right on, sir!' I grinned back at him and we drank.

'Now, my boy, what did you want to talk to me about?'

I found a message that Sherry had gone to visit Missus Chubby when I arrived back at the shack, so I went out on to the veranda with a cold beer. I went over my meeting with President Biddle, reviewing it word for word, and found myself satisfied. I thought I had covered all the openings – except the ones I might need to escape through.

Three wooden cases marked 'Canned Fish. Produce of Norway' arrived on the ten o'clock plane from the mainland addressed to Coker's Travel Agency.

'Eat your liver, Alfred Nobel,' I thought when I saw the legend as Fred Coker unloaded them from the hearse at Turtle Bay and I placed them in the rear of the pick-up under the canvas cover.

'Until the end of the month then, Mister Harry,' said Fred Coker, like the leading man from a Shakespearian tragedy.

'Depend upon it, Mister Coker,' I assured him and he drove away through the palms.

Sherry had finished packing away the stores. She looked so different from yesterday's siren, with her hair scraped back, dressed in one of my old shirts, which fitted her like a night-dress, and a pair of faded jeans with raggedy legs cut off below the knees.

I helped her carry the cases out to the pick-up, and we climbed into the cab.

'Next time we come back here we'll be rich,' I said, and started the motor, forgetting to make the sign against the hex.

We ground up through the palm grove, hit the main road below the pineapple fields and climbed up the ridge.

We came out on the crest above the town and the harbour.

'God damn it!' I shouted angrily, and hit the brakes hard, swinging off the road on to the verge so violently that the pineapple truck following us swerved to avoid running into our rear, and the driver hung out of his window to shout abuse as he passed.

'What is it?' Sherry pulled herself off the dashboard where my manoeuvre had thrown her. 'Are you crazy?'

It was a bright and cloudless day, the air so clear that every detail of the lovely white and blue ship stood out like a drawing. She lay at the entrance to Grand Harbour on the moorings usually reserved for visiting cruise ships, or the regular mail ship.

She was flying a festival burst of signal flags and I could see her crew in tropical whites lining the rail and staring at the shore. The harbour tender was running out to her, carrying the harbour master, the customs inspector and Doctor MacNab.

'*Mandrake?*' Sherry asked.

'*Mandrake* and Manny Resnick,' I agreed, and swung the truck into a U-turn across the road.

'What are you going to do?' she asked.

'One thing I'm not going to do is show myself in St Mary's while Manny and his fly lads are ashore. I've met most of them before in circumstances which are likely to have burned my lovely features clearly into even their rudimentary brains.'

Down the hill at the first bus stop beyond the turn off to Turtle Bay was the small General Dealers' Store which supplied me with eggs, milk, butter and other perishables. The proprietor was delighted to see me and he flourished my outstanding bill like a winning lottery ticket. I paid him, and then closed the door of his back office while I used the telephone.

Chubby did not have a phone, but his next-door neighbour called him to speak to me.

267

'Chubby,' I told him, 'that big white floating brothel at the mail ship mooring is no friend of ours.'

'What you want me to do, Harry?'

'Move fast. Cover the water cans with stump nets and make like you are going fishing. Get out to sea and come around to Turtle Bay. We'll load from the beach and run for Gunfire Reef as soon as it's dark.'

'I'll be in the bay in two hours,' he said and hung up.

He was there in one hour forty-five minutes. One of the reasons I liked working with him is that you can put money on his promises.

As soon as the sun set and visibility was down to a hundred yards we slipped out of Turtle Bay, and we were well clear of the island by the time the moon came up.

Huddled under the tarpaulin, sitting on a case of gelignite, Sherry and I discussed the arrival of *Mandrake* in Grand Harbour.

'First thing Manny will do, he will send his lads out with a pocketful of bread to ask a few questions around the shops and bars. "Anyone seen Harry Fletcher?" and they'll be queueing up to tell him all about it. How Mister Harry chartered Chubby Andrews' stump boat, and how they been diving looking for seashells. If he gets really lucky somebody will point him in the direction of Frederick Coker Esquire – and Fred will fall over himself to tell all, as long as the price is right.'

'Then what will he do?'

'He will have an attack of the vapours when he hears that I didn't drown in the Severn. When he recovers from that, he will send a team out to ransack and search the shack at Turtle Bay. He will draw a dud card there. Then the lovely Miss Lorna Page will lead them all to the alleged site of the wreck off Big Gull. That will keep them happy and busy for two or three days – until they find they have nothing but the ship's bell.'

'Then?'

'Well, then Manny is going to get mad. I think Lorna is in line for some unpleasantness – but after that I don't know what will happen. All we can do is try to keep out of sight and work like a tribe of beavers to get the Colonel's goodies out of the wreck.'

The next day the state of the tides was such that we could not navigate the channel before the late morning. It gave us time to make preparations. I opened one of the cases of gelignite and took out ten of the waxy yellow sticks. I reclosed the case and buried it with the other two in the sandy soil of the palm grove, well away from the camp.

Then Chubby and I assembled and checked the blasting equipment. It was a home-made contraption, but it had proved its efficiency before. It consisted of two nine-volt transistor batteries in a simple switchbox. We had four reels of light insulated copper wire, and a cigar-box of detonators. Each of the lethal silver tubes was carefully wrapped in cotton wool. There was also a selection of time-delayed detonators of the pencil type in the box.

Chubby and I isolated ourselves while we worked with them, clamping the electric detonators to the handmade terminals that I had soldered for the purpose.

The use of high explosives is simple in theory, and nerve-racking in practice. Even an idiot can wire it up and hit the button, but in its refined form it becomes an art.

I have seen a medium-sized tree survive a blast of half a case, losing only its leaves and some of its bark – but with half a stick I can drop the same tree neatly across a road to block it effectively, without removing a single leaf. I consider myself something of an artist, and I had taught

Chubby all I knew. He was a natural, although he could never be termed an artist – his glee in the proceedings was too frankly childlike. Chubby just naturally loved to blow things up. He hummed happily to himself as he worked with the detonators.

We took up position in the pool a few minutes before noon and I went down alone, armed only with a Nemrod captive air spear gun with a barbed crucifix head I had designed and made myself. The point was needle-sharp, and it was multi-barbed for the first six inches. Twenty-four small sharp barbs, like those used by Batonka tribesmen when they spear catfish in the Zambezi River. Behind the barbs was the crucifix, a four-inch cross-piece which would prevent the victim slipping down the shaft close enough to attack me when I held the reverse end. The line was five-hundred-pound blue nylon and there was a twenty-foot loop of it under the barrel of the spear gun.

I finned down on to the overgrown heap of wreckage and I settled myself comfortably beside the gunport and closed my eyes for a few seconds to accustom them to the gloom, then I peered cautiously into the dark square opening, pushing the barrel of the spear gun ahead of me.

The dark slimy coils of the Moray eel slithered and unwound as it sensed my presence, and it reared threateningly, displaying the fearsome irregular yellow fangs. In the gloom the eyes were black and bright, catching the feeble light like those of a cat.

He was a huge old mugger, thick as my calf and longer than the stretch of both my arms. The waving mane of his dorsal fin was angrily erected as he threatened me.

I lined him up carefully, waiting for him to turn his head and offer a better target. It was a scary few moments, I had one shot and if that was badly placed he would fly at me. I had seen a captive Moray chew mouthfuls out of the woodwork of a dinghy. Those fangs would tear easily through rubber suit and flesh, right down to the bone.

He was weaving slowly, like a flaring cobra, watching me, and the range was extreme for accurate shooting. I waited for the moment, and at last he went into the second stage of aggression. He blew up his throat and turned slightly to offer me a profile.

'My God,' I thought, 'I once used to do this for fun,' and I took up the slack in the trigger. The gas hissed viciously and the plunger thudded to the end of its travel as it threw the spear. It flew in a long blur with the line whipping out behind it.

I had aimed for the dark earlike marking at the back of the skull, and I was an inch and a half high and two inches right. The Moray exploded into a spinning, whipping ball of coils that seemed to fill the whole gunport. I dropped the gun and with a push of my fins I shot forward and got a grip of the hilt of the spear. It kicked and thumped in my hands as the eel wound its thick dark body around the shaft. I drew him out of his lair, pinned by a thick bite of skin and rubbery muscle to the barbed head.

His mouth was opened in a silent screech of fury, and he unwound his body and let it fly and writhe like a pennant in a high wind.

The tail slapped into my face, dislodging my mask. Water flooded into my nose and eyes and I had to blow it clear before I could begin the ascent.

Now the eel twisted its head back at an impossible angle and closed the dreadfully gaping jaws on the metal shaft of the spear. I could hear the fangs grinding and squeaking in the steel, and there were bright silver scratches where it had bitten.

I came out through the surface holding aloft my prize. I heard Sherry squeal with horror at the writhing snake-like monster, and Chubby grunted, 'Come to papa, you beauty,' and he leaned out to grasp the spear and lift the eel aboard. He was showing his plastic gums in a happy grin for Moray eel was Chubby's favourite food. He held the neck against the gunwale and, with an expert sweep of his bait-knife, lopped the monstrous head cleanly away, letting it fall into the pool.

'Miss Sherry,' he said, 'you going to love the taste of him.'

'Never!' Sherry shuddered, and drew herself farther away from the bleeding, wriggling carcass.

'Okay, my children, let's have the gelly.' Angelo had the underwater carry-net ready to pass to me, and Sherry slid in over the side prepared to dive. She had the reel of insulated wire and she paid it out smoothly as we went down.

Once again I went directly to the now untenanted gunport and crept into it. The breech of the cannon was jammed solidly against the mass of debris beyond.

I chose two sites to place my shots. I wanted to kick the cannon aside, using it like a giant lever to tear out a slab of the petrified planking. The second shot fired simultaneously would blow into the wall of debris that barred entry to the gun-deck.

I wired the shots firmly into place. Sherry passed the end of the line in to me and I snipped and bared the copper wire with the side-cutters before connecting it up to the terminals.

I checked the job once it was finished and then backed out of the port. Sherry was sitting cross-legged on the hull with the reel on her lap and I grinned at her around my mouthpiece and gave her the thumbs up before I retrieved my spear gun from where I had dropped it.

When we climbed over the side of the whaleboat Chubby had the battery switchbox beside him on the thwart and it was wired up. He was scowling with anticipation, as he crouched possessively over the blaster. It would have taken physical force to deprive him of the pleasure of hitting the button.

'Ready to shoot, skipper,' he growled.

'Shoot her then, Chubby.' He fussed with the box a little longer, drawing out the pleasure, then he turned the switch.

The surface of the pool bounced and shivered and we felt the bump come up through the bottom of the boat. Many seconds later there was a surge and frothing of bubbles, as though somebody had dropped a ton of Alka Seltzer into the pool. Slowly it cleared.

'I want you to put the trousers of your suit on, my sweeting,' I told Sherry, and predictably she took the order as an invitation to debate its correctness.

'Why, the water is warm?'

'Gloves and bootees also,' I said, as I began to pull on my own rubber full-length pants. 'If the hull is open we may penetrate her on this dive. You'll need protection against snags.'

Convinced at last, she did what she should have done without question. I still had a lot of work to do before she was properly trained, I thought, as I assembled the other equipment I needed for this descent.

I took the sealed unit underwater torch, the jemmy bar and a coil of light nylon line and waited while Sherry completed the major task of wiggling her bottom into the tight rubber pants, assisted faithfully by Angelo. Once she had them hoisted and had buttoned the crotch piece, we were set to go.

When we were halfway down, we came upon the first dead fish floating belly up in the misty blue depths. There were hundreds of them that the explosions had killed or maimed, and they ranged in size from fingerlings to big striped snapper and reef bass as long as my arm. I felt a pang of remorse at the massacre I had perpetrated, but consoled myself with the thought I had killed less than a bluefin tunny would in a single day's feeding.

We went down through this killing ground, and the light caught the eddying and drifting carcasses so they blinked and shone like dying stars in a smoky azure sky.

The bottom of the pool was murky with particles of sand and other material stirred up by the shock of the blast. There was a hole torn in the cover of sea bamboo and we went down into it.

I saw at once that I had achieved my purpose. The explosion had kicked the massive cannon out of the hull, tearing it like a rotten tooth from the black and ancient maw of the gunport. It had fallen to the bed of the pool surrounded by the debris that it had brought away with it.

The upper lip of the gunport had been knocked out, enlarging the opening so that a man might stand almost upright in it. When I flashed the torch into the darkness beyond, I saw that it was a turgid fog of suspended dirt and particles which would take time to settle. My impatience would not allow that, however, and as we settled on the hull I checked my time elapse and air reserves. Quickly I calculated our working time, allowing for my two previous descents which would necessitate additional decompression. I reckoned we had seventeen minutes' safe time before beginning the ascent and I set the swivel ring on my wristwatch before preparing for the penetration.

I used the jettisoned cannon as a convenient anchor point on which to fix the end of the nylon line and then rose again to the opening, paying it out behind me as I went.

I had to remove Sherry North from the gunport, in the few seconds while I was busy with the line she had almost disappeared into the hole in the hull. I made angry signs at her to keep clear, and in return she made an unladylike gesture with two fingers which I pretended not to see.

Gingerly I entered the gunport and found that the visibility was down to about three feet in the murky soup.

The shots had only partially moved the blockage beyond the spot where the cannon had lain. There seemed to be a gap beyond but it needed to be enlarged before I could get through. I used the jemmy bar to prise a lump of the wreckage away and discovered that it was the heavy gun carriage that was causing most of the blockage.

Working in freshly blasted wreckage is a delicate business, for it is impossible to know how critically balanced the mass may be. Even the slightest disturbance can bring the whole weight of it sliding and crashing down upon the trespasser, pinning and crushing him beneath it.

I worked slowly and deliberately, ignoring the regular thumps on my rump with which Sherry signalled her burning impatience. Once when I emerged with a section of shattered planking, she took my slate and wrote on it 'I am smaller!!' and underlined the 'smaller' twice in case the double exclamation mark was not noticed when she thrust the slate two inches from my nose. I returned her Churchillian salute and went back to my burrowing.

I had now cleared the area sufficiently to see that my only remaining obstacle was the heavy timber bulk of the gun carriage which was hanging at a drunken angle across the entry to the gundeck. The jemmy bar was totally ineffective against this mass, and I could abandon the effort and return with another charge of gelignite tomorrow or I could take a chance.

I glanced at my time elapse and saw that I had been busy for twelve minutes. I reckoned that I had probably been using air more wastefully than usual during my recent exertions. Nevertheless, I decided to take a flier.

I passed the torch and jemmy bar out to Sherry, and worked my way carefully back into the opening. I got my shoulder under the upper end of the gun carriage, and moved my feet around until I had a firm stance. When I was solidly placed, I took a good breath of air and began to lift.

Slowly I increased the strain until I was thrusting upwards with all the strength of my legs and back. I felt my face and throat swelling with pumping blood and my eyes felt ready to jump out of their sockets. Nothing moved, and I took another lungful of air and tried again, but this time throwing all my weight on the timber beam in a single explosive effort.

It gave way, and I felt like Samson who had pulled the temple down on his own head. I lost my balance and tumbled backwards in a storm of falling debris that groaned and grated as it fell, thudding and bumping around me.

When silence had settled, I found myself in utter darkness, a thick pea soup of swirling filth that blotted out the light. I tried to move, and found my leg pinned. Panic rushed through me in an icy wave and I fought frantically to free my leg. I took only half-a-dozen terrified kicks before I realized that I had escaped with great good luck. The gun carriage had missed my foot by a quarter of an inch, and had fallen across the rubber swimming fin. I pulled my foot out of the shoe, abandoning it, and grouped my way out into the open.

Sherry was waiting eagerly for news, and I wiped the slate and wrote 'OPEN!!' underlining the word twice. She pointed into the gunport, demanding permission to enter and I checked my time elapse. We had two minutes, so I nodded and led the way in.

Flashing the beam of the torch ahead I had visibility of eighteen inches, enough to find the opening I had cleared. There was just sufficient clearance to allow me through without fouling my air bottles or breathing hose.

I paid out the nylon line behind me, like Theseus in the

labyrinth of the Minotaur, so as not to lose my direction in the *Dawn Light*'s warren of decks and companionways.

Sherry followed me along the line. I could feel her hand touch my foot and brush my leg as she groped after me.

Beyond the blockage, the water cleared a little, and we found ourselves in the low wide chamber of the gun-deck. It was murky and mysterious, with strange shapes strewn about us in profusion. I saw other gun carriages, cannonballs strewn loosely or in heaps against angles and corners, and other equipment so altered by long immersion as to be unrecognizable.

We moved slowly forward, our fins stirring up fresh whirlpools of dirt and mud. Here also there were dead fish floating about us, although I noticed some of the red reef crayfish scrambling away like monstrous spiders into the depths of the ship. They at least had survived the blast in their armoured carapaces.

I played the beam of the torch on the deck above our heads, looking for the entry point to the lower decks and the holds. With the ship lying upside down, I had to keep trying to relate the existing geography of the wreck to the drawing I had studied.

About fifteen feet from our entry point I found the forecastle ladder, another dark square opening above my head, and I rose into it, my bubbles blowing upwards in a silver shower and running like liquid mercury across the bulkheads and decking. The ladder was rotted so that it fell to pieces at my touch, the pieces hanging suspended in the water around my head as I went on into the lower deck.

This was a narrow and crowded alleyway, probably serving the passenger cabins and officers' mess. The claustrophobic atmosphere reminded me of the appalling conditions in which the crew of the frigate must have lived.

I ventured gingerly along this passage, attracted power-fully to the doorways on either hand which promised all manner of fascinating discoveries. I resisted their temptation and finned on down the long deck until it ended abruptly against a heavy timber bulkhead.

This would be the outer wall of the well of the forward hold, where it pierced the deck and went down into the ship's belly.

Satisfied with what we had achieved, I turned the beam of the torch on to my wrist and realized with a guilty thrill that we had overrun our working time by four minutes. Every second was taking us closer to the dreaded danger of empty air bottles and uncompleted decompression stops.

I grabbed Sherry's wrist and gave her the cut-throat hand signal for danger before tapping my wristwatch. She understood immediately, and followed me meekly on the long slow journey back through the hull along the guiding line. Already I could feel the stiffening of the demand valve, as it gave me air more reluctantly now that the bottles were almost exhausted.

We came out into the open and I made certain that Sherry was by my side before I looked upwards. What I saw above me made my breathing choke in my throat, and the horror I felt turned to a warm oily liquid sensation in my bowels.

The pool of Gunfire Break had been transformed into a bloody arena. Attracted by the tons of dead fish that had been killed by the blast, the deep-water killer sharks had arrived in their scores. The scent of flesh and blood, together with the excited movements of their fellows transmitted to them through the water, had driven them into that mindless savagery known as the feeding frenzy.

Quickly I drew Sherry back into the gunport and we cowered there, looking up at the huge gliding shapes so clearly silhouetted against the light source of the surface.

Amongst the shoals of smaller sharks there were at least

278

two dozen of the ugly beasts that the islanders called Albacore shark. They were barrel-bodied and swing-bellied, big powerful fish with rounded snouts and wide grinning jaws. They swirled about the pool like some grotesque carousel, with their tails waggling and their mouths opening mechanically to gulp down shreds of flesh. I knew them for greedy but stupid animals, easily discouraged by any aggressive display when not in feeding frenzy. Now they were in intense excitation they would be dangerous, yet I would have accepted the risk of a decompression ascent if it had been for them alone.

What truly appalled me were two other long lithe shapes that sped silently about the pool, turning with a single powerful flick of the long swallow tail, so that the pointed nose almost touched the tip of the tail, then gliding away again with all the power and grace of an eagle in flight.

When either one of these terrible fish paused to feed, the sickle-moon mouth opened and the multiple rows of teeth came erect like the quills of a porcupine and flared outwards.

They were a matched pair, each about twelve feet in length from nose to tail-tip, with the standing blade of the dorsal fin as long as a man's arm; they were slaty blue across the back and with snowy white bellies and dark tips to tail and fins, they could bite a man in half and swallow the pieces whole.

One of them saw us crouching in the mouth of the gunport, and it turned sharply and came down over us, planing a few feet above us as we cowered back into the gloom so that I could clearly see the long trailing spikes of the male reproductive organs.

These were the dreaded white death sharks, the most vicious fish of all the seas, and I knew that to attempt to ascend in the clear and decompress adequately with limited air and no protection would be certain death.

If I were to get Sherry out alive I would have to take risks that in any other circumstances would be unthinkable.

Quickly I scribbled on the slate: 'STAY!! I am free ascending for air and gun.'

She read the message and immediately shook her head in refusal and made urgent signs to prevent me, but already I had pulled the pin out of the quick release buckle of my harness and I took the last deep, chest-swelling breath before I thrust my scuba set into her hands. I dropped my weight belt to give myself buoyancy and slid down the side of the hull, using the wreck to cover me as I finned swiftly for the cover of the cliff.

I had left Sherry what remained of my air supplies, perhaps five or six minutes' breathing if she used it sparingly, and now with only the air that I held in my lungs I had to run the gauntlet of the pool and try for the surface.

I reached the cliff and began to go up, close in against the coral, hoping that my dark suit would blend with the shades. I went up with my back to the coral, facing out into the open pool where the great sinister shapes still swirled and milled.

Twenty feet from the bottom and the air in my lungs was expanding rapidly as the pressure of water decreased. I could not hold it in or it would rupture the tissue of my lungs. I let it trickle from my lips, a silver beacon of bubbles that one of the white death sharks noticed immediately.

He rolled and turned, dashing across the pool with slashing strokes of his tail, bearing down upon me.

Desperately I glanced up the cliff and found six feet above me one of the small caves in the rotten coral. I dived into it just as the shark flashed past me, turned and sped back for a second pass as I shrank into my shallow shelter. The shark lost interest and swirled away to pick up the falling-leaf body of a dead snapper, gulping it down convulsively.

My lungs were throbbing and pumping now for the oxygen had all been absorbed from the air I held, and the carbon dioxide was building up in my blood. Soon I would begin to black out into anoxia.

I left the shelter of the cave, but, still following the cliff, I drove upwards as hard as I could with the single swimming fin, wishing bitterly for the use of the other still trapped under the gun carriage.

Again I had to release expanding air as I rose, and I knew that in my veins nitrogen was also decompressing too rapidly and soon it would turn to gas and bubble like champagne in my blood.

Above me I saw the silvery moving mirror of the surface and the black cigar shape of the whaleboat's hull suspended upon it. I was coming up fast and I glanced down again. Far below me I could see the shark pack still milling and turning. It looked as though I had escaped their notice.

My lungs burned with the craving for air, and the blood pounded in my temples as I decided that the time had arrived when I must forsake the shelter of the cliff and cross the open pool to the whaleboat.

I kicked out and shot towards the whaleboat where it lay a hundred feet from the reef. Halfway across I glanced down and saw one of the white deaths had seen me and was chasing. It came up from the blue depths with incredible speed, and terror gave me new strength as I drove for the surface and the boat.

I was looking down, watching the shark come. It seemed to swell up in size as it rushed towards me. Every detail was burned into my mind in those frantic seconds. I saw the hog's snout with the two slitted nostrils, the golden eyes with the black pupils like arrowheads, the broad blue back from which stood the tall executioner's blade of the dorsal fin.

I came out through the surface so fast that I broke clear

to my waist, and I turned in the air and got my good arm over the gunwale of the boat. With all my strength I swung my body forward and jack-knifed my legs up under my chin.

In that instant the white death struck, the water exploded about me as he burst through the surface, I felt the harsh gritty skin tear across the legs of my suit as he brushed against me, then there was a shuddering crash as he struck the hull of the whaleboat.

I saw Chubby and Angelo's startled faces as the boat heeled over and rocked wildly. My violent contortions had thrown the shark off his run, and he had missed my legs and collided with the hull.

Now with one more desperate kick and heave I tumbled over the gunwale and fell into the bottom of the whaleboat. Again the shark crashed into the hull as I went over, missing me again by inches.

I lay there pumping air into my aching lungs, great sweet gulps of it that made me light-headed and giddy as on strong wine.

Chubby was yelling at me, 'Where is Miss Sherry? That big Johnny Uptail get Miss Sherry?'

I rolled on to my back, panting and sobbing for the precious air.

'Spare lungs,' I gasped. 'Sherry waiting in the wreck. She needs air.'

Chubby leaped into the bows and dragged the canvas sheet off the extra scuba sets stacked there. In a crisis he is the kind of man I like to have covering for me.

'Angelo,' he growled, 'get them Johnny pills.' They were a pack of copper acetate shark repellent pills which I had ordered from an American sports goods catalogue and for which Chubby had professed a deep and abiding scorn. 'Let's see if those fancy things are any bloody good.'

I had breathed enough to drag myself off the floorboards and to tell Chubby: 'We've got problems. The pool is full of big Johnnys, and there are two really mean uptails with them. That one that charged me and another.'

Chubby scowled as he fitted the demand valves to the new sets.

'Did you come straight up, Harry?'

I nodded. 'I left my bottles for Sherry. She's waiting down there.'

'You going to bend, Harry?' He looked up at me and I saw the worry in his eyes.

'Yes,' I nodded, as I dragged myself to my tackle box and lifted the lid. 'I've got to get down again fast – got to put pressure on my blood again before she fizzes.'

I picked out the bandolier of explosive heads for my hand spear. There were twelve of them, and I wished for more as I strapped the bandolier around my thigh. Each head was hand-tapped to screw on to the shaft of a ten-foot stainless steel spear. It contained explosive charge equivalent to that of a 12-gauge shotgun shell and I could fire the charge with a trigger on the handle. It was an effective shark-killer.

Chubby hoisted one of the scuba sets on to my back and clinched the harness, and Angelo knelt before me to strap the shark repellent tablets in their perforated plastic containers to my ankles.

'I'll need another weight belt,' I said, 'and I lost a fin. There is a spare set in—' I did not finish the sentence. Blinding burning agony struck me in the elbow of my bad arm. Agony so fierce that I cried aloud, and my arm snapped closed like the blade of a clasp knfe. It was an involuntary reaction, the joint doubling as the pressure of bubbles in the blood pressed on nerve and tendons.

'He's bending,' snarled Chubby. 'Sweet Mary, he's bending.' He leapt to the motors and gunned them, taking me in close to the reef. 'Work fast, Angelo,' Chubby shouted, 'we got to get him down again.'

283

The pain struck again, a fiery cramping agony in my right leg. The knee doubled under me and I whimpered like an infant. Angelo strapped the weight belt around my waist, and thrust the swimming fin on to my crippled leg.

Chubby cut the motors and we coasted in under the lee of the reef, while Chubby scrambled back to where I crouched on the thwart. He stooped over me to thrust the mouthpiece between my lips and open the cocks on the air bottles.

'Okay?' he asked, and I sucked from the set and nodded.

Chubby leaned over the side and peered down into the pool. 'Okay,' he grunted, 'Johnny Uptail gone somewhere else.'

He lifted me like a child, for I had lost the use of arm and leg, and he lowered me into the water between boat and reef.

Angelo hooked the harness of the extra scuba set for Sherry on to my belt, then he passed me the ten-foot spear and I prayed that I would not drop it.

'You go get Miss Sherry out of there,' said Chubby, and I rolled over in a clumsy one-legged duck dive and went down.

Even in the cramping agony of the bends my first concern was to search for the sinister gliding shapes of the white deaths. I saw one of them, but he was deep down, amongst the pack of lumbering Albacore sharks. Clinging to the shelter of the reef, I kicked and wriggled downwards like a maimed water beetle. Thirty feet under the surface the pain began to recede. Renewed pressure of water was reducing the size of the bubbles in my bloodstream, my limbs straightened and I had use of them.

I went down faster, and the relief was swift and blessed. I felt new courage and confidence flooding away my earlier despair. I had air and a weapon. I had a fighting chance now.

I was ninety feet down, in clear sight of the bottom. I could see Sherry's bubbles rising from the smoky blue depths, and the sight cheered me. She was still breathing, and I had a fully charged extra scuba set for her. All I had to do was get it to her.

One of the fat ugly Albacore sharks saw me as I slid down the dark cliff face, and he swerved towards me. Already gorged with food, but endlessly hungry, he came in at me grinning horribly and paddling his wide tail.

I backed up and hung in the water against the cliff, facing him. I had the spear with its explosive head extended towards him, and as I finned gently to hold myself ready the streamers of bright blue dye from the shark repellent tablets smoked out in a cloud around me.

The shark came on in, and I lined up to hit him fairly on the snout, but the instant his head and gills encountered clouds of blue dye he spun away, flapping his tail in shock and dismay. The copper acetate had burned his gills and eyes, and he retreated hurriedly.

'Eat your liver, Chubby Andrews,' I thought. 'They work!'

Down again I went, almost to the tops of the bamboo forest, seeing Sherry still crouched in the gunport thirty feet away watching me. She had exhausted her own air bottles and was using mine – but I could tell by the volume and scanty rate of flow of bubbles that she had only seconds of breathing time left to her.

I started towards her, leaving the cliff – and only her frantic hand signals alerted me. I turned and saw the white death coming like a long blue torpedo. He was skimming the tops of the bamboo, and from one corner of his jaws hung a tattered streamer of flesh. He opened that wide maw to gulp down the morsel, and the rows of fangs gleamed whitely, like the petals of some obscene flower.

I faced him as he charged, but at the same time I fell

back kicking my fins in his direction and laying a thick smoke-screen of blue dye between us.

With hard slashing strokes of his tail, he arrowed in the last few yards, but then he hit the blue dye and swirled, altering the direction of his charge as he sheered away.

He passed me so close that his tail struck me a heavy blow on the shoulder, sending me tumbling end over end. For seconds I lost my bearings, but as I recovered my balance and looked wildly about me I found the great shark circling.

He swept around me, forty feet away, and in his full length he seemed to my heated eye as long as a battleship and as blue and as vast as a summer sky. It seemed impossible to believe that these fish grew to almost twice this size. This one was still a baby – I was thankful for that.

Suddenly the slim steel spear in which I had placed so much faith seemed futile, and the shark regarded me with a cold yellow eye across which the pale nictitating membrane flicked occasionally in a sardonic wink, and once he opened his jaws in a convulsive gulp, as though in anticipation of the taste of my flesh.

He continued in those wide racing circles, with myself always at the centre, turning with him and paddling frantically with my fins to match his smooth unforced speed.

As I turned, I unhooked the spare lung from my belt and slung it by the harness on my left shoulder like the shield of a Roman legionary, and I tucked the hilt of the spear under my arm and kept the head pointed at the circling monster.

My whole body tingled with the warm flush of adrenalin in the bloodstream, and my senses were enhanced and sharpened by the adrenalin high – the intensely pleasurable sensation of acute fear to which a man can become an addict.

Each detail of the deadly fish was etched indelibly on my memory, from the gentle pulsing of the multiple gill behind the head to the long trailing ribbons of the remora fish holding by their suckers to the smooth snowy expanse of his belly. With a fish of this size, it would only infuriate him further if I went for a hit with the explosive spear on his snout. My only chance was for a hit on the brain.

I recognized the moment when the shark's distaste for the blue mist of repellent was overcome by his hunger and his anger. His tail seemed to stiffen and it gave a series of rapid strokes, driving his speed up sharply.

I braced myself, lifting the spare scuba protectively, and the shark turned hard and fast, breaking the wide circle and coming in directly at me.

I saw the jaws open like a pit, lined with the wedge-shaped fangs, and at the moment of strike I thrust the twin steel bottles of the scuba into it.

The shark closed its jaws on the decoy and it was torn from my grasp, while the impact of the attack tossed me aside like a floating leaf. When I had gathered myself again I looked around frantically and found the white death was twenty feet away, moving only slowly but worrying the steel bottles the way a puppy chews a slipper.

It was shaking its head in the instinctive reaction which tears lumps of flesh from a victim – but which was now inflicting only deep scratches on the painted metal of the scuba.

This was my chance, my one and only chance. Kicking hard, I spurted above the broad blue back, brushing the tall dorsal fin and I sank down over him, coming in on his blind spot like an attacking fighter pilot from high astern.

I reached out with the steel spear and pressed the tip of it firmly on to the curved blue skull, directly between those cold and deadly yellow eyes – and I squeezed the spring-loaded trigger on the hilt of the spear.

287

The shot fired with a crack that beat in upon my eardrums, and the spear jumped heavily in my grip.

The white death shark reared on its tail like a startled horse, and once again I was tossed lightly aside by his careless bulk, but I recovered to watch him go into a terrible frenzy. The muscles beneath the smooth skin twitched and rippled at random impulse from the damaged brain, and the shark spun and dived, rolling wildly on its back, arrowing downwards to crash snout first into the rocky bottom of the pool, then it stood on its tail and scooted in aimless parabolas through the pale blue waters.

Still watching it, and keeping a respectful distance, I unscrewed the exploded head off the spear and replaced it with a fresh charge.

The white death still had Sherry's air supply clamped in his jaws. I could not leave it. I trailed his violent, unpredictable manoeuvres warily, and when at last he hung stationary for a moment nose down, suspended on the wide flukes of his tail, I shot in again and once more pressed the explosive charge to his skull, holding it firmly against the cartilaginous dome, so that the full shock of the charge would be transmitted directly to the tiny brain.

I fired the shot, cracking painfully in my own ears, and the shark froze rigidly. It never moved again but still in that frozen rigour it rolled over slowly and began to sink towards the floor of the pool. I darted in and wrested the damaged scuba from his jaws.

I saw immediately the air hoses had been torn and shredded by the shark's teeth, but the bottles were only extensively scratched.

Carrying the lung with me I sprinted across the tops of the bamboo towards the wreck. There were no longer air bubbles rising from the gunport, and as I came in sight of her I saw that Sherry had discarded the last empty scuba set. They were empty, and she was dying slowly.

Yet even in the extremes of slow suffocation she had not made the suicidal attempt to rise to the surface. She was waiting for me, dying slowly, but trusting me.

As I came down beside her, I pulled out my own mouthpiece and offered it to her. Her movements were slow and uncoordinated. The mouthpiece slipped from her grasp and floated upwards, spewing out a torrent of air. I grabbed it and forced it into her mouth, holding it there while lowering myself slightly below her level to induce a readier flow of air.

She began to breathe. Her chest rose and fell in long deep draughts of the precious stuff, and almost immediately I saw her regaining strength and purpose. Satisfied I turned my attention to removing a demand valve from one of the abandoned lungs from which the air supply was exhausted and using it to replace the one damaged by the shark.

I breathed off it for half a minute, before strapping it on to Sherry's back and retrieving my own mouthpiece.

We had air now, enough to take us through the long period of slow decompression ahead of us. I knelt facing Sherry in the gunport and she grinned lopsidedly around the mouthpiece and lifted her thumb in a high sign and I returned it. You okay, me okay, I thought, and unscrewed the expended head from the spear and renewed it from the bandolier on my thigh.

Then once more I peered from the safety of the gunport out into the open waters of the pool.

As the supply of dead fish was depleted so the shark pack seemed to have dispersed. I saw one or two of the ungainly dark shapes still searching and sniffing the tainted waters, but their frenzy was reduced. They moved in a more leisurely fashion, and I felt happier about taking Sherry out now.

I reached for her hand and was surprised at how small

and cold it felt in mine, but she answered my gesture with a squeeze of her fingers.

I pointed to the surface and she nodded. I led her out of the gunport and we slid down the hull and under cover of the bamboo crossed quickly to the shelter of the reef.

Side by side, still holding hands and with our backs to the cliff, we rose slowly up out of the pool.

The light strengthened and when I looked up I could see the whaleboat high above. My spirits rose.

At sixty feet I stopped for a minute to begin decompressing. A fat old Albacore shark swam past us, blotched and piebald like a pig, but he paid us no attention and I lowered the spear as he drifted away into the hazy distance.

Slowly we rose to the next decompression stop at forty feet, where we stayed for two minutes, allowing the nitrogen in our blood to evaporate out through our lungs gradually. Then up to twenty feet for the next stop.

I peered into Sherry's face-mask and she rolled her eyes at me, clearly she was regaining her courage and cheek. It was all going smoothly now. We were as good as home, and drinking whisky – just another twelve minutes.

The whaleboat was so close it seemed that I could touch it with the spear. I could quite clearly see Chubby's and Angelo's brown faces hanging over the side as they waited anxiously for us to emerge.

I looked away from them, making another careful search of the water about us. At the extreme range of my vision, where the haze of water shaded away to solid blue, I saw something move. It was just a suspicion of a shadow that had come and gone before I had really seen it, but I felt the returning prickle of fear and apprehension.

I hung in the water, completely alert once more, searching and waiting while the last few slow minutes dragged by like crippled insects.

The shadow passed again, this time clearly seen, a swift

and deadly movement that left me in no doubt that it was not an Albacore shark. It was the difference between the shape of the prowling hyena in the shadows around the campfire and that of the lion when he hunts.

Suddenly, through the misty blue curtains of water, came the second white death shark. He came swiftly and silently, passing fifty feet away, seeming to ignore us and going on almost to the range of our vision and then turning steeply and returning to pass us again, like a caged animal back and forth along the bars.

Sherry cowered close to me and I disengaged my hand from the death grip in which she had it. I needed both hands now.

On the next pass the shark broke the pattern of its movements and went into the great sweeping circles which always precede attack. Around and around it went, with that pale yellow eye fastened hungrily upon us.

Suddenly my attention was distracted by the slow descent from above of a dozen of the blue plastic shark repellent containers. Seeing our predicament Chubby must have emptied the entire boxful over the side. One of them passed closely enough for me to snatch it up and hand it to Sherry.

It smoked blue dye in her hand, and I transferred my attention back to the shark. It had sheered off a little from the blue dye, but it was still circling swiftly and grinning loathsomely at us.

I glanced at my watch, three minutes more to be safe, but I could risk sending Sherry out ahead of me. Unlike myself she had not already had a nitrogen fizz in her blood, she would probably be safe in another minute.

The shark tightened its circle, boring in relentlessly on us. Close – so very close that I looked deep into the black spear-headed pupil of his eye, and read his intention there.

I glanced at the watch. It was cutting it fine – very fine,

but I decided to send Sherry up. I slapped her shoulder and pointed urgently to the surface. She hesitated, but I slapped her again and repeated my instruction.

She began to rise, going up slowly, the right way, but her legs dangled invitingly. The shark left me and rose slowly in time with her, following her.

She saw it and began to rise faster, smoothly the shark closed in on her. Now I was under them both, and I finned out fast to one side just as the shark went into the stiff-tailed attitude which signalled the instant of his attack.

I was directly under him, as he turned to maul Sherry. I reached up and pressed the spear-head into the softly obscene throat, and I hit the trigger.

I saw the shock kick into the bloated white flesh, and the shark reared away with a convulsive beat of its tail. It shot upwards and went out through the surface, leaping out high and clear, and falling back heavily in a creaming froth of bubbles.

Immediately it began to spin and fly in maddened, crazy circles, as though beset by a swarm of bees. Repeatedly its jaws opened and snapped closed.

Torn with terrible anxiety, I watched Sherry maintain her mental discipline and rise leisurely towards the whale-boat. A pair of huge brown paws were thrust down through the surface to welcome her. As I watched, she came within reach of them. The brown fingers closed on her like steel grab-hooks and she was plucked with miraculous strength from the water.

I could now employ all my attention on the problem of staying alive through the next few minutes before I could follow her. The shark seemed to recover from the shock of the charge, and it exchanged its mindless crazy gyrations for the terrible familiar circling.

It began again on the wide circumference, closing in steadily with each circuit. I glanced at my wristwatch and saw that at last I could begin to rise through the final stage.

I drifted upwards slowly. The agony of the bends was fresh in my memory – but the white death shark was pressing closer and closer.

Ten feet below the whaleboat, I paused again and the shark was suspicious, probably remembering the recent violent explosion in its throat. It ceased its circling and hung motionless in the pale water on the wide pointed wings of his pectoral fins. We stared at each other across a distance of fifteen feet, and I could sense that the great blue beast was gathering himself for the final rush.

I extended the spear to the full reach of my arm, and gently, so as not to trigger him, I finned towards him until the explosive charge was an inch from the nostril slits below the snout.

I hit the trigger and he reared back in shock as the explosive cracked. He whirled away in a wide angry turn and I dropped the spear and shot for the surface.

He was angry as a wounded lion, goaded by the hurts he had received, and he charged for me with his humped back large as a blue mountain and his wide jaws gaping open. I knew there was no turning him this time, nothing short of death would stop him.

As I shot for the surface I saw Chubby's hands waiting for me, the fingers like a bunch of brown bananas, and I loved him at that moment. I lifted my right arm above my head, offering it to Chubby and as the shark flashed across the last few feet that separated us I felt Chubby's fingers close on my wrist.

Then the water exploded about me. I felt the enormous drag on my arm and the powerful disruption of the water as the shark's bulk tore it apart. Then I was lying on my back upon the deck of the whaleboat, dragged from the very jaws of that dreadful animal.

'You got some nice pets, Harry,' said Chubby in a disinterested tone that I knew was forced, and I looked about quickly for Sherry.

'You okay?' I called, as I saw her wet and pale-faced in the stern. She nodded; I doubted she could speak.

I jerked out the quick release pin on my harness, freeing myself of the weight of the scuba.

'Chubby, set up a stick of gelly ready to shoot,' I called, as I rid myself of mask and fins and peered over the side of the whaleboat.

The shark was still with us, circling the whaleboat in a fury of hurt and frustration. He came up to show the full length of his dorsal fin above the surface. I knew he could easily attack and stove in the planking of the whaleboat.

'Oh God, Harry, he's horrible.' Sherry found her voice at last, and I knew how she felt. I hated that loathsome fish with the full force of my recent terror – but I had to distract it from direct attack.

'Angelo, give me that Moray and a bait-knife,' I shouted and he handed me the cold slimy body. I hacked off a ten-pound lump of the dead eel and tossed it into the pool.

The shark swirled and raced for the scrap, gulping it down and scraping the hull of the whaleboat as it passed so close. We rocked violently at its passing.

'Hurry up, Chubby,' I shouted, and fed the shark another lump. It took it as readily as a hungry dog, dashing past under the hull and again bumping the boat so that it swayed unpleasantly and Sherry squeaked and grabbed the gunwale.

'Ready,' said Chubby, and I passed him a two-foot section of the eel with its empty belly cavity hanging open like a pouch.

'Put the stick in there, and tie it up,' I instructed him, and he began to grin.

'Hey, Harry,' he chortled, 'I like it.'

While I fed the monster with scraps of eel, Chubby

trussed up the stick of gelignite in a neat parcel of eel flesh, with the insulated copper wire protruding from it. He passed it to me.

'Connect her up,' I instructed, as I coiled a dozen loops of the wire into my left hand.

'Ready to shoot,' grinned Chubby, and I threw the bundle of meat and explosive into the path of the circling shark.

It raced for it, and its glistening blue back broke the surface as it swallowed the offering. Immediately the wire began to stream away over the side and I paid out more from the reel.

'Let him eat it down,' I said and Chubby nodded happily.

'Okay, Chubby, blow the bastard to hell,' I snarled as the fish came to the surface, fin up, and swung around us in another circle, with the copper wire trailing from the corner of the sickle-moon mouth.

Chubby hit the switch, and the shark erupted in a tall burst of pink spray, like a bursting water melon, as his pale blood mingled with the paler flesh and purple contents of the belly cavity, spurting fifty feet into the air and splattering the pool and whaleboat. The shattered carcass wallowed like a bleeding log upon the surface, then rolled over and began to sink.

'Goodbye, Johnny Uptail,' hooted Angelo, and Chubby grinned like a cherub.

'Let's go home,' I said, for already the oceanic surf was breaking over the reef, and I thought I was going to throw up.

However, my indisposition responded miraculously to a treatment of Chivas Regal whisky, even though taken from an enamel mug, and much later in the cave Sherry said: 'I suppose you want me to thank you for saving my life, and all that crap?'

I grinned at her and opened my arms. 'No, my sweeting,

295

just show me how grateful you are,' which she did, and afterwards there were no ugly dreams to spoil my sleep for I was exhausted in body and spirit.

I think all of us were coming to regard the pool at Gunfire Break with a superstitious dread. The series of accidents and mishaps to which we had been subject appeared to be the result of some deliberate malevolent scheme.

It seemed as though each time we returned to the pool it had grown more sinister in its aspect and that an aura of menace was growing about it.

'You know what I think,' Sherry said laughingly, but not completely as a joke. 'I think the spirits of the murdered Mogul princes have followed the treasure to act as guardians—' Even in the bright sunshine of a glorious morning I saw the expressions on the faces of Angelo and Chubby. 'I think the spirits were in those two big Johnny Uptails that we killed yesterday.' Chubby looked as though he had breakfasted off a dozen rotten oysters, he blanched to a waxy golden brown and I saw him make the sign with his right hand.

'Miss Sherry,' said Angelo severely, 'you must never talk like that.' I could see gooseflesh on his forearms. Both he and Chubby had an attack of the ghostlies.

'Yes, cut it out,' I agreed.

'I was joking,' protested Sherry.

'Good joke,' I said, 'you really slayed us.' And we were all silent during the passage of the channel and until we had taken station in the shelter of the reef.

I was sitting in the bows, and when all three of them looked at me I saw by the expressions on their faces that I had a crisis of morale on my hands.

'I will go down alone,' I announced, and there was a small stir of relief.

'I'll go with you,' Sherry volunteered half-heartedly.

'Later,' I agreed, 'but first I want to check for Johnnies, and recover the equipment we lost yesterday.'

I went down cautiously, hanging just under the boat for five minutes while I scrutinized the depths of the pool for those evil dark shapes, and then finning down quietly.

It was cold and eerie in the deeper shades, but I saw that the night tide had scoured the pool and sucked out to sea all the carrion and blood that had attracted the shark pack the previous day.

There was no sign of the huge white death carcasses, and the only fish I saw were the multitudinous shoals of brilliant coral dwellers. A glint of silver from below led me to the spear I had abandoned in my rush for the boat, and I found the empty scubas and the damaged demand valve where we had left them in the gunport.

I surfaced with my load, and there were smiles amongst my crew for the first time that day when I reported the pool clear.

'All right,' I capitalized on the rise of their spirits, 'today we are going to open up the hold.'

'You going in through the hull?' Chubby asked.

'I thought about that, Chubby, but I reckoned that it would need a couple of heavy charges to get in that way. I've decided to go in through the passenger deck into the well.' I sketched it on my slate for them as I explained. 'The cargo will have shifted, it will be lying in a jumble just beyond that bulkhead and once we pop her open here, we can drag it out item by item into the companionway.'

'It's a long haul from there to the gunport.' Chubby lifted his cap and massaged his bald dome thoughtfully.

'I'll rig a light block and tackle at the gun-deck ladder and another at the gunport.'

'A lot of work,' Chubby looked sad.

'The first time you agree with me – I'm going to begin worrying that I may be wrong.'

'I didn't say you were wrong,' said Chubby stiffly, 'I just said it was a lot of work. You can't let Miss Sherry haul on a block and tackle, can you now?'

'No,' I agreed. 'We need somebody with beef,' and I prodded his bulging rock-hard gut.

'That's what I thought,' said Chubby mournfully. 'You want me to get geared up?'

'No.' I stopped him. 'Sherry can come down with me to set the charges now.' I wanted her to test her nerves after the previous day's horrors. 'We will blast the well open and then go home. We aren't going to work again immediately after blasting. We are going to let the tide clean the pool of dead fish before going down. I don't want an action replay of yesterday.'

We crept in through the gunport and followed the nylon guide line we had placed on our first visit, along the gun-deck, up through the companion ladder to the passenger deck, and then along the dark forbidding tunnel to the dead-end bulkhead of the forward well.

While Sherry held the torch for me, I began to drill a hole through the partition with the brace and bit that I had brought from the surface. It was awkward working without a really firm stance on which to anchor myself, but the first inch and a half was easy going. This layer of wood had rotted to a soft corky consistency, but beyond that I encountered iron hard oak planking and I had to abandon my efforts. I would have been a week at the task.

Unable to place my explosive in prepared shot holes, I would now have to use a larger charge than I really wanted and rely on the tunnel effect of the passageway for a secondary shock to drive the panel inwards. I used six half sticks of gelignite, placed on the corners and in the centre of the bulkhead, and I secured them to bolts driven into the woodwork with a slap hammer.

It took almost half an hour to set up the blast, and afterwards it was a relief to leave the claustrophobic confines of the ancient hull and to rise up through clean clear water to the silver surface, trailing the insulated wires behind us.

Chubby fired the shots while we stripped off our equipment. The shock was cushioned by the hull of the wreck so that it was hardly noticeable to us on the surface.

We left the pool immediately afterwards and ran home with rising spirits to the prospect of a lazy day while we waited for the tide to clean the pool of carrion.

In the afternoon Sherry and I went on a picnic down to the south tip of the island. For provisions we took a wicker-covered two-litre bottle of Portuguese *vinos verde*, but to supplement this we dug out a batch of big sand clams which I wrapped in seaweed and reburied in the sand. Over them I built an open fire of driftwood.

By the time we had almost finished the wine, the sun was setting and the clams were ready to eat. The wine and the food and the glorious sunset had a softening effect on Sherry North. She became doe-eyed and melting, and when the sunset faded at last and made way for a fat yellow lovers' moon, we walked home barefooted on the wet sand.

The next morning Chubby and I worked for half an hour bringing down the equipment we needed from the whaleboat and stacking it on the gun-deck of the wreck before we were able to penetrate deeper into the hull.

The heavy charges I had set against the well had wrought the sort of havoc I feared. They had torn out the decking and smashed in the bulkheads of the passenger cabins, blocking the passage for a quarter of its length.

We found a good anchor point for our block and tackle and while Chubby rigged it, I left him and floated back to the nearest cabin. I played my torch through the shattered panelling. The interior was, like everything else, smothered in a thick furring of marine growth but I could make out the shape of the simple furniture beneath it.

I eased myself through the gap, and moved slowly across the cluttered deck, fascinated by the objects which I found scattered and heaped about the cabin. There were items of porcelain and china, a shattered washbasin and a magnificent chamber pot with a pink floral design showing through the film of accumulated sediment. There were cosmetic pots and scent bottles, smaller indefinable metal objects and mounds of rotted and amorphous material which may have been clothing, curtaining or mattresses and bedclothing.

I glanced at my watch and saw that it was time to leave and surface for a change of air bottles. As I turned, a small square object caught my attention and I played the torch-beam upon it while I gently brushed it clear of the thick layer of muddy filth. It was a wooden box, the size of a portable transistor radio, but the lid was beautifully inlaid with mother-of-pearl and tortoiseshell. I picked it up and tucked it under my arm. Chubby had finished rigging the block and tackle and he was waiting for me beside the gun-deck ladder. When we surfaced beside the whaleboat I passed the box up to Angelo before climbing aboard.

While Sherry poured coffee for us and Angelo charged the demand valves to the fresh scuba bottles, I lit a cheroot and examined the box.

It was in a sorry state of deterioration, I saw at once. The inlay was rotten and falling out of its seating, the rosewood was swollen and distorted and the lock and hinges half eaten away.

Sherry came to sit beside me on the thwart and examined my prize with me. She recognized it immediately.

'It's a ladies' jewel box,' she exclaimed. 'Open it, Harry. Let's see what's inside.'

I slipped the blade of a screwdriver under the lock and at the first pressure the hinges snapped and the lid flew off.

'Oh, Harry!' Sherry was first into it, and she came out with a thick gold chain and a heavy locket of the same material. 'This stuff is so in fashion, you'd never believe it.'

Everyone was dipping into the box now. Angelo ripped off a pair of gold and sapphire earrings which immediately replaced the brass pair he habitually wore, while Chubby picked an enormous necklace of garnets which he hung around his neck and preened like a teenage girl.

'For my missus,' he explained.

It was the personal jewellery of a middle-class wife, probably some minor official or civil servant – none of it of great value, but in its context it was a fascinating collection. Inevitably Miss North acquired the lion's share – but I managed to snatch away a thick plain gold wedding band.

'What do you want with that?' she challenged me, reluctant to yield a single item.

'I'll find a use for it,' I told her, and gave her one of my looks of deep significance, which was completely wasted for she had returned to ransacking the jewel box.

Nevertheless I tucked the ring safely away in the small zip pocket of my canvas gear bag. Chubby by this stage was bedecked with chunky jewellery like a Hindu bride.

'My God, Chubby, you're a dead ringer for Liz Taylor,' I told him and he accepted the compliment with a graceful inclination of his head.

I had a difficult job getting him interested in a return to the wreck, but once we were in the passenger deck again, he worked like a giant amongst the shattered wreckage.

We hauled out the panelling and timber baulks that

blocked the passage by use of the block and tackle and our combined strength, and we dragged it down to the gun-deck and stacked it out of the way in the recesses of that gloomy gallery.

We had reached the well of the forward hold by the time our air supplies were almost exhausted. The heavy planking had broken up in the explosion and beyond the opening we could make out what appeared to be a solid dark mass of material. I guessed that this was a conglomerate formed by the cargo out of its own weight and pressure.

However, it was afternoon the following day before I found that I was correct. We were at last into the hold, but I had not expected such a Herculean task as awaited us there.

The contents of the hold had been impregnated with sea water for over a century. Ninety per cent of the containers had rotted and collapsed, and the perishable contents had coalesced into a friable dark mass.

Within this solid heap of marine compost, the metal objects, the containers of stronger and impervious material and other imperishable objects, both large and small, were studded like lucky coins in a Christmas pudding. We would have to dig for them.

At this point we encountered our next problem. At the slightest disturbance of this rotted mass the water was immediately filled with a swirling storm of dark particles that blotted out the beams of the torches and plunged us into clouds of blinding darkness.

We were forced to work by sense of touch alone. It was painfully slow progress. When we encountered some solid body in the softness we had to drag it clear, manoeuvre it down the passage, lower it to the gun-deck and there try to identify it. Sometimes we were obliged to break open what remained of the container, to get at the contents.

If they were of little value or interest, we tucked them away in the depths of the gundeck to keep our working field clear.

At the end of the first day's work we had salvaged only one item which we decided was worth raising. It was a sturdy case of hard wood, covered with what appeared to be leather and with the corners bound in heavy brass. It was the size of a large cabin trunk.

It was so heavy that Chubby and I could not lift it between us. The weight alone gave me high hopes. I believed it could very readily contain part of the golden throne. Although the container did not look like one that had been manufactured by an Indian village carpenter and his sons in the middle of the nineteenth century, yet there was a chance that the throne had been repacked before it was shipped from Bombay.

If it did contain part of the throne, then our task would be simplified. We would know what type of container to look for in the future. Using the block and tackle Chubby and I dragged the case down the gun-deck to the gunport and there we shrouded it in a nylon cargo net to prevent it bursting open or breaking during the ascent. To the eyes spliced into the circumference of the net we attached the canvas flotation bags and inflated them from our air bottles.

We went up with the case, controlling its ascent by either spilling air from the bags, or adding more from our bottles. We came out beside the whaleboat and Angelo passed us half a dozen nylon slings with which we secured the case before climbing aboard.

The weight of the case defeated our efforts to lift it over the side, for the whaleboat heeled dangerously when the three of us made the attempt. We had to step the mast and use it as a derrick, only then did our combined efforts suffice and the case swung on board, spouting water from its seams.

The moment that it sank to the deck Chubby scrambled back to the motors and ran for the channel. The tide pressed closely on our heels as we went.

The case was too weighty and our curiosity too strong to allow us to carry it up to the caves. We opened it on the beach, prising the lid open with a pair of jemmy bars. The elaborate locking device in the lid was of brass and had withstood the ravages of salt sea water. It resisted our efforts bravely, but at last with a rending of woodwork the lid flew back and creaked against the heavily corroded hinges.

My disappointment was immediate, for it was clear that this was no tiger throne. It was only when Sherry lifted out one of the large gleaming discs and turned it curiously in her hands that I began to suspect that we had been awarded an enormous bonus.

It was an entrée plate she held, and my first thought was that it was of solid gold. However, when I snatched a mate from its slot in the cunningly designed rack and turned it to examine the hallmarks, I realized that it was silver and gold gilt.

The gold plating had protected it from the sea so that it was perfectly preserved, a masterpiece of the silversmith's art with a raised coat of arms in the centre and the rim wondrously chased with scenes of woods and deer, of huntsmen and birds.

The plate I held weighed almost two pounds and as I set it aside and examined the rest of the set I saw the weight of the chest fully accounted for.

There were servings for thirty-six guests in the set; soup bowls, fish plates, entrée plates, dessert bowls, side plates and all the cutlery to go with it. There were serving dishes, a magnificent chafing dish, wine coolers, dish covers and a carving dish almost the size of a baby's bath.

Every piece was wrought with the same coat of arms,

and the ornamental scenes of wild animals and huntsmen, and the case had been designed to hold this array of plate.

'Ladies and gentlemen,' I said, 'as your chairman, it behoves me to assure you, one and all, that our little venture is now in profit.'

'It's just plates and things,' said Angelo, and I winced theatrically.

'My dear Angelo, this is probably one of the few complete sets of Georgian banquet silverware remaining anywhere in the world – it's priceless.'

'How much?' asked Chubby, doubtfully.

'Good Lord, I don't know. It would depend of course on the maker and the original owner – this coat of arms probably belongs to some noble house. A wealthy nobleman on service in India, an earl, a duke perhaps, even a viceroy.'

Chubby looked at me as though I was trying to sell him a spavined horse.

'How much?' he repeated.

'At Messrs Sothebys on a good day,' I hesitated, 'I don't know, say, a hundred thousand pounds.'

Chubby spat into the sand and shook his head. You couldn't fool old Chubby.

'This fellow Sotheby, does he run a loony house?'

'It's true, Chubby,' Sherry cut in. 'This stuff is worth a fortune. It could be more than that.'

Chubby was now torn between natural scepticism and chivalry. It would be an ungentlemanly act to call Sherry a liar. He compromised by lifting his hat and rubbing his head, spitting once more and saying nothing.

However, he handled the case with new respect when we dragged it up through the palms to the caves. We stored it behind the stack of jerrycans, and I went to fetch a new bottle of whisky.

'Even if there is no tiger throne in the wreck, we aren't going to do too badly out of this,' I told them.

Chubby sipped at his whisky mug and muttered, 'A hundred thousand – they've got to be crazy.'

'We've got to go through that hold and the cabins more carefully. We are going to leave a fortune down there if we don't.'

'Even the little items, less spectacular than the silver plate, they have enormous antique value,' Sherry agreed.

'Trouble is when you touch anything down there it stirs up such a fog you can't see the tip of your nose,' gloomed Chubby, and I refilled his mug with good cheer.

'Listen, Chubby, you know the centrifugal water pump that Arnie Andrews has got out at Monkey Bay?' I asked, and Chubby nodded.

'Will he lend it to us?' Arnie was Chubby's uncle. He owned a small market garden on the southern side of St Mary's island.

'He might,' Chubby answered warily. 'Why?'

'I want to try and rig a dredge pump,' I explained and sketched it for them in the sand between my feet. 'We set the pump up in the whaleboat, and we use a length of steam hose to reach the wreck – like this.' I roughed it out with my finger. 'Then we use it like a vacuum cleaner in the hold, suck out all that muck and pump it to the surface—'

'Hey, that's right,' Angelo burst out enthusiastically. 'When it spills out of the pump we run it through a sieve, and we will be able to pick up all the small stuff.'

'That's right. Only muck and small light items will go up the spout – anything large or heavy will be left behind.'

We discussed it for an hour working out details and refinements on the basic idea. During that time Chubby tried manfully to show no signs of enthusiasm, but finally he could contain himself no longer.

'It might work,' he muttered, which from him was a high accolade.

'Well, you better go fetch that pump then, hadn't you?' I asked.

'I think I will have one more drink,' he procrastinated, and I handed him the bottle.

'Take it with you,' I suggested. 'It will save time.'

He grunted, and went to fetch his overcoat.

Sherry and I slept late, gloating on the lazy day ahead and at the feeling of having the island entirely to ourselves. We did not expect Chubby and Angelo to return before noon.

After breakfast we crossed the saddle between the hills and went down to the beach. We were playing in the shallows, and the rumble of the surf on the outer reef and our own splashing and laughter blanketed any other sounds. It was only by chance that I looked up and saw the light aircraft sweeping in from the landward channel.

'Run!' I shouted at Sherry, and she thought I was joking until I pointed urgently at the approaching aircraft.

'Run! Don't let him see us,' and this time she responded quickly. We floundered naked from the water, and went up the beach at top speed.

Now I could hear the buzz of the aircraft engines and I glanced over my shoulder. It was banking low over the southernmost peak of the island and levelling over the long straight beach towards us.

'Faster!' I yelled at Sherry, as she ran long-legged and full-bottomed ahead of me with the wet tresses of her sable hair dangling down her darkly tanned back.

I looked back and the aircraft was headed directly at us, still about a mile distant, but I could see that it was twin-engined. As I watched, it sank lower towards the snowy expanse of coral sands.

We snatched up our discarded clothing at full run, and sprinted the last few yards into the palm grove. There was a mound formed by a fallen palm tree and the fronds torn off the trees by the storm. It was a convenient shelter and I grabbed Sherry's arm and dragged her down.

We rolled under the shelter of the dead fronds and lay side by side, panting wildly from the run up the beach.

I saw now that it was a twin-engined Cessna. It came down the beach and swept past our hideaway only twenty feet above the water's edge.

The fuselage was painted a distinctive daisy yellow and was blazoned with the name 'Africair'. I recognized the aircraft. I had seen it before at St Mary's Airport on half a dozen occasions, usually discharging or picking up groups of wealthy tourists. I knew that Africair was a charter company based on the mainland, and that its aircraft were for hire on a mileage tariff. I wondered who was paying for the hire on this trip.

There were two persons in the forward seats of the aircraft, the pilot and a passenger, and their faces were turned towards us as it roared past. However, they were too far from us to make out the features and I could not be sure if I knew either of them. They were both white men, that was all that was certain.

The Cessna turned steeply out over the lagoon and, one wing pointed directly down into the crystal water, it swept around and then levelled for another run down the beach.

This time it passed so closely that for an instant I looked up into the face of the passenger as he peered down into the palm grove. I thought I recognized him, but I could not be certain.

The Cessna then turned away, rising slowly, and set a new course for the mainland. There was something about her going that was complacent, the air of someone having achieved his purpose, a job well done.

308

Sherry and I crawled from our hiding-place and stood up to brush the sand from our damp bodies.

'Do you think they saw us?' she asked timidly.

'With that bottom of yours flashing like a mirror in the sunlight, they could hardly miss.'

'They might have mistaken us for a couple of native fishermen.'

I looked at her, not at her face, and I grinned: 'Fisherman? With those great beautiful boobs?'

'Harry Fletcher, you are a disgusting beast,' she said. 'But seriously, Harry, what is going to happen now?'

'I wish I knew, my sweeting, I wish I knew,' I answered, but I was glad that Chubby had taken the case of silverware back to St Mary's with him. By now it was probably buried behind the shack at Turtle Bay. We were still in profit – even if we had to run for it soon.

The visit by the aircraft instilled in us all a new sense of urgency. We knew now that our time was strictly rationed, and Chubby brought news with him when he returned that was equally disturbing.

'The *Mandrake* cruised for five days in the south islands. They saw her nearly every day from Coolie Peak, and she was messing about like she didn't know what she was doing,' he reported. 'Then on Monday she anchored again in Grand Harbour. Wallys says that the owner and his wife went up to the hotel for lunch, then afterwards they took a taxi and went down to Frobisher Street. They spent an hour with Fred Coker in his office, then he drove them down to Admiralty Wharf and they went back on board *Mandrake*. She weighed and sailed almost immediately.'

'Is that all?'

'Yes,' Chubby nodded, 'except that Fred Coker went straight up to the bank afterwards and put fifteen hundred dollars into his savings account.'

'How do you know that?'

'My sister's third daughter works at the bank.'

I tried to show a cheerful face, although I felt ugly little insects crawling around in my stomach. 'Well,' I said, 'no use moping around. Let's try and get the pump assembled so we can catch tomorrow's tide.'

Later, after we had carried the water pump up to the caves, Chubby returned alone to the whaleboat and when he came back he carried a long canvas-wrapped bundle.

'What have you got there, Chubby?' I demanded, and shyly he opened the canvas cover. It was my FN carbine and a dozen spare magazines of ammunition packed into a small haversack.

'Thought it might come in useful,' he muttered.

I took the weapon down into the grove and buried it beside the cases of gelignite in a shallow grave. Its proximity gave me a little comfort when I returned to assist in assembling the water pump.

We worked on into the night by the light of the gas lanterns, and it was after midnight when we carried the pump and its engine down to the whaleboat and bolted it to a makeshift mounting of heavy timber which we placed squarely amidship. Angelo and I were still working on the pump when we ran out towards the reef in the morning. We had been on station for half an hour before we had it assembled and ready to test.

Three of us dived on the wreck – Chubby, Sherry and myself – and we manhandled the stiff black snake of the hose through the gunport and up into the breach through the well of the hold.

Once it was in position, I slapped Chubby on the shoulder and pointed to the surface. He replied with a high sign and finned away, leaving Sherry and me in the passenger deck.

We had planned this part of the operation carefully and we waited impatiently while Chubby went up, decompressing on his way, and climbed into the whaleboat to prime the pump and start the motor.

We knew he had done so by the faint hum and vibration that was transmitted to us down the hose.

I braced myself in the ragged entrance to the hold, and grasped the end of the hose with both hands. Sherry trained the torchbeam on to the dark heap of cargo, and I swung the open end of the hose slowly over the rotted cargo.

I saw immediately that it was going to work, small pieces of debris vanished miraculously into the hose, and it caused a small whirlpool as it sucked in water and floating motes of rubbish.

At this depth and with the RPM provided by the petrol engine, the pump was rated to move thirty thousand gallons of water an hour, which was a considerable volume. Within seconds I had cleared the working area and we still had good visibility. I could start probing into the heap with a jemmy bar, breaking out larger pieces and pushing them back into the passage behind us.

Once or twice I had to resort to the block and tackle to clear some bulky case or object, but mostly I was able to advance with only the hose and the jemmy bar.

We had moved almost fifty cubic foot of cargo before it was time to ascend for a change of air bottle. We left the end of the hose firmly anchored in the passenger deck, and went up to a hero's welcome. Angelo was in transports of delight and even Chubby was smiling.

The water around the whaleboat was clouded and filthy with the thick soup of rubbish we had pumped out of the hold, and Angelo had retrieved almost a bucketful of small items that had come through the outlet of the pump and fallen into the sieve – it was a collection of buttons, nails, small ornaments from women's dresses, brass military insignia, some small copper and silver coins of the period, and odds and ends of metal and glass and bone.

Even I was impatient to return to the task, and Sherry was so insistent that I had to donate my half-smoked cheroot to Chubby and we went down again.

We had been working for fifteen minutes when I came upon the corner of an up-ended crate similar to others that we had already cleared. Although the wood was soft as cork, the seams had been reinforced with strips of hoop iron and iron nails so I struggled with it for some time before I prised out a plank and pushed it back between us. The next plank came free more readily, and the contents seemed to be a mattress of decomposed and matted vegetable fibre.

I pulled out a large hunk of this and it almost jammed the opening of the hose, but eventually disappeared on its way to the surface. I almost lost interest in this box and was about to begin working in another area – but Sherry showed strong signs of disapproval, shaking her head, thumping my shoulder and refusing to direct the beam of the torch anywhere but at the unappetizing mess of fibre.

Afterwards I asked her why she had insisted and she fluttered her eyelashes and looked important.

'Female intuition, my dear. You wouldn't understand.'

At her urging, I once more attacked the opening in the case, but scratching smaller chunks of the fibre loose so as not to block the hose opening.

I had removed about six inches of this material when I saw the gleam of metal in the depths of the excavation. I felt the first deep throb of certainty in my belly then, and I tore out another plank with furious impatience. It enlarged the opening so I could work in it more easily.

Slowly I removed the layers of compacted fibre which I

realized must have been straw originally used as packing. Like a face materializing in a dream, it was revealed.

The first tiny gleam opened to a golden glory of intricately worked metal and I felt Sherry's grip on my shoulder as she crowded down close beside me.

There was a snout, and lips below that were drawn up in a savage snarl, revealing great golden fangs and an arched tongue. There was a broad deep forehead as wide as my shoulders, and ears flattened down close upon the burnished skull – and there was a single empty eye-socket set fairly in the centre of the wide brow. The lack of an eye gave the animal a blind and tragic expression, like some maimed god from mythology.

I felt an almost religious awe as I stared at the huge, wonderfully fashioned tiger's head we had exposed. Something cold and frightening slithered up my spine, and involuntarily I glanced about me into the dark and forbidding recesses of the hold, almost as if I expected the spirits of the Mogul prince guardians to be lurking there.

Sherry squeezed my shoulder again and I returned my attention to the golden idol, but the sense of awe was so strong upon me that I had to force myself to return to the task of clearing the packing from around it. I worked very carefully for I was fully aware that the slightest scratch or damage would greatly reduce the value and the beauty of this image.

When our working time was exhausted we drew back and stared at the exposed head and shoulders, and the torch beam was reflected from the brilliant surface in arrows of golden light that lit the hold like some holy shrine. We turned then and left it to the silence and the dark, while we went up into the sunlight.

Chubby was aware immediately that something significant had happened, but he said nothing until we had climbed aboard and in silence shed our equipment. I lit a cheroot and drew deeply upon it, not bothering to mop the droplets of seawater that ran from my sodden hair down my cheeks. Chubby was watching me but Sherry was withdrawn from us, wrapped in secret thoughts, turned inward upon herself.

'You found it?' Chubby asked at last, and I nodded.

'Yes, Chubby, it's there.' I was surprised to hear that my own voice was husky and unsteady.

Angelo who had not sensed the mood looked up quickly from where he was stacking our equipment. He opened his mouth to say something, but then slowly closed it as he became aware of the charged atmosphere.

We were all silent, moved beyond speech. I had not expected it would be like this, and I looked at Sherry. She met my gaze at last and her dark eyes were haunted.

'Let's go home, Harry,' she said and I nodded at Chubby. He buoyed the hose and dropped it overboard to be retrieved on the following day. Then he threw the motors into gear and swung our bows to face the channel.

Sherry moved across the whaleboat and came to sit beside me on the thwart. I placed my arm about her shoulders but neither of us spoke until the whaleboat slid silently up on to the white beach of the island.

In the sunset Sherry and I climbed to the peak above the camp and we sat close together staring out across the reef, and watching the light fade on the sea and plunge the pool at Gunfire Reef into deeper shadow.

'I feel guilty in a way,' Sherry whispered, 'as though I have committed some dreadful sacrilege.'

'Yes,' I agreed, 'I know what you mean.'

'That thing – it seemed to have a life of its own. It was strange that we should have exposed its head, before any other part of it. Just suddenly to have that face glaring out at one,' she shuddered and was silent for a few moments, 'and yet I felt also a deep satisfaction, a good quiet feeling inside myself. I don't know if I can explain it properly – for the two feelings were so opposite, and yet mingled.'

'I understand. I had the same feelings.'

'What are we going to do with it, Harry, what are we going to do with that fantastic animal?'

Somehow I did not want to talk about money and buyers at that moment – which in itself was a measure of how profound was my involvement with the golden idol.

'Let's go down,' I suggested instead. 'Angelo will be waiting dinner for us.'

Sitting in the firelight with a good meal filling and warming the cold empty place in my belly, and with a mug of whisky in one hand and a cheroot in the other, I felt at last able to tell the others about it.

I explained how we had come upon it, and I described the fearsome golden head. They listened in complete and intent silence.

'We have cleared the head down to the shoulder. I think that is where it ends. It is notched there, probably to fit into the next section. Tomorrow we should be able to lift it clear, but it's going to be ticklish work. We can't just haul it out with the block and tackle. It has to be protected from damage before we can move it.'

Chubby made a suggestion, and for a while we discussed in detail how the head should be handled to minimize the risk of damage.

'We can expect that all five cases containing the treasure were loaded together. I hope to find them in the same part of the hold, probably similarly packed in wooden crates and reinforced with hoop iron—'

'Except for the stones,' Sherry interrupted. 'In the court-martial evidence, the Subahdar described how they were packed in a paymaster's chest.'

'Yes, of course,' I agreed.

'What would that look like?' Sherry asked.

'I saw one on display in the arsenal at Copenhagen which would probably be very similar. It's like a small iron safe – the size of a large biscuit bin.' I sketched the size with the spread of my hands like a fisherman boasting of his catch. 'It is ribbed with iron bands and has a locking rod and a pair of head padlocks at each corner.'

'It sounds formidable.'

'After a hundred-odd years in the pool it will probably be soft as chalk – even if it's still in one piece.'

'We'll find out tomorrow,' Sherry announced with confidence.

We tramped down to the beach in the morning with rain drumming on our oilskins and cascading from them in sheets. The cloud was right down on the peaks, oily dark banks that rolled steadily in from the sea to loose their bomb loads of moisture upon the island.

The force of the rain lifted a fine pearly spray from the surface of the sea, and the moving grey curtains reduced visibility to a few hundred yards so that the island disappeared in a grey haze as we ran out to the reef.

Everything in the whaleboat was cold and clammy and running with water. Angelo had to bale regularly and we huddled miserably in our oilskins while Chubby stood in the stern and slitted his eyes against the slanting, driving rain as he negotiated the channel.

The flourescent orange buoy still bobbed close in beside the reef and we picked it up and dragged in the end of the hose and connected it to the pump head. It served as an anchor cable and Chubby could cut the motors.

It was a relief to leave the boat, escape from the cold

needle lances of the rain and go down into the quiet blue mists of the pool.

After withstanding considerable pressure from Chubby and me, Angelo had at last succumbed to veiled threats and open bribes, and relinquished his ticking mattress stuffed with coconut-fibre. Once the mattress was thoroughly soaked with seawater, it sank readily, and I took it down with me in a neat roll, tied with line.

Only when I had manoeuvred it through the gunport, down the gun-deck and into the passenger deck did I cut the line and spread the mattress.

Then Sherry and I returned to the hold where the tiger's head still snarled blindly into the torchlight.

Ten minutes' work was all that was necessary to free the head from its nest. As I suspected, this section ended at shoulder level, and the junction area was neatly flanged – clearly it would mate with the trunk section of the throne, and the flange would engage the female slot to form a joint that would be strong and barely perceivable.

When I rolled the head carefully on to its side I made another discovery. Somehow I had taken it for granted that the idol was made from solid gold, but now I saw that in fact it was a hollow casting.

The actual thickness of metal was only about an inch, and the interior was rough and knobbly to the touch. I realized immediately that a solid idol would have weighed hundreds of tons, and that the cost of such construction would have been prohibitive even to an emperor who could support the construction of a temple as vast as the Taj Mahal.

The thinness of the metal skin had naturally weakened the structure, and I saw immediately when I turned it that the head had already suffered damage.

The rim of the neck cavity was flattened and distorted,

probably during its secret journey through the Indian forests in an unsprung cart – or possibly during the wild death struggles of the *Dawn Light* during the cyclone.

Bracing myself in the entrance to the hold, I stooped over it to test its weight, and I cradled the head in my arms like the body of a child. Gradually I increased the strength of my lift and was pleased, but not surprised, when it came up in my arms.

It was, of course, tremendously weighty, and it required all of my strength from a carefully selected stance – but I could lift it. It weighed not much more than three hundred pounds, I thought, as I turned awkwardly under the oppressive load of gleaming gold and laid it gently on the coir mattress that Sherry was holding ready to receive it. Then I straightened up to rest and massage those parts where the sharp edges of metal had bitten into my flesh. While I did so I tried a little mental arithmetic: 300 pounds avoirdupois at 16 ounces to the pound was 4800 ounces, at 150 to the ounce was almost three-quarters of a million dollars. That was the intrinsic value of the head alone. There were three other sections to the throne, all were probably heavier and larger – then there was the value of the stones. It was an astronomic total, but could be doubled or even trebled if the artistic and historical value of the hoard were taken into account.

I abandoned my calculations. They were meaningless at this time, and instead I helped Sherry to fold the mattress around the tiger's head and to rope it all into a secure bundle. Then I could use the block and tackle to drag it down to the companion ladder and lower it to the gundeck.

Laboriously we dragged it to the gunport and there we struggled to pass it through the restricted opening, but at last it was accomplished and we could place the nylon cargo net around it and inflate the airbags. Again we had to step the mast to lift it aboard.

But there was no suggestion that the head should remain covered once we had it safely in the whaleboat, and with what ceremony and aplomb I could muster in the streaming tropical rain, I unveiled it for Chubby and Angelo. They were an appreciative audience. Their excitement superseded even the miserable sodden conditions, and they crowded about the head to fondle and examine it amid shouted comment and giddy laughter. It was the festive gaiety which our first discovery of the treasure had lacked. I had taken the precaution of slipping my silver travelling flask into my gearbag, and now I laced the steaming mugs of black coffee with liberal portions of Scotch whisky and we toasted each other and the golden tiger in the steaming liquor, laughing while the rain gushed down upon us and rattled on the fabulous treasure at our feet.

At last I swilled out my mug over the side and checked my watch.

'We'll do another dive,' I decided. 'You can start the pump again, Chubby.'

Now we knew where to continue the search, and after I had broken out the remains of the case that had contained the head, I saw, in the opening beyond, the side of a similar crate and I pressed the hose into the area to clear it of dirt before proceeding.

My excavations must have unbalanced the rotting heap of ancient cargo, and it needed only the further disturbance caused by suction of the hose to dislodge a part of it. With a groaning and rumbling it collapsed around us and instantly the swirling clouds of muck defeated the efforts of the hose to clear them and we were plunged into darkness once more.

I groped quickly for Sherry through the darkness, and she must have been searching for me, for our hands met and held. With a squeeze she reassured me that she had not been hit by the sliding cargo, and I could begin to clear out the fouled water with the suction hose.

Within five minutes I could make out the yellow glow of Sherry's torch through the murk, and then her shape and the vague jumble of freshly revealed cargo.

With Sherry beside me, we moved farther into the hold again.

The slide had covered the wooden crate on which I had been working, but in exchange it had exposed something else that I recognized instantly, despite its sorry condition, for it was almost exactly as I had described it to Sherry the previous evening, even down to the detail of the rod that ran through the locking device and the double padlocks. The paymaster's chest was, however, almost eaten through with rust and when I touched it my hand came away smeared with the chalky red of iron oxide.

In each end of the case were heavy iron carrying rings, which had most likely swivelled at one time but were now solidly rusted into the metal side – but still they enabled me to get a firm grip and gently to work the chest out of the clutching bed of muck. It came free in a minor storm of debris, and I was able to lift it fairly easily. I doubt that the total weight exceeded a hundred and fifty pounds, and I felt certain that most of that was made up by the massive iron construction.

After the enormously heavy head in its soft bulky mattress, it was a minor labour to get the smaller lighter chest out of the wreck, and it needed only a single airbag to lift it dangling out of the gunport.

Once again the tide and surf were pouring alarmingly into the pool, and the whaleboat tossed and kicked impatiently as we lifted the chest inboard and laid it on the canvas-covered heap of scuba bottles in the bows.

Then at last Chubby could start the motors and take us

out through the channel. We were still all high with excitement, and the silver flask passed from hand to hand.

'What's it feel like to be rich, Chubby?' I called, and he took a swallow from the flask, screwing up his eyes and then coughing at the sting of the liquor before he grinned at me.

'Just like before, man. No change yet.'

'What are you going to do with your share?' Sherry insisted.

'It's a little late in the day, Miss Sherry – if only I had it twenty years ago, then I have use for it – and how.' He took another swallow. 'That's the trouble – you never have it when you're young, and when you're old, it's just too damned late.'

'What about you, Angelo?' Sherry turned to him as he perched on the rusted pay-chest, with his gipsy curls heavy with rain dangling on to his cheeks and the droplets clinging in the long dark eyelashes. 'You're still young, what will you do?'

'Miss Sherry, I've been sitting here thinking about it – and already I've got a list from here to St Mary's and back.'

It took two trips from the beach to the camp before we had both the head and the chest out of the rain and into the cave we were using as the store room.

Chubby lit two gas lanterns, for the lowering sky had brought on the evening prematurely, and we gathered around the chest, while the golden head snarled down upon us from a place of honour, an earthen ledge hewn into the back of the cave.

With a hacksaw and jemmy bar, Chubby and I began work on the locking device and found immediately that the decrepit appearance of the metal was deceptive, clearly it had been hardened and alloyed. We broke three hacksaw blades in the first half hour and Sherry professed to be severely shocked by my language. I sent her to fetch a bottle of Chivas Regal from our cave to keep the workers in good cheer and Chubby and I took the Scottish equivalent of a tea break.

With renewed vigour we resumed our assault on the case, but it was another twenty minutes before he had sawn through the rod. By that time it was dark outside the cave. The rain was still hissing down steadily, but the soft clatter of the palm fronds heralded the rising westerly wind that would disperse the storm clouds by morning.

With the locking rod sawn through, we started it from its ringbolts with a two-pound hammer from the tool-box. Each blow loosened a soft patter of rust scales from the surface of the metal, and it required a number of goodly blows to drive the rod from the clutching fist of corrosion.

Even when it was cleared, the lid would not lift. Although we hammered it from a dozen different directions and I treated it with a further laying on of abuse, it would not yield.

I called another whisky break to discuss the problem.

'What about a stick of gelly?' Chubby suggested with a gleam in his eye, but reluctantly I had to restrain him.

'We need a welding torch,' Angelo announced.

'Brilliant,' I applauded him ironically, for I was fast losing my patience. 'The nearest welding set is fifty miles away – and you make a remark like that.'

It was Sherry who discovered the secondary locking device, a secret pinning through the lid that hooked into recesses in the body of the chest. It obviously needed a key to release this, but for lack of it I selected a half-inch punch and drove it into the keyhole and by luck I caught the locking arm and snapped it.

Chubby started on the lid again, and this time it came up stiffly on corroded hinges with some of the rotting evil-smelling contents sticking to the inside of it and tearing away from the main body of aged brown cloth. It was woven cotton fabric, a wet solid brick of it, and I guessed that it

322

had been cheap native robes or bolts of cloth used as packing.

I was about to explore further, but suddenly found myself in the second row looking over Sherry North's shoulder.

'You'd better let me do this,' she said. 'You might break something.'

'Come on!' I protested.

'Why don't you get yourself another drink?' she suggested placatingly, as she began lifting off layers of sodden fabric. The suggestion had some merit, I thought, so I refilled my mug and watched Sherry expose a layer of cloth-wrapped parcels.

Each was tied with twine that fell apart at the touch, and the first parcel also disintegrated as she tried to lift it out. Sherry cupped her hand around the decaying mass and scooped it on to a folded tarpaulin placed beside the chest. The parcel contained scores of small nutty objects, varying in size from slightly larger than a matchhead to a ripe grape and each had been folded in a wisp of paper, which, like the cotton, had completely rotted away.

Sherry picked out one of these lumpy objects and rubbed away the remnants of paper between thumb and forefinger to reveal a large shiny blue stone, cut square and polished on one face.

'Sapphire?' she guessed, and I took it from her and examined it quickly in the lantern light. It was opaque and I contradicted her.

'No, I think it's probably lapis lazuli.' The scrap of paper still adhering to it was faintly discoloured with a blue dye. 'Ink, I should say.' I crumpled it between my fingers. 'At least Roger, the Colonel, took the trouble to identify each stone. He probably wrapped each piece in a numbered slip of paper which related to a master sketch of the throne to enable it to be reassembled.'

'There is no hope of that now,' said Sherry.

'I don't know,' I said. 'It would be a hell of a job, but it would still be possible to put it all together again.'

Amongst our stores was a roll of plastic packets, and I sent Angelo to ferret it out. As we opened each parcel of rotted fabric we superficially cleaned the stones it contained and packed each lot in a separate plastic packet.

It was slow work even though we all contributed and after almost two hours of it we had filled dozens of packets with thousands of semi-precious stones – lapis lazuli, beryl, tiger's eye, garnets, verdite, amethyst, and half a dozen others of whose identity I was uncertain. Each stone had clearly been lovingly cut and exactingly polished to fit into its own niche in the golden throne.

It was only when we had unpacked the chest to its last layer that we came upon the stones of greater value. The old Colonel had obviously selected these first and they had gone into the lowest layer of the chest.

I held a transparent plastic packet of emeralds to the lantern light, and they burned like a bursting green star.

We all stared at it as if mesmerized while I turned it slowly to catch the fierce white light.

I laid it aside and Sherry dipped once more into the chest and after a moment's hesitation brought out a smaller parcel. She rubbed away the damp crumbling material, that was wound thick about the single stone it contained.

Then she held up the Great Mogul diamond in the cupped palm of her hand. It was the size of a pullet's egg, cut into a faceted cushion shape, just as Jean Baptiste Tavernier had described it so many hundred years ago.

The glittering array of treasure we had handled before in no way dimmed the glory of this stone, as all the stars of the firmament cannot dull the rising of the sun. They paled and faded away before the brilliance and lustre of the great diamond.

Sherry slowly extended her cupped hand towards

Angelo, offering it to him to hold and examine, but he snatched his hands away and clasped them behind his back, still staring at the stone in superstitious awe.

Sherry turned and offered it to Chubby, but with gravity he declined also.

'Give it to Mister Harry. Guess he deserves to be the one.'

I took it from her, and was surprised that such unearthly fire could be so cold to touch. I stood up and I carried it to where the golden tiger's head stood snarling angrily in the unwavering light of the lanterns and I pressed the diamond into the empty eye socket.

It fitted perfectly, and I used my bait-knife to close the golden clasps that held it firmly in place, and which the old Colonel had probably opened with a bayonet a century and a quarter ago.

I stood back then, and I heard the small gasps of wonder. With the eye returned to its socket the golden beast had come to life. It seemed now to survey us with an imperial mien, and at any instant we expected the cave to resound to its crackling wicked snarl of anger.

I went back and took my place in the squatting circle around the rusted chest, and we all stared up at the golden tiger head. We seemed like worshippers in some ancient heathen rite, crouched in awe before the fearsome idol.

'Chubby, my old well beloved and trusted buddy, you will earn yourself an entry on the title page of the book of mercy if you pass me that bottle,' I said, and that broke the spell. They all recovered their voices competing fiercely for a turn to speak – and it wasn't long before I had to send Sherry to fetch another bottle to lubricate dry throats.

We all got more than a little drunk that night, even Sherry North, and she leaned against me for support as we finally made a riotous way through the rain to our own cave.

325

'You really are corrupting me, Fletcher,' she stumbled into a puddle, and nearly brought me down. 'This is the first time ever I have been stoned.'

'Be of good cheer, my pretty sweeting, your next lesson in corruption follows immediately.'

When I woke it was still dark and I rose from our bed, careful not to disturb Sherry who was breathing lightly and evenly in the darkness. It was cool so I pulled on shorts and a woollen jersey.

Outside the cave the west wind had broken up the cloud banks. It had stopped raining and the stars were showing in the breaks of the heavens, giving me enough light to read the luminous dial of my wristwatch. It was a little after three o'clock.

As I sought my favourite palm tree, I saw that we had left the lantern burning in the storage cave. I finished what I had to do and went up to the lighted entrance.

The open chest stood where we had left it, as did the priceless golden head with its glittering eye – and suddenly I was struck with the consuming terror that the miser must feel for his hoard. It was so vulnerable.

' – where thieves break in—' I thought, and it was not as though there were any shortage of them in the immediate vicinity.

I had to get it all stowed away safely, and tomorrow would be too late. Despite the pain in my head and the taste of stale whisky in the back of my throat, it must be done now – but I needed help.

Chubby roused to my first soft call at the entrance of his cave, and came out into the starlight, resplendent in his striped pyjamas and as wide awake as if he had drank nothing more noxious than mother's milk before retiring.

I explained my fears and misgivings. Chubby grunted in agreement and went with me back to the storage cave. The plastic bags of gem stones we repacked casually into the iron chest and I secured the lid with a length of nylon line. The golden head we shrouded carefully in a length of green canvas tarpaulin and we carried both down into the palm grove, before returning for spades and the gas lantern.

By the flat white glare of the lantern we worked side by side, digging two shallow graves in the sandy soil within a few feet of where the gelignite and the FN rifle with its spare ammunition were already buried.

We laid the chest and the golden head away and covered them. Afterwards I brushed the soil over them with a palm frond to wipe out all trace of our labours.

'You happy now, Harry?' Chubby asked at last.

'Yeah, I'm happier, Chubby. You go and get some sleep, hear.'

He went away amongst the palms carrying the lantern and not looking back. I knew I would not be able to sleep again, for the spadework had cleared my head and roused my blood. It would be senseless to return to the cave and try to lie quietly beside Sherry until dawn.

I wanted to find some quiet and secret place where I could think out my next moves in this intricate game of chance in which I was involved. I chose the path that led to the saddle between the lesser peaks and as I climbed it, the last of the clouds were blown aside and revealed a pale yellow moon still a week from full. Its light was strong enough to show me the way to the nearest peak and I left the path and toiled upwards to the summit.

I found a place protected from the wind and settled into it. I wished that I had a cheroot with me for I think better with one of them in my mouth. I also think better without a hangover – but there was nothing I could do about either.

After half an hour I had firmly decided that we must consolidate what we had gained to this point. The miser's fears, which had assailed me earlier, still persisted and I had been given clear warning that the wolf pack was out hunting. As soon as it was light we would take what we had salvaged so far – the head and the chest – and run down the island to St Mary's to dispose of them in the manner which I had already so carefully planned.

There would be time later to return to Gunfire Reef and recover what remained in the misty depths of the pool. Once the decision had been made I felt a lift of relief, a new lightness of spirit, and I looked forward to the solution of the other major puzzle that had troubled me for so long.

Very soon I would be in a position to call Sherry North's hand and have a sight of those cards which she concealed so carefully from me. I wanted to know what caused those shadows in the blue depths of her eyes, and the answers to many other mysteries that surrounded her. That time would soon come.

There was a paling of the sky at last, dawn's first pearling light spread across from the east and softened the harsh dark plain of the ocean. I rose stiffly from my seat amongst the rocks, and picked my way around the peak into the wicked eye of the west wind. I stood there on the exposed face above the camp with the wind raising a rash of goose bumps along my arms and ruffling my hair.

I looked down into the sheltering arms of the lagoon, and in the feeble glimmer of dawn, the darkened ship that was creeping stealthily into the open arms of the bay looked like some pale phantom.

Even as I stared I saw the splash at her bows as she let go her anchor, and she rounded up into the wind showing her full silhouette so that I could not doubt that she was the *Mandrake*.

Before I had recovered my wits, she had dropped a boat which sped in swiftly towards the beach.

I started to run.

I fell once on the path, but the force of my headlong descent from the peak carried me on and with a single roll I was on my feet again, still running.

I was panting wildly as I burst into Chubby's cave, and I shouted, 'Move, man, move! They are on the beach already.'

The two of them tumbled from their sleeping bags. Angelo was tousle-haired and blank-eyed from sleep, but Chubby was quick and alert.

'Chubby,' I snapped, 'go get that piece out of the ground. Jump, man, they'll be coming up through the grove in a few minutes.' He had changed while I spoke, pulling on a shirt and belting his denim breeches. He grunted an acknowledgement. 'I'll follow you in a minute,' I called as he ran out into the feeble light of dawn.

'Angelo, snap out of it!' I grabbed his shoulder and shook him. 'I want you to look after Miss Sherry, hear?'

He was dressed now and he nodded owlishly at me.

'Come on.' I half dragged him as we ran across to my cave. I dragged her out of bed and while she dressed I told her.

'Angelo will go with you. I want you to take a can of drinking water and the two of you get the hell down to the south of the island, cross the saddle first though and keep out of sight. Climb the peak and hide out in the chimney where we found the inscription. You know where I mean.'

'Yes, Harry,' she nodded.

'Stay there. Don't go out or show yourself under any circumstances. Understand?'

329

She nodded as she tucked the tail of her shirt into her breeches.

'Remember, these people are killers. The time for games is over, this is a pack of wolves that we are dealing with.'

'Yes, Harry, I know.'

'Okay then,' I embraced and kissed her quickly. 'Off you go then.' And they went out of the cave, Angelo lugging a five-gallon can of drinking water, and they trotted away into the palm grove.

Quickly I threw a few items into a light haversack, a box of cheroots, matches, binoculars, water bottle and a heavy jersey, a tin of chocolate and of survival rations, a torch – and I buckled my belt around my waist with the heavy bait-knife in the sheath. Slinging the strap of the haversack over my shoulder, I also ran from the cave and followed Chubby down into the palm grove towards the beach.

I had run fifty yards when there was the thud, thudding of small-arms fire, a shout and another burst of firing. It was directly ahead of me and very close.

I paused and slipped behind the bole of the palm tree while I peered into the lightening shades of the grove. I saw movement, a figure running towards me and I loosened the bait-knife in its sheath and waited until I was sure, before I called softly, 'Chubby!'

The running figure swerved towards me. He was carrying the FN rifle and the canvas bandolier with spare magazines of ammunition, and he was breathing quickly but lightly as he saw me.

'They spotted me,' he grunted. 'There are hundreds of the bastards.'

At that moment I saw more movement amongst the trees.

'Here they come,' I said. 'Let's go.'

I wanted to give Sherry a clear run, so I did not take the path across the saddle, but turned directly southwards to

330

lead the pursuit off her scent. We headed for the swamps at the southern end of the island.

They saw us as we ran obliquely across their front. I heard a shout, answered immediately by others, and then there were five scattered shots and I saw the muzzle flashes bloom amongst the dark trees. A bullet struck a palm trunk high above our head, a woody thunk, but we were going fast and within minutes the shouts of pursuit were fading behind us.

I reached the edge of the salt marsh, and swung away inland to avoid the stinking mudflats. On the first gentle slope of the hills I halted to listen and to regain our breath. The light was strengthening swiftly now. Within a short while it would be sunrise and I wanted to be under cover before then.

Suddenly there were distant cries of dismay from the direction of the swamps and I guessed that the pursuit had blundered into the glutinous mud. That would discourage them fairly persuasively, I thought, and grinned.

'Okay, Chubby, let's get on,' I whispered, and as we stood there was a new sound from a different direction.

The sound was muted by distance and by the intervening heights of the ridge, for it came from the seaward side of the island, but it was the unmistakable ripping sound of automatic gunfire.

Chubby and I froze into listening attitudes and the sound was repeated, another long tearing burst of machine-gun fire. Then there was silence, though we listened for three or four minutes.

'Come on,' I said quietly, we could delay no longer and we ran on up the slope towards the southernmost peak.

We climbed quickly in the fast-growing morning light, and I was too preoccupied to feel any qualms as we negotiated the narrow ledge and stepped at last into the deep rock crack where I had arranged to meet Sherry.

The shelter was silent and deserted but I called without hope, 'Sherry! Are you there, love?'

There was no reply from the shadows, and I turned back to Chubby.

'They had a good lead on us. They should have been here,' and only then did that burst of machine-gun fire we had heard earlier take on new meaning.

I removed the binoculars from the haversack and then thrust it away into a crack in the rock.

'They've run into trouble, Chubby,' I told him. 'Come on. Let's go and find out what happened.'

Once we were off the ledge we struck out through the jumble of broken rock towards the seaward side of the island, but even in my haste and dreadful anxiety for Sherry's safety, I moved with stealth and we were careful not to show ourselves to a watcher in the groves or on the beaches below us.

As we crossed the divide of the ridge a new vista opened before us, the curve of the beach and the jagged black sweep of Gunfire Reef.

I halted instantly and pulled Chubby down beside me, as we crouched into cover.

Anchored in a position to command the mouth of the channel through Gunfire Reef was the armed crash boat from Zinballa Bay, flagship of my old friend Suleiman Dada. Returning to it from the beach was a small motor-boat, crowded with tiny figures.

'God damn it,' I muttered, 'they really had it planned. Manny Resnick has teamed up with Suleiman Dada. That's what took him so long to get here. While Manny hit the beach, Dada was covering the channel, so we couldn't make a bolt for it like we did before.'

'And he had men on the beach – that was the machine-gun fire. Manny Resnick sailed *Mandrake* into the bay to flush us, and Dada had the back door covered.'

'What about Miss Sherry and Angelo? Do you think they got away? Did Dada's men catch them when they crossed the saddle?'

'Oh God!' I groaned, and cursed myself for not having stayed with her. I stood up and focused the binoculars on the motor-boat as it crawled across the clear waters of the outer lagoon to the anchored crash boat.

'I can't see them.' Even with the aid of the binoculars, the occupants of the dinghy were merely a dark mass, for the morning sun was rising beyond them and the glare off the water dazzled me. I could not make out separate figures, let alone recognize individuals.

'They may have them in the boat – but I can't see.' In my agitation I had left the cover of the rocks, and was seeking a better vantage point, moving about on the skyline. Out in the open I must have been highlit by the same sun rays that were blinding me.

I saw the familiar flash, and the long white feather of gunsmoke blow from the mounted quick-firer on the bows of the crash boat, and I heard the shell coming with a rushing sound like eagles' wings.

'Get down!' I shouted at Chubby, and threw myself flat amongst the rocks.

The shell burst in very close, with the bright hot glare like the brief opening of a furnace door. Shrapnel and rock fragments trilled and whined around us, and I jumped to my feet.

'Run!' I yelled at Chubby, and we jinked back over the skyline just as the next shell passed over us, making us both flinch our heads at the mighty crack of passing shot.

Chubby was wiping a smear of blood from his forearm as we crouched behind the ridge.

'Okay?' I asked.

'A scratch, that's all. Bit of a rock fragment,' he growled.

'Chubby, I'm going down to find out what happened to

the others. No point both of us taking a chance. You wait here.'

'You're wasting time, Harry, I'm coming with you. Let's go.' He hefted the rifle and led the way down the peak. I thought of taking the FN away from him. In his hands it was about as lethal as a slingshot when fired with his closed-eyes technique. Then I left it. It made him feel good.

We moved slowly, hugging any cover there was and searching ahead before moving forward. However, the island was silent except for the sough and clatter of the west wind in the tops of the palms and we saw nobody as we moved up the seaward side of the island.

I cut the spoor left by Angelo and Sherry as they crossed the saddle, above the camp. Their running footsteps had bitten deep into the fluffy soil, Sherry's small slim prints were overlapped by Angelo's broad bare feet.

We followed them down the slope, and suddenly they shied off the track. They had dropped the water-can here and, turning abruptly, had separated slightly, as though they had run side by side for sixty yards.

There we found Angelo, and he was never going to enjoy his share of the spoils. He had been hit by three of the soft heavy-calibre slugs. They had torn through the thin fabric of his shirt, and opened huge dark wounds in his back and chest.

He had bled copiously but the sandy soil had absorbed most of it, and already what was left was drying into a thick black crust. The flies were assembled, crawling gleefully into the bullet holes and swarming on the long dark lashes around his wide open and startled eyes.

Following her tracks I saw where Sherry had run on for twenty paces, and then the little idiot had turned back and gone to kneel beside where Angelo lay. I cursed her for that. She might have been able to escape if she had not indulged in that useless and extravagant gesture.

They had caught her as she knelt beside the body and dragged her down through the palms to the beach. I could see the long slide marks in the sand where she had dug her feet in and tried to resist.

Without leaving the shelter of the trees, I looked down the smooth white sand, following their tracks to where the marks of the motor-boat's keel still showed in the sand of the water's edge.

They had taken her out to the crash boat, and I crouched behind a pile of driftwood and dried palm fronds to stare out at the graceful little ship.

Even as I watched she weighed anchor, picked up speed and passed slowly down the length of the island to round the point and enter the inner lagoon where *Mandrake* was still lying at anchor.

I straightened up and slipped back through the grove to where I had left Chubby. He had laid the carbine aside and he sat with Angelo's body in his arms, cradling the head against his shoulder. Chubby was weeping, fat glistening tears slid wearily down the seamed brown cheeks and fell from his jaw to wet the thick dark curls of the boy in his arms.

I picked up the rifle and stood guard over them while Chubby wept for both of us. I envied him the relief of tears, the outpouring of pain that would bring surcease. My own grief was as fierce as Chubby's, for I had loved Angelo as much, but it was down deep inside where it hurt more.

'All right, Chubby,' I said at last. 'Let's go, man.' He stood up with the boy still in his arms and we moved back along the ridge.

In a gully that was choked with rank vegetation we laid Angelo in a shallow grave that we scraped with our hands, and we covered him with a blanket of branches and leaves that I cut with my bait-knife before filling the grave. I could not bring myself to throw sand into his unprotected face, and the leaves made a gentler shroud.

Chubby wiped away his tears with the open palm of his hand and he stood up.

'They got Sherry,' I told him quietly. 'She is aboard the crash boat.'

'Is she hurt?' he asked.

'I don't think so, not yet.'

'What do you want to do now, Harry?' he asked, and the question was answered for me.

Somewhere far off towards the camp, we heard a whistle shrill, and we moved up the ridge to a point where we could see down into the inner lagoon and landward side of the island.

Mandrake lay where I had last seen her and the Zinballa crash boat was anchored a hundred yards closer to the shore. They had seized the whaleboat and were using her to land men on the beach. They were all armed, and uniformed. They set off immediately into the palm trees and the whaleboat ran back to *Mandrake*.

I put the binoculars on to *Mandrake* and saw that there were developments taking place there also. In the field of the glasses I recognized Manny Resnick in a white openneck shirt and blue slacks as he climbed down into the whaleboat. He was followed by Lorna Page. She wore dark glasses, a yellow scarf around her pale blonde hair and an emerald green slack suit. I felt hatred seethe in my guts as I recognized them.

Now something happened that puzzled me. The luggage that I had seen loaded into the Rolls at Curzon Street was brought out on to the deck by two of Manny's thugs and it also was passed down into the whaleboat.

A uniformed crew member of *Mandrake* saluted from the deck, and Manny waved at him in a gesture of airy dismissal.

The whaleboat left *Mandrake*'s side and moved in towards the crash boat. As Manny, his lady friend, body-guards and luggage were disembarked on to the deck of the crash boat, *Mandrake* weighed anchor, turned for the entrance of the bay, and set out in a determined fashion for the deep-water channel.

'She's leaving,' muttered Chubby. 'Why is she doing that?'

'Yes, she's leaving,' I agreed. 'Manny Resnick has finished with her. He's got a new ally now, and he doesn't need his own ship. She's probably costing him a thousand nicker a day – and Manny always was a shy man with a buck.'

I turned my glasses on to the crash boat again and saw Manny and his entourage enter the cabin.

'There is probably another reason,' I muttered.

'What's that, Harry?'

'Manny Resnick and Suleiman Dada will want as few witnesses as possible to what they intend doing now.'

'Yeah, I see what you mean,' grunted Chubby.

'I think, my friend, that we are about to be treated to the kind of nastiness that will make what they did to Angelo seem kind, by comparison.'

'We've got to get Miss Sherry off that boat, Harry.' Chubby was coming out of the daze of grief into which Angelo's killing had thrown him. 'We've got to do something, Harry.'

'It's a nice thought, Chubby, I agree. But we aren't going to help her much by getting ourselves killed. My guess is that she will be safe until they get their hands on the treasure.'

His huge face creased up like that of a worried bulldog.

'What we going to do, Harry?'

'Right now we are going to run again.'

'What do you mean?'

337

'Listen,' I told him, and he cocked his head. There was the shrill of the whistle again and then faintly we heard voices carried up to us on the wind.

'Looks like their first effort will be brute strength. They've landed the entire goon squad, and they are going to drive the island and put us up like a brace of cock pheasant.'

'Let's go down and have a go,' Chubby growled, and cocked the FN. 'I got a message for them from Angelo.'

'Don't be a fool, Chubby,' I snapped at him angrily. 'Now listen to me. I want to count how many men they have. Then, if we get a good chance, I want to try and get one of them alone and take his piece off him. Watch for an opportunity, Chubby, but don't have a go yet. Play it very cautious, hear?' I didn't want to refer to his markmanship in derogatory tones.

'Okay,' Chubby nodded.

'You stay this side of the ridge. Count how many of them come down this side of the island. I'll cross over and do the same on the other side.' He nodded. 'I'll meet you at the spot where the crash boat shelled us in two hours.'

'What about you, Harry?' He made a gesture of handing me the FN – but I didn't have the heart to deprive him.

'I'll be okay,' I told him. 'Off you go, man.'

It was a simple task to keep ahead of the line of beaters for they called to each other loudly to keep their spirits up, and they made no pretence at concealment or stealth, but advanced slowly and cautiously in an extended line.

There were nine of them on my side of the ridge, seven of them were blacks in naval uniform, armed with AK47

338

assault rifles and two of them were Manny Resnick's men. They were dressed in casual tropical gear and carried sidearms. One of them I recognized as the driver of the Rover that night so long ago, and the passenger in the twin-engined Cessna that had spotted Sherry and me on the beach.

Once I had made my head count, I turned my back on them and ran ahead to the curve of the salt marsh. I knew that when the line of beaters ran into this obstacle, it would lose its cohesion and that it was likely that some of its members would become isolated.

I found an advanced neck of swampland with stands of young mangrove and coarse swamp grass in dense shades of fever green. I followed the edge of this thicket and came upon a spot where a fallen palm tree lay across the neck like a bridge – offering escape in two directions. It had collected a dense covering of blown palm fronds and swamp grass which provided a good hide from which to mount an ambush.

I lay in the back of this shaggy mound of dead vegetation and I had the heavy bait-knife in my right hand ready to throw.

The line of the beaters came on steadily, their voices growing louder as they approached the swamp. Soon I could hear the rustle and scrape of branches as one of them came directly down to where I lay.

He paused and called when he was about twenty feet from me, and I pressed my face close to the damp earth and peered under the pile of dead branches. There was an opening there and I saw his feet and his legs below the knees. His trousers were thick blue serge and he wore grubby white sneakers without socks. At each step his naked ankles showed very black African skin.

It was one of the sailors from the crash boat then, and I

was pleased. He would be carrying an automatic weapon. I preferred that to a pistol, which was what Manny's boys were armed with.

Slowly I rolled on to my side and cleared my knife arm. The sailor called again so close and so loud that my nerves jumped and I felt the tingling flush of adrenalin in my blood. His call was answered from farther off, and the sailor came on.

I could hear his soft footfalls on the sand, padding towards me.

Suddenly he came into full view, as he rounded the fall of brushwood. He was ten paces from me.

He was in naval uniform, a blue cap on his head with its gay little red pom-pom on the top, but he carried the vicious and brutal-looking machine-gun on his hip. He was a tall lean youngster in his early twenties, smooth faced and sweating nervously so there was a purple black sheen on his skin, against which his eyes were very white.

He saw me and tried to swing the machine-gun on to me, but it was on his right hip and he blocked himself awkwardly in the turn. I aimed for the notch where the two collarbones meet, that was framed by the opening of his uniform at the base of his throat. I threw overhand, snapping my wrist into it at the moment of release so the knife leapt in a silvery blur and thudded precisely into the mark I had chosen. The blade was completely buried and only the dark walnut handle protruded from his throat.

He tried to cry out, but no sound came, for the blade had severed all his vocal chords as I intended. He sank slowly to his knees facing me in a prayerful attitude with his hands dangling at his sides and the machine-gun hanging on its strap.

We stared at each other for a moment that seemed to last for ever. Then he shuddered violently and a thick burst of bubbling blood poured from his mouth and nose, and he pitched face forward to the ground.

Crouched low, I flipped him on to his back and withdrew the knife against the clinging drag of wet flesh, and I cleaned the blade on his sleeve.

Working swiftly I stripped him of his weapon and the spare magazines in the bandolier on his webbing belt, then, still crouching low, I dragged him by his heels into the gluey mud of the creek and knelt on his chest to force him below the surface. The mud flowed over his face as slowly and thickly as molten chocolate, and when he was totally submerged I buckled the webbing belt around my waist, picked up the machine-gun and slipped back quietly through the breach that I had made in the line of beaters.

As I ran doubled over and using all the cover there was, I checked the load on the AK47. I was familiar with the weapon. I had used it in Biafra and I made sure that the magazine was full and that the breech was loaded before I slipped the strap over my right shoulder and held it ready on my hip.

When I had moved back about five hundred yards I paused and took shelter against the trunk of a palm while I listened. Behind me, the line of beaters seemed to have run into trouble against the swamp, and they were trying to sort themselves out. I listened to the shouts and the angry shrill of the whistle. It sounded like a cup final, I thought, and grinned queasily, for the memory of the man I had killed was still nauseatingly fresh.

Now that I had broken through their line I turned and struck directly across the island towards my rendezvous with Chubby on the south peak. Once I was out of the palm groves on to the lower slopes, the vegetation was thicker, and I moved more swiftly through the better cover.

Halfway to the crest I was startled by a fresh burst of

gunfire. This time it was the distinctive whipcracking lash of the FN, a sharper slower beat than the storm of AK47 machine-gun fire that answered it immediately.

I judged by the volume and duration of the outburst that all the weapons involved had emptied magazines in a continuous burst. A heavy silence followed.

Chubby was having a go, after all my warnings. Although I was bitterly angry, I was also thoroughly alarmed by what trouble he had got himself into. One thing was certain – Chubby had missed whatever he had aimed at.

I broke from a trot into a run, and angled upwards towards the crest, aiming to reach the area from which the gunfire had sounded.

I burst out of a patch of goose-bush into a narrow overgrown path that followed the direction I wanted, and I turned into it and went into a full run.

I topped the rise and almost ran into the arms of one of the uniformed seamen coming in the opposite direction, also at a headlong run.

There were six of his comrades with him in Indian file, all making the best possible speed on his heels. Thirty yards farther back was another who had lost his weapon and whose uniform jacket was sodden with fresh blood.

On all their faces were expressions of abandoned terror, and they ran with the single-minded determination of men pursued closely by all the legions of hell.

I knew instantly that this rabble were the survivors of an encounter with Chubby Andrews, and that it had been too much for their nerves. They were hell-bent and homeward-bound – Chubby's shooting must have improved miraculously, and I made him a silent apology.

So much were the seamen involved with the devil behind them that they seemed not to notice me for the fleeting instant which it took for me to slip the safety-catch on the machine-gun on my hip, brace myself with knees bent and feet spread.

I swung the weapon in a short kicking traverse aimed low at their knees. With a rate of fire like that of an AK47, you must go for the legs, and rely on another three or four hits in the body as the man drops through the sheet of fire. It also defeats the efforts of the short barrel to ride up under the thrust of the recoil.

They went downward in a sprawling shrieking mass, punched backwards into each other by the savage strike of the soft heavy-calibre slugs.

I held the trigger down for the count of four, and then I turned and plunged off the path into the thick wall of goose-bush. It hid me instantly and I doubled over as I jinked and dodged under the branches.

Behind me, a machine-gun was firing, and the bullets tore and snapped through the thick foliage. None came near me and I settled back into a quick trot.

I guessed that my sudden and completely unexpected attack would have permanently acounted for two or three of the seamen, and may have wounded one or two others.

However, the effect on their morale would be disastrous – especially coming so soon after Chubby's onslaught. Once they reached the safety of the crash boat, I guessed that the forces of evil would debate long and hard before setting foot on the island again. We had won the second round decisively, but they still had Sherry North. That was the major trump in their hands. As long as they held her they could dictate the course of the game.

Chubby was waiting for me amongst the rocks on the saddle of the peak. The man was indestructible.

'Jesus, Harry, where the hell you been?' he growled. 'I've been waiting here all morning.'

I saw that he had retrieved my haversack from the cleft

in the rocks where I had left it. It lay with two captured AK47 rifles and bandoliers of ammunition at his feet.

He handed me the water bottle, and only then did I realize how thirsty I was. The heavily chlorinated water tasted like Veuve Clicquot, but I rationed myself to three swallows.

'I got to apologize to you, Harry. I had a go. Just couldn't help it, man. They were bunched up and standing out in the open like a Sunday-school picnic. Just couldn't help myself, gave them a good old squirt. Dropped two of them and the others run like hens, shooting their pieces straight up in the air as they go.'

'Yeah,' I nodded. 'I met them as they crossed the ridge.'

'Heard the shooting. Just about to come and look for you.'

I sat down on the rock beside him, and found my cheroots in the haversack. We each lit one and smoked in grateful silence for a moment which Chubby spoiled.

'Well, we lit a fire under their tails – don't reckon they'll come back for more. But they have still got Miss Sherry, man. Long as they got her, they are winning.'

'How many were there, Chubby?'

'Ten.' He spat out a scrap of tobacco and inspected the glowing tip of the cheroot. 'But I took out two – and I think I winged another.'

'Yeah,' I agreed. 'I met seven on the ridge. I had a go at them also. Aren't more than four left now – and there are eight more out of my bunch. Say a dozen, plus those left on board – another six or seven. About twenty guns still against us, Chubby.'

'Pretty odds, Harry.'

'Let's work on it, Chubby.'

'Let's do that, Harry.'

I selected the newest and least abused of the three

344

machine-guns and there were five full magazines of ammunition for it. I cached the discarded weapons under a slab of flat rock and loaded and checked the other.

We each had another short drink from the water bottle and then I led the way cautiously along the ridge, keeping off the skyline, back towards the deserted camp.

From the spot at which I had first spotted the approach of the *Mandrake* we surveyed the whole northern end of the island.

As we guessed they would, Manny and Suleiman Dada had taken all their men off the island. Both the whaleboat and the smaller motor-boat were moored alongside the crash boat. There was much confused and meaningless activity on board, and as I watched the scurrying figures I imagined the scenes of terrible wrath and retribution which were taking place in the main cabin.

Suleiman Dada and his new protégé were certainly wreaking a fearful vengeance on their already badly beaten and demoralized troops.

'I want to go down to the camp, Chubby. See what they left for us,' I said at last, and handed him the binoculars. 'Keep watch for me. Three quick shots as a warning signal.'

'Okay, Harry,' he agreed, but as I stood up there was a renewed outbreak of feverish activity on board the crash boat. I took the glasses back from Chubby and watched Suleiman Dada emerge from the cabin and make a laborious ascent to the open bridge. In his white uniform, bedecked with medals that glittered in the sunlight and attended by a host of helpers he reminded me of a fat white queen termite being moved from its royal cell by swarming worker ants.

The transfer was effected at last and as I watched through the binoculars I saw an electronic bullhorn handed to Suleiman. He faced the shore, lifted the hailer to his mouth and through the powerful lens I saw his lips moving. Seconds later the sound reached us clearly, magnified by the instrument and carried by the wind.

'Harry Fletcher. I hope you can hear me.' The deep well-modulated voice was given a harsher sound by the amplifier. 'I plan to put on a demonstration this evening which will convince you of the necessity of co-operating with me. Please be in a position where you can watch. You will find it fascinating. Nine o'clock this evening on the afterdeck of this ship. It's a date, Harry. Don't miss it.'

He handed the bullhorn to one of his officers and went below.

'They're going to do something to Sherry,' muttered Chubby and fiddled disconsolately with the rifle in his lap.

'We'll know at nine,' I said, and watched the officer with the bullhorn climb from the deck into the motor-boat. They set off on a slow circuit of the island, stopping every half mile to shout a repetition of Suleiman Dada's invitation to me at the silent tree-lined shore. He was very anxious for me to attend.

'All right, Chubby,' I glanced at my watch. 'We have hours yet. I'm going down to the camp. Watch out for me.'

The camp had been ransacked and plundered of most items of value, equipment and stores had been smashed and scattered about the caves – but still some of it had been overlooked.

I found five cans of fuel and hid them along with much other equipment that might be of value. Then I crept cautiously down into the grove, and learned with relief that the hiding-place of the chest and the golden tiger's head and the other stores was undisturbed.

Carrying a five-gallon can of drinking water and three cans of corned beef and mixed vegetables I climbed again to the ridge where Chubby waited. We ate and drank and I said to Chubby: 'Get some sleep if you can. It's going to be a long hard night.'

He grunted and curled up in the grass like a great brown bear. Soon he was snoring softly and regularly.

I smoked three cheroots slowly and thoughtfully, but it was only as the sun was setting that I had my first real stroke of genius. It was so clear and simple, and so delightfully apt that it was immediately suspect and I re-examined it carefully.

The wind had dropped and it was completely dark by the time I was certain of my idea and I sat smiling and nodding contentedly as I thought about it.

The crash boat was brightly lit, all her ports glowed and a pair of floods glared whitely down upon the afterdeck, so it looked like an empty stage.

I woke Chubby and we ate and drank again.

'Let's go down to the beach,' I said. 'We'll have a better view from there.'

'It might be a trap,' Chubby warned me morosely.

'I don't think so. They are all on board, and they are playing from strength. They've still got Sherry. They don't have to try any fancy tricks.'

'Man, if they do anything to that girl—' he stopped himself, and stood up. 'All right, let's go.'

We moved silently and cautiously down through the grove with our weapons cocked and our fingers on the triggers, but the night was still and the grove deserted.

We halted amongst the trees at the top of the beach. The crash boat was only two hundred yards away and I leaned my shoulder against the trunk of a palm and focused my glasses on her. It was so clear and close that I could read the writing on the lid of a packet from which one of the sentries took and lit a cigarette.

We had a front row seat for whatever entertainment

Suleiman Dada was planning, and I felt the stir of apprehension and knowledge of coming horror blow like a cold breeze across my skin.

I lowered the glasses and whispered softly to Chubby, 'Change your piece for mine,' and he passed me the long-barrelled FN and took the AK47.

I wanted the accuracy of the FN to command the deck of the crash boat. Naturally there was nothing I could do to intervene while Sherry was unharmed, but if they did anything to her – I would make sure she didn't suffer alone.

I squatted down beside the palm tree, adjusted the peep sights of the rifle, and drew a careful bead on the head of the deck guard. I knew I could put a bullet through his temple from where I sat and when I was satisfied I laid the rifle across my lap and settled down to wait.

The mosquitoes from the swamp whined around our ears but both Chubby and I ignored them and sat quietly. I longed for a cheroot to soothe the tension of my nerves, but I was forced to forgo that comfort.

Time passed very slowly, and new fears came to plague me and make the waiting seem even longer than it was – but finally, a few minutes before the promised hour, there was a renewed stirring and bustle on board the crash boat and once more Suleiman Dada was helped up the ladder by his men and he took his place at the bridge rail looking down over the after-deck. He was sweating heavily and it had soaked the area around the armpits and across the back of his white uniform jacket. I guessed that he had passed his own period of waiting by frequent recourse to the whisky bottle, probably from my own stock that had been plundered from the cave.

He laughed and joked with the men around him, his vast belly shaking with mirth and his men echoed the laughter slavishly. The sound of it carried across the water to the beach.

Suleiman was followed by Manny Resnick and his blonde lady friend. Manny was well groomed and cool-looking in his expensive casual clothing. He stood slightly apart from the others, his expression aloof and disinterested. He reminded me of an adult at a children's party, seeing out a boring and mildly unpleasant duty.

In contrast, Lorna Page was excited and shiny-eyed as a girl on her first date. She laughed with Suleiman Dada and leaned expectantly over the rail above the deserted deck. Through the powerful glasses I could see the flush on her cheeks which was not rouge.

I was concentrating on her so that it was only when I felt Chubby move suddenly and restlessly, and heard his grunt of alarm that I swung the glasses downwards on to the deck.

Sherry was there, standing between two of the uniformed sailors. They held her arms and she looked small and frail between them.

She still wore the clothes she had thrown on so hurriedly that morning and her hair was dishevelled. Her face was gaunt and her expression strained – but it was only when I studied her carefully that I saw that what looked like sleepless dark rings below her eyes were in fact bruises. With a cold chill of anger, I realized that her lips were swollen and puffed up as though they had been stung by bees. One of her cheeks was also fatly distorted and bruised.

They had beaten her and knocked her about badly. Now that I looked for it I could see dark splotches of dried blood on her blue shirt, and when one of the guards dragged her around roughly to face the shore I saw that one of her hands was bandaged roughly – and that either blood or disinfectant had stained the bandages.

She looked tired and ill, nearly at the end of her strength. My anger threatened to wipe out my reason. I wanted to inflict hurt upon those that had treated Sherry like this, and I had already begun to lift the rifle with hands that shook with the force of my hatred before I could control myself. I closed my eyes tightly and took a long deep breath to steady myself. The time would come – but it was not now.

When I opened my eyes again and refocused the binoculars, Suleiman Dada had the bullhorn to his lips.

'Good evening, Harry, my dear friend, I am sure you recognize this young lady.' He made a wide gesture towards Sherry and she looked up at him wearily. 'After questioning her closely, a procedure which alas caused her a little discomfort, I am at last convinced that she does not know the whereabouts of the property in which my friends and I are interested. She tells me that you have hidden it.' He paused and mopped his streaming face with a towel handed to him by one of his men before he went on.

'She is no longer of any interest to me – except possibly as a medium of exchange.'

He made a gesture, and Sherry was hustled away below. Something cold and slimy moved in my guts at her going. I wondered if I would ever see her again – alive.

On to the deserted deck filed four of Suleiman's men. Each of them had stripped to the waist and the floodlights rippled on their smooth darkly muscled bodies.

Each of them carried the hickory wooden handles of a pickaxe, and silently they formed up at the points of a star about the open deck. Next a man was led into the open centre by two guards. His hands were tied behind his back. They stood on each side of him and slowly forced him to turn in a circle and show himself while Suleiman Dada's voice boomed through the bullhorn.

'I wonder if you recognize him?' I stared at the stooped creature in canvas prison overalls that hung in filthy grey tatters from his gaunt frame. His skin was pale and waxy with deep-set dark eyes, long scraggly blond hair hung in greasy snakes about his face and his half-grown beard was thin and wispy.

He had lost teeth, probably knocked from his mouth with a careless blow.

'Yes, Harry?' Suleiman laughed fruitily over the loud hailer. 'A sojourn in Zinballa prison does wonders for a man, does it not – but the regulation garb is not as smart as that of an Inspector of Police.'

Only then did I recognize ex-Inspector Peter Daly – the man who I had pitched from the deck of *Wave Dancer* into the waters of the outer lagoon just before I had escaped from Suleiman Dada by running the channel at Gunfire Reef.

'Inspector Peter Daly,' Suleiman confirmed with a chuckle, 'a man who let me down badly. I do not like men who let me down, Harry. I really take it very hard. I brought him along for just such an eventuality. It was a wise precaution, for I believe that a graphic demonstration is so much more convincing than mere words.'

Once again he paused to mop his face and to drink deeply from a glass offered him by one of his men. Daly fell to his knees and looked up at the man on the bridge. His expression was of abject terror, and his mouth dribbled saliva as he pleaded for mercy.

'Very well, we can proceed if you are ready, Harry,' he boomed, and one of the guards produced a large black cloth bag which he pulled over Peter Daly's head and secured with a drawn string around his neck. They dragged him roughly to his feet again.

'It's our own variation on the game of blind man's bluff.'

Through the glasses I saw the liquid flood soak through the front of Peter Daly's canvas trousers, as his bladder emptied in anguished terror. Obviously he had seen this game played before during his stay in Zinballa prison.

'Harry, I want you to use your imagination. Do not see

this snivelling filthy creature – but in his place imagine your lovely young lady friend.' He breathed heavily, but when the man beside him offered him the towel again Suleiman struck him a passionless backhanded blow that sent him sprawling across the bridge, and he continued evenly, 'Imagine her lovely young body, imagine her delicious fear as she stands in darkness not knowing what to expect.'

The two guards began to spin Daly between them, as they do in the children's game, around and around he went and now I could faintly hear his muffled shrieks and cries of fear.

Suddenly the two guards stepped away from him, and left the circle of half-naked men with their pick handles. One of them placed the butt of his weapon in the small of Daly's back and shoved him, reeling and staggering across the circle and the man opposite was waiting to drive the end of his club into Daly's belly.

Back and forth he staggered, driven by the thrust of the clubs. Slowly his tormentors increased the savagery of their attack, until one of them hefted his club and swung it like an axe at a tree. It smashed into Daly's ribs.

It was the signal to end it, and as Peter Daly fell to the deck they crowded about him, the clubs rising and falling in a fearsome rhythm and the blows sounding clearly across the lagoon to where we watched in disgust and revulsion.

One after the other they tired, and stepped back to rest from their grim work and Peter Daly's crumpled and broken body lay in the centre of the deck.

'Crude, you will say, Harry – but then you will not deny that it is effective.'

I was sickened by the barbaric cruelty of it, and Chubby muttered beside me, 'He's a monster – I've never heard of nothing like that before.'

'You have until noon tomorrow, Harry, to come to me

352

unarmed and reasonable. We will talk, we will agree on certain matters, we will make an exchange of assets and we will part friends.'

He stopped speaking to watch while one of his men secured a line to Peter Daly's ankle, and they hoisted him to the masthead of the crash boat where he dangled grotesquely, like some obscene pennant. Lorna Page was looking up at him, her head thrown back so the blonde hair hung down her back and her lips were slightly parted.

'If you refuse to be reasonable, Harry, then at noon tomorrow I shall sail around this island with your lady friend hanging like that—' He pointed up to the corpse whose masked head swung slowly back and forth only a few feet above the deck, '—from the mast. Think about it, Harry. Take your time. Think about it well.'

Suddenly the floodlights were switched off, and Suleiman Dada began his laborious descent to the cabin. Manny Resnick and Lorna Page followed him. Manny was frowning slightly, as though he was pondering a business deal, but I could see that Lorna was enjoying herself.

'I think I'm going to throw up,' muttered Chubby.

'Get it over then,' I said, 'because we have a lot of work to do.'

I stood up and quietly led the way back into the palm grove. We took it in turns to dig while the other stood guard amongst the trees. I would not use a light for fear of attracting attention from the crash boat and we were both exaggeratedly careful to maintain silence and not to let the clank of metal sound through the grove.

We lifted the remaining cases of gelignite and blasting equipment, then we did the same with the rusted pay chest and carried it to a carefully chosen site below the steeply sloping ground of the peak. Fifty yards up the slope was a fold in the ground thickly screened with goose-bush and salt grass.

353

We dug another hole for the chest, going deep into the soft soil until we struck water. Then we repacked the pay chest and reburied it. Chubby climbed up to the hidden fold above us and made his arrangements there.

In the meantime I reloaded the machine-gun and wrapped it lightly in one of my old shirts, the five full magazines placed with it, and I buried the lot under an inch of sand, next to the stem of the nearest palm tree where the recent rain waters had cut a shallow dry runnel down the slope.

The water-torn trench and the tree were forty paces from the spot where the chest was buried, and I hoped it was far enough. The trench was little more than two feet deep and would provide scanty cover.

The moon came out after midnight and it gave us enough light to check our arrangements. Chubby made sure I was in full view from his hideaway up the slope when I stood beside the shallow runnel. Then I climbed up to him and double-checked him. We lit a cheroot each, sheltering the match and screening the glowing tips with cupped hands, while we went over our planning once again.

I was particularly anxious that there should be no misunderstanding in our timing and signals, and I made Chubby repeat them twice. He did so with long-suffering and theatrical patience, but at last I was satisfied. We dumped the cheroot butts and scraped sand over them and when we went down the slope we both carried palm-frond brooms to sweep out all signs of activity.

The first part of my planning was complete, and we returned to where the golden tiger and the rest of the gelignite was cached. We reburied the tiger and then I prepared a full case of gelignite. It was a massive overdose of explosive, sufficient for a tenfold over-kill – but I have never been a man to stint myself when I have the means to indulge.

I would not be able to use the electric blaster and insulated wire, and I must rely on one of the time-pencil detonators. I have a strong distaste for these temperamental little gadgets. They operate on the principle of acid eating through a thin wire which holds the hammer on a powder cap. When the acid cuts the wire the cap explodes, and the delay in the detonation is governed by the strength of the acid and the thickness of the wire.

There can be a large latitude of error in this timing which on one occasion caused me a nearly fatal embarrassment. However, in this case I had no choice in the matter – and I selected a pencil with a six-hour delay and prepared it for use with the gelignite.

Amongst the equipment overlooked by the looters was my old oxygen rebreathing underwater set. This diving set is almost as dangerous to use as the time pencils. Unlike the aqualung which uses compressed air, the rebreather employs pure oxygen which is filtered and cleansed of carbon dioxide after each breath and then cycled back to the user.

Oxygen breathed at pressures in excess of twice atmospheric becomes as poisonous as carbon monoxide. In other words, if you rebreathe pure oxygen below underwater depths of thirty-three feet, it will kill you. You have to have all your wits together to play around with the stuff – but it has one enormous advantage. It does not blow bubbles on the surface to alarm a sentry and give away your position to him.

Chubby carried the prepared case of gelignite and the rifle when we went back to the beach. It was after three o'clock when I had donned and tested the oxygen set, and then I carried the gelignite down to the water and tested that for buoyancy. It needed a few pounds of lead weights to give it a neutral buoyancy and make it easier to handle in the water.

We had reached the water from the beach around the horn of the bay from the anchored crash boat. The point of sand and palm trees covererd us as we worked, and at last I was ready.

It was a long tiring swim. I had to round the point and enter the bay – a distance of almost a mile – and I had to tow the case of explosive with me. It dragged heavily through the water and it took me almost an hour before I could see the lights of the crash boat glimmering above me through the clear water.

Hugging the bottom I crept forward slowly, terribly aware that the moonlight would silhouette me clearly against the white sand of the lagoon bed, for the water was clear as gin and only twenty-five feet deep.

It was a relief to move slowly into the dark shadow cast by the crash boat's hull and to know that I was safe from discovery. I rested for a few minutes, then I unrolled the nylon slings that I had on my belt and secured them to the case of gelignite.

Now I checked the time on my wristwatch, and the luminous hands showed ten minutes past four o'clock.

I crushed the glass ampoule of the time pencil, releasing the acid to begin its slow eroding attack on the wire, and I returned it to its prepared slot in the case of explosive. In six hours, more or less, the whole lot would go up with the force of a two hundred pound aerial bomb.

Now I left the floor of the lagoon and rose slowly to the hull of the crash boat. It was foul with a hanging slimy beard of weed and the hull itself was thick with a rough scale of shellfish and goose-neck mussels.

I moved slowly along the keel, searching for an anchor point – but there was none and at last I was forced to use the shank of the rudder. I bound the case in position with all the nylon rope I had – and when I was finished I was

356

certain that it would resist even the drag of water when the crash boat was travelling at the top of her speed.

Satisfied at last, I sank once more to the bed of the lagoon and moved off quietly on my return. I made much better speed through the water now without the burden of the gelignite case and Chubby was waiting for me on the beach.

'Fixed up?' he asked quietly, as he helped me shed the oxygen set.

'Just as long as that pencil does its job.'

I was so tired now that the walk back through the grove seemed like an eternity and my feet dragged in the loose footing. I had slept little the previous night, and not at all since then.

This time Chubby watched over me while I slept, and when he shook me gently awake it was after seven o'clock and the daylight was growing swiftly.

We ate a breakfast cold from the can, and I finished it with a handful of high-energy glucose tablets from the survival kit and washed them down with a mug of chlorinated water.

I drew the knife from the sheath on my belt and threw it underhand to pin into the trunk of the nearest palm. It stood there shivering with the force of the impact.

'Show off!' muttered Chubby, and I grinned at him, trying to look relaxed and easy.

'Look, just like the man said – no weapons,' and I spread my empty hands.

'You ready?' he asked, and we both stood up and looked at each other awkwardly. Chubby would never wish me good luck – which was the worst of all possible hex to put on someone.

'See you later,' he said.

'Okay, Chubby.' I held out my hand. He took it and

squeezed it hard, then he turned away, picked up the FN rifle and plodded off through the grove.

I watched him out of sight, but he never looked back and I turned away myself and walked down unarmed to the beach.

I walked out from amongst the trees and stood at the water's edge, staring across the narrow strip of water at the crash boat. The dangling corpse had been removed from the masthead, I saw with relief.

For many seconds none of the sentries on deck noticed me, so I raised both hands above my head and gave them a loud 'Halloo'. Instantly there was a boil of activity and clamour of shouted orders on board the crash boat. Manny Resnick and Lorna appeared at the rail and stared across at me, while half a dozen armed seamen dropped into the whaleboat and headed for the beach.

As the boat touched, they leaped out on to the sand and surrounded me with the muzzles of the AK47s pressed eagerly into my back and belly. I kept my hands hoisted at half-mast and tried to maintain an expression of disinterest as a petty officer searched me with deliberate thoroughness for any weapon. When he was at last satisfied, he placed his hand between my shoulder-blades and gave me a hearty shove towards the whaleboat. One of the more eager of his men took this as a licence and he tried to rupture my kidneys with the butt of his AK47 – but the blow landed six inches high.

I made briskly for the whaleboat to forestall any further martial displays and they crowded into the boat around me pressing the muzzles of their fully loaded weapons painfully into various parts of my anatomy.

Manny Resnick watched me come in over the side of the crash boat.

'Hallo again, Harry,' he smiled without mirth.

'The pleasure is all yours, Manny,' I returned the death's head grin, and another blow caught me between the shoulder-blades and drove me across the deck. I ground my teeth together to control my anger, and I thought about Sherry North. That helped.

Commander Suleiman Dada was sprawled on a low couch covered with plain canvas cushions. He had removed his uniform jacket and it hung heavy with all the braid and medals from a hook on the bulkhead beside him. He wore only a sweat-soaked and greyish sleeveless vest, and even this early in the morning he held a glass of pale brown liquid in his right hand.

'Ah, Harry Fletcher – or should it be Harry Bruce?' he grinned at me like an enormous coal-black baby.

'You take your pick, Suleiman,' I invited him, but I didn't feel like playing word games with him now. I had no illusions about how dangerous was the position in which Sherry and I were placed, and my nerves were painfully tight and fear growled like a caged animal in my belly.

'I have learned so much more about you from my good friends,' he indicated Manny and the blonde Lorna who had followed me into the main cabin. 'Fascinating, Harry. I never dreamed you were a man of such vast talent and formidable achievement.'

'Thanks, Suleiman, you really are a brick, but let's not get carried away with compliments. We have important business – don't we?'

'True, Harry, very true.'

'You have raised the tiger throne, Harry, we know that,' Manny cut in, but I shook my head.

'Only part of it. The rest has gone – but we salvaged what there was.'

'All right, I'll buy that,' Manny agreed. 'Just tell us what there is.'

359

'There is the head of the tiger, about three hundred pounds weight in gold—' Suleiman and Manny glanced at each other.

'Is that all?' Manny asked, and I knew instinctively that Sherry had told them everything she knew during the beating they had given her. I did not hold that against her. I had expected it.

'There is also the jewel chest. The stones removed from the throne were placed in an iron pay chest.'

'The diamond – the Great Mogul?' demanded Manny.

'We've got it,' I said, and they murmured and smiled and nodded at each other. 'But I'm the only one who knows where it is—' I added softly, and immediately they were tense and quiet again.

'This time I've got something to trade, Manny. Are you interested?'

'We are interested, Harry, very interested,' Suleiman Dada spoke for him, and I was aware of the tension growing between my two enemies now that the loot was almost in view.

'I want Sherry North,' I said.

'Sherry North?' Manny stared at me for a moment, and then let out a brief cough of amusement. 'You're a bigger fool than I thought you were, Harry.'

'The girl is of no further interest to us.' Suleiman took a swallow from his glass, and I could smell his sweat in the rising warmth of the cabin. 'You can have her.'

'I want my boat, fuel and water to get me off the island.'

'Reasonable, Harry, very reasonable,' Manny smiled again as if at a secret joke.

'And I want the tiger's head,' and both Manny and Suleiman laughed out loud.

'Harry! Harry!' Suleiman chided me, still laughing.

'Greedy Harry,' Manny stopped laughing.

360

'You can have the diamond and about fifty pounds weight of other gem stones—' I tried to sell the idea with all the persuasion I could muster. It was the understandable thing to do for a man in my position, ' – in comparison the head is nothing. The diamond is worth a million – the head would just cover my expenses.'

'You are a hard man, Harry,' Suleiman chuckled. 'Too hard.'

'What will I get out of it, then?' I demanded.

'Your life, and be grateful for it,' Manny said softly, and I stared at him. I saw the coldness in his eyes, like those of a reptile and I knew beyond all doubt what his intentions were for me, once I had led them to the treasure.

'How can I trust you?' I went through the motions however, and Manny shrugged indifferently.

'Harry, how can you not trust us?' Suleiman intervened. 'What could we possibly gain by killing you and your young lady?'

'And what could you possibly lose,' I thought, but I nodded and said, 'Okay. I don't have much choice.'

They relaxed again, smiling at each other and Suleiman lifted his glass in a silent salute.

'Drink, Harry?' he asked.

'It's a little early for me, Suleiman,' I declined, 'but I would like to have the girl with me now.'

Suleiman motioned one of his men to fetch her.

'I want the whaleboat loaded with fuel and water and left on the beach,' I went on doggedly, and Suleiman gave the orders.

'The girl goes with me when we go ashore and after I have shown you the chest and the head, you'll take it and go.' I stared from one to the other. 'You'll leave us on the island unharmed, do we agree?'

'Of course, Harry.' Suleiman spread his hands disarmingly. 'We are all agreed.' I was afraid that they would see the disbelief in my expression – so I turned with relief to Sherry as she was led into the cabin.

My relief faded swiftly as I stared at her.

'Harry,' she whispered through her swollen purple lips. 'You came – oh God, you came.' She took a faltering step towards me.

Her cheek was bruised and swollen horribly, and from the extent of the oedema I thought perhaps the bone was cracked. The bruising under her eyes made her look sick and consumptive, and blood had dried in a black crust on the rims of her nostrils. I didn't want to look at her injuries, so I took her in my arms and held her to my chest.

They were watching the pair of us with amusement and interest, I felt their eyes upon us, but I did not want to face them and let them see the murderous hatred that must show in my eyes.

'All right,' I said, 'let's get it over with.' When at last I turned to face them, I hoped that my expression was under control.

'Unfortunately, I shall not be going with you,' Suleiman made no effort to rise from the couch. 'Climbing in and out of small boats, walking great distances in the sun and through the sand are not my particular pleasures. I shall say farewell to you here, Harry, and my friends—' again he indicated Manny and Lorna, '—will go with you as my representatives. Of course, you will also be accompanied by a dozen of my men – all of them armed and operating under my instructions.' I thought that this warning was not entirely for my benefit alone.

'Goodbye, Suleiman. Perhaps we'll meet again.'

'I doubt it, Harry,' he chuckled. 'But God speed and my blessings go with you.' He dismissed me with one great pink-palmed paw and with the other he raised his glass and drained the last half-inch of liquor.

Sherry sat close beside me in the motor-boat. She leaned

against me, and her body seemed to have shrivelled with the pain of her ordeal. I put my arm about her shoulders, and she whispered wearily, 'They are going to kill us, Harry, you know that, don't you?'

I ignored the question and asked softly, 'Your hand,' it was still wrapped in the rough bandage, 'what happened?'

Sherry looked up at the blonde girl beside Manny Resnick, and I felt her shiver briefly against me.

'She did it, Harry.' Lorna Page was chatting animatedly to Manny Resnick. Her carefully lacquered hairstyle resisted the efforts of the breeze to ruffle it, and her face was meticulously made up with expensive cosmetics. Her lipstick was moist and glossy and her eyelids were silvery green, with long mascaraed lashes around the cat's eyes.

'They held me – and she pulled out my fingernails.' She shuddered again, and Lorna Page laughed lightly. Manny cupped his hands around a gold Dunhill lighter for her while she lit a cigarette. 'They kept asking me where the treasure was – and each time I couldn't answer she pulled out a nail with the pliers. They made a tearing sound as they came out.' Sherry broke off and held her injured hand protectively against her stomach. I knew how near she was to breaking completely and I held her close, trying to transmit strength to her by physical contact.

'Gently, baby, gently now,' I whispered, and she pressed a little closer to me. I stroked her hair, and tried once again to control my anger, bearing down hard upon it before it clouded my wits.

The motor-boat ran in and grounded on the beach. We climbed out and stood on the white sands while the guards ringed us with levelled weapons.

'Okay, Harry,' Manny pointed. 'There's your boat all ready for you.' The whaleboat was drawn up on the beach. 'The tanks are full and when you've shown us the goods – you can take off.'

He spoke easily, but the girl beside him looked at us with hot predatory eyes – the way a mongoose looks at a chicken. I wondered what way she had chosen for us. I guessed that Manny had promised us to her for her pleasure without reservations – just as soon as he was through with us.

'I hope we aren't going to play games, Harry. I hope you're going to be sensible – and not waste our time.'

I had noticed that Manny had surrounded himself with his own men. Four of them, all armed with pistols, one of them my old acquaintance who had driven the Rover on our first meeting. To balance them there were ten black seamen under a petty officer, and already I sensed that the opposition was divided into two increasingly hostile parties. Manny further reduced the number of seamen in the party by detailing two of them to stay with the motor-boat. Then he turned to me, 'If you are ready, Harry, you may lead the way.'

I had to help Sherry, holding her elbow and guiding her up through the grove. She was so weak that she stumbled repeatedly and her breathing was distressed and ragged before we reached the caves.

With the mob of armed men following us closely, we went on along the edge of the slope. Surreptitiously I glanced at my watch. It was nine o'clock. One hour to go before the case of gelignite under the crash boat blew. The timing was still within the limits I had set.

I made a small show out of locating the precise spot where the chest was buried, and it was with difficulty that I refrained from glancing up the slope to where the fold of ground was screened by vegetation.

'Tell them to dig here,' I said to Manny, and stepped back. Four seamen handed their weapons to a comrade and assembled the small folding army-type shovels they had brought with them.

The soil was soft and freshly turned so they went down

364

at an alarming speed. They would expose the chest within minutes.

'The girl's hurt,' I said to Manny, 'she must sit down.' He glanced at me, and I saw his mind work swiftly. He knew Sherry could not run far and I think he welcomed the opportunity to distract some of the seamen – for he spoke briefly to the petty officer and I led Sherry to the palm tree and sat her down against the stem.

She sighed with weary relief, and two of the seamen came to stand over us with cocked weapons.

I glanced up the slope, but there was no sign of anything suspicious there, although I knew Chubby must be watching us intently. Apart from the two guards, everyone else was gathered expectantly around the four men who were already knee-deep in the freshly dug hole.

Even our two guards were consumed with curiosity, their attention kept wandering and they glanced repeatedly at the group forty yards away.

I heard quite clearly the clang as a spade struck the metal of the chest – and there was a shout of excitement. They all crowded around the excavation with a babble of rising voices, beginning to pull and elbow each other for the opportunity to look down on to it. Our two guards turned their backs on us, and took a step or two in the same direction. It was more than I could have hoped for.

Manny Resnick shoved two seamen aside roughly, and jumped down into the hole beside the diggers. I heard him shouting, 'All right then, bring those ropes and let's lift it out. Carefully, don't damage anything.'

Lorna Page was leaning out over the hole also. It was perfect.

I lifted my right hand and wiped my forehead slowly in the signal I had arranged with Chubby, and as I dropped my hand again, I seized Sherry and rolled swiftly backwards into the shallow rain-washed runnel.

It caught Sherry by surprise, and I had handled her roughly in my anxiety to get under cover. She cried out as I hurt her already painful injuries.

The two guards whirled at the cry, lifting their machine-guns and I knew that they were going to fire – and that the shallow trench provided no cover.

'Now, Chubby, now!' I prayed and threw myself on top of Sherry to shield her from the blast of machine-gun fire and I clapped both hands over her ears to protect them.

At that instant Chubby switched the knob on the electric battery blaster, and the impulse ran down the insulated wire that we had concealed so carefully the night before. There was half a case of gelignite crammed into the iron pay chest – as much explosive as I dared use without destroying Sherry and myself in the blast.

I imagined Chubby's fiendish glee as the case blew. It blew upwards, deflected by the sides of the excavation – but I had packed the sticks of gelignite with sand and handfuls of semi-precious stones to serve as primitive shrapnel and to contain the blast and make it even more vicious.

The group of men around the hole were lifted high in the air, spinning and somersaulting like a troupe of insane acrobats, and a column of sand and dust shot a hundred feet into the air.

The earth jarred under us, slamming into our prone bodies – then the shock wave tore across us. It knocked sprawling the two guards who had been about to fire down on us, ripping their clothing from their bodies.

I thought my eardrums had both burst, I was completely deafened but I knew that I had saved Sherry's ears from damage. Deafened and half blinded by dust, I rolled off Sherry and scratched frantically in the sandy bottom of the trench. My fingers hit the machine-gun buried there and I dragged it out, pulling off the protective rags and coming swiftly to my knees.

Both the guards nearest me were alive, one crawling to his knees and the other sitting up dazedly with blood from a burst eardrum trickling down his cheek.

I killed them with two short bursts that knocked them down in the sand. Then I looked towards the broken heap of humanity around the excavation.

There was small, convulsive movement there and soft moans and whimpering sounds. I stood up shakily from the trench – and I saw Chubby standing up on the slope. He was shouting, but I heard nothing for the ringing buzzing din in my ears.

I stood there, swaying slightly, peering stupidly around me and Sherry rose to her feet beside me. She touched my shoulder, saying something, and with relief I heard her voice as the ringing in my ears subsided slightly.

I looked again towards the area of the explosion and saw a strange and frightening sight. A half-human figure, stripped of clothing and most of its skin, a raw bleeding thing with one arm half torn loose at the shoulder socket and dangling at its side by a shred of flesh rose slowly from beside the excavation like some horrible phantom from the grave.

It stood like that for the long moment which it took me to recognize Manny Resnick. It seemed impossible that he should have survived that holocaust, but more than that he began walking towards me.

He tottered step after step, closer and closer, and I stood frozen, unable to move myself. I saw then that he was blinded, the flying sand had scorched his eyeballs and flayed the skin from his face.

'Oh God! Oh God!' Sherry whispered beside me, and it broke the spell. I lifted the machine-gun and the stream of bullets that tore into Manny Resnick's chest were a mercy.

I was still dazed, staring about me at the shambles we had created when Chubby reached me. He took my arm

367

and I could hear his voice as he shouted, 'Are you okay, Harry?' I nodded and he went on, 'The whaleboat! We have got to make sure of the whaleboat.'

'I turned to Sherry. 'Go to the cave. Wait for me there,' and she turned away obediently.

'Make sure of these first,' I mumbled to Chubby, and we went to the heap of bodies about the shattered iron chest. All of them were dead or would soon be so.

Lorna Page lay upon her back. The blast had torn off her outer clothing and the slim pale body was clad only in lacy underwear, with shreds of the green slack suit hanging from her wrists and draped about her torn and still bleeding legs.

Defying even the explosion, her hairstyle retained its lacquered elegance except for the powdering of fine white sand. Death had played a macabre joke upon her – for a lump of blue lapis lazuli from the jewel chest had been driven by the force of the explosion deep into her forehead. It had embedded itself in the bone of her skull like the eye of the tiger from the golden throne.

Her own eyes were closed while the third precious eye of the stone glared up at me accusingly.

'They are all dead,' grunted Chubby.

'Yes, they're dead,' I agreed, and tore my eyes away from the mutilated girl. I was surprised that I felt no triumph or satisfaction at her death, nor at the manner of it. Vengeance, far from being sweet, is entirely tasteless, I thought, as I followed Chubby down to the beach.

I was still unsteady from the effects of the explosion, and although my ears had recovered almost entirely, I was hard-pressed to keep up with Chubby. He was light on his feet for such a big man.

I was ten paces behind him as we came out of the trees and stopped at the head of the beach.

The whaleboat lay where we had left her, but the two

seamen detailed to guard the motor-boat must have heard the explosion and decided to take no chances.

They were halfway back to the crash boat already, and when they saw Chubby and me, one of them fired his machine-gun in our direction. The range was far beyond the accurate limits of the weapon, and we did not bother to take cover. However, the firing attracted the attention of the crew remaining aboard the crash boat – and I saw three of them run forward to man the quick-firer in the bows.

'Here comes trouble,' I murmured.

The first round was high and wide, cracking into the palms behind us and pitting their stems with the burst of shrapnel.

Chubby and I moved quickly back into the grove and lay flat behind the sandy crest of the beach.

'What now?' Chubby asked.

'Stalemate,' I told him, and the next two rounds from the quick-firer burst in futile fury in the trees above and behind us – but then there was a delay of a few seconds and I saw them training the gun around.

The next shot lifted a tall graceful spout of water from the shallows alongside the whaleboat. Chubby let out a roar of anger, like a lioness whose cub is threatened.

'They are trying to take out the whaleboat!' he bellowed, as the next round tore into the beach in a brief spurt of soft sand.

'Give it to me,' I snapped, and took the FN from him, thrusting the short-barrelled AK47 at him and lifting the strap of the haversack off Chubby's shoulder. His marksmanship was not equal to the finer work that was now necessary.

'Stay here,' I told him, and I jumped up and doubled away around the curve of the bay. I had almost entirely recovered from the effects of the blast now – and as I reached the horn of the bay nearest the anchored crash boat I fell flat on my belly in the sand and pushed forward the long barrel of the FN.

The gun crew were still blazing away at the whaleboat, and spouts of sand and water rose in rapid succession about it. The plate of frontal armour of the gun was aimed diagonally away from me, and the backs and flanks of the gun crew were exposed.

I pushed the rate of fire selector of the FN on to single shot, and drew a few long deep breaths to steady my aim after the long run through the soft sand.

The gun-layer was pedalling the traversing and elevating handles of the gun and had his forehead pressed hard against the pad above the eye-piece of the gunsight.

I picked him up in the peepsight and squeezed off a single shot. It knocked him off his seat and flung him sideways across the breech of the gun. The untended aiming handles spiralled idly and the barrel of the gun lifted lazily towards the sky.

The two gun-loaders looked around in amazement and I squeezed off two more snap shots at them.

Their amazement was altered instantly to panic, and they deserted their posts and sprinted back along the deck, diving into an open hatchway.

I swung my aim across and up to the open bridge of the crash boat. Three shots into the assembled officers and seamen produced a gratifying chorus of yells and the bridge cleared miraculously.

The motor-boat from the beach came alongside, and I hastened the two seamen up the side and into the deck-house with three more rounds. They neglected to make the boat fast and it drifted away from the side of the crash boat.

I changed the magazine of the FN and then carefully and deliberately I put a single bullet through each porthole on the near side of the boat. I could hear clearly the shattering crack of glass at each side.

This proved too much provocation for Commander Suleiman Dada. I heard the donkey winch clatter to life and the anchor chain streamed in over the bows, glistening with sea-water, and the moment the fluked anchor broke out through the surface, the crash boat's propellers churned a white wash of water under her stern and she swung round towards the opening of the lagoon.

I kept her under fire as she moved slowly past my hiding-place lest she change her mind about leaving. The bridge was screened by a wind shield of dirty white canvas, and I knew the helmsman was lying behind this with his head well down. I fired shot after shot through the canvas, trying to guess his position.

There was no apparent effect so I turned my attention to the portholes again, hoping for a lucky ricochet within the hull.

The crash boat picked up speed rapidly until she was waddling along like an old lady hurrying to catch a bus. She rounded the horn of the bay, and I stood up and brushed off the sand. Then I reloaded the rifle and broke into a trot through the palm grove.

By the time I reached the north tip of the island, and climbed high enough up the slope to look out over the deep-water channel, the crash boat was a mile away, heading resolutely for the distant mainland of Africa, a small white shape against the shaded greens of the sea, and the higher harsher blue of the sky.

I tucked the FN under my arm and found a seat from where I could watch her further progress. My wristwatch showed seven minutes past ten o'clock, and I began to wonder if the case of gelignite below the crash boat's stern had, after all, been torn loose by the drag of the water and the wash of the propellers.

The crash boat was now passing between the submerged outer reefs before entering the open inshore waters. The reefs blew regularly, breathing white foam at each surge of the sea as though a monster lay beneath the surface.

The small white speck of the crash boat seemed ethereal and insubstantial in that wilderness of sea and sky, soon she would merge with the wind-flecked and current-chopped waters of the open sea.

The explosion when it came was without passion, its violence muted by distance and its sound toned by the wind. There was a sudden soft waterspout that enveloped the tiny white boat. It looked like an ostrich feather, soft and blowing on the wind, bending when it reached its full height and then losing its shape and smearing away across the choppy surface.

The sound reached me many seconds later, a single unwarlike thud against my still-tender eardrums, and I thought I felt the flap of the blast like the puff of the wind against my face.

When the spray had blown into nothingness the channel was empty, no sign remained of the tiny vessel and there was no mark of her going upon the wind-blown waters.

I knew that with the tide the big evil-looking albacore sharks hunted inshore upon the flood. They would be quick to the taint of blood and torn flesh in the water, and I doubted that any of those aboard the crash boat who had survived the blast would long avoid the attentions of those single-minded and voracious killers. Those that found Commander Suleiman Dada would fare well, I thought, unless they recognized a kindred spirit and accorded him professional privilege. It was a grim little joke, and it gave me only fleeting amusement. I stood up and walked down to the caves.

I found my medical kit had been broken open and scattered during the previous day's looting, but I retrieved sufficient material to clean and dress Sherry's mutilated fingers. Three of the nails had been torn out. I feared that the roots had been destroyed, and that they would never grow again – but when Sherry expressed the same fears, I denied them stoutly.

Once her injuries were taken care of I made her swallow a couple of codeine for the pain and made a bed for her in the darkness of the back of the cave.

'Rest,' I told her, kneeling to kiss her tenderly. 'Try and sleep. I will fetch you when we are ready to leave.'

Chubby was already busy with the necessary tasks. He had checked the whaleboat and, apart from a few shrapnel holes, found her in good condition.

We filled the holes with Pratleys putty from the tool-chest, and left her on the beach.

The hole in which the chest had been buried served as a communal grave for the dead men and the woman lying about it. We laid them in it like sardines, and covered them with the soft sand.

We exhumed the golden head from its own grave with its glittering eye still in the broad forehead, and staggering under its weight we carried it down to the whaleboat and padded it with the polythene cushions in the bottom of the boat. The plastic packets of sapphires and emeralds I packed into my haversack and laid it beside the head.

Then we returned to the caves and salvaged all the undamaged stores and equipment – the jerrycans of water and petrol, the scuba bottles and the compressor. It was late afternoon before we had packed it all into the whaleboat and I was tired. I laid the FN rifle on top of the load and stood back.

'Okay, Chubby?' I asked, as I lit our cheroots and we took our first break. 'Reckon we can take off now.'

Chubby drew on the cheroot and blew a long flag of blue smoke before he spat on the sand. 'I just want to go up and fetch Angelo,' he muttered, and when I stared at him he went on, 'I'm not going to leave the kid up there. It's too lonely here, he'll want to be with his own people in a Christian grave.'

So while I went back to the caves to fetch Sherry, Chubby selected a bolt of canvas and went off into the gathering darkness.

I woke Sherry and made sure she was warmly dressed in one of my jerseys, then I gave her two more codeine and took her down towards the beach. It was dark now, and I held the flashlight in one hand and helped Sherry with the other. We reached the beach and I paused uncertainly. There was something wrong, I knew, and I played the torch over the loaded vessel.

Then I realized what it was, and I felt a sick little jolt in my belly.

The FN rifle was no longer where I had left it in the whaleboat.

'Sherry,' I whispered urgently, 'get down and stay there until I tell you.'

She sank swiftly to the sand beside the beached hull, and I looked around frantically for a weapon. I thought of the spear-gun, but it was under the jerrycans, my bait-knife was still pegged into a palm tree in the grove – I had forgotten about it until this moment. A spanner from the toolbox, perhaps – but the thought was as far as I got.

'All right, Harry, I've got the gun.' The deep throaty voice spoke out of the darkness close behind me. 'Don't turn around or do anything stupid.'

He must have been lying up in the grove after he had taken the rifle, and now he had come up silently behind me. I froze.

'Without turning around – just toss that flashlight back here. Over your shoulder.'

I did as he ordered and I heard the sand crunch under his feet as he stooped to pick it up.

'All right, turn around – slowly.' As I turned, he shone the powerful beam into my eyes, dazzling me. However, I could still vaguely make out the huge hulking shape of the man beyond the beam.

'Have a good swim, Suleiman?' I asked. I could see that he wore only a pair of short white underpants, and his enormous belly and thick shapeless legs gleamed wetly in the reflected torchlight.

'I am beginning to develop an allergy to your jokes, Harry,' he spoke again in that deep beautifully modulated voice, and I remembered too late how a grossly overweight man becomes light and strong in the supporting salt water of the sea. However, even with the turn of the tide to help him, Suleiman Dada had performed a formidable feat in surviving the explosion and swimming back through almost two miles of choppy water. I doubted any of his men had done as well.

'I think it should be in the belly first,' he spoke again, and I saw that he held the stock of the rifle across his left elbow. With the same hand he aimed the torch beam into my face. 'They tell me that is the most painful place to get it.'

We were silent for moments then, Suleiman Dada breathing with his deep asthmatic wheeze and I trying desperately to think of some way in which to distract him long enough to give me a chance to grab the barrel of the FN.

'I don't suppose you'd like to go down on your knees and plead with me?' he asked.

'Go screw, Suleiman,' I answered.

'No, I didn't really think you would. A pity, I would have enjoyed that. But what about the girl, Harry, surely it would be worth a little of your pride—'

We both heard Chubby. He had known there was no way he could cross the open beach undetected, even in the dark. He had tried to rush Suleiman Dada, but I am sure he knew that he would not make it. What he was really doing was giving me the distraction I so desperately needed.

He came fast out of the darkness, running in silently with only the squeak of the treacherous sand beneath his feet to betray him. Even when Suleiman Dada turned the rifle on to him, he did not falter in his charge.

There was the crack of the shot and the long lightning flash of the muzzle blast, but even before that, I was halfway across the distance that separated me from the huge black man. From the corner of my eye I saw Chubby fall, and then Suleiman Dada began to swing the rifle back towards me.

I brushed past the barrel of the FN and crashed shoulder first into his chest. It should have staved his ribs in like the victim of a car smash – instead I found the power of my rush absorbed in the thick padding of dark flesh. It was like running into a feather mattress, and although he reeled back a few paces and lost the rifle, Suleiman Dada remained upright on those two thick tree-trunks of his legs, and before I could recover my own balance I was enfolded in a vast bear hug.

He picked me up off my feet, and pulled me to his mountainously soft chest, trapping both my arms and lifting me so that I could not brace my legs to resist his weight and strength. I experienced a chill of disbelief when I felt the strength of the man, not a hard brutal strength – but something so massive and weighty that there seemed no end to it, almost like the irresistible push and surge of the sea.

I tried with my elbows and knees, kicking and striking to break his hold, but the blows found nothing solid and made no impression upon the man. Instead, the enfolding grip of his arms began to tighten with the slow pulsing power of a giant python. I realized instantly that he was quite capable of literally crushing me to death – and I experienced a sense of panic. I twisted and struggled frantically and unavailingly in his arms, but as he brought more of his immense power to bear upon me, so his breathing wheezed more harshly and he leaned, forward, hunching his great shoulders over me and forcing my back into an arc that must soon snap my spine.

I bent back my head, reached up with an open mouth and I locked my teeth into the broad flattened nose. I bit in hard, with all my desperation, and quite clearly I felt my teeth slice through the flesh and gristle of his nose and instantly my mouth filled with the warm salty metallic flood of his blood. Like a dog at a bull-baiting, I worried and tugged at his nose.

The man bellowed a roar of agony and anger and he released his crushing grip from around my body to try and tear my teeth from his face. The instant my arms were free I twisted convulsively and got a purchase with both feet in the firm wet sand, so I could put my hip into him for the throw. He was so busy attempting to dislodge the grip of my teeth from his nose that he could not resist the throw and as he went over backwards my teeth tore loose, cutting away a lump of his living flesh.

I spat out the horrid mouthful but the warm blood streamed down my chin and I resisted the temptation to pause and wipe it clean.

Suleiman Dada was down on his back, stranded like some massive crippled black frog, but he would not remain helpless much longer, I had to take him out cleanly now and there was only one place where he might be vulnerable.

I jumped up high over him and came down to knee-drop into his throat, to drive my one knee with the full weight and momentum of my body into his larynx and crush it.

He was swift as a cobra, throwing up both arms to shield his throat and to catch me as I descended on to him. Once again, I was enmeshed by those thick black arms, and we rolled down the beach, locked chest to chest into the warm shallow water of the lagoon.

In a direct contrast of weight for weight like this, I was outmatched, and he came up over me with blood streaming from his injured nose, still bellowing with anger, and he pinned me into the shallows forcing my head below the surface and bearing down upon my chest and lungs with all his vast weight.

I began to drown. My lungs caught fire, and the need to breathe laced my vision with sparks and whorls of fire. I could feel the strength going out of me and my consciousness receding into blackness.

The shot when it sounded was muted and dull. I did not recognize it for what it was, until I felt Suleiman Dada jerk and stiffen, felt the strength go out of him and his weight slip and fall from me.

I sat up coughing and gasping for air, with water cascading from my hair and streaming into my eyes. In the light of the fallen torch I saw Sherry North kneeling on the sand at the edge of the water. She had the rifle still clutched in her bandaged hand and her face was pale and frightened.

Beside me, Suleiman Dada floated face down in the shallow water, his half-naked body glistening blackly like a stranded porpoise. I stood up slowly, water pouring from my clothing and she stared at me, horrified with what she had done.

'Oh God,' she whispered, 'I've killed him. Oh God!'

'Baby,' I gasped. 'That was the best day's work you've ever done,' and I staggered past her to where Chubby lay.

He was trying to sit up, struggling feebly.

'Take it easy, Chubby,' I snapped at him, and picked up the torch. There was fresh blood on his shirt and I unbuttoned it and pulled it open around the broad brown chest.

It was low and left, but it was a lung hit. I saw the bubbles frothing from the dark hole at each breath. I have seen enough gunshot wounds to be something of an authority and I knew that this was a bad one.

He watched my face. 'How does it look?' he grunted. 'It's not sore.'

'Lovely,' I answered grimly. 'Every time you drink a beer it will run out of the hole.' He grinned crookedly, and I helped him to sit up. The exit hole was clean and neat, the FN had been loaded with solid ammunition, and it was only slightly larger than the entry hole. The bullet had not mushroomed against bone.

I found a pair of field dressings in the medical chest and bound up the wounds before I helped him into the boat. Sherry had prepared one of the mattresses and we covered him with blankets.

'Don't forget Angelo,' he whispered. I found the long heartbreaking canvas bundle where Chubby had dropped it, and I carried Angelo down and laid him in the bows.

I shoved the whaleboat out until I was waist-deep, then I scrambled over the side and started the engines. My one concern now was to get proper medical attention for Chubby, but it was a long cold run down the islands to St Mary's.

Sherry sat beside Chubby on the floorboards, doing what little she could for his comfort – while I stood in the stern between the motors and negotiated the deep-water channel before turning southwards under a sky full of cold white stars, bearing my cargo of wounded, and dying and dead.

We had been going for almost five hours when Sherry

stood up from beside the blanketed form in the bottom of the boat and made her way back to me.

'Chubby wants to talk to you,' she said quietly, and then impulsively she leaned forward and touched my cheek with the cold fingers of her uninjured hand. 'I think he is going, Harry.' And I heard the desolation in her voice.

I passed the con to her. 'You see those two bright stars,' I showed her the pointers of the Southern Cross, 'steer straight for them,' and I went forward to where Chubby lay.

For a while he did not seem to know me, and I knelt beside him and listened to the soft liquid sound of his breathing. Then at last he became aware. I saw the starlight catch his eyes and he looked up at me, and I leaned closer so that our faces were only inches apart.

'We took some good fish together, Harry,' he whispered.

'We are going to take a lot more,' I answered. 'With what we've got aboard now we will be able to buy a really good boat. You and I will be going for billfish again next season – that's for sure.'

Then we were silent for a long time, until at last I felt his hand grope for mine and I took it and held it hard. I could feel the callouses and the ancient line burns from handling heavy fish.

'Harry,' his voice was so faint I could just hear it over the sound of the motors when I laid my ear to his lips, 'Harry, I'm going to tell you something I never told you before. I love you, man,' he whispered. 'I love you better than my own brother.'

'I love you too, Chubby,' I said, and for a little longer his grip was strong again, and then it relaxed. I sat on beside him while slowly that big horny paw turned cold in my hands, and dawn began to pale the sky above the dark and brooding sea.

During the next three weeks, Sherry and I seldom left the sanctuary of Turtle Bay. We went together to stand awkwardly in the graveyard while they buried our friends, and once I drove alone to the fort and spent two hours with President Godfrey Biddle and Inspector Wally Andrews – but the rest of that time we were alone while the wounds healed.

Our bodies healed more quickly than did our minds. One morning as I dressed Sherry's hand, I noticed the pearly white seeds in the healing flesh of her fingertips and I realized that they were the nail roots regrowing. She would have fingernails once more to grace those long narrow hands – I was thankful for that.

They were not happy days, the memories were too fresh and the days were dark with mourning for Chubby and Angelo and both of us knew that the crisis of our relationship was at hand. I guessed what agonies of decision she must be facing, and I forgave her the quick flares of temper, the long sullen silences – and her sudden disappearances from the shack when for hours at a time she walked the long deserted beaches or made a remote and lonely figure sitting out on the headland of the bay.

At last I knew that she was strong enough to face what lay ahead for both of us. One evening I raised the subject of the treasure for the first time since our return to St Mary's.

It lay now buried beneath the raised foundations of the shack. Sherry listened quietly as we sat together upon the veranda, drinking whisky and listening to the sound of the night surf upon the beach.

'I want you to go ahead to make the arrangements for the arrival of the coffin. Hire a car in Zürich and drive down to Basle. I have arranged a room for you at the Red Ox Hotel there. I have picked that hotel because they have an underground parking garage and I know the head porter there. His name is Max.' I explained my plans to her. 'He will arrange a hearse to meet the plane. You will play the part of the bereaved widow and bring the coffin down to Basle. We will make the exchange in the garage, and you will arrange for my banker to have an armoured car to take the tiger's head to his own premises from there.'

'You've got it all worked out, haven't you?'

'I hope so.' I poured another whisky. 'My bank is Falle et Fils and the man to ask for is M. Challon. When you meet him you will give him my name and the number of my account – ten sixty-six, the same as the battle of Hastings. You must arrange with M. Challon for a private room to which we can invite dealers to view the head—' I went on explaining in detail the arrangements I had made, and she listened intently. Now and then she asked a question but mostly she was silent, and at last I produced the air ticket and a thin sheaf of traveller's cheques to carry her through.

'You have made the reservations already?' she looked startled, and when I nodded she thumbed open the booklet of the air ticket. 'When do I leave?'

'On the noon plane tomorrow.'

'And when will you follow?'

'On the same plane as the coffin, three days later – on Friday. I will come in on the BOAC flight at 1.30 p.m. That will give you time to make the arrangements and be there to meet me.'

That night was as tender and loving as it had ever been, but even so I sensed a deeper mood of melancholia in Sherry – as at the time of leave-taking and farewell.

In the dawn, the dolphins met us at the entrance of the bay, and we romped with them for half the morning and then swam in slowly to the beach.

I drove her out to the airport in the old pick-up. For most of the ride she was silent and then she tried to tell me something, but she was confused and she did not make sense. She ended lamely, '—if anything ever happens to us, well, I mean nothing lasts for ever, does it—'

'Go on,' I said.

'No, it's nothing. Just that we should try to forgive each other – if anything does happen.' That was all she would say, and at the airport barrier she kissed me briefly and clung for a second with both arms about my neck, then she turned and walked quickly to the waiting aircraft. She did not look back or wave as she climbed the boarding ladder.

I watched the aircraft climb swiftly and head out across the inshore channel for the mainland, then I drove slowly back to Turtle Bay.

It was a lonely place without her, and that night as I lay alone under the mosquito net on the wide bed, I knew that the risk I was about to take was necessary. Highly dangerous, but necessary. I knew I must have her back here. Without her, it would all be tasteless. I must gamble on the pull I would be able to exert over her outweighing the other forces that governed her. I must let her make the choice herself, but I must try to influence it with every play in my power.

In the morning I drove into St Mary's and after Fred Coker and I had argued and consulted and passed money and promises back and forth, he opened the double doors to his warehouse and I drove the pick-up in beside the hearse. We loaded one of his best coffins, teak with silver-gilt handles, and red velvet-lined interior, into the back of the truck. I covered it with a sheet of canvas and drove back to Turtle Bay. When I had packed the coffin and screwed down the lid it weighed almost five hundred pounds.

When it was dark, I drove back into town and it was almost closing time at the Lord Nelson before I had completed my arrangements. I had just time for a quick drink and then I drove back to Turtle Bay to pack my battered old canvas campaign bag.

At the noon of the next day, twenty-four hours earlier than I had arranged with Sherry North, I boarded the aircraft for the mainland and that evening caught the BOAC connection onwards from Nairobi.

There was no one to meet me at Zürich airport, for I was a full day early, and I passed quickly through customs and immigration and went out into the vast arrivals hall.

I checked my luggage before I went about tidying up the final loose threads of my plan. I found a flight outwards leaving at 1.20 the following day which suited my timing admirably. I made a single reservation, then I drifted over to the inquiries desk and waited until the pretty little blonde girl in the Swissair uniform was not busy, before engaging her in a long explanation. At first she was adamant, but I gave her the old crinkled eyes and smiled that way, until at last she became intrigued with it all – and giggled in anticipation.

'You sure you'll be on duty tomorrow?' I asked anxiously.

'Yes, Monsieur, don't worry, I will be here.'

We parted as friends and I retrieved my bag and caught a cab to the Zürich Holiday Inn just down the road. The same hotel where I had sweated out the survival of the Dutch policeman so long ago. I ordered a drink, took a bath and then settled down in front of the television set. It brought back memories.

A little before noon the following day I sat at the airport café pretending to read a copy of the *Frankfurter Allgemeine Zeitung* and watching the arrivals hall over the top of the page. I had already checked my baggage and my ticket. All I had to do was to go through into the final departure lounge.

I was wearing a new suit purchased that morning of such

a bizarre cut and mousy shade of grey, that no one who knew him could believe that Harry Fletcher would be seen in public wearing it. It was two sizes too large for me, and I had padded myself with hotel towels to alter my shape entirely. I had also self-barbered my hair into a short and ragged style and dusted it with talcum powder to put fifteen years on my age. When I peered at my image through gold-rimmed spectacles in the mirror of the men's room, I did not even recognize myself.

At seven minutes past one, Sherry North walked in through the main doors of the terminal. She wore a suit of grey checked wool, a full length black leather coat and a small matching leather hat with a narrow businesslike brim. Her eyes were screened by a pair of dark glasses, but her expression was set and determined as she strode through the crowd of tourists.

I felt the sick slide and churn of my guts as I saw all my suspicions and fears confirmed and the newspaper shook in my hands. Following a pace behind and to her side, was the small neatly dressed figure of the man she had introduced to me as Uncle Dan. He wore a tweed cap and carried an overcoat across his arm. More than ever he exuded an air of awareness, the hunter's alert and confident tread as he followed the girl.

He had four of his men with him. They moved quietly after him, quiet, soberly dressed men with closed watchful faces.

'Oh, you little bitch,' I whispered, but I wondered why I should feel so bitter. I had known for long enough now.

The group of girl and five men stopped in the centre of the hall and I watched dear Uncle Dan issuing his orders. He was a professional, you could see that in the way he staked out the hall for me. He placed his men to cover the arrivals gate and every exit.

Sherry North stood listening quietly, her face neutral

385

and her eyes hidden by the glasses. Once Uncle Dan spoke to her and she nodded abruptly, then when the four strong-arm men had been placed, the two of them stood together facing the arrivals gate.

'Get out now, Harry,' the little warning voice urged me. 'Don't play fancy games. This is the wolf pack all over again. Run, Harry, run.'

Just then the public address system called the outward flight on which I had made a reservation the previous day. I stood up from the table in my cheap baggy suit and shuffled across to the Inquiries Desk. The little blonde Swissair hostess did not recognize me at first, then her mouth dropped open and her eyes flew wide. She covered her mouth with her hand and her eyes sparkled with conspiratory glee.

'The end booth,' she whispered, 'the end nearest the departures gate.' I winked at her and shuffled away. In the telephone booth I lifted the receiver and pretended to be speaking, but I broke the connection with a finger on the bar and I watched the hall through the glass door.

I heard my accomplice paging.

'Miss Sherry North, will Miss North please report to the inquiries desk.'

Through the glass I saw Sherry approach the desk and speak with the hostess. The blonde girl pointed to the booth beside mine and Sherry turned and walked directly towards me. She was screened from Uncle Dan and his merry men by the row of booths.

The leather coat swung gracefully about her long legs, and her hair was glossy black and bouncing on her shoulders at each stride. I saw she wore black leather gloves to hide her injured hand, and I thought she had never looked so beautiful as in this moment of my betrayal.

She entered the booth beside me and lifted the receiver. Swiftly I replaced my own telephone and stepped out of the booth. As I opened her door she looked around with impatient annoyance.

'Okay, you dumb cop – give me a good reason why I shouldn't break your head,' I said.

'You!' Her expression crumpled, and her hand flew to her mouth. We stared at each other.

'What happened to the real Sherry North?' I demanded, and the question seemed to steady her.

'She was killed. We found her body – almost unrecognizable – in a quarry outside Ascot.'

'Manny Resnick told me he had killed her—' I said. 'I didn't believe him. He also laughed at me when I went on board to do a deal with him and Suleiman Dada for your life. I called you Sherry North and he laughed at me and called me a fool.' I grinned at her lopsidedly. 'He was right – wasn't he? I was a fool.'

She was silent then, unable to meet my eyes. I went on talking, confirming what I had guessed.

'So after Sherry North was killed, they decided not to announce her identity – but to stake out the North cottage. Hoping that the killers would return to investigate the new arrival – or that some other patsy would be sucked in and lead them home. They chose you for the stake-out, because you were a trained police diver. That's right, isn't it?'

She nodded, still not looking at me.

'They should have made sure you knew something about conchology as well. Then you wouldn't have grabbed that piece of fire coral – and saved me a lot of trouble.'

She was over the first shock of my appearance. Now was the time to whistle for Uncle Dan and his men, if she was going to. She remained silent, her face half-turned away, her cheek flushed with bright blood beneath the dark golden tan.

'That first night, you telephoned when you thought I was asleep. You were reporting to your superior officer that

387

a sucker had walked in. They told you to play me along. And – oh baby – how you played me.'

She looked at me at last, dark blue eyes snapping with defiance, words seemed to boil behind her closed lips, but she held them back and I went on.

'That's why you used the back entrance to Jimmy's shop, to avoid the neighbours who knew Sherry. That's why those two goons of Manny's arrived to roast your fingers on the gas-ring. They wanted to find out who you were – because you sure as hell weren't Sherry North. They had killed her.'

I wanted her to speak now. Her silence was wearing my nerves.

'What rank is Uncle Dan – Inspector?'

'Chief Inspector,' she said.

'I had him tabbed the moment I laid eyes on him.'

'If you knew all this, then why did you go through with it?' she demanded.

'I was suspicious at first – but by the time I knew for certain I was crazy stupid in love with you.'

She braced herself, as though I had struck her, and I went on remorselessly.

'I thought by some of the things we did together that you felt pretty good about me. In my book when you love someone, you don't sell them down the river.'

'I'm a policewoman,' she flashed at me, 'and you're a killer.'

'I never killed a man who wasn't trying to kill me first,' I flashed back, 'just the way you hit Suleiman Dada.'

That caught her off-balance. She stammered and looked about her as if she were in a trap.

'You're a thief,' she attacked again.

'Yes,' I agreed. 'I was once – but that was a long time ago, and since then I worked hard on it. With a bit of help, I'd have made it.'

388

'The throne—' she went on, 'you are stealing the throne.'

'No, ma'am,' I grinned at her.

'What is in the coffin then?'

'Three hundred pounds of beach sand from Turtle Bay. When you see it, think of the times we had there.'

'The throne – where is it?'

'With its rightful owner, the representative of the people of St Mary's, President Godfrey Biddle.'

'You gave it up?' she stared at me with disbelief that faded slowly as something else began to dawn in her eyes. 'Why, Harry, why?'

'Like I said, I'm working hard on it.' Again we were staring hard at each other, and suddenly I saw the clear liquid flooding her dark blue eyes.

'And you came here – knowing what I had to do?' she asked, her voice choking.

'I wanted you to make a choice,' I said, and she let the tears cling like dewdrops in the thick dark eyelashes. I went on deliberately, 'I'm going to walk out of this booth and go out through that gate. If nobody blows the whistle I will be on the next flight out of here and the day after tomorrow, I will swim out through the reef to look for the dolphins.'

'They'll come after you, Harry,' she said, and I shook my head.

'President Biddle has just altered his extradition agreements. Nobody will be able to touch me on St Mary's. I have his word for it.'

I turned and opened the door of the booth. 'I'm going to be lonely as all hell out there at Turtle Bay.'

I turned my back on her then and walked slowly and deliberately to the departures gate, just as they called my flight for the second time. It was the longest and scariest walk of my entire life, and my heart thumped in time to my footsteps. Nobody challenged me and I dared not look back.

389

As I settled into the seat of the Swissair Caravelle and fastened my seat belt, I wondered how long it would take her to screw up her nerve enough to follow me out to St Mary's, and I reflected that there was much I still had to tell her.

I had to tell her that I had contracted to raise the rest of the golden throne from Gunfire Break for the benefit of the people of St Mary's. In return President Godfrey Biddle had undertaken to buy me a new deep-sea boat from the proceeds – just like *Wave Dancer* – a token of the people's gratitude.

I would be able to keep my lady in the style to which I was accustomed, and of course there was always the case of Georgian silver gilt plate buried behind the shack at Turtle Bay for the lean and hungry off season. I hadn't reformed *that* much. There would be no more night runs, however.

As the Caravelle took off and climbed steeply up over the blue lakes and forested mountains, I realized that I did not even know her real name.

That would be the first thing I would ask her when I met her at the airport of St Mary's island – Pearl of the Indian Ocean.

GOLDEN FOX

This book is dedicated to
Danielle Antoinette,
who transformed my life into
a joyous adventure

A cloud of butterflies rose into the sunlight, the breeze smeared them across the summer sky and a hundred thousand young faces shining with wonder turned upwards to watch them drift overhead.

In the forefront of that vast concourse sat a girl, the girl that he had been stalking for ten days now. A hunter studying his prey, he had come to know with a peculiar intimacy her every gesture and movement, the turn and lift of her head as something caught her attention, the way she cocked it to listen, or tossed it in annoyance or impatience. Now in a new attitude she lifted her face to the glorious cloud of winged insects, and even at this distance he could see the sparkle of her teeth, and her lips formed a soft pink 'O' of wonder.

On the high stage above her the figure in the white satin shirt held up yet another box and, laughing, shook from it a fresh burst of fluttering wings. Yellow and white and iridescent, they bore aloft, and the crowd gasped and 'oohed' afresh.

One of the butterflies toppled and dived; and, though a hundred hands were held out to catch it, it swerved and wobbled down to alight at last on the girl's upturned face. Even above the swelling murmur of the crowd, he heard the girl's happy cry of laughter, and he found himself smiling in sympathy with her.

She reached up to where it sat on her forehead and took it gently, almost reverently, in the cup of her hands. For a moment she held it close to her face, studying it with those indigo-blue eyes that he had come to know so well. Her expression was suddenly wistful, and her lips moved as she whispered to it, but he could not hear the words.

Her sadness was fleeting, and then those lovely lips smiled again and she leapt to her feet and held both hands high above her head, standing on tiptoe. The butterfly hesitated,

7

perched on her outstretched fingertips, pulsing its wings softly on the point of flight, and he heard her voice.

'Fly! Fly for me!' And those around her took up the cry. 'Fly! Fly for peace!'

For a moment she had usurped the limelight, and all eyes were fastened on her rather than on the flamboyant single figure in the centre of the stage.

She was tall and lithe, her bare limbs tanned and glowing with health. She wore her skirt so short, in the fashion of the day, that as she reached upwards the hem rose high above the circular creases where her cocky little buttocks joined her thighs in a froth of white lace.

For a moment, poised like that, she seemed to epitomize her generation, wild and free and fey, and he sensed the instant accord of spirit of all those who watched her. Even the man on the stage leant forward to see her better, and his lips, thick and livid as though stung by bees, split in a smile and he called out: 'Peace!' And his voice was magnified a thousand times by the great banks of amplifiers that rose high on each side of the stage.

The butterfly flew from her hands, and she pressed all her fingers to her lips and blew a wide kiss after it as it fluttered aloft and was lost in the swirling cloud of insects.

The girl sank down on to the grass, and those seated close to her reached out to touch and embrace her.

On the stage Mick Jagger held his arms wide, commanding silence. Once he had it, he spoke into the microphone. Distorted by the amplifiers, his voice was slurred and incoherent; his accent so thick that the watcher could barely understand the stumbling tribute he read out to the member of his band, who only days previously had drowned in a swimming-pool during a wild weekend party.

The whisper was that the victim had been almost comatose with drugs when he entered the water. It was a hero's death, for this was the age of drugs and sexual excess, of pot and Pill, of freedom and peace and overdosing.

Jagger ended his little speech. It had been so brief that it had not dulled the buoyant mood of the gathering. The electric guitars struck a discord, and Jagger hurled himself into 'Honky Tonk Women' with every fibre of his being. Within seconds he had a hundred thousand hearts racing in time to his, a hundred thousand young bodies jerking and pulsing, and two hundred thousand arms held high, swaying like a field of wheat in a high wind.

The music was cosmic, brutal as an artillery bombardment; painful to the ear, it penetrated the skull and seemed to numb and crush the brain. Swiftly it reduced the audience to a mindless frenzy, transformed the multitude into a single organism, like a gigantic amoeba that throbbed and undulated in the act of reproduction, fraught with a passion that was overtly sexual; and from it rose the stench of dust and sweat, the sickly odour of cannabis smoke and the heady overpowering musk of young bodies physically aroused.

The watcher was alone in the midst of the throng, isolated and detached, unmoved by the blasts of sound that swept over him. He studied the girl, awaiting his moment.

She swayed to the primeval rhythm, moved in time to the bodies that pressed close about her, but with a singular grace that set her apart. Her hair was glistening jet with highlights of ruby that glinted in the sun, piled on top of her head; but thick tresses of it had come down in smoky coils, enhancing the elegant line of her neck and the set of her head upon it, like a tulip on its stem.

Directly below the stage, an area had been cordoned off with a low picket fence, a tiny enclave for a privileged few. Marianne Faithfull, in a flowing caftan but with bare feet, sat here with the other wives and camp-followers. Her beauty was remote and ethereal. Her eyes seemed dreamy and sightless as those of a blind woman, and her movements slow and somnolent. Children crawled about her feet, and they were guarded and protected by a phalanx of Hell's Angels.

In black Wehrmacht steel helmets, hung with chains and Nazi iron crosses, chest hair curling out from under gilets of black leather studded with silver metal, steel-shod motor-cycle boots, arms covered with intricate tattoos, they struck menacing poses, arms akimbo, billy-clubs in their belts, and their clenched fists heavy with sharp-edged steel rings. They surveyed the crowd with brooding insolent stares, watching for trouble, hoping for trouble.

The music pounded on and on, an hour and then another, the heat built up, and the smell of humanity was like that of an animal-cage, for some of the audience, both men and women, hemmed in and reluctant to miss a moment of it, had urinated where they sat.

The watcher was disgusted by the decadence, by the wild abandon and the gross indulgence of it all. It offended everything that he believed in. His eyes felt gritty and sensitive, and his head ached, throbbing in time to the driving rhythm of the guitars. It was time to leave. Another day wasted, another day spent waiting for the opportunity that never came. However, he was a hunter with all the patience of the predator. There would be other days; he was in no hurry. The moment must be exactly right for his purpose.

He began to move, working his way across the low knoll where he had stood through the dense throng of bodies, shouldering through them; they were in such a mesmeric trance that they seemed neither to see nor to feel him push past them.

He glanced back, and his eyes narrowed as he saw the girl speak to the boy beside her, smile and shake her head in response to his reply and rise to her feet. Then she also began to work her way through the crowd, stepping over the seated ranks, steadying herself with a hand on a shoulder, laughing an apology as she went.

The watcher changed direction, angling down the gentle slope to intercept her, the hunter's instinct warning him that unexpectedly the moment for which he had waited had arrived.

Behind the stage were the television-trucks, row upon row of them, each as tall as a double-decker bus, parked so close together that there were only inches between them.

The girl moved back, circling the low picket fence, working her way around the side of the stage trying to get clear of the throng; but it was so dense that it blocked her further progress, and her expression was desperate as she glanced around her, caught in the press of bodies.

Suddenly she turned directly towards the fence, pushed her way to it, and then with a swift athletic bound jumped over it and scuttled into the narrow space between two of the high television-trucks. One of the Hell's Angels saw her dart away into the forbidden area, and he shouted and followed her at a run, twisting his shoulders to squeeze into the narrow passage down which she had disappeared; and, as he turned, the watcher had a flash of the grin on his face.

It took the watcher almost two minutes to force his way to the point on the fence where the girl had crossed. Somebody reached out to stop him, but he struck the hand away and went over it, and slipped into the space between the high steel sides of the parked trucks.

He moved sideways, the gap too narrow to accommodate the width of his shoulders, and he was level with the door of the driver's cab when he heard the muffled cries of protest just ahead of him. The sound spurred him, and as he came around the side of the bonnet, he checked for an instant as he took in what was happening just in front of him.

The Hell's Angel had caught the girl, and now he had her held against the front wing of the truck. He had one of her arms twisted up behind her back, at almost the level of her shoulder-blades. She was facing him, but he pressed her backwards against the steel wing with his hips and his pot belly. He bent over her, trying to reach her mouth with his. The girl's back was arched, and she rolled her head violently from side to side trying to avoid his mouth. He was laughing, his mouth wide open, flicking his tongue out at her, trying to force it into her mouth.

With his right hand he had hoisted the tiny skirt up to her waist, and his hairy fingers, stained with motor-cycle grease, were hooked into the waistband of her lace panties. The girl was striking and clawing at him with her free hand, but he hunched his shoulders so that she could not reach his face with her nails, and her blows fell on studded black leather and on thick shoulders padded with muscle and fat. The

Angel's laughter was thick and guttural, and the lace of her panties tore with a sharp crackling sound as he forced them over her hips and down the smooth tanned thighs.

The watcher stepped forward and touched the Angel's shoulder, and the man froze and twisted his head round. His eyes were glazed, but they cleared instantly and he flung the girl sideways so viciously that she sprawled on the torn muddy grass between the trucks. The Angel reached for the club in his belt.

The watcher reached out and touched him again, under the ear, just below the rim of his steel helmet. He pressed with two fingers, and the Angel froze and stiffened; all his limbs went rigid, and he made a glottal cawing sound deep in his throat, his entire body convulsed and he collapsed in a heap and, like an epileptic, lay twitching and jerking spasmodically. The girl was on her knees, pulling up her torn underclothes, and watching in fascinated horror. The watcher stepped over the sprawling Angel and lifted the girl to her feet without apparent effort.

'Come,' he said softly. 'Before his friends arrive.'

Swiftly he led her away by the hand, and she followed as trustingly as a child.

Beyond the parked trucks was a maze of narrow pathways through the rhododendron bushes. As they ran down one of these paths, she asked breathlessly: 'Did you kill him?'

'No.' He did not even glance round. 'He'll be on his feet again in less than five minutes.'

'You flattened him. How did you do that? You hardly touched him.'

He did not answer, but round the next bend in the path he stopped and turned back to face her.

'Are you all right?' he asked, and she nodded jerkily without speaking.

He studied her, still holding her hand. He knew she was twenty-four years old, a young woman who had just experienced a violent attempted rape, but the gaze of her dark blue eyes was level and appraising. There were no tears, no hysterics, not even a tremor of those pink lips, and the hand in his was slim and firm and warm.

The psychiatrist's report on her which he had studied had been correct in at least this much: she was resilient and self-assured; already she was almost fully recovered from the attack. Then he saw the colour mount softly in her cheeks and at the base of her long elegant throat, and her breath quickened perceptibly. She was experiencing another strong emotion.

'What's your name?' she asked, her eyes fastened on his with an intensity which he recognized. Women, on first encounter, usually looked at him like that.

'Ramón,' he replied.

'Ramón,' she repeated softly, relishing the sound of it. God, he was beautiful. 'Ramón who?'

'You won't believe it if I tell you.' His English was perfect, too perfect. He must be foreign, but the voice matched his face, beautiful, deep and grave.

'Try me,' she invited, and heard the catch in her own voice.

'Ramón de Santiago y Machado.' He made it sound like music; it was impossibly romantic. It was the most beautiful name she had ever heard, perfect for that face and voice.

'We must go,' he said, while she still stared at him.

'I can't run,' she said. 'Don't make me run.'

'If you don't, you might end up as a mascot on the handlebars of a motor-cycle.'

She laughed, and then bit her lower lip to stop herself.

'Don't do that,' she protested. 'Don't make me laugh. I need a loo. My condition is critical.'

'Ah, so that's where you were headed when Prince Charming fell in love with you.'

'I warned you, don't do that.' With an effort she smothered her giggle, and he took pity on her.

'There is a public loo at the gate to the park. Can you make it that far?'

'I don't know.'

'The alternative is the rhododendrons.'

'No, thanks. No more public performances today.'

'Let's go, then.' He took her arm.

They skirted the Serpentine, and Ramón glanced back. 'Your boyfriend's ardour must have cooled,' he said. 'No sign of him. What a fickle fellow.'

'Pity. I'd love to watch you do that trick of yours again. How much further is it?'

'Here it is.' They had reached the gate, and she dropped his arm and started for the small red-brick building that nestled discreetly in the shrubbery beside the path; but at the door she hesitated.

'My name is Isabella, Isabella Courtney, but my friends call me Bella,' she said over her shoulder, and darted through the doorway.

'Yes,' he murmured softly, 'I know.'

Even while she was in the cubicle she could hear the music, barely muted by the distance and the brick walls, and then the clatter of a helicopter passing low over the roof, but it was unimportant. She was thinking about Ramón.

At the washbasins she studied herself in the mirror. Her hair was a mess; she tidied it quickly. Ramón's hair was thick and dark and wavy. He wore it long, but not too long. She wiped off her pale pink lipstick on a Kleenex and then re-painted her mouth. Ramón's mouth was full but masculine, soft but strong; she wondered how it would taste.

She dropped the lipstick back into her bag and leant close to the mirror to appraise her own eyes. They didn't need drops. The whites were so clear they had a bluish sheen, like those of a healthy baby. She knew her eyes were her best feature, that Courtney blue, something between cornflower and sapphire. Ramón's eyes were green. They were the first thing that had struck her about him. That clear startling green, beautiful but – she searched for the adjective – beautiful but deadly. That was it exactly. She didn't need the demonstration that had felled the Hell's Angel. One look at those eyes and she had known he was a dangerous man. She felt the back of her neck prickle with a delicious thrill of fear and of anticipation. Perhaps this was the one, at last. Beside his image all the others seemed to pale and fade. Perhaps this was the one she had searched for so long.

'Ramón de Santiago y Machado.' She said it in a throaty purr, savouring the taste of it in her mouth, watching her own lips form the words. Then she straightened up and turned to the doorway. She prevented herself from hurrying. Slowly, languidly, on the tall stiletto heels that made her hips roll as she walked and her bottom swing like a metronome, lace flashing under the abbreviated skirt, she went to the door.

She pouted slightly and let her long thick eyelashes droop over the blue as she stepped out into the slanting golden sunlight and she stopped dead.

He was gone. She caught her breath and felt the cold quick slide of her stomach as though she had swallowed a stone. She looked around her in disbelief. 'Ramón,' she said uncertainly, and ran into the pathway. There were hundreds of others coming down the tarmac path towards her, the first escapees from the concert trying to avoid the human avalanche that would soon follow, but none of them was the elegant figure she sought.

'Ramón,' she said, and hurried to the park gates. The traffic boomed down the Bayswater Road, and she looked frantically right and left. She was overcome with a sense of disbelief. He had gone and left her. It was beyond her experience. She had shown him that she wanted him – she couldn't possibly have made it plainer – and he had walked away.

Her next emotion was outrage. Nobody did that to Isabella Courtney, not ever. She felt slighted and insulted and very angry.

'Damn him,' she said. 'Damn the man.'

Her anger lasted only seconds, and then it slumped. She felt lost and bereft. It was an alien sensation for her.

'He can't just leave like that,' she said aloud, and recognized in her own voice the self-pitying whine of a spoilt child, so she said it again differently, trying to recapture her anger, but it was unconvincing.

Behind her, she heard a shout of raucous laughter and she glanced back. A bunch of Hell's Angels was swaggering down the pathway, still a hundred yards away but coming directly towards her. She couldn't remain here.

The concert was over, the crowds were breaking up. The helicopter she had heard must have come in to pick up Jagger and his Rolling Stones. There was little chance of her rejoining her friends now; they would be lost in the multitude. She looked around her just once more, swiftly but despairingly. Still no sign of that dark wavy head of hair. She tossed her own head and lifted her chin.

'Who needs him anyway, damned dago?' she muttered furiously, and struck out down the pavement.

Behind her there was a chorus of whistles and catcalls, and someone, one of the Angels, began calling the step for her. 'Left, right, left – shake, rattle and roll.'

She knew that her high heels were making her bottom waggle furiously. She hopped on one foot and then the other as she pulled off her shoes and then fled barefoot down the pavement. She had left her car at the embassy carpark in the Strand, so she had to take the Tube from Lancaster Gate station to reach it.

Her car was a brand-new Mini-Cooper, the very latest 1969 model. Daddy had given it to her for her birthday, and had had it customized for her by the same body shop that had done Antony Armstrong-Jones's Mini. They had souped up its engine, upholstered it in white Connolly leather like a Rolls and resprayed it the same glitter silver as Daddy's new Aston Martin with her initials in gold leaf on the door. All the swinging set were driving Minis; there were more of them than Rollses or Bentleys parked outside Annabel's on a Saturday night.

Bella threw her shoes into the tiny back seat and revved the engine until the needle went into the red; the tyres squealed and left black smears on the ramp of the carpark.

As she glanced back at them in the rear-view mirror it gave her a dark satanic pleasure.

She drove with abandon, protected from the wrath of the Metropolitan Police by her diplomatic plates. She wasn't really entitled to them, but Daddy had wangled them for her.

She beat her own record back to Highveld, the ambassador's residence in Chelsea, and Daddy's official Bentley with its pennants on the wings was parked at the entrance and Klonkie, the chauffeur, grinned and saluted her. Daddy had brought most of his own staff from Cape Town.

Bella controlled her mood long enough to give Klonkie her sweetest smile and toss him the keys. 'Put my car away for me, there's a dear, Klonkie.' Daddy was tremendously strict about the way she treated the servants. She could take her moods out on anyone but them. 'They are part of the family, Bella.' And most of them had indeed been at Weltevreden, the family home at the Cape of Good Hope, since before she was born.

Daddy was at his desk in his study on the ground floor overlooking the garden. He had discarded his coat and tie, and the desk-top was piled with official documents, but he tossed down his pen and swivelled his chair towards her as she came in. His face lit up at the sight of her.

Bella dropped into his lap and kissed him. 'God,' she murmured, 'you are the most beautiful man in the world.'

'Far be it from me to question your good judgement,' Shasa Courtney smiled, 'but may I ask what has brought this on?'

'Men are either boars or bores,' she said. 'All except you, of course.'

'Ah! And what has young Roger done to arouse your ire? To me, he seemed fairly inoffensive, if not actually insipid.'

Roger was the one who had escorted her to the concert. She had left him on the crowded lawn in front of the stage, but now it took her a moment to remember him.

17

'I'm off men for life,' Isabella declared. 'I shall probably hie me to a nunnery.'

'Could you possibly eschew holy orders at least until tomorrow? I do need a hostess for dinner this evening, and we haven't yet arranged the seating.'

'All done, long ago,' she said. 'Before I left for the concert.'

'The menu?'

'Chef and I settled that last Friday. Don't panic, Papa. All your favourites: Coquilles St Jacques and lamb from Camdeboo.' Shasa served only lamb reared on his own farms in the Karoo. The desert scrub gave the flesh a distinctive herby flavour. All the embassy beef came from his extensive ranches in Rhodesia, and the wines from the vineyards of Weltevreden where for the last twenty years Shasa's German winemaker had laboured with rare skill and dedication to raise the quality of the vintage to the point where now Shasa would back it against nearly any of the second *crus* of Burgundy. His ambition was still to make a wine that would compare with some of the great and noble houses of the Côte d'Or.

When it came to transporting this fare from the Cape of Good Hope to London, Courtney shipping lines ran a weekly refrigerated vessel on the Atlantic route.

' . . . *and* I picked up your dinner-jacket from the cleaner's this morning, *and* I had Budds in Piccadilly Arcade make you three more dress-shirts and a dozen new eye-patches. Your others were all getting so tatty. I've thrown them out.'

Still sitting in his lap, she adjusted his eye-patch. Shasa had lost his left eye flying Hurricanes against the Italians in Abyssinia during the Second World War. The black silk eye-patch gave him a dashing piratical air.

Now Shasa smiled complacently. When he had first invited Bella to come to London with him, she had only recently turned twenty-one years of age, and he had thought long and hard before foisting the onerous task of official embassy hostess on to one so young. He need not have worried. After all, she had been trained by her grandmother. Added to which they had brought the chef and butler and half the staff from the Cape with them, so she started with her own highly trained team.

In three years, Isabella had built up a reputation in the diplomatic circle, and her invitations were sought after, except by those embassies whose countries no longer maintained relations with South Africa.

'Do you want me to cover for you while you sneak off with your Israeli pal for half an hour after dinner to build an atom bomb?'

'Bella!' Shasa frowned quickly. 'You know I don't like remarks like that.'

'Joke, Daddy. There is nobody to hear us.'

'Even in private and in fun, Bella.' Shasa shook his head severely. That had been uncomfortably close to the truth. The Israeli military attaché and Shasa had been involved in a courtship dance for almost a year now, and they had gone far beyond the stage of flirtation already.

She kissed him, and his expression softened. 'I must go and bath.' She stood up from his lap. 'The invitations are for eight-thirty. I'll come and do your tie for you at ten past.' Shasa had tied his own bow for forty years, until Isabella had decided that he was incapable of doing so.

Shasa's eyes dropped to her legs. 'If your skirts get any shorter, mademoiselle, your belly-button will be winking at the moon.'

'You really must try not to be an old fogey. It's most unbecoming in one of the swingingest papas of the twentieth century.' She headed for the door, deliberately accentuating the movement of her lower body under the offending article of clothing, and Shasa sighed as the door closed.

'That's a load of dynamite with a very short fuse,' he murmured. 'Perhaps, in a way, it's a good thing that we are going home.'

In September, Shasa's three-year ambassadorial stint would be up. Isabella would once more go under the control and discipline of Centaine Courtney-Malcomess, her grandmother. Shasa realized that his own efforts in that direction had been less than totally successful, and he would hand over the responsibility with relief.

Thinking of their imminent return to Cape Town, Shasa glanced back at the papers on his desk. The years in the London embassy had been a political penance for him. When the prime minister, Hendrik Verwoerd, had been assassinated in 1966, Shasa had made a serious miscalculation and backed the wrong man to succeed to the premiership. The result of that mistake had been that once John Vorster had become prime minister, Shasa had been shunted into this political backwater; but, as so many times before, he had turned disaster into triumph.

Using all his gifts and natural abilities, his shrewd business acumen, his presence and good looks, his charm and powers of persuasion, he had done much to deflect from his homeland the building wrath and contempt of the world, particularly that of Britain's Labour government and her Commonwealth, most of whose members were nations headed by black or Asian premiers. John Vorster had taken these achievements into account. Before leaving South Africa, Shasa had been intimately concerned with Armscor, and Vorster had offered him the job of chairman of Armscor on his return home.

Armscor was, put simply, the largest industrial undertaking that had ever existed on the African continent. It was the country's answer to the arms boycott, begun by America's President Dwight Eisenhower and now being extended rapidly by other nations in an attempt to leave South Africa defenceless and vulnerable. Armscor – Armaments Development and Production Company – was the entire defence industry of the country under single management, state-sponsored to the extent of billions upon billions of dollars.

It was an enormous and exciting challenge, especially since the multifarious companies that made up the Courtney financial and business empire were being well managed. During the three years of his ambassadorial duties, Shasa had allowed the management and control to pass gradually, in an orderly fashion, into the hands of his son Garry Courtney. Garry was making an amazing success of it for one so young; but, then, Shasa had not been much older when he had become chairman of Courtney Enterprises.

Then, again, Garry had the day-to-day backing of his grandmother, Centaine Courtney-Malcomess, the founder and dowager empress of the empire. He also had, working under him, the management team of experts that Centaine and Shasa between them had meticulously assembled over the previous forty years.

This in no way detracted from Garry's achievements, not least of which was the fashion in which he had steered them all through the recent collapse of the Johannesburg Stock Exchange which had stripped up to sixty per cent of the value off some share prices. In some remarkable fashion that would have done credit to either Shasa or Centaine, Garry had anticipated the end of the wild bull run that had preceded the collapse. Far from being damaged or destroyed, Courtney Enterprises had come through the ordeal even more powerful and cash-liquid, and in a better position to take advantage of the bargains that the market was now offering.

No – Shasa smiled and shook his head – Garry was doing great things, and it would be bitterly unfair to come in above him again. However, Shasa was still a young man, not much over fifty years of age. When he got home he would need something to keep his wits sharp and his juices flowing. The Armscor job was perfect.

Of course, he would keep his seat on the Courtney board, but he could devote most of his time and energy to Armscor. Many of the subcontracts could be steered in the direction of the Courtney companies. Both enterprises might benefit enormously from this mutual association, and Shasa would have the additional pleasure and comfort of warming his patriotic ardour at the fire of capitalistic rewards.

Isabella's remark that he had objected to earlier was directly related to his new appointment. He had used his diplomatic connections with the Israeli embassy to initiate and then pursue the idea of a joint nuclear project between the two states. Tonight he would be handing over another batch of documents to the Israeli attaché to be forwarded in the diplomatic bag to Tel Aviv.

He glanced at his wristwatch. He still had twenty minutes before he must go up to change for dinner, and he switched all his concentration back to the papers in front of him.

*   *   *

Nanny had laid out the Zandra Rhodes couture model and run Isabella's bath.

'You are late, Miss Bella. And I still have to do your hair.' She was a Cape Coloured, her Hottentot blood mixed with that of most of the world's seafaring nations.

'Don't fuss so, Nanny,' Isabella protested, but Nanny swept her off to the bathroom with as little ceremony as she had when Isabella was five years old.

While Isabella sank with a luxurious sigh chin-deep into the steaming foam, Nanny gathered up her discarded clothes.

'Your dress is stained with grass, child, and your new panties are torn. What you been up to?' Nanny washed all Isabella's underclothes by hand; she would trust no laundry with them.

'I've been playing touch-rugby with a Hell's Angel, Nanny. Our team won thirty–love.'

'You'll get yourself in bad trouble. All the Courtneys got hot blood.' Nanny held up the torn panties and examined them with heavy disapproval. 'Long past time you were safely married.'

'You've got a dirty mind. Now tell me what's been happening today. What about Klonkie's new girl-friend?' Isabella knew how to distract her.

Nanny was an inveterate gossip, and this was the time of day when she brought Isabella up to date on the doings and undoings of the entire household. While she chattered, Isabella made little murmurs of encouragement, but she was listening with only half her attention, and when she stood up to soap herself she examined her body in the steamy full-length mirror across the room.

'Do you think I'm getting fat, Nanny?'

'You are so skinny, that's why no boy married you yet,' Nanny sniffed, and went through to the bedroom.

Isabella tried to be completely objective as she studied herself. Was there any way in which her body could be improved? Should her bosom be a little bigger? And did the tips point outwards at too acute an angle? Were her hips too wide or should her bottom be smaller? After critical reflection, she shook her head. It all looked just about perfect from where she stood. 'Ramón de Santiago y Machado,' she whispered, 'you will never know what you missed.' And why did that make her feel so miserable?

'You are talking to yourself again, child.' Nanny came back with a bath-towel the size of a bed-sheet and held it open for her. 'Out you get now. We are running out of time.' She enveloped Isabella in the towel as she stepped out of the bath, and vigorously began to rub her back dry. It was no good trying to convince Nanny that she could dry herself.

'Don't be so rough.' Isabella had been making the same protest for twenty years, and Nanny ignored it.

'How many times have you been married, Nanny?'

'You know well that I been married four times, but I only been churched just once.' Nanny checked and looked at her with new attention. 'Why you ask about marrying? Did you find something interesting, that's why the torn panties?'

'You vulgar old woman!' Isabella avoided her eyes and snatched up her Thai-silk gown on the way to the bedroom.

She picked up the hairbrush and made one stroke through her hair before Nanny took it away from her.

'That's my job, child,' she said firmly; and Isabella sat down and closed her eyes giving herself up to the familiar comfort of having Nanny brush out her hair for her.

'Do you know, I think I'll have a baby, just so you'll have someone else to fuss over, and get you off my back.'

Nanny missed a stroke, taken by the attractions of that proposal, and then she said sternly, 'You get yourself married first before we talk babies.'

The Zandra Rhodes creation was an ethereal cloud of subtle colour, spangled with sequins and seed pearls. Even Nanny nodded and looked complacent as Isabella pirouetted in front of her.

Isabella was halfway down the staircase on her way to a last-minute conference with Chef when a thought occurred to her and she stopped abruptly. The Spanish *chargé d'affaires* was one of tonight's dinner-guests, and it took only a second for her to rearrange the table-seating in her mind.

'Yes, of course.' The Spanish *chargé* nodded immediately she mentioned the name. 'An old Andalusian family. As I recall, the Marqués de Santiago y Machado left Spain and went to Cuba after the Civil War. He had considerable sugar and tobacco interests on the island at one time, but I imagine Castro changed all that.'

A marqués – the reply silenced Isabella for a moment. Her knowledge of Spanish nobility was less than elementary, but she imagined that a marqués ranked just below a duke.

'The Marquesa Isabella de Santiago y Machado.' With awe she allowed herself to consider the prospect, and she saw again in her mind's eye those deadly green eyes and for a moment she had difficulty breathing. Her voice was still ragged as she asked: 'How old is the marqués?'

'Oh, he would be getting on a little now. That is, if he is still alive. He must be in his late sixties or early seventies.'

'He had a son perhaps?'

'That I don't know.' The *chargé* shook his head. 'But it would be easy to find out. If you wish, I will make some enquiries for you.'

'Oh, that would be so kind of you.' Isabella laid her

hand on his arm and gave him her most brilliant smile.

Marqués or not, you don't get away from Isabella Courtney that easily, she thought smugly.

*   *   *

'It took you almost two weeks to make contact, and then
when you had at last done so you immediately allowed the
subject to escape.' The man seated at the head of the table
stubbed out his cigarette in the overflowing ashtray in front
of him and immediately lit another. The first two fingertips
of his right hand were stained dark yellow, and the smoke
from the oval Turkish cigarettes that he smoked incessantly
had already tarred the air in the small room to a blue fog.
'Was that in accordance with your orders?' he asked.

Ramón Machado shrugged lightly. 'It was the only certain way of getting and holding her attention. You must
realize that this woman is accustomed to male adulation.
She has only to lift a finger and men come swarming about
her. I think you must trust my judgement in this matter.'

'You allowed her to get away.' The older man knew he
was repeating himself, but this fellow needled him.

He did not like him, and did not know him well enough
yet to trust him. Not that he ever fully trusted any one of
his operatives. However, this one was too self-assured, too
disrespectful. He had turned aside the rebuke with a shrug,
where another might have cringed. He had blatantly set
his own judgement above that of a superior officer.

Joe Cicero hooded his eyes. They were as opaque as
puddles of old engine oil, startlingly black against the pallor
of his skin and the silver-white hair that hung limply over
his ears and forehead.

'Your orders were to make contact and to maintain it.'

'With respect, Comrade Director, my orders were to
inveigle myself into the woman's confidence, not to rush
at her barking like a mad dog.'

No, Joe Cicero did not like him. His attitude was offensive, but that was not the only reason. He was a foreigner.

25

Joe Cicero considered any non-Russian a foreigner. No matter what the concept of international socialism dictated, East Germans, Yugoslavs, Hungarians, Cubans and Poles – they were all foreigners to him. It infuriated him to have to pass on responsibility for so much of the section that he had headed for almost thirty years to others. Especially people like this.

Not only was Machado a foreigner, but also his very roots and origins were corrupt. He was no scion of the proletariat, not even of the despised bourgeoisie, but was a full member of that hated and outdated system of class and privilege, an aristocrat.

True, Machado disparaged and despised his origins, and used his title now only to achieve his goals, but to Joe Cicero his blood-lines were tainted and his aristocratic manners and affectations were an insult to all he, Cicero, believed in.

Furthermore he had been born in Spain, a fascist country historically ruled by a Catholic monarchy which was the enemy of the people, even more so now under the monstrous Franco who had put down the communist revolution. He might call himself a Cuban socialist, but to Joe Cicero he stank of Spanish fascism and aristocracy.

'You let her get away,' he persisted. 'After all this time and money wasted.' He realized that he was being ponderous and heavy-handed, and he knew that his powers were failing. The sickness was already slowing his wits.

Ramón smiled, that condescending smile that Joe Cicero hated so well. 'She is on the line, like a fish; she may swim and dive only until I am ready to reel her in.'

Again he had contradicted his superior, and Joe Cicero considered the last but the most poignant reason for his dislike of the man. His youth and comeliness and health. It made him painfully aware of his own mortality, for Joe Cicero was dying.

Since childhood he had chain-smoked these rank Turkish cigarettes, and on his last visit to Moscow the doctors had at last diagnosed the cancer in his lungs and offered him treatment in one of the sanatoria reserved for officers of his seniority. Instead Joe Cicero had elected to continue in service, to see his department securely handed over to his successor. He had not then known that this Spaniard was to be that successor. If he had known, perhaps he might have chosen the sanatorium.

He felt tired now and discouraged. His store of energy and enthusiasm was all used up, just as only a few years ago his hair had been jet black and dense, and now was white, tinged only with yellow like sun-dried seaweed, and he could not walk a dozen paces without wheezing and coughing like an asthmatic.

Recently he had been waking in the night, drenched with those terrible night-sweats, and when he fought for his breath he lay awake in the darkness and was assailed with terrible doubts. Had it been worth it, a lifetime of dedicated painstaking work? What did he have to show for it? What little solid success had he achieved?

For almost thirty years he had served in the African department of the fourth directorate of the KGB. For the last ten of those years, he had been head of station South, the division responsible for the African continent below the equator, and quite naturally most of his attention and that of his department had been devoted to the most developed and richest country in his region, the Republic of South Africa.

The other man at the table was a South African. Up until this time, he had remained silent, but now he said softly: 'I do not understand why we are spending so much time discussing this woman. Explain it to me.' Both the white men at the table diverted their attention to him. When Raleigh Tabaka spoke, other men usually listened. He had about him a peculiar intensity, a charged air of purpose that held the attention of others.

All his life, Joe Cicero had worked with black Africans, the nationalist leaders of the forces of liberation and the socialist struggle. He had known them all, Jomo Kenyatta and Kenneth Kaunda, Kwame Nkrumah and Julius Nyerere.

27

Some of them he had come to know intimately: men like Moses Gama, who had been sent to a martyr's death, and Nelson Mandela, who was still languishing in the prison of white racism.

Cicero placed Raleigh Tabaka in the forefront of that illustrious company. In fact Raleigh had been Moses Gama's nephew, and Raleigh had been present the night the South African police murdered his uncle. He seemed to have inherited Moses Gama's tremendous personality and force of character, and he had stepped squarely into the wide gap left by Gama. He was thirty years old, but already he was deputy director of Umkhonto we Sizwe, 'The Spear of the Nation', the military wing of the South African National Congress, and Joe Cicero knew that he had proved himself time and again in the field and in the councils of the ANC. He had the talent, the guts and the verve to rise as high as any other man in Africa.

Joe Cicero preferred him to the white Spanish aristocrat, but he recognized that despite their difference in colour and lineage they were men cast in the same mould. Hard and dangerous men, well versed in death and violence, adepts in the subtle shifting world of political power and intrigue. These were the men to whom Joe Cicero must hand over the reins, and he resented them and hated them for it.

'The woman,' he said heavily, 'could be of extraordinary value, if she is controlled and developed to her full potential, but I will let the marqués explain that to you. It is his case, and he has studied the subject fully.'

Abruptly Ramón Machado's smile thinned, and his eyes turned flat and hostile.

'I would prefer the Comrade Director not to use that title,' he said coldly. 'Even in jest.'

Joe Cicero had learnt that it was probably the only way he could penetrate the Spaniard's slick armour-plating.

'I beg your pardon, comrade.' Joe inclined his head in mock contrition. 'But please do not let my little lapse interrupt your recitation.'

Ramón Machado opened the loose-leaf binder that lay

on the table in front of him, but he did not even glance at it. He knew every word it contained by heart.

'We have assigned the woman the case-name "Red Rose", and we have had our psychiatrists develop a detailed profile of her. The evaluation is that she is highly susceptible to skilful recruitment. She is uniquely placed to become an extremely valuable field-operative.'

Raleigh Tabaka leant forward attentively. Ramón noted that he did not interject question or comment at this stage, and he approved of that restraint. They had not yet worked together extensively, this was only their third meeting, and both of them were still evaluating each other.

'Red Rose can be placed in an emotional dilemma. On her father's side she is a member of the white ruling class in South Africa. Her father is just finishing a term as his country's ambassador to Britain, and he returns now to take up an appointment as the chairman of the national armaments industry. He has enormous holdings in mining, land and finance; after the Oppenheimers and their Anglo-American Company, the family is probably the most wealthy and influential in southern Africa. In addition, the father has conduits to the very highest levels of the ruling racist régime. Most important, however, is the fact that the father dotes on Red Rose. She is able to obtain from him, with little effort, anything she sets her heart upon. This would include an *entrée* to any level of government and any information of whatever classification, even that relating to his new appointment on the armaments corporation.'

Raleigh Tabaka nodded. He knew the Courtney family, and could find no fault with this assessment. 'I have met Red Rose's mother, but she is on our side of the political fence,' he murmured, and Ramón nodded.

'Precisely. Shasa Courtney has been divorced from his wife Tara for seven years. She was an accomplice of your uncle, Moses Gama, in his bomb attack on the white racist parliament, for which he was imprisoned and subsequently murdered. She was also Gama's mistress and bore his bastard son. Tara Courtney fled from South Africa with Gama's child

29

after the failure of the bomb plot. She lives now in London where she is very active in the anti-apartheid movement. She is also a member of the ANC, but she is not considered sufficiently competent or emotionally stable for any but junior rank and routine assignments. At present she operates a safe house for ANC personnel here in London and occasionally undertakes courier work or assists in the organization of rallies and demonstrations. Her real potential value lies in her influence over Red Rose.'

'Yes,' Raleigh agreed impatiently. 'I know all about this, especially about her relationship to my uncle, but does she in fact have any influence over her daughter? It appears that Red Rose's sympathies lie heavily on her father's side?'

Again Ramón nodded. 'At present this is the case. But, apart from her mother, there is another member of the family who holds radical views: her brother Michael, who has a much greater influence on her. And there are other ways of turning her.'

'What are those?' Tabaka asked.

'One of them is the honey trap,' Joe Cicero said. 'The marqués – forgive me – Comrade Machado has made the initial contact to that end. The honey trap is one of his many specialities.'

'You will keep me informed of progress.' Raleigh made a statement, and neither of them replied immediately. Although Raleigh Tabaka was an executive of the ANC and a member of the Communist Party, he was not, unlike the other two, an officer of the Russian KGB. Joe Cicero was, on the other hand, a KGB officer first and foremost, although his promotion from colonel to colonel-general had been confirmed only a month previously, at the same time that the Moscow clinic had diagnosed carcinoma of both his lungs. Joe Cicero suspected that the promotion had been given to him merely to allow him to retire at the higher pension, after a lifetime of loyal service to the department. Nevertheless, he was an officer in the ANC only after his loyalty to Mother Russia, his lines of allegiance were not diluted, and the ANC would receive only what information it was necessary for them to have.

Ramón Machado's lines of allegiance were also clear-cut. He had been born in Spain, and his title of nobility was Spanish, but his mother had been a Cuban woman, sloe-eyed and raven-haired. She had met Ramón's father when she was a young housekeeper on the Machado estates near Havana in Cuba. After the marriage, the marqués had taken his beautiful commoner bride back to Spain.

During the Spanish Civil War, the marqués had opposed General Francisco Franco's Nationalists. Despite his noble background and inherited wealth, Ramón's father had been an enlightened and liberal man. He joined the Republican army and commanded a battalion at the siege of Madrid where he was severely wounded. After the war, the Machado family found oppression and discrimination under the Franco régime intolerable. The marquesa prevailed on her husband to take her and her young son back to her native island in the Caribbean. Although they had been stripped of most of their Spanish property and possessions, the family still owned the Cuban estates. However, the Machado family found that life under the dictatorship of Batista was no great improvement on that under Francisco Franco.

Ramón's mother was an aunt of the young left-wing student firebrand Fidel Castro and one of his avid admirers. She became active in the campaign of agitation and intrigue against the Batista régime, and young Ramón gleaned his own first political convictions from her and from her celebrated nephew.

After Fidel Castro was imprisoned for leading the gallant but abortive attack on the Santiago barracks on 26 July 1953, both Ramón's father and mother were arrested along with the rebels.

Ramón's mother died under interrogation in a police cell in Havana, and his father died in the same prison only a few weeks later of ill-treatment and a broken heart. Once again the family estates were confiscated, and Ramón's only inheritance was the derelict title of marqués, void of all property or fortune. At the time he was fourteen years old. The Castro family took him in and cared for him.

When Fidel Castro was released from prison under amnesty, Ramón went with him to Mexico, and at sixteen years of age was one of the first recruits to the Cuban army of liberation in exile.

It was in Mexico that he first learnt how to exploit his extraordinary good looks and to develop his natural winning ways with women. By the age of seventeen his companions had nicknamed him El Zorro Dorado, 'The Golden Fox', and his reputation as an irresistible lover was established.

Up to the time of his father's arrest and death in Batista's prison, Ramón had been given the benefit of the finest education available to the only son of a wealthy aristocratic family. He had attended an exclusive preparatory school in England, and spent two years at Harrow, so he spoke English like a native, as well as his own Spanish. During his schooldays, he had demonstrated superior academic ability and had become proficient in the manners and pastimes of a young gentleman. He had a good seat on a horse, learnt to keep a straight bat and cast a salmon fly. He was also a phenomenal shot at Spanish red-legged partridge or Mexican white-winged dove. He could shoot and ride and dance and sing, and he was beautiful, and when he returned to Cuba with Fidel Castro and the eighty-two heroes on 2 December 1956, he proved his valour in the fighting which left most of the valiant band dead on the beaches.

He was with the survivors that escaped with Castro into the mountains. During the years of the guerrilla warfare that followed El Zorro was sent down into the towns and villages to practise his arts on scores of women, young and not so young, beautiful and plain. In Ramón's arms they became enthusiastic daughters of the revolution. With every conquest he became more skilled and confident until his band of female recruits contributed significantly to the eventual triumph of the revolution and the overthrow of the Batista régime.

By this time, Castro was fully aware of the potential value of his young relative and protégé, and once in power he rewarded him by sending him to further his education on the American mainland. While he studied political history and social anthropology at the University of Florida, Ramón used his amatory skills to infiltrate the band of Cuban exiles who, with the collusion of the American CIA, were planning the counter-revolution and the invasion of the island.

It was largely Ramón's intelligence that pinpointed the time and place of the Bay of Pigs landing, and resulted in the annihilation of the traitors. By this time, his extraordinary gifts had been recognized not only by his own countrymen but also by their allies.

When he graduated *cum laude* from the University of Florida and returned to Havana, the head of the KGB in Cuba prevailed upon Castro and the director of the DGA to send Ramón to Moscow for further training. While in Russia, Ramón exceeded the estimates that the KGB had made of his capabilities and his potential value. He was one of those remarkable creatures who could pass easily in any stratum of society, from the crude guerrilla-camps of the jungle to the drawing-rooms and private clubs of the most sophisticated capitals of the world.

With the knowledge and blessing of Fidel Castro, he was recruited into the KGB. Given his connections, it was only natural that he should be appointed director of the joint committee co-ordinating Russian and Cuban interests in Africa.

In this job, Ramón made a special study of the African socialist liberation movements and he was responsible for selecting those organizations that were to receive full Russian and Cuban backing. He initiated the policy under which Cuba came to act as a surrogate for Mother Russia in southern Africa, and he was soon responsible for the supply of arms and the training of African resistance groups. In that capacity, he became a member of the ANC.

In a very short time, he had visited all of the African countries under his jurisdiction, using his Spanish passport

33

and his title, posing as a capitalist investor and merchant banker with credentials supplied by the fourth directorate. He was accepted without reservation by the white colonial administrations, and was received cordially and entertained by everyone from the governors of Portuguese Angola and Mozambique to the British Governor-general of Rhodesia. He even dined with that notorious architect of apartheid, the South African leader, Hendrik Verwoerd.

When it became necessary to appoint a new station head for the African division to replace the ailing General Cicero, Ramón's qualifications and experience made him the natural choice.

So as he sat now in the back room of the Russian consulate in Bayswater Road, with the man he was about to replace and this black African guerrilla leader, his loyalties were as clear-cut as those of his superior.

When Raleigh Tabaka said, 'You will keep me informed of progress,' he was being naïve. He would be informed only on a "need to know" basis. In Ramón's view and that of his government, the installation of this man and the organization which he represented as the ruling élite in South Africa was merely a single step along the road to the eventual goal of universal socialism throughout the length and breadth of the African continent.

'Naturally, you will be kept right up to date with this as with all other matters of joint interest,' Ramón assured him in a tone of such total sincerity that the black man settled more comfortably in his chair and returned Ramón's smile. Very few persons, male or female, were immune to his charms. It gave Ramón a solid sense of satisfaction to see the magic work on even such a tough and uncompromising subject as this one.

Raleigh Tabaka was fully aware of the white man's smug self-satisfaction, although no sign of it showed on his face. There had been that flat spot in the Cuban's otherwise clear green gaze. Only someone with Raleigh's developed powers of observation would have noticed that. Raleigh had worked with these whites from Russia and Cuba for many years now, and he had come to understand that in dealing with them only one principle was fixed and certain. They were never to be trusted, not in any circumstances or in even the smallest detail.

He had learnt to fake his acceptance, to give them false signals of compliance, such as the deliberate physical relaxation and the frank trusting smile. However, he never forgot for one instant that they were white. Like most Africans, Raleigh was a natural racist and a tribalist. He hated these white men who patronized and condescended to him across the conference-table with the same passion as he hated the white policemen who had fired the bullets at Sharpeville.

He had never forgotten for a single waking minute that dreadful day when under a blue African sky he had held in his arms the girl he loved, the lovely black maiden who was to be his wife. He had held her and watched her die, and then before her flesh cooled he had thrust his fingers deep into the bullet wounds in her chest and made his vow of vengeance.

The vow had been made not only against the assassins but against them all, every white face and every bloody white hand that had forced slavery and subjugation upon his tribe down the centuries. Hatred was the fuel on which Raleigh Tabaka's life ran.

He watched the white faces across the table and smiled and drew strength and resolve from his hatred. 'So,' he said, 'you will take care of the woman, it is agreed. Now let us move on . . .'

'A moment.' Ramón lifted his hand to restrain him and turned back to Joe Cicero. 'If I am to proceed with Red Rose, then there is the matter of the budget for the operation.'

'We have already allocated two thousand British sterling—' General Cicero protested.

'Just sufficient for the preliminary stage. The budget will have to be upgraded. Red Rose is the daughter of a wealthy capitalist, and to impress her I will have to maintain my rôle as a Spanish grandee.'

They argued for a few minutes more, while Raleigh Tabaka tapped his pencil impatiently on the table-top. The African division was the Cinderella of the fourth directorate, and every rouble had to be counted.

It was degrading, Raleigh thought, as he listened to them haggle. They were more like a pair of old women selling pumpkins beside a dusty African road than two men planning the overthrow of an evil empire and the liberation of fifteen million oppressed black souls.

At last they agreed, and Raleigh found it difficult to conceal his disgust as he repeated: 'Can we move on to discuss my itinerary for the African tour?' He had believed that this was the reason for today's meeting. 'Has the authorization been received from Moscow?'

The discussions went on into the afternoon. They ate a frugal lunch sent up from the consulate canteen as they worked, and the fog of Joe Cicero's cigarette smoke dulled the shaft of sunlight through the single high window. The room was a high-security unit on the top floor, regularly swept for electronic listening devices and safe from outside surveillance.

At last Joe Cicero closed the file in front of him and looked up. His dark eyes were bloodshot from the smoke and the strain. 'I think that covers all points for discussion, unless there is anything new?'

They shook their heads.

'As usual Comrade Machado will leave first,' said Joe Cicero. It was an elementary rule of procedure that they should never be seen in public in each other's company.

Ramón left the consulate by the entrance to the visa section, the busiest part of the building where he would be less noticeable in the crowd of students and others applying for travel documents to the Soviet Union.

There was a bus-stop directly outside the walled consulate. He took a number 88 bus but left it at the next stop and hurried through the Lancaster Gate entrance to Kensington Gardens. He lingered in the rose garden until he was certain he was not being followed, and then crossed the park.

His flat was in a narrow side-street off Kensington High Street. It had been rented specifically for the Red Rose operation and, although it contained only a single bedroom, the living-room was spacious and the locality was fashionable.

During the two weeks that he had been in residence, Ramón had managed to create an air of permanence. His personal chests had come from Cuba in the diplomatic bag. They had contained the few good pictures his father had left him and other small items of furnishing, including family photographs in silver frames of his parents and the family castle and estates in Andalusia when these had been in their heyday. The glassware and porcelain were incomplete sets, but they bore the Machado coat of arms: the stag and the boar rampant on either side of the quartered shield. His golf-clubs were displayed casually in the corner of the tiny entrance-hall, the plain leather Hermès bag well used, the discreetly embossed coat of arms almost obscured by wear. From what he had learnt about Red Rose, he knew that she would have an eye for such detail.

He glanced at the venerable gold Cartier, another family heirloom, that felt unfamiliar on his wrist. He would have to hurry. His growth of beard was heavy and dark. He shaved it off quickly but carefully and then showered and washed the stink of Joe Cicero's Turkish cigarettes out of his hair.

He checked himself automatically in the mirror as he went through to the bedroom. He had been in peak physical condition when he had returned from Russia three weeks previously. The refresher course for senior officers at the KGB training college on the shores of the Black Sea had honed his body and, although he had managed to take little physical exercise since then, the lack was not yet apparent. His body was still sleek and hard, his belly flat and his body hair crisp and curly black. The scrutiny he directed at his image was completely without vanity. Face and body were simply implements, tools to be used to accomplish the tasks that he was set. He had no illusions about the fleeting nature of his physical attributes, but he worked to prolong it in the same way that a warrior cared for his weapons.

'Gym tomorrow,' he promised himself. Ramón had the use of a martial arts studio in Bloomsbury run by a Hungarian refugee. Two hours of hard work a couple of times a week would maintain him in fit condition for the Red Rose operation.

His riding-breeches were cavalry whipcord, and he wore a sage-coloured Trevira woollen shirt with a green tie under his tweed hacking-jacket. His riding-boots fitted him like a second skin, with a supple gloss of dubbined leather that flexed into perfect creases over his ankles as he moved. No amount of craftsmanship or money, only years of loving attention, could achieve that effect.

He knew that Red Rose was a horsewoman; in her world horses were a major part of existence. She would recognize those boots as a badge of membership of the same exclusive and élite group to which she belonged.

He checked his watch again; he had timed it nicely.

He locked the flat and went down into the street. The rain-clouds that had threatened earlier in the afternoon had dispersed, and it had turned into a glorious summer evening. Even the elements seemed to conspire to assist him.

The riding-stables were in a narrow mews behind the Guards barracks. The stable-manager recognized him. As Ramón signed the register he ran his eye down the immediately preceding entries, and saw that his good fortune was persisting. Red Rose had signed for her mount twenty minutes previously.

He went down to the stalls, and the groom had the saddle on his mount. She was a bay filly that Ramón had chosen with care and for which he had paid five hundred pounds from his expense budget. However, she had been a bargain, and he knew that he would recoup the cost and probably make some profit whenever he chose to sell her on. He checked the girth and harness, speaking softly to the filly, soothing her with hands and voice, and then thanked the groom with a nod and went up into the saddle.

On an evening like this there were fifty or so other riders out in Rotten Row. Ramón walked the filly under the oaks, while groups of horsemen cantered past him in both directions. The girl was not amongst them.

As soon as she had warmed a little, he pressed the filly with his toes and she moved up into a trot. She had an elegant action, and he rode her like a centaur, his superior horsemanship obvious even in that expert company. They made a striking pair, and more than a few of the women they passed turned in the saddle to look back after them.

At the Park Lane end of the Row, Ramón turned and moved the filly up into an easy canter; galloping was forbidden. A hundred yards ahead, a group of four riders were coming towards him, two couples, young people well mounted and turned out, but the girl stood out amongst them like a sunbird in a flock of sparrows.

From under her riding-hat her hair undulated like the wing of a bird in flight, and glistened in the buttery sunshine. When she laughed her teeth were very white, and her colour was vivid from the exercise and the wind in her face.

Ramón recognized the man riding beside her. He had been her companion on most occasions that he had observed Red Rose over the previous two weeks. Ramón had requested information on him from records. He was the second son of an extremely wealthy family of brewers, an effete upper-class playboy of the type known in London society as a 'Deb's Delight' or 'Hooray Henry', and he had been with her at the Rolling Stones concert four days ago. Since then Red Rose had spent two evenings in his company, party-hopping around Knightsbridge and Chelsea. Ramón had noticed that she treated him with a type of amused condescension, as though he were an over-affectionate St Bernard puppy, and that on no occasion that he had followed them had she been alone in his company except when he drove her in his MG from one party to the next. Ramón was almost certain that they were not sleeping with each other, which was unusual in this summer of 1969 when sexual licence was a raging epidemic.

He knew also that Isabella Courtney was not a simpering virgin. In the three years that she had been living at Highveld, it was documented that she had indulged in at least three explosive, if short-lived, liaisons.

As the gap between them closed, Ramón transferred his attention to the horse under him and leant forward to pat her neck. 'There, my darling.' He spoke to her in Spanish, while from the corner of his eye he was watching the girl. It was a trick that he had of deflecting his gaze so that he seemed not to be looking while he missed not the smallest detail.

They were almost past each other when he saw the girl's chin snap up and her eyes fly wide open, but he ignored her and rode on.

'Ramón!' Her cry was high and imperative. 'Wait!'

He checked the filly, and glanced back with a little frown of annoyance. She had wheeled her own mount and was riding after him, and he let his expression remain reserved and slightly frosty as though he resented her scraping acquaintance.

She drew up beside him, reining her horse down to a walk. 'Don't you remember me? Isabella Courtney. You were my saviour.' Her smile was uncertain and awkward. Men always recognized her, no matter how fleeting or distant their last meeting. 'At the concert in the park,' she ended lamely.

'Ah!' Ramón allowed his smile to bloom at last. 'The motorcycle mascot. Forgive me. You were dressed rather differently then.'

'You didn't wait for me to thank you,' she accused him. She suppressed the urge to laugh out loud with relief that he had recognized her at last.

'No thanks were necessary. Besides which you had rather urgent business elsewhere, as I recall.'

'Are you on your own?' She changed the subject quickly. 'Why don't you join us? Let me introduce you to my friends.'

'Oh, I don't want to impose myself.'

'Please,' she insisted. 'You'll enjoy them; they are good fun.' And Ramón bowed slightly in the saddle.

'How can I refuse such a kind invitation from such a lovely lady?' he agreed, and Isabella felt as though her chest was in a vice. She had difficulty breathing as she looked into those green eyes in the face of a dark angel.

The other three had reined in and were waiting for them. Even before she came up to him, she saw that Roger was already sulking, and it gave her a vindictive little pleasure to say: 'Roger, may I introduce the Marqués de Santiago y Machado? Ramón, this is Roger Coates-Grainger.'

She noticed Ramón glance at her quizzically and only then realized that she had made a gaffe by using his title; he had not mentioned it at their first meeting.

However, her momentary discomfort was forgotten when she introduced Ramón to Harriet Beauchamp and saw how Harriet reacted to him. She actually licked her lips like the cat in the television advertisement for pet food. Harriet was Isabella's best friend in London, more out of symbiotic consideration than out of genuine mutual affection. Lady Harriet was Isabella's entrance-ticket to the inner circles of London society. As the daughter of a belted earl, she was welcome where Isabella despite her looks and family wealth would have been considered a *nouveau riche* interloper with a funny accent. Harriet on the other hand had found that wherever Isabella Courtney was there swiftly assembled a superabundance of males. Beneath Harriet's plump, bland and colourless blonde exterior flourished a ravenously amorous nature, and Isabella was happy to pass on her rejects to her.

Usually the arrangement worked perfectly, but Ramón was definitely no reject, not yet anyway, and smoothly Isabella interposed her horse between them and flashed a silent warning at Harriet. Harriet was enormously flattered.

41

She knew that she could never aspire to become Isabella's rival, but it was gratifying to be treated like one.

'Marqués?' Ramón murmured as they rode on. 'You know considerably more about me than I do about you.'

'Oh, I must have seen your photo in one of the slosh columns,' Isabella suggested airily as she thought: God, don't let him think I have been that interested.

'Ah, the *Tatler* of course . . .' Ramón nodded. His photograph had never appeared anywhere, except possibly in the files of the CIA and a few other intelligence agencies around the world.

'Yes, the *Tatler*, that's it.' Gratefully Isabella jumped at the escape he offered her, and then set herself out to captivate him, without making her interest too obvious or oppressive. It was easier than she had anticipated. Ramón had a relaxed charm, a *savoir-faire* that fitted in with their group. Soon all of them, except Roger who was still sulking monumentally, were chatting and laughing together as though they were old chums.

As the dusk gathered and they turned back towards the stables, Isabella kneed her mount closer to Harriet's and hissed at her: 'Invite him to the party tonight!'

'Who?' Harriet opened her vacuous pansy eyes in feigned incomprehension.

'You know damned well who, you randy little witch. You've been rolling your eyes and ovaries at him for the last hour!'

★   ★   ★

Lady Harriet Beauchamp had the run of the family house in Belgravia during the week when her parents were in the country. She put together some of the best bashes in town.

Tonight most of the cast of *Hair*, the current musical hit, pitched up after the show. They were still in costume and stage make-up, and the four-piece Jamaican band that Harriet had hired burst into a calypso version of 'Aquarius' to welcome them.

It bode fair to becoming one of Harriet's more memorable parties. It was so crowded that those couples with serious business in mind took up to twenty minutes to get from the ballroom up the staircase to the bedrooms; even there they were forced to wait their turn. Isabella wondered sourly what Harriet's papa, the tenth Earl, would think if he knew of the flow of traffic through his four-poster bed.

In the midst of all the gaiety and laughter, Isabella was determinedly insular. She had found a perch halfway up the sweeping marble staircase from which she could keep an eye on all arrivals at the front door, as well as on the action in the ballroom and the front drawing-room into which the dancing had overflowed.

She steadfastly refused to dance herself, despite an incessant string of invitations to do so. She had been so icily dismissive of Roger Coates-Grainger's ponderous attention and callow humour that, discouraged, he had wandered away to the champagne-bar on the terrace. By now he was probably pissed out of his gourd, she thought with gloomy relish.

Such was the success of the evening that none of the guests could tear themselves away to move on to any other venue. All the traffic through the teak double front doors from the square was one-way, and the noise and crush increased with every passing minute.

Another group arrived squealing and shouting tipsy greetings, and Isabella felt a fleeting lift of her spirits as she saw amongst them a head of dark wavy hair, but almost immediately she realized that the man was too short, and when he turned so she could see his face, he was sallow and jowly. She actively hated him, whoever he was.

As a kind of masochistic penance she had made her single glass of champagne last all evening, and now the wine was flat and warm from her fingers on the stem. She looked around to find Roger and send him for another glass but saw that he was dancing with a tall thin girl with false eyelashes and a high penetrating giggle that carried even to where Isabella sat.

God, she's awful, Isabella thought. And Roger looks such a ponce, slobbering all over her like that.

She glanced at the ormolu and porcelain French clock above the door to the drawing-room. The time was twenty minutes to one, and she sighed.

At half-past noon today, Daddy was having an important lunch for a group of influential Conservative Members of Parliament and their wives. As usual Isabella was to be hostess. She should get some sleep to be at her best, but still she lingered.

Where the hell is he? she thought bitterly. He promised he'd come, damn him. (Actually, he had said that he would try to drop in later.) But we were getting on so well, it was as good as a promise.

She dismissed another invitation to dance without even looking up, and tasted the champagne. It was awful.

'I'm not going to wait a minute after one o'clock,' she promised herself firmly. 'And that is absolutely final.'

Then abruptly her pulse checked and then raced away again. In her ears the music took on a sweeter, more cheerful note, the oppressive crowds and the noise seemed to recede, her dark mood evaporated miraculously, and she was borne up on a wave of excitement and wild anticipation.

There he was, standing in the front doorway. He was so tall that he towered half a head above those around him. A single lock of hair had fallen like a question-mark on to his forehead, and his expression was remote, almost contemptuous.

She wanted to shout his name. 'Ramón, here I am!' But she restrained herself, and set aside her glass without looking. It toppled over, and the girl on the step below her exclaimed as lukewarm champagne cascaded down her bare back. Isabella did not even hear her protest. She came to her feet in one fluid movement, and instantly, Ramón's cool green gaze was on her.

They looked at each other over the heads of the swirling, gyrating dancers, and it was as though the two of them were completely alone. Neither of them smiled. It seemed

44

to Isabella that this was a solemn moment. He had come, and in some vague way she sensed the significance of what was happening. She was certain that in that instant her life had changed. Nothing would ever be the same again.

She began to descend, and she did not stumble over the sprawling, embracing couples that clogged the staircase. They seemed to open before her, and her feet found their own way between them.

She was watching Ramón. He had not moved to meet her. He stood very still in the giddy throng. His stillness reminded her of one of the great predatory African cats, and she felt a tiny thrill of fear, an exhilaration of the blood as she went down to him.

When she stood before him, neither of them spoke, and after a moment she lifted her tanned bare arms towards him and as he took her to his chest she wound her arms around his neck. They danced, and she found every movement of his body transmitted to her own like a current of electricity.

The music was superfluous; they moved to a rhythm of their own. As she flattened her breasts against the hard rubbery muscle of his chest, she could feel his heart beating, and her own nipples swelled and hardened. She knew he could feel them pressing into him, for the beat of his heart quickened and the colour of green darkened in his eyes as she stared up into them.

She arched her back, a slow voluptuous movement that made the ridges of hard muscle stand proud along each side of her spine. His fingertips traced them down, moving lightly over the crests of her spine as though he were playing a musical instrument. She shivered under his touch, and pressed her hips forward instinctively, welding them against his, and she felt his flesh harden and swell just as hers had done.

For her he was a great tree and she was the vine that entwined it, he was a rock and she the current of a tropical ocean that washed about it, he was a mountain peak and she was the cloud that softly enfolded it. Her body was

45

light and free, she seemed to float in his arms, and that was all of reality. They were alone in the universe, and transported far beyond all the natural laws of space and time; even gravity was suspended, and her feet no longer made contact with the earth.

He moved her towards the door, and she saw Roger mouthing something at her across the room. The tall girl was gone, and he was flushed with outrage, but she left him caught helplessly in the press of bodies like a fish in a net.

They went down the front steps, and she took the key of the Mini-Cooper from her sequinned evening bag and pressed it into Ramón's hand.

He drove very fast through the deserted streets, and she leant as close to him as the bucket seats would allow and watched his face with such a fierce concentration that she did not see or care where he was taking her. She did not think she could endure another moment without touching him, without feeling his hands on her body again. She found that she was shivering once more.

Then, abruptly, he pulled into the kerb and parked the Mini. He came round to her side with long strides, and she knew his need was almost as great as her own. She clung to his arm, and she could not feel the ground beneath her feet as they crossed the pavement and went to the entrance of the red-brick house in a row of similar buildings. He led her up the stairs to the second floor.

As soon as he closed the door of the flat he turned to her, and for the first time she felt his mouth on hers. His face was as rough as shark-skin with new beard, but his lips were soft and hot, and sweet as ripe fruit, and his tongue was like a live thing deep in her mouth.

She felt something burst within her, and all reason and restraint were washed away on the flood. There was a sound in her ears like a gale-force wind over a turbulent sea, and a madness descended on her.

She twisted out of his embrace and tore at her own clothing in a frenzy of impatience, letting it fall around her feet on the polished wooden floor of the small hallway. He

46

stripped his own clothing as swiftly, facing her, and she stared hungrily as every exquisite detail of his body was revealed.

She had never dreamt that a man's body could be so beautiful. Where other men were gross and hairy, inflamed and knotted with veins, he was smooth and perfect. She felt that she could stare at him forever, but at the same time she knew that if she did not instantly feel him against her she would scream aloud with frustration, and she flung herself naked against his naked chest.

She pressed hard to him, and his body was firm and sleek and hot. Yet the hair on his chest was unbearably harsh against the sensitive engorged tips of her breasts. She moaned and covered his lips with hers to prevent herself screaming out her desperate need.

He picked her up, and she felt herself weightless in his arms, and he carried her to the bed without breaking the clinging suction of their mouths, one upon the other.

✶   ✶   ✶

As she came awake, Isabella was aware of an overwhelming sense of well-being. She felt as though she might burst with joy. Her body tingled as though every separate muscle and nerve had a life of its own.

For long moments, she could not understand what had happened to her. She lay with her eyes closed, clinging to the moment. She knew that such a magical sensation must be evanescent, but she did not want it ever to end. Then slowly she was aware of the man musk in her nostrils and the taste of his mouth that still lingered on her tongue. She felt the ache where he had been deep in her body and the heat of the pink rash that his beard had raised on the sensitive skin around her lips. She savoured it all, small pain transmuted into deep and fulfilling pleasure.

Then, with a sense of fresh wonder, the thought imploded into her consciousness: I'm in love! And she came fully awake. Her joy was almost delirious.

She sat up quickly, and the sheet dropped to her waist.

'Ramón,' she said, and the indentation of his head was impressed upon the pillow beside hers. A single strand of dark body hair was coiled like a watch-spring on the white sheet. She reached for it and discovered that the sheet was cool, the heat of his body long since dissipated, and she felt her joy sink into despair.

'Ramón.' She slipped from the bed and padded on bare feet to the bathroom. The door was ajar, and the bathroom was empty. Once again he had gone, and she stood naked in the middle of the floor and looked around her with dismay.

He was like a cat. His stealth was eerie, and a rash of tiny goose-pimples arose around her nipples. She hugged herself and shivered.

Then she saw the note on the bedside table. It was a single sheet of expensive cream-coloured paper embossed with his family crest. He had weighted it down with her key-ring, the keys to her Mini. She snatched it up eagerly. There was no salutation.

You are an extraordinary woman, and yet when you sleep you look like a child, a beautiful innocent child. I could not bear to wake you. I could hardly bear to leave you, but I must.

If you can come to Málaga with me for the weekend, meet me here at nine tomorrow morning. You will need your passport, but do not bother with pyjamas.

Ramón

She chuckled with delight and relief, all the lightness of her waking mood recaptured. She reread the note; the paper was smooth and cool as marble and had a sensuous feel under her fingertips. His skin had been as smooth, and her eyes turned dreamy and reflective as tiny disjointed episodes from the night replayed in her mind.

He had been far beyond all her previous experience. With the others, even the most skilled and patient and perceptive of them, she had always been aware of their separate bodies, their divergent existences, of the deliberate attempts to please and to reciprocate. With Ramón, there

48

had been no division. It was almost as though he had taken over her mind as well as her body. They had blended into each other in some semi-divine osmotic process; their flesh and their minds had become one.

So many times during the night, she had believed that they had reached the pinnacle together, only to discover that they were still upon the foothills and before them towered an alp and then another and another. Each higher and more magnificent than the last. There had been no end to it, only at last the oblivion of sleep so deep that it had been like dying, and a resurrection into this new charmed and joyous existence.

'I'm in love,' she whispered in almost religious awe, and she looked down on her own body, amazed that such a frail vessel could contain so much happiness, such abundant emotion.

Then she noticed her wristwatch lying beside her car keys on the bedside table.

'Oh my God!' she breathed. It was half-past ten. 'Daddy's lunch!' And she leapt to her feet and flew to the bathroom. On the washbasin, Ramón had placed a brand-new toothbrush still in its sealed plastic container for her, and this small kindness touched her out of all proportion.

She hummed the lyric of 'Faraway Places' through a mouthful of foaming toothpaste.

She decided there was just time for a quick bath, and she lay in the hot water and thought about Ramón and found there was a great void in her body aching for him to fill it.

'Enough of that, girl,' she laughed at herself. 'With a wave of his magic wand, he has transformed you into a shameless little raver.'

She jumped out of the bath and reached for the towel. It was still damp from his body, and she pressed a fold of it over her mouth and nose, and inhaled the faint but distinctive aroma of his skin. It excited her all over again.

'Stop it!' she commanded herself in the steamy mirror. 'You have to be at Trafalgar Square in an hour.'

She was just about to let herself out of the flat when she exclaimed again, and darted back into the bathroom. She rummaged in her sequinned handbag for the Ovanon pills in their calendar-marked pack and broke one out of its sealed compartment.

She placed the tiny white capsule on her tongue while she ran half a tooth-mug of water from the tap and then saluted her image in the mirror with the raised glass.

'To life, love and freedom,' she said, 'and to many happy returns.' And washed down the pill.

★   ★   ★

Blood sports did not revolt Isabella Courtney. Her father had always been a hunter, and the walls of Weltevreden, their home at the Cape of Good Hope, were decorated with trophies of the chase. Amongst the family assets was a safari company that owned a huge hunting concession in the Zambezi valley. Only the previous year she had spent an idyllic fortnight in that enchanted wilderness with her elder brother, Sean Courtney, who was a licensed professional hunter and ran the outfit for Courtney Enterprises. On a number of occasions Isabella herself had ridden to hounds at Harriet Beauchamp's invitation. Isabella was a passable shot with the lovely little gold-engraved Holland & Holland 20-gauge shotgun that her father had given her for her seventeenth birthday. With it she had shot snipe in the Okavango Delta, sand grouse in the Karoo, duck and geese on the great Zambezi, grouse on the highland moors, and pheasant, woodcock and partridge on some of the great English estates to which she and the ambassador had been invited.

She felt no offence at the sight of blood deliberately spilled, and in addition she had inherited her fair share of the family's gambling instinct, so the contest intrigued her.

This was the second day, and the original field of nearly three hundred contestants had been whittled down to two, for it was a 'one miss and out' and a 'winner take all' competition. The entrance fee was one thousand US dollars a head, so there was well over a quarter of a million in the pot, and the tension was as hot and thick as minestrone soup as the American went to the plate.

He and Ramón Machado were the only two remaining contestants and they had shot level for the last twenty-three rounds. Finally, to break the deadlock and decide the winner, the Spanish judges had decreed that double birds must be taken from now on.

The American was a full-time professional. He followed the circuit in Spain and Portugal and Mexico and South America, and until last year in Monaco. Now, however, the tournaments had been banned in that tiny principality, after a mortally wounded pigeon had escaped from the stadium and winged its way over the palace walls to crash at last on to Princess Grace's tea-table, spraying the lace table-cloth and the ladies' tea-gowns with its blood. Prince Rainier had heard the screams halfway across his tiny realm, and that was the end of live pigeon tournaments in Monaco.

The American was Isabella's age, not yet twenty-five years old, but his income was reputed to be well over a hundred thousand dollars a year. He was shooting a 12-gauge 'side by side' that had been made by that legendary gunsmith James Manton almost a century ago. Of course, the weapon had been rebarrelled and proofed to accommodate the longer modern cartridges and smokeless powders. However, the stock and action, complete with the engraved hammers, were original and retained the marvellous balance and pointability that old man James had built into it.

The young American took his stance on the plate, cocked the hammers, tucked the butt-stock under his right armpit, and pointed the double muzzles just over the centre of the semicircle of five woven wicker baskets that were placed thirty yards from where he stood.

Each basket contained a live pigeon. They were the feral birds of the type that live in flocks in the centre of most large cities. Big robust birds of variegated colours, bronze and blue and iridescent green, some of them with dark bands around their necks or patches of white in their wings.

To ensure a supply of birds, the shooting club had built a feeding-shed on the premises, a structure containing trays that were replenished daily with crushed maize and enclosed by drop-sides that could be released by remote control and trap the feeding birds within. Often a pigeon that escaped untouched from the killing-ground would head straight back for the feeding-shed. Many birds had been shot at numerous times before, and these were wily creatures who had learnt subtle little tricks to disturb the aim of the marksmen. In addition the bird-handlers who loaded them into the baskets knew how to pluck a feather or two from wing or tail to make them fly an erratic unpredictable course.

The baskets were operated by a random mechanism, with a delay of up to five seconds after the shooter had called 'Pull' for the release of a bird. Five seconds, for a man with sweaty palms, a racing heart and tens of thousands of dollars at stake, could seem like all eternity.

The baskets were thirty yards out, and the effective range of a 12-gauge shotgun was generally reckoned to be forty yards. Thus, the birds were released at almost extreme range, and in addition the retaining circle was a mere ten yards beyond the line of baskets.

The retaining circle was a low wooden wall, only eight inches high, painted white, which demarcated the boundary of the killing-ground. To qualify as a hit the carcass of the bird or, in the event of the blast of pellets tearing a bird into more than one piece, the largest portion of the carcass, calculated by weight, had to fall inside the low wooden wall. In this way, the shooter had to kill his bird as it rose from the release-basket within the ten yards before it passed over the periphery of the killing-ground.

The baskets were fanned out over a semicircle of forty-five degrees in front of him, there was no indication as to which lid would fly open at the command 'Pull' and no way to predict which direction the bird would take once it was released. It could cross either left or right, bear directly away, or sometimes – the most disconcerting of all – race straight towards the gunner's face.

Added to all this, the pigeons were fast noisy fliers, that could jink and swerve in full flight, and now the judges had decided that instead of a single bird two pigeons would be released simultaneously.

The American braced himself at the plate, crouching a little, left foot leading slightly like a boxer, and Isabella reached for Ramón's hand and squeezed it lightly. They sat in the front bottom row of the covered grandstand in the padded leather chairs reserved for contestants and club officials.

'Pull!' said the American, and his Texan twang rang in the silence like a hammer on a steel anvil.

'Miss!' whispered Isabella. 'Please miss!'

For a second and then another second, nothing happened. Then, with a crash, the lids of two of the baskets snapped open, numbers two and five, half left and full right from where the American stood, and both birds, hit by compressed-air jets from nozzles in the bottom of the baskets, launched into instant flight.

Number two went straight out, keeping low and going very fast. The American swung smoothly on to him, mounting the shotgun to his shoulder, and as it touched he fired. Five yards out from the basket, the silhouette of the pigeon was distorted by the rush of pellets. Its wingbeats froze in mid-stroke, and it died instantaneously in the air, and fell in a puff of feathers to hit well inside the ring and lie without further movement on the bright green turf.

The American swung on to the second bird. It had broken away towards his right, a glistening streak of burnished bronze, but at the sound of the first shot it jinked back inside the American's swing so swiftly that he could not correct his aim in time. The shot was left of centre, but only inches out. Instead of slicing into heart and brain, the blast of pellets from the fully choked barrel tore away the bird's right wing, and the horribly maimed creature tumbled and fluttered, streaming a trail of feathers through the air.

53

It struck only a foot inside the low white wooden wall, and a sigh went up from the watchers in the grandstand. Then, incredibly, the bird, one wing gone, pumped frantically with its remaining wing and found its feet. It tottered towards the wall, beating at the air ineffectually with one wing, uttering an agonized cawing sound in its puffed-out throat.

The spectators gasped and rose to their feet as one, and in the centre the American froze with the empty shotgun still mounted to his shoulder. He was allowed only two cartridges. If he reloaded now and killed the bird with a third shot, he would be instantly disqualified and would forfeit the prize money.

The pigeon reached the barricade and leapt weakly at it. It struck the wood with its chest only an inch from the top and fell back, leaving a splash of brilliant ruby blood on the white paint.

Half the spectators screamed, 'Die!' while those who had bet against the American screamed: 'Go! Go for it, bird!'

The pigeon gathered itself groggily, and leapt once more at the barrier. This time, it reached the top and balanced there uncertainly, swaying back and forth.

Isabella was on her feet howling wildly with the others. 'Jump!' she pleaded. 'Don't – oh, please don't die, pigeon! Get over, please!'

Suddenly the dying bird stiffened into a convulsive rigor, its neck arched backwards and it flopped from the wall and lay still and dead on the green lawn.

'Thank you!' Isabella breathed, and dropped back into the seat.

The pigeon had fallen forward and died outside the circle, and the loudspeakers above their heads boomed out the verdict in the Spanish phrases that Isabella had come to understand so well in the past two days.

'One kill. One miss.'

'My heart won't stand the strain.' Isabella clutched her bosom in a theatrical gesture, and Ramón smiled at her with those cool green eyes.

'Look at you!' she cried. 'The original ice man. Don't you even feel a thing?'

'Not outside your bed,' he murmured, and before she could find a suitable reply the loudspeakers interrupted her.

'Next gun up! Number one hundred and ten!'

Ramón stood up, and while he adjusted the protectors over his ears his expression was still cold and remote. He had taught Isabella not to wish him luck, so she said nothing more as he moved to the long rack at the gate on which his was the only weapon still standing. He took it down, and broke it open and placed it over the crook of his arm and walked out into the bright Iberian sunshine.

To Isabella he looked so beautiful and romantic. The sunlight sparkled in his hair, and the sleeveless shooting-vest with suede leather shoulder-patches was tailored to his lean torso, fitting so smoothly that the butt of the shotgun could not catch on a fold or tuck of cloth as he swung it up to mount.

At the plate, he loaded the 'under and over' barrels of the Perazzi 12-gauge and snapped the breeches closed. Only then he glanced back over his shoulder at Isabella as he had done every time he had shot over the past two days. She had anticipated it, and now she held up both hands, clutching her own thumbs hard, and showed him her clenched fists.

Ramón turned back, and his whole body went still. Once again he reminded her of an African cat, that peculiar stillness of the wild leopard as it fixed on its prey. He did not crouch as the American had done, but stood tall and lean and graceful, and said softly, 'Pull!'

Both birds bounded from the open baskets on wildly clattering wings, and Ramón mounted the gun with such elegant economy of movement that he seemed casual and unhurried.

When he had been in Mexico with his cousin Fidel Castro he had provided much of the funds of the embryo army of liberation's war-chest with his shotgun in the live pigeon rings of Guadalajara. So he also was a professional with the marvellous eye and reflexes needed for the job.

The first bird was going obliquely out, speeding on shining green wings for the wall, and he had to drop that one first. He took it cleanly with a charge of number six shot from the fully choked bottom barrel, and it exploded in a puff of feathers like a burst pillow.

He turned for the other bird, pirouetting like a dancer. This pigeon was a veteran; it had been shot at a dozen times before, and it kept low at basket-level. The handler had plucked its tail unevenly, and although it was going at sixty miles an hour it slid to one side and wobbled in flight.

Instead of going for the wall, it came straight at Ramón's head, reducing the range to less than ten feet and, in doing so, making the shot many times more difficult. As it flashed towards his eyes, he had only a hundredth part of a second to react, and the extreme shortness of range would not give the charge of shot an opportunity to spread. It was as though he were firing a single ball, and an error of a mere fraction of a minute of angle would mean a miss.

He hit the pigeon squarely in the head with the full charge at point-blank range, and the bird disintegrated. Its body was blown away in a flurry of bloodied feathers, and only the two separate wings remained intact. They spiralled down and fell at Ramón's feet.

Isabella screamed wildly and came to her feet; then, with a single bound, she vaulted the barrier. Although the range-master called sternly to her in unintelligible Spanish, she flouted range discipline and ran out on long denim-clad legs to throw her arms around Ramón's neck.

The crowd was already excited and volatile from the tensions of the contest. Now they laughed and applauded as Ramón and Isabella embraced in the centre of the stadium. They made a splendid couple, almost impossibly handsome, both tall and athletic, shining with health and youthful vigour, and that spontaneous display of affection touched a chord in those that watched them.

★   ★   ★

They drove into the city in the Mercedes that Isabella had hired at the airport. Ramón opened an account at the Banco de España in the main square and deposited the winner's cheque into it.

In a strange fashion, they shared a common attitude to money. Isabella seemed never even to consider price or value. Ramón had noticed that if a frock or a trinket took her fancy she never even bothered to ask the price. She merely flipped one of her vast collection of plastic credit cards on to the counter, then signed the slip and crumpled her copy into her handbag without as much as glancing at it. When she emptied her handbag in the hotel room, she screwed the accumulated receipts into a ball and, still without reading them, tossed them disdainfully into the waste-basket or dropped them into the nearest ashtray for the chambermaid to dispose of.

As a convenience, she also carried a fist-sized wad of banknotes, crammed into her large leather shoulder-bag. However, it was obvious that she had not concerned herself with the rate of exchange of sterling into Spanish pesetas. To pay for a cup of coffee or a glass of wine, she selected a banknote whose size and colour she deemed appropriate to the occasion and dropped it on to the table, often leaving a waiter staring after her in speechless astonishment.

Ramón had a similiar contempt for money. At one level he abhorred it as the symbol and the foundation of the capitalist system. He hated to be dictated to by the laws of economics and wealth which he had dedicated his entire life to tearing down. He felt besmirched and demeaned when he had to wheedle and haggle with Moscow for the cash with which to perform his duties. Yet very early on in his career he had become aware of the particular approbation that he earned from his superiors when he personally provided funds to finance his own operations.

In Mexico he had shot live pigeon. While he was at the University of Florida he had imported drugs from South America and sold them on campus. In France he had run weapons for the Algerians. In Italy he had smuggled currency and had arranged and executed four lucrative kidnappings. All the profits of these operations had meticulously been accounted for to Havana and Moscow. Their approval was reflected in the rapid promotion he had enjoyed, and the fact that a man of his age had been selected to replace General Cicero as head of a full section of the fourth directorate.

It had been quite obvious to Ramón from the outset that the paltry operating expenses that General Cicero had allocated for the Red Rose project were totally inadequate. He had been obliged to make up the shortfall as expeditiously as possible, and of course this little jaunt to Spain also provided an ideal opportunity to begin the second phase of the operation.

That evening, to celebrate Ramón's win, they dined at a tiny seafood restaurant, jealously concealed from the tourist hordes in one of the back alleys where Isabella was the only foreigner amongst the dinner-guests. The meal was an exquisite paella cooked in the classical tradition and accompanied by a wine from one of the estates that had once belonged to Ramón's family, and whose tiny production was never sold outside Spain. It was crisp and perfumed, and had a pale green luminosity in the candlelight.

'What happened to your family estates?' Isabella asked, after she had tasted and exclaimed over the wine.

'My father lost them all after Franco came to power.' Ramón lowered his voice as he said it. 'He was an antifascist from the very beginning.'

And Isabella nodded with approval and understanding. Her own father had fought against the fascists, and she subscribed to the comfortable and fashionable belief of her generation in the essential goodness of all mankind and the fervent if rather hazy ideal of universal peace of which she was aware that fascism was the antithesis. She carried a 'Ban the Bomb' button in her handbag, although it would have been crassly non-U to wear it actually pinned on her clothing.

'Tell me about your father and your family,' she invited

him. She realized that, although she had been with him almost a week, she actually knew very little about him, apart from what the Spanish *chargé* had told her over the dinner-table.

She listened with fascination as Ramón recounted a little of the family history. One of his ancestors had received the title after he had sailed with Columbus to the Americas and Caribbean in 1492, and Isabella was vastly impressed by the antiquity of his lineage.

'We go back as far as Great-Grandfather Sean Courtney,' she deprecated her own ancestry. 'And he died sometime in the nineteen twenties.' As she said it, she realized for the first time that if Ramón was the father, then her own son might one day be able to boast of such distinguished blood-lines. Until that moment, she had been content simply to be with Ramón, but now, as she leant close to him and watched his eyes in the candlelight, the horizons of her ambitions widened. She wanted him as she had never wanted anything in her life before.

'And so you see, Bella, despite all of this, I am not a rich man.'

'Oh, yes you are. I saw you pay over two hundred thousand dollars into your bank this afternoon,' she told him gaily. 'You can afford to buy me another bottle of wine, at the very least.'

'If you didn't have to fly back to London tomorrow morning, I would have used some of that money to take you up to Granada. I could have accompanied you to the bullfight, and shown you my family castle in the Sierra Nevada . . .'

'But you have to go back to London as well,' she protested, 'don't you?'

'A few days – I could have managed a few days. Any sacrifice to be with you.'

'You know, Ramón, I don't even know what you do. How do you earn your crust?'

'Merchant banking,' he shrugged dismissively. 'I work for a private bank and I am responsible for African affairs.

We arrange loans for developing companies in central and southern Africa.'

By now Isabella's mind was accelerating up to racing speed. Ramón's lack of fortune was fully compensated for by his august origins, and he was a banker. There would certainly be a place for a merchant banker in the top ranks of Courtney Enterprises. It was all beginning to look marvellously exciting.

'I would like more than anything in this world to see your castle, Ramón darling,' she whispered huskily, and she thought: I wonder how much a castle would cost, and if I could talk Garry into it. Her brother Garry was the chairman and financial head of Courtney Enterprises. He was no more proof to Isabella's charms and wiles than any of the other male members of the family. Like most of the family, he was also a terrible snob. A marquesa needed a castle – he might just fall for it.

'What about your father?' Ramón asked. 'I thought that you promised you'd be back on Monday.'

'You leave my father to me,' she said firmly.

*   *   *

'Bella, this is the most ridiculous hour to wake an old man,' Shasa protested as he answered her telephone call. 'What time is it, in the name of all that's holy?'

'It's after six, and we have already been for a swim, and you are not old. You are young and beautiful, the most beautiful man I know,' Isabella cooed over the international line.

'This sounds ominous,' Shasa murmured. 'The more extravagant the compliment, the more outrageous the request. What do you want, young lady? What are you up to now?'

'You really are an awful old cynic, Pater,' said Isabella, and traced patterns in Ramón's chest hair with her forefinger. He sprawled naked beside her on the double bed; his body was still sticky, damp and salty from their dip in the Mediterranean. 'I just rang you to tell you how much I love you.'

Shasa chuckled. 'What a dutiful little mouse. I certainly trained you well.' He lay back on the pillows and slipped his free arm around the shoulders of the woman who lay beside him. She sighed sleepily and wriggled closer to him, nuzzling against his chest.

'How is Harriet?' Shasa asked. Harriet Beauchamp had agreed to provide cover for Isabella's expedition to Spain.

'She's fine,' Isabella assured him. 'She's right here now. We have been having a wonderful time.'

'Give her my love,' Shasa ordered.

'Oh, I will,' she agreed and, covering the mouthpiece, she leant over and kissed Ramón full on the lips. 'She sends her love back to you, Papa, but she refuses to catch the London plane this morning.'

'Ah!' said Shasa. 'Now we come to the true reason for all this filial consideration.'

'It's not me, Daddy, it's Harriet. She wants to go up to Granada. There is a bullfight. She wants me to go with her.' Isabella let her voice trail into silence.

'You and I are flying to Paris on Wednesday. Had you forgotten that? I am addressing the Club Dimanche.'

'Daddy, you speak so well; the French ladies adore you. I'm sure you don't really need me.'

Shasa did not reply. He knew that silence was the one sure way in which he could disconcert his wayward daughter. He covered the mouthpiece and asked the woman cuddled against him: 'Kitty, can you come to Paris on Wednesday?'

She opened her eyes. 'You know I am leaving for the OAU conference in Ethiopia on Saturday.'

'I'll have you back by then.'

She raised herself on one elbow and looked down at him thoughtfully. 'Get thou behind me, Satan.'

'Daddy, are you still there?' Isabella's voice floated between them.

'So my own flesh and blood are determined to desert

61

me, are they?' Shasa asked in his most injured tones. 'All by myself in the least romantic city in the world?'

'I can't let Harriet down,' Isabella explained. 'I'll make it up to you, I promise.'

'You'd better, young lady,' Shasa warned her. 'I shall remind you of your indebtedness at a future date.'

'Granada will probably be deadly dull – and I'll miss you awfully, dear Papa,' said Isabella contritely, and traced her forefinger down Ramón's body, past his navel and into the thick bush of hair below it; she twirled a dark curl around her fingertip.

'And I will be desolated without you, Bella,' Shasa agreed, and dropped the handset of the telephone on to its cradle and pushed Kitty back gently on to the pillows.

'I said get thou behind me, Satan,' she protested huskily. 'Not get thou on top of me.'

★   ★   ★

Isabella drove as fast and as well as any man he had known. Ramón lay back in the leather bucket seat of the hired Mercedes and studied her openly. She basked in his attention and every few minutes, when a straight section of road allowed it, she glanced sideways at him or reached across to touch his hand or his thigh.

Unlike many of the assignments that he had been given over the years, Ramón did not find it difficult to act out his part with this woman. He sensed a strength in her, an untapped reservoir of courage and determination that intrigued him.

He recognized that she was as yet unfulfilled and restless, dissatisfied with and rebellious against her easy undemanding existence, ripe for excitement and challenge, searching for something, some cause to which to dedicate herself.

Physically she was immensely attractive, and he had no difficulty faking that tender concern towards her that was the hallmark of the accomplished lover. When he looked at her like this, it was a deliberate device. He knew the

62

appeal of his gaze, that cold green contemplation like the stare of the serpent that mesmerizes a wild bird, and yet he enjoyed looking at her as at an exquisite work of art. Although he knew from her file that she had been with other men, he had learnt in these last few days that the core of her being was still untouched and there was a strange virginal quality about her that aroused him.

As with so many legendary male lovers, Ramón experienced that condition known as satyriasis. The name derived from those woodland godlings of Roman mythology which were half-man and half-goat and whose sexual appetite was insatiable. Although Ramón Machado was quite abnormally responsive to any woman, whether she was attractive to him or otherwise, yet it was unusual for him to be able to achieve orgasm. He was in most cases simply indefatigable, able to outlast a partner with even the most tardy libido and to drive a normal woman on and on until she at last screamed for mercy. Then he was able to continue at the very first indication that she wished to do so, and he was so sensitively attuned to feminine sexuality that he would usually recognize that indication before she did herself.

However, this woman was one of those rare creatures who was able to bring him on without too much difficulty. With her he had already achieved true orgasm a number of times and he knew he would again. It was, of course, essential to his plans that he did so.

Driving up from the coast on that sultry summer's day, Isabella was as happy and exhilarated as she had ever been. She was in love. Now there was not the least shadow of doubt in her mind that this was the grand passion of her life. There had never been, and there could not conceivably be again, anyone to match him. She would never experience any emotion to exceed what she felt for him now. His presence beside her and those green eyes upon her made the sunlight brighter and the high dry air of the Sierra taste sweeter on her lips.

The wide plains and the mountains beyond were so like her own beloved land. They transported her back to the open horizons of the great Karoo, for there were the same lion-coloured earth and sepia rockscapes. Looking upon them, her mood was carried upwards even higher and she laughed aloud with joy and had to strive hard to prevent herself crying out: 'Oh, Ramón my darling, I love you. I love you with all my heart and with all my soul for ever.'

Even in her giddy exhilaration, she was determined that he must say it first. That way she could be doubly certain that what she already knew was true – that he loved her as much as she loved him.

Ramón knew these mountains and he directed her over dusty back-roads to vistas of grandeur and beauty hidden far from the usual tourist routes. They stopped in one of the little villages, and he joked with the locals in their patois. He came away with a slab of the pink *serrano* ham cured in the snow, a loaf of rough peasant bread and a goatskin full of the sweet dark Malaga wine.

Beyond the village, they left the Mercedes parked beside an ancient stone bridge and followed the stream up through the olive groves into the foothills of the Sierra Nevada. While a bearded billy-goat watched them in astonishment from the cliff above, they plunged naked into a secret pool of the river. Then, still naked, they ate their picnic lunch seated on the smooth black rocks above the water.

Ramón demonstrated how to hold the wine-skin at arm's length and direct a hissing jet into the back of his open mouth. When she tried, the wine spurted over her cheeks and dribbled from her chin, and at her request he licked the ruby droplets from her face and from her taut white bosom. This was such fun that they forgot about the rest of their lunch and made love, Isabella still perched on her rock and Ramón standing knee-deep in the pool facing her.

'You are incredible,' she whispered. 'My legs are jelly. You'll probably have to carry me back to the car.'

They spent so much of the afternoon beside the pool that the sun was on the tops of the mountains, turning the snows to incandescent gold, when they came in sight of the castle.

It was not as large or as grand as Isabella had expected it to be. It was simply a gaunt dark building high on the slopes above the higgledy-piggledy pink-tiled roofs of the village. As they approached, Isabella saw that part of the parapet had collapsed and that the grounds were overgrown and neglected.

'Who does it belong to now?' she asked.

'The State.' Ramón shrugged. 'There was talk some years ago of turning it into a tourist hotel, but nothing came of it.'

The caretaker was an old man who remembered Ramón's family, and he led them through the ground-floor rooms. They were empty; all the furniture had been sold to pay the family debts, and the chandeliers were thick with dust and cobwebs. The walls of the hall were stained with rain-water from the leaks in the roof.

'It's so sad to see something once so lovely ruined by neglect,' Isabella whispered. 'Doesn't it make you sad, too?'

'Do you want to go?' he asked.

'Yes, I don't want to be sad today.'

As they went down the hairpin track into the village, the last of the sunset was so splendid on the mountain-tops that Isabella recaptured her bubbling mood.

At the inn in the village, the innkeeper recognized the family name. He ordered his two daughters up to change the bed-linen in the front room, and sent his wife back to her kitchen to prepare one of the Andalusian specialities for their dinner, *cocido Madrileño*, a stew of chicken and the spicy little *chorizo* sausages on a bed of *cabello de ángel*, noodles so fine that they deserved their name of Angel's Hair.

'In Spain, sherry is the drink of the people,' Ramón explained to her as he filled her glass. It was cold enough here in the mountains to warrant a fire in the stone fireplace, and the light of the flames played over his features making him even more improbably handsome.

'We always seem to be doing one of three things' – she contemplated the golden wine in her glass – 'eating or drinking or . . .' She sipped the wine.

65

'Are you complaining?' he asked.

'Gloating, actually.' She slanted her eyes at him. 'Eat your *cocido* and drink your sherry, señor, you are going to need your strength.'

She awoke with the sunlight streaming in through the open window and experienced a moment's dread that he had gone again. However, he was there beside her in the wide soft bed, watching her with that cool enigmatic expression; she felt another moment's chill of doubt, but as she reached for him, almost diffidently, she found that he was already hard and swollen for her.

'Oh God!' she whispered joyously. 'You are incredible!' No man had ever wanted her as much as he did. He made her feel like the most desirable woman in the universe.

The innkeeper had laid a breakfast of purple figs and goat's cheese for them in the walled courtyard. They sat under the trellised vines, and Isabella peeled the figs with her long painted nails and placed the globules of succulent flesh between his lips. Her father was the only other man she had ever done that for.

When one of the daughters brought a pot of steaming coffee out to them, Ramón excused himself and went up to their bedroom. Through the tiny bathroom window, he could see Isabella sitting in the courtyard below and heard her voice and her laughter as she tried to make herself understood in her newly acquired Spanish.

Earlier he had watched her swallow a birth-control pill as she stood beside him at the washbasin. She had made a silly little ritual of it, toasting him with the glass of water. 'Many happy returns!' However, the pack of remaining pills was no longer in her toilet-bag on the ledge above the basin.

He went back into the bedroom. The bed occupied almost the entire floor-space, and their luggage was crammed into the curtained alcove beside the door. Isabella's big squashy leather shoulder-bag was thrown carelessly on top of her suitcase.

He paused to listen again, and heard her voice faintly through the open window. He took the bag to the bed and

66

began to unpack it swiftly, laying out the contents in careful sequence so that he could repack it in exactly the same order. He had searched her sequinned handbag and checked the brand of birth-control pills she was using on that first morning in the Kensington flat while she was still asleep. Later he had discussed them with the doctor at the embassy.

'If the woman discontinues treatment before the tenth day of her cycle, she will almost certainly experience a fertility backlash effect and become considerably more susceptible to impregnation when she ovulates,' he had assured Ramón.

The slim pack of pills was in one of the compartments of her black crocodile-skin purse near the bottom of the bag. Once again, Ramón straightened up to listen. There was no sound of voices from the courtyard, and he darted back to the window. He saw that Isabella still sat at the table and that the innkeeper's black cat now had all her attention. The supercilious creature had settled in her lap and was allowing her to tickle behind his ears.

Ramón stepped back into the bedroom. There were seven pills missing from the separate date-marked compartments in the packet. From his inside pocket Ramón slipped the identical Ovanon packet with which the embassy doctor had provided him. He removed the first seven pills from their compartments and dropped them into the toilet-bowl. Then he placed the two packages side by side and compared them. Now they were identical in every respect, except that the second package contained only aspirin tablets cunningly coated to resemble birth-control pills.

He slipped the packet of placebo tablets into Isabella's purse and replaced her shoulder-bag in the alcove. He pocketed the original package and flushed the toilet, making sure that the seven pills were gone before he washed his hands and went down the narrow staircase to where Isabella waited in the courtyard.

*　　　*　　　*

In Granada, Ramón took her to the *corrida de toros* and exulted in their great good fortune that they were to be able to watch El Cordobes work.

Had not Ramón's father been a patron of this most famous of all matadors when he was a mere *novillero*, they would never have procured tickets to the performance at such short notice. As it was, two tickets were delivered to their hotel on the morning after their arrival. Not only were they seated at the ringside directly to the right of the president's box, but also before the spectacle they were invited to watch El Cordobes dress for the *corrida*.

Of course, Isabella had read Hemingway's *Death in the Afternoon*, and she realized the honour of that invitation. Nevertheless, she was unprepared for the obvious depth of Ramón's respect as he greeted Manuel Benitez, El Cordobes, or for the semi-religious solemnity of the ritual of dressing.

'You have to be Spanish to understand the bulls,' Ramón told her as they took their reserved seats, and indeed she had never seen him so moved and emotional. His involvement was so powerful and infectious that she found herself as wrought-up as he was.

The trumpets of the entry parade sent thrills down her spine, and the spectacle was magnificent: the horses and the costumes encrusted with silver and gold and seed pearls, and the matadors strutting in their short embroidered jackets and skin-tight trousers that blatantly emphasized their buttocks and their bunched genitalia. Even the flaring coral pink and incarnadine satins of the capes glistened with the lubricious tones of intimate feminine flesh and served to underscore the essentially lascivious nature of the frenzy that descended upon the tiered ranks of spectators.

When the bull surged into the ring, horned head high, the great hump of his shoulders swollen with rage, white sand dashing from under his hoofs and his engorged scrotum swinging to the pounding rhythm of his charge, Isabella came to her feet and screamed with the crowd.

As El Cordobes performed the initial passes, Ramón gripped her arm and leant close to her, describing and explaining the significance of each graceful evolution, from the pure elegance of the simple *verónica* to the more complicated *quite*. Through Ramón's eyes, she came to see it as the beginning of some movingly beautiful ritual, steeped in ancient tradition, which did not attempt to disguise its cruel and darkly tragic essence.

When the trumpets saluted the entrance of the picadors, Isabella moaned aloud and pressed her knuckles against her teeth, for she had been dreading the horses. She had read of the horror of the disembowelled horses with their entrails tangled about their legs. To calm her fears, Ramón pointed out to her the thick armour of compressed cotton and canvas and leather that protected them. In the end none of the horses was harmed even when the bull hooked viciously into their padded bodies and drove them up against the barriers.

The picador leant from the saddle and worked the steel into the bull's hump, and the blood sprayed up in a roseate nimbus of light, and then slicked down over the bull's shoulders so that its hide gleamed like metal in the sun.

Isabella shuddered with awful fascination, and Ramón murmured: 'The blood is real, everything you see here is real, as real as life. This *is* life, my darling, with all life's beauty and cruelty and passion.'

She understood it then, accepted it and allowed herself to be carried along on the flood.

El Cordobes took his own *banderillas*. He posed in the sunlight and held high the long darts wrapped in coloured paper streamers. He called to the bull, and when it came he ran to meet it with light dancing strides. As they came together, Isabella gasped, and then the master had planted the *banderillas* and pirouetted away. The bull dropped his head and bucked at the sting of the barbs high in his withers, but his momentum had carried him out of goring range.

The trumpets sounded the final *tercio*, the hour of truth, and a new mood descended upon the stadium. El Cordobes

69

and the bull engaged each other in the stately intimate dance of death. With only the floating cape between them, the passes were so close and dangerous that the bright blood from the beast's shoulders smeared the matador's thighs as it swept by.

At last El Cordobes stood below the president's box and lifted his *montera* cap decorated with black silk pompons to ask permission to dedicate the bull. Isabella was overwhelmed when he came to where she sat and dedicated the bull to her beauty. He tossed his *montera* up to her and turned and went back to face the bull.

El Cordobes performed the final passes in the centre of the ring, each one more graceful and closer to the horns than the last. Every time the crowd erupted with one primeval voice, a great burst of sound that punctuated the aching silences in which each separate pass was performed.

In the end, he prepared for the kill directly below where Isabella sat. As he sighted the bull over the long silver blade, Ramón gripped her arm hard and whispered to Isabella: 'Look! He will take it *recibiendo*, the most dangerous manner of all!' When the bull made its last desperate rush, instead of running to meet it, El Cordobes stood four-square and went in over the top of the horns. The bright point of the *estoque* severed the great artery of the heart, and the blood gushed up in a fountain.

On the return from the bull-ring to the hotel, neither of them spoke. They were entranced, caught up in a rapture which was mystic and semi-religious. The cruelty and the blood, the tragic beauty of the spectacle had not wearied or jaded their emotions, but had enhanced them to the threshold of a kind of spiritual agony, which cried out for release. Isabella sensed that Ramón's need was even greater and more uncontrollable than her own.

In their bedroom whose double doors and wrought-iron balcony overlooked the gardens of the old Moorish palace, Ramón stood her in the centre of the floor. While the blades of the old-fashioned fan on the high ceiling revolved overhead, he undressed her. It seemed that in doing so, he performed another ritual as ancient as that of the *corrida*. When she was naked, he knelt at her feet, clasped her around the hips and buried his face in the dense warm pillow of hair in the basin of her pelvis.

She caressed his head with a tenderness that she had never felt for another human being, yet it was tinged with a great sadness and humility. She felt that a love like this was divine, and that she was not worthy of it. It was too great for any mortal being to bear.

At last he rose and took her up like a child in his arms and carried her to the bed. It was as though it had never happened before, as though he had broken through to such secret depths of her physical and spiritual being that even she had not suspected their existence.

The laws of time and space were redefined while she was in his arms. It lasted an instant and a flaming eternity. Like a comet she was transported through the full circle of the heavens. When she looked up into his green eyes, she knew with a lambent joy that his spirit was locked into hers as deeply as his flesh was entrapped within her throughout all that incredible odyssey. When she believed that she could reach no higher, survive no longer, there was an outpouring within her, as hot and copious as a flood of volcanic lava.

As the last light of day faded and their room filled with shadows, she found that she was so devastated that she could no longer speak or move; she had only the strength left to weep, and while she wept with exhaustion and fulfilment sleep overcame her.

★   ★   ★

Her entire world was a brighter, more joyous place now that she had Ramón.

London, that most fascinating and vital of cities, transcended itself and became for her an earthly paradise. She saw it all through a shimmering golden mist of excitement. Each minute spent in his company was like a precious jewel set in that gold.

71

When they had come to London three years earlier, Isabella had resumed her studies and gained her bachelor's degree. Surprised at her sudden studiousness, her father had encouraged her to enrol in the School of Oriental and African Studies at London University, and she had embarked on her doctoral thesis. She had chosen as her subject 'A Dispensation for Post-Colonial Africa'. Her thesis was advancing well, and she had hoped to complete most of it before her father's term as ambassador ended and they returned to Cape Town.

However, all that had been before Ramón entered her life. Since then she had become a shameless truant. In the weeks since they had returned from Spain, she had not visited her tutor once, and had barely had time to open a book.

Rather than labouring on her thesis, she rose before dawn and slipped away to ride with Ramón in the park or to jog with him along the Embankment. Sometimes they worked out together in the shabby little gym in Bloomsbury run by a Hungarian expatriate who had fled his own country after the abortive rising.

There Ramón began to instruct her in the mysteries of judo and self-defence, arts in which he was frighteningly adept. Sometimes they wandered hand-in-hand through the galleries and museums. They dreamt in front of the Turners in the Tate, or disparaged the new acceptances at the Royal Academy. Always they ended up in the bed in Ramón's flat in Kensington. She didn't care to ask him how he was able to spend so much time with her instead of at his bank. She simply accepted it gratefully.

'You've turned me into a junkie,' she accused him. 'I have to have my regular fix.'

Indeed, when he left London for eight days on some mysterious business for his bank, she moped and pined and truly sickened, even to the point of throwing up when she rose in the morning.

She kept half a dozen changes of clothing and a full range of perfumes and cosmetics at his flat and made it her duty to arrange the flowers and replenish the refrigerator daily. She was a talented cook and she loved to prepare food for him.

She began to neglect her duties at the embassy. She wormed her way out of official invitations and often left the chef and his staff to work on their own. Her father taxed her with her changed behaviour.

'You are never at home any more, Bella. I can't rely on you for a single thing. Nanny says that you slept in your bed only twice last week.'

'Nanny is a little tell-tale – and a fibber.'

'What's going on, young lady?'

'I'm over twenty-one years of age, Pater darling, and it was part of our agreement that I don't have to account to you for my private life.'

'It was also part of our agreement that you show your face at my receptions once in a while.'

'Cheer up, Papa.' She kissed him. 'We'll be going back to Cape Town in a few months' time. Then you won't have to fret about me any longer.'

However, that evening she asked Ramón if he wouldn't come to a cocktail-party that Shasa was holding at the embassy in Trafalgar Square to welcome the celebrated South African author Alan Paton to London.

Ramón thought about it carefully for a full minute before he shook his head. 'It is not the right time to meet your father yet.'

'Why not, darling?' Up to that moment, it had not been important to her, but now his refusal piqued her.

'There are reasons.' He was often so damnably mysterious. She wanted to draw him out, but she knew she was wasting her time. He was the only man she had ever met who could resist her. There was a lining of steel beneath that beautiful façade.

'Therein lies much of his appeal,' she laughed at herself ruefully. It was not that she wanted to share him with any other person, not even her father. She was more than content to be entirely alone with him; their love was so totally engrossing that they avoided other people.

73

True, they occasionally dined at Les A or the White Elephant with Harriet or some of the myriad other acquaintances that Isabella had made over the past three years. Once or twice they went on with the party to dance at Annabel's, but mostly they sneaked away from the others to be alone. Ramón did not seem to have friends of his own or, if he did, he never invited her to meet them. It troubled her not at all.

On the weekends when she could wriggle out of the official ambassadorial arrangements, she and Ramón threw their overnight bags and tennis-rackets into the back of the Mini-Cooper and escaped into the country. They were usually very late back to town on Sunday night.

At the beginning of August, they departed from their solitary habits and caught the train up to Scotland. On the opening day of the grouse season, they were Harriet Beauchamp's guests on the moors of the family estate. The earl was a stickler for correct form, and the ladies were not invited to shoot on the opening day. They were, however, allowed to pick up or join the line of beaters. The earl wasn't very keen on foreigners, either, especially those who shot 'under and over' rather than 'side by side' and who favoured Italian guns over English.

On the first drive, he placed Ramón out on the end of the line. Unexpectedly three coveys came through on the right, sliding low over the tops of the heather, going like furies on a thirty-mile-an-hour tail-wind. Isabella was loading for Ramón. He killed four birds from each covey. He took a double out in front. Then as the covey swept overhead Isabella passed him the second gun. With it he took another double behind the line of butts. Twelve birds with twelve shots fired. Even the head keeper shook his grizzled old head. 'In thirty-three seasons, I've no' seen the likes,' he told the earl lugubriously. 'He kills his bird like de Grey or Walsingham – dead in the air with nary a flutter.' High praise to be compared to the best shots in English history.

The earl promptly abrogated custom, and on the second

drive, Ramón found himself in one of the favoured butts in the centre of the line. At the long dinner-table that evening, he was elevated to within conversational range of the earl who addressed most of his remarks to him over the heads of the bishop and the baronet between them. The weekend was off to a great start. Harriet had arranged for Ramón and Isabella to occupy adjoining rooms at the furthest end of the huge rambling old country house.

'Papa suffers from insomnia,' she explained. 'And you and Ramón in action sound like the Berlin Philharmonic performing Ravel's "Bolero".'

'You vulgar little slut,' Isabella protested.

'Talking of sluts, lovey. Have you sprung your little surprise on Ramón yet?' Harriet asked sweetly.

'I'm waiting for the right moment.' Isabella was immediately defensive.

'In my vast experience, there ain't no right moment for that sort of news.'

Harriet was right for once. No opportunity presented itself that weekend. They were halfway back to London when Isabella abandoned any further attempt at subtlety. Fortunately, they had the first-class compartment to themselves.

'Darling, I went to see a doctor last Wednesday – not the embassy doctor, but a new one that Harriet recommended. He did a test, and we got the result on Friday . . .' She paused and watched his expression. There was no change; he regarded her with that remote green gaze, and she felt a sudden illogical dread. Surely nothing could tarnish their feelings for each other, nothing could spoil the perfection of their love, and yet she sensed a wariness in him, a spiritual drawing away from her. She found herself blurting it out in a rush.

'I'm almost two months pregnant. It must have been in Spain, probably that day in Granada, after the bullfight . . .' She felt breathless and shaky, and she hurried on. 'I just can't explain it. I mean, I've been taking the Pill religiously, I swear it, you've seen me . . .' She realized that she was beginning to gabble out her explanations in an undignified and uncontrolled rush. 'I know I've been an awful chump, darling, but you don't have to worry. It's all in hand. Harriet also made a little slip last year. She went to see a doctor in Amsterdam; he took care of it with absolutely no muss and no fuss. She caught the evening flight on a Friday and was back in London on Sunday – as good as new. She's given me the address, and she's even offered to come with me to hold my hand—'

'Isabella!' he cut in sharply. 'Stop it. Stop talking. Listen to me!' And she broke off and stared at him fearfully.

'You don't know what you are saying.' His voice cut her cruelly. 'What you suggest is monstrous!'

'I'm sorry, Ramón.' She was confused. 'I shouldn't have bothered you with it. Harriet and I could have . . .'

'Harriet is a shallow asinine little tramp. When you place the life of my child in her hands, then you make yourself every bit as culpable as she is.'

Isabella stared at him. This was not what she had expected from him at all.

'This is a miracle, Isabella, the greatest miracle and mystery of the universe. You talk of destroying it. This is our child, Isabella. This is life, new beautiful life, that you and I have created in love. Don't you understand that?'

He leant across and took her hands, and she saw the coldness of his eyes fade. 'This is something that we have made together, our own wondrous creation. It belongs to both of us, to our love.'

'You aren't angry?' she asked hesitantly. 'I thought you would be angry.'

'I am proud and humble,' he whispered. 'I love you. You are infinitely precious to me.' He turned her hands, holding them by the wrists, and laid them on her own stomach. 'I love what you have here; it also is infinitely precious to me.' He had said it at last. 'I love you,' he had said.

'Oh, Ramón,' her vision blurred, 'you are so wonderful, so tender, so kind. The true miracle is that I was ever able to meet somebody like you.'

76

'You will give birth to our child, my darling Bella.'

'Oh, yes! Oh, a thousand times yes, my darling. You have made me so proud, so happy.' All her uncertainty was gone, replaced by an excitement and anticipation that seemed to drive all else into insignificance.

★   ★   ★

This euphoria buoyed her up over the days that followed. It laid a new rich texture on her love for Ramón; something that up until that time had been engrossing but random now had direction and purpose. A dozen times she had been on the point of telling Nanny, and had only succeeded in preventing herself when she realized that the old woman's excitement would be so uncontained that the entire embassy, including her father, would know of the coming event within twenty-four hours. This brought her at last to sober consideration of the prosaic details that had to be arranged. She was already over two months, and Nanny had an eagle eye and an earthy instinct. At home on the family estate of Weltevreden she called the shots on the maids and house-servants and field-girls with an uncanny accuracy. Nanny bathed her when she was at home, and the only surprise was that she hadn't already latched on to Isabella's change of condition.

That evening Ramón had tickets for the Festival of Flamenco at Drury Lane, but she rang him at his private number at the bank.

'Ramón darling, I don't feel like going out tonight. I just want to be alone with you. I'll cook dinner. I'll have it ready by the time you get back to the flat, and we can listen to the new von Karajan disc.'

She could hear the reluctance in his voice. He had been looking forward to the flamenco dancing all week. He was so aggressively Spanish at times. He had even insisted that she begin learning the language, and had given her a set of Linguaphone records. However, she wheedled him shamelessly, and finally he succumbed.

On the way from the embassy to the flat, Isabella double-parked the Mini and picked up a bottle of Pol Roger and another of Montrachet from her father's private bin at Berry Brothers, the wine merchants in St James's Street. Then in the food-hall at Harrods she selected two dozen Whitstable oysters and a pair of perfect veal cutlets.

She was watching from the front window as Ramón turned the corner and came striding down the pavement towards the front door. He looked so English in his three-piece suit. While in London, he even carried a rolled black brolly and sported a bowler, the epitome of the young merchant banker. It was a peculiar gift he had of fitting perfectly into any environment, no matter how diverse, as though he were born to it.

She opened the champagne and as soon as she heard his key in the front door she poured their glasses and placed them beside the silver tray of crushed ice on which she had arranged the open oysters. She restrained herself from rushing wildly through into the tiny hall and instead met him as he came into the living-room. Then her restraint faded and her kiss was long and melting.

'Special occasion?' he asked, with his arm still around her waist, as he saw the tray of oysters and the two long-stemmed tulip glasses softly seething with the yellow wine. She went to fetch a glass and placed it in his hand, and then she looked at him over the rim of her own glass.

'Welcome home, Ramón. I wanted to give you just a little taste of what it's going to be like when you are married to me.'

She saw his eyes flinch; it was more poignant in that she had never seen it happen before. His gaze was always level and steady.

He did not taste the wine and set his glass aside, and she felt an awful premonition of disaster.

'Ramón, what is it?' she asked.

Before she could drink, he took the champagne-glass from her hand and placed it upon the walnut table.

'Bella.' He turned back to face her, and took her hands

78

in his. 'Bella,' he said again, softly, with deep regret, and he turned her hands and kissed the open palms.

'What is it, Ramón?' She could barely draw breath, so tight was her chest with dread.

'I can't marry you, my darling.' She stared at him, and felt her legs tremble and go weak with the shock. 'I can't marry you, at least not yet, my darling.'

She drew her hands out of his grasp and turned away from him. She went slowly to the armchair and sank into it.

'Why?' she asked softly, without looking at him as he came and knelt in front of her. 'You want me to bear your child, then why can't you marry me?'

'Bella, there is nothing I want more in this life than to have you as my wife, and to be father of our child, but . . .'

'Then, why?' she repeated almost listlessly.

'Please listen to me, my darling. Don't say anything more until you have heard me out.'

Now she lifted her eyes and looked at his face, but she was very pale.

'Nine years ago, I married a Cuban girl in Miami.'

Isabella shuddered, and closed her eyes.

'The marriage was a disaster from the very beginning. We spent only a few months together before we parted, but we are both Catholics . . .' He broke off, and touched her pale cheek. She pulled back from his caress, and he sighed softly.

'I'm still married to her,' he said simply.

'What is her name?' Isabella asked without opening her eyes.

'Why do you want to know that?'

'Tell me.' Her voice firmed.

'Natalie.' He shrugged.

'Children?' she asked. 'How many children do you have?'

'None,' he replied. 'You will be the mother of my firstborn.' And he watched the petals of rose return to her cheeks. After a moment she opened her eyes again, but they were shadowed with such despair that the blue had turned to black.

'Oh, Ramón! What are we going to do?'

'I have already begun to do all I can,' he told her. 'When we returned from Spain, I knew then, even before you told me about the baby, I knew that above all else in my life I must have you as my wife.'

'Oh, Ramón.' She blinked hard, and tightened her grip on his hands.

'Natalie is still living in Miami, with her family. I was able to contact her. We spoke on the telephone, more than once. She is very devout. There is nothing, she said, that would persuade her to divorce me.'

Isabella was staring at him hard, and now she shook her head miserably.

'I called her again, on three consecutive evenings. At last, we found something that was more important to her than her God and her confessor.'

'What was that?'

'Money,' he said, with a shade of contempt in his voice. 'I still have most of the winnings from the pigeon shoot. For fifty thousand dollars, she finally agreed to move to Reno and file for divorce.'

'Darling!' Isabella whispered, joy blooming in her eyes again. 'Oh, thank God! When? When will she go?'

'That is the catch. It takes time. I can't push her too hard. I know Natalie. If she found out about you, and guessed why I wanted the divorce, she would exploit her advantage to the utmost. She promised to leave for Reno at the beginning of next month. She says that she has her job and her family to consider. Her mother is not well.'

'Yes, yes,' Isabella cut in impatiently. 'But how long will it take?'

'There is provision in the Nevada state laws for the period of residency in Reno. Three months before they will grant the divorce.'

'I'll be six months gone by then.' Isabella bit her knuckles, then her expression changed. 'And Daddy and

I are booked to leave for Cape Town. Oh, Ramón, what a mess!'

'You can't go back to Cape Town,' Ramón told her flatly. 'I couldn't live without you and, besides, your pregnancy will be obvious to all your family and friends.'

'What do you want me to do?'

'Stay with me until my divorce is final. I love you too much to let you go. I don't want to miss a day of my son's life.'

She smiled at last. 'So it's definitely a son, is it?'

'Of course.' He nodded with mock gravity. 'We must have an heir to the title, must we not? You will stay with me, won't you, Bella?'

'What will I tell my father, and my grandmother? Papa is a pushover, but my grandmother . . .!' Isabella rolled her eyes. 'Centaine Courtney-Malcomess is the family dragon. She actually breathes fire and crunches up the bones of her victims.'

'I will tame your dragon,' he promised.

'I truly believe that you might.' Isabella felt gay and light-headed with relief. 'If anyone can charm Nana, it would be you, my darling.'

*   *   *

The fact that Centaine Courtney-Malcomess was six thousand miles away did make the task a little easier. Isabella prepared the ground with great care. She worked on her father first. Overnight she became once more the dutiful daughter and consummate hostess. She plunged headlong and with all her previous panache into organizing the final few weeks of social engagements that marked the end of Shasa Courtney's ambassadorial term.

'Welcome back from wherever it was you disappeared to,' Shasa told her drily at the end of one of her more successful dinner-parties. 'I missed you, you know.'

They were standing arm-in-arm on the front steps of

Highveld, watching the limousine pull away, bearing the last departing guest.

'One o'clock in the morning.' Shasa glanced at his wrist-watch, but Isabella forestalled him.

'Too early for bed.' She squeezed his arm. 'Let me fix a nightcap and a final cigar for you. We haven't had a chance to talk all evening.'

That afternoon Davidoffs had delivered a dozen of his cigars from the stock they kept for him in their specially humidified storage in St James's. She held one to her ear as she rolled it between her fingers.

'Perfect,' she murmured.

Shasa lolled in the buttoned-leather armchair across the room. Earlier the company had done full justice to the claret and the port, but his single eye was still clear and bright. The black silk patch over the other eye was as pristine as the perfectly constructed bow at the throat of his snowy shirt-front.

He watched her with undiluted pleasure, as though she were a blood filly from his stables or the gem of his art collection. She was the most beautiful of all the Courtneys, he arrived at that considered verdict.

In her youth his own mother had been a celebrated beauty. The years had dimmed Shasa's memory of the zenith of her beauty, but there was a portrait of her in her prime by Annigoni in the drawing-room of Weltevreden. Even allowing for the artist's kindly eye, she must have been an extraordinary woman. The force of her character shone out of the portrait's dark eyes. She was still, at sixty-nine years of age, a magnificent woman, handsome and vigorous, but at no time in her life could she have equalled her grand-daughter who now stood in the bright noonday of her youth.

Isabella cut the tip of the cigar with the gold cutter from her father's desk. She lit the cedarwood taper from the fire and held it for him until the cigar was drawing evenly. Then she extinguished the taper and went to dribble a little Cognac into the crystal balloon glass.

'Professor Symmonds read the latest section of my thesis this morning.'

'Ah, you are still gracing the University with your presence, are you?' Shasa studied his daughter's bare shoulders in the soft light of the fire. She had inherited that skin from her mother, as lustrous and unblemished as ivory.

'He thinks it is good.' Isabella ignored the jibe.

'If it is up to the same standard as the first hundred pages that you let me read, then Symmonds is probably correct.'

'He wants me to stay on here to finish it.' She was not looking at him. Shasa felt the sick little slide of dread in his chest.

'Here in London, on your own?' His response was instantaneous.

'On my own? With five hundred friends, the staff of Courtney Enterprises' London office, my mother . . . !' She brought the brandy balloon to him. 'Not really abandoned completely in a strange city, Papa.'

Shasa made a noncommittal noise in his throat and tasted the Cognac, searching desperately for some better reason why she should accompany him back to the Cape.

'Where would you stay?' he grumped.

'That wasn't even a good try,' she laughed at him openly, and took the cigar from his hand. She drew upon it with pursed red lips, and then blew a feather of smoke into his face. 'In Cadogan Square there is a flat which cost you almost a million pounds. It is standing empty.' She gave him back the cigar.

She was right of course. Since the official ambassadorial residence went with the job, the family flat had been unused. He was silent, driven to the ropes, and Isabella gathered herself for the *coup de grâce*.

'You are the one who was so frightfully keen on my doctorate, Pater. You won't deprive me of it now, will you?'

Shasa rallied gamely. 'Since you have obviously thought this all out so carefully, you must already have spoken to your grandmother.'

Isabella stooped over him as he sat in the armchair and kissed the top of his head.

'I was hoping that you would speak to Nana for me, my darling Daddy.'

Shasa sighed. 'Witch,' he murmured. 'You make me a party to my own undoing.'

She could rely on her father to take care of Nana, but there was still Nanny to consider. However, Isabella softened her up for a day or two beforehand by reciting the names and virtues of all seventeen of the grandchildren who so eagerly awaited her return to Weltevreden. Nanny had been away from home for three years, and three long English winters.

'Just think of it, Nanny. It will be spring at the Cape when the boat docks, and Johannes will be waiting on the pier.' Johannes was the head groom at Weltevreden and Nanny's favourite son. The old woman's eyes shone. So when Isabella finally broke the news Nanny threw her hands around and wailed about ingratitude and the decay of the modern generation's sense of duty. Then she sulked for two days but without real venom.

Isabella went down to Southampton to see them all off. Shasa's new Aston Martin was hoisted on board the Union Castle liner by one of the giraffe-necked cranes, and then the servants lined up on the pier for their farewells. She embraced them all, from the Malay chef to Klonkie the chauffeur. Nanny burst into tears when Isabella kissed her.

'You'll probably never see this old woman again. You'll miss me when I've gone. Think of how I nursed you when you was a baby . . .'

'Go on with you, Nanny. You'll be there to nurse all my babies for me.' It was a dangerous subject to broach, but Nanny's perceptions were dulled. The promise drove off the shadow of her imminent demise, and she cheered noticeably.

'You come home soon now, child, you hear, where old Nanny can keep an eye on you. All that hot Courtney blood – we'll find you a good clean South African boy.'

When Isabella came to say goodbye to Shasa, unexpectedly she found herself also dissolving into a salty wash of tears. Shasa handed her the crisp white handkerchief from the pocket of his double-breasted blazer. When she had dried up and given it back to him, he blew his own nose loudly and then dabbed at his single eye.

'Damned wind!' he explained. 'Got a bit of grit in it.'

As the liner pulled away from the wharf and headed down-river, he was a tall and elegant figure at the ship's rail, high above her; but he stood alone, slightly separated from the other passengers. He had never remarried since the divorce. She knew that since then he had been seeing literally dozens of women, all elegant and talented and nubile, but he always walked on alone.

'Doesn't he ever feel lonely?' she wondered, and waved until he was an indistinguishable speck on the ship's deck.

On the drive back to London, the road kept dissolving before her eyes in a glassy mirage of tears.

'It's the baby,' she tried to excuse herself. 'He's making me all gooey and sentimental.' And she clasped her belly and tried to find a lump, and was vaguely disappointed that her muscles were still flat and hard. 'God, what if it's all just a false alarm!'

The possibility heightened her melancholy, and she reached for the packet of Kleenex in the cubby-hole of the Mini.

However, when she climbed the stairs to the flat, the door opened before she touched it and Ramón reached out and drew her into his arms. Her tears were forgotten.

*   *   *

The family flat in Cadogan Square occupied the first two floors of a listed red-brick Victorian house. There were five double bedrooms, and the walls of the master suite were clad with powder-blue and antique silver panelling that had reputedly graced the boudoir of Madame de Pompadour. The *plafond* was decorated with dancing circles of

85

naked wood-nymphs and leering satyrs. Much to Shasa's chagrin, Isabella referred to the décor as 'Louis Quinze bordello'.

She used it merely as an accommodation address, and called round on Fridays to pick up her mail and have tea with the full-time housekeeper in the ground-floor pantry. The housekeeper was an ally and fielded all the long-distance telephone calls from Weltevreden and other parts afar.

Isabella made her true home in Ramón's tiny flat. When the wardrobe that he allocated to her proved to be inadequate, she rotated her clothes between it and the cavernous storage at Cadogan Square. She found a dainty little lady's writing-bureau in an antique shop in Kensington Church Street which just fitted into the corner beside the bed, and made that her study.

Like a married couple, they settled into a routine. They were up before dawn for gym or riding; Isabella's gynaecologist had forbidden jogging. 'It's a foetus not a milk-shake that you are brewing, my dear.' Then, when Ramón left for the bank, she settled down at her bureau and worked steadily on her thesis until lunchtime. They met at Justin de Blank or the health bar at Harrods, for Isabella had given up alcohol and put herself on a strict diet for the baby's sake.

'I refuse to let myself swell up like a toad. I don't want to revolt you.'

'You are the most desirable woman in existence, and pregnancy has brought you to full bloom,' he contradicted her, and touched her bosom. It was magnificent.

'I asked the gyney, and he said it's quite OK; we don't have to hold back at all,' she giggled. 'I do hope the ambulance that takes me to the maternity home has a comfortable double stretcher so that we can fit in a quickie on the way.'

After lunch she went on to visit her tutor or to spend the rest of the afternoon in the reading-room of the British Museum. Finally there was a mad dash back to the flat in the Mini in time to start preparing Ramón's dinner. Fortunately, Papa had arranged for her to retain her diplomatic plates, and she parked at the kerb right outside the front door and smiled winningly at the hovering traffic warden.

In the evenings they went out less and less frequently, apart from an occasional theatre or an early dinner with Harriet and her latest beau. Usually they piled all the cushions on the floor and sprawled in front of the television, arguing and discussing and billing and cooing and ignoring the inane burble of 'Coronation Street' and the game-shows.

When at last the taut flat plain of her belly began to bulge she opened the front of her silk dressing-gown and exhibited it proudly. 'Feel it!' she urged Ramón. 'Isn't it wonderful?'

He palpated it solemnly. 'Yes,' he nodded sagely. 'Definitely a boy.'

'How do you know?'

'Here.' He took her hand. 'Can't you feel it?'

'Ah, it does stick out a bit. He must take after his papa. Funny how thinking about that makes me feel like bed.'

'Sleepy?' he asked.

'Hardly,' she replied.

Shasa had left her with her Harrods charge-card, and she acquired most of her maternity clothes there, although Harriet kept discovering newly fashionable boutiques that specialized in clothes for the swinging young mother-to-be. Wearing one of her flowing new caftans, she enrolled in the ante-natal classes that her gynaecologist recommended. Suddenly the company and conversation of the other gravid classmates that would once have bored her to distraction was fun and fascination.

At least once a month, Ramón had to fly out of town on bank business, and each time he was away for a week or more. However, he telephoned her whenever he had an opportunity. Although she missed him more painfully than

87

she would admit even to herself, when he returned her joy was enhanced a hundredfold.

After one such trip, she met him at Heathrow and drove him directly back to the flat. He dropped his travel-bag in the hall and threw his jacket over the back of the chair before he went into the bathroom.

His Spanish passport slipped from the inner pocket of his jacket and plopped on to the carpet. She picked it up and riffled through it until she found his photograph. It wasn't bad, but no camera could do him full justice. She flipped the page and saw the date of birth. That reminded her that his birthday was only two weeks away. She had determined to make it a wonderful occasion. She had already seen a glass statuette in an antique-shop in Mayfair, an exquisite little glass nude by René Lalique. She recognized the body as so similar to her own, even to the exaggerated length of leg and tight boyish buttocks. But for the fact that it had been sculptured at the height of Lalique's popularity during the 1920s, Isabella could easily have been the model. However, the price daunted even her, and she was still plucking up sufficient courage to buy it for him.

She flipped over a few pages more of his passport, and the visa caught her eye. It had been stamped in Moscow that morning, and she blinked with surprise.

'Darling,' she called through the bathroom door. 'I thought you were in Rome. How did you end up in Moscow?' Everything she had ever learnt, every facet of her South African upbringing, had always pointed to Russia as the great Antichrist. Even the symbol of hammer and sickle and the Cyrillic script stamped in his passport made the fine hairs on her forearms rise in repugnance.

There was silence for a full minute beyond the locked door, and then it was flung open abruptly, and Ramón strode out in his shirt-sleeves and snatched the booklet from her hand. His expression was one of cold fury, and his eyes terrified her.

'Don't ever pry into my affairs again,' he said softly.

Although he never mentioned the incident later, it was almost a week before she felt that he had forgiven her. It had so intimidated her that thereafter she tried to put it completely out of her mind.

Then, in early November, when she called round at the Cadogan Square flat, the housekeeper handed her her mail. As always, there was a letter from her father, but under it was another envelope franked in Johannesburg, and with a lift of pleasure she recognized her brother Michael's handwriting.

Each of her three brothers was so distinctly different in looks and character and personality that it was impossible for her to have a favourite.

Sean, the eldest, was the flamboyant adventurer. A wild spirit who, until she met Ramón, had been the most impossibly beautiful man she had ever known. Sean was the soldier and the hunter. He had already been decorated with the Silver Cross for valour in Rhodesia's grim little bush war. When he wasn't tracking down terrorists, he ran the vast hunting concession in the Zambezi valley for Courtney Enterprises. Isabella adored him.

Garrick was her second brother, the ugly duckling, the myopic asthmatic who during his unhappy childhood had always been referred to as 'Poor Garry'. However, although born deficient in most physical areas, he had inherited his full measure of the Courtney spirit and determination and shrewdness. He had worked on his puny body until it was almost grotesquely muscular with such a barrel of a chest and powerful arms that all his clothes had to be tailored for him. With near-sighted eyes behind thick horn-rimmed spectacles, and no natural sporting ability, he had developed such powers of concentration that he made himself into a four-goal polo-player, a scratch golfer and an extraordinary shot with rifle and shotgun.

In addition he had succeeded his father as chairman and chief executive officer of Courtney Enterprises. Not yet thirty years of age, he ran a multi-billion-dollar complex of companies with the same formidable application to detail and insatiable appetite for hard work that he brought to all his other endeavours. Yet he never forgot her birthday, and responded instantly to any call that Isabella made on him no matter how onerous or how trivial. She called him 'Teddy Bear' because he was so big and hairy and cuddly, and she loved him dearly.

Then there was Michael, sweet, gentle Michael, the family peacemaker, the thoughtful, compassionate, poetic creature, and the only Courtney who, despite the encouragement and example of his father and his two brothers, had never killed a wild bird or animal in his life. Instead, he had written and published three successful books, one a collection of poems and the other two on South African history and politics. The last two had both been banned by South Africa's industrious censors for their unseemly treatment of racial matters and their radical political flavour. He was also a highly considered journalist and the deputy editor of the *Golden City Mail*, a large-circulation English-language newspaper which was stubbornly and outspokenly opposed to the Nationalist Afrikaner government of John Vorster and its policy of apartheid. Of course, Courtney Enterprises owned eighty per cent of the *Mail*'s stock, otherwise he might not have achieved such a responsible position at such a tender age.

During all of Isabella's childhood, Michael had been her protector and adviser and confidant, and after Nana her favourite story-teller. She trusted Michael more than anybody else in her life, and if Sean hadn't been so wonderful and Garrick so lovable and cuddly, then Michael would definitely have been her favourite brother. It was a dead heat between the three of them for her affections, but she loved Michael as much as any of them, and now his handwriting on the envelope gave her a warm glow of pleasure and a prickle of guilt. She hadn't written to him since she had met Ramón, almost six months ago.

The second paragraph of the first page caught her eye the instant she unfolded it, and she skipped the salutation and went straight to it.

Pater tells me that you are cosily ensconced in Cadogan Square and labouring mightily on your thesis. Good for you, Bella. However, I am sure that you are not presently occupying all five of the bedrooms, and I was hoping that you could fit me in somehow. I plan to be in London for three weeks from the fifteenth of the month. I will be out all day, every day. I have a full schedule of interviews and meetings, so I promise not to be a nuisance and interfere with your studies . . .

It was a complication in that she would be forced to take up physical residence at Cadogan Square for the period of Michael's visit. However, most fortunately, it coincided with one of Ramón's periodic travels abroad. She would have been alone anyway. Now at least she would have Michael's company.

She sent him a cable addressed to the *Mail*'s offices in Johannesburg, and set about making Cadogan Square look as though it was being permanently lived in. She had a week to prepare for Michael's arrival.

'There will have to be some explanations,' she told Ramón, and clasped the neat little bulge of her tummy. 'Luckily Michael is so understanding. I'm sure that the two of you would get on well together. I wish you could meet him.'

'I will try to complete my business ahead of time and get back to London while your brother is still here.'

'Oh, Ramón darling, I would love that. Please do try.'

She was waiting for Michael as he pushed his luggage-trolley through the international-arrivals barrier at Heathrow, and she let out a squeal of glee as she recognized him. He swung her off her feet, and then his expression changed as he felt her stomach against him, and he set her down again with exaggerated gentleness.

As she drove him into town in the Mini, she kept darting glances at him. He was tanned – when you lived in London you noticed that immediately – and he had grown his hair fashionably long. It curled over the collar of his bottle-green

91

corduroy hacking-jacket. However, his smile was still boy-ish and frank, and the blue Courtney eyes lacked the hard acquisitive sparkle of all the other Courtneys, and were instead mild and thoughtful.

She pumped him for news of home, partly to satisfy her curiosity but mostly to keep the conversation away from her fecund belly. According to Michael, Pater had en-grossed himself in his new duties as chairman of Armscor. Nana was growing more vigorous and more imperious every day, ruling Weltevreden with an iron fist. She had even taken up breeding retrievers and training them for gun-dog trials. Sean was still killing platoons of guerrillas and droves of buffalo. He had recently been promoted to a reserve captain in the Ballantyne Scouts, one of the crack Rhodesian regiments. Garry had just presented his share-holders with record company profits, for the sixth year in succession. His wife, Holly, was about to produce another infant. Everybody was holding thumbs for a girl this time.

As he said this, Michael glanced at her midriff signifi-cantly, but Isabella concentrated all her attention on the traffic to avoid an explanation and at last parked the Mini in the mews garage at the back of the square.

Michael was suffering from jet-lag, so she ran him a foam bath and brought him a whisky and soda. While he was soaking, she sat on the closed lid of the toilet-seat and chatted. She would never have contemplated sharing a bathroom with either Sean or Garry, but between Michael and herself nudity was natural and unremarked.

'Do you remember that silly little nonsense rhyme?' Michael asked at last. 'How did it go again?

' "Dum de dum-dum,
And her father said, 'Nelly,
There is more in your belly
Than ever went in through your mouth!' " '

Isabella chuckled unashamedly. 'Is that what they call "the trained journalistic eye"? You don't miss anything, do you, Mickey?'

'Miss it?' he laughed with her. 'Your tummy damn near knocked out my trained journalistic eye!'

'Pretty, isn't it?' Isabella pushed it out as far as it would go, and patted it proudly.

'Stunning!' Michael agreed. 'And I am sure that Pater and Nana would agree if they could see it.'

'You won't tell, will you, Mickey?'

'We don't tell each other's secrets, you and me. Never have, never will. But what are you going to do with the eventual, ah, result?'

'My son, your nephew – you call that a *result*? Shame on you, Mickey. Ramón calls it the greatest miracle and mystery of the universe.'

'Ramón! So that is the culprit's name. I hope he's wearing bullet-proof knickers when Nana catches up with him toting her trusty old shotgun, loaded with buckshot.'

'He's a marqués, Mickey. The Marqués de Santiago y Machado.'

'Ah, that might make a difference. Nana is enough of a snob to be impressed. She will probably reduce the charge from buckshot to birdshot.'

'By the time Nana finds out about it, I'll be a marquesa.'

'So the nefarious Ramón intends making an honest woman out of you, does he? When?'

'Well, there is a little bit of a hitch,' she admitted.

'You mean he's married already.'

'How did you know that, Mickey?' She gaped at him.

'And his wife won't give him a divorce?'

'Mickey!'

'My love, that's the hoariest old chestnut in the packet.' Michael stood up, cascading soapy bath water, and reached for the towel.

'You don't know him, Mickey. He's not like that.'

'May I take that as an impartial and totally unbiased opinion?' Michael stepped out of the bath, and began to towel himself down.

'He loves me.'

'So I see.'

93

'Don't be flippant.'

'Make me a promise, Bella. If anything goes wrong, come to me first. Will you promise me that?'

She nodded. 'Yes, I promise. You are still my very best friend. I promise, but nothing is going to go wrong. You just wait and see.'

She took him to dinner at Ma Cuisine in Walton Street. The restaurant was so popular that they would never have got a table had not Isabella made the reservation the very day that she heard Michael was coming to London.

'I like escorting a pregger,' Michael remarked as they settled at the table. 'Everybody smiles at me, as though I am responsible.'

'Nonsense. It's simply because you are so handsome.' They talked about their work. Isabella made him promise to read her thesis and make suggestions. Then Michael explained that the main reason he was in London was to write a series of articles on the anti-apartheid movement, and the South African political exiles living in Britain.

'I have arranged interviews with some of the leading lights: Oliver Tambo, Denis Brutus . . .'

'Do you think our censors will let you publish the article?' Isabella asked. 'They'll probably ban the entire edition again, and Garry will be furious. Anything that affects the profits makes Garry furious.'

Michael chuckled. 'Poor old Garry.' That title was habitual but no longer appropriate. 'Life is so simple for him – not the black and white of morality, but the black and red of the bank statement.'

With the dessert Michael asked suddenly, 'How is Mater? Have you seen her lately?'

'Not Mater, nor Mother, nor even Mummy,' Isabella corrected him tartly. 'You know that she thinks those terms terribly bourgeois. But to answer your question – no, I haven't seen Tara for some time.'

'She is our mother, Bella.'

'She might have thought of that when she deserted Pater

and the rest of us and ran off with a black revolutionary and bore him a little brown bastard.'

'And you might be a shade more charitable when it comes to bearing bastards,' Michael said mildly, and then saw the hurt in her eyes. 'I'm sorry, Bella, but as in your case there are reasons for all things. We shouldn't judge her too harshly. Pater can't be the easiest man in the world to be married to, and not everybody can play the game to the rules that Nana lays down. Some of us don't have the killer instincts finely enough developed. I don't think Tara fitted into the family at all, not from the very beginning. She never was an élitist. Her sympathies were always with the underdog, and then Moses Gama came into her life . . .'

'Mickey darling' – Isabella leant across the table and took his hand – 'you are the most compassionate, understanding person in the world. You spend your life making excuses for us, protecting us from the Fates. I do love you so much. I don't even want to fight or argue with you.'

'Good.' He squeezed her hand. 'Then, you'll come along to see Tara with me. She writes to me regularly. She adores you, Isabella, and she misses you terribly. It hurts her when you avoid her.'

'Oh, Mickey, you set a trap for me, you devil.' She thought furiously for a second. 'But what about my condition? I was hoping to be a little more discreet.'

'Tara is your mother, she loves you, and they don't come any more broad-minded than our Tara. She's not going to do anything to hurt you, you know that.'

'To please you,' she sighed, and capitulated. 'Only to please you, Mickey.'

So on the following Saturday morning they walked down Brompton Road, and Michael had to stretch his long legs to match her flowing athletic stride.

'Are you training to have a sprog-bod, or for the next Olympics?' he asked with a grin.

'You smoke too much,' Isabella scoffed at him.

'My only vice.'

Tara Courtney, or Tara Gama as she now called herself, was the manageress of a small residential hotel off Cromwell Road, and her clientele was composed almost exclusively of expatriates and new immigrants from Africa and India and the Caribbean.

It always amazed Isabella that an area like this existed only twenty minutes' walk from the grandeur of Cadogan Square. The Lord Kitchener Hotel was as shabby and run-down as its manageress. Again it amazed Isabella that her mother was the same person who had once presided over the great château of Weltevreden. Isabella's earliest memories were of her mother in a full-length ball-gown, with yellow diamonds from the Courtney mine at H'ani glittering at her smooth white throat and on her earlobes, her dark auburn hair piled high on her lovely head as she came down the sweep of the marble staircase. Isabella had never suspected the terrible dissatisfaction and misery that must have festered beneath that regal façade.

Now Tara's magnificent head of hair had greyed, and she had touched it up with a cheap home-dye job that came up in variegated tones of ginger and brazen plum. Her skin that Isabella had inherited in all its silken perfection had withered and bagged and wrinkled with neglect. There were little blackheads lodged in the enlarged pores around the creases between her nose and cheeks, and her false teeth were too large for her mouth, distorting the sweet line of her lips.

She rushed down the front steps of the hotel to embrace Isabella in a cloud of pungent Cologne. Isabella returned her hug with the strength of a guilty conscience.

'Let me look at my darling daughter.' She held Isabella at arm's length, and her eyes dropped immediately. 'You have grown more beautiful, Bella, if that were possible, but the reason is pretty obvious. I see you are carrying a little bundle of fun and joy.'

Isabella's smile crooked with annoyance, but she ignored the reference.

'You look well, Mummy – Tara, I mean.' Tara wore

the self-conscious uniform of the militant left-winger: a shapeless grey cardigan over a full-length granny-print shift and men's open brown sandals.

'It's been months,' Tara complained, 'almost a year, and you live just down the road. How can you neglect your old mum so?'

Michael intervened smoothly, deflecting Tara's self-pity, embracing her with unfeigned warmth and enthusiasm. She turned to him with theatrical mother-love.

'Mickey, you were always the sweetest and most loving of all my children.'

And Isabella's smile began to hurt her lips. She wondered just how long she had to stay and when she could escape. She knew it wasn't going to be easy, and that for once she could expect little support from Michael. Tara linked her arms through theirs. Michael on one side of her and Isabella on the other, she led them into the hotel.

'I've got tea and biscuits ready for you. I've been in an absolute tizz ever since Michael called to say you were coming.'

On a Saturday morning the Lord Kitchener's public lounge was filled with Tara's guests. The air was thick with tobacco smoke and the cadences of Swahili and Gujarati and Xhosa. Tara introduced them to everybody in the room, even though Isabella had met many of them on her previous visits.

'My son and daughter from Cape Town in South Africa.' And she saw how some of the eyes flicked at the name of her country.

The hell with them, too, Isabella decided defiantly. Funny how at home she thought of herself as a liberal, but when she was abroad and encountered that reaction she thought of herself as a patriot.

At last Tara seated them in a corner of the lounge, and while she poured the tea, she asked in a bright and cheery tone that carried clearly to everybody in the large room: 'So now, Bella, tell me about the baby. When are you expecting it and who is the father?'

'This is hardly the time or the place, Tara.' Isabella paled with irritation, but Tara laughed.

'Oh, we are all just one big family here at the Lordy. You can talk freely.'

This time Michael murmured gently: 'Bella really doesn't want all the world to know her private business. We'll talk about it later, Tara.'

'You funny old-fashioned thing.' Tara reached across and tried to hug Isabella again, but spilled some of her tea on her granny-print skirt and gave up the attempt. 'None of us here worries our head over bourgeois conventions.'

'That's enough, Tara,' Michael said firmly, and then to divert her: 'Where is Benjamin and how is he doing?'

'Oh, Ben is my pride and joy.' Tara took the bait. 'He just popped out for a few minutes. He had to go down to the school to hand in an essay. He's such a clever boy, he's taking his A-levels this year, only sixteen and his headmaster says he is the most brilliant, the cleverest child he has had in Ryham Grammar for the last ten years. All the girls adore him. He's so good-looking.' Tara chattered on, and Isabella was relieved not to have to make conversation. Instead she listened to the recital of her half-brother's virtues.

Benjamin Gama was one of the many reasons that Isabella felt uncomfortable in this other world in which her mother lived. So deep had been the disgrace and so poisonous the scandal that Tara had brought on the Courtney family that her name was never mentioned at Weltevreden. Nana had forbidden it.

Only Michael had ever discussed it with her, and then in the most general terms. 'I'm sorry, Bella. I'm not going to repeat cruel rumour and hearsay. If you want that, you'll have to go elsewhere. I'll only tell you the facts, and those are that when Tara left South Africa after Moses Gama was arrested and imprisoned no charges were ever brought against her and no proof was ever offered to implicate her in any criminal activity.'

'But didn't Pater arrange it that way to protect the family reputation?'

'Why don't you ask Pater himself?' She had indeed tentatively broached the subject with her father; but Shasa, for once cold and aloof, had dismissed the enquiry. In an odd way Isabella had been relieved by his refusal to talk about it. Isabella was honest enough to recognize her own cowardice. She didn't truly want to know the extent of her mother's guilt. Deep down, she didn't really want to know if her mother had indeed been a party to the notorious 'Guy Fawkes' plot of her lover, Moses Gama, to blow up the South African Houses of Parliament, the attempt which had resulted in the death of Isabella's grandfather, Tara's own father. Perhaps her mother was a traitor and a murderess guilty of patricide. At the very least she was certainly a blatant adulteress and a miscegenist, which was a crime under South African law, and once again Isabella wondered just what she was doing here.

Suddenly Tara's features brightened, and for an instant she recaptured a faint glimmer of her lost beauty.

'Ben!' she cried. 'Look who have come to see us, Benjamin. Your brother and sister. Isn't that nice?'

Isabella swivelled in her chair, and her half-brother stood in the doorway of the hotel lounge behind her. He had grown again in the year since last she had seen him and obviously he had made that leap from puberty into manhood.

'Hello, Benjamin,' she cried too enthusiastically, and although he smiled she sensed the reserve in him, and saw the wariness in his dark eyes.

Tara had not been completely prejudiced by her maternal instincts. Benjamin was indeed a fine-looking lad. His natural African grace had combined well with his mother's more delicate features. His skin had a coppery tone, and his hair was a neat woolly cap of tight dark curls.

'Hello, Isabella.' The south London accent on the tongue of this son of Africa startled her. She made no move to embrace him. From their very first meeting there had been a tacit agreement between them: no displays of simulated affection. They shook hands quickly, and then both stepped back. Before Isabella could think of anything further to say, Benjamin had turned to Michael. Now his smile was a flash of perfect teeth and the sparkle of dark eyes.

'Mickey!' he said, and he took two quick light steps to meet his older brother. They clasped each other around the shoulders.

Isabella envied Michael that exceptional ability to evoke trust and liking in everybody around him. Benjamin seemed truly to accept him as a brother and a friend without any of the reserve that he showed towards Isabella. Soon all three of them, Tara, Ben and Mickey, were chatting away with animation. Isabella felt herself excluded from their intimate little circle.

At last one of the black South African students crossed the lounge and spoke to Tara. She looked up in consternation and then glanced at her watch.

'My goodness, thank you for reminding me, Nelson.' She smiled up at the student. 'We were having such a good natter that we completely forgot about the time.' Tara jumped to her feet. 'Come on, everybody! If we are going to Trafalgar Square, we had better leave now.'

There was a general exodus from the lounge, and Isabella edged across to Michael.

'What's this all about, Mickey? You seem to know what's going on. Fill me in.'

'There is a rally in Trafalgar Square.'

'Oh God, no! Not another one of those anti-apartheid jamborees. Why didn't you warn me?'

'It would have given you an excuse to duck out,' Michael grinned at her. 'Why don't you come along?'

'No, thanks. I've lived with that nonsense for the past three years, ever since Pater took over the embassy. What are you getting mixed up in that ridiculous business for?'

'It's my job, Bella my sweeting. That's what I came to

London for, to write about this ridiculous business, as you call it. Come with us.'

'Why should I bother?'

'See the world from the other side of the fence for a change – you might find it refreshing – and to be with me. We could have fun together.' She wavered uncertainly. Despite her disdain for the subject, she loved his company. They truly did have fun together, and with Ramón away she was lonely.

'Only if we ride on the top of a bus, not on the Tube. You know I can never resist a bus ride.'

They were a party of twenty or so from the Lordy, including Nelson Litalongi, the South African student. Michael found a seat for her on the upper deck of the red bus, and then he and Nelson squeezed in beside her. Tara and Benjamin were in the seat directly in front of them, but they faced around to join in the laughter and the joking. The mood was gay and carefree, and despite herself Isabella found she was indeed having fun. Michael was the centre of everything, and he and Nelson began to sing. They both had fine voices, and the others joined in with the chorus of 'This Is My Island in the Sun'. Nelson could mimic Harry Belafonte to the life and resembled him except that the tone of his skin was lustrous charcoal. He and Michael had hit it off together from the beginning.

When they climbed off the bus in front of the National Gallery, the demonstrators were already assembling on the open square beneath the tall column, and Michael made a joke about Nelson and Horatio. Everybody laughed, and they trooped across the road into the square, and the pigeons rose in fluttering clouds from around their feet.

There was a temporary platform erected at the end of the square, directly in front of South Africa House, and an area had been roped off, in which a few hundred demonstrators had already assembled. They joined the back ranks, and Tara produced a hand-drawn banner from her plastic shopping-bag and held it aloft.

'Apartheid is a crime against humanity.'

Isabella edged away from her and tried to pretend they were not related. 'She really doesn't mind making a spectacle of herself, does she?' she whispered to Michael, and he laughed.

'That's the whole object of the exercise.'

Nevertheless, Isabella did find it interesting to be a part of this motley gathering. With distaste she had viewed many others like it from the high windows of the ambassador's office across the road, but this gave her a totally new perspective. The crowd was good-natured and well behaved. Four blue-uniformed bobbies stood by to see fair play, and smiled in avuncular fashion when one of the speakers referred to London as a police state every bit as bad as Pretoria. To show her support and to dissociate herself from the remark, Isabella blew the nicest-looking copper a kiss, and his indulgent smile stretched into a delighted grin.

The speeches from the platform droned on against the rumble of the traffic and the passing scarlet buses. Isabella had heard it all before, and so had the others in the crowd to judge by their phlegm and apathy. The best laugh of the day came when a pigeon wheeling high overhead ejected a spurt of whitewash which hit the speaker of the moment fairly on his shiny bald pate and Bella called out: 'Fascist bird, agent of the racist Pretoria régime!'

The meeting ended with a vote on the motion that John Vorster and his illegal régime should immediately resign and hand over power to the Democratic People's Government of South Africa. The motion was declared carried unanimously and Michael remarked: 'Which should make John Vorster tremble in his boots.' The meeting broke up more peaceably than a crowd from a football match.

'Let's find a pub,' Michael suggested. 'All that toppling of fascist governments has made me thirsty.'

'There is a good one in the Strand,' Nelson Litalongi suggested.

'Lead the way,' Michael encouraged him. When they bellied up to the bar-counter, he bought the first round.

'Well,' Isabella gave her judgement as she sipped her ginger beer, 'that was a fair old waste of time. Two hundred little people spouting hot air aren't going to change anything.'

'Don't be too sure of that.' Michael wiped the froth off his upper lip with the back of his hand. 'Maybe it's the first little ripple lapping at the foot of the dam wall – soon that ripple could become a wavelet, and then a rip-tide and finally a tidal wave.'

'Oh, nonsense, Mickey,' Isabella dismissed the idea brusquely. 'South Africa is too strong, too rich. America and Britain have too much invested in her. They won't let us down; they can't expect us to hand over our birthright to a pack of Marxist savages.' She repeated the obvious truths that she had heard her father as ambassador voice so often over the last three years. She was discomfited by the acrimony and logic with which she was assailed by her mother and her half-brother, and by Nelson Litalongi and the twenty other coloured residents from the Lord Kitchener Hotel. It was not a happy experience. That evening when she and Michael returned to Cadogan Square, she was shaken and subdued.

'They are so bitter and angry, Mickey,' she lamented.

'It's the new wave, Bella. If we are to survive it, we should try to understand and come to terms with it.'

'It's not as though they are badly treated. Just think about Nanny and Klonkie and Gamiet and all our people at Weltevreden. I mean, Mickey, they are a damned sight better off than most of the whites living in this country.'

'I know how you feel, Bella. You can drive yourself mad pondering on the rights and wrongs, but you've got to come back to one thing in the end. They are human beings, just like us. Some of them a hell of a lot better and nicer. By what right, divine or infernal, can we prevent them sharing all that the country of our birth has to offer?'

'That's very well in theory, but this afternoon they were talking about armed struggle. That means blowing women and children to pieces. That means blood and death,

Mickey. Just like the Irish. How do you feel about that?'

'I don't know what I feel about that, Bella. Sometimes I feel – No! Killing and maiming and burning are never justified. Then at other times I feel – Sure, why not? Man has been killing his fellow-men for a million years to protect himself and his birthright. Pater, who rants and roars at the thought of an armed struggle in South Africa, is the same person who climbed into a Hurricane in 1940 and went off to machine-gun Ethiopians and Italians and Germans with gay old abandon in defence of what he saw as his freedom. Nana, that stalwart of the rule of law and the sanctity of private property, and defender of the free-market system, was the one who nodded happily and murmured, "Quite right, too!" when she heard the news of the most appalling violence of all mankind's bloody and violent history, the bombs on Hiroshima and Nagasaki. So how immoral and bloodthirsty are Tara and Benjamin and Nelson Litalongi compared to us and our own family? Who is right and who is wrong, Bella?'

'You've given me a terrible headache.' Bella stood up. 'I'm going to bed.'

★   ★   ★

The telephone woke her at six in the morning, and as she heard Ramón's voice the dark shadow over her life evaporated.

'Darling, where are you?'

'Athens.'

'Oh.' Her spirits plunged. 'I hoped you might be at Heathrow.'

'I've been delayed. I will be here for at least three more days. Why don't you come across and join me?'

'To Athens?' She was still half-asleep.

'Yes, why not? You can still catch the ten o'clock flight on BEA. We could steal three days together. How about the Acropolis in the moonlight? We can get out to the islands, and there are some important people I would like you to meet.'

'Yes!' she cried. 'Why not! Give me your telephone number. I'll ring you back as soon as I have a seat on the plane.' All the lines to British European Airways reservations were busy, and she was running out of time, so Michael drove her out to Heathrow in the Mini and dropped her at the terminal entrance.

'I'll wait until you get a confirmed reservation,' he suggested.

'No, Mickey, you're a darling, but I won't have any trouble at this time of year; the holiday season is over. You go off to your interview, and I'll call you at the flat when Ramón and I are on our way home.'

As she walked into the terminal she realized that she had been over-optimistic. Hordes of dejected and weary travellers blocked the aisles with their luggage. When she finally got to the head of the queue at the information-desk, she was told that a wildcat strike by the French air-traffic controllers had delayed all flights by up to five hours, and that the Athens flight was fully booked. She would have to join the waiting list, even for a seat in first class.

She stood in another queue to use a public telephone and finally got through to Ramón at the number he had given her in Athens. He sounded as disappointed as she felt.

'I was looking forward to your arrival. I have lauded you to the skies to the people I want you to meet here.'

'I'm not going to give up,' she declared. 'Even if I have to sit here all day.'

It was a day of discomfort and misery and frustration. When the flight was finally called at five o'clock that evening, she stood at the check-in counter praying for a seat on the waiting-list. However, there were half a dozen other hopefuls ahead of her. In the end, the booking clerk shook her head regretfully.

'I'm so sorry, Miss Courtney.'

The next flight to Athens was scheduled for ten the

following morning, but there would certainly be delays and another waiting-list. Finally Isabella gave up, and went dejectedly to place another call to Athens. Ramón was not available, so she left a message for him with someone on the other end who spoke atrocious English. She hoped that Ramón would understand that she was aborting the journey.

There were no taxis available: hundreds of other passengers like her had abandoned hope and were trying to get home. She lugged her bag down the pavement and queued for a bus to take her into town. It was after eight when she reached it and at last found a taxi to take her back to Cadogan Square.

Her back ached from the baby, and she was close to tears of frustration when at last she let herself into the flat. There was the delicious aroma of cooking, and she realized how hungry she was. She dumped her bag in the lobby, kicked off her shoes and went through to the kitchen. It was obvious that Michael had made himself dinner. The used dishes on the table in the breakfast-nook were still warm, and there were generous leftovers in the warmer. Like her, Michael was an excellent cook. She helped herself to the breasts of chicken Kiev and a slice of the cheesecake that remained. She noticed that there were two used wine-glasses and an empty bottle of Pater's Nuits St Georges 1961 on the draining-board of the sink. The significance of this did not really occur to her. She was too weary and dejected and she wanted Michael to cheer her up.

She heard music coming from his bedroom suite upstairs, the sentimental strains of Mantovani, one of Michael's favourites. She climbed the stairs on stockinged feet, went down the passage and pushed open the door to Michael's room.

For a long moment, she did not comprehend what she was seeing; it was too distant from her wildest expectations or imaginings.

Then she thought that Michael was being attacked, and a scream rushed up her throat. She had to cover her mouth with both hands to contain it. At last understanding flooded over her.

Naked, Michael knelt on hands and knees in the centre of the double bed. The satin eiderdown and bed-sheets had spilled over on to the floor, and the bed was in disarray. She knew his body so well, lithe and elegantly muscled, tanned by the African sun to the colour of ripe tobacco leaf except where his bathing-trunks had left his skin pale and vulnerable-looking.

Also naked, Nelson Litalongi knelt beside him. In contrast his torso shone with sweat like newly mined coal, so bright that it seemed to have been freshly oiled.

Michael's dearly beloved features were contorted with a deep and particular anguish. His mouth was twisted into a savage rictus that struck her to the depth of her being. For a moment, he reminded her of a stricken animal on the very point of a dreadful death.

Then his vision cleared and focused and he saw her. Before her eyes, his face seemed to dissolve and run like molten wax, and re-form in an expression of terror and deadly shame. With a violent twist of his body, he broke the grip of the man who held him and rolled away from him, reaching for a crumpled pillow to cover his own groin.

Isabella whirled and rushed from the room.

Despite her exhaustion, she slept fitfully and with disjointed and confused dreams, in which she saw Michael struggling naked and terrified in the grip of some fearsome dark monster and once she shouted out in her sleep so wildly that she woke herself.

Before dawn, she abandoned all further attempts at resting and went down to the kitchen. She saw immediately that the dishes and cutlery of the previous evening's meal had been washed and packed away. The empty wine-glasses and bottle had disappeared, and the kitchen was spotless.

She switched on the coffee-percolator and went to check the letter-box. It was too early for the newspaper to have been delivered, so she went back and poured a cup of coffee. She knew the caffeine was bad for the baby, but this morning she needed fortification.

She had taken her first sip when she smelt cigarette smoke and looked up quickly. Michael stood in the doorway with the inevitable cigarette between his lips, slanting his eyes against the spiral of smoke.

'I say, the coffee smells good.' He was dressed in a silk dressing-gown. His eyes were underscored with leaden smudges, and there were shadows, sickly with guilt, in the blue of his eyes. Uncertainty and diffidence puckered at the corners of his mouth as he said: 'I thought you were in Athens – I'm sorry.'

They stared at each other across the kitchen for only a few seconds, but which seemed like an age. Then Isabella stood up and crossed to him. She reached up on tiptoe to embrace him, and kissed him full on the mouth.

Then she held him close and pressed her cheek against his cheek that was raspy with new beard.

'I love you, Mickey. You are the dearest, sweetest person in my life. I love you without reservation or qualification.'

He sighed deeply. 'Thank you, Bella. I should have known that you would be generous and understanding, but I was afraid. You'll never know how terrified I've been that you might reject me.'

'No, Mickey. You had no reason to worry.'

'I was going to tell you. I've been waiting for the right moment.'

'You don't have to tell me, or anybody. It's your business alone.'

'No, I wanted you to know. We've never had any secrets between us. I knew you would find out sooner or later. I wanted – oh God, I would have given anything for you not to have found out the way you did. It must have been a terrible shock for you.'

She closed her eyes tightly and pressed her face harder to his, so that he could not see her expression. She tried to shut the image of what she had witnessed from her mind. However, Michael's face in that contorted rapture of

108

anguish still floated before her like a reel from a horror movie.

'It doesn't matter, Mickey. It makes no difference to us or to anything.'

'Yes, it does, Bella,' he contradicted her, and then gently held her away from him so that he could study her face. What he saw there made him sadder. With an arm around her shoulders he led her back to her seat at the table in the breakfast-nook, and sat beside her on the banquette.

'Strange,' he said. 'In a way it's a relief that you know. I still hate the way you found out, but at last there is one person in the world with whom I can be my true self; somebody for whom I no longer have to lie and dissemble.'

'Why hide it, Mickey? This is nineteen sixty-nine. If that's the way you are, why not be open? Nobody cares any more.'

Michael fished a packet of Camels out of his dressing-gown pocket and lit one. For a moment, he studied the burning tip, and then he said: 'That might be true for others, but not for me.' He shook his head. 'Not for me. Like it or not, I'm a Courtney. There are Nana and Pater, Garry and Sean, the family, the name.'

She wanted to deny it, but then she saw that it was futile.

'Nana and Pater,' Michael repeated. 'It would destroy them. Don't think that I haven't considered it – coming out of the closet.' He grinned wryly. 'God, what an awful expression.'

She squeezed his hand hard, beginning at last to have some faint understanding of her brother's predicament. She knew he was right. He could never let Nana and Pater know. For them it would be as bad – no, it would be worse than Tara. Tara had been a foreigner; Michael was Courtney blood. They would not survive it. It would destroy part of them, and Michael was too kind, too un-selfish, too loyal ever to let that happen. 'How long have you known – about your nature?' she asked quietly.

'Since prep school,' he answered frankly. 'Since those first pre-pubescent gropings and explorations in the showers and the bog shop . . .' He broke off. 'I've tried to deny myself. I've tried not to let it happen. Sometimes for months, a year even – but it's like a beast inside me, Bella, a ravaging beast over which I have no control.'

She smiled softly, indulgently. 'As Nanny would say, it's the hot Courtney blood, Mickey. We all have it; none of us can control it very well, not Pater and Garry and Sean – nor you and I.'

'You don't mind talking about it?' he asked diffidently. 'I've kept it bottled up so long.'

'You talk as much as you like. I'm here to listen.'

'I've lived with it for fifteen years now and I suppose I'll have to live with it for another fifty. The strange thing – something that would make it even worse as far as the family is concerned – is that I am attracted by coloured men. That would aggravate my guilt and degradation in the eyes of Nana and Pater, in the eyes of our courts at home. God, the scandal if I were discovered and charged under that Immorality Act of our enlightened government!' He shuddered, and stubbed out the cigarette, and immediately lit another from the crumpled pack.

'I don't know why black men attract me so powerfully. I've thought about it a great deal. I suppose I'm like Tara, in a way. Perhaps it's a kind of racial guilt, a subconscious desire to appease and mollify their anger.' He chuckled sardonically. 'We've been screwing them for so long. Why not give them a chance to get their own back?'

'Don't!' Isabella said softly. 'Don't degrade and belittle yourself by talking like that, Mickey. You are a fine and decent person. We are, none of us, responsible for our instincts.'

Isabella remembered Michael as the gentle shy boy, self-effacing but with boundless affection and concern for every being around him, yet always with that wistful air of sadness about him. She understood now the source of that sadness. She realized what spiritual agony he must have been suffering, that he still suffered. Her heart went out to him as it never had before. The last vestiges of her physical repugnance faded. She knew she would never again hate what she had seen taking place in the room upstairs. She would think only of the agonies which still lay in wait for this dear person, and her instincts became fiercer and more protective.

'My poor darling Mickey,' she whispered.

'Poor no longer,' he denied it. 'Not with your love and understanding.'

*   *   *

Two days later, while Michael was out on one of his interviews and Isabella's desk was a jumble of open books and scattered papers, the telephone rang. She reached for it distractedly and for a moment she did not recognize the husky voice, or understand the words.

'Ramón? Is that you? Is something wrong? Where are you? Athens?'

'I'm at the flat . . .'

'Here in London?'

'Yes. Can you come quickly? I need you.'

Isabella pushed the Mini through the lunch-hour traffic, and when she reached his flat went up the stairs two at a time and arrived on the landing flushed and breathless. She fumbled with the key and at last threw the door open.

'Ramón!' There was no reply, and she ran through to the bedroom. His valise was open on the bed, and a crumpled shirt lay in the middle of the floor. It was stained with blood – patches of old dried blood, almost mulberry black in colour, and also newer brighter blood.

'Ramón! Oh God! Ramón! Can you hear me?'

She ran to the bathroom door. It was locked from inside. She stood back and kicked the lock with her heel. It was one of the judo kicks he had taught her, and the flimsy lock snapped and the door flew open.

Ramón lay on the tiled floor beside the toilet. He must have grabbed at the shelf above the washbasin as he fell, and her cosmetics had cascaded down into the basin and across the floor. He was naked from the waist up, but his chest was heavily strapped with bandages. She could tell at a glance that the bandages had been tied by a professional hand. Like his abandoned shirt, the white bandages were soaked with concentric rings of blood, some dark and old, some fresh and wet.

She dropped on to her knees beside him, and turned his head. His skin was pale, almost opalescent, with a sheen of nauseous sweat upon it. She lifted his head into her lap. Then she snatched up the face-cloth that hung over the edge of the bath. She could just reach the cold-water tap from where she sat. She soaked the cloth and wiped his face and neck.

His eyelids quivered and opened, and he looked up at her.

'Ramón.'

His eyes focused. 'I keeled over,' he murmured.

'My darling, what happened to you? You've been badly hurt.'

'Help me to the bed,' he said.

Kneeling beside him, she propped him into a sitting position. She was almost as strong as a man, with arms and torso trained by riding and tennis. However, she knew that even she could not lift him unaided.

'Can you stand, if I steady you?'

He grunted and made the effort, but halfway to his feet he winced and clutched at the blood-stained bandages as the pain knifed him.

'Take it easy,' she whispered, and for a minute he remained doubled over, then he straightened slowly.

'All right.' He gritted his teeth, and she led him through, taking most of his weight on her shoulder, and lowered him on to the bed.

'Did you come all the way from Athens in this condition?' she asked incredulously.

He nodded the lie. He had summoned Isabella to Athens to act as a courier. The need had risen urgently and unexpectedly. There had been no other agent available immediately, and it was time for her to be blooded in the field. She was ripe for it. By now she had been conditioned to accept his orders without question, and it was an easy first assignment that he planned for her. She was the perfect innocent, an attractive and pregnant female who would instantly evoke sympathy. She was unmarked, unknown to any of the world's intelligence organizations, including Mossad. In the jargon of the trade, she was a virgin. In addition, she carried a South African passport, and Israel had cordial, indeed intimate, relations with that country.

The plan was for her to catch the flight from Athens to Tel Aviv, make the pick-up and leave by the same route. It would have been a day's work. The plan had foundered when she had not been able to make the flight to Athens. The pick-up was crucial. It involved details of the co-operation between Israeli and South African scientists in the development of tactical nuclear weapons systems. Even though there was a high probability that he was marked by Mossad, Ramón had been forced to make the pick-up in person.

He had disguised his appearance as best he was able, and of course he had gone unarmed. It was madness to attempt to carry a weapon through an Israeli security check. He had used his Mexican passport in an assumed name. However, they must have got on to him at Ben Gurion Airport and tailed him to the pick-up.

He had spotted the tail and taken emergency evading procedure, but they had cornered him. He had broken the neck of one Mossad agent and in return had taken this hit. Even severely wounded, he had made it to the PLO safe house in Tel Aviv. Within twelve hours they had smuggled him out on their pipeline to Syria.

However, London was his safe ground. Despite the risks and his injuries, he had too much in play to remain in Damascus. The local KGB head of station had escorted him on to the Aeroflot flight to London. He had made the call to Isabella as he staggered into the flat. Then he had just managed to reach the bathroom before he collapsed.

'I must call a doctor,' she said.

'No doctor!' Despite his weakness, his voice took on that cold sibilant tone which she was so conditioned to obey.

'What must I do?' she asked.

'Get me the telephone,' he ordered, and she hurried to bring the instrument through from its jack in the sitting-room.

'Ramón, you look awful. At least let me get you something – a bowl of soup, darling?'

He nodded agreement, but did not look up from the telephone as he dialled. She went through to the kitchen and heated up a can of thick vegetable soup. As she worked she could hear him speaking to somebody in Spanish on the telephone. However, her recent exercise with the Linguaphone course was insufficient to allow her to follow the conversation. She took the tray of soup and Pro-Vita biscuits through to him as he hung up.

'Darling, what has happened to you? Why won't you let me call the doctor?'

He grimaced. If a British doctor saw that injury, he would be bound to report it. If the Cuban embassy doctor came to the flat, it would almost certainly compromise this address and Ramón's cover. So he had made alternative arrangements. However, he did not answer her question directly.

'I want you to go out immediately. Go to the westbound platform of Sloane Square Underground station and walk the full length of it slowly. Somebody will put an envelope in your hand . . .'

'Who? How will I recognize him?'

'You won't,' he answered brusquely. 'He will recognize you. You will not speak nor acknowledge the messenger in any way. In the envelope will be a doctor's prescription and a detailed list of instructions to treat my injury. Take the prescription to the all-night chemist in Piccadilly Circus and bring the supplies back here.'

'Yes, Ramón, but you haven't told me how you hurt yourself.'

'You must learn to do as you are told – without all those tiresome questions. Now, go!'

'Yes, Ramón.' She picked up her jacket and scarf and then stooped over the bed to kiss him.

'I love you,' she whispered. Halfway down the stairs, she stopped suddenly. Nobody, with the possible exception of Nana, had ever spoken to her in such forceful terms since childhood. Even her father made requests; he did not give her orders. Yet here she was scampering breathlessly as a schoolgirl to obey. She pulled a face and ran on down into the street.

She had not reached the end of the Underground platform when, from behind, she felt a light touch on her wrist and an envelope was slipped into her hand. She glanced over her shoulder, but the messenger was already walking away. He wore a blue wool cap and dark overcoat, but she could not see his face.

At the chemist's the dispenser read the prescription and remarked: 'You have somebody badly injured?' But she shook her head.

'I'm just Doctor Alves' receptionist. I don't know.'

And he made up the package of medicines without further comment.

Ramón seemed to be sleeping, but he opened his eyes immediately she entered the bedroom. All her previous fears for him returned in full force when she saw his face. His eyes seemed to have sunk into dark bruised cavities, and his skin had the pallor of a two-day corpse. However, she thrust aside her personal misgivings and steeled herself to act calmly.

While she was at university she had taken a course in first aid with the Red Cross. At Weltevreden she had often assisted the visiting doctor at his weekly clinic for the coloured employees. She had seen enough missing fingers and crushed feet and other injuries inflicted by farm machinery to have overcome any squeamishness.

She laid out the supplies from the chemist and read swiftly through the simple typed instructions from the envelope. She washed in the bathroom basin, adding half a cup of Dettol to the water; then sat Ramón upright and began unwrapping the bandages.

The blood had dried, and the dressing stuck to the edges of the wound. He closed his eyes, and a light sweat dewed his forehead and chin as she worked it loose.

'I'm sorry,' she whispered. 'I'm trying not to hurt you.'

The dressing came away at last, and she suppressed an exclamation as she saw the wounds. There was a deep puncture low down in the side of his chest and a second corresponding ragged aperture in the smooth muscles of his back that was clogged with a black plug of clotted blood. The skin around the wounds was hot and inflamed, and there was the faint sickly smell of infection.

She knew instantly how those injuries had been inflicted. On her last visit to her brother Sean's hunting concession in the Zambezi valley, they had answered a call for assistance from a nearby Batonka village that had been attacked by terrorists. That was where she had first seen the distinctive entry puncture and enlarged exit of a through-and-through bullet wound. Ramón was watching her face, so she made no comment and tried to keep her expression neutral as she cleaned the area around the wounds with disinfectant, and then strapped fresh dressings in place with crisp white bandages.

She knew that she had done a proficient job, and he murmured as she eased him back on the pillows: 'Good. You know what you are doing.'

'Not finished yet. I have to give you a jab. Doctor's orders.' And then in an attempt at humour; 'Show me your gorgeous bum, chum!'

She stood at the foot of the bed and removed his shoes and socks, then took a grip on the turn-ups of his trousers and, while he arched his back and lifted himself slightly, she pulled them off.

'Now your underpants.' She drew them down, and sighed with mock relief. 'At least you didn't damage any of my special goodies. That would have made me really mad.' This time he smiled, and then rolled cautiously on to his side.

She filled the disposable syringe and injected an ampoule of broad-spectrum antibiotic into the smooth hard swell of his buttock. Then she covered him carefully with the down-filled duvet.

'Now,' she said firmly, 'two of these pills – and rest.'

He did not protest and when he had taken the sleeping pills she kissed him and switched out the bedside light.

'I'll be in the sitting-room if you need me.'

* * *

In the morning his colour was much improved and obviously the antibiotic had done its work. His temperature was down, and his eyes were clear.

'How did you sleep?' she asked.

'Those pills are dynamite. It was like falling over a cliff, and now I could use a bath.'

She ran the bath and helped him through. Once he was seated waist-deep, she used the sponge to clean around the edges of the bandage, and then her attentions moved lower and she plied the soapy sponge with cunning.

'Ah, you may be damaged on top, but down below things are all working very satisfactorily, I am glad to report.'

'Merely as a matter of interest, Nurse, is what you are doing at the moment business or pleasure?'

'A little of one and considerably more of the other,' she confessed.

Back on the bed, he protested half-heartedly when she filled the syringe with another measure of antibiotic, but she told him sternly: 'Why are men such cowards? Bottoms up!' And he rolled over obediently. 'Good boy,' she nodded as she withdrew the needle and swabbed the puncture mark with alcohol. 'Now you've earned your breakfast, and I've got you a kipper as a reward.'

She enjoyed nursing him. For once she was in a position to give him orders and have them obeyed. While she was busy in the kitchen, she heard him on the telephone, talking Spanish that was too rapid and complicated for her to follow. She listened, trying, despite her limitations, to make sense of it, and the misgivings that had troubled her most of the night returned in full force. To fend them off she slipped down the stairs and ran to the flower and fruit stall on the corner opposite the entrance to the Tube station.

She chose a dark red Papa Meillon rosebud and a perfect golden peach, and ran all the way back. Ramón was still speaking on the telephone when she let herself in.

She arranged the rose and the peach on the breakfast-tray. When she took them through to him he looked up from the telephone and rewarded her with one of his rare and treasured smiles.

She sat on the edge of the bed and carefully forked the succulent flesh off the kipper bone and fed it to him, a mouthful at a time, while he continued his telephone conversation. When he had finished, she took the tray back to the kitchen, and while she was washing up she heard him hang up the telephone receiver.

Quickly she returned to the bedroom and settled down on her own side of the bed with her legs curled up sideways under her in that feminine double-jointed fashion impossible for a man to emulate.

'Ramón,' she said quietly and seriously, 'that is a bullet wound.'

His eyes went cold and deadly green, and he stared back at her without expression.

'How did it happen?' she asked, and he was silent, watching her. She felt her resolution fade, but she steeled herself to continue.

'You are not a banker, are you?'

'I am a banker most of the time,' he said softly.

'And at other times, what are you then?'

'I am a patriot. I serve my country.'

She felt a hot rush of relief. During the night she had imagined a hundred horrid possibilities: that he was a

118

drug-smuggler, or a bank-robber, or a member of some criminal syndicate involved in a gang war.

'Spain,' she said. 'You are a member of the Spanish secret service, is that it?'

He was silent again, watching her with careful calculation. He was the master of progressive revelation. She must be drawn in gradually, a little at a time, so that she was neither unwilling nor resistant, an insect being entrapped and slowly engulfed in a puddle of honey.

'You must realize, Bella, that if that were indeed the case I would not be able to tell you.'

'Of course.' She nodded happily. She had known another man from this dangerous and exciting world of espionage and intrigue. He was the only man before Ramón with whom she had believed herself to be in love. He had been a brigadier in the South African security police, another powerful ruthless one who could match her spirit and control her wilder emotional excesses. She had lived as man and wife with Lothar De La Rey in the Johannesburg flat for six marvellously stormy months. When he had ended it suddenly and without warning, she had been shattered. Now she realized that it had been shallow infatuation, nothing to compare even remotely with what she had found in Ramón Machado. 'I understand completely, Ramón darling, and you can trust me. I won't ask any more silly questions.'

'I have trusted you with my life already,' he said. 'You were the first person I called upon for help.'

'I'm proud of that. Because you are Spanish and because you are my lover and the father of my baby, I feel myself to be in a large part Spanish as well. I want to help you any way I am able.'

'Yes,' he nodded. 'I understand that. I have thought about the baby.' He reached out and touched her stomach, and his hand felt cool and hard. 'I want my son to be born in Spain, so that he, too, will be a Spaniard and his claim to the title will be secured.'

She was startled. She had taken it for granted that she

would have her baby here in London. The gynaecologist had already made a tentative reservation at the maternity home.

'Will you do that for me, Bella? Will you make my son a full Spaniard?' he asked, and she hesitated not a moment longer.

'Yes, of course, my darling. I will do whatever you wish.' She leant over him and kissed him. Then she snuggled down on the pillow beside him, careful not to jostle his injuries. 'If that is what you want, then we will have to start making arrangements,' she suggested.

'I have already done so,' he confessed. 'There is an excellent private clinic just outside Málaga. I have a friend at the bank's head office in Málaga who will find us a flat and a maid. I have arranged a transfer to the head office, so that I will be with you when the baby is born.'

'It sounds so exciting,' she agreed. 'And if you get to choose where the baby is to be born, then I choose where we marry when we eventually can. That's fair, isn't it?'

He smiled. 'Yes, that is fair.'

'I want to be married at Weltevreden. There is an old slave church on the estate, built a hundred and fifty years ago. My grandmother, Nana, had it completely restored and renovated for my brother Garry's wedding. It's exquisite, and Nana filled it with flowers for Garry and Holly. I will have arum lilies. Some people believe that they are unlucky, but they are my favourite flowers and I'm not superstitious, or not much anyway . . .'

Patiently he let her ramble on, occasionally murmuring encouragement, awaiting the precise moment for his next revelation, and she gave him the opening.

'But we are cutting things a little fine, Ramón darling. Nana will want at least six weeks to make all the arrangements, and by then I am going to be the size of a house. They'll play the "Baby Elephant Walk" as I come down the aisle.'

'No, Bella,' he contradicted her. 'At your wedding, you

will be slim and beautiful – because you will no longer be pregnant.'

She sat bolt upright on the bed. 'What are you trying to tell me, Ramón. Something has happened, hasn't it?'

'Yes. You are right. There is bad news, I'm afraid. I have heard from Natalie. She's still in Florida. She is being obstinate, and there are legal delays.'

'Oh, Ramón!'

'I am as unhappy as you are about it. If there was anything I could do, believe me, I would do it.'

'I hate her,' she whispered.

'Yes, sometimes I feel that way. But truly it is not a disaster, only an inconvenience at the most. We will still be married, and you will still have your little slave church and your arum lilies. It is just that our son will be born before that happens.'

'Promise me, Ramón, swear it to me – that we will be married as soon as you are free.'

'I swear it to you.'

She settled down beside him, cradling her head on his good shoulder, hiding her face so that he could not guess how disappointed she truly was.

'I hate her, but I love you,' she said, and Ramón gave a grim little smile of satisfaction that she could not see.

*   *   *

He was confined to the flat by his wound for another week, and there was time to talk. She told Ramón about Michael, and was flattered by the interest he showed in her brother.

She expanded on Michael's virtues, and on their special relationship. Ramón listened and drew her out gently. He was so easy to talk to. She looked upon him as an extension of herself. She found herself going on to tell him about the rest of her family, about what lay behind the public mask that they as a group presented to the world; about their secrets and their weaknesses and their scandals, about Shasa and Tara's divorce. She even told him about the dark suspicion that Nana had once given birth to a bastard son in the wild southern deserts of Africa.

'Of course, nobody has ever proved it. I don't think anybody would dare. Nana is a formidable force.' She laughed. 'And that is understating the fact. However, there was definitely some very fishy business back there in the nineteen twenties.'

In the end, Ramón brought the conversation back to Michael. 'If he's here in London, why haven't you introduced us? Are you ashamed of me?'

'Oh, may I? May I bring him round here, Ramón? I've told him a little about you, about us. I know he'd love to meet you, and I'm sure you will like him. He's the only truly sweet and good Courtney. The rest of us . . .!' She rolled her eyes comically.

Michael arrived with a bottle of his father's burgundy under his arm. 'I thought of bringing flowers,' he explained, 'but then I decided to get something useful instead.'

He and Ramón scrutinized each other carefully as they shook hands. Isabella watched them anxiously, willing them to like each other.

'How are your ribs?' Michael asked. Isabella had told him that Ramón had taken a toss from his horse and broken three ribs.

'Your sister is holding me prisoner. There is nothing wrong with me – nothing that a glass of that excellent burgundy won't cure.' Ramón displayed that rare warmth and special charm of his which were irresistible. Isabella felt quite giddy with relief. Her two most favourite and important people were going to like each other.

She took the burgundy through to the kitchen to find a corkscrew. When she returned with the open bottle and two glasses, Michael was settled in the chair beside the bed and they were already engrossed in conversation. 'We get the airmail edition of your paper, the *Golden City Mail*, at the bank,' Ramón was telling him. 'I particularly like your financial and economic coverage.'

'Ah, you are in banking,' Michael nodded. 'Bella didn't tell me that.'

'Merchant banking. We specialize in sub-Saharan Africa.' And they were away at a conversational gallop. Bella kicked off her flat shoes, rolled up the bottoms of her blue jeans and perched up on the bed beside Ramón. Although she took no part in the conversation, she listened avidly.

She had no idea that Ramón had such a grasp of African facts and realities, such a deep knowledge of the personalities and places and events which made up the rich and fascinating mosaic of her native land. Compared to this discussion, all her previous conversations with him had been shallow and trivial. Listening to the two of them, she learnt new facts and heard ideas expressed that were totally fresh to her.

Michael was obviously as impressed as she was. His pleasure at finding a challenging and stimulating intellect on which to try out his own interpretations and beliefs was evident.

It was after midnight; the original bottle of wine and another that Isabella had dug out of her tiny stock in the kitchen were empty. The bedroom was thick with the smoke of Michael's Camels before she looked at her watch and exclaimed: 'You were invited for one drink, Mickey, and Ramón is an invalid. Away with you, now.' She went to fetch his overcoat.

While she helped him into it, Ramón said softly from the bed: 'If you are doing a series on the political exiles, it wouldn't be complete without one on Raleigh Tabaka.'

Mickey laughed ruefully. 'I'd give my chance of salvation for a crack at Tabaka, the mystery man. It just ain't possible, as old Rudyard put it, "if you know the track of the morning mist, then you know where his pickets are".'

'I've met him in the line of duty at the bank. We keep tabs on all the players. I might be able to arrange for you to meet him,' Ramón told him, and Michael froze and stared at him with one arm in the sleeve of his coat.

'I've been trying to get hold of him for five years,' he said. 'If you could . . .'

'Call me tomorrow, around lunchtime,' Ramón told him. 'I'll see what I can do.'

At the door Michael kissed Isabella. 'I take it that you are not coming home tonight?'

'This is home.' She hugged him. 'My temporary residence at Cadogan Square was just to impress you, but I don't have to do that any longer.'

'He's a knockout, your Ramón,' Michael said, and she felt a sudden shocking stab of jealousy, as though another woman had challenged her for Ramón's affection. She tried to suppress it. It was the only ugly feeling she had ever harboured towards Mickey, but the pain persisted as she went back to the bedroom and deepened again as Ramón said: 'I like him. Your brother is one of the superior beings – they are rare enough.'

She felt ashamed of her unkind feelings towards Mickey. How could she harbour the slightest doubt that Ramón was a man, a natural man. She knew that he liked Michael only for his charm and fine intellect, and because he was her brother – and yet, and yet that dirty sneaking feeling persisted.

She stooped over the bed and kissed Ramón with a passion that surprised even her. After the first moment of shock, his mouth opened and their tongues slithered and rolled around each other, slippery as mating eels.

She broke away at last and looked up at him. 'You swan around Europe for weeks on end, leaving me pining, and when you do come home you lie around in bed, hogging food and sleeping,' she accused him in a husky voice, tight with her need of him. 'And never a thought for the maid or the nurse. Well, Master Ramón, I'm here to tell you it's pay-day, and I've come to collect.'

'I'll need some help,' he warned her.

'You just lie still. Don't do a thing. Nurse's orders. We'll take care of the details.'

She drew back the bed-sheets and reached down under

them, and her voice was a languorous coo. 'We'll take care of things, he and I. You keep out of it.'

She straddled him gently, taking care not to touch his bandaged chest. As she sank down on top of him, she saw her own deep need reflected in the green mirror of his eyes, and felt all her doubts evaporate. He belonged to her and to her alone.

Afterwards she lay at his good side, close and secure and happy, and they talked drowsily, hovering on the edge of sleep in the darkness. When he mentioned Michael again, she felt a twinge of remorse at her earlier doubts. She was so relaxed, so much off-guard, and she trusted Ramón as she did herself. She wanted to explain and share it with him.

'Poor Mickey, I never suspected the agony he has had to endure all these years. I am closer to him than any person in the world, and yet even I did not know about it. A few days ago, I found out, quite by accident, that he is a practising homosexual . . .'

The words were out before she could stop them, and suddenly she was appalled by what she had done. Mickey had trusted her, and she shivered, waiting for some reaction from Ramón. However, it was not what she had expected.

'Yes,' he agreed calmly. 'I knew that. There are some indications which are unmistakable. I knew it within the first half-hour.'

She felt a rush of relief. Ramón had known, so there was no betrayal on her part.

'You are not repelled by it?'

'No, not at all,' Ramón answered. 'Many of them are creative and intelligent and productive people.'

'Yes, Mickey is like that,' she agreed eagerly. 'I was shocked at first, but now it means little to me. He is still my darling brother. However, I do worry about him being caught up in a criminal prosecution.'

'I don't think there is much chance of that. Society has accepted—'

'You don't understand, Ramón. Michael likes black boys and he lives in South Africa.'

'Yes,' Ramón agreed thoughtfully. 'That could present some problems.'

★   ★   ★

Michael phoned the flat from a pay-booth in Fleet Street a little before noon, and Ramón answered on the second ring.

'The news is good,' Ramón assured him. 'Raleigh Tabaka is in London and he knows of you. Did you write a series of newspaper articles back in nineteen sixty under the title "Rage"?'

'Yes, a series of six for the *Mail*; it got the paper banned by the security police.'

'Tabaka read them and liked them. He has agreed to meet you.'

'My God, Ramón. I can't tell you how grateful I am. This is the most marvellous break—'

Ramón cut short his thanks. 'He'll meet you this evening, but he has laid down some conditions.'

'Anything,' Michael agreed quickly.

'You are to come to the meeting alone. No weapons, of course, and no tape-recorder or camera. He does not want his voice or appearance on record. There is a pub in Shepherd's Bush.' He gave Michael the address. 'Be there at seven this evening. Carry a bunch of flowers – carnations. Someone will meet and take you to the rendezvous.'

'Right, I've got that.'

'One other condition. Tabaka wants to read all your copy on the interview before you print it.'

Michael was silent for a slow count of five. The request contravened all his journalistic principles. It amounted to a form of censorship and cast a slur on his professional ethics. However, the price was an interview with one of the most wanted men in Africa.

'All right,' he agreed heavily. 'I'll give him first read.'

And then his tone brightened. 'I owe you a favour, Ramón. I'll come around and tell you all about it tomorrow evening.'

'Don't forget the bottle of wine.'

Michael rushed back to Cadogan Square. As soon as he reached the telephone he cancelled all the rest of the day's appointments, and then settled down to plan his strategy for the interview. His questions had to be searching, but not so barbed as to cool Tabaka's co-operative mood. He had to be sincere and sympathetic, and yet at the same time, severe, for he was dealing with a man who had deliberately chosen the path of violence and bloodshed. To achieve credibility his questions must be balanced and neutral, and at the same time designed to draw the man out. In particular he did not want a mere recital of all the radical slogans and revolutionary jargon.

'The term "terrorist" is generally applied to a person who for reasons of political coercion commits an act of violence on a target of a non-military nature during which there is a high probability of injury or death being inflicted on innocent bystanders. Do you accept that definition and, if so, does the label "terrorist" apply to Umkhonto we Sizwe?'

He worked that out as his first question, and lit another Camel as he studied it.

'Good.' That was what you called jumping straight in with both feet, but perhaps it needed a little honing and polishing. He worked on steadily, and by five-thirty he had prepared twenty questions that satisfied him. He made himself a smoked-salmon sandwich and drank a bottle of Guinness while he reviewed and rehearsed his script.

Then he shrugged on his overcoat, armed himself with the bunch of carnations which he had bought at the corner stall. It was drizzling rain. He flagged down a taxi in Sloane Street.

The pub was steamy with body heat. The condensation ran down the stained-glass windows in rainbow rivulets. Michael displayed the carnations ostentatiously and peered through the soft blue mist of tobacco smoke. Almost immediately a neatly dressed Indian in a three-piece blue wool suit left the bar-counter and made his way down the crowded room.

'Mr Courtney, my name is Govan.'

'From Natal.' Michael recognized the accent.

'From Stanger.' The man smiled. 'But that was six years ago.' He glanced at the shoulders of Michael's coat. 'Has it stopped raining? Good, we can walk. It's not far.'

His guide struck out down the main thoroughfare. Within a hundred yards he turned abruptly into a narrow alleyway and increased his pace. Michael had to trot to match him. He was wheezing when they reached the exit to the alley.

'Damned fags – I must cut down.'

Govan turned out of the alley, and stopped abruptly round the corner. Michael was about to speak, but Govan gripped his arm to silence him. They waited for five minutes. Only when it was certain that they were not being followed did he relax his grip.

'You don't trust me,' Michael smiled, and dumped the carnations in the rubbish-bin that bore a warning of the penalties for littering.

'We do not trust anybody.' Govan led him away. 'Especially not the Boers. They are learning new kinds of nastiness each day.'

Ten minutes later they stopped again outside a modern block of flats, in a broad well-lit street. There was a rank of Mercedes and Jaguars parked at the kerb. The lawn and small garden in front of the apartment-block was carefully groomed. It was clearly an expensive residential enclave. 'I will leave you here,' said Govan. 'Go in. There is a porter in the lobby. Tell him that you are a guest of Mr Kendrick, Flat 505.'

The lobby was in keeping with the façade of the building, Italian marble floor, wood-panelled walls and gilded doors to the lift. The uniformed porter saluted him. 'Yes, Mr Courtney, Mr Kendrick is expecting you. Please go up to the fifth floor.'

When the lift doors opened, there were two unsmiling young coloured men waiting for him.

'Come this way, Mr Courtney.'

They led him down the carpeted passage to number 505 and let him into the flat.

As the door closed, they stepped in on each side of him and swiftly but thoroughly patted him down. Michael lifted his arms and spread his legs co-operatively. As they searched him, he looked around him with the journalist's eye. The flat had been decorated with flair and taste, and money.

His escorts stepped back satisfied, and one of them opened the double doors ahead of him.

'Please,' he said, and Michael went through into a spacious and beautifully decorated room. The sofas and easy chairs were covered with cream-coloured Connolly leather. The thick pile of the wall-to-wall carpet was a soft cocoa. The tables and the cocktail-bar were in crystal and chrome. On the walls hung four large Hockney paintings, from his swimming-pool series.

Fifty thousand quid each, Michael estimated, and then his eyes flicked to the figure who stood in the centre of the room.

There had been no recent photograph of this man, but Michael recognized him instantly from a blurred press picture in the *Mail*'s archives which dated back years to the Sharpeville era and the subsequent enquiries.

'Mr Tabaka,' he said. He was as tall as Michael, probably six foot one, but broader in the shoulder and narrower in the waist.

'Mr Courtney.' Raleigh Tabaka came forward to offer his hand. He moved like a boxer, fluidly in balance, poised and aggressive.

'You live in style?' Michael put a question in his voice, and Raleigh Tabaka frowned slightly.

'This is the apartment of a sympathizer. I have no call for such frippery.' His voice was firm and deep, melodious with the unmistakable echoes of Africa. Despite the denial, his suit was of pure new wool and draped elegantly over his warrior's frame. There were the tiny stirrups of the Gucci motif on his silk tie. He was an impressive man.

'I am grateful for this opportunity to meet you,' Michael said.

'I read your "Rage" series,' Raleigh told him, studying Michael with those black onyx eyes. 'You understand my people. You examined their aspirations with a fair and impartial eye.'

'Not everybody would agree with you – especially those in authority in South Africa.'

Raleigh smiled. His teeth were even and white. 'I have very little to tell you that will comfort them now. But first may I offer you a drink?'

'A gin and tonic.'

'Ah, yes, the fuel on which the journalistic mind functions.' Raleigh's tone was scornful. He went to the bar and poured the clear liquid from a crystal decanter, and squirted the tonic from a hand-held nozzle connected to the bar by a chrome-sheathed hose.

'You don't drink?' Michael asked, and Raleigh frowned again.

'With so much work to be done, why should I cloud my mind?' He glanced at his wristwatch. 'We have only an hour, then I must go.'

'I mustn't waste a minute of it,' Michael agreed. As they settled facing each other in the cream Connolly-leather chairs, he said: 'I have all the background I need: your place and date of birth, your education at Waterford School in Swaziland, your relationship to Moses Gama, your present position in the ANC. May I go on from there?' And Raleigh inclined his head in assent.

'The term "terrorist" is generally applied to . . .' Michael repeated his definition, and Raleigh's features tightened with anger as he listened.

'There are no innocent bystanders in South Africa,' he cut in brusquely. 'It is a war. Nobody can claim to be a neutral. We are all combatants.'

'No matter how young, how old? No matter how sympathetic to your people's aspirations?'

'There are no bystanders,' Raleigh repeated. 'From the cradle to the grave, we are all in the battlefield. We all fall into one of two camps, either the oppressed or the oppressors.'

'No man or woman or child has a choice?' Michael asked.

'Yes, there is a choice – to take one or the other side. Neutrality is not an option.'

'If a bomb explodes in a crowded supermarket, some of your own people, your own sympathizers may die or be maimed. Would you feel remorse?'

'Remorse is not a revolutionary emotion, just as it is not an emotion of the perpetrators of apartheid. Those who die are either enemy casualties or courageous and honourable sacrifices. In war both are unavoidable, even desirable.'

Michael's pen dashed across the sheets of his notepad as he attempted to capture these frightful pronouncements. He felt shaken and aroused, both excited and terrified by what he heard. He had the feeling that, like a moth that circled the flame too closely, he would be scarred by the white heat of this man's rage. He knew that he could faithfully record the words, but he could never reproduce the fierce spirit in which they were uttered.

The allotted hour sped away too fast, as Michael tried to use every second to the full, and when at last Raleigh glanced at his wristwatch and stood up he tried desperately to prolong it.

'You have spoken of your child warriors,' he said. 'What age, how young are they?'

'I will show you children of seven who will bear arms, and commanders of sections who are ten years old.'

'You will show me?' Michael asked. 'Is that possible – that you will show me?'

Raleigh studied him for a long moment. The intelligence that Ramón Machado had passed on to him seemed to be valid. Here was a useful tool. One that could be fitted to his hand and his purpose. He might be well worth the effort that would be needed to develop him fully. He was one of Lenin's 'useful idiots' who, to begin with, could be made to serve the cause unwittingly. Later, of course, it would be different. At first, he would be the spade and the ploughshare; only later, when the time was ripe, would he be forged into the sword of war.

'Michael Courtney,' he said softly, 'I am disposed to trust you. I think that you are a decent and enlightened man. If you keep my trust, I will open doors for you into places you have never dreamt existed. I will take you into the streets and hovels of Soweto. Into the hearts of my people – and, yes, I will show you the children.'

'When?' Michael demanded anxiously, aware that his time was running out.

'Soon,' Raleigh promised, and at that moment they heard the front door open.

'How will I find you?' Michael persisted.

'You won't. I will find you when I am ready.'

The double doors to the sitting-room swung open and a man stood at the threshold. Even in his preoccupation with Raleigh Tabaka's promise, Michael was struck, his attention was diverted. He recognized the newcomer instantly, even in his street clothes. The name Kendrick should have alerted him.

'This is our host who owns this apartment,' Raleigh Tabaka introduced them. 'Oliver Kendrick, this is Michael Courtney.'

'I saw you dance Spartacus,' Michael said, his voice subdued with awe. 'Three times. Such virility and athleticism.'

Oliver Kendrick smiled and crossed the room with the springing gait of the ballet-dancer, and offered Michael his hand. It was surprisingly narrow and cool, and his bones felt light as those of a bird. It was appropriate, for they called him 'the Black Swan'. His neck was long and elegant, as that of the bird, and his eyes were as luminous as a mountain pool reflected in the moonlight. His skin had the same dark lustre.

Michael thought that close up he was more beautiful even than he had appeared in the romantic lighting of the stage set, and his breathing cramped. The dancer left his hand in Michael's grip, as he turned his head to Raleigh. 'Don't rush away, Raleigh,' he pleaded in that musical West Indian lilt.

'I must go.' Raleigh shook his head. 'I'm afraid that I have a plane to catch.'

Oliver Kendrick turned back to Michael, still holding his hand. 'I have had a beastly day. I swear I could simply curl up and die. Don't leave me alone, Michael. Do stay and distract me. You can be entertaining and distracting, can't you, Michael?'

Raleigh Tabaka left him and let himself out of the flat. One of his men was waiting for him outside the door, but they did not leave the building. Instead the man led Raleigh only a short distance down the passageway to a less ostentatious doorway. This second flat, beyond it, was much smaller and starkly furnished. Raleigh went through to the inner room, and the second of his men made to stand up from the chair beside the lit window in the side-wall.

Raleigh gestured to him to remain seated and crossed to the window. It was of unusual shape, tall and narrow, like a full-length dressing-mirror. The glass was shaded with that slightly opaque tone that was characteristic of a two-way mirror viewed from the reverse side.

The room beyond was a bedroom, lavishly furnished like the rest of Oliver Kendrick's apartment. The colour theme was pale oyster and mushroom, and the satin bedspread matched exactly the shade of the deep pile of the carpet. Hidden lighting glimmered and glowed on the mirrored tiles of the ceiling. Set in an alcove facing the bed was an ancient phallic symbol, carved from amber-coloured obsidian, a precious antique from a Hindu temple.

The room was empty, and Raleigh turned his attention to the camera equipment that stood ready, aimed through the two-way mirror.

The apartment and the camera equipment belonged to

Oliver Kendrick. He had loaned it to Raleigh on previous occasions. It was odd that a man of Kendrick's talent and fame would consent to take part in an arranged tableau such as this. However, not only did he do so willingly, but he had also actually offered his equipment and his services to Raleigh. He participated with such unfeigned enthusiasm and inventive delight that it was obvious that this was very much to his particular taste. His only stipulation was that Raleigh hand over to him a copy of the videotapes and photographs to add to his huge private collection. The video equipment was of the very finest professional standard. Raleigh had been impressed by the quality of reproduction even in this low-light environment.

Raleigh glanced at his wristwatch again. He could safely leave the rest of it to his two bodyguards. They had done this before. However, a perverse curiosity made him linger. It was almost half an hour before the door to the bedroom opened. Kendrick and Michael Courtney entered. Raleigh's two assistants moved quickly to their positions, one to the video-recorder and the other to the big black Hasselblad camera on its tripod. The still camera was loaded with monochrome theatrical film, rated at 3000 ASA which rendered crisp prints in the poorest light conditions.

In the room beyond, the two men embraced, a long lingering kiss with open mouths, and the video-recorder emitted a faint electric hum. The sound of the shutter of the Hasselblad was much louder, almost explosive in the quiet dark room.

At one stage, as the white man lay expectantly in the centre of the oyster satin bedspread, Kendrick crossed naked to stand in front of the two-way mirror. He pretended to examine his own body, in reality flaunting it before the men who, he knew, were watching on the far side of the glass. His musculature was extraordinarily developed by long hours at the practice *barre*. His calves and thighs were disproportionately massive.

He gazed arrogantly into the mirror, and the diamond ear-rings in his lobes glittered as he turned his head on its long swan's neck, striking a theatrical pose. He ran the tip of his tongue along the inside of his parted lips and stared through the darkling mirror into Raleigh Tabaka's eyes. It was the lewdest gesture he had ever witnessed, with a chill of evil to it that made even Raleigh shiver briefly. Kendrick turned away and sauntered back towards the bed. His velvety black buttocks swayed in that stylized mincing gait, and the man on the bed raised both arms to greet him.

Raleigh turned away and left the apartment. He rode down in the lift and walked out into the chill of evening. He drew his overcoat tighter across his chest and took a slow breath of clean cold air. Then he gathered himself and walked away with the long determined stride of a man with important work to do.

★   ★   ★

When Michael left London he took with him a little of the special joy that had filled Isabella's life over these last weeks.

She drove him out to Heathrow. 'We always seem to be saying goodbye, Mickey,' she whispered. 'I shall miss you so, as I always do.'

'I'll see you at the wedding.'

'There will probably be a christening before that,' she answered, and he held her at arm's length.

'You didn't tell me,' he accused.

'His wife,' she explained. 'We are moving to Spain at the end of January. Ramón wants the baby to be born there. He will adopt it under Spanish law.'

'You must let me know where you are – at all times – and remember your promise.'

She nodded. 'You'll be the very first one that I'll call on for help, if I need it.'

At the doors to the departure-hall, he looked back and blew her a kiss. When he disappeared she felt chilled with loneliness.

This was a feeling that evaporated swiftly in the Iberian sunlight.

The apartment that Ramón found was in a tiny fishing village a few miles down the coast from Málaga. It occupied the top two floors, and had a wide paved terrace that looked out over the tops of the pines to the blue Mediterranean beyond. During the day, while Ramón was at the bank, Isabella in her tiniest bikini lay out on a protected corner of the terrace where the cold wind could not reach her and the sun tanned her face and body to the colour of dark amber while she wrote the final section of her thesis. Born in Africa, she was a child of the sun, and she had missed it desperately during the London years.

Ramón was called upon by his bank to travel as frequently as when they had lived in London. She hated to see him go, but between his trips there were lyrical interludes spent together. While in Málaga his bank duties were light and he could slip away for the entire afternoon and take her to secret and unfrequented coves along the seashore, or to out-of-the-way restaurants that served the local seafood specialities and country wines.

His wound had healed cleanly. 'It was the expert nurse I had,' he told her. It left a pair of dimpled scars on his chest and back that were glossy with a pink cicatrice. The sun tanned the rest of his body to a much darker tone than hers, like oiled mahogany. In contrast to the tan, his eyes seemed a lighter brighter green.

While Ramón was away she had Adra for company. Where Ramón had found her she was never able to ascertain. However, the choice was a master-stroke, for Adra Olivares was a marvellous substitute for Nanny. In some ways, she surpassed the original, for she was not as garrulous and prying and domineering as the old woman.

Adra was a slim but physically robust woman in her early forties. She had jet hair with just a few strands of dead white that she wore sleeked back into a bun the size of a cricket ball behind her head. Her face was dark and solemn, but at the same time kind and humorous. Her hands were brown and square and powerful when she performed the housework, but quick and light when she cooked or ironed Isabella's clothes to a crisp crackling perfection, or again they were gentle and infinitely comforting when she massaged Isabella's aching back or anointed her bulging sun-browned belly with olive oil to keep the muscles supple and the skin smooth and young and free of stretch-marks.

She took over Isabella's tuition in the Spanish language, and their progress was so rapid that it surprised Ramón. Within a month, Isabella was reading the local newspapers with ease, and arguing fluently with the plumber and the television repair man, or supporting Adra as she haggled with the stall-holders in the local marketplace.

Although she loved to question Isabella about her family and Africa, Adra was not forthcoming about her own origins. Isabella presumed that she was a local woman, until one morning she noticed amongst the mail in their postbox an envelope addressed to her that was stamped and franked in Havana, Cuba.

When she remarked, 'Is it from your husband or family, Adra? Who is writing to you from Cuba?' the woman was brusque.

'It's only a friend, señora. My husband is dead.' And for the rest of the day she was withdrawn and taciturn. It took until the end of the week for her to return to normal, and Isabella was careful not to mention the Cuban letter again.

As the weeks passed, and the time of Isabella's parturition drew closer, so Adra's anticipation of the event increased. She took an intense interest in the layette that Isabella was assembling. Michael had made the original contribution. An airmail parcel arrived from Johannesburg with a set of six cot-sheets and pillow-slips in finest cotton piped with blue silk ribbon, and an exquisite pair of woollen baby-jackets. Each day Isabella added to the collection and

137

Adra helped her with her selections. Together they scoured every possible source of babywear within a radius of an hour's drive in the Mini.

Whenever Ramón returned from his business trips, he always brought a further contribution. Although the clothing was often large enough to fit a teenager, Isabella was so touched by his concern that she could not bring herself to point out the discrepancy. On one occasion, he returned with a pram whose capacity, suspension and glistening paintwork were worthy of the Rolls-Royce workshops in Crewe. Adra presented Isabella with a silk christening-robe that she had made herself with antique lace that she told Isabella came from her grandmother's wedding-dress. Isabella was so touched that she broke down and wept. Her tears seemed to come closer to the surface as her pregnancy progressed, and she thought often of Weltevreden. When she telephoned her father and Nana, it was difficult to prevent herself blurting out something about Ramón or the baby. They believed that she had merely gone into retreat in Spain to finish the thesis.

On several occasions before her pregnancy made it unwise for her to travel, Ramón asked her to undertake errands for him during his absence. In each case, she had merely to fly to a foreign destination in Europe, North Africa or the Middle East, there to make a rendezvous, receive an envelope or small packet and return home. When she flew to Tel Aviv, she used her South African passport, but in Benghazi and Cairo she showed her British passport. All these trips lasted only a day and a night and were uneventful, but served to vary her lifestyle and give her a fine opportunity to shop for the baby. Only a week after her trip to Benghazi, the monarchy of King Idris I was overthrown by a military *coup d'état* led by Colonel Muammar al-Qaddafi, and Isabella was appalled when she realized how close she and her baby had come to being caught up in the revolution. Ramón shared her concern and promised not to ask her to undertake another errand until after the baby was born. She never asked him if her journeys were in connection with bank business or the darker clandestine side of his life.

Once a week, she went for a check-up at the clinic that Ramón had selected for her. Adra always accompanied her. The gynaecologist was a suave and cultured Spaniard with an austere aristocratic face and pale competent hands that felt cool against her skin as he examined her.

'Everything proceeds perfectly, señora. Nature is doing her work, and you are young and healthy and well formed for the task of childbirth.'

'Will it be a boy?'

'Of course, señora. A beautiful healthy boy. I give you my personal guarantee.'

The clinic was a former Moorish palace, restored and renovated, and equipped with the most modern medical equipment. After the doctor had taken her on a tour of the facilities, Isabella realized the wisdom of Ramón's choice. She was sure that it was the finest available.

During one of her visits, when the doctor had finished his examination and Isabella was dressing in the curtained cubicle, she overheard him discussing her condition with Adra in the waiting-room. Isabella's Spanish was by this time good enough for her to appreciate that the exchange was technical and specific, like that of two professionals. It surprised her.

On the drive home, she stopped at a sea-front restaurant and, as was their established custom, ordered ice-cream and chocolate sauce for both of them.

'I heard you talking to the doctor, Adra,' Isabella said, with a mouthful of ice-cream. 'You must once have been a nurse, you know so much about it – all those technical words.'

Once again, she encountered that strangely hostile reaction from the woman.

'I am too stupid for that. I am just a maid,' she said harshly, and retreated into a sullen silence from which Isabella could not dislodge her.

The doctor anticipated that the baby would arrive during

the first week in April, and she made a spurt on her thesis to finish it before that time. She typed the final pages on the last day of March and sent it off to London. She was undecided whether it was arrant nonsense or sheer genius. After it had gone she agonized endlessly over fancied omissions and possible improvements which she could have made to the text.

However, within a week she had a reply from the university inviting her to defend her thesis during a viva with the examiners of the faculty.

'They like it,' she exulted, 'or they wouldn't bother.'

Despite her advanced pregnancy she flew to London for three days to attend the viva. It went better than she could have hoped but by the time she got back to Málaga she was exhausted.

'They promised to let me know as soon as possible!' she told Ramón. 'But I think it's going to be all right – hold thumbs for me.'

She made Ramón give his solemn promise not to leave her alone from now onwards. Thus, she was lying in his arms, both of them naked under the sheet in the moonlight, the doors to the terrace wide open to catch the faintest breeze off the sea, when the first pain woke her.

She lay quietly, not waking him, while she timed the intervals between contractions, feeling smug and accomplished as she entered the final stages of the long fascinating process. When at last, she shook Ramón awake, he was most gratifyingly solicitous. He hurried away in his pyjamas to fetch Adra from the servant's room on the lower floor.

Isabella's suitcase was ready, and the three of them climbed into the Mini. With Isabella seated in splendid isolation on the tiny rear seat, Ramón drove them out to the clinic.

As her doctor had predicted, it all went forward naturally and rapidly. Although the baby was large and Isabella's hips were relatively narrow, there were no complications. When the doctor called upon her from between her raised knees for a final effort, she thrust down with all her strength and then as she felt the enormous slippery rushing release within her she uttered a joyous and triumphant cry.

Anxiously she struggled up on one elbow and brushed the sweaty tangle of hair out of her eyes. 'What is it?' she demanded. 'Is it a boy?' And the doctor held the skinny glistening red body high, and they all laughed at the petulant birth-wail.

'There you are.' Still holding him dangling by the ankles, the doctor turned the infant so that Isabella could see him better.

The child's face was scarlet and creased, the eyelids swollen tightly closed. His hair was dense and jet black, plastered wetly over the skull. His penis stuck out half as long as her forefinger in what seemed to be, to Isabella's partisan appraisal, a full and impressive erection.

'It's a boy!' she gasped, and then with a chuckle of wonderment: 'He's a boy and a Courtney!'

Isabella was unprepared for the overwhelming strength of her maternal instincts as they laid her firstborn son at her breast and he took her engorged nipple between his rubbery little gums and tugged at it with an animal strength that aroused sympathetic contractions in her distended womb and a deeper, more primeval pain in her heart.

He was the most beautiful creature she had ever touched, as beautiful as his father. In those first days, she could not take her eyes off him, often rising in the night to bend over his cot and examine his tiny face in the moonlight, or while he suckled, opening his pink fists and studying each perfect little finger with an almost religious awe.

'He's mine. He belongs to me,' she kept telling herself, not yet able to overcome the wonder of it.

Ramón spent most of those first three days with them in the big sunny private room of the clinic. He seemed to share her fascination with the child. They discussed, as they had during the previous months, what names they would christen him. In the end, by a slow and painful process of elimination, they struck out Shasa and Sean from her side of the family, and Huesca and Mahon from Ramón's side. They settled for Nicholas Miguel Ramón de Santiago y Machado. Miguel was a compromise for the Michael which Isabella had suggested.

On the fourth day, when Ramón came to her room in the clinic, he was accompanied by three sober gentlemen in dark suits, all of them bearing important-looking briefcases. One was an attorney, another was an official from the State Registrar's office and the third was the local magistrate.

The magistrate bore witness as Isabella signed the order of adoption, relinquishing her guardianship of Nicholas to the Marqués de Santiago y Machado, and he placed his official seal on the document. The birth certificate provided by the registrar showed Ramón as the father.

After the officials had toasted the mother and child with a large glass of sherry and left, Ramón took Isabella tenderly in his arms.

'Your son's claim to the title is secure,' he whispered.

'Our son,' she whispered in reply, and kissed him. 'My men, Nicky and Ramón.'

When Ramón fetched them from the clinic and brought them back to the flat, Isabella insisted on carrying Nicky up the stairs herself. Adra had filled bowls of flowers to welcome them.

She took the child out of Isabella's arms. 'He is wet. I will change him.' And Isabella felt like a lioness deprived of her cub.

Over the days that followed an unspoken but nevertheless intense competition developed between the two women. Although Isabella acknowledged Adra's obvious expertise in dealing with the infant, she found herself resenting the intrusion. She wanted Nicky all to herself, and she tried to anticipate his needs and to get to him ahead of Adra.

The florid birth-tones of Nicky's face soon faded into a peachy perfection, and his thick dark hair curled. When he opened his eyes for the first time, they were that exact same shade of pale green as Ramón's. Isabella considered this one of the great miracles of the universe.

'You are as beautiful as your father,' she told him as she suckled him. At least that was one service that Adra could not render him.

In the months that they had lived in the village, Isabella had become a local favourite. Her loveliness and her easy engaging manner, her pregnancy and her sincere efforts to master the language had delighted the tradespeople and the stall-holders in the market-place.

In response to their entreaties, when Nicky was barely ten days old, she laid him in the pram and paraded him through the village. It was a triumphant progress, and they returned to the flat laden with small gifts and with their ears ringing with praises.

When she phoned home on Easter Day her grandmother asked severely: 'What is so important in Spain that you cannot come home to Weltevreden?'

'Oh, Nana, I love you all, but it is just impossible. Please forgive me.'

'If I know you, young lady, which I do, you are up to no good and it wears trousers.'

'Nana, you are an absolute shocker. How can you believe that of me?'

'Twenty years of experience,' Centaine Courtney-Malcomess told her drily. 'Just don't get into any more trouble, child.'

'I won't, I promise,' Isabella told her sweetly, and hugged the infant at her bosom. Oh, if you only knew, she thought. He doesn't wear trousers; not yet anyway.

'How is the thesis going?' her father asked, when he came on the line. She could not tell him that she had already submitted it, for that was her excuse for remaining in Spain.

'Almost done,' she compromised. She hadn't thought about it since Nicky had come along.

143

'Good luck with it.' And then Shasa was silent for a moment. 'Do you remember our talk, the promise you gave me?'

'Which one?' she procrastinated guiltily. She knew very well what he was referring to.

'You promised that if you were ever in any trouble, any trouble at all, you wouldn't try to go it alone, you would come to me.'

'Yes, I remember.'

'Are you all right, Bella baby?'

'I'm fine, wonderful, just marvellous, Daddy.'

He heard the ring of it in her voice and sighed with relief.

'Happy Easter, my bright and beautiful daughter.'

With Michael it was a relief to let it all out of her. They were on the telephone for forty-five minutes, Málaga to Johannesburg, and she tickled Nicky to make him gurgle for his distant uncle.

'When are you coming home, Bella?' Michael asked at last.

'Ramón's divorce will be through by June, that's definite. We will have a civil marriage here in Spain and the church wedding at Weltevreden. I expect you to be at both functions.'

'Try to stop me,' he challenged her.

★ ★ ★

They celebrated Easter dinner at their favourite seaside restaurant with Nicky's pram parked at the table. The patron's wife had knitted a jacket for the baby.

Adra was with them. She was part of their small family by now, and she wheeled the pram when they walked home to the flat. Isabella clung to Ramón's arm. She felt very married and maternal, and as happy as she had ever been in her entire life.

When they arrived at the flat, Adra took Nicky away to change him. For once Isabella did not resent it.

In the front bedroom she lowered the shutters, and then came to Ramón.

'It's three weeks since Nicky was born. I'm not made of glass, you know. I won't break.'

He was too gentle, too considerate for her mood. She had been without him for too long.

'I think you've forgotten how to do this,' she said, and pushed him over on his back. 'Let me refresh your memory, sir.'

'Don't hurt yourself,' he cautioned anxiously.

'If anybody gets hurt around here, it is more likely to be you, my friend. Now, fasten your seatbelt. We are ready for take-off.'

Afterwards, in the shuttered room, she lay against him in languorous exhaustion, their bodies sticking lightly together with the sweat of their loving and he said: 'I have to go away for four days next week.'

She sat up quickly. 'Oh, Ramón, so soon!' she protested, and then realized that she was being possessive and unreasonable.

'You'll phone me every day, won't you?' she demanded.

'I'll do better than that. I'll be in Paris and I'll try to arrange for you to join me there. We will have dinner at Laserre.'

'That would be lovely, but what about Nicky?'

'Nicky has got Adra to look after him,' Ramón chuckled. 'Nicky will be all right, and Adra will love the opportunity to have him all to herself.'

'I don't know . . .' she said dubiously. The thought of being parted from her wondrous achievement for even an hour appalled her.

'It will be for one night only, and you have really earned a little reward. Besides, I need you, too, you know.'

'Oh, my darling.' His appeal touched her. Her flow of milk was copious. She could express enough to cover the feeds that Nicky would need during such a short absence. 'Of course, I'd love to be with you. You are right. Nicky and Adra will survive a night without me. I'll come as soon as you call me.'

★   ★   ★

'The woman gave birth to her brat almost a month ago,' General Joseph Cicero whispered hoarsely. 'What has been the delay? You should have terminated the operation immediately. The cost has been out of all proportion!'

'The general will recall that I am meeting the cost out of funds that I have provided, not out of the departmental budget,' Ramón reminded him quietly.

Cicero coughed and rustled the copy of *France Soir* which he held before his face. They sat side by side in a second-class coach of the Paris Métro. Cicero had entered the coach at the Concorde station and taken the seat beside Ramón. Neither of them had shown any sign of recognition. The rush of the train through the underground tunnel would foil any eavesdropper. Both of them used open newspapers to cover their face as they talked. This was one of their regular procedures for short meetings.

'I was not referring only to the cost in roubles,' Cicero wheezed. 'You have spent nearly a year on this project, an incalculable cost to the other work of the department.'

Ramón was fascinated by the rapid course of the disease that was destroying his superior. It seemed that at every meeting Joseph Cicero had deteriorated visibly. It would not be much longer, months rather than years.

'These few months of work will pay us back enormous dividends over the years and, yes, over the decades ahead.'

'Work,' snorted Cicero. 'Stirring the honey-pot with your spoon. If that is work, how do you define pleasure, Marqués? And why are you prolonging termination month after month?'

'If the woman is to be of the utmost value to us, then it is absolutely necessary that she bond to the child before we proceed to the next step in the operation.'

146

'When will that be?' Cicero demanded.

'It has happened already. The fruit is ripe for picking. Everything is in place. I need your co-operation in the final resolution. That is why I chose Paris for this meeting.'

Cicero nodded. 'Go on,' he invited.

And Ramón spoke quietly for another five minutes. Cicero listened without comment, but grudgingly he admitted to himself that the plan was airtight. Once again, he acceded privately that his successor seemed to have been well chosen, despite the original prejudice he had fostered towards him.

'Very well,' he whispered at last. 'You have approval to proceed. And, as you request, I will monitor proceedings at this end.' Cicero folded his newspaper and stood up as the coach slid into the Métro station at Bastille on its silent rubber wheels.

As the doors opened, he stepped down on to the platform and walked away without looking back.

★ ★ ★

The notification from London University arrived the afternoon that Ramón left. It took the form of an express letter with the University's coat of arms embossed on the flap of the envelope.

'The Chancellor and the faculty members of the University of London take pleasure in informing Isabella Courtney that she has been awarded the degree of Doctor of Philosophy of the University.'

Isabella telephoned Weltevreden immediately. There was little time-difference between Málaga and Cape Town, and Shasa had just returned from the polo-field. He was still in boots and breeches, and he took the call in the downstairs study whose french windows overlooked the field.

'Son of a gun!' he let out a whoop when she told him. Such an uncharacteristic display was proof to her of her father's deep delight. 'When will they cap you, darling?'

'Not till June or July. I'll have to stay until then.' It was the excuse she had been looking for.

'Of course,' Shasa agreed immediately. 'I'll come over.'

'Oh, Daddy, it's such a long way.'

'Nonsense, Doctor Courtney, I wouldn't miss it for the world. Your grandmother will probably want to come with me.' Strangely the prospect did not alarm her as it might have. She realized that it was probably the ideal occasion for both her father and Nana to meet Ramón, and Nicky. Centaine Courtney-Malcomess off her home ground was not such a daunting prospect as she was when installed in all the splendour and tradition of Weltevreden.

More than anything at that moment, Isabella wanted to share her joy in her achievement with Ramón, but he did not telephone that night, nor even the following day. By Thursday morning, she was almost frantic with worry. It was so unlike Ramón; usually he telephoned every day that they were apart.

When finally the telephone rang she was in the tiny kitchen in a heated argument with Adra as to how many cloves of garlic should go into the paella.

'You would inject the stuff into your veins if you were given the chance,' she accused in her now fluent Spanish.

'We are making paella, not Irish stew.' Adra held her ground, and then the telephone rang and Isabella dropped the spoon with a clatter and knocked over the chair in the hall in her haste to reach it.

'Ramón darling, I was so worried. I missed your call.'

'I'm sorry, Bella.' The rich dark tones of his voice soothed her, so her own voice became a purr.

'Do you still love me?'

'Come to Paris, and I will prove it to you.'

'When?'

'Now. I have made a reservation for you on the Air France flight at eleven o'clock. They are holding your ticket at the airport. You'll be here by two o'clock.'

'Where will I meet you?'

'At the Plaza Athénée. We have a suite.'

'You spoil me, Ramón darling.'

'No less than you deserve.'

She left the flat immediately. However, the Air France take-off was delayed by forty minutes. In Paris the baggage-handlers were working to rule, so she stood fuming and fretting at the baggage-carousel for almost an hour before her overnight case made its leisurely appearance. It was after five o'clock in the evening before her taxi pulled up in the Avenue Montaigne before the elegant façade of the Plaza Athénée with its scarlet awnings.

She half-expected Ramón to be waiting for her in the marbled and mirrored foyer and looked about eagerly as she came in through the revolving glass doors. He was not there. She paid no heed to the gaunt figure who sat in one of the gilt and brocade armchairs opposite the reception-desk. The man lifted his head of lank white hair and for a moment regarded her with strangely lifeless tar-black eyes. Then he coughed harshly and returned his attention to the newspaper he was reading.

Isabella crossed quickly and expectantly to the concierge's counter.

'You have a guest, the Marqués de Santiago y Machado. I am his wife.'

'A moment, madame.' The uniformed concierge consulted the guest-list, and then shook his head and frowned as he started again at the head of the list.

'I'm sorry, Marquesa. The Marqués is not staying with us at the moment.'

'Perhaps he has registered as Monsieur Machado.'

'I'm afraid not. We have nobody of that name.'

Isabella looked confused. 'I don't understand. I spoke to him this morning.'

'I will make further enquiry.' The concierge left her for a moment to consult the booking-clerk, and returned almost immediately. 'Your husband is not with us, and there is no reservation for him.'

'He must have been delayed.' Isabella tried to look unconcerned. 'Do you have a room for me?'

'The hotel is fully booked.' The concierge spread his hands apologetically. 'It's spring, you understand. I am desolated, Marquesa. Paris is overflowing.'

'He must be coming,' Isabella insisted brightly. 'Do you mind if I wait for my husband in the gallery?'

'Of course not, Marquesa. The waiter will bring you coffee and whatever refreshment you wish. The porter will guard your baggage in his store.'

As she moved towards the long gallery, which at the cocktail hour was the fashionable meeting-place for 'le tout Paris', the white-haired gentleman rose from his armchair. He moved stiffly with the gait of a frail and sick old man, but Isabella in her consternation did not even glance in his direction. Cicero went out into the street, and the doorman hailed a taxi for him and it dropped him in rue Grenelle. He walked the last block to the Soviet embassy, and the guard at the night-desk recognized him as he approached.

From the office of the military attaché on the second floor, Joe Cicero phoned a number in Málaga.

'The woman is waiting at the hotel,' he whispered huskily. 'She cannot return before noon tomorrow. You may proceed as planned.'

A little before seven o'clock, the concierge came and found Isabella in the gallery.

'There has been a cancellation, Marquesa. We have a room for you now. I have already sent your baggage up.'

She could have kissed him, but instead tipped him a hundred francs.

From the room, she rang the flat in Málaga. She hoped that Ramón might have left a message with Adra, now that the arrangements had so obviously gone awry. Although she let the telephone ring for a counted one hundred peals, there was no reply. That truly alarmed her. Adra should have been there; the telephone was in the hallway just outside her bedroom door. Isabella telephoned again twice more during the night, each time without success.

'The telephone is out of order,' she told herself with conviction, but she hardly slept at all.

As soon as the airline reservations office opened, she booked a flight back to Málaga, and despite her distress she managed to sleep for an hour during the journey. It was after midday when they landed at Málaga airport.

The taxi dropped her at the front door of the apartment-block, and she dragged her bag to their front door. With fingers that shook with fatigue and agitation she finally got the key into the lock.

The apartment was strangely silent, and her voice rang through the open doorway.

'Adra, I'm back. Where are you?'

She glanced into the kitchen as she hurried to Adra's room. The room was empty, and she started up the stairs at a run, and then stopped abruptly at the door to her bedroom. It was wide open.

Nicky's cot still stood in the alcove opposite the window. It was stripped of sheets and pillows and blankets, that exquisite layette that Michael had sent her from home. The table beside the cot, on which had stood Nicky's platoon of soft toys, the teddies and bunnies and Disney creatures which she had showered on him, was bare.

She stepped to the terrace door and glanced out. His pram was gone.

'Adra!' she cried, and heard the high thin tone of panic in her own voice. 'Where are you?'

She raced through the other rooms. 'Nicky! My baby! Oh God, please. Where have you taken Nicky?'

She found herself back in the main bedroom beside his empty cot.

'I don't understand,' she whispered. 'What has happened?'

On a sudden impulse, she whirled and jerked open the drawers of Nicky's bureau. They were all empty. The nappies and vests and jackets were all of them gone.

'The hospital.' Her voice was a sob. 'Something has happened to my baby!'

She rushed down the stairs and seized the telephone and

then froze as she saw the envelope taped to the cradle of the instrument. She dropped the telephone receiver and ripped open the envelope. Her hands shook so that she could barely read the words on the single sheet of note-paper.

However, she recognized Ramón's handwriting instantly and felt a treacherous rush of relief, which evaporated swiftly as she read the words:

Nicholas is with me. He is safe for the time being. If you wish to see him again, you must follow these instructions exactly. Do not speak to anybody in Málaga. I repeat do not speak to anybody. Leave the flat immediately and return to London. You will be contacted at Cadogan Square. Tell nobody what has happened, not even your brother Michael. Follow these instructions implicitly. Your disobedience will have dire consequences for Nicky. You may never see him again. Destroy this note.

R

Her legs went soft and boneless under her, and she sank down against the wall and sat on the tiled floor with them sprawled out loosely in front of her as though they were disjointed at the hips. She read the note again, and then again, but it didn't make sense.

'My baby,' she whispered. 'My little Nicky.' And then she read the terrible words aloud. ' "Your disobedience will have dire consequences for Nicky. You may never see him again." '

She let the hand holding the note drop into her lap and she stared at the wall opposite. She felt as though the world and her entire existence had been swept away. It left her as blank and meaningless as that empty expanse of brickwork in front of her.

She did not know how long she sat there, but at last with a supreme effort she roused herself. Using the wall as a support, she regained her feet. Once more, she climbed the stairs to their bedroom and went directly to Ramón's cupboard. She threw the doors open, and found that it also was empty. Even the coat-hangers were gone. She moved listlessly to his chest of drawers, and opened each empty drawer. Ramón had left nothing.

She wandered back to Nicky's alcove, moving like the survivor of a bomb blast, dazed and unco-ordinated, and knelt beside the empty cot.

'My baby,' she whispered. 'What have they done with you?'

Then she saw that something had slipped down between the baby mattress and the wooden bars of the cot. She eased it free, and held it in both hands. Kneeling at the cot as though it were the high altar, she held the sacrament in her hands. It was one of Nicky's bootees, a scrap of soft knitted wool with a blue satin ribbon as the drawstring for his chubby pink ankle. She lifted it to her face and inhaled the perfumed baby-smell of her son.

Only then she began to weep. She wept with a bitter ferocity that drained her strength and left her exhausted. By that time, the terrace and the bedroom were filled with the shades of evening and she had only the strength left to crawl to the double bed and curl up on it. As she fell asleep she held the woollen bootee pressed to her cheek.

It was still dark when she awoke. She lay for long seconds with the dark sense of doom overpowering her, uncertain of its origin or cause. Then suddenly it all came back to her and she struggled upright and looked about her with horror.

Ramón's note lay on the table beside the bed. She took it up and reread it, still trying to make sense of it.

'Ramón my darling, why are you doing this to us?' she whispered. Then, obedient to his instructions, she carried the note to the bathroom and standing over the toilet-bowl tore it into tiny scraps. She dropped these into the bowl and flushed them away. She knew that every word would be graven on her mind for ever; she had no need nor wish to conserve that dreadful sheet of paper.

She showered and dressed and made herself a slice of toast and a pot of coffee. They were without taste. Her mouth felt numb as though it had been scalded with boiling water.

Then she set herself to search the apartment thoroughly. She began in Adra's room. There was no trace left of Adra Olivares, not a shred of clothing, not a pot or a tube of ointment or cosmetics in her bathroom, not even a single hair from her head on the pillow of her bed.

Then she went over the living-room and kitchen; again there was nothing, except the hired furniture and crockery and the remains of food in the refrigerator.

She went up to the bedroom. There was a small wall-safe in the back of Ramón's cupboard, but the steel door was ajar and all the documents were missing. Nicky's birth certificate and adoption papers were gone with them.

She sat down on the bed and tried to think clearly, attempting desperately to find a reason for this madness. She went round and round, trying to examine it from every possible angle.

She was driven remorselessly to a single conclusion. Ramón was in deep trouble. It was some horror from his clandestine life which had overtaken them. She knew that under extreme duress he had been forced to leave with Nicky. She understood that she must do everything in her power to help them, Ramón and Nicky, the two most important elements in her life. She knew that she must do as he ordered her. Their safety and possibly their lives depended upon it. Yet she could not leave it like that. She had to learn more; any morsel of knowledge might be of value.

She left the apartment and went downstairs. There was a small bakery shop across the street, and over the months Isabella had become friendly with the baker's wife. The woman was opening the shutters over the shop window as Isabella hurried across the road.

'Yes,' the baker's wife told her, 'after you left on Thursday, Adra went out with Nicholas in the pram. They went down towards the beach and returned just before I closed

154

the shop. I saw them go up to your apartment, but I didn't see them again, not after that.'

Isabella went up the street, stopping to question all the tradespeople whose businesses were within sight of the apartment-block. Some of them had seen Adra and Nicky return on Thursday evening, but not one of them had seen them again since then. Her last resort was the shoeshine urchin on the corner of the park. Ramón always allowed the lad to polish his shoes and over-tipped him exorbitantly. He was one of Isabella's favourites on the street.

'Sí, señora,' he grinned at Isabella, as he squatted over his box. 'On Thursday night I work late, because of the cinema and the arcade. At ten o'clock I see the marqués. He came in a big black car with two men. They park in the street and go upstairs.'

'What did the other men look like, *chico*? Do you know them? Had you see them before?'

'Never. They two tough *hombres* – policemen, I think. Much trouble. I don't like police. They all go upstairs, and then soon they come down. They all carry suitcases, big suitcases. Adra come with them. She carry baby Nico; they get into the car, all of them, and they drive away. That is all. I don't see them again.'

The two tough *hombres* confirmed what Isabella had suspected: that Ramón was acting under coercion. She realized that the only source of action open to her was to follow the instruction that Ramón had given her in the note. She went back to the apartment and began to pack up. Her redundant maternity clothes she left lying on the bedroom floor, and her good clothes filled only two cases.

When she came to the drawer that contained her cosmetics she found that the fat album of snapshots that she had accumulated since Nicky's birth was missing, together with the envelopes of negatives. It came as a shock to realize that she had no record of her baby, no photograph or souvenir, apart from the single woollen bootee that she had retrieved from his cot.

She lugged her bulging cases downstairs and packed them into the back of the Mini. Then she crossed the street and spoke to the baker's wife.

'If my husband comes back and asks for me, tell him I have gone back to London.'

'What about Nico? Are you all right, señora?' The woman was sympathetic, and Isabella smiled brightly.

'Nico is with my husband. I'll meet them in London soon. Muchas gracias por su ayuda, señora. Adiós.'

* * *

The drive northwards seemed endless. Each episode of the last few days since last she had seen her son played over and over in her mind until she felt that she was going slowly mad.

On the cross-Channel ferry, she forsook the loud bonhomie of the crowded saloon and went up on to the boat-deck. It was a cold grey day, with the north wind kicking the tops off the swells in dashing white spurts of spray. The wind and her despair chilled her through, until she was shivering uncontrollably even in her padded anorak. However, in the end it was the ache in her swollen breasts that drove her below. In the women's toilet she used the express pump to draw off the flow that should have been for her son.

'Oh, Nicky, Nicky!' she cried silently, as she discharged the rich creamy liquid into the toilet-bowl, and she imagined once again his hot little mouth on her nipples and the smell and the feel of him against her breast.

She found herself weeping, and with a huge effort controlled herself. 'You're losing your grip on reality,' she warned herself. 'You've got to be strong now. You can't let go. For Nicky's sake, you must be strong. No more crying and moping – no more.'

It was raining when she drove into Cadogan Square, and the flat seemed chilly and uninviting. While she unpacked she thought about the promise that she had made her father. Suddenly she threw down the dress that she held and ran through to the drawing-room.

'International, I want to place a call to Cape Town, South Africa.'

At this time of night, the delay was less than ten minutes, and she heard the peals of the telephone at the other end. One of the servants answered it, and as she opened her mouth to ask for her father Ramón's strict injunction came back to her with all its force and threat. 'Your disobedience will have dire consequences for Nicky.'

She replaced the receiver on its cradle without speaking, and resigned herself to wait for the promised contact.

Nothing happened for six days. She never left the flat, not daring to put herself beyond the reach of the telephone. She rang nobody, spoke to nobody except the housekeeper, and tried to keep herself occupied by reading and watching television. The uncertainty aggravated her despair, and she found that, although she stared at the pages of her book or at the small flickering screen of the television set, the printed words and the images were meaningless. Only her agony was real. Only her loss had poignant meaning. Only her pain abided.

She could barely bring herself to eat, and within three days her milk-flow had dried up. She lost weight dramatically. Her hair, which was one of the high points of her beauty, turned dull and dry. Her face in the mirror was gaunt, her eyes sank into bruised-looking cavities and her golden amber Mediterranean tan became sallow and yellow like the skin of a malaria sufferer.

She waited, and the waiting was torture. Each hour was an insupportable eternity. Then, on the sixth day, the telephone rang. She snatched it up with desperate haste, before the second peal.

'I have a message from Ramón.' It was a woman's voice with an elusive accent, probably mid-European. 'Leave now, immediately. Take a taxi to the junction of Royal Hospital Road and the Embankment. Walk down the Embankment towards Westminster. Somebody will greet you with the name Red Rose. Follow their orders,' said the caller. 'Repeat these instructions, please.'

Breathlessly Isabella obeyed. 'Good,' said the woman, and broke the connection.

Isabella had not walked further than a hundred yards along the Embankment above the Thames when a small unmarked van passed her, travelling slowly in the same direction. It pulled into the kerb ahead of her, and as she drew level with it the rear door opened to reveal a middle-aged woman in grey overalls sitting on the side-bench of the body of the van.

'Red Rose,' she said and Isabella recognized her voice from their telephone conversation. 'Get in!'

Quickly Isabella slipped into the van and sat on the bench opposite the woman. She slammed the door, and immediately the van pulled away.

The body of the van was without windows or any opening except for the ventilator in the roof above Isabella's head. She could not see out and, though she tried to track their course by the turns and stops, she was soon totally confused and abandoned the attempt.

'Where are you taking me?' she asked the woman opposite her.

'Silence, please.' And Isabella resigned herself. She pulled her collar up around her ears, and thrust her hands deep into the pockets of her anorak. They drove for twenty-three minutes by her wristwatch, and then the van stopped again and the rear door was opened from outside.

They were in a parking garage. She judged from the unpainted concrete pillars that supported the low roof and from the steep access-ramp at the far end of the long narrow chamber that it was an underground parking facility.

The woman in the grey overalls took her arm and helped her down from the van. The touch of her hand made Isabella aware of just how powerful she was. The hand felt like the paw of a gorilla, and she towered above Isabella with wide meaty shoulders under the grey cloth.

'This way,' she ordered. Still holding her arm, she led

Isabella to the lift doors opposite the van. Despite the painful grip, Isabella glanced around her quickly. There were a dozen or so other vehicles parked in the bays alongside the van; at least two of them had diplomatic number-plates.

The doors of the lift opened, and the woman pushed Isabella into it. A glance at the control panel showed Isabella that her assumption had been correct. The lighted stage-indicator showed that they were at 'Basement Level II'. The woman pushed the button for the third floor and they rode up in silence, until the lift stopped with the stage-indicator at 'Level III' and her escort urged her out into a bare corridor with cork flooring. They walked down it side by side, and still in silence. The corridor was empty and the doors on each side closed.

As they approached the end of the corridor, the facing door slid open. Another large female with flat Slavic features, dressed also in grey overalls, ushered them into what appeared to be a small lecture-room or an intimate movie-theatre. A double row of easy chairs faced the raised dais and the screen that covered the far wall.

Isabella's escort led her to the chair in the front row centre.

'Sit down,' she said, and Isabella sank down on the smooth cold plastic padding. The two women moved around and took up their position, standing behind Isabella. For several minutes, there was silence. Then the small door to the right of the dais opened and a man came through.

He moved slowly, stiffly, like a frail and sick old man. His hair was dead white, with a yellowish tinge, and hung over his forehead and ears. His features were very pale, lined and seamed with age and suffering, so that Isabella felt a twinge of sympathy for him, until the light caught his eyes.

With a small jolt of intense distaste she recognized those eyes. Once she had been with her father on a chartered fishing-boat out of Black River. Shasa had been trolling a live bonito along the oceanic drop-off under the shadow of Le Morne Brabant on the island of Mauritius when he had hooked into a gigantic mako shark. After a battle which lasted two hours, he had dragged the creature alongside. As its pointed snout broke through the surface, Isabella had been leaning over the rail and she had looked into its eyes. They were black and pitiless, without definite iris or pupil, two holes that seemed to reach down into hell itself. Those were the same eyes that studied her now.

She held her breath under their implacable scrutiny, until at last the man spoke. Then his voice came as a surprise. It was low and hoarse. She had to lean forward slightly to make sense of the words.

'Isabella Courtney, from now on we will never use that name again in any communication. You will be referred to and you will refer to yourself only as Red Rose. Do you understand?'

She nodded, not trusting her voice to reply. He lifted the cigarette that smouldered between his fingers and drew deeply upon it. He spoke again through a cloud of exhaled smoke.

'I have a message for you, in the form of a video-tape recording.' He stepped down from the dais and took the chair at the end of the row furthest from her.

As he settled into it, the overhead lights dimmed. She heard the faint hum of electronic equipment, and then the screen lit up. The scene it displayed was a bare white-tiled room – a laboratory or an operating-theatre, she decided.

There was a table in the centre of the room, and on it was a glass-sided tank much like one of the aquariums in which ornamental tropical fish were displayed in a pet shop. The tank was filled with water to within a few inches of the top. On the table-top beside the tank stood some sort of electronic cabinet and an array of instruments and medical paraphernalia. She recognized a portable oxygen-cylinder and an oxygen-mask. The mask was a diminutive model suitable for infants and very small children.

A man was busy at the table. His back was towards the

camera and his features were hidden. He wore some type of white laboratory-coat. He turned to face the camera, and Isabella saw that he wore a cloth theatre-cap and surgical mask.

His voice was dispassionate as he began to speak, and his accent was foreign, east European. He seemed to be addressing Isabella directly out of the screen.

'Your orders were to speak to nobody, not in Malaga or elsewhere. You deliberately disobeyed those orders.' He was staring at her from the screen with disembodied eyes.

'I'm sorry,' she replied, as though he could hear her. 'I was so worried. I couldn't—'

'Silence!' hissed one of the women behind her chair. A hand fell on her shoulder, fingers dug into her flesh with a strength that made her wince.

On the screen, the man was still speaking. 'You were warned that your disobedience would have dire consequences for your son. You chose to ignore that warning. What you are about to witness is a first demonstration of the seriousness of those instructions.'

He made a gesture to somebody off-camera and a figure entered from the side. It was impossible to tell whether it was male or female, for it also wore a cloth cap and surgical mask that covered all the face and head except for the narrow strip across the eyes. A full-length surgical gown fell to below the knees and was tucked into the tops of white rubber boots.

'This is a qualified doctor who will monitor all the proceedings,' he explained.

The figure carried a bundle in its arms. Only when it deposited the bundle on the table beside the glass-sided tank and a tiny bare leg kicked free of the swaddling cloth, Isabella realized that it was a child. With quick trained hands, the doctor unwrapped the infant, and the video-camera zoomed in on Nicky as he lay naked on the table-top kicking his legs in the air, and his gurgles sounded in the quiet room.

Isabella thrust the fingers of one hand into her mouth

and bit down on them hard to prevent herself crying out again.

The doctor placed two small black suction cups on Nicky's bare chest. Thin wires dangled from them, and the doctor connected them to the electronic cabinet and switched it on. The digital figures in the panel lit with a green glow, and the narrator explained in a neutral voice: 'The child's breathing and heartbeat will be recorded.'

The doctor looked up from his equipment and nodded. The narrator moved around behind the table and faced the camera.

'You are Red Rose,' he said with peculiar emphasis on the name. 'And in future you will obey all orders given to you by that name.'

He reached down and took both of Nicky's ankles in one hand and lifted him. Nicky let out a squawk of surprise as he hung head-down like a small pink wingless bat.

'You are about to witness the consequences of dis-obedience.'

He swung the child and held him head-down over the glass-sided tank. Nicky arched his back and tried to lift his head, he waved his arms and clenched and unclenched his fists, making small noises of uncertainty and alarm. Slowly the narrator lowered the child head-first into the water, and the sounds of his little voice were cut off abruptly. The video-camera zoomed in through the glass side of the tank and focused on his face below the surface of the water. The colour resolution of the film was true to life.

Isabella screamed wildly and tried to struggle out of her chair. The two women seized her from behind and forced her down again.

On the screen Nicky struggled in the narrator's grip. Underwater his face was contorted and silver bubbles streamed from his nostrils. His face seemed to swell and darken.

Isabella was still screaming and fighting when on the screen the masked doctor looked up quickly from the heart monitor and said sharply in Spanish: 'Stop! That is enough, comrade!'

Immediately the man lifted the child clear of the tank. Water streamed from Nicky's nostrils and open mouth, and for long seconds he could not utter a sound, except for his tiny gasping breaths.

The narrator laid him down on the table, and the doctor clapped the oxygen-mask over his swollen face and pressed down on his chest with the palm of his hand to induce regular breathing. Within a minute the digital readout on the cabinet had settled back to normal and Nicky's movements were stronger. He howled into his mask with shock and outrage, his voice becoming louder and stronger with each cry.

The doctor removed the mask and stepped back from the table. He nodded at the narrator. Once again he seized Nicky's ankles and lifted him over the tank. Nicky seemed to realize what was coming. His cries of protest reached a higher terrified pitch, he kicked and writhed in the man's grip.

'He's my son!' Isabella screamed. 'You can't – you mustn't do this to my baby!'

The narrator lowered Nicky's head once again below the surface, and the child fought with all his strength. His frenzied exertions racked the tiny body, water splashed over the edge of the tank, and once again his face changed colour swiftly.

Isabella screamed at him. 'Stop it! I'll do anything you say, just stop torturing my baby! Please! Please!'

Once again the doctor intervened with a sharp warning, and this time when Nicky was lifted clear of the water his movements were weaker. He made little choking, cawing sounds, and a mixture of water and vomit erupted from his open inverted mouth and silver strings of mucus slid down from his flared nostrils.

The doctor worked swiftly, his alarm apparent, and he said something to the other man. The narrator looked up at the camera, seeming to stare directly at Isabella.

'We almost miscalculated that time. We exceeded the limit of safety.' He and the doctor put their heads closer together and spoke so softly that Isabella could not catch the words, and then the narrator addressed her again. 'That concludes our demonstration for the time being. I sincerely hope that it will not be necessary for you to witness another like it. It would be harrowing for you to have to watch the amputation of the child's limbs without anaesthetic, or eventually his strangulation in front of the camera. Of course, it will depend on you, and the degree of co-operation that you are prepared to afford us.'

The image faded, and the screen went blank. There was no sound in the darkened theatre except Isabella's sobs. These lasted for a long time. When they finally quietened the lights were raised slowly and Joseph Cicero came to stand over Isabella.

'I assure you that none of us takes any particular pleasure in this sort of thing. We will try to avoid any repetition.'

'How could he do it!' Isabella whispered brokenly. She was huddled down in the large chair. 'How could any human being do that to a child?'

'I repeat, we do not enjoy the necessity. You must blame yourself, Red Rose. It was your disobedience that caused your son's discomfort.'

'Discomfort! Is that what you call the torture of an innocent . . .?'

'Control yourself,' Cicero warned her sharply. 'For your child's sake, control your insolence.'

'I'm sorry.' Isabella dropped her voice. 'It won't happen again. Just don't hurt Nicky again, please.'

'If you co-operate, your son will not have to suffer further. He is in the care of a highly trained paediatric sister. He will receive the type of professional care that even you would not be able to give him. Later he will be given the best education that any boy or young man could hope for.'

Isabella stared up at him, her face twisted with misery.

'You speak as though he has been taken away from me for ever, as though I will never see my baby again.'

Cicero coughed and shook his head, struggled to regain his breath and then whispered hoarsely: 'This is not the case, Red Rose. You will be allowed to earn the privilege of access to your son. To begin with you will receive regular reports of his progress. You will be shown video recordings of how he develops, when he first sits up unaided, when he begins to crawl, to walk.'

'Oh no!' she whispered. 'You can't keep him from me that long. It will be months.'

Cicero went on as though she had not spoken. 'Later you will be allowed to spend some time with him each year. It is possible that some time in the future, if your conduct is satisfactory, you will be allowed to spend holidays together – days, even weeks in your son's company.'

'No.' Her voice was a pitiful sob. 'You can't be so cruel as to keep us apart.'

'Who knows, it is not beyond the bounds of possibility that one day we may remove all restrictions and allow you free access. For that to happen you would have to earn our complete trust and gratitude.'

'Who are you?' Isabella asked in a small subdued voice. 'Who is Ramón Machado? I thought I knew him so well and yet I did not know him at all. Where is Ramón? Is he part of all this monstrous . . .?' Isabella's voice broke, and she could not continue.

'You must put aside all thoughts of that nature. You must not seek to find the answer to the question of who we are,' Cicero warned her. 'Ramón Machado is under our control. Do not expect help from him. The child is his also. He is under the same constraint as you are.'

'What must I do? What do you want of me?' Isabella asked. And Cicero nodded with satisfaction. There had been a remote chance that the woman might prove headstrong and uncontrollable. The psychiatrist's report on her had mentioned that possibility, but Cicero had never placed much credence in it. The hook on which they had hung her was sharp and fiercely barbed. Even if the child died, they would find a replacement to act in the video games and keep her dangling on the hook. No, he had expected her to be compliant, and those expectations had been vindicated.

'First, I must congratulate you, Red Rose, on your doctorate. It will make your work for us easier.'

Isabella stared at him. It was difficult for her to make the mental leap from this terrifying world of torture and espionage back to the prosaic consideration of her studies and academic honours. She had to concentrate to keep up with what he was saying.

'You will return as soon as possible to Cape Town and your family, after making arrangements at the University to receive your doctorate *in absentia*, do you understand?'

Isabella nodded, not yet trusting herself to speak.

'On your return home, you will begin to take more interest in all the family activities. You will work to make yourself indispensable to your father. You will make yourself his assistant and confidante in all things, but especially in his new position as head of the armaments corporation. What is more, you will begin to take an active interest in South African politics.'

'My father is a self-contained man. He does not need me.'

'You are wrong, Red Rose. Your father is a very lonely and a basically unhappy man. He is incapable of a lasting relationship with any woman, except your grandmother, his mother, Centaine Courtney-Malcomess, and with you, his daughter. He needs that relationship very deeply – and you will give it to him.'

'You want me to use my own father?' she whispered, horror blending with fresh horror in her eyes.

'For the survival of your son,' Cicero agreed softly. 'No harm will come to your father, but your son stands full in harm's way unless you co-operate.'

Isabella took a handkerchief from her handbag and blew

her nose. Her voice was soggy. 'You want me to inveigle myself into my father's confidence to gain information on the national armaments programme and pass it on to you?'

'You learn quickly, Red Rose. However, that is not all. You will use your father's political contact within the South African Nationalist régime to foster your own political career within the party.'

She shook her head. 'I am not a political creature.'

'You are now,' Cicero contradicted her. 'You have a doctorate in political theory. Your father will introduce you to the corridors of power.'

Again she denied it. 'My father is in political eclipse. He backed the wrong horse when John Vorster came to power in South Africa. That was why he was shunted into the ambassadorial post here, into political oblivion.'

'Your father has exonerated himself by the way he performed his duties here in London. His appointment to such a responsible position as head of Armscor is indication of that. We anticipate that soon he will be totally reinstated within the party. We deem it highly probable that within two years he will be once more a member of the Cabinet. You, Red Rose, will ride upon his back. In twenty years from now you yourself could be a minister of the Government.'

'Twenty years!' Isabella echoed in disbelief. 'Is that how long I must be your slave?'

'You still don't understand?' Cicero asked, shaking his head. 'Let me explain it to you. You belong to us, Red Rose, you, your lover Ramón Machado, and your son, for ever.'

For many minutes Isabella stared sightlessly at the blank screen, contemplating the enormity of the vision that he had conjured up for her.

Joe Cicero broke the silence. His voice was almost gentle. 'You will be taken back now. They will leave you where they found you, on the Embankment. Follow your orders, Red Rose, and in the long run it will work out well for you and your son.'

The women attendants helped Isabella to her feet and led her to the door.

When she had gone, the side-door to the lecture-theatre opened and Ramón Machado stepped through. 'You were watching?' Joe Cicero asked, and Ramón nodded. 'I congratulate you,' Joe murmured reluctantly. 'It has been well run. We may reap much of value from this operation. How is the child?'

'He suffered no ill-effects. He and his nurse have arrived in Havana.'

Joe Cicero lit another cigarette and coughed and sat down heavily in one of the plastic chairs.

Perhaps . . . he thought, just perhaps I will be able to leave the department in capable hands.

★　　　★　　　★

Amber Joy was about to 'fail to find'. They could all see it. A palpable air of tension and expectation hung over the entire field of the trial.

The South African retriever championship trial was being conducted over the foothills of the Kabonkel Berg along the western end of the Weltevreden estate. The terrain was testing, and over the two days of the trials the field of dogs had been whittled down to these four still in the hunt.

The birds were mallard ducks, pen-reared on Weltevreden and placed in the field under the supervision of the judges prior to each retrieve. This would probably be the last occasion on which they would be allowed to use mallards, Shasa Courtney reflected. The conservationists were kicking up such a terrible stink about unshot mallards escaping into the wild. There these exotic birds were highly attractive to the indigenous yellow-billed ducks. Avian Don Juans, he smiled.

The progeny of these illicit unions were hybrids, and the Department of Nature Conservation had proclaimed a ban on the release of mallards which would become effective at the end of the month. Thereafter they would be forced to use ring-necked doves or guinea-fowl, which was a pity, they all agreed. These terrestrial birds did not float well on the water-retrieves.

Shasa Courtney switched his full attention back to the retrieve in progress. Amber Joy was the main competition to Weltevreden's hopes of carrying off the cup for the first time. Amber Joy was a splendid yellow Labrador. His sire had been American field-trial champion for three years in a row. Up until now every single retrieve that he had made during the last two days had been SOB, straight out and back. This time fortune had turned against him. The mallard had risen from its cage and flashed away along the edge of the dam. Garry Courtney and Shasa were the field-guns, chosen for the task because both of them were renowned shots. The mallard was flying left, Garry's side, and he had let it go to fifty yards before killing it so cleanly that it folded its wings and went in head-first like a kamikaze. It fell close in to the reed-beds, amongst the lily-pads and 'water blommetjies', the flowering aquatics that infested most dams in the Cape of Good Hope. The mallard's plunge drove it deep, and it had not re-emerged. Probably it was entangled with the plant stems below the surface of the muddy brown water.

The judge had called Amber Joy's number, and Bunty Charles, his owner and handler, had sent him away. While the spectators crowded the dam wall to watch, the dog had taken to the water and swum out towards the spot where the mallard had disappeared. However, he had deviated from the true line as he swam, going up above the bird where any blood would drift away from him on the faint current set up by the in-flowing river and the gusty south-easter which was sweeping across the open water.

Now Amber Joy was paddling around amongst the reeds in erratic circles, occasionally ducking his head below the surface but each time coming up with empty jaws, and a little further from the spot where the duck had plunged.

His efforts were causing consternation on the bank.

Bunty Charles was dancing from one leg to the other in frustration. If he whistled and redirected Amber Joy on to the fall of the bird he would lose points. There was still no guarantee that Amber Joy would find even with this assistance. On the other hand, time was running out. The three judges were already consulting their stop-watches. Amber Joy had been in the water for over three minutes.

Bunty Charles flashed an anxious glance at the next handler and dog in the line. Centaine Courtney-Malcomess and Dandy Lass of Weltevreden were his most bitter rivals. Up to now he and Amber Joy had managed to hold them off, but only by ten points. If they failed to find, they would certainly forfeit their hard-won lead.

Centaine Courtney was also under intense strain. She did not have Bunty's thirty years of field-trial experience. She had taken to the sport only recently. Yet she had brought all her immense energy and powers of concentration to it. Dandy Lass was the progeny of champions, a leggy golden retriever. She was bred for speed as a working gun-dog, strong and wiry, unlike the heavier show-dogs with their classical points of breed but with their working instincts bred out of them. Dandy Lass had the heart and instinct to enter the heaviest cover or coldest water and work through it like a heroine. She had a fine nose to pick up the faintest scent of feather on the air, and her intelligence was uncanny. She and Centaine had developed an almost telepathic rapport.

Although she stood erect and utterly still, with her face calm and imperturbable, inwardly Centaine was seething with agitation, and Dandy Lass picked it up from her. The judges would notice any word or gesture of restraint between them and mark them down immediately. However, Dandy Lass was sitting on the live coals of her eagerness. Her fluffy golden bottom barely came in contact with the ground, and she switched from haunch to haunch with tiny excited movements, not quite sufficient to incur the judges' wrath and penalty points. Whining or barking were grounds for instant elimination. With huge effort,

Dandy prevented herself from giving tongue as she watched Amber Joy's frenzied efforts to find the bird. Yet her entire body shivered with eagerness, and the suppressed cries of excitement rumbled in her throat as she awaited her turn. Every few seconds she glanced up at Centaine with imploring eyes, begging for the command to go.

Shasa Courtney watched his mother from his place in the gun-line. As always she evoked in him the most profound sense of admiration. Centaine Courtney-Malcomess had turned seventy years old last New Year's Day. She had been named for her birth on the first day of the twentieth century, and yet she was as slim and straight as a teenage boy. The outline of her legs and buttocks under fine woollen cloth was aristocratic and elegant.

Who else would wear Chanel slacks to a field-trial? he smiled, and her boots were of ostrich skin, hand-made by Hermès of Paris.

Single-handed, she had raised Shasa from infancy when Shasa's father had been killed in action in France before his birth. Alone in the desert, she had discovered the first diamond that led to the establishment of the fabulous H'ani mine. For thirty years she had run the mine and built up the sprawling financial empire that was to become Courtney Enterprises. Even though the chairmanship had passed to Shasa and then to her grandson Garry Courtney, Centaine still regularly took her seat on the board. Every word she uttered from that seat, every thought she expressed was received with the utmost attention and respect. Every member of the family, from Shasa himself to Garry's brood of her great-grandchildren aged between four years and a few months stood in total awe of Centaine Courtney. She was the only one who could give orders to Bella Courtney and have them obeyed without argument or question.

She stood bare-headed in the bright sunshine of a golden day of Cape spring with the pedigree bitch squatting beside her, and the sunlight sparkled on her hair. Her hair was one of her finer points, dense and thick and curling still, cut into a short cap, the colour of gun-metal touched with bright inlays of pure platinum. She held her chin high and the set of her head alert.

The years had not eroded her beauty but had transformed it into a dignified serenity. Time may have withered that flawless skin, but had been unable to affect the strong line of her jaw, the proud cheekbones and the high intelligent forehead. Nor had it dimmed those dark eyes; eyes that could one moment reflect the ferocity of a cruel predator and the next moment shine with humour and wisdom.

One hell of a lady, Shasa thought. Just look at her, as hungry to win as she was fifty years ago.

One of the judges blew a single sharp blast on his whistle, and Bunty Charles's shoulders slumped with disappointment. Amber Joy had failed and was being recalled. Bunty Charles reinforced the recall with a blast on his own whistle and a brusque hand-signal. Amber Joy came in obediently to the bank and lunged up out of the water. He shook himself, throwing a crystal curtain of water droplets into the sunlight, and then to the horror of his owner and the amusement of the spectators lifted one leg and gave the nearest clump of reeds a contemptuous squirt, succinct expression of Amber Joy's opinion of the duck, the dam and the judges.

Such an unbridled display while under judges' orders was considered very poor form, and would certainly attract penalty points. However, Amber Joy was the picture of nonchalance as he trotted back to his owner, lolling his tongue and wagging his sodden tail.

By this stage, Dandy Lass was in a turmoil of eagerness. She was shivering wildly, rolling her eyes like a berserker. She knew she would be called next, and the effort of keeping her backside pressed to the ground and maintaining her seat was destroying her from within.

Without looking down at her, Centaine exerted all her powers of telepathic communication to hold the bitch under control. The judges were sadistically relishing the delay, making a pretence of consulting each other and writing up their notes, but in reality testing Dandy Lass to the outside

172

limit of her endurance. If she broke now, she would be instantly eliminated; a whine or a bark would penalize her cruelly.

Bastards! Centaine thought bitterly. I hate every last man-jack of you. Let my darling go. Let her go!

A faint choking whine escaped through Dandy's lips, a sound as though a bullfrog was being attacked by a swarm of bees under a blanket, and without seeming to move Centaine extended her forefinger down the side-seam of her Chanel slacks and Dandy suppressed her next utterance.

The senior judge looked up from his notebook.

'Thank you, Number Three,' he called across the water, and Centaine said sharply: 'Fetch!' And Dandy Lass went away like a golden javelin launched from the sling.

As she came to the water, she folded her forelegs under her chest and went out from the bank in a stylish leap, like a thorough-bred steeplechaser, and hit the water three paces out, clear of the weeds. She came up swimming, and Centaine's chest swelled with pride – only a true champion committed to water with such dash.

Dandy Lass swam like an otter, snaking through the water, leaving a broad V of ripples across the surface. Then the swelling in Centaine's chest turned to a cold weight of dread as she realized that Dandy was making the same mistake as Amber Joy. Perhaps the long delay had unsighted her, but she was veering slightly across the wind and the current, up into the blind spot where the scent would be carried away from her.

For an instant, Centaine considered forfeiting points by redirecting her bitch. If Dandy found, even with assistance, she would still have wiped Amber Joy's eye, but they needed every single point if they were to win, and Centaine could already taste the sweetness of victory on the back of her tongue. She stood motionless, her whistle dangling on the loop around her neck.

Dandy Lass judged the length of the retrieve to within feet, and she circled once on the edge of the far reed-bank, but she was too high by three yards. Where Amber Joy had ploughed on, getting ever further from the bird, Dandy Lass stopped and, treading water, looked back to where Centaine stood on the far bank.

Deliberately Centaine thrust her left hand into the hip pocket of her slacks. Not even the strictest judge with the eyes of an eagle could have construed that tiny movement as a signal, but Shasa picked it up.

'The old girl hasn't changed.' He shook his head, grinning. 'Anything to win, any weapon in the arsenal, and the only sin is being caught out.'

In the water Dandy Lass immediately turned left, down-current, paddling hard, and two seconds later her nose went up as she acknowledged scent. She made one more circle, with the scent of blood rich and hot in her nostrils, as she placed the fallen mallard, then she ducked her head into the cold brown water.

A roar of approval went up from the bank as she lifted her head again, streaming water, ears flat against her skull, but the carcass of the mallard held in her jaws.

She left an arrow-head of ripples behind her as she headed back to the bank, the bird held neatly, wings folded, keeping it high to avoid drag through the water. As her feet touched bottom, Dandy Lass flew up the bank. She did not even pause to shake herself. Not wasting a second, she went in to make her delivery.

As she dropped to sit in front of her mistress, Shasa felt a choke in his throat and his vision misted over. It was beautiful, he thought, to see that kind of rapport between a woman and a dog. Centaine took the carcass from Dandy's mouth, and the iridescent patches in the wings burnt like sapphires in the sunlight.

She handed it to the judge, and he examined it carefully, parting the feathers to check for teeth-marks, for any sign of 'hard mouthing', and Centaine held her breath until the judge looked up again and nodded.

'Thank you, Number Three.'

*   *   *

Not only had Centaine Courtney-Malcomess provided the venue for the trials, but she was in addition the hostess for the prize-giving ceremony.

The candy-striped marquee tent, able to accommodate five hundred guests, was set up on the main polo-field of the estate, and from Weltevreden's kitchens had come the gargantuan array of fine foods. The rock lobster had been caught by the fishing boats of Courtney Fishing and Canning Company at Lambert's Bay; the turkey had been raised on Weltevreden; the succulent Karoo lamb came from Dragon's Fountain, the Courtney sheep station on the Camdeboo plains of the Karoo; and the wines were from the vineyards that began at the edge of the polo-field outside the marquee tent.

The prime minister, John Vorster, had agreed to present the prizes. This was the fruit of Centaine's machinations over the years, a less than subtle hint to the world that the Courtneys were no longer a spent political force, that the days of their eclipse were ending.

Shasa Courtney had been a member of the faction within the Verwoerd cabinet that had opposed John Vorster's elevation to the premiership and in consequence he had been sent into political exile. But over the years that he had been in London Centaine had laboured with all her finesse and skill within the party to seek her son's rehabilitation. Of course, the fact that Shasa's term in London had been such an unequivocal triumph had reinforced her efforts. However, much of the credit for the Armscor appointment redounded directly to Centaine's tireless lobbying, her refusal to accept defeat and the blatant wielding of all her political and financial influence in her son's favour.

She would see to it that John Vorster's presence on the Weltevreden estate heralded a new golden era for the Courtneys. His round red face was the rising sun of their hopes and aspirations, Centaine thought comfortably as she looked around the crowded marquee. They were all gathered here at Weltevreden once again, all the power-brokers and the power-wielders. Although none of them had ever been so foolish or so reckless as to give Centaine Courtney-Malcomess direct offence or to write her off completely, there had been a period of cooling off while Shasa had been serving his term in London. Some had been cooler than others, Centaine reflected with a steely glint in her eye as she picked them out amongst the crowd, and she would remember them.

'Now is the winter of our discontent made glorious summer,' she thought with deep satisfaction, and almost as if to echo her sentiment the chairman of the South African Kennel Union rose to his feet and called for silence from the dais at the far end of the marquee. After welcoming the prime minister and spending a few minutes discussing the field-trial scene in general, the chairman began calling the prize-winners to the stand, and the line of glistening silver trophies dwindled until only one remained in the centre of the green baize-covered table, but it was the tallest and most ornate of them all with a statuette of a gun-dog on point surmounting the pinnacle.

'We come at last to the champion dog of trial.' The chairman beamed round the tent until he picked out Centaine standing at the back of the tent surrounded by her family. 'And it gives me much pleasure to call to the champion's berth for the first time a lady who in the few short years since she has taken to our sport has brought to it so much energy and enthusiasm that her contribution equals and in many cases surpasses those who have spent a lifetime working with gun-dogs. Ladies and gentlemen, I ask you to welcome Mrs Centaine Courtney-Malcomess and Dandy Lass of Weltevreden.'

Isabella had been waiting outside the tent with Dandy Lass on leash and now she came in with her, and while the crowd applauded Isabella handed the dog over to her grandmother.

Dandy Lass wore a fitted blanket in daffodil yellow, Centaine's racing colours, and with the Courtney insignia, a stylized silver diamond, embroidered in one corner. She fell in beside her mistress, heeling perfectly as Centaine started up towards the dais. The crowd laughed and applauded. Woman and dog made an elegant pair of thoroughbreds, and Dandy Lass grinned and lolled her tongue and wagged her tail at the fun of it.

On the dais, Dandy Lass curtsied politely in front of the prime minister, and at a word from Centaine offered him her right paw. The crowd loved it when John Vorster stooped to shake the proffered paw.

As he handed Centaine the enormous silver trophy, the prime minister smiled at her. For a man with such a formidable reputation for ruthless strength and granite resolve, his smile was boyishly infectious and his blue eyes twinkled.

As he shook Centaine's hand, he leant a little closer, so that she alone could hear his words.

'Don't you and your family find that unbroken success in everything you do becomes monotonous, Centaine?' he asked. They had come to first-name terms only in the last year or so.

'We try to be brave about enduring it, Uncle John,' she assured him gravely.

The prime minister made a short and uncontroversial speech of congratulation, and then circulated around the marquee with the alacrity of an adroit political gamesman. Smiling and shaking hands and passing on, he reached the end of the tent where Centaine was holding court.

'Once again my congratulations, Centaine. I wish I could stay longer to help you celebrate your famous victory.' He glanced at his wristwatch.

'You have been generous with your time,' Centaine agreed. 'But, before you leave, may I introduce the only one of my grandchildren whom you have not met?' She beckoned to Isabella, who was hovering close by. 'Isabella has been in London serving as hostess to Shasa during his term at South Africa House.'

As Isabella came forward, Centaine was watching the prime minister's craggy bulldog features attentively. She knew that Vorster was no philanderer; he could never have reached his position in the iron Calvinistic coils of his party if he had been. But despite the fact that for thirty years he had been happily and securely married he was still very much a man, and no man could remain unmoved when he looked at Isabella Courtney for the first time. Centaine saw the shift in his gaze, and the way he hid his quick flare of attention behind that formidable frown.

Centaine and Isabella had planned for this meeting with care, ever since Isabella had amazed both Centaine and Shasa by her sudden declared intention to enter the political arena.

'She'll get over it,' Shasa predicted, but Centaine had shaken her head.

'Bella has changed. Something has happened to her since she went to London with you. She went as a flighty spoiled little bitch—'

'Oh, come, Mater.' Predictably Shasa had risen to his precious daughter's defence, but Centaine went on without check.

'But she has returned a mature woman. However, there is more than that to it. She has steel now. She has a cutting edge, and there is something else.' Centaine had hesitated as she tried to define it. 'She has shed her romantic view of life; it is as though she has experienced a revelation, as though she has suffered and learnt to hate, as though she has come through some portentous crisis and armed herself for whatever lies ahead.'

'It's not like you to make these fanciful flights of imagination,' Shasa had chaffed her, but Centaine had insisted.

'You mark my words, Bella has found her direction and she will prove herself as tough and ruthless as any of us.'

'Surely not as tough and ruthless as you, Mater?'

'Have your little joke, Shasa Courtney, but time will prove me right.' Centaine's eyes had gone out of focus and squinted slightly. Shasa knew that expression so well, when his mother indulged in furious concentration. He called them her scheming eyes. Then her eyes came back into focus. 'She is going far, Shasa, probably further than even you and I could dream – and I am going to help her.'

And so, Centaine had arranged this meeting, and now she watched her grand-daughter acquit herself with all the aplomb that she had expected of her.

Vorster asked Isabella: 'So how did you enjoy the English winters?' And it was clear that he expected a trivial response, but Isabella said: 'It was worth putting up with them, if only to meet Harold Wilson and to have a first-hand account of the Labour government's attitude and intentions towards all of us who live in southern Africa.'

Vorster's expression changed as he realized that there was a brain behind that lovely young face. He dropped his voice, and they talked quietly for a few minutes longer before Centaine intervened again.

'Isabella has just received her doctorate in political theory from London University.' Artlessly she tossed out a little more ground bait.

'Oh so!' Vorster nodded. 'Do we have a budding Helen Suzman in our midst?' He was referring to the only woman member of the South African parliament, the staunchest champion of human rights and the only really galling liberal thorn in the complacently thick hide of the Nationalist majority.

Isabella laughed, that husky sexual chuckle which she knew could stir even the most hidebound misogynist. 'Perhaps,' she agreed. 'A seat in the house might be my ultimate ambition, but that is still far ahead, and I don't think I would be as naïve as Mrs Suzman, Prime Minister. My politics is very much in tune with that of my father and my grandmother.' Which of course made her a conservative, and now Vorster's regard was sharp blue and attentive as he studied her.

'The world is changing, Prime Minister.' Centaine seized

the moment. 'One day, there may even be a place in your cabinet for a woman, don't you think?'

Vorster smiled and switched easily from English into Afrikaans.

'Even Doctor Courtney agrees that day is still far ahead. However, I do concede that such a pretty face would do much to lighten the deliberations of us ugly old men.'

The change of language was, of course, a test. Nobody in South Africa with political aspirations could survive without fluency in Afrikaans, the language of the politically dominant group.

Isabella switched as easily as he had done. Her vocabulary was wide, her grammar perfect and her accent rang sweetly, even in the ear of a born Afrikaner.

Vorster smiled again, this time with pleasure, and continued the conversation for a few minutes more before glancing pointedly at his wristwatch and speaking to Centaine.

'I must go now. I have another function to attend.' He turned back to Isabella. '*Totsiens*, Doctor Courtney, until we meet again. I will be watching your progress with interest.'

Centaine and Shasa walked with him from the marquee to where his official car and driver waited on the edge of the polo-ground.

'*Totsiens*, Centaine.' Vorster shook her hand. 'I congratulate you on the rearing of your grand-daughter. I recognize many traits which she can only have inherited from you.'

When Centaine returned to the marquee, she looked around quickly. Isabella was already the centre of a circle of eager males.

'She has them panting like puppy dogs.' Centaine suppressed a smile and caught her grand-daughter's eye. Isabella left her admirers and came to her immediately, and Centaine took her arm in a comfortable proprietorial gesture.

'Well done, missy. You behaved like a veteran. Uncle John likes you. I rather think that we are on our way.'

*　　　*　　　*

That evening, only the family sat down to dinner at the long table in Weltevreden's main dining-room. However, Centaine had ordered the antique Limoges dinner service and the best silver. The table was resplendent in candlelight and a massed display of yellow roses.

As was usual on these family evenings, the women wore long dresses and the men were in black tie.

Only Sean was missing.

Sean had been invited – or, rather, Centaine had summoned him – but he was hunting with one of his most valuable clients on the Rhodesian concession and had sent his humble apologies. Centaine had accepted them reluctantly. She had wanted them all to celebrate her triumph with Dandy Lass, but she conceded that business came first.

The German industrialist that Sean was guiding paid for sixty-three days of hunting each year at five hundred dollars a day. Of course, his vast business commitments in Germany would not allow him to spend that much time in the hunting-veld. He was lucky if he could fit in two weeks in any one year. However, he paid for the additional days to secure the right to hunt three elephant instead of one. Sean had to be on call for him, even though he usually gave only a few days' notice of his intended arrival.

Centaine missed her eldest grandson. Sean was the handsomest and wildest of the three of them, but his presence was always stimulating. He seemed to charge the very air around him with the static electricity of danger and excitement. It had cost her and the family tens of thousand of dollars to bail him out of the various scrapes that his tempestuous nature led him into. Although she always expressed her outrage at these expenditures in the severest terms, secretly she did not grudge them. Her only fear was that one day Sean would go too far and get himself into real trouble from which even Centaine would be unable to extricate him. She dismissed that thought.

Tonight was not the night for morbid fancies.

The tall silver trophy glittered in the centre of the long table. It stood on a pyramid of yellow roses. It was strange what satisfaction that bauble gave her. It had cost her countless hours of hard work in the field, but the winning had made it all worthwhile. It had always been like that for her. The burning need to excel was in her blood. She had passed on that divine contagion to those she loved.

At the far end of the table Shasa tapped the crystal glass in front of him with a silver spoon and in the ensuing silence rose to his feet. He was tall and elegant in his impeccable dinner-jacket and black tie. He began one of those speeches for which he was renowned – easy and flowing, the wit and sentiment so cleverly timed and blended that he could at one moment raise a storm of laughter and at the next moisten every eye with a skilfully turned phrase.

Although he heaped her with praise and turned the attention of every person in the room full upon her, Centaine found her own mind wandering to her other grandchildren. They were all hanging on their father's lips, so engrossed by his words that they were unaware of Centaine's appraisal.

Garry sat at her right hand as befitted his importance in the family hierarchy. From the runt of the litter, myopic, weedy and asthmatic, he had transformed himself with little or no help from her or any of them into this bull of power and confidence. Now he was the helmsman of the family fortune, chairman of Courtney Enterprises. His bulk threatening the fragile legs of the genuine Chippendale chair, his thumbs were hooked into the pockets of his discreetly brocaded waistcoat. His dress shirt was a snowy expanse over the great chest, and the starched wing collar too tight for a neck swollen not with fat but with muscle and sinew. His dense black hair stood up in a cockscomb at the crown, and his thick horn-rimmed spectacles glittered in the candlelight. His laughter rocked the room; full and unrestrained, it greeted each of Shasa's sallies and it was so infectious that it transformed even his father's mildest remarks into wild hilarity.

Centaine switched her gaze to Garry's wife. Holly sat beside Shasa at the far end of the table. She was almost ten years Garry's senior. Centaine had opposed the union with all her power and cunning. Of course, she had not succeeded in preventing the marriage. She admitted to herself now that it had been a serious error of judgement to attempt to do so. She would now have had more control and influence over Holly had she not made the attempt. Instead she had raised barricades of mistrust in Holly's mind that she might never be able to pull down.

She had been wrong about Holly. She had proved the perfect wife for Garry. Holly had recognized those qualities in him that none of them, not even Centaine, had fully perceived. She had brought them to full flower and carefully nurtured his self-confidence. In large measure she was responsible for Garry's success. She had given him strength and unflagging support. She had given him love and happiness, and she had given him three sons and a daughter. Centaine smiled as she thought of those little scamps asleep in the nursery wing upstairs, and then sighed and frowned. The reserve that Holly still felt towards her was a barrier between her and her great-grandchildren. Garry and Holly lived in Johannesburg, the nation's financial centre, a thousand miles from Weltevreden.

The head office of Courtney Enterprises was in Johannesburg, as was the Stock Exchange. Garry was one of the main players; he had to be at the centre of the arena. Thus there was every reason for him and Holly to have left Weltevreden, but Centaine felt that Holly was keeping the children from her. Although it was only a three-hour flight in the company jet which Garry loved to pilot himself, yet these days Centaine very seldom saw them at Weltevreden. She wanted desperately to have the children close to her to guide and influence them, to protect and train them as she had their father, but Holly was the key. She would have to redouble her efforts to win her round. Now she deliberately caught her eye down the length of the long table, and smiled at her with all the warmth and affection she could convey. Holly smiled back, blonde and serene, her beauty given an extraordinary dimension by those particoloured eyes, one blue, the other a startling violet.

'I'll make you like and trust me yet,' Centaine promised silently. 'You'll not be able to hold out for ever, not against me. I'll have those children. This family is mine, those children are mine. You'll not keep them from me much longer.'

Shasa had said something about her that she had missed in her preoccupation. Now every head at the table was turned towards Centaine, and they were all applauding with enthusiasm. She smiled and nodded her acknowledgement of whatever compliment Shasa had paid her, and as the applause faded Shasa continued.

'You may have thought to yourselves as you watched her handling Dandy Lass today that it was a remarkable accomplishment. For any other woman, it might have been so, but here we have the lady who faced down a man-eating lion with me as an infant strapped upon her back . . .' Shasa was reciting once again all the old stories about her that were the weft and the warp of the family legend. In itself this recitation at every important occasion had become tradition and, though they had all heard them a hundred times, their enjoyment was as fresh as ever.

Only one person at the table looked faintly embarrassed by the extravagance of Shasa's eulogy.

Centaine felt a chill little breeze of annoyance ruffle the silken surface of her self-satisfaction. Of all her grandchildren the one for whom she felt the least warmth and concern was Michael. He sat near the centre of the long table at the lowliest position, not simply because he was the youngest of her grandsons. Michael did not fit into Centaine's scheme of things. There were secret depths and hidden places in his nature that she had not yet fathomed, and which therefore annoyed her.

She had never been able to wean Michael away from his natural mother. Even the thought of Tara Courtney sent a scalding acidic rush of hatred through Centaine's bowels. Tara had outraged every principle and concept of decency and morality that Centaine held sacrosanct. She was a Marxist and a miscegenist, a traitor and a patricide. A portion of Centaine's feelings towards Tara were passed on to this one of her sons.

The force of her gaze must have been fierce enough for Michael to sense it. He glanced up at her suddenly and paled under Centaine's dark eyes, then looked away again hurriedly, almost guiltily.

At Shasa's insistence, and over her objections, the family had acquired a controlling interest in the media company which counted amongst its assets the *Golden City Mail* newspaper. Shasa's motive had been to secure a place for Michael at the top of his chosen profession. His idea had been to build up the *Mail* as a powerful and conservative voice of reason, and for Michael, once he had earned his spurs, to take over as publisher and editor. That day had not yet dawned, and Michael was still only a deputy editor. If it had been left to Shasa, he would have pushed Michael earlier. However, both Garry and Centaine had kept his paternal indulgence in check. The two of them had reasoned that Michael was not yet ready for the job. His financial and administrative instincts were under-developed and his political judgement was naïve, perhaps irreparably flawed. It was Michael's influence on editorial policy that continually nudged the *Mail* off the centre of the road, slanting it dangerously to the left, so that the newspaper had become distrusted not only by Government but also by the establishment of finance and mining and industry, those who paid for advertising space.

On three previous occasions the *Mail* had been banned by government decree, each time at a financial cost that infuriated Garry and with a loss of prestige and influence that made Centaine uneasy.

He's not a true Courtney, Centaine thought, as she studied Michael's pretty features. Even Bella has more steel in one of her little fingers than he has in his entire body. Michael is a waverer and a bleeder. His concern is for strangers and for the losers, not for the family. For Centaine that was the most heinous form of treachery. He doesn't take after any of us; he takes after his mother. And that was her most damning judgement. He has even tried to corrupt Bella. Centaine knew about the presence of her two grandchildren at the anti-apartheid rally in Trafalgar Square. They had been photographed by South African intelligence from the windows of South Africa House, and Centaine had received a warning call from one of her important contacts in the Government.

Fortunately, Centaine had been able to smooth things over. Bella had done some undercover work for South African intelligence during her passionate love-affair with Lothar De La Rey. Lothar had been a colonel in the police at the time, and he was now a Member of Parliament and a deputy minister in the Ministry of Law and Order.

Centaine had called upon Lothar personally. She had enormous influence over him; there were secrets that involved Lothar's father and other mysteries which Lothar could only guess at. In addition Lothar had been Bella's lover and, Centaine suspected, was still more than a little in love with her.

'I will include a full explanation of her presence at the rally in Isabella's file,' Lothar assured her. 'We know that she is a patriot, she has worked for us before, but I can't promise anything for Michael, Tantie.' Lothar used the respectful term of address which meant more than simply 'Aunt'. 'Michael has too many black marks on his file already, I'm afraid.'

Yes, thought Centaine grimly, Michael has accumulated black marks like a dog picks up fleas, and some of them hop off on to all of us.

At that moment Shasa finished his speech and all of them turned towards Centaine's end of the table expectantly. As a speaker she was every bit as good as her son, but there was often a little more of a sting in her words, and a little more directness in her views. They waited with anticipation for the customary fireworks as she began her reply, but tonight they were disappointed.

Centaine seemed in an unusually mild and benevolent mood. Rather than censure, she had praise and appreciation for all of them. Garry's financial results, Isabella's academic achievements, Holly's architectural plans for the new Courtney luxury hotel on the Zululand coast and her forthcoming birthday.

'So sorry you won't be able to stay over with us for the big day, Holly darling.'

Even Michael came in for praise, albeit much fainter praise, with the publication of his most recent book. 'One doesn't have to agree with your conclusions or with the solutions which you suggest, Mickey dear, to appreciate just how much thought and hard work went into the writing of it.'

When she asked them to rise and drink a toast to 'our family and every single person in it' they responded with gusto. Then Shasa came to the head of the table to take her arm and lead her through into the blue drawing-room where coffee and liqueurs and cigars were waiting. Centaine would never accede to the barbarous custom of leaving the men alone with their cigars after dinner. If there was anything worth talking about, then she wanted to be part of those discussions.

Quickly Michael crossed to Isabella as she rose from her seat at the table and took her arm.

'I've missed you, Bella. Why didn't you answer my letters? There is so much I want to know. Ramón and Nicky—' He saw her expression change, and his alarm was quick.

'Is something wrong, Bella?'

'Not now, Mickey,' she warned him quickly. This was

the first time they had spoken in almost six months, since Nicky had gone. She had not telephoned him or answered his letters. Moreover, she had avoided being alone with him ever since he had arrived at Weltevreden that morning.

'There is something wrong,' Michael insisted.

'Smile!' she ordered him, smiling herself. 'Don't make a fuss. I'll come to your room later. No questions now.' She squeezed his arm, and laughed gaily as they all trooped through to the blue drawing-room and clustered round attentively while Centaine settled herself in her customary place on the long sofa facing the roaring log fire in the Adam fireplace.

'Let me have my girls with me tonight,' she decided, and picked out Holly. 'Come and sit this side, my dear.' She patted the sofa beside her. 'Bella, you on this side of me, please.'

Centaine seldom did anything without good reason, and as soon as the servants had given them coffee and Shasa had poured Cognac for the men she played her high card.

'I've been waiting for a chance to do this, Holly,' she said in a voice that commanded all their attention. 'And I suppose your birthday is the best excuse I'll ever have. You are my eldest grand-daughter, so I'm going to establish a little family tradition tonight.'

Centaine reached up behind her own neck and unclasped the necklace she wore and held it in her hands, a glittering treasure, over a thousand carats of perfect yellow diamonds. Each stone had personally been selected by Centaine Courtney from the production of her fabulous H'ani mine in the far north. It had taken ten years for her to accumulate them, and Garrards of London had designed and manufactured the setting in pure platinum.

'Something so lovely should only be worn by a beautiful woman,' Centaine whispered regretfully, and the tears that sparkled in her dark eyes were genuine. 'Alas, I no longer fulfil that requirement, so it is time for me to pass them on to somebody who does.'

She turned to Holly. 'Wear these with joy,' she said and hung them at her throat.

Holly sat as though stunned, and everybody in the room was silent with awe. They all knew what that necklace meant to Centaine; they knew that she placed a far higher value on it than the mere two million sterling which the Lloyd's assessors had recently decided was its intrinsic worth.

Holly lifted her right hand and stroked the bright stars at her throat with a look of total disbelief on her delicate features, then she choked and sobbed and turned to Centaine and embraced her. The two women clung together for a moment before Holly could find her voice. It was muffled and small, but all of them heard it clearly.

'Thank you, Nana.' Only close members of the family called Centaine that, and Holly had never done so before.

Centaine held her tightly, closing her eyes and pressing her face against Holly's golden head so that none of them would see the little smile of triumph on her lips and the satisfied gleam through the tears in her eyes.

★   ★   ★

Nanny was waiting in Isabella's suite.

'It's after one o'clock,' Isabella exclaimed. 'I've told you not to wait up for me, you silly old woman.'

'I've been waiting up for you twenty-five years.' Nanny came to unhook the back of her dress.

'It makes me feel terrible,' Isabella protested.

'It makes me feel good,' Nanny grunted. 'I don't feel happy 'less I know what you been up to, missy. I'll run your bath – didn't do it before, didn't want it to turn cold.'

'A bath at one o'clock in the morning!' Isabella dismissed the idea strenuously. She had not allowed Nanny to see her naked since her return. The old woman's eyes were much too sharp. She would pick up the tiny changes that childbirth had wrought on Isabella's body: the darkening and enlarging of her nipples, the faint stria where the skin had stretched across her hips and lower belly.

She sensed that Nanny was becoming suspicious at this change of behaviour, and to divert her she said: 'Off with you now, Nanny. Go and warm Bossie's bed for him.'

Nanny looked shocked. 'Who's been telling you scandal stories?' she demanded.

'You're not the only one who knows what's going on at Weltevreden,' Isabella informed her gleefully. 'Old Bossie has been after you for years. About time you took pity on him. He's a good man.' Bossie was the estate blacksmith who had come to work for Centaine as an apprentice thirty-five years ago. 'You go off and hammer his anvil for him.'

'That's dirty talk,' Nanny sniffed. 'A real lady don't talk dirty.' Nanny tried to hide her confusion behind a prim expression, but backed off towards the door, and Isabella sighed with relief as it closed behind her.

She went through to her bathroom and swiftly removed her make-up, tossed her evening-dress over the back of the sofa for Nanny to deal with in the morning, and slipped into a silk bathrobe. As she belted the robe, she crossed her bedroom and then paused with her fingers on the door-handle.

'What am I going to tell Mickey?' If she had asked herself that question only three days ago, the answer would have been obvious, but since then circumstances had changed. The packet had arrived.

The last communication she had received from Joe Cicero had been on the day before she left London to return to the Cape of Good Hope. He had telephoned her at Cadogan Square while she was in the process of packing.

'Red Rose.' She had recognized the husky wheeze of his voice instantly, and as always it had frozen her with dread and loathing. 'I am going to give you your contact address. Use it only in an emergency. It is an answering service, so do not waste time and energy checking it. A telegram or letter addressed to Hoffman, care of Mason's Agency, 10

Blushing Lane, Soho, will find me. Memorize that address. Do not write it down.'

'I have it,' Isabella whispered.

'On your return home, you will hire a post-office box at a location not associated with Weltevreden. Use a fictitious name and inform me at the Blushing Lane address when it is established. Is that clear?'

Within days of arriving back at Weltevreden, Isabella had driven over the Constantiaberg Pass to the sprawling suburb of Camps Bay on the Atlantic seaboard of the Cape peninsula. The post office there was far enough removed from Weltevreden for none of the postal staff to recognize her. She hired the box in the name of Mrs Rose Cohen, and sent a registered letter to Blushing Lane with this box number.

She checked the box for a letter each evening as she returned from her office in Centaine House in central Cape Town, driving the Mini over the neck between Signal Hill and the mountain, the more circuitous route around the back of Table Mountain to reach Weltevreden. Even though the box remained empty day after day and week after week, she never varied her routine.

The lack of news of Nicky ate away at the fabric of her soul. The day-to-day events of her life seemed all a sham and a pretence. Although she channelled all her energy into her work as Shasa's assistant, the effort was not the opiate for her pain that she had hoped it might be.

She smiled and laughed, she rode with Nana and at the weekends played tennis or sailed with her old friends. She worked and played as though everything was the same, but it was all acting.

The nights were long and lonely. In the midnight hours, she would resolve to go to Shasa and describe in detail the web in which she was enmeshed, but then in daylight she would ask herself: 'What can Pater do? What can anybody do to help me?' And she remembered Nicky's swollen face and the silver bubbles streaming from his nose as he drowned, and she knew she could not risk that ever happening again. Strangely, the passage of time did not reduce the pain of her loss; instead it seemed to inflame her wounds, and the lack of news of Nicky aggravated them still further. Each day her suffering was harder to bear alone.

Then she heard that Michael was coming down from Johannesburg to Weltevreden for the trials, and it seemed fortuitous. Michael was the perfect confidant. She would not expect him to do anything except share her suffering and lighten the terrible load which up until now she had carried alone.

On the Friday before Michael's arrival, she had driven over the neck to Camps Bay and parked the Mini in the street beyond the post office. She walked back slowly and glanced into the side-hall that housed the tiers of tiny steel post-boxes. It was almost six in the evening, and the main post office was long ago closed. There were a couple of teenagers necking in the corner of the postal hall, but they scurried away guiltily as she glared at them. Isabella took the precaution of never approaching or opening her box while a stranger was in the hall.

She glanced back at the entrance to make sure she was alone, and then inserted her key in the lock of the tiny steel door in the fifth row of tiered boxes. The shock was greater for the fact that she was expecting the box to be empty. Adrenalin squirted into her bloodstream, and she felt her cheeks burn and her breathing choke.

She snatched up the thick brown envelope and crammed it into her sling bag. Then, as guilty as a thief, she slammed and locked the box and ran back to where the Mini was parked. She was trembling so that she had difficulty fitting the key in the door-lock. She was breathing as hard as though she had played a long rally on the tennis-court as she started the Mini and U-turned back across the road.

She parked above the beach under the palms that line the drive. At this hour the beach was almost deserted. An elderly couple exercised an Irish setter at the edge of the water, and a single bather braved the south-easter and the icy green waters of the Benguela current.

Isabella rolled up the windows and locked both doors of the Mini before she took the envelope out of her bag and held it in her lap.

The address was typed, Mrs Rose Cohen, and the Queen's-head postage-stamps had been franked at Trafalgar Square post office. She turned the envelope over, reluctant to open it, terrified of what it might contain. There was no return address on the reverse. Still delaying the moment, she searched for the gold lady's penknife in her bag and carefully slit the flap of the envelope with its razor-edged blade.

A coloured photograph slid out, and every nerve in her body tingled as she turned it face-up and recognized her son.

Nicky sat on a blue blanket on a garden lawn. He wore only a napkin. He was sitting up unsupported, and she reminded herself that he was nearly seven months old. He had grown, his cheeks were not so chubby, his limbs longer and sleeker. His hair was thicker and longer, curling darkly on to his forehead. His expression was quizzical, but there was a smile hovering at the corners of his mouth, and his eyes were bright and green as emeralds.

'Oh God. He's more beautiful!' she gasped, holding the photograph up to the light to study every tiny detail of his face. 'He's grown so big already, and sitting up on his own. My clever little manikin.' She touched the image and then saw with consternation that she had left a fingerprint on the glossy surface of the photograph. She wiped it off carefully with a Kleenex.

'My baby,' she whispered, and felt her loss tear at her heart with renewed ferocity. 'Oh, my baby!'

The sun had sunk to touch the line of the horizon far out on the Atlantic before she could rouse herself. Only then, as she returned the photograph to the envelope, did she realize that she had overlooked the other items it contained.

193

First, there was a photostat copy of a page from what was obviously a medical register at some children's clinic, but the name and address of the clinic had been obliterated. It was written in Spanish.

His name was at the head of the sheet, 'Nicholas Miguel Ramón de Machado', followed by his date of birth and a record of weekly visits to the clinic. Each dated entry was in a variety of handwritings and signed by the clinic's doctors or sisters.

It showed his weight and diet and dental records. She saw that on 15 July he had been treated for a rash that the doctor diagnosed as prickly heat and two weeks later for a mild oral thrush. Otherwise he was healthy and normal. With a rush of maternal pride, she read that his first two teeth had erupted at four months, and he weighed almost sixteen kilos.

Isabella turned to the last folded sheet of paper that the envelope contained and immediately recognized the handwriting. It was in Spanish, in Adra's firm restrained hand.

Señorita Bella,
Nicky grows every day stronger and cleverer. He has a temper like one of the bulls of the *corrida*. He can crawl on hands and knees almost as fast as I can run, and I expect that at any day now he will rise up on his back legs and walk.

The first word he spoke was 'Mamma', and I tell him each day how beautiful you are and how one day you will come to him. He does not yet understand, but one day he will.

I think of you often, señorita. You must believe that I will care for Nicky with my own life. Please do not do anything to endanger him.

Respectfully,
Adra Olivares

The warning contained in the last line twisted like a knife between her ribs, and was more urgent and poignant for being so mildly expressed. She knew then that she could never risk telling anyone, not Pater or Nana or even Michael.

She hesitated now with her hand on the handle of her bedroom door. 'I have to lie to you, Mickey. I'm sorry. Perhaps, one day, I will tell you the truth.' She listened for a moment, but the great house was silent, and she turned the handle and quietly swung the door open.

The long gallery was deserted with only the night lights burning in their brackets on the wood-panelled walls. On bare feet, Isabella slipped silently over the Persian carpets scattered on the parquet floor. Since he was so seldom at Weltevreden, Michael kept his old room in the nursery wing.

He was sitting up in bed reading. As soon as she pushed the door open, he dropped the book on the bedside table and lifted the bedclothes for her.

As she climbed in beside him, he tucked the eiderdown around her shoulders and she clung to him, shivering with misery. They held each other for a long time in silence before Michael invited her gently.

'Tell me, Bella.' Even then she could not say it immediately. Her good intentions wavered, she felt the desperate temptation to ignore Adra's warning. Mickey was the only one of the family who knew that Ramón and Nicky even existed. She wanted desperately to blurt it all out to him and have his gentle warming comfort to help fill the terrible void in her soul.

Then the image of Nicky that she had watched on the video film flashed before her eyes once more. She drew a deep breath and pressed her face to Michael's chest. 'Nicky is dead,' she whispered, and felt him flinch in her embrace. He did not reply at once.

'It's true,' she consoled herself silently. 'Nicky is dead to all of us now.' And yet the words seemed a dreadful betrayal of Michael and of Nicky. She did not, dare not, trust him. She had denied the existence of her own son to him, and the falsehood seemed to increase her own misery and isolation, if that were possible.

'How?' Michael asked at last, and she had anticipated the question.

'Cot death,' she whispered. 'I went to wake him for his feed, and he was cold and dead.'

She felt Michael shiver against her. 'Oh God! My poor Bella! How horrible! How cruel!'

The reality was crueller and more horrible than he could imagine, but she could not share it with him.

After a long minute, he asked: 'Ramón? Where is Ramón? He should be here to comfort you.'

'Ramón,' she repeated the name, trying to keep fear out of her voice. 'When Nicky was gone, Ramón changed completely. I think he blamed me. His love for me died with Nicky.' She found herself weeping now, hard tearing sobs that expressed all the grief and terror and loneliness that had haunted her for so long. 'Nicky is gone. Ramón is gone. I will never see either of them again, not as long as I live.'

Michael hugged her tightly. His body was hard and warm and strong. Masculine strength that was completely devoid of sexuality was what she needed most. She felt it flowing into her like water filling the depleted dam of her courage and fortitude, and she clung to him silently.

After a while, he began to talk. She lay and listened, her ear pressed to his chest so that his voice was a reverberating murmur. He talked of love and suffering, of loneliness and of hope, and at last, of death.

'The true terror of death is its finality. The ending so abrupt, the void beyond so irrevocable. You cannot challenge death, or appeal against it. You only break your heart if you try.'

Platitudes, she thought, old clichés, the same ones with which man has tried to console himself for tens of thousands of years. Yet, like most clichés, they were true, and they were the only comfort that she had available to her. More important than the sense of the words, was the soft lulling music of Michael's voice, the warmth and strength of his body, and his love for her.

At last, she fell asleep.

She awoke before dawn and was immediately aware that he had lain all night without moving so as not to disturb her, and that he was awake also.

'Thank you, Mickey,' she whispered. 'You'll never know how alone I have been. I needed that badly..'

'I do know, Bella. I know what loneliness is.' And she felt her heart go out to him, her own pain temporarily assuaged. She wanted to be there for him now. It was his turn.

'Tell me about your new book, Mickey. I haven't read it yet – I'm sorry.' He had sent her a pre-publication copy, lovingly inscribed, but she had been totally engrossed with her own suffering. There had been no time for anybody else, not even Mickey. So this time, while she listened, he talked about the book and then about himself and his view of the world around them.

'I have spoken to Raleigh Tabaka again,' he said suddenly, and she was startled. She had not thought of that name since she left London.

'Where? Where did you meet him?'

Michael shook his head. 'I did not meet him. We spoke on the telephone, very briefly. I think he was calling from another country, but he will be here soon. He is a will-o'-the-wisp, a Black Pimpernel. He comes and goes across borders like a shadow.'

'You have arranged to meet him?' she asked.

'Yes. He is as good as his word.'

'Be careful, Mickey. Please promise me you will be careful. He is a dangerous man.'

'There is nothing for you to worry about,' he assured her. 'I'm no hero. I'm not like Sean or Garry. I'll be careful, very careful, I promise you.'

*   *   *

Michael Courtney parked his battered Valiant in the car-park of a drive-in restaurant on an off-ramp of the main Johannesburg-to-Durban highway.

He switched off the ignition, but the engine continued running on pre-ignition for a few unsteady beats. It had been missing badly all the way down from the offices of the *Golden City Mail* in central Johannesburg. The car had clocked up over seventy thousand miles and should have been sold two years previously.

As deputy editor his contract stipulated that he was entitled to a new 'luxury' vehicle every twelve months. However, Michael had developed an affection for the old Valiant. All its scars and scrapes had been honourably acquired, while over the years the driver's seat had taken on the contours of his body.

He studied the other vehicles in the carpark, but none of them answered the description he had been given. He glanced at his wristwatch, a Japanese digital for which he had paid five dollars on a trip to Tokyo for the newspaper the previous year. He was twenty minutes early at the rendezvous, so he lit a cigarette and slumped down in the comfortable shabby old seat.

Thinking about the car and the watch made him smile. He really was the odd man out in his family. From Nana down to Bella, they were all obsessed with material possessions. Nana had her daffodil-coloured Daimlers; the colour was always the same, although the model changed each year. Pater kept a garage filled with classic cars, mostly British sports-cars like the SS Jaguar and the big six-litre touring Bentley in racing green. Garry had his fancy Italian Maseratis and Ferraris. Sean bolstered his tough-guy image with elaborately outfitted four-wheel-drive hunting vehicles, and even Bella drove a souped-up little thing that cost twice as much as a new Valiant.

Not one of them would have worn a digital wristwatch, not Nana with her diamond Piaget nor Sean with his macho gold Rolex. 'Things.' Michael's smile turned down at the corners of his mouth. 'All they see are things, not people. It's the sickness of our country.'

There was a tap on the side-window of the Valiant and Michael started and looked round, expecting his contact.

There was nobody there.

He was startled. Then a small black hand with a pink palm came into view and diffidently tapped on the glass with one finger.

Michael rolled down the window and stuck his head out. A black urchin grinned up at him. He could not have been more than five or six years of age. He was barefoot, and his singlet and shorts were ragged. Although his nostrils were crusted with white flakes of dried snot, his smile was radiant.

'Please, Baas,' he piped, and cupped his hands in a beggar's gesture. 'Me hungry. Please give one cent, Baas!'

Michael opened the door, and the child backed away uncertainly. Michael picked up his cardigan which he had thrown on the seat beside him and slipped it over the child's head. It hung down almost to his ankles, and the sleeves drooped a foot beyond his fingertips. Michael rolled them up for him and said in fluent Xhosa: 'Where do you live, little one?'

The boy was obviously flabbergasted, not only by this attention but also to hear a white man speak Xhosa. Six years before, Michael had realized that it was impossible to understand a man unless you spoke his language. He had been studying and practising since then. Not one white in a thousand went to those lengths. All blacks were expected to learn either English or Afrikaans; otherwise they were virtually unemployable. Now Michael spoke both Xhosa and Zulu. These languages were closely related and between them covered the vast majority of the black population of southern Africa.

'I live at Drake's Farm, Nkosi.'

Drake's Farm was the sprawling black township which almost a million souls called home. From here it was out of view to the east of the highway, but the smoke from the thousands of cooking-fires hazed the sky to a dirty leaden grey. The wage-earners of Drake's Farm commuted daily by train or bus to their work-places in the homes and factories and businesses of the white areas of the Witwatersrand.

The huge commercial and mining complex of greater Johannesburg was surrounded by these dormitory townships, Drake's Farm and Soweto and Alexandria. Under the bizarre conditions of the Group Areas Act, the entire country was divided up into areas reserved for each of the racial groups.

'When did you last eat?' Michael asked the child gently.

'I ate yesterday, in the morning, great chief.'

Michael took a five-rand banknote from his wallet. The child's eyes seemed to expand into a pair of luminous pools as he stared at it. He had almost certainly never possessed so much money at one time in his short life.

Michael proffered the note. The child snatched it and turned and ran, tripping over the skirts of the dangling cardigan. He gave no thanks, and his expression was one of desperate terror lest the gift be taken back from him before he could escape.

Michael laughed with delight at his antics and then suddenly his amusement turned to outrage. Was there another country in the modern First World, he wondered, where little children were still forced to beg upon the streets? Then mingled with his anger was a sense of utter hopelessness.

Was there any other country that embraced both the members of the First World, like his own family with its vast estates and stunning collection of treasures, and the desperate poverty of the Third World epitomized here in the townships? The contrast was all the crueller for being so closely juxtaposed.

'If only there was something I could do,' he lamented, and drew so hard on his cigarette that a full inch of ash glowed and a spark fell unnoticed on to his tie and scorched a spot the size of a pinhead. It did not make much difference to the general appearance of his attire.

A small blue delivery-van turned off the main highway

into the carpark. It was driven by a young black man in a peaked cap. The sign-writing on the body read: 'Phuza Muhle Butchery. 12th Avenue, Drake's Farm.' The name promised 'good eating'.

Michael flashed his lights as he had been instructed to do. The van pulled into the parking-bay directly in front of him. Michael climbed out and locked the Valiant before he crossed to the blue van. The rear doors were unlocked. Michael climbed in and slammed them behind him. The body of the van was more than half-filled with baskets containing packages of raw meat, and the skinned carcasses of a number of sheep hung from hooks in the roof.

'Come this way,' the driver called to him in Zulu, and Michael crawled down the length of the body. The hanging carcasses brushed against him, and the drippings stained the knees of his corduroy bags. The driver had prepared a niche for him between two of the meat-baskets where he would be hidden from casual inspection.

'There will be no trouble,' the driver assured him in cheerful Zulu. 'Nobody ever stops this van.'

He pulled away, and Michael settled down on the grubby floor. These theatrical precautions were annoying but necessary. No white was allowed into the township without a permit issued by the local police station in consultation with the township management council.

In the ordinary course of events this permit was not difficult to obtain. However, Michael Courtney was a marked man. He had three previous convictions for contravention of the Publications Control Act for which he and his newspaper had been heavily fined.

Under the Act, the government censors had been given almost unlimited powers of banning and suppression of any material or publication, and they were encouraged by the full caucus of the ruling National Party not to flinch from exercising those powers to uphold the Calvinistic moral views of the Dutch Reformed Church and to protect the political *status quo*.

What chance, then, did Michael's writings have against

their vigilance? Michael's application for a permit to enter Drake's Farm township had been summarily rejected.

The blue van entered the main gates of the township without a check, and the indolent uniformed black guards did not even glance up from their game of African Ludo, played with Coca-Cola crown tops on a carved wooden board.

'You can come up front now,' the driver called, and Michael clambered over the meat-baskets to reach the passenger-seat in the cab.

The township always fascinated him. It was almost like visiting an alien planet.

It was back in 1960, almost eleven years ago, that he had last visited Drake's Farm. At that time, he had been a cub reporter for the *Mail*. That was the year in which he had written the 'Rage' series of articles that were the foundation on which his journalistic reputation was built, and incidentally the grounds for his first conviction under the Publications Control Act.

He smiled at the memory and looked around him with interest as they drove through the old section of the township. This dated from the previous century, the Victorian era during which the fabulous golden reefs of the Witwatersrand had first been discovered close by.

The old section was a maze of lanes and alleys and higgledy-piggledy buildings, shacks and shanties of unburnt brick and cracked plaster, of corrugated-iron roofs painted all the shades of an artist's palette. Most of the original colours had faded and were running with the red leprosy of rust.

The narrow streets were rutted and studded with potholes and puddles of indeterminate liquid. Scrawny chickens scurried and scratched in the litter of rubbish. A huge sow with a pink hide that looked as though it had been parboiled wallowed in one of the puddles and grunted irritably as the van passed. The stink was wondrous. The sour stench of ripening garbage mingled with that of the open drains and the earthen toilets that stood like sentry-boxes behind each of the hovels.

The government health inspector had long ago abandoned all hope of ever regulating the old section of Drake's Farm. One day the bulldozers would arrive and the *Mail* would run front-page photographs of the distraught black families crouching on the pathetic piles of their worldly possessions, watching the brutal machines demolishing their homes. A white civil servant in a dark suit would make a statement on the state television network about 'this festering health hazard making way for comfortable modern bungalows'. The anticipation of that day made Michael angry all over again.

The blue van bumped and weaved over the rutted lanes, passing the dismal shebeens and whorehouses, and then crossed the invisible line from the old into the new section that the same civil servant would describe as comfortable modern bungalows. Thousands of identical brick boxes with grey corrugated-asbestos roofs stood in endless lines upon the treeless veld. They reminded Michael of the rows of white wooden crosses that he had seen in the military cemeteries of France.

Yet, somehow, the black residents had managed to imprint their character and individuality upon this forbidding townscape. Here and there a house had been repainted a startling colour in the monotonous grubby white lines. Pink or sky blue or vivid orange, they bore witness to the African love of bright colour. Michael noticed one that had been beautifully decorated in the traditional geometric designs of the Ndebele tribe from the north.

The tiny front gardens were a mirror of the personal style of the occupants. One was a square of dusty bare earth; another was planted with rows of maize plants and had a milking goat tethered at the front door; yet another boasted a garden of straggly geranium plants in old five-gallon paint-tins; while still another was fenced with high barbed wire and the weed-clogged yard was patrolled by a bony but ferocious mongrel guard-dog.

Some of the plots were separated from each other by ornamental walls of concrete breeze blocks or old truck tyres painted gaudy colours and half-buried in the brick-hard earth. Most of the cottages had extraneous additions tacked on to them, usually a lean-to of salvaged lumber and rusty corrugated iron into which a family of the owners' relatives had overflowed. There were abandoned motor-vehicles, sans engine or wheels, parked at the kerb. Hill-ocks of old mattresses, disintegrating cardboard boxes and other discarded rubbish which the refuse removal service had overlooked stood on the street-corners.

Across this stage moved the people of the townships. These were the people whom Michael loved more than his own race or class, the people with whom he empathized and for whom he agonized. They delighted him endlessly. They amazed him endlessly with their strength and forti-tude and will to survive.

The children were everywhere he looked, the crawlers and totterers and squawkers who rolled and roistered in the streets like litters of glossy black Labrador puppies or rode high, strapped to their mothers' backs in the tra-ditional style. The older children played their simple games with wire and empty beer-cans which they had fashioned into toy automobiles. The little girls played with skipping-ropes in the middle of the road, or imitated the games of hopscotch and catch that they had seen the white children play. They were tardy and reluctant to give way and clear the roadway when the driver of the blue van hooted at them.

When they saw Michael's white face they danced beside the slow-moving van with cries of 'Sweetie! Sweetie!' Michael had come prepared and he tossed them the hard sugar candy with which he had stuffed his pockets.

Though most of the adult population had made the long daily journey to their work-place in the city, the mothers and the old people and the unemployed had been left behind.

Gangs of street-youths stared at him expressionlessly as

he passed, gathered in idle groups on the littered street-corners. Though he knew that these teenagers were the jackals of the townships who preyed upon their own kind, Michael's sympathy went out to them. He understood their despair. He knew that even before they had fairly embarked on life's journey they were aware that it held nothing for them, no expectation or hope of better things or kinder times.

Then there were the women at their chores, hanging the long lines of laundry to dry like prayer-flags on the breeze; or stooped over the black three-legged pots in the back-yards, cooking the staple maize porridge of their diet over open fires in the traditional way, preferring that to the iron stoves in the tiny cottage kitchens. The smoke of the fires mingled with the blown dust to form the perpetual cloud that hung over the township.

The illegal hawkers or *spouzas*, who had eluded the Afrikaner government's passion for regulations and licens-ing, wheeled their barrows and shouted their wares in the busy streets. The housewives bartered with them for a single potato or cigarette or orange or slice of white bread, depending on their circumstances.

Despite these dreary surroundings and all the evidence of poverty and neglect, Michael heard in every street and at every corner they turned the sound of laughter and music. The laughter was spontaneous and merry. Their shouted greetings and repartee were carefree. Wherever he looked were those lovely African smiles that filled his heart and then squeezed it to the point of pain.

The music rang and echoed from the bleak little cottages and, in the streets, from the transistor radios that men and women carried in hand or balanced on their heads as they walked. The children played their penny whistles and banjos made from paraffin-tins and wood and pieces of wire. They danced and they sang in a spontaneous expression of the sheer joy of living, even in these most insalubrious circum-stances.

For Michael the laughter and the music depicted the

indomitable spirit of the black African in the face of all hardship. For him there could not be another race on earth quite like them. Michael loved them, every one of them, no matter what age or sex or tribe or condition. He was of Africa, and these were his people.

'What can I do for you, my brothers?' he whispered. 'What can I do to help you? I wish I knew. Everything I have attempted so far has failed. All my efforts have died like a hopeless shout upon the desert air. If only I could find the way.'

Then abruptly he was distracted. They topped a rise in the gently undulating veld and Michael straightened in his seat.

Eleven years ago when last he had passed this way there had been nothing but open grassland here, with a few scrawny goats grazing amongst the red wounds with which erosion and neglect had raked the earth.

'Nobs Hill.' The driver of the van chuckled at his surprise. 'Beautiful, hey?'

Such is the determination and fortitude of men that even in the face of the most adverse circumstances there are those few who will not only survive, but who with courage and ingenuity far beyond the average will flourish and rise high above the obstacles and pitfalls with which their path is strewn. Along the low ridge of ground, standing above the huddled shacks and cottages of Drake's Farm, were the homes of the black élite. There were a hundred or so of these successful men set apart from all the million inhabitants of Drake's Farm. Through business acumen and natural ability and hard work they had wrested material success from the hands of their white political masters, from those who had attempted to dictate their fate through the monumental framework of interlocking laws and regulations which was the Verwoerd-inspired policy of apartheid in action.

Yet their victory over circumstances was hollow. No matter that they could afford to make their home in any part of this land, they were constrained by the Group Areas

Act to live only in these areas which those architects of apartheid had set aside for them. The homes that these black businessmen and doctors and lawyers and successful criminals had built for themselves would have graced the elegant suburbs of Sandton or La Lucia or Constantia where their white counterparts lived.

'See!' the driver of the van pointed proudly. 'The pink house with big windows. It is the home of Josia Nrubu, the famous witchdoctor. He sells his charms and potions and spells by mail order all over Africa, even to Nigeria and Kenya. He sells a charm to make all men and women love you, and lion bones to give you success in business and money matters. He can give you the fat of vultures for your eyesight and another potion made from the hymen of a virgin that will make your meat-plough hard as granite and tireless as a war assegai. He has four new Cadillac motor-cars and his sons go to university in America.'

'I'll take the lion bones,' Michael chuckled. The *Golden City Mail* had run at a loss for the last four years, much to the chagrin of Nana and Garry.

'See! The house with the green roof and the high wall. There lives Peter Ngonyama. His tribe grows the weed that we call dagga or boom and which you whites call cannabis. They harvest the dagga in the secret places in the hills and send it by the truckload to Cape Town and Johannesburg and Durban. He has twenty-five wives and is very rich.'

They left the crumbling surface of the old road for the smooth blue asphalt expanse of the newly laid boulevard. The driver accelerated down between the green lawns and high brick walls of Nobs Hill, officially designated Drake's Farm Extension IV.

Suddenly he braked and turned off to pause before the steel gates of one of the more luxurious mansions. The electric gates slid aside silently and then closed again behind them as they drove through into a garden of planted shrubs and green lawns. There was a free-form swimming-pool below the terrace with a rock fountain at the centre. Sprinklers played upon the lawns, and Michael noticed two black gardeners in overalls working amongst the flowering plants.

The building was of ultra-modern design with plate-glass picture-windows and exposed woodwork. The roof was split into various levels and planes. The driver parked below the main terrace, and a tall figure came down the steps to welcome Michael as he stepped out of the van.

'Michael!' Raleigh Tabaka's greeting took him unprepared, as did the friendly smile and hand-clasp. It was so different from the spirit of their last meeting in London.

Raleigh wore casual slacks and a white open-necked shirt which emphasized his fine unblemished skin and his romantic African features. Michael felt a charge of sexual electricity ripple across his fingertips as they shook hands. Raleigh was still one of the most impressive and attractive men that he had ever met.

'You are welcome,' he said, and Michael looked around him and lifted an eyebrow.

'Not bad, Raleigh. You are still keeping fine style.'

'This does not belong to me.' Raleigh shook his head. 'I own nothing other than the clothes on my back.'

'Who does all this belong to, then?'

'Questions, always questions,' Raleigh chided him with an edge to his voice.

'I am a journalist,' Michael pointed out. 'Questions are my meat and drink.'

'Of course. This house was built by the Trans Africa Foundation of America for the lady you are about to meet.'

'Trans Africa – that's an American civil rights group?' Michael asked. 'Isn't it run by the coloured evangelist preacher from Chicago, Doctor Rondall?'

'You are well informed.' Raleigh took his arm and led him up on to the wide terrace.

'It must have cost half a million dollars,' Michael persisted, and Raleigh shrugged and changed the subject.

'I promised to show you the children of apartheid, Michael, but first I want you to meet their mother, the mother of the nation.'

He led Michael across the terrace. There were beach umbrellas spread in the sunshine, like a field of brightly coloured mushrooms. A dozen black children sat at the white plastic tables drinking Coca-Cola from the cans and listening to one of the ubiquitous portable transistor radios from which blared the driving rhythms of African jazz.

They were boys ranging in age from eight or nine years to the late teens. All of them wore canary-yellow T-shirts with the legend 'Gama Athletics Club' printed across the chest. None of them stood up as Michael passed, but they watched him with flat incurious stares.

The glass doors of the main building stood open to the terrace, and Raleigh led the way into a split-level living-room whose walls were decorated with carved wooden masks and fetish statuettes. The stone floor was covered with animal-skin rugs.

'Something to drink, Michael?' Raleigh asked. 'Coffee or tea?'

Michael shook his head. 'Nothing, but do you mind if I smoke?'

'I remember your habit,' Raleigh smiled. 'Go ahead. I'm sorry I can't offer you a match.'

Michael paused with the lighter in his hand and glanced towards the upper level of the spacious room.

A woman came down the steps towards them. Michael took the unlit cigarette from his lips and stared at her. He knew who she was, of course. They called her the black Evita, the mother of the nation. However, none of the photographs had been able to capture her particular dark beauty and regal presence.

'Victoria Gama,' Raleigh introduced them. 'This is Michael Courtney, the newspaperman I told you about.'

'Yes,' Vicky Gama said. 'I know who Michael Courtney is.'

She swept towards him with a stately dignity. She wore a full ankle-length caftan in striking green and yellow and black, the colours of the banned African National Congress. Around her head was an emerald-green turban; the caftan and the turban were her trademarks.

She held out her hand to Michael. It was fine-boned, but the grip of her long tapered fingers was firm and cool, almost cold. Her skin was velvety smooth and the colour of dark amber.

'Your mother was my husband's second wife,' she told Michael softly. 'She bore Moses Gama a son, as I did. Your mother is a fine woman, one of us.'

Michael was always astounded by the total lack of jealousy between the wives of an African man. His wives regarded each other not as rivals, but rather as sisters with family ties and loyalties.

'How is Tara?' Vicky persisted, as she led Michael to one of the sofas and seated him comfortably. 'I have not seen her for many years. Is she still living in England? And how is Moses's son, Benjamin?'

'Yes, they are living in England,' Michael told her. 'I saw them both in London recently. Benjamin is a big lad now. He is doing very well. He is studying chemical engineering at Leeds University.'

'I wonder if he will ever return to Africa.' Vicky sat down beside him. They chatted easily for a while, and Michael found himself coming under the spell of her charming personality.

At last she asked: 'So you want to meet some of my children, the children of apartheid?'

It struck Michael that this was the only title for his article or perhaps series of articles that he would write.

'The children of apartheid,' he repeated. 'Yes, Mrs Gama, I would like to meet your children.'

'Please call me Vicky. We are of the same family, Michael. Dare I also hope that our dreams and hopes are the same?'

'Yes, I think that we have a great deal in common, Vicky.'

She led him back to the terrace and she called the

children and youths around her and introduced them to Michael.

'He is our friend,' she told them. 'You may speak freely to him. Answer his questions. Tell him whatever he wants to know.'

Michael threw off his jacket and tie and sat under one of the umbrellas. The boys crowded around him. With Vicky Gama's endorsement and assurance they seemed to accept him immediately and were delighted that Michael spoke their language. Michael knew how to draw them out. Soon they were competing for his attention. He did not use his notepad to write down what they told him, for he knew that would inhibit them. He valued their spontaneity and frankness. Besides which, he did not need notes. He would not forget their words, and the sound of their young voices.

They told him stories that were funny and others that were harrowing. One of the boys had been at Sharpeville on that fateful day. As an infant he had been strapped to his mother's back. The same police bullet that had killed her had shattered one of his legs. The bone had set crookedly, and the other children called him 'Cripple Pete'. Michael wanted to weep as he listened to his story.

The afternoon passed too swiftly. Some of the boys left the group to swim in the pool. They stripped naked and plunged into the clear bright waters. They shrieked with laughter and splashed each other as they played.

Raleigh sat aside with Vicky Gama and watched the scene. He saw the way that Michael looked at the naked children and he said to Vicky: 'I want you to keep him here tonight.' She nodded, and he went on: 'He likes boys. Do you have one for him?'

She laughed softly. 'He can take his pick. My boys will do whatever I tell them to do.'

She stood up and walked across to where Michael sat and placed her hand on his shoulder.

'Why don't you write your articles here? Stay with us tonight. I have a typewriter upstairs that you can use. Spend tomorrow with us also. The boys like you, and there are so many stories to hear . . .'

Michael's fingers flew over the typewriter keys in an exuberant *allegro*, and the words appeared on the blank white page in serried ranks like warriors of the mind, ready to charge into the battle. The story wrote itself. It was not the smoke that spiralled up from the cigarette between his lips that made Michael's eyelids prickle as he read what he was writing. Very seldom did he have this conviction of the vital worth and weight of his own composition. He knew, deep in his guts, that this was good, really good. This was the story of the 'children' as the world should hear it.

He finished the article which he knew now was only the first of a triumphant series and found that he was trembling with excitement. He glanced at his watch and saw that it was a few minutes before midnight, but he knew he could not sleep. The story still fizzed in his blood and seethed in his brain like some heady champagne.

There was a demure tap on the door that startled him. He called softly in Xhosa: 'It is open. Enter!' And one of the boys slipped into the bedroom. He was dressed only in a pair of blue soccer-shorts.

'I heard you typing,' he said. 'I thought that you might like me to bring you some tea.'

He was the youth whom Michael had most admired in the swimming-pool. He had told Michael that he was sixteen years old. His body was sleek and inviting to stroke as a black cat.

'Thank you.' Michael found that his voice was husky. 'I would like that very much.'

'What are you writing?' The youth came to stand behind his chair and leant over him to read the page. 'Is this what I told you today?'

'Yes,' Michael whispered, and the boy placed his hand on Michael's shoulder and turned his head to smile shyly into Michael's eyes. His breath was warm on Michael's face. 'I like you,' he said.

★　　　★　　　★

Raleigh Tabaka read the article as they sat together beside the pool in the early-morning sunlight. When he finished he held the sheaf of pages in both hands and was silent for a long while.

'You have a special genius,' he said at last. 'I have never read anything so powerful. But it is too powerful. You dare not publish this.'

'Not in this country,' Michael agreed. 'The *Guardian* in London has invited me to submit it to them.'

'It would have the greatest effect there,' Raleigh agreed. 'I congratulate you. Something like this turns the bullets of the oppressor to water. You must finish the series as soon as possible. Stay here another night at least. You seem to work so well when you are close to your subjects.'

★　　　★　　　★

As Michael came awake he was not certain what had disturbed him. He reached out and touched the warm smooth body of the boy who lay beside him. The boy muttered and rolled over in his sleep. One of his arms was flung out across Michael's chest.

Then the sound that had woken Michael came again. It was faint, from the floor below in the far reaches of the house. It sounded like a cry of terrible pain.

Michael lifted the arm of the sleeping boy from his chest and slipped out from under it. There was a glimmer of moonlight through the open window, sufficient for him to find his underpants. He moved quietly across the bedroom and let himself out into the passageway. He crept towards the head of the stairs and stood there listening. The sound came up to him again much louder, another wild cry like the voice of a seabird, and it was punctuated by a sharp snapping sound that Michael could not place.

He started down the stairs, but had not reached the bottom before a voice arrested him.

'Michael. What are you doing?' Raleigh Tabaka's voice was sharp and accusing, and Michael started guiltily and looked back up the stairs. Raleigh stood on the landing in his dressing-gown.

'I heard something,' Michael said. 'It sounded like—'

'It is nothing. Go to your room, Michael.'

'But I thought that I heard—'

'Go to your room!' Raleigh spoke softly, but it was not an order that Michael could disobey. He turned and went back up the stairs. Raleigh reached out to touch his arm as he passed.

'Sometimes one's hearing plays strange tricks in the night. You heard nothing, Michael. It was a cat, perhaps – or the wind. Go to sleep now. We will talk in the morning.'

Raleigh waited until Michael had returned to his bedroom and closed the door before he ran down the stairs. He went directly to the kitchen door and threw it open.

Victoria Gama, the black Evita, the mother of the nation, stood in the centre of the tiled floor. She was naked to the waist. Her breasts were beautifully shaped. Smooth as velvet, black as the fur of sable, large as the ripe tsama melons of the Kalahari desert.

In her right hand she held a supple whip made of cured hippo hide, the terrible African sjambok. It was slim as one of Vicky's elegant fingers and as long as her arm. In her other hand she held a glass. She was drinking from it as Raleigh burst into the room. The gin-bottle stood on the sink behind her.

There were two members of the Gama Athletics Club in the kitchen with her. They were the eldest and biggest of all her bodyguards. Both of them were in their late teens. They were also bared to the waist. They stood at either

214

end of the long kitchen table and held a naked body pinioned down upon the table.

The flogging must have been in progress for some considerable time. The whip-weals were latticed closely across the shiny black skin, raised and purple. Some of them had cut through into the flesh and were bleeding. The blood formed a puddle under the body and spilled over to drip on to the tiled kitchen floor.

'Are you mad?' Raleigh hissed at her. 'With the journalist in the house?'

'He is a police spy,' Vicky snarled at him. 'He is a traitor. I have to teach him a lesson.'

'You are drunk again.' Raleigh struck the glass from her hand, and it spun into the corner and shattered against the wall. 'Can't you enjoy your little boys without having to warm yourself up to it?'

Her eyes blazed with fury, and she lifted the whip to slash at his face. He caught her wrist and held it easily. He twisted the whip out of her fingers and flung it into the sink. Still holding her wrist, he spoke to her young bodyguards.

'Get rid of this.' He indicated the bleeding figure on the table. 'Then clean the place up. No more of this sort of thing while the white man is in the house. Do you understand?'

They lifted the boy off the table, and he moaned and blubbered as they half-carried him to the door.

As soon as they were alone, Raleigh turned back to Vicky. 'You bear an illustrious name. If you bring dishonour upon it, I will kill you myself. Now, go to your room.'

She marched from the room. Despite the gin, her step was regal. She carried her liquor well. If only she could carry her fame and the adulation of the media as well, he thought grimly.

He had watched her change over a few short years. When Moses Gama married her, she had been a bright and pure flame, committed to her husband and the struggle. Then the American left had discovered her, and the media had showered praise and money upon her to the point where she believed all they said about her.

From there the disintegration had been swift. Of course, the struggle was fierce. Of course, freedom must be won through rivers of blood. However, for Vicky Gama the spilling of blood had become a pleasure and not a duty, and her personal glory had eclipsed the call of freedom. It was time to consider carefully what must be done about her.

★   ★   ★

They took Michael back to the carpark where he had left his old Valiant. Raleigh Tabaka sat up beside the driver in the front seat of the butchery-van while Michael crouched in the back. Michael was surprised to see that his car was still standing where he had left it.

'Nobody took the trouble to steal it,' he remarked.

'No,' Raleigh agreed. 'It was guarded by our people. We look after our own.'

They shook hands, and Michael began to turn away, but Raleigh was not yet ready to let him go.

'I believe you own an aircraft, Michael?' he asked.

'Of a sort,' Michael laughed. 'It's an old Centurion that has already flown over three thousand hours.'

'I have a favour to ask of you.'

'I owe you one,' Michael agreed. 'What do you want me to do?'

'Will you fly to Botswana for me?' Raleigh asked.

'With a passenger?'

'No. Fly there on your own – and return on your own.'

Michael hesitated a moment longer. 'Is it to do with your struggle?'

'Of course,' Raleigh replied frankly. 'Everything in my life is to do with the struggle.'

'When do you want me to go?' Michael asked, and Raleigh did not let his relief show in his expression.

Perhaps, after all, it might not be necessary to use the

216

material that they had filmed in the ballet-dancer's flat in London.

'When can you get away for a few days?' he asked.

★   ★   ★

Unlike his father or his brothers, Michael had not taken to flying early in life. Looking back on it, he realized it was because of their passionate love of aircraft that he had shied away from them. Instinctively he had resented his father's efforts to interest him and to instruct him. He didn't want to be like them. He refused to be forced into the mould his father had prepared for him.

Later, when he moved outside the cloying family influence, he discovered the fascination of flight all for himself. He had bought the Centurion out of his own savings. Despite its age, the aircraft was fast and comfortable. She cruised at 210 knots and took him up to Maun in northern Botswana in a little over three hours.

He loved Botswana. It was the only truly democratic country in all of Africa. It had never been colonized by any of the European powers, although Britain had been its protector from the 1880s when the Boer Republic had threatened to muscle in and take the land from the Tswana tribe.

After Britain had relinquished her status as protector and handed the country back to the people, it had swiftly transformed itself into a model for the rest of the continent. It was a multi-party democracy with universal suffrage and regular elections. The Government was truly responsible to the electorate. There were no tyrants or dictators. By African standards, very little corruption existed. The minority white population was accepted as a useful and productive section of the population. There was little inverse racism or tribalism. After South Africa, it was the most prosperous state in all of Africa. In fact it had achieved almost effortlessly the condition that Michael prayed his own country would some day be able to arrive at, after all the suffering and strife. Michael loved Botswana and was happy to be going back there.

At Maun he cleared the formalities in the small single-roomed building that housed both Customs and Immigration and then took off again for a short northern leg into the Okavango delta.

The delta was an extraordinary wetland area where the mighty Okavango river debouched into the northern Kalahari desert and formed a vast swamp. It was not a swamp of reeking black mud and dreary wastes. The waters were clear as a trout stream. The sandbanks and bottoms of the maze of waterways were of sugary white sands. The islands were decked with palms and luxuriant growth. The wild fig trees were loaded with yellow fruit, and the fat green pigeons swarmed in their branches. Strange and rare fishing owls, seeming more like apes than like birds, nested in the tall African ebony trees.

The fabled lions of the Okavango with manes like russet haystacks were quick as otters in the lambent waters. Great herds of buffalo grazed in the reed-beds with a canopy of snowy egrets hovering over them. Weird sitatunga antelope with elongated hoofs, corkscrew horns and shaggy coats spent their entire amphibian lives in the tall papyrus, and clouds of duck and geese and waterfowl shaded the blazing orange sunsets.

Michael landed the Centurion on an airstrip on one of the larger islands. There were two river bushmen in a dugout canoe to ferry him across a lagoon perfumed with water-lilies to the camp.

The camp was called the Gay Goose Lodge, and catered for up to forty guests who lived in picturesque little reed huts. The ostensible reason for their visit was to study and photograph the animals and birdlife of the delta or to troll for the glittering striped tigerfish that shoaled in the waterways. Each morning and evening expeditions of guests ventured out in the primitive canoes, to be poled silently through the reed-beds and channels by one of the black boatmen.

However, the guests were almost exclusively male, and the name Gay Goose had been chosen with good reason. All of the staff were good-looking young Tswana lads who were also chosen with good reason. The camp was run by a political refugee from South Africa. Brian Susskind was a striking-looking fellow in his mid-thirties. He had long blond hair, bleached almost white by the sun. He wore ear-rings in his pierced ear-lobes, gold chains around his neck that tinkled on his bare muscular chest, and bangles of ivory and plaited elephant hair at his wrists.

'God, darling,' he greeted Michael, 'it's just so lovely to meet you. Raleigh has told me all about you. You are going to absolutely love it here. We've got such fun people with us. They are in an absolute tizz to meet you, too.'

Michael spent a long and exciting weekend at Gay Goose Camp, and when it was time to leave Brian Susskind came across the lagoon in the Makorro canoe to see him off.

'It's been such fun, Mickey.' He squeezed Michael's hand. 'I think we'll be seeing a lot more of each other. Don't forget to trim your plane. You may be a touch tail-heavy on take-off.'

Michael took off without looking in the hidden compartment below the passenger-seats, but he noticed the small alteration in trim that Brian had warned him of. The cargo that Brian had loaded must be very heavy for its bulk. He had been told not to touch it or try to examine it. He followed his instructions strictly.

As he cleared Customs on his arrival at Lanseria Airport his nerves were stretched tight and he puffed on his cigarette. He need not have worried. The Customs officer recognized him from many previous occasions and did not even bother to examine his luggage, let alone traipse out on to the tarmac to inspect the Centurion.

That night one of the black nightwatchmen in the Lanseria hangar unloaded a heavy box from under the Centurion's back seat and passed it through the fence to the driver of a small blue butcher's delivery-van.

In the kitchen at Nobs Hill in Drake's Farm township,

Raleigh Tabaka inspected the seals on the crate. They were all intact. Nobody had tampered with the cargo. Raleigh nodded with satisfaction and unscrewed the lid. The crate contained seventy copies of the Holy Bible. Michael Courtney had passed another test.

Michael flew up to Gay Goose Camp five weeks later. This time, on his return the crate contained twenty mini-limpet mines of Russian manufacture. He paid another nine visits to Gay Goose over the following two years, and each time the entry through the South African Customs at Lanseria was easier on his nerves.

Five years after he had first met Raleigh Tabaka, Michael was invited to join the African National Congress as a member of its military wing, Umkhonto we Sizwe, 'the Spear of the Nation'.

'I've been thinking about this a lot recently,' he answered Raleigh, 'and reluctantly I've already reached the conclusion that sometimes the pen alone is not enough. At last I've come to realize that, even though it goes against my deeply ingrained feelings, there comes a time when a man must take up the sword. Even a year ago I would have refused what you are offering me, but now I accept the dictates of my conscience. I am ready to join the armed struggle.'

*   *   *

'All right, Bella,' Centaine Courtney-Malcomess nodded firmly. 'You will begin at the far end of the street – and I'll take this end.' Then she transferred her attention to the back of the chauffeur's head. 'Klonkie, drop us round the corner, then you can pick us up again at lunchtime.'

Obediently Klonkie slowed the yellow Daimler, eased it around the corner and pulled into the pavement.

The two women climbed out and watched the limousine pull away. 'You don't want the voters to see you in a great luxury wagon with a chauffeur,' Centaine explained. 'Envy is a corrosive emotion, and you'll find it at every level of society.' She turned her full attention upon her grand-daughter and inspected her carefully from head to foot.

Isabella's hair was freshly shampooed and gleaming with ruby highlights in the sunshine. However, Centaine had insisted that she pull it back into a severe bun behind the head. Her make-up was limited to a moisturizing cream that gave her a scrubbed schoolgirl complexion. She wore no lipstick, although her lips were a natural youthful pink.

Centaine nodded, and ran her eyes downwards. Bella wore a classic cashmere outfit with low-heeled sensible shoes. Centaine nodded again with complete satisfaction. She smoothed the tweed skirt over her own hips.

'All right, Bella. Remember we are aiming at the ladies this morning.' They had timed their visit for mid-morning, when the men were out of the house, the children were at school, and the main chores were behind the lower-middle-class house-wives who lived in this area below the slopes of Signal Hill, overlooking the city and the harbour of Cape Town.

The previous evening Isabella had addressed a predominantly male audience in the Sea Point Masonic Hall. Most of them had come out of curiosity to listen to the first ever female National Party candidate in their constituency.

On that occasion Bella's dress and make-up had evoked a chorus of wolf-whistles from the body of the hall when she stood up to speak. They had heckled her good-naturedly for the first few minutes while she struggled to overcome her nervousness. However, the horseplay had roused her anger, and she had flushed and snapped at them.

'Gentlemen, your behaviour does none of us credit. If you have any sense of fair play, you'll give me a sporting chance.'

They grinned shamefacedly, shuffled their feet and re-lapsed into a silence that grew more attentive as she spoke. She and Centaine had studied the issues that concerned them most, and they listened as she addressed herself to them.

It had been a good baptism of fire, and Centaine was proud of her, without making it too obvious.

'All right,' she said now. 'You'll do, missy. Here we go for St George, for Harry, and for England.'

The war-cry was entirely inappropriate to the occasion, Isabella smiled wryly, and misquoted to boot, but who would dare tell Nana that? They separated and went to their respective ends of the street.

Number twelve was a semi-detached cottage with bull-nosed corrugated-iron roof and a Victorian fretwork cast-iron trellis beneath the eaves. The front garden was five paces deep, but the dahlias were in full bloom. Isabella went up the path and quietened the yapping fox terrier on the stoep with a sharp word. She had always been good with dogs and horses.

The housewife came to the door and peered suspiciously at Isabella through the fly-screen. Her hair was in yellow plastic curlers.

'Yes? What do you want?'

'My name is Isabella Courtney and I am your National Party candidate for next month's by-election. May I talk to you for a few minutes?'

'Hold on.' The woman disappeared, and came back a minute later with a headscarf over her curlers.

'We are United Party supporters,' she declared her allegiance, but Isabella distracted her.

'What beautiful dahlias!'

This was an opposition party stronghold. Isabella was a political fledgling. Her own party would never have allowed her to contest a safe Nationalist seat. Those were reserved for others who had already proven their worth. As it was, it had taken all Nana's influence and persuasive ability, together with Isabella's own personality and present-ability, to win the opportunity from the party machine to make this foredoomed attempt. The very best Isabella could hope for was a good showing and a gallant defeat. Nana had set their objective. In the last general election the United Party had taken this seat with a five thousand majority.

'If we can cut the majority to three thousand, then in

the next election we can force them to give you a better constituency to contest.'

Now the housewife softened with gratification as Isabella looked at her prize-winning dahlias and wavered.

'May I come in?' Isabella smiled her sweetest and most winning smile, and the woman stood aside reluctantly.

'Well, just for a few minutes.'

'What work does your husband do?'

'He's a motor mechanic.'

'What does he think about trade fragmentation and black trade unions?' Isabella struck hard, and the woman looked grave. Isabella was talking about family survival and the bread in her children's mouths.

'May I get you a cup of coffee, Mrs Courtney?' she asked and Isabella did not correct her form of address.

Fifteen minutes later she shook the housewife's hand and went back down the short garden path. She had followed Nana's maxim: 'Be forceful, but be brief.'

She felt a flush of achievement. Her victim had begun as a definite 'No' and gradually mellowed under Isabella's persuasive logic to a tentative 'Maybe'. Isabella marked her so on her copy of the voters' roll.

'One down,' she whispered. 'Two thousand more to go.'

She marched across the street to the door of number eleven, and a child opened the door.

'Is your mummy at home?'

The child was a freckle-faced little boy with curly blond hair and sticky lips. He held a half-devoured slice of bread and jam in one hand, and smiled at her shyly. He was at least five years old, but she thought of Nicky, and her resolve hardened.

'I am Isabella Courtney,' she said, as the mother came to the door, 'and I am your National Party candidate in next month's by-election.'

After the third call she found to her astonishment that she was starting to enjoy herself. She was seeing a side of life that she had never imagined existed. She found herself warming to these ordinary simple folk, and developing an understanding and concern for their problems and fears and their way of life which was so alien from her own existence.

'Privilege carries responsibilities.' She had heard her father say it so often. 'Noblesse oblige.' She had not thought deeply about it, but believed that she understood the concept. Not that she had ever intended doing anything about it, of course. Up until now, life had been too busy. Her own needs and desires had been too pressing to care or worry about other, insignificant, people such as these.

Now she felt herself drawn to them. She felt a genuine warmth for them, a sympathy and a desire to understand and protect them.

Perhaps motherhood has mellowed me a little, she thought, and the ache of her loss immediately followed the thought. Was this some displacement emotion, a diversion of her frustrated maternal instincts? She did not know, and also she did not really care. All that was important was that she wanted to do this, she truly wanted to help these people. She wanted very strongly to win a seat in Parliament, and to put her time and her talents to good unselfish use.

She felt a genuine regret when after the eighth call she checked her wristwatch and found that it was time to meet Nana and call it a day.

Centaine was waiting for her at the rendezvous at the street-corner. She looked fresh and alert, bubbling with the energy of a much younger woman.

'How did you go, Bella?' she demanded briskly. 'How many calls?'

'Eight,' Bella told her with satisfaction. 'Two "Yesses" and a "Maybe". How about you, Nana?'

'Fourteen calls and five "Yesses". I don't count "Maybes" or "Might have beens". Never have.'

She took Isabella's arm as the yellow Daimler came into view and slowed to pick them up.

'Now, as soon as we get home you will send them each a personal handwritten note – I hope you noted their children's names and ages, and some personal details about each of them.'

'Do I have to write to all of them?'

'All of them,' Centaine confirmed. '"Yesses", "Noes" and "Maybes". Then we will follow it up with another note a few days before polling, just to remind them.'

'You make it such hard work, Nana,' Isabella protested mildly.

'Nothing of value is ever achieved without hard work, missy.' She stepped into the Daimler and settled on to the cream leather seat. 'And don't forget the meeting this evening. Have you got your speech written yet? We'll go over it together.'

'Nana, I've still got a pile of work to do for Pater.'

'Keep you out of mischief,' Centaine agreed complacently. 'Home to Weltevreden, Klonkie,' she told the chauffeur.

Isabella cheated a little. She had her secretary type a standard letter to all of the constituents that she and Nana had visited, but she checked and signed each of these personally. By exercising these little economies of time she was able to discharge her political aspirations and also keep abreast of the work that her father piled upon her desk.

*   *   *

Shasa had given her a corner suite of offices in Centaine House. Her new secretary was one of the stalwarts who had worked for Courtney Enterprises for twenty years. She occupied the outer office of the suite. Isabella's inner office was panelled in indigenous yellow wood that Shasa had salvaged from a two-hundred-year-old building that had been demolished to make way for a block of modern apartments in Sea Point. The wood had a glorious buttery glow. Shasa had loaned her four paintings from his collection, two Pierneefs and a pair of landscapes by Hugo Naudé. Their colours stood out very well on the light-toned panels. All the books on the shelves were fully bound in royal blue calf leather, though Isabella doubted that she would have much call for thirty years' worth of Hansard's parliamentary reports.

The windows of her suite looked out on to the park and St George's Cathedral, with a backdrop of Table Mountain beyond. There was a saying that you hadn't arrived in Cape Town unless you had a view of the mountain from your window.

She signed the last of her form letters to her prospective constituents and carried the batch through to her secretary's office. The secretary's office was empty, and the cover was on the Underwood typewriter. Isabella checked her wristwatch.

'Good grief – it's after five already.'

She felt a quick relief in the fact that time had passed so swiftly and painlessly. It hadn't always been like that since she had lost Nicky. She had come to rely on hard work and long hours as the opiate for the deep gnawing pain of her bereavement.

Dinner at Weltevreden was at eight-thirty sharp, cocktails thirty minutes before. She had time to fill, so she went back to her own desk. Shasa had left a draft copy of his report on her desk with a note: 'I need it back tomorrow a.m. Love you, Pater.'

During their time together at the embassy they had fallen into this routine in which she checked his speeches and written reports for style and syntax. Shasa did not truly need such assistance. He could craft a telling phrase with the best of them. However, the custom gave them both pleasure, and Shasa occasionally went over the top with a metaphor or let an unseemly cliché creep into his compositions. At the very least he enjoyed her praises.

She read the twelve-page report through carefully, and suggested one change. Then she wrote 'What a clever father I chose!' on the foot of it, and took it down to his office at the end of the long carpeted corridor.

His office was locked. She had a key and let herself in.

Shasa's office was four times larger and grander than

hers was. His desk was reputed to have come from the Dauphin's apartments at Versailles. He had an original auctioneer's receipt dated 1791 which showed that provenance.

Isabella placed the corrected report in the centre of the delicate marquetry desk-top, and then changed her mind. The report was destined to be read only by the prime minister and members of his cabinet. Some of the facts and figures that it contained were highly confidential, and crucial to the nation's security. Shasa should not have left it unprotected on her desk but, then, he was often careless with important documents.

She retrieved the report and took it to his personal safe. The safe was concealed behind a false bookcase. The mechanism was incorporated into the lamp on its wall-bracket above the bookcase. The release was in the shape of a bronze nymph in art deco style, holding the lightbulb above her head like a torch.

Isabella rotated the bracket on its hinge, and the false bookcase slid noiselessly aside, revealing the massive green-painted steel Chubb door.

Shasa's choice of numerals for the combination lacked either subtlety or originality. It was simply his own birth-date in inverted sequence. Apart from Shasa himself, Isabella, in her capacity as his personal assistant, was the only one who had the combination. He had not even given it to Nana or Garry.

She set the combination, swung the heavy steel door open and walked into the cavernous strongroom. She often had to nag her father to keep the room tidy, and now she clucked her tongue with disapproval as she saw two green Armscor files piled haphazardly on the central table. She tidied up quickly, locked the strongroom and then stopped in the ladies' washroom on her way back to her own office.

As she settled into the driving-seat of the Mini, she sighed. It had been a long day, and she still had the election meeting after dinner. She wouldn't be in bed until long after midnight.

For a moment she considered the shortest route back to Weltevreden. However, the Mini took the road up the slope of the mountain almost of its own volition, and fifteen minutes later she parked in the side-street round the corner from the Camps Bay post office.

She felt that familiar heavy rock of dread in the pit of her stomach as she approached her post-box. Would it be empty, as it had been for so many weeks? Would she never have word of Nicky again?

She opened the box, and her heart seemed to bounce against her ribs with a single wild lunge. Like a thief she snatched out the slim envelope and thrust it deep into her jacket pocket.

As was her habit she parked above the beach, under the palms, and read the four lines of typewritten instruction with a mixture of dread and anticipation.

This was something new.

In strict accordance with her standing instructions she memorized the contents of the letter and then burnt it and crushed the ashes to dust.

*　　　*　　　*

On the Friday morning three days after receiving the Red Rose letter, Isabella left the Mini in the carpark of the new Pick 'n' Pay supermarket in the suburb of Claremont.

She locked the driver's door, but left the side-window open an inch at the top as she had been instructed. She entered the back door of the bustling supermarket. It was the last Friday of the month, and pay-day for tens of thousands of office workers and civil servants. The queues at the checkout tills were scores long.

Isabella passed quickly out through the front entrance into the main street of the suburb and turned left. She pushed her way along the crowded pavements until she reached the new post office building. There was a pair of teenage girls in the glass cubicle of the first public telephone booth from the left. They giggled into the receiver and jangled their fake gold ear-rings and rolled their eyes at each other as they listened to the boy on the other end of the line, sharing the earpiece of the telephone.

Isabella checked her watch. It was five minutes short of the hour, and she felt a stab of anxiety. She tapped imperiously on the glass door, and one of the girls pushed out her tongue at her and went on speaking.

A minute later Isabella tapped again. With ill grace the pair hung up the receiver and flounced away angrily. Isabella darted into the booth and closed the door. She did not lift the receiver, but made a show of searching for small change in her purse. She was watching the minute-hand of her wristwatch. As it touched the pip at the top of the dial the telephone rang and she snatched it up.

'Red Rose,' she whispered breathlessly, and a voice said: 'Return immediately to your vehicle.' The connection was broken and the burr of the dialling tone echoed in her ears. Even in her perplexity, Isabella thought she had recognized the heavy accent of the large powerful woman who had picked her up in the closed van on the Thames Embankment almost three years previously.

Isabella dropped the receiver back on to its cradle and fled from the booth. It took her three minutes to reach the Mini in the Pick 'n' Pay carpark. As she inserted the key in the door-lock she saw the envelope lying on the driver's seat, and she understood. She had read the books of Le Carré and Len Deighton, and she realized that this was a dead-letter drop.

She knew that she was almost certainly under observation at that moment. She glanced around the carpark furtively. It was almost two acres in extent, and there were several hundred other vehicles parked around her. Dozens of shoppers pushed their laden shopping-trolleys to the waiting motor-cars, and beggars and off-duty schoolchildren loitered and idled about the carpark. Cars pulled in and out of the gates in a steady two-way stream. It would be impossible to pick out the watcher from this crowd.

She slipped behind the wheel and drove carefully back

to Weltevreden. The letter was obviously too important to be entrusted to the postal service. This was an ingenious form of hand delivery. Locked in the safety of her own private bedroom suite she at last opened the envelope.

First, there was a recent colour photograph of Nicky. He was dressed in bathing-trunks. He had developed into a sturdy and beautiful child of nearly three years of age. He stood on a beach of white coral sand with the blue ocean behind him.

The letter that accompanied the photograph was terse and unequivocal:

As soon as possible, you will acquire full technical specifications of the new Siemens computer-linked coastal radar network presently being installed by Armscor at Silver Mine naval headquarters on the Cape peninsula.

Inform us in the usual way once these plans are in your possession. After you have delivered, arrangements will be made for your first meeting with your son.

There was no signature.

Standing over the toilet-bowl in her bathroom, Isabella burnt the letter and, as the flames scorched her fingertips, dropped it into the bowl and flushed the ashes away. She closed the toilet-cover and sat upon it, staring at the tiled wall opposite.

So it had come at last – as she had known it must. For three years she had waited for the order to commit an act that would finally put her beyond the pale.

Up until now she had been instructed merely to inveigle herself into her father's complete confidence. She had been told to make her self indispensable to him, and she had done so. She had been ordered to join the National Party and seek election to parliamentary office. With Nana's help and guidance, she had done so.

However, this was different. She recognized that she had at last reached the point of no return. She could turn back from treason – and abandon her son; or she could go forward into the dangerous unknown.

'Oh, God help me,' she whispered aloud. 'What can I do – what must I do?'

She felt the great serpentine coils of dread and guilt tighten about her. She knew what the answer to her question must be.

A copy of the Siemens radar installation report was in her father's strongroom in Centaine House at this moment. On Monday the file would be returned by special courier to naval headquarters in the nuclear-proof bunker complex built into Silver Mine mountain.

However, her father was flying up to the sheep ranch at Camdeboo over the weekend. She had already refused the invitation to accompany him on the excuse that she had so much work to catch up on. On Saturday and Sunday, Nana was judging the Cape gun-dog trials. Garry was in Europe with Holly and the children. Isabella would have the top floor of Centaine House to herself for the entire weekend. She had full security clearance, and the guards at the front door knew her well.

★　　　★　　　★

The wind was out of the north. The first snowflakes eddied down, silver bright against the grey sow's belly of the sky.

There were a dozen men at the graveside, no women. There had been no women in Joe Cicero's life, just as now there was none at his death. All the mourners were officers from the department. They had been delegated to this duty. They stood stolidly to attention in a single rank. All of them wore uniform greatcoats and scarlet-piped dress caps. All their noses were red, with cold rather than with grief. Joe Cicero had no friends. He had seldom evoked any emotion in his peers other than envious admiration or fear.

The honour guard stepped smartly forward and, at the order, raised their rifles and pointed them to the sky. The volleys rang out, punctuated by the rattle of the bolts. At the next order they shouldered their weapons and marched away, boots slamming into the gravel path and clenched fists swinging high across the chest.

The official mourners broke their ranks, shook hands briefly and expressionlessly then hurried to the waiting vehicles.

Ramón Machado was the only one left at the graveside. He also wore the full-dress uniform of a KGB colonel, and beneath his greatcoat the gaudy lines of his decorations reached below his ribcage.

'And so, you old bastard, for you the game is over at last – but it took you long enough to clear the stage.' Although Ramón had been head of section for two years now, he had never truly felt that he had succeeded to the title while Joe Cicero was still alive.

The old man had died grudgingly. He had held the cancer in remission for long agonizing months. He had even kept his office in the Lubyanka right up to the last day. His gaunt spectral presence had presided at every meeting of section heads, his will and his enmity had inhibited Ramón at every turn, right to the last.

'Goodbye, Joe Cicero. The devil can have you now.' Ramón smiled, and his lips felt as though they might tear in the cold.

He turned away from the grave. His car was the last one remaining under the row of tall dark yews. With his rank, Ramón now rated a black Chaika and a corporal driver. The driver opened the door for him. As Ramón settled into the back seat he brushed the snowflakes from his shoulders with his gloves.

'Back to the office,' he said.

The corporal drove fast but skilfully, and Ramón relaxed and watched the streets of Moscow unfold ahead of the departmental pennant on the shining black bonnet of the Chaika.

Ramón loved Moscow. He loved the broad boulevards that Joseph Stalin had built after the Great Patriotic War. He loved the pure classical lines of some of the buildings and the brilliant contrast that they struck with those in the

232

rococo style alongside the skyscrapers that Stalin had built and topped with their red stars. The concept of Soviet giantism excited him. They drove past the massive bronze statues of the heroes of the people, the monstrous figures of men and women marching forward together brandishing submachine-guns and sickles and hammers, raising high the socialist banner and the red star.

There were no commercial advertisements, no exhortations to drink Coca-Cola or to smoke Marlboros or invest with Prudential Insurance and read the *Sun*. That was the most striking difference between the cities of Mother Russia and those of the crass and avaricious capitalistic West. It offended Ramón's instinct that the appetites of the people should be stimulated for such shoddy and indulgent goods, that a nation's productive capacity should be diverted from the essential to the trivial.

From the back seat of the Chaika he looked upon the Russian people and he felt a glow of righteous approval. Here was a people organized and committed to the good of the State, to the betterment of the whole not the individual parts. He observed them, patient and obedient, standing at the bus-stops, standing in the food-queues, orderly and regimented.

In his mind he compared them to the American people. America, that fractious childlike nation, where each man pulled against the other; where avarice was considered the greatest virtue; where patience and subtlety were considered the greatest vice. Was there any other nation in history which had perverted the ideal of democracy to the point where the freedom and the rights of the individual had become a tyranny on the rest of society? Was there any other nation which so glorified its criminals – Bonnie and Clyde, Al Capone, Billy the Kid, the Mafia, the black drug-lords? Would Russia or any other sensate government emasculate and shackle its armed forces with such rules of disclosure and publicly debated budget allocations?

The Chaika stopped at a set of traffic-lights. It was the only vehicle on the broad thoroughfare apart from two public buses. Where every American had his own automobile, there was no such wasteful ownership in Russian society. Ramón watched the pedestrians cross the street in an orderly stream in front of his vehicle. The faces were handsome and intelligent, the expressions patient and reserved. Their dress had none of the wild eccentricity that would be evident in any American street. Apart from the predominance of military uniforms, the clothing of both men and women was sober and conservative.

Compared to this educated and scholarly people, the Americans were illiterate oafs. Even the workers in the Russian fields could quote Pushkin. The classic books were amongst the most sought-after items on the black market. Any day that one visited the cemetery at the monastery of Alexander Nevsky in Leningrad you would find the graves of Dostoevsky and Tchaikovsky piled with fresh flowers, daily tributes from ordinary people. By contrast, half the American high-school graduates, especially the blacks, had reading skills barely adequate to follow the captions in a Batman comic-book.

Here, then, was the reward for almost sixty years of the socialist revolution. A structured and delicately layered society, secretive and protected in depth. Ramón often compared it to the Matryoshka dolls in the Beriozka tourist stores, those cunningly carved nests of human figures which fitted one within the other, the outer layers protecting and hiding the precious centre.

Even the Russian economy was deceptive to the Western eye. The Americans looked at the food-queues and the lack of consumer goods in the gigantic GUM departmental stores, and in their naïve and simple-minded way they saw this as the sign of a failed or at least an ailing system. Hidden from them was the internal economy of the military productive machine. A vast, highly efficient and powerful structure which not only matched but far outstripped its American capitalistic counterpart.

Ramón smiled at the story of the American astronaut perched in the nose capsule of his rocket waiting for the blast-off who, when asked by ground control if he was nervous, answered: 'How would you like to be sitting on top of the efforts of a thousand low-bidders?' There were no low-bidders in the Russian armaments industry. There was only the best.

In much the same way there were no siftings from the 'equal opportunity' school of employment, or rejects from IMB and GM, in the upper echelons of the Russian military. There were only the best. Ramón was aware that he was one of them, one of the very best.

He straightened up in his seat as the Chaika entered Dzerzhinsky Square and passed the heroic statue of the founder of the organization of state security on its raised plinth, and moved up the hill towards the elegant but substantial edifice of the Lubyanka.

The driver pulled into the narrower street which ran behind the headquarters and parked with the rows of other official KGB vehicles in the rank reserved for them. Ramón waited for him to open the door and then he crossed the road to the rear entrance and entered the building through the massive cast-iron grille doors.

There were two other KGB officers ahead of him at the security-desk. He waited his turn for clearance. The captain of the security guard was thorough and painstaking. He compared Ramón's features to those of the photograph on his identity document the regulation three times before allowing him to sign the register.

Ramón mounted to the second floor in the antique lift of etched glass and polished bronze. The lift and the chandeliers were relics from pre-revolutionary times when the building had been a foreign embassy.

His secretary stood to attention beside her desk when he entered his office and greeted him as he hung his greatcoat at the door.

'Good morning, Comrade Colonel.' He saw that overnight she had set her hair with hot curling-tongs into crisp tight curls. He preferred it loose and soft. Katrina's eyes were almond-shaped and hooded, a legacy from some distant Tartar ancestor. She was twenty-four years old, the widow of an air-force test pilot who had died flying a prototype of the new MiG-27 series.

Katrina indicated the cardboard box on the corner of her desk. 'What should I do with these, Comrade Colonel?'

She opened the lid, and Ramón glanced at the contents. They were all that remained of General Cicero's presence. She had cleared the drawers of the desk that now, at last, belonged to Ramón alone.

Apart from a gold-plated Parker ballpoint pen and a leather wallet, there were no personal items in the box. Ramón picked out the wallet and opened it. There were half a dozen photographs in the compartments. In each of them Joe Cicero posed with a prominent African leader, Nyerere, Kaunda, Nkrumah.

He dropped the wallet back into the box, and his hand brushed against Katrina's soft pale fingers. She trembled slightly, and he heard her catch her breath.

'Take it all down to Archives. Get a receipt from them,' he ordered.

'Immediately, Comrade Colonel.'

She was an attractive placid woman, with a narrow waist and wide comfortable hips. Of course, she had the highest security clearance, and Ramón had meticulously recorded their relationship in his daybook. Their relationship had the tacit sanction of the head of department. Her flat was a convenient base for him while he was in Moscow, even though she shared the two rooms with her elderly parents and her three-year-old son.

'There is a green-flash despatch on your desk, Comrade Colonel,' Katrina said huskily as she picked up the cardboard box. Her cheeks were still lightly flushed from the brief physical contact. Ramón felt a shaded regret that he would be leaving Moscow at midnight. On the average he spent only a few days in the mother city in any one month. He saw so little of Katrina that her appeal was still fresh, even after two years.

She must have read his mind, for she dropped her voice

to a whisper. 'Will you dine at the flat tonight, before you leave? Mamma has found an excellent sausage and a bottle of vodka.'

'Very well, little one,' he agreed, and then went through to his own office.

The green-flash box was on his desk, and he unbuttoned his tunic and split the security seal that the cipher department had affixed.

As he read the code Red Rose he felt a sharp elevation of his pulse rate. That annoyed him.

Red Rose was merely an agent like a hundred others under his control. If he allowed personalities to intrude, his own efficiency was diminished. Even so, as he lifted the Red Rose folder from the box he was struck suddenly by a mental image of a naked girl perched on a black boulder in a Spanish mountain stream. The picture was extraordinarily vivid, even down to the deep indigo blue of her eyes.

He opened the file and saw at a glance that it was the report on the South African naval radar chain that he had called for. It had come in via the London embassy bag. He nodded with satisfaction and then consulted his daybook. With the log open before him he lifted the handset of his departmental intercom and dialled Records.

'A printout. Reference "Protea", item number 1178. Urgent, please.'

While he waited for the printout to be delivered, he rose from his desk and crossed to the windows. The view was novel enough to engage his interest. Over the statue of the founder he looked across the stately forest of buildings to the colourful onion-shaped domes of the Cathedral of St Basil the Blessed, and the walls of the Kremlin.

He was still disturbed by the memories that the Red Rose despatch had evoked. On a logical train of thought his mind went on to the journey that would begin for him at midnight from Sheremetyevo Airport, and the child who would be waiting for him at the journey's end.

He had not seen Nicholas for over two months. He

would have grown again and he would be speaking even more fluently. His vocabulary was quite unusual for his age. Paternal pride was a bourgeois emotion, and Ramón sought to suppress it. He should not be standing dreaming out of the window while there was so much work to be done. He checked his wristwatch. In forty-eight minutes there was a meeting scheduled, the result of which would vitally affect his career over the next decade.

He returned to his desk and took his notes for the meeting from the top drawer. Katrina had typed them out in double spacing. He flipped through the pages, and found that he still knew every word by heart. His presentation was memorized word-perfect. Further study would only affect the spontaneity of his delivery. He set the report aside.

At that moment there was a knock on the door and Katrina ushered the records clerk into his office. Ramón signed for the computer printout in the records-book, and after Katrina and the clerk had left he slit the envelope and spread the printout on his desk.

Protea was the code-name of another of his South African agents. His real name was Dieter Reinhardt, a German national, born in Dresden in 1930. His father had commanded one of Admiral Doenitz's U-boats with distinction. After the partition of Germany, Reinhardt had enrolled as a cadet officer in the fledgling navy of the German Democratic Republic, and two years later had been recruited by the KGB.

Subsequently, his 'escape' over the Berlin Wall to the West had been carefully stage-managed by Joe Cicero personally. Reinhardt and his wife had emigrated to South Africa in 1960, and after he had become a naturalized South African citizen he had joined the South African navy and worked his way up to the rank of kommandant. He was presently chief of signals on headquarters staff at Silver Mine command bunker.

The printout was a copy of the report that he had filed three weeks previously concerning the Siemens radar chain at Silver Mine.

Ramón laid the Red Rose report of the same installation alongside Protea's and began comparing them item by item, paragraph by paragraph. Within ten minutes he was satisfied that they were in total agreement, in general and in detail.

The integrity of Protea was of the highest order. It had been tested repeatedly over a decade and long ago rated Class I, the highest-category source.

Red Rose had just survived her first security check. She could now be considered as active and given a Class III rating. After almost four years of carefully executed preparation, Ramón considered the price acceptable. He smiled at the portrait of Leonid Brezhnev on the opposite wall, and the general secretary stared back at him solemnly from under beetling brows.

Katrina rang through on his private line. 'Comrade Colonel, you are expected on the top floor in six minutes.'

'Thank you, comrade. Please come through to witness destruction of documents.'

She stood at his side while he fed the printout of the Protea report into the paper-shredder and then countersigned the entry in his daybook to attest to the destruction.

She watched him button his tunic and adjust the block of medal ribbons on his chest in the small wall-mirror. Then she handed him the sheaf of notes for the meeting.

'Good luck, Comrade Colonel.' She stood close to him with face upturned.

'Thank you.' He turned away without touching her: never in the office.

* * *

Ramón waited alone in the secure conference-room on the top floor. They kept him waiting for ten minutes. The walls of the room were bare plaster, painted white. There was no panelling that might conceal a microphone. Apart from the obligatory portraits of Lenin and Brezhnev, there was no decoration. There were a dozen chairs at the long conference-table, and Ramón stood for the full ten minutes at the lower end.

At last the door from the director's suite opened.

General Yuri Borodin was head of the fourth directorate. In his new capacity Ramón reported directly to him. He was a chunky grey-haired septuagenarian, a cautious devious man, in a shiny striped suit. Ramón admired him and held him in awe.

The man that followed him into the conference-room deserved even greater respect. He was younger than Borodin, not much over fifty, and yet he was already a member of the Praesidium of the Supreme Soviet and a deputy minister at the Department of Foreign Affairs.

Ramón's report had drawn a much heavier reaction than he had anticipated. He was being invited to defend his thesis in front of one of the hundred most influential men in Russia.

Aleksei Yudenich was short and slight in stature but he had the fierce penetrating gaze of a mystic. He shook Ramón's hand briefly and stared into his eyes for a moment while Borodin introduced them, and then he took the seat at the head of the table with his aides on each side of him.

'You have novel ideas, young man,' he began abruptly, and his choice of adjectives was not necessarily complimentary. Youth was not a commodity by which the Department of Foreign Affairs set as much store as they did by traditional and well-tried policies. 'You wish to abandon our long-standing support for the liberation movements in southern Africa – the African National Congress and the South African Communist Party – and for the armed struggle in southern Africa in general.'

'With respect, Comrade Director,' Ramón replied carefully, 'that is not my intention.'

'Then, I have misread your paper. Have you not stated that the ANC has proved to be the most inept and unproductive guerrilla organization in modern history?'

'I have pointed out the reasons for this, and the manner in which previous mistakes may be rectified.'

Yudenich grunted and turned a sheet of his copy of the report. 'Continue. Explain to me why the armed struggle should not succeed in South Africa as it did in, for instance, Algeria.'

'There are basic differences, Minister. The settlers in Algeria, the *pieds-noirs*, were Frenchmen, and France was a short boat-ride away across the Mediterranean. The white Afrikaner has no such escape-route. He stands with his back to the Atlantic Ocean. He must fight. Africa is his motherland.'

'Yes,' Yudenich nodded. 'Continue.'

'The FLN guerrillas in Algeria were united by the Muslim religion and a common language. They were waging a holy war, a *jihad*. On the other hand, the black Africans are not so inspired. They are splintered by language and tribal enmities. The ANC, as an example, is an almost exclusively Xhosa tribal organization which excludes the most numerous and powerful tribe, the Zulu nation, from its ranks.'

Yudenich listened for fifteen minutes without interruption. His gaze never left Ramón's face. When at last Ramón finished speaking he asked softly: 'So what is the alternative that you propose?'

'Not an alternative.' Ramón shook his head. 'The armed struggle must, of course, continue. There are younger, brighter and more committed men coming forward in its ranks, men like Raleigh Tabaka. From them we may see greater successes in future. What I propose is an adjunct to the struggle, an economic onslaught, a series of boycotts and mandatory sanctions. . . .'

'We do not have economic contacts with South Africa,' Yudenich pointed out brusquely.

'I propose that we let our arch-enemy do the job for us. I propose that we orchestrate in America and Western Europe a campaign to destroy the South African economy. Let our enemies prepare the ground for us, and plant the seeds of revolution. We will harvest the fruits.'

'How do you suggest we go about this?'

'You know that we have excellent penetration of the American Democratic Party. We have access at the highest-possible levels to the American media. Our influence in such organizations as the NAACP and the Trans Africa Foundation is pervasive. I propose that we make South Africa and apartheid a rallying cry for the American left. They are looking for a cause to unite them. We will give them that cause. We will make South Africa a domestic political issue in the United States of America. The black Americans will flock to the standard and, to secure their votes, the Democratic Party will follow them. We will orchestrate a campaign in the ghettos and on the campuses of America for comprehensive mandatory sanctions that will destroy the South African economy and bring its government crashing down in ruins, unable any longer to protect itself or to keep its security forces in the field. When that happens we will step in and place our own surrogate government in power.'

They were silent awhile, contemplating this startling vision. Aleksei Yudenich coughed and asked quietly: 'How much will this cost – in financial terms?'

'Billions of dollars,' Ramón admitted and, when Yudenich's expression tightened, he went on: 'Billions of *American* dollars, Comrade Minister. We will let the Democratic Party call the tune for us and the American people pay the piper.'

Minister Yudenich smiled for the first time that afternoon. The discussions lasted another two hours before Yuri Borodin rang the bell to summon his aide.

'Vodka,' he said.

It came on a silver tray, the bottle thickly crusted with frost from the freezer.

Aleksei Yudenich gave them the first of many toasts.

'The Democratic Party of America!' And they laughed and drained their glasses and shook hands and clapped each other's back.

Director Borodin moved slightly, until he and Ramón Machado were standing shoulder to shoulder. It was a gesture that was not lost on any of them. He was aligning himself with his brilliant young subordinate.

★   ★   ★

Katrina's flat was in one of the more pleasant sections of the city. From her bedroom window there was a view of Gorky Park and the amusement-ground. On the skyline the big Ferris wheel, lit with myriad fairy-lights, revolved slowly against the cold grey clouds as Ramón stepped out of the Chaika and went in through the front entrance of the apartment-building.

It was a relic from pre-revolutionary Tsarist Russia, a wedding-cake of a building in rococo style. There was no lift, and Ramón climbed the stairs to the sixth floor. The exercise helped clear the vodka fumes from his brain.

Katrina's mother had lovingly prepared the thick pork sausage with a side-dish of cabbage – always cabbage. The entire apartment-block smelt of boiled cabbage.

Katrina's parents treated Ramón with servile and fawning respect. Her mother served Ramón with the greater portion of the sausage, while Katrina poured pepper vodka into his tumbler. When they had eaten, Katrina's parents took the child with them and went to watch television in a neighbour's apartment, discreetly leaving Ramón and Katrina to say their farewells.

'I shall miss you,' Katrina whispered, as she led him to the single bed in her tiny room and let the skirt of her tunic fall around her ankles. 'Please return soon.'

They had an hour before Ramón had to leave for the airport. Her skin was velvety smooth and warm to his touch. There were tiny blue veins radiating out from around her large rosy brown nipples. There was plenty of time for Ramón to make it really good for her.

He left her with barely enough strength to totter to the door. The threadbare dressing-gown was clutched around her flawless shoulders, and her crisp curls were in tangled disarray.

At the door, she leant heavily against him and kissed him deeply. 'Come back to me soon, please. Oh, please!'

At this time of night there was very little traffic on the airport road, only a few rumbling military trucks. The journey took less than half an hour.

Ramón travelled so often that he had his own régime for minimizing the adverse effects of jet-lag. He neither ate nor touched alcohol during the flight, and he had trained himself to sleep in any circumstance. A man who could fall asleep on a bed of jagged Ethiopian rock in a temperature of forty-two degrees, or in the hothouse of a dripping Central American rainforest with centipedes crawling over his skin, could do so even in the torturous seat of an Ilyushin passenger-jet.

Although the sun burnt down with a peculiar brilliance and dampened his open sports-shirt along the spine and at the armpits, it was by his reckoning a Moscow winter midnight and not a balmy Caribbean noon when he stepped off the plane at Havana's José Marti Airport. He made the local connection on a scheduled flight, an old prop-driven Dakota that flew him down to Cienfuegos.

Lugging his own valise from the airport building, he bargained with the driver of one of the vintage Detroit model taxis standing at the 'Piqueras' rank and took the ride out to the military cantonment of Buenaventura.

On the way they skirted the sparkling water of the Bahía de Cochinos and passed the museum dedicated to the battle of the Bay of Pigs. It always gave him a satisfied glow of achievement when he recalled his own rôle in that salutary humiliation of the American barbarians.

It was late afternoon when the taxi dropped him at the gates of the Buenaventura camp. The day's activity was coming to an end, and columns of the Che Guevara para-trooper regiment were marching back to barracks. These were crack troops in brown fatigues, trained especially for an assault rôle in any theatre of the world, but since the last meeting of the Politburo in Havana they had been exercising and training for deployment in Africa.

Ramón paused to watch a unit of them pass by. Young men and women, they were singing one of the revolutionary songs that he remembered so well from the bitter days in the Sierra Maestra. 'Land of the Landless' was the title and the lyric made his skin prickle even though it was all so long ago. He showed his pass at the gate to the married officers' quarters.

Ramón was dressed in sports-shirt and light cotton slacks with open sandals on his feet, but the sergeant of the guard saluted him deferentially when he recognized his name and rank. Ramón was one of the eighty-two heroes. Their names were recited in the schoolrooms and sung in the *bodegas*.

His cottage was one in a row of identical two-bedroomed flat-roofed adobe-walled dwellings set amongst the palms above the beach. The calm waters of the Bay of Pigs sparkled between the long curved stems of the palms.

Adra Olivares was sweeping the narrow front veranda, but when he was still a hundred paces distant she looked up and saw him and her expression smoothed into neutrality.

'Welcome, Comrade Colonel,' she said quietly, as he stepped up on to the veranda, and although she cast down her gaze she could not conceal the fear in her eyes.

'Where is Nicholas?' he asked as he dropped his valise on the concrete floor, and in reply she looked away down towards the beach.

There was a group of children frolicking at the edge of the water. Their shrill excited cries carried above the clatter of the trade wind in the palm fronds. The children were all wearing bathing-suits, and their bodies were brown and sleek with sun and water.

Nicholas stood a little apart from the other children, and Ramón felt his heart turn over as he recognized his son. It was only within the last year that he had begun to think of him that way. Before that it had always been 'the child' and in his departmental reports it had been 'the child of Red Rose'. Insidiously it had become 'my son', but only

245

in his mind. The words were never spoken or written down.

Ramón left the veranda of the cottage and drifted down through the palms to the beach. At the high-water mark he sat on the low sea-wall and watched his son.

Nicholas was just three years of age. He was precocious and physically well developed for his age. He would grow to be tall; already his limbs were long and coltish without any trace of baby fat. He stood with one hip thrust out, his weight all on one leg, his hand upon the hip in a pose that called to mind Michelangelo's 'David'.

Ramón's interest in the child had been awakened only after it became clear that he was exceptionally intelligent. The reports from his teacher at the camp nursery school had been euphoric. His drawings and his speech were those of a child many years older. Until that time Ramón had taken no active part in the child's upbringing. He had arranged this accommodation for Adra Olivares and Nicholas through the DGA in Havana. Adra was now a lieutenant in the organization of state security.

Ramón had arranged that also. It was necessary for her to have officer's rank in order to qualify for one of the Buenaventura cottages, and to enable Nicholas to attend the military crèche and nursery school.

For the first two years Ramón had not seen the child, although the various reports from the military clinic and the education department had passed over his desk when he prepared despatches for Red Rose. Eventually these reports and the accompanying photographs had piqued his interest. He had made the journey down to Buenaventura from the capital.

It seemed that the child recognized him immediately. He had hidden behind Adra's legs and peered out at Ramón fearfully. The last time he had seen his father was in that white-tiled operating-theatre in the Buenaventura military clinic when Ramón had staged his partial drowning in front of the camera to coerce Red Rose into accepting his authority. Nicholas had been only a few weeks old at the time. It was impossible that he could remember the incident – and yet his reaction to Ramón had been too intense to be merely coincidental.

Ramón had been taken unawares by his own response to the child's terror. He was accustomed to other people's trepidation in his presence. It seldom needed one of his ruthless demonstrations to instil fear in those around him, but this had been different.

Apart from his own mother and his cousin Fidel, he had felt no deep sympathetic response to any of his fellow human beings. He had always deemed this to be one of his great strengths. He was almost impervious to sentimental or emotional considerations. This allowed him to make his decisions and base his actions entirely upon logical and intellectual judgement. When necessary he was able to sacrifice a comrade of many years' standing without flinching and with no futile and debilitating regrets later. He could make tender and unselfish love to a beautiful woman and only hours later, without a moment's hesitation, order her execution. He had trained himself to be above all feeble mundane considerations. He had forged and tempered himself into one of Lenin's steely men, and honed the edges of his strength and resolve into a terrible shining weapon – and then, unexpectedly, he had found this flaw in the metal of his soul.

'A tiny flaw,' he consoled himself, as he sat on the sea-wall in the bright Caribbean sunshine and watched the child. 'Only a hairline crack in the blade, and then only because this is part of me. Blood of my blood, flesh of my flesh, and my hope for immortality.'

He cast his mind back to that episode in the military clinic. In his imagination he saw once again the infant squirming in the doctor's grip and heard the outraged terrified squeals and the painful choking breath as he lifted the sodden little head from the waters of the tank. He did not flinch from the memory.

At the time, it was necessary, he thought. Never regret the strong, the necessary action, the deed of steel.

247

The child stooped and picked a shell from the sand at his feet. He turned it in his hands, and bowed his head to examine the iridescent pearly fragment.

Nicholas's curls were dark and dense, and, although damp with sea-salt, the sun struck little reddish sparks from them. He had inherited many features from his mother. Even Ramón could recognize that chiselled classical nose and the clean sweet line of his jaw. However, the green eyes were Ramón's eyes.

Suddenly the child threw back his arm and sent the shell skimming out. It hopped across the still water leaving a series of tiny dimples where it touched the surface. Then Nicholas turned away and began to walk alone along the edge of the water, but at that moment there came an anguished squeal from the group of children further up the beach. One of the little girls had been knocked over in the rough and tumble, and she sprawled on the white sand and howled.

'Nicholas!'

With a patient sigh Nicholas turned back to her and lifted her to her feet. She was a pretty little imp, with sand on one cheek and tears welling from her huge dark eyes. Her costume had slid halfway down to her knees revealing the cleft between her chubby pink little buttocks.

Nicholas hauled up her costume for her, restoring her modesty but almost lifting her off her feet in the process, then he led her by the hand to the water. He washed the sand off her cheek and wiped the tears from her eyes. The girl gave one last convulsive sniff and stopped howling.

She took Nicholas's hand and trotted beside him as he led her up the beach.

'I will take you back to your mamma,' Nicholas was telling her, and then he looked up and saw his father. He stopped abruptly and stared at him.

Ramón saw the flare of terror in his eyes that was instantly hidden. Then Nicholas lifted his chin in a defiant gesture, and his expression went dead.

Ramón liked what he saw. It was good that the boy felt

248

fear, for fear was the basis of respect and obedience. It was good also that he could control and hide that fear. The ability to conceal fear was one of the qualities of leadership. Already he showed a strength and resolve far beyond his tender years.

He is my son, Ramón thought, and raised one hand in a gesture of command.

'Come here, boy,' he said.

The little girl shrank away from him. Then she released Nicholas's hand and fled up the beach, bawling once again, but this time for her mother. Ramón did not even glance in her direction. He often had that effect on children.

Nicholas steeled himself visibly and then came to his father's bidding. 'Good day, Padre.' He held out his hand solemnly.

'Good day, Nicholas.' Ramón took the proffered hand. He had schooled the child to shake hands like a man, but Adra had taught him the term of address. 'Padre.' He should not have allowed it, but was pleased that in the end he had done so. It gave him another little twinge of sentimentality to be addressed as Father, but that was an indulgence he could afford. There were few enough that he allowed himself.

'Sit here.' Ramón indicated the wall beside him, and Nicholas scrambled up and sat with his little legs dangling.

They were silent for a while. Ramón did not approve of childish chatter. When he asked finally, 'What have you been doing?' Nicholas considered the question gravely.

'I have been to school every day.'

'What do they teach you at school?'

'We learn the drills and the songs of the revolution.' Nicholas thought about it a little longer. 'And we paint.'

They were silent again until Nicholas added helpfully: 'In the afternoons we swim and play soccer, and in the evenings I help Adra with the housework. Then we watch the TV together.'

He was three years old, Ramón reminded himself. A Western child who was asked the same question might have replied 'Nothing' or 'Just stuff'. Nicholas had spoken like a man, a little old man.

'I have brought you a present,' Ramón told him.

'Thank you, Padre.'

'Don't you want to know what it is?'

'You will show it to me,' Nicholas pointed out. 'And then I will know what it is.'

It was a plastic model of an AK 47 assault-rifle. Although it was a miniature, it was perfect in detail with a removable magazine that was loaded with metallic painted bullets. Ramón had bought it at a toyshop on his last visit to London.

Nicholas's eyes shone as he raised it to his shoulder and aimed it down towards the beach. Apart from the first flash of fear, it was the only real emotion he had displayed since Ramón's arrival. When he pulled the trigger the toy rifle made a satisfying warlike clatter.

'It is very beautiful,' Nicholas said. 'Thank you, Padre.'

'It is a good toy for a brave son of the revolution,' Ramón told him.

'Am I a brave son of the revolution?'

'One day you will be,' Ramón told him.

'Comrade Colonel, it is time for the child's bath,' Adra intervened diffidently.

She took Nicholas and led him from the veranda into the cottage. Ramón put aside the temptation to follow them. It was unseemly for him to participate in such a bourgeois domestic ritual. Instead he went to the small table at the end of the veranda where Adra had set out a jug of lime-juice and a bottle of Havana Club rum, indisputably the finest rum in the world.

Ramón mixed himself a *mojito* and then selected a cigar from the box on the table. He smoked only when he was at home in Cuba and then only the premium cigars of Miguel Fernandez Roig, and Adra knew this. Like the Havana Club, they were the finest in the world. He took the tall sugared glass and the cigar back to his seat and watched the sunset turn the waters of the bay to bloodied gold.

From the bathroom, he heard the splashing and the happy cries of his son, and Adra's soft replies.

Ramón was a warrior and a wanderer on the face of the earth. This was the closest he would ever come to a home of his own; perhaps the child had made it so for him.

Adra served a meal of chicken and *Moros y Cristianos*, or 'Moors and Christians', a mixture of black beans and white rice. Through the DGA, Ramón had arranged a preferential ration-book for the little household. He wanted the boy to grow up strong and well nourished.

'Soon you are going on a journey with me,' he told Nicholas as they ate. 'Across the sea. Would you like that, Nicholas?'

'Will Adra come with us?'

The question irritated Ramón. He did not recognize his annoyance as jealousy. He answered shortly: 'Sí.'

'Then, I will like that,' Nicholas nodded. 'Where will we go?'

'To Spain,' Ramón told him. 'To the land of your ancestors and the land of your birth.'

After dinner Nicholas was allowed to watch the television for one hour. When his eyelids drooped, Adra took him to his bedroom.

When she returned to the small, starkly furnished living-room she asked Ramón: 'Do you want me to-night?'

Ramón nodded. She was over forty years of age. However, her belly was flat, and her thighs were firm and powerful. She had never given birth, and she had extraordinary muscular control. At his request she often excited him with a little trick. He would hold one end of a lead pencil while she snapped it in half with a spasmodic constriction of her vaginal sphincter.

She was an adept, one of the most natural and intuitive

251

lovers he had ever known – furthermore she was terrified of him, which enhanced both her pleasure and his.

*   *   *

In the dawn Ramón swam down to the head of the bay and then made the hard two-mile return against the tide, ploughing in a crawl through the choppy water.

When he came up from the beach, Nicholas was ready for school and there was an army jeep and driver waiting at the back door of the cottage. Ramón was dressed in plain brown paratrooper fatigues and soft cap. This was revolutionary uniform, so different from the flamboyant Russian braid and scarlet piping and tiers of medal ribbons. Nicholas sat proudly beside him in the jeep for the short ride until they dropped him off at the nursery school near the main gate.

The drive up to Havana took a little over two hours, for the sugar harvest was in progress. The sky over the hills was smudged with smoke from the cane fires, and the road was congested with behemoth trucks piled high with cargoes of cut cane *en route* to the mills.

When they reached the city, the driver dropped Ramón at the far end of the vast Plaza de la Revolución, with its 350-foot obelisk to the memory of José Marti, hero of the people, who founded the Cuban Revolutionary Party way back in 1892.

The square was the scene of many of the moving rallies of the party, where a million and more of the Cuban people gathered to listen to Fidel Castro's speeches. The president's office was in the building of the Central Committee of the Communist Party of Cuba, of which El Jefe was the first secretary.

The office in which he welcomed Ramón was as austere as the revolutionary principle dictated. Under the revolving ceiling-fan, the massive desk was piled with working documents and reports. However, the white walls were bare of all ornament, except for the portrait of Lenin on the wall behind his desk. Fidel Castro came to embrace Ramón.

'Mi Zorro Dorado,' he chuckled with pleasure. 'My Golden Fox. It is good to see you. You have been away too long, old comrade. Much too long.'

'It is good to be back, El Jefe.' Ramón truly meant it. Here was one man he respected and loved above all others. He was always startled by the size of the man he called the Leader. Castro towered over him, and smothered Ramón in his embrace. Then he held him at arm's length and studied his face.

'You look tired, comrade. You have been working hard.'

'With excellent results,' Ramón assured him.

'Come, sit down by the window,' Castro invited him. 'Tell me about it.'

He selected two Roig cigars from the box on the corner of his desk and gave one to Ramón. He held the burning taper for him; then lit his own before he settled into the straight-backed chair and leant forward with the cigar stuck out of the corner of his mouth, puffing smoke around it.

'So tell me what is the news from Moscow. You saw Yudenich?'

'I saw him, El Jefe, and the meeting went well . . . ' Ramón launched into his report. It was typical of them that there was no small-talk, no preamble to serious discussions. Neither of them had to manoeuvre for position or advantage. Ramón could speak with total honesty, without worrying about giving offence or trying to improve his own position. His position was unassailable. They were brothers of the blood and of the soul.

Of course, Castro could be changeable. His affections could shift. It had been that way with Che Guevara, another of the eighty-two heroes who came ashore from *Granma*. Che had fallen from grace after he had disagreed with Castro's economic policies and he had been driven out to become a wandering knight of the revolution, a Walt Whitman with grenade and AK 47. Yes, it had happened to Che, but it could never happen to Ramón.

'Yudenich has agreed to back our new export drive,'

Ramón told him, and Castro chuckled. It was a little joke between them. Castro was an inspired political genius with that rare gift of being able to communicate his passionate vision to the masses of the people. However, although he was an educated man, a qualified lawyer who had practised his profession before the revolution had swept him up, he was no economist.

His grasp of the whole arcane science of economics was weak. He could not bother himself with the balance of payments and employment and productivity. His vision was sweeping and transcended those petty aspects of the body politic. He liked the bold and the big. Ramón had conceived the entire plan to appeal to El Jefe. It was bold and it was direct.

The problem was that Cuba's island wealth was based on three staples: sugar and tobacco and coffee. These were insufficient to provide the hard currency to fuel Castro's ambitious plans for urban renewal and social welfare, let alone to provide full employment for an exploding population.

Since the revolution the population had doubled. According to the forecasts it would double again in the next ten years. Ramón's plan had been devised to counter these problems. It would provide hard cash, and go far to ending unemployment on the island.

The 'new export drive' was simply the export of men, of fighting men and women. They would be sent out in their tens of thousands as mercenaries to pursue the revolution at the ends of the earth. Perhaps as many as a hundred thousand, nearly ten per cent of the island's total workforce, could be exported. At one stroke they would end unemployment and swell the public coffer with the fees of a mercenary army.

Castro had liked the plan from the first day that Ramón had propounded it to him. It was the kind of economics that he could understand and applaud.

'Yudenich will recommend it to Brezhnev,' Ramón assured him, and Castro stroked his beard as though it were a shaggy black cat.

'If Yudenich recommends it, then we have no worries.' He leant forward with his hands on his knees. 'And we both know where you want them sent.'

'I have meetings this afternoon, at the Tanzanian embassy,' Ramón said.

There were seventeen African embassies in Havana, all of them representatives of socialist governments newly liberated from colonial oppression.

Tanzania under Julius Nyerere was amongst the most Marxist of them all. Already Nyerere had declared that any person who owned more than one acre of property was a 'capitalist and enemy of the people' and that they would be punished by having all their property confiscated by the State. The Tanzanians were active in their support for those others struggling for liberation in the colonial slave states in the rest of Africa. They provided shelter for the freedom fighters from Portuguese Angola and Mozambique, from that racist pariah South Africa, and from the medieval serfdom of the ancient tyrant Emperor Haile Selassie of Ethiopia. In all those countries there would be work for the army of Cuban mercenaries.

'I am meeting officers of the Ethiopian army who are dedicated to the cause of Marxist socialism, and who are prepared to risk their lives to break the yoke of the oppressor.'

'Yes,' Castro nodded. 'Ethiopia is ripe for us.'

Ramón considered the ash of his cigar; it was firm and crisp, almost two inches long.

'We both know that destiny has dictated that you play a rôle beyond the shores of this lovely island. Africa awaits you.'

Castro leant back with satisfaction and placed his huge powerful hands on his knees, as Ramón went on: 'The Africans have a natural distrust of Mother Russia. The Russians in the Kremlin are all Caucasians – the word originates in that country. It is an unfortunate fact that despite all their other virtues most Russians are racists. We cannot escape that fact. Many of the African leaders, especially the young ones, have studied in Russia. They have heard the name *obezyana*, "monkey", whispered as they pass in the corridors of Patrice Lumumba University. The Russians are white men and racists – deep in his heart the African does not trust them.'

Ramón drew evenly on his cigar, and they were silent awhile. Castro broke the silence.

'Go on.'

'On the other hand you, El Jefe, are a great-grandson of Africa . . .' but Castro shook his head.

'I am Spanish,' he contradicted.

Ramón smiled and went on. 'If you were to claim that your forefathers were sold on the slave block in Havana – who would doubt it?' he suggested delicately. 'And how vast might your influence become in Africa?'

Castro was silent, contemplating that vision, and Ramón went on softly: 'We must arrange a tour for you. A triumphant cavalcade beginning in Egypt and going southwards through twenty nations in which you could declare your concern, your commitment to the African people. If you could demonstrate your Africanism to two hundred million Africans, how great might your influence become.' Ramón leant forward and touched his wrist. 'No longer the president of a tiny beleaguered island. No longer the plaything of America, but a statesman of world influence and power.'

'My Golden Fox,' Castro said softly. 'No wonder that I love you.'

*   *   *

The Tanzanian embassy was temporarily accommodated in one of the Spanish colonial buildings in the old city.

There the Ethiopians were waiting for Ramón. There were three of them, all young officers in the imperial army of Emperor Haile Selassie. Only one of the three interested Ramón Machado. He had met Captain Getachew Abebe on several previous visits to Addis Ababa.

In Ethiopia ethnic lines cannot be distinguished. A thousand years of invasion and interbreeding between Caucasian tribes from across the Red Sea and those from the heartland of the African continent have resulted in a *mélange* that cannot be separated. Definitions such as Galla and Amhara refer to linguistic and cultural groupings rather than to blood-lines.

However, in Captain Getachew Abebe the pure African ancestral influence dominated. He was very dark-skinned with full lips and pock-marked skin. He was a product of the University of Addis Ababa. Joe Cicero had succeeded in infiltrating a strong cadre of American and British Marxists into the university in the rôles of professors and lecturers. As one of their star students, Getachew Abebe had been transformed into a dedicated Marxist Leninist.

Ramón had studied and courted him over the years until now he judged that he was the right man. At the very least, he was intelligent, hard and ruthless – and totally committed to the cause. Although he was only in his middle thirties, he was Ramón's provisional choice for the next leader of Ethiopia.

As they shook hands in the shuttered sitting-room at the back of the Tanzanian embassy, Ramón cautioned him with a glance and a small gesture towards the collection of African tribal masks that covered the walls. Any one of these could conceal a microphone.

The conversation that followed was trivial and inconclusive and lasted less than half an hour. As they shook hands, Ramón leant close to Abebe and whispered four words – a place and a time.

The two of them met again an hour later in the Bodeguita del Medio. It was the most famous bar in the old city. There was sawdust on the floor, and the tables and chairs were scarred and battered. The walls were pitted and scratched with the graffiti and signatures of the famous and the ordinary: from Hemingway to Spencer Tracy and Edward, Duke of Windsor, they had all drunk here. Their faded yellowed photographs were tacked into plain wooden frames that hung, fly-spotted and askew, upon the grubby walls. The long narrow room was thick with smoke. The cacophony of a portable radio blaring 'Bembé' folk music and the shouted tiddly conversation of the customers covered their own quiet discussion.

They sat in the furthest corner, with a *mojito* on the table in front of each of them. The condensation ran down the glasses and formed wet rings on the wood, but neither of them touched the drinks.

'Comrade, the time is almost ripe,' Ramón said, and Abebe nodded.

'The lion of Amhara has grown old and toothless; his son is a weak indulgent idiot. The nation groans under his tyranny and hungers in the worst famine and drought for a hundred years. The time is ripe.'

'There are two things we must avoid,' Ramón cautioned. 'The first is an armed revolution. If the army rises and executes the emperor immediately, you will be passed over. You are still too junior in rank. One of the generals will seize power.'

'So?' Abebe asked. 'What is the solution?'

'A creeping revolution,' Ramón told him, and it was the first time Abebe had ever heard the term used, though he would not admit it.

'I see,' he murmured, and Ramón went on to enlighten him.

'The Derg must call Haile Selassie to account and demand his abdication. As you say, the old lion has lost his teeth. He is isolated and out of touch. He must comply. You will use all your influence in the Derg, and I will exert all of mine.'

The Derg was the Ethiopian parliament, an assembly of all the tribal and army chiefs, the heads of government departments and the religious elders. The entire body had been infiltrated by the Marxist products of the University of Addis Ababa. Most of them were under the direct influence of Ramón's fourth directorate. All of them had accepted Getachew Abebe as their leader.

'Then we will put in place a provisional military-based junta and I will arrange to move in a considerable Cuban force. With this we will consolidate your position. When it is secure we will be ready for the next step.'

'What will that be?' Abebe asked.

'The emperor must be eliminated,' Ramón told him. 'To prevent a royalist backlash.'

'Execution?'

'Executions are too public and too emotional.' Ramón shook his head. 'He is a sick old man. He will simply die, and then . . .'

'And then an election?' Abebe interjected, and Ramón looked at him sharply. Only when he saw the cynical smile on the Ethiopian's thick purple lips did he smile thinly.

'You startled me, comrade,' Ramón admitted. 'For a moment I thought you were serious. The very last thing we want is an election before we have chosen the new president and the form of government. Nowhere have the masses ever been capable of governing themselves; even less have they been able to choose the persons who should govern them. It is our duty to make that choice for them. Later, much later, after you are declared president of a Marxist socialist government, we will hold a controlled and orderly election to confirm our choice.'

'I will need you in Addis, comrade,' Abebe told him. 'I will need your guidance and the strong right hand of Cuba to see the struggle through the dangerous and exciting days ahead.'

'I will be there, comrade,' Ramón promised him. 'Together, you and I will show the world how a revolution should be conducted.'

*　　　*　　　*

There were always risks, Ramón thought, but they had to be weighed carefully against the possible rewards. Then all possible precautions must be taken to minimize those risks.

It was time for Red Rose to be given access to the child,

just as she had been given time to make the initial bonding after Nicholas's birth. She had been allowed then to feel the child feeding at her breast, and to come to know every exquisite detail of the tiny body, but that had been three years ago, and the bond would be weakening. Ramón had used the threat video, the photographs and the reports from clinic and nursery school to reinforce her maternal instincts. However, three years was a long time, and he sensed that his control over Red Rose was weakening.

She must be rewarded for delivering the authentic Siemens radar report, and taught that co-operation was the only possible avenue open to her. On the other hand, she must not be stimulated to attempt some wild endeavour. She was a strong and wilful personality. She possessed a dangerous spirit, a core of strength that Ramón sensed would be difficult to shatter. She could be cowed, but could she ever be completely subjugated? He was not yet certain. She had to be played with extreme delicacy.

She must not be tempted to believe that this meeting with Nicholas was an indication of leniency. She must be taught that she was held in the trap by bands of steel.

Ramón had considered all the possible adverse reactions that the visit might generate. The most likely was that Red Rose might conceive some foolhardy idea of escaping with the child or planning a rescue.

He had taken precautions against this. The *hacienda* was remote. It was the property of a member of the Spanish Communist Party who was on a visit to New York with all his family. Ramón had moved a section of KGB staff in to cover the meeting.

There were twelve guards strategically placed in and around the *hacienda*. All of them were armed. The weapons had come in the diplomatic bag to Madrid, along with the two-way radios and the drugs that might be needed if Red Rose became dangerously hysterical on seeing her son.

He had chosen Spain for the meeting for a good reason. Red Rose must never be allowed to know where Nicholas was being kept. Ramón was fully aware of the power and influence of the Courtney family. If Red Rose went to her father, and they knew where the child was being held, then they might hire mercenaries or prevail upon the South African security services to mount some kind of kidnap attempt.

She must be led to believe that Nicholas was being held here in Spain.

It was quite logical, of course. Nicholas had been born here. She knew Ramón was Spanish. The last time she had seen the boy was in Spain. She had no reason to think that he had been transferred to another country, especially not across the Atlantic Ocean.

They had come in on the Aeroflot flight from Havana to London and transferred to Iberian Airways from Heathrow. After the meeting, Adra and the child would return the same way with two KGB bodyguards, while Ramón flew south to Ethiopia.

Ramón stood at the shuttered window in the bell-tower of the *hacienda*. Through the slats he looked down at the red-tiled roof that was mellowed and spotted with a century's accumulation of lichen and mosses. The building was of traditional design. Its thick white plastered walls were built around a central courtyard. In the centre of the lawned courtyard was a swimming-pool. An ornamental date palm stood at each corner of the pool. Below the long graceful fronds of each palm hung bunches of ripening yellow fruit.

From his position in the tower Ramón could survey not only the courtyard, but also the fields and vineyards surrounding the *hacienda*. However, he was concealed by the wooden shutters. There were vehicles concealed in the walled lanes that divided the vineyards. They were ready to react to his radio command and cut off any escape-route. Ramón had placed eight guards around the estate and at windows overlooking the courtyard. One of these was armed with a sniper's rifle, and another with a dart-gun, but he did not really believe there would be a call for them.

What with air fares and the personnel involved, the entire operation had been extremely costly. However, he had been able to use guards and vehicles from the Russian embassy in Madrid, and the owner of the *hacienda* had not required any payment. Ramón felt again that sour burn in his stomach when he thought of the parsimony of the finance section and the time that he had to spend filling in expense-sheets and justifying each item to one of the accountants.

How could an accountant ever understand the necessities and priorities of field-operations? How much more could be achieved without this continuous audit to which he was subjected? What price could they place on a nation brought into the fold of Soviet socialism?

The soft crackle of the radio interrupted these unpleasant speculations.

'Da? Yes?' He spoke Russian into the microphone.

'This is Number Three. The vehicle is visual.' That was the guard at the far end of the lane on the south side of the estate.

Ramón crossed to the southern window in the tower. He could see the pale yellow dust of the approaching car spreading over the vineyards.

'Very well.' He went back to his original position, and nodded to the female signals clerk from the embassy. She sat at the electronic console, with the directional microphone trained down into the courtyard. Every word or sound uttered in the courtyard would be recorded, and the meeting would be filmed on videotape.

There were, of course, voice-activated microphones and concealed cameras in every room of the *hacienda* that Red Rose might enter, including the toilets and bathroom. Ramón had requisitioned this equipment from the embassy in Madrid. The voice-prints and up-to-date photographs would be a nice little spinoff from the main object of the operation.

The car came into view as it turned into the gates of the estate. It was a blue Cortina with diplomatic plates, and it drew up at the front door of the *hacienda*.

Isabella Courtney was the first to alight, followed by the

female embassy guard who had escorted her from the airport. Isabella paused on the paved driveway and looked up at the shuttered windows of the tower, almost as though she sensed his gaze upon her. Ramón picked up his binoculars and studied her upturned face.

She had changed quite dramatically in the years since he had last seen her. There were few vestiges of the silly flighty girl remaining. She was a mature woman now. There was poise and determination in the way she carried herself. Her features seemed to have firmed. She was thin, too thin. There were dark smudges below her eyes. Even from this distance he could make out the first faint chiselling of life's hardship and care at the corners of her mouth, and a new hard line to her jaw. There was a tragic air about her, a sense of suffering that appealed to him. She was not as pretty, but considerably more attractive and interesting than he remembered her.

Quite unexpectedly the thought that this was Nicholas's mother occurred to him, and in the next instant he felt a stab of pity for her. The treachery of his emotion made him angry, and he crushed down the sense of pity. He could not remember ever having such a soft and enervating feeling towards a subject before, not even when they were in the interrogation-cells below the Lubyanka, or on the torture-racks in the Congo jungle. His anger turned upon himself, and then upon her. She was responsible for inducing that momentary weakness. He shielded his anger, the way he might cup his hands around a match-flame on a windy night.

Isabella thought she had glimpsed an obscure movement beyond the shuttered window in the high tower, but it must have been her imagination.

The woman who had escorted her touched her arm and said in only slightly accented English: 'Come. We will go in.'

Isabella lowered her gaze from the bell-tower to the carved teak front door just as it swung open. There was another female waiting for them. Isabella buttoned the jacket of her grey business-suit as though it might protect her like a coat of mail. She drew back her shoulders and went in through the doorway.

The interior was gloomy and cool. There were worn sombre-coloured rugs on the flagged floor and dark heavy furniture. The doors were black oak studded with iron. The windows were shuttered and barred. The house had a brooding and forbidding atmosphere that made her pause in the entrance-hall.

'This way!' The woman led her into a small antechamber off the main hall. Her escort followed her, carrying the single suitcase and the large parcel that Isabella had brought with her. She placed the suitcase and parcel on a heavy oak table then locked the door.

'Keys.' She held out her hand, and Isabella searched in her handbag and gave them to her.

Methodically the two women went through the contents of the suitcase. It was obvious that they had been trained for the task. They unfolded each item of clothing and examined the seams and linings. They opened each jar of cosmetics and probed the creams and ointments they contained with a knitting-needle. They palpated every tube and removed the batteries from the electric shaver which Isabella used on her under-arm hair. They tested the heels on her spare pair of shoes and the lining of the case. Then they turned their attention to the wrapped parcel. It contained the gift that she had brought for Nicholas. One of them reached for her handbag, and Isabella handed it over. They went through it with as much care.

'Please to remove clothes.' Isabella shrugged and began to undress. They took each item as she removed it and examined it minutely. They removed the shoulder-pads from her jacket and examined the lining of her bra.

When she was entirely naked one of the women ordered: 'Lift the arms.'

She obeyed, and then to her horror one of the women slipped a surgical rubber glove on to her right hand and dipped two fingers into a pot of Vaseline.

'Turn around,' she ordered.

'No.' Isabella shook her head.

'Do you want to see the boy?' the woman asked heavily, holding up her two gloved fingers glistening with Vaseline. 'Turn around.'

Isabella shivered and felt the goose-pimples rise on her arms.

'Please,' she whispered. 'I give you my word. I'm not hiding anything. This isn't necessary.'

'Turn around.' The woman's voice did not change. Slowly Isabella turned her back.

'Bend over,' the woman said. 'Put your hands on the table.'

She leant forward and gripped the edge of the table hard.

'Move your feet apart.'

Isabella realized that she was being deliberately humiliated. She knew that it was all part of the process. She tried to close her mind to it, but she gasped as she felt the woman's fingers slide into her and she started to pull away.

'Stay still.'

She bit down on her lip, and closed her eyes. The examination was leisurely and thorough.

'All right.' The woman stepped back. 'Get dressed.'

Isabella found tears upon her cheeks. She took a Kleenex from the pocket of her jacket and wiped them away. They were tears of fury.

'Wait here.' The woman stripped the glove from her hand and threw it into the wastepaper-bin.

The two of them left the room and locked the door.

Isabella dressed quickly and sat down on the bench. Her hands were shaking. She clenched them into fists and thrust them into the pockets of her jacket.

They kept her waiting for almost an hour.

$$\star \qquad \star \qquad \star$$

Ramón had watched the search and the physical examination on the small screen of the remote video-camera.

265

The camera had been carefully positioned to give him a full view of Isabella's face during the entire process. What he could see of her expression gave him cause for disquiet. He had hoped, but not truly expected, to cow her completely. Instead he saw that cold fury in her eyes, the stubborn reckless line of her clenched jaw. He studied her carefully, leaning closer to the screen. Was that fury murderous or suicidal? He could not be certain.

At that moment Isabella glanced up and looked directly at the lens of the concealed camera. She recognized the camera for what it was, and he saw her take control of herself. A veil fell over those glittering dark blue eyes, and her expression smoothed into blank neutrality.

Ramón straightened up. He sighed. As he had suspected all along, this subject could not be pushed beyond a certain point. He sensed that the point was very close now. She was on the very edge of rebellion. It called for a change of tactics. Very well; he was prepared for that. A change was often good procedure; it confused and unsettled the subject. Ramón was always flexible and versatile.

He turned away from the screen and called softly: 'Bring the child.'

Adra came through from the next room, leading Nicholas by the hand.

Ramón studied him as carefully as he had the boy's mother. Adra had washed his hair for him that morning. His curls, shiny and springing, tumbled on to his forehead. She had dressed him in a plain short-sleeved shirt and short cotton trousers. His limbs were slim and smoothly tanned, his lips were a sensitive pink and his brows were darkly curved over his huge solemn eyes. He would break any mother's heart.

'Do you remember what I told you, Nicholas?'

'Sí, Padre.'

'You will meet a very kind lady. She likes you very much. She has a present for you. You will be nice to her and you will call her "Mamma".'

'Is she going to take me away from Adra?'

'No, Nicholas. She has come only to talk to you for a while and give you a present. Then she will go away. Will you be nice to her? If you are, Adra will let you watch a Woody Woodpecker video this evening. Would you like that?'

'Yes, Padre.' Nicholas smiled happily at the promise.

'Off you go now.'

Ramón turned back to the shuttered window and looked through the slats. In the courtyard below one of the KGB women was leading Isabella out into the sunlight. She pointed to the bench beside the swimming-pool, and her voice was amplified through the directional microphone that the signals clerk trained on her.

'Please to wait here. The child will come to you.'

The woman turned away, and Isabella went to the bench. She sat down, took a pair of sunglasses from her handbag and placed them over her eyes. From behind the dark lenses she studied her surroundings covertly.

Ramón depressed the transmit button on his two-way radio. 'All stations, this is Number One. Full alert. The contact is in progress.'

Apart from the electronic surveillance equipment, Isabella now had a 7.62-millimetre Dragunov sniper's rifle and a dart-gun aimed at her. The dart-gun was loaded with Tentanyl and would immobilize a human victim within two minutes. Ramón had two 10-milligram phials of Nalorphine on hand as an antidote. Even as a last resort, he did not want to risk losing such a potentially valuable operative as Red Rose.

Abruptly Isabella leapt to her feet and stared across the courtyard. Ramón glanced down. Directly below the tower Adra and Nicholas had appeared. He could see the tops of their heads.

With a supreme effort Isabella prevented herself from rushing across the lawn and sweeping her son into her arms. She knew intuitively that such an action on her part would confuse and distress the child. He was at the age when any boy hated to be treated like a baby. Isabella had studied her copy of Dr Spock until it was tired and dog-eared.

Slowly she removed her sunglasses and remained still. Nicholas hung on to Adra's hand and studied his mother with great interest.

Isabella had thought she was prepared for his physical appearance. The last photograph she had of him was only two months old, but it was nothing like the reality. It could not capture his colouring, nor the texture of his skin, nor those curls – and those eyes. Oh, those eyes!

'Oh God,' she whispered. 'He's the loveliest child. There could never be another like this. Please, God, help him to like me.'

Adra tugged gently at Nicholas's hand, urging him forward, and they skirted the swimming-pool and stopped in front of her.

'Buenos días, Señorita Bella,' Adra said softly in Spanish. 'Nicholas likes to swim. There is a costume for both you and Nicholas if you want to swim with him. They are in the *cabaña*.' She pointed to the shuttered door of the bath-house. 'You may change in there.'

Then she looked down at Nicholas. 'Greet the lady, your mother,' she instructed him gently, and released his hand. She turned and hurried from the courtyard leaving them alone together.

Nicholas had not smiled or taken his eyes from Isabella's face. Now he stepped forward dutifully and held out his right hand.

'Good day, Mamma, my name is Nicholas Machado and I am pleased to meet you.'

Isabella wanted to drop on her knees and hug him with all her strength. The word 'Mamma' had stabbed through her heart like a bayonet. Instead she took his hand and shook it carefully.

'You are a fine young man, Nicholas. I hear that you are doing very well at nursery school.'

'Yes,' Nicholas agreed. 'And next year I am to join the young pioneers.'

'That will be nice for you,' Isabella nodded. 'Who are the young pioneers, Nicholas?'

'Everybody knows.' He was obviously amused by her ignorance. 'They are the sons and daughters of the revolution.'

'That's wonderful,' Isabella went on hastily. 'I have brought a present for you.'

'Thank you, Mamma.' Uncontrollably Nicholas's eyes slid towards the package.

Isabella sat on the bench and handed him the gift, and Nicholas squatted in front of her and unwrapped it carefully. Then he was silent.

'Do you like it?' Isabella asked nervously.

'It's a soccer ball,' Nicholas pronounced.

'Yes. Do you like it?'

'It's the best gift anybody has ever given me,' he said.

He looked up at her, and she saw in his eyes that despite his formal stilted speech he truly meant it. What a reserved self-possessed little old man he is, she thought. What terrible events and nightmares have made him like this?

'I have never played soccer,' Isabella told him. 'Will you teach me?'

'You're a girl.' Nicholas looked doubtful.

'Still, I'd like to try.'

'All right.' He stood up with the ball under one arm. 'But you'll have to take your shoes off.'

Within minutes all the child's reserves evaporated. He shrieked with excitement as he dribbled and darted after the ball. He was nimble as a field-mouse, and Isabella raced after him, laughing with him, obeying his instructions and allowing him to score five goals between the legs of the bench.

When at last they both collapsed on the lawn, Nicholas informed her between gasps: 'You are quite good – for a girl.'

They changed into swimming-costumes, and Nicholas gave her an exhibition of his prowess. First he swam a length dogpaddle, and her praises were so fulsome that he declared: 'I can do a width underwater. Watch me.' He almost made it across, and surfaced just short of the bar, blowing and huffing and red-faced.

Sitting waist-deep on the shallow-end steps, Isabella felt a moment of physical revulsion as she remembered the last time she had seen her son immersed, but she managed to smile and sound enthusiastic.

'Oh, well done, Nicholas.'

He came to her, still puffing for breath, and without warning climbed into her lap.

'You are pretty,' he said. 'I like you.'

Carefully, as though he might shatter like a precious crystal, she wrapped her arms around him and held him. Through the cool water his body was warm and slippery and she could feel her heart twist and tear within her.

'Nicholas,' she mumbled. 'Oh, my baby. How I love you. How I miss you.'

The afternoon passed like a flash of sheet-lightning in a summer sky and then Adra came to fetch him. 'It is time for Nicholas's dinner. Do you wish to eat with him, señorita?'

They ate *al fresco*, at a table that Adra set for them in the courtyard. They shared a baked *besugo*, a sea-bream from the Atlantic, and salads. There was a glass of fresh orange juice for Nicholas and a sherry for her. Isabella shredded the flesh of the bream to remove any bones, but Nicholas fed himself.

As Nicholas was finishing his ice-cream, Isabella's vision began to swim. She heard a rushing in her ears and Nicholas's face seemed to expand and blur.

Adra caught her before she slipped from the chair, and Ramón stepped into the courtyard from the doorway behind her. The two KGB women followed him.

'You have been a good boy, Nicholas,' Ramón said. 'Now, go off to bed with Adra.'

'What is wrong with the nice lady?'

'There is nothing wrong,' Ramón told him. 'She is just very sleepy. You are sleepy, too, Nicholas.'

'Yes, Padre.' At the suggestion he yawned and rubbed his eyes with the backs of his fists. Adra led him away, and Ramón nodded at the waiting women.

'Take her to the room.'

While they lifted Isabella out of the chair, Ramón picked up the empty sherry-glass from the dinner-table and wiped out the last traces of the drug with his handkerchief.

$$\star \qquad \star \qquad \star$$

Isabella woke in a strange bedroom. She felt rested and at peace. The early sun streamed in through the slats of the shuttered window. She blinked drowsily and pulled the single sheet up around her naked shoulders. She wondered without any real urgency where she was, but her memory was fuzzy.

She was suddenly aware that she was totally nude under the sheet. She lifted her head. Her clothing was neatly folded on the chair beside the open bathroom door. Her suitcase was on the luggage-rack.

Then out of the corner of her eye she caught a movement and she stiffened and came fully awake. There was a man in the bedroom with her. She opened her mouth to scream, but he signalled her urgently to silence.

'Ram—' she started to say his name, but with two rapid paces he reached the bedside and laid his open hand on her lips to keep her from speaking.

She stared at him, stunned and completely bemused. Ramón! Joy rose in her like a spring tide.

He left her and crossed quickly to the nearest wall of the bedroom. On it hung a dark oil painting in the style of Goya. Ramón swivelled the painting to one side to reveal a hidden microphone the size of a silver dollar attached to the wall.

Once again, he made a gesture to silence her and came back. He lifted the shade off the lamp on the bedside table, and showed her the second microphone taped to the stand below the bulb.

Then he leant so close to her that his warm breath fanned her cheek.

'Come.' He touched her bare shoulder through the sheet. It had been so long that despite her happiness she felt strange and shy in his presence.

'I will explain – come.' His eyes were so full of pain and suffering that she felt her joy waver.

He took her hand that held the sheet to her chin and drew her, suddenly unresisting, from the bed. Still holding her hand, he led her, stark naked, to the bathroom. She was unaware of her nudity, and she staggered a little from the after-effects of the drug.

In the bathroom Ramón flushed the toilet, opened the taps in the handbasin and in the bath, and switched on the shower in the glass-walled cabinet.

Then he came back to her. She drew away from him, afraid to touch him. Her naked back was pressed to the cold tiles.

'What is happening to us? Are you one of them, Ramón? I am so confused. Please tell me what is happening.'

His marvellous features contorted with agony. 'I am like you. I have to co-operate, for Nicky's sake. I can't explain now – forces greater than we are. We have been caught up, all three of us. Oh, my darling, how I have wanted to hold you and explain it all to you, but I have so little time.'

'Ramón, tell me you still love me,' she whispered timidly.

'Yes, my darling. More than I ever did. I know what hell you must have lived through. I have shared it with you, every moment of it. I know what you must have thought of me. One day you will understand that everything I have done has been for Nicky and for you.'

She wanted to believe him, desperately, wildly she wanted it to be true.

'Soon,' he whispered, taking her face between his cupped hands. 'Soon we'll be together, just the three of us – you and Nicky and me. You must trust me.'

'Ramón!' It came out as a choking sob, and she wound

both arms around his neck and clung to him with all her strength. Against all reason or logic she believed him completely.

'We have only a few minutes together. We dare not risk more. It is so dangerous. You can never know what terrible danger Nicky is in.'

'And you also,' her voice quavered.

'My life does not matter. It's Nicky . . .'

'Both of you,' she denied it. 'You are both so precious.'

'Promise me that you will do nothing to harm Nicky.' He kissed her mouth. 'Please do whatever they say. It will not be for much longer. I will get us free of this thing, if you will help me. But you must trust me.'

'Oh, my love. Oh, my darling. I knew deep down. I knew there must be a reason. Of course, I trust you, my heart.'

'Be strong for all of us.'

'I swear it to you,' she nodded violently, her face smeared with tears. 'Oh God, how I love you. I have suppressed it so long.'

'I know, my darling. I know.'

'Please, please, make love to me, Ramón. I've been without you for so long. I have been withering away. Make love to me before you have to go.'

He took her quickly, and yet it crashed over her like the winds of a hurricane and left her shattered.

When he was gone, breaking away with a last long lingering kiss, her legs could no longer support her. She sank slowly down the tiled wall, and sat on the floor with her legs sprawled jointlessly under her. The taps roared and billows of steam filled the room. She didn't understand it all. She didn't have to and she didn't care any more. All that mattered was Nicky and Ramón.

'Oh, thank God,' she whispered. 'It wasn't true. None of the horrors was true. Ramón loves me still. We will be all right, the three of us. We'll come through this together. Somehow. Sometime.'

She dragged herself to her feet. 'Now I must pull myself

273

together. They mustn't suspect. . . .' She staggered to the shower.

She was still in bra and panties when, without a knock, the door opened and the large heavy-featured woman who had escorted her from the airport and had conducted that dreadful body-search entered the room. She looked at Isabella's body in a way that made Isabella's flesh crawl and she stepped hurriedly into the skirt of her grey suit.

'What do you want?'

'You leave in twenty minutes to airport.'

'Where is Nicky? Where is my son?'

'Child has gone.'

'I want to see him, please.'

'Is not possible. Child has gone.'

Isabella felt the ebullient mood of hope, which her brief interlude with Ramón had raised, begin to evaporate.

The nightmare begins again, she thought, and tried to steel herself against the creeping sense of despair.

'I must trust Ramón. I must be strong.'

The woman sat beside Isabella in the back seat of the Cortina on the drive back to the airport. It was a hot morning, and the car was not air-conditioned. The woman's body odour was rank as a man's. Isabella felt she was going to be ill, and she opened the side-window and let the wind blow in her face.

The driver of the Cortina stopped outside the international departures terminal and, while he went to unlock the boot and lift out Isabella's suitcase, the woman spoke for the first time since leaving the *hacienda*.

'Is for you,' she said, and handed over a sealed unaddressed envelope.

Isabella opened her handbag and secreted the envelope. The woman was staring straight ahead through the windscreen. She offered no word of farewell. Isabella stepped out of the Cortina and picked up her suitcase. The driver slammed the door and drove away.

Standing on the pavement, in the midst of the throng of package-tour travellers, Isabella felt alone, more alone and

274

frightened than she had been before she had seen Nicky and Ramón again.

'I must trust him,' she repeated to herself as a litany of faith, and went to the Iberian check-in desk.

In the first-class lounge, she went to the women's washroom and locked herself in one of the cubicles. She sat on the closed lid of the toilet and tore open the envelope.

Red Rose,
You will ascertain precisely what stage the development of a nuclear explosive device by Armscor and the nuclear research institute at Pelindaba has reached. You will report on the test site that has been selected and the date for the preliminary testing of the device.

On receipt of this data a further meeting with your son will be arranged. The duration of this meeting will depend on the depth and scope of information that you deliver.

There was, as usual, no signature, and the message was typed on a sheet of plain paper. She stared at it sightlessly.

'Deeper and deeper,' she whispered. 'First the radar report.' That had not seemed so bad. Radar was a defensive weapon – but this? An atomic bomb? Would there ever be an end to it?

She shook her head. 'I can't – I'll tell them, I can't.'

Her father had never even hinted at any interest in the Pelindaba Institute. She had never seen any file or even a single letter that addressed the subject of a nuclear explosive device. She had read in the press that the research at Pelindaba was directed towards refinement and processing of the country's huge uranium production, and towards the development of a reactor for industrial and urban electrical power. The prime minister had given repeated assurances that South Africa was not developing the bomb.

Despite that, her instructions were not to ascertain if production were in progress. That was taken as a fact. She had been ordered to find out where and when the first device would be tested.

She began to shred the message between nervous fingers. 'I can't,' she whispered. She stood up and raised the

275

toilet-seat. She dropped each tiny scrap of paper into the bowl separately, and then flushed them away.

'I'll tell them I can't.' But already her mind was busy.

I'll have to work on Pater, she thought, and immediately began to plan it.

★　　　★　　　★

Isabella had been out of the country on her visit to Spain for only five days. Nevertheless, Nana was angry, and sniffed at her weak excuse for leaving in the middle of her election campaign. The Friday before polling day, the prime minister, John Vorster, addressed a meeting in the Sea Point town hall in support of the National Party candidate.

It had taken all Centaine Courtney-Malcomess's wiles and wit to get him to cancel two other important engagements to make the speech. The party machine realized that Sea Point was a safe opposition seat and that they were simply going through the motions. They were reluctant to wheel out their big gun; but Centaine prevailed, as she usually did.

With the promise of hearing the prime minister speak, the town hall was jam-packed. The meeting began with the usual heckling from the body of the hall, but it was fairly good-natured.

Isabella spoke first. She kept it short, ten minutes. It was her best speech of the entire campaign. She had gathered valuable experience and confidence over the preceding weeks, and her jaunt to Spain seemed to have revitalized her. Both Nana and Shasa had gone over the text with her, and she had rehearsed her delivery in front of them. These two shrewd old political warhorses had given her valuable tips and suggestions.

Standing on the platform in front of the crowded hall, Isabella cut a slim determined figure, and the heart of the audience seemed to go out to her youth and loveliness. They gave her a standing ovation at the end, while John

276

Vorster stood beside her, red-faced and benign, nodding and clapping his approval.

The following Wednesday evening Shasa and Nana were standing on either side of Isabella, wearing huge party rosettes and straw boaters with the party colours, when the results of the polling were read out.

There were no upsets. The Progressive Party regained the seat, but Isabella had cut their majority to a mere twelve hundred votes. Her supporters chaired her shoulder-high from the hall as though she were the victor and not the vanquished.

A week later John Vorster invited her to a meeting in his office in the parliament building. Isabella knew the building intimately. When her father had been a cabinet minister in Hendrik Verwoerd's government, his office had been on the same floor only a few doors down the corridor from the prime minister's office.

During his tenure Shasa had given her the run of his office, and she had used it as a club whenever she was in central Cape Town. It brought back so many memories to walk once again down the wide corridor. As a teenager she had not in any way appreciated the aura of history with which the magnificent old building was imbued.

Now, with political aspirations thrust upon her against her will, she was entranced by portraits of great men, both good and evil, which decorated the panelled walls.

The prime minister kept her waiting only a few minutes. When she went through into his office he came round his desk to greet her.

'It's so good of you to want to see me, Oom John,' Isabella said in flawless Afrikaans. It was naughty of her to use such familiar address without being invited to do so. However, the term 'Oom', or 'Uncle', was one of great respect and the gamble paid off. Vorster's blue eyes twinkled in acknowledgement of her nerve.

'I wanted to congratulate you on your showing at Sea

277

Point, Bella,' he replied, and she felt a thrill of acceptance. Use of her pet name was an unusual accolade.

'I'm having a coffee-break.' Vorster waved at the silver and porcelain service on a side-table. 'Will you pour a cup for both of us?

'Now, young lady,' he addressed her sternly over the rim of his cup. 'What are you going to do with yourself? Since you aren't going to be an MP.'

'Well, Oom John, I am working for my father—'

'Of course, I know that,' he interrupted her. 'But we can't let all that fresh young political talent go begging. Have you considered a seat in the Senate?'

'The Senate?' Isabella gulped, and the coffee scalded her tongue. 'No, Prime Minister, I haven't. Nobody ever suggested—'

'Well, somebody is suggesting it now. Old Kleinhans is retiring next month. I have to nominate somebody to take his seat. It will do until we can find a safe seat in the lower house for you.'

The Senate was the upper of the two legislative houses of the Republic of South Africa. Its duties were similar to those of the House of Lords, and it had the power to hold up dubious legislation and refer it back to the lower house. It had been considerably expanded back in the 1950s when the then prime minister, Malan, had set out to disfranchise those coloured voters who had the vote. He had packed the upper house with senators nominated by himself in order to force through the distasteful Act that stripped the coloureds of their vote. Some of the seats in the upper house were still in the prime minister's gift, and Vorster was offering her one of these.

Isabella set down her coffee-cup and stared speechlessly at him. Her mind was racing to keep up with this new development.

'Will you accept the nomination?' Vorster asked.

It was a marvellous short-cut, one that none of them – not Shasa nor even Nana – had dreamt of.

Hendrik Verwoerd himself had started his political

278

career in the Senate. At twenty-eight years of age, she would almost certainly be the youngest, brightest and certainly the most attractive senator in the upper house.

Appointments to various commissions and house committees would certainly follow her nomination. If she was only half as good as she knew she was, the National Party would turn her into their prime feminist political figure. Her entry to the innermost circles of power, to the innermost state secrets would come very swiftly.

'You do me great honour, Prime Minister.' Her voice was a whisper.

'I know that you will serve your country with even greater honour.' Vorster held out his hand. 'Congratulations, Senator.'

As Isabella took his hand, she felt an icy finger of guilt trace down her spine, the chill of treason and treachery. She forced it back. The reaction followed swiftly – with a great surge of her spirits she realized that Red Rose was now invaluable to her masters. Soon she could set her own terms and demand her own rewards from them.

Nicky and Ramón, she thought. Ramón and Nicky – it will be soon now. Much sooner than we could ever have believed. We will be together again.

★   ★   ★

Isabella had come to love the austere grandeur of the Karoo.

Shasa had purchased the vast sheep-ranch while she was still a child. On her first visit she had hated the grim stony kopjes and forbidding plains that spread aimlessly to a distant horizon blurred by sun and dust until the juncture of earth and a milky luminous sky was obscured. Then as a teenager she had read Eve Palmer's *The Plains of Camdeboo* and she had begun to understand just what a wondrous world the Karoo really was.

With her father, she had hunted for fossils in the up-thrust sedimentary beds that had been a vast antediluvian swamp in the age of the great reptiles, and she had stood amazed and filled with awe by their petrified bones and fangs.

The homestead was named Dragon's Fountain in memory of those terrible creatures, and for the spring of clear sweet water that gushed ceaselessly from a grotto at the base of one of the table-topped mountains. The sheer wall of red rock towered above the sprawling mansion with its green lawns and lush gardens nurtured by the spring. Vultures and eagles nested in the crags, and their droppings whitewashed the weathered precipice.

The sheep-ranch spread over sixty thousand acres of this fascinating wilderness. Mingled with the flocks of merino sheep were vast herds of springbok. These graceful little antelope danced upon the plains like puffs of wind-driven dust. Their delicate bodies were pale cinnamon slashed with bars of chocolate and blazing white. Their lovely patterned heads and lyre-shaped horns made them Isabella's favourite amongst all the multitudinous life-forms that inhabited the plains of Camdeboo. Both sheep and antelope flourished on the low wiry desert bush, and the diet flavoured their flesh with the taste of sage and wild herbs.

Each winter, at the commencement of the hunting season, Shasa invited a party to Dragon's Fountain to join the annual springbok cull. Anything over four inches of rainfall in the Karoo was considered a good year, and in such a season the springbok ewes lambed twice. The resulting explosion of the herds had to be controlled. In a year such as this it is necessary to cull a thousand head of springbok to protect the fragile desert growth from their ravages.

Garry brought a party of his friends and their families down from Johannesburg. The landing-strip at Dragon's Fountain had been extended and macadamized to accommodate the new Lear jet. Shasa brought the rest of the guests up from Cape Town in the twin-engined Queen Air.

Isabella had not been able to leave Cape Town until the

Senate went into recess. Then she drove up with Nana in the silver-grey Porsche that her father had given her on her twenty-ninth birthday to replace the aged Mini. She enjoyed having Nana as a passenger. The old lady's stories whiled away the hours of the long drive. Unlike Shasa, Nana did not watch the speedometer. At one stage on the arrow-straight stretch of road between Beaufort West and the ranch, Isabella had wound the Porsche up to almost 160 miles per hour without a word of protest from Nana.

It was mid-afternoon when they pulled into the kitchen yard at Dragon's Fountain. Servants and dogs came pouring from the kitchen and outbuildings to give them a riotous welcome. When at last Isabella escaped to her own room, Nanny was already running her bath and unpacking her three suitcases.

'God, I'm bushed, Nanny. I'm going to sleep for a week.'

'Thou shall not take the name of the Lord thy God in vain,' Nanny warned her darkly.

'Don't come that with me, Nanny. You're a Muslim.'

'We got the same rules,' Nanny sniffed haughtily.

'Where are all the men?' Isabella flopped on to the bed.

'Out hunting, of course.'

'Are there any nice ones, Nanny?'

'Yes, but they are all married. You shoulda brought your own, Miss Bella.' Nanny paused. 'Come to think of it, there is a new one that got no wife.' Then she shook her head. 'You won't like him.'

'Why not?'

'He got no hair on his head,' Nanny cackled merrily. 'What you'd call an eggshell blond.'

Nanny was correct. He didn't tickle Isabella's fancy, although he had a kind and rather sensitive face and beautiful Jewish sloe eyes. His bald head was a damper. It was tanned and freckled like a plover's egg with a thick fringe of dark curls around the back in the style of Friar Tuck. He was talking to Garry on the wide front stoep.

Isabella felt good when she came down for pre-dinner cocktails. She had managed an hour's sleep after the hot bath. She was wearing a deceptively simple blue silk sheath with a risqué *décolletage* whose cunning cut and drape caught the eye of every man present, married or not.

She went to Garry immediately. She hadn't seen him for months. 'My big teddy bear.' She hugged him.

With his arm still around her waist, Garry introduced them. 'Bella, this is Professor Aaron Friedman. Aaron, this is my baby sister, Senator Doctor Isabella Courtney.'

'Oh, come on, Garry!' she protested modestly at his use of all her titles, and took Aaron Friedman's hand. It was fine-boned but strong, the hand of a pianist or a surgeon.

'Aaron is on a sabbatical from the University of Jerusalem.'

'Oh, I love Jerusalem,' Isabella told him politely. 'In fact, I love Israel. It's such an exciting vibrant country, so steeped in history and religion.'

She gave him another minute of her attention, then she moved down the veranda to find her father. He had three of the prettiest wives grouped around him, giggling at his wit.

'My beautiful daddy.' She kissed him, and then took her place beside him with her arm linked through his in a proprietorial fashion. She knew just how good they looked together. As usual the two of them swiftly became the centre of the elegant little gathering.

They sipped their champagne and laughed and chatted and flirted, while a flamboyant Karoo sunset lit the gaunt kopjes with a ruddy glow and set the clouds on fire.

One of the men mentioned casually: 'I was listening to the radio while I dressed. It seems that the Ethiopians have forced Haile Selassie to abdicate.'

'Damned fuzzy-wuzzies, bunch of bandits and Shufta,' said another. 'I was there with the Sixth Division during the war – we went the hard way, on foot, while Shasa was swanning around in his Hurricane.'

Shasa touched the black eye-patch. 'We called it Abyssinia then. We went to keep an eye on them, and dashed if I didn't leave one of mine behind.'

282

They laughed, and somebody else remarked: 'Haile Selassie was a marvellous old fellow really. Wonder what will happen now.'

'The same as the rest of black Africa – chaos and confusion and communism, murder and mayhem and Marxism.'

There was a general murmur of agreement, and they dismissed the subject and turned their attention to the splendour of the final moments of the sunset.

The night fell with the suddenness of a stage curtain, and immediately the evening chill struck through their light clothing. With perfect timing, the dinner-gong chimed. Centaine rose from her seat at the end of the veranda to lead the entire party through the french windows into the long dining-room, where candlelight glinted on silver and crystal, and polished walnut glowed with a precious antique lustre.

Isabella found her place-card and checked those on each side of her: Garry and Aaron Friedman.

Damn, she thought. She had noticed him mooning after her ever since Garry had introduced them. It was natural that Nana would pair her with the only single male in the company.

Aaron hurried across to hold her chair for her. As he seated her, she set herself the task of being pleasant. She soon discovered that he was a delightful conversationalist with a droll sense of humour that amused her. She no longer noticed his bald head.

Garry had been occupied with his dinner partner but now he turned and leant forward to speak to Aaron across Isabella.

'By the way, Aaron, if you really have got to be back at Pelindaba by Monday afternoon, I'll fly you up in the Lear.'

As the significance of the casual mention of that name struck her, Isabella felt her cheeks chill. The nuclear research institute was based at Pelindaba.

'Are you all right, Bella?' Garry was watching her with concern.

'Of course I am.'

'For a moment you looked quite strange.'

'Nonsense, Garry. You are imagining things.' But she was thinking furiously as Garry and Aaron made their arrangements. By the time Garry turned his attention back to his own partner, she had gathered herself.

'I have neglected to ask you what discipline you teach, Professor.'

'Won't you call me Aaron, Doctor?'

She smiled. 'Only if you call me Isabella, Professor.'

'I am a physicist, Isabella, a nuclear physicist. Very boring, I'm afraid.'

'That's not fair on yourself, Aaron.' She touched his wrist lightly. 'It's the science of the future, in war and in peace.'

Still touching him, she turned one shoulder and leant towards him so that the sheer silk of her *décolletage* fell away from her bosom. She wore no bra. When his eyes changed their direction of gaze and opened very wide, she knew that he was staring at her nipple. She gave him two seconds more before she straightened up, ending the show, and she lifted her fingers from his wrist.

In those two seconds Aaron Friedman had undergone a profound change. He was now a man bewitched.

'Where is your wife, Aaron?' she asked.

'My wife and I were divorced almost five years ago.'

'Oh, I'm so sorry.' She lowered her voice to a husky murmur and let her sympathy show in her eyes, staring deeply into his.

Later that evening, while preparing for bed, Isabella sat in front of her dressing-table and regarded herself in the mirror as she creamed away the last traces of her make-up.

'Israel, Pelindaba, nuclear physics . . .' she murmured. 'It just has to add up to one big bang.'

Not a month had passed during the past two years in which she had not been able to send some intelligence to her masters. Most of it was routine reports and minutes of meetings. But this could at last hasten her next meeting with Nicholas.

During dinner Aaron had professed a great love of horses and riding – but, then, he would probably have declared a fascination with polar exploration and munching razorblades if he thought that was what she wanted to hear. She would soon see how well he sat a horse. They had a date to ride out at dawn tomorrow morning.

'How far will you go?' Isabella asked herself in the mirror. She thought about it carefully before she answered. 'Well, he is terribly amusing and quite sweet, and they do say that men with bald heads have a tremendous libido.' She pulled a face at herself in the mirror. 'You are a terrible little tart, aren't you? A regular Mata Hari.'

When she was fourteen years old her brother Sean had taught her a smutty rhyme about Mata Hari. How did it go? She cast her mind back.

'She learnt the location
Of a very secret station
On the point of emission
In the twenty-third position.'

When she had asked him what 'emission' meant, Sean had sniggered dirtily and darkly. She had been obliged to look it up in the dictionary, which didn't do much to clarify the issue. She smiled at her unintended pun.

'Would you actually go that far?' she demanded of herself and grinned again. 'Well, perhaps not as far as the twenty-third. The second or third position should do the trick quite nicely.' Beneath the flippancy she knew she would do anything for Nicky and Ramón.

Dawn was still only a pale promise in the east when she went down to the stables the following morning, but already Aaron was waiting for her. He wore jodhpurs and riding-boots. That he had his own riding-gear was encouraging.

The syce was already walking the saddled horses. The animals at Dragon's Fountain were seldom exercised sufficiently, and there were always fields full of lucerne and oats irrigated from the spring. They were usually full of pep. However, she had ordered the quietest old gelding in the stables for Aaron. She hoped he could manage him, and she watched uneasily as he approached his mount. She need not have worried. Aaron went up into the saddle, and she saw immediately that he had a good solid seat and gentle hands.

They skirted the kopje as the sun burst over the horizon. It was cool enough to make her grateful for the waxed cotton Barbour hacking-jacket she wore. The still air had that peculiar desert lambency that made her believe that she could see to the very ends of the earth.

The vultures left their shaggy nests in the rock-cliff above them and soared on wide graceful wings overhead. Out on the plain the springbok herds were still nervous and jittery from the previous day's hunting. In their alarm they erected the snowy plumes of mane from the pouches of skin along their spines and flashed them in the bright morning sunlight as they blew away, lightly as smoke, into the purple blossoming sage. The sweet clean air seemed to fizz like champagne in her head, and she felt gay and reckless.

Once the horses had warmed up, Isabella urged her mare into a gallop, and led them on a wildly exhilarating charge along the old dry riverbed and down to the dam. Huge flocks of Egyptian geese rose honking from the muddy brown water as they reined up on the bank.

Isabella slid from the saddle and dabbed in theatrical distress at her eye with the end of her silk scarf. Aaron tumbled from the saddle with gratifying concern.

'Are you all right, Isabella?'

'I seem to have something in my eye.'

'May I look?'

She turned her face up to him. He cupped it gently in his hands and stared into her eye.

'I don't see anything.'

She blinked her long dark lashes, and the early sunlight

splintered into myriad pinpoints of pure sapphire in the depths of her iris.

'Are you sure?' she asked. His breath was sweet, and his body odour was clean and manly. She stared back into his eyes. They were dark and shining as burnt wild honey.

He touched her lower lid, gently massaging the eyeball through the skin.

'How does that feel?' he asked, and she blinked again.

'You have a magic touch. That's much better, thank you.' And she kissed him with wet and open lips.

Aaron shuddered with shock, then recovered swiftly and seized her round the waist. She pressed her hips forward and let him explore the inside of her mouth with his tongue for a few seconds. Then the moment she felt the flare of his loins she broke away.

'I'll race you back to the stables.' She laughed her husky sexy laugh at him and went up into the saddle with a lithe bound. The gelding was no match for her chestnut mare and, besides, she had two hundred yards' start.

Over the next three days, she made Aaron Friedman's life an exquisite torment. She touched his thigh under the dinner-table. She let him have a good grope while they were playing water polo in the swimming-pool that was fed directly from the spring. Innocently she adjusted her bikini top in front of him while they lay on the lawn and he read Shelley to her. When he helped her up into the back of the hunting Land-rover she gave him a glimpse of the transparent Janet Reger panties that she had donned for the occasion. When they danced on the veranda, she rotated and oscillated her hips in lewd and lazy circles. Trapped between them was something that felt like the handle of a cricket bat.

On the night before he left Dragon's Fountain to fly back to the Transvaal with Garry, she allowed him to see her up to her room and say goodnight to her in the corridor outside the door of her suite. Without breaking the kiss he manoeuvred her until her back was pressed firmly against

287

the wall and her skirt was up around her waist. Once he hit his stride he was really rather masterful.

Isabella liked that and soon found she was almost as breathless as he was. She didn't really want him to stop. Her first impression had been intuitive; with those fingers he should have been a concert pianist, his touch was light and artistic. Unwittingly she found herself on the very threshold.

'Won't you leave your door unlocked tonight?' he whispered into her ear. With an effort she roused herself from a trance of lust and pushed him away.

'Are you crazy?' she whispered back, smoothing down her skirt with trembling fingers. 'The house is crawling with my family – my father, my brother, my grandmother, my nanny.'

'Yes, I'm going crazy – you're driving me mad. I love you. I want you. It's torture, Bella. I can't go on like this.'

'I know,' she said. 'Me, too. I'll come up to Johannesburg.'

'When? Oh, tell me when, my darling.'

'I'll telephone you. Leave me your number.'

★   ★   ★

Isabella was serving on the Senate committee of inquiry into civil service pensions. She and the two other members of the committee were taking evidence in the Transvaal the following month. She drove up to Johannesburg in the Porsche. She stayed with Garry and Holly in their lovely new home in Sandton and telephoned Aaron at the Pelindaba Institute the morning she arrived.

She drove out to fetch him, and they dined at a chic little restaurant. Over the crayfish cocktails she sounded him out discreetly about his work at the nuclear research institute.

'Oh, it's all terribly boring really. Anti-particles and quarks.' He was genially evasive. 'Did you know that the name originated from a James Joyce quotation, "Three

288

Quarks for Muster Mark", and should be pronounced "Quart"?'

'How fascinating.' She touched his thigh under the table, and he seized her hand. 'What you do must be very hard,' she said.

'Yes.' He moved her fingers a few inches higher. 'It is, rather.'

'I see what you mean.' She widened her eyes. 'Do you really want to go dancing after dinner?'

'We could go back to my place for coffee.'

'I'm not all that hungry. The crayfish was very filling. Let's skip the second course,' she suggested.

'Waiter. The bill, please.'

Aaron had a flat in the apartment-block in the residential compound of the institute. Although the security was not nearly so strict as in the main research and reactor area of the facility, Aaron was obliged to show his pass at the gate and Isabella had to go with him into the security office to sign the visitors' book and fill in all her particulars, including telephone number and residential address. The guard looked knowing and smug as he issued her a visitor's pass.

She had been much too long without love, and Aaron was an immensely satisfying lover. At first he was gentle and patient. Then as her passion mounted under his lips and cunning fingers, he became forceful and demanding. He pushed her to the edge half a dozen times and then held her back at the very brink until she screamed with exquisite frustration.

When at last she plunged over the top he went with her, and let her down softly on the other side. He held her and caressed her and murmured flatteries until she glowed with contentment and asked with a happy little sigh: 'What is your birth-sign?'

'Scorpio.'

'Ah, yes – Scorpios are always wonderful lovers. What date?'

'November the seventh.'

In the morning they made breakfast together, scrambled

eggs and laughter. When she saw him off to work at the door of the flat, she was dressed in one of his pyjama-tops with the sleeves rolled up and the shirt trailing to her knees.

'I'll sort things out with the guard at the main gate – you don't have to leave until you are ready.' He kissed her. 'In fact, if you were still here at lunchtime, I wouldn't mind a bit.'

'No chance.' She shook her head. 'I've got work to do today.'

As soon as he was gone she double-latched the door. The safe was in his study. She had looked for it as soon as she entered the flat the previous evening. There had been no attempt to conceal it behind panelling. It stood four square beside his desk. It was a heavy expensive jeweller's-quality Chubb with a six-numeral combination lock.

She sat cross-legged in front of it.

'November the seventh,' she mumbled, 'and he's about forty-three or forty-four years old. That makes it 1931 or 1932.'

She got it on the fourth try. Aaron hadn't even been as cunning as Shasa, who had at least inverted his birthdate.

'Why are so many truly brilliant men such naïve idiots?' she wondered. Before she swung the thick steel door open, she ran her finger around the door-seal. There was a tiny scrap of Sellotape across one hinge. 'Not such an idiot.'

Aaron obviously liked working at home. The safe was neatly packed with files, most of them the familiar Armscor green.

From the day that Red Rose had been given this assignment at Madrid Airport, Isabella had begun a study of nuclear weapons and their development.

She had stopped over for two extra days in London and spent them in the reading-room at the British Museum. She still had her card from her student days. She had requested and read every book that was listed under the subject in the library catalogue and filled two notebooks with her scribbles. For a lay person, she was now exceptionally well versed in the mysteries of the most dreadful process that man's infernal intelligence had yet devised.

The green Armscor file on top of the pile was stamped with the highest security-clearance. The copies were limited to eight, of which this was number four. The eight names with clearance to the files were listed on the cover and included the Minister of Defence and the commander-in-chief of the defence forces, her father as chairman of Armscor, Professor A. Friedman and four others who, judging by their scientific qualifications, were all scientists. One of the names she recognized as the head electrical engineer at Armscor who was often a guest at Weltevreden. No wonder her father had never allowed her to see one of these files.

The code-name on the green cover was 'Project Skylight'. She lifted it out, careful not to disturb anything else in the safe. She opened the file and began to scan the contents. While she had been assembling material for her thesis, she had taught herself the technique of speed reading, and now she turned the pages at a steady tempo.

The vast bulk of the material was so technical as to be utterly meaningless to her, even with the benefit of all her study. But she understood sufficient of it to realize that this was a series of reports on the progress being made at Pelindaba in the process of massively enriching the common uranium isotope, Uranium 238, with the highly fissionable Uranium 235. She knew that this was the basic step in the production of nuclear-fission weapons.

The reports were filed in chronological order, and before she reached the last page she realized that success had been achieved almost three years previously and that sufficient Uranium 235 had already been manufactured for the production of approximately 200 fissionable explosive devices with a yield of up to fifty kilotons. Much of this seemed to have been exported to Israel in return for technical assistance with the manufacture of the uranium. She blinked as she digested that information. At twenty kilotons the Hiroshima bomb had been less than half as powerful as one of these weapons.

She laid the file aside and reached for the next. She was at pains to note the exact order and position of each file in the safe, so that she could replace them without arousing suspicion that they had been tampered with. She read on. The main object of Project Skylight was the development of a series of tactical nuclear warheads of varying power and application, suitable for delivery not only by aircraft but also by ground artillery.

She knew that Armscor was already building a 155-millimetre howitzer designated G5 which would be capable of firing a 47-kilo shell with an 11-kilo payload and a maximum sea-level range of 39 kilometres. This would, she realized, make an ideal delivery system for a nuclear warhead. The report gave high priority to developing a nuclear artillery round for the G5.

The basic principles of the nuclear weapon were common knowledge. They consisted of assembling two subcritical masses of fissionable enriched uranium. One was a female charge with a vaginal recess. The second, male, charge was propelled by a conventional explosive to implode into the female recess with such velocity as instantly to render the entire mass supercritical and set off the fission reaction.

However, there were many technical pitfalls and obstacles to the actual manufacture of a viable device, particularly in the making of a warhead that weighed less than eleven kilos and was able to be contained in the casing of a 155-millimetre artillery round.

Isabella raced through the series of reports and working papers with a sense of rising excitement. She felt a strange proprietorial pride in the ingenuity and dedication of the development team. A dozen times she recognized her father's touch and influence as she read how each pitfall had been circumvented and the whole massive project gathered momentum and rolled towards its climax.

The last report in the file was dated only five days previously. She read it quickly, and then read it again.

The first South African atomic bomb would be tested in a little less than two months from today.

'But where?' she whispered desperately, and the next file she opened gave her the answer to that question.

She replaced the files in their exact order and remembered to stick the scrap of Sellotape over the hinge and to reset the combination of the lock in the same sequence she had found it.

*　　*　　*

Two years' study and deliberation had gone into choosing the site for the test. The prime consideration had been that of contamination by radioactive fallout.

South Africa maintained a weather station at Gough Island in the Antarctic. They had considered an Antarctic site, but had swiftly rejected that idea. Not only would contamination be difficult to control, but also detection before or after the test would be a foregone conclusion. There were too many others, notably the Australians, who were interested in that bleak and beautiful continent at the foot of the world.

For security, then, the test must be conducted on national soil or within South African air-space. The idea of an aerial test was soon abandoned. Again, detection would be a serious threat and the risk of contamination from fallout would be suicidal.

It had come down at the end to an underground test. The South African gold mines are the deepest underground workings in the world. For sixty years the South Africans have been the leaders in deep-mining techniques, and associated with the mines is the art and science of deep drilling.

Courtney Enterprises owned Orion Explorations, a specialist drilling company. The gnarled old magicians at Orion were able to sink a borehole two miles below the surface of the earth and bring up cores of rock from that depth. They could drive a straight hole or incline it at any angle they chose, or they could go straight down a mile and a half and then kick the bit off at an angle of forty-five degrees.

It was this incredible skill that filled Shasa Courtney with a sense of awe and deep respect as he stood at the test site in the middle of a bright sunlit day and looked around him at the gargantuan machines that between them comprised the drilling rig.

The entire rig was self-propelled. One truck the size of a modern fire-engine carried the power-plant. It was a diesel engine that could have driven an ocean liner. Another truck housed the control-room and electronic monitoring equipment. A third incorporated the actual drill and base-plate for the shot-hole. A fourth was the hydraulic lift and crane for the steel bore-rods.

The drill site was surrounded by a community of residential caravans and supply-trucks. The rods were piled in a storage area many acres in extent. At night the entire area was lit by the brutal blue-white glare of the arc lamps, for the work continued around the clock. When completed, the hole would have cost almost three hundred thousand US dollars to sink.

Shasa lifted his hat and wiped his brow with his forearm. It was hot.

This was the fringe of the Kalahari desert, which the little yellow Bushmen call 'The Great Dry Place'.

The low undulating red dunes rolled like the waves of a turbulent ocean into the monotonous distance. The desert grasses were sparse and silver dry. In the troughs between the dunes stood isolated desert camel-thorn trees. The foliage was dark green, and the bark was rough as a crocodile's back. In the nearest tree a colony of social weavers had built their communal nest. Hundreds of pairs of the drab little brown birds had combined their labours. The result was a shapeless edifice the size of a haystack that dwarfed the tall thorn tree which supported it. Each pair of birds occupied a separate chamber in the nest and helped to keep the whole structure in good repair the year round. One nest near Upington on the Orange river had been continuously occupied by successive generations of weavers for over a hundred years.

This district was a vast, sparsely populated wilderness. Courtney Mineral Exploration Company owned the 150,000-acre concession on which the drilling rig now stood. The entire property was posted and fenced. There were guards at every access-point and gate. Nobody outside the company would ever see this encampment -- and if they did . . . well, it was simply another mineral-exploration drill in progress.

Shasa glanced up at the sky. There was not a single cloud to sully the high, achingly blue bowl. This section of the Kalahari was a restricted military zone and overflight by either commercial or private aircraft was forbidden. It was often used for military exercises by the artillery and tank school based at Kimberley only a few hundred miles to the south.

Still Shasa worried. They were at D minus eight. The hole should be completed by the weekend. On Saturday evening the heavily guarded convoy would leave Pelindaba to arrive on Sunday at noon. It would bring the team of scientists and the bomb.

The test bomb would be positioned in the hole by Monday evening. The Minister of Defence and General Malan would fly up from Cape Town on D minus one.

He shook his head. 'It's all going just beautifully,' he assured himself, and climbed the steel steps into the mobile control-room.

The chief drilling engineer had worked for Orion for twelve years. He rose from his seat and offered Shasa a broad callused hand.

'How is it going, Mick?'

'Bak gat, Mr Courtney!' The driller used a coarse Afrikaans expression of ultimate approbation. 'We hit the three-thousand-metre mark at nine this morning.'

He indicated the plot on the display-screen. It graphically

illustrated the dog-leg in the line of the hole which would help to contain the blast.

'Don't let me bother you.' Shasa took the seat beside the engineer. 'Get on with it, man.'

Mick turned his full attention back to the control-console.

Shasa lit a cheroot and imagined that flexible steel worm gnawing its way down into the earth below where he sat, down to the edge of the earth's crust, far below the subterranean water-table, down to the very edge of the magma where the earth's temperature would approximate to that of a domestic oven.

A telephone rang in the control-room, but Shasa was wrapped up in his imagination. The junior technician who answered the phone had to call him twice.

'Mr Courtney, it's for you.'

'Ask who it is,' Shasa snapped irritably. 'Take a message.'

'It's Mr Vorster, sir.'

'Which Mr Vorster?'

'The prime minister, sir. In person.'

Shasa snatched the receiver out of his hand. He had a sudden sickening premonition of disaster.

'Ja, Oom John?' he asked.

'Shasa, within the last hour the ambassadors of Britain, America and France have all presented notes of protest from their respective governments.'

'What about?'

'At nine o'clock this morning an American satellite photographed the drill site. Ons is in die kak – we are in deep shit. They have somehow tumbled to Skylight and they are demanding that we abandon the test immediately. How long will it take you to get back to Cape Town?'

'My jet is standing on the strip. I'll be in your office in four hours.'

'I've called a full cabinet meeting. I want you to brief them.'

'I'll be there.'

296

Shasa had never seen John Vorster so worried and angry. As they shook hands he growled, 'Since I spoke to you the Russians have called an emergency meeting of the UN Security Council. They are threatening immediate mandatory sanctions if we proceed with the test.'

Shasa realized that they all had very good reason to be worried.

'The Americans and the Brits have warned that they won't use their veto to save us if we test.'

'You haven't admitted anything, Prime Minister?'

'Of course not,' Vorster snarled at him. 'But they want to inspect the drill site. They have aerial photographs – and they know the code-name Skylight.'

'They have our code?' Shasa stared at him, and Vorster nodded heavily.

'Ja, man, they have the code-name.'

'You know what that means, Prime Minister? We have a traitor – and at a very high level. At the very top.'

*   *   *

In the United Nations the representatives of Third World and non-aligned nations rose one after the other in the General Assembly to castigate and condemn South Africa and her attempt to join the nuclear club. She was judged guilty as soon as the accusation was levelled. Both India and China had tested nuclear bombs in the previous year or two, but that was different. Despite assurances from the South African prime minister that no test had been conducted, the ambassadors of Great Britain and the United States insisted on a personal inspection of the site. They were flown up into the Kalahari in an air-force Puma helicopter. By the time they had arrived, the drilling rig and every other vehicle had been removed. There was only a borehole casing capped with fresh concrete left standing forlornly in an area of rutted and trampled earth.

'What was the purpose of the drilling?' the British ambassador asked Shasa, not for the first time. Sir Percy was

297

an old friend who had dined at Weltevreden and hunted at Dragon's Fountain.

'Oil-prospecting,' Shasa answered him with a straight face, and the ambassador lifted an eyebrow and made no further comment. However, three days later Great Britain vetoed the sanctions proposed in the Security Council, and the storm began to blow over.

Aaron Friedman telephoned Isabella to tell her of his immediate departure for Israel. He wanted her to go with him. He didn't, however, mention to her that the United States had put enormous pressure on the Israeli government for his recall to Jerusalem.

'You are a darling, Aaron,' she told him, 'and I wouldn't have missed it for the world, but you have your life and I have mine. Perhaps we'll meet again some day.'

'I'll never forget you, Bella.'

The South African Bureau for State Security began a witch-hunt for the traitor that dragged on for months without any conclusive results. In the end it was accepted that one of the four Israeli scientists who had by that stage all left the country must have been responsible.

When Shasa read the secret report of the investigation he was embarrassed to learn that his darling daughter had signed into the Pelindaba residential compound and had apparently stayed overnight as a guest of the good professor.

'Well, you didn't think she was a virgin?' Centaine asked, when he mentioned it to her. 'Did you?'

'Hardly,' Shasa admitted. 'But, still, one doesn't like having one's nose rubbed in it, does one?'

'One has not had one's nose rubbed in it,' she corrected him. 'Bella seems to have been uncharacteristically discreet, for a change.'

'Still, it's a good thing he's gone.'

'He might have been quite a catch,' Centaine teased him, and he looked shocked.

'Good Lord, he was old enough to be her father.'

'Bella is thirty,' Centaine pointed out. 'Almost an old maid.'

298

'Is she that old?' Shasa looked startled. 'I often forget how the years go by.'

'We must seriously do something about finding her a husband.'

'There is no desperate hurry.' Shasa did not relish the prospect of losing her. He had become accustomed to things just the way they were.

*   *   *

Isabella's reward came swiftly. Within months she was promised a holiday with Nicky and instructed to make arrangements to be absent from the country for two weeks.

'Two weeks!' she exalted. 'With my baby! I can hardly believe it's happening at last.'

Her euphoria was enough to banish the crippling sense of guilt that she had lived with since the Skylight furore had made world headlines. She tried to appease her conscience by assuring herself that she had helped to avert an escalation of the nuclear menace and that her treachery would, in the long run, yield beneficial results for all mankind.

Naturally, she registered a patriotic sense of outrage when she discussed the subject with her family or with other senators in the halls of the parliament building, but the truth haunted her in the night. She was a traitor – and the penalty was death.

She told Nana and Shasa that she was meeting Harriet Beauchamp in Zurich. They planned to hire a kombi and cruise around Switzerland for two weeks, going wherever the snow was good, eating fondue and trying all the most famous runs.

'Don't expect to hear from me until I get back,' she warned them.

'Have you got enough money, Bella?' Shasa wanted to know.

'That's a silly question, Pater.' She kissed him. 'Wasn't it you who set up my trust fund – who gives me a ridiculous salary each month, twice as much as my pay from the Senate?'

'Well, I'll give you the name of somebody at Crédit Suisse in Lausanne, just in case you run short.'

'You are sweet, but I'm not sixteen any more.'

'Sometimes I wish you were, my love.'

Isabella caught the Swissair flight for Zurich, but left the aircraft at Nairobi. She checked in at the Norfolk Hotel and the following morning telephoned Weltevreden and spoke to Nana, pretending that she was calling from Zurich.

'Have fun and keep your eyes open for a nice millionaire,' Nana told her.

'For you or for me, Nana?'

'That's enough of your sauce, missy.'

As she had been instructed, Isabella caught the Air Kenya flight to Lusaka in Zambia and the airline bus from the airport to the Ridgeway Hotel. She found that a single room had been reserved for her. This was as far as her instructions took her.

Before dinner she sat on the swimming-pool terrace and ordered a gin and tonic. A few minutes later, a tall good-looking black man sitting at the bar sauntered across to her table.

'Red Rose,' he said.

'Sit down,' she nodded, her heart pounding and her palms damp.

'My name is Paul.' He refused the drink she offered him. 'I will not trouble you any longer than necessary. Will you please be ready at nine o'clock tomorrow morning? I will meet you with transport at the front entrance of the hotel.'

'Where are you taking me?'

'I don't know,' he said as he stood up. 'And you shouldn't ask.'

She was waiting for him as he had instructed. He drove her back to the airport in a battered Volkswagen, but bypassed the commercial terminal and drove on to the gates of the restricted military area.

The remains of Zambia's squadron of MiG fighters stood on the apron in the sunlight. There had been four crashes in the last month alone. Not only had Zambian pilots been inadequately trained in East Germany, but also they had not adjusted well to the complexity of supersonic flight. In addition, the MiGs had done almost twenty years of service in eastern Europe before being sold to Zambia. Zambia's copper-based economy had been sent reeling by the fall in the price of the metal, and by two decades of gross mismanagement. Costs had been pruned in the maintenance of the fighter squadron, and they were familiarly known as 'The Flying Bombs'.

Beyond the fighters was parked an enormous unmarked aircraft with four turbo-fan engines and a tail-fin taller than a two-storey house. Although Isabella did not recognize it as such, it was an Ilyushin Il-76 with the NATO reporting name 'Candid'. It was the standard Russian military heavy freight-carrying transport.

Paul, her escort, spoke to the guards at the gate and showed them a document from his brief-case. The guard commander studied the paper and then went into his kiosk. He spoke on the telephone to a superior and then handed Paul back his papers, opened the gates and saluted as they drove through.

Two pilots in flying-overalls were supervising the refuelling of the huge Candid. Paul parked the Volkswagen alongside the main hangar and walked across to the aircraft. He spoke to one of the pilots and then beckoned to Isabella to follow. They watched her struggling with her suitcase, but none of them offered to help her.

'You will go with the aircraft,' Paul told her.

'What about my luggage?' she asked, and the chief pilot shrugged and answered in a heavy accent: 'Leave here. Me fix. Come.'

Isabella looked round, but Paul was already halfway back to the Volkswagen. She followed the pilot up the loading-ramp of the Candid.

The hold was filled with cargo. It was packed on wooden

pallets under heavy nylon netting. There were literally hundreds of wooden cases of various sizes. Most of them were stencilled in black paint with letters and numerals in Cyrillic script. The pilot led her down the side-aisle of the cavernous compartment and up the ladder to the flight-deck.

'Sit.' He pointed at one of the folding jump-seats in the rear bulkhead of the flight-deck.

There were no formalities when the Candid took off an hour later.

From her seat in the rear of the compartment Isabella had a clear view of the instrument-panel over the pilot's shoulder. The Candid levelled out into a cruise altitude of thirty thousand feet and settled on a course of 300 degrees magnetic.

Surreptitiously, she checked the time on her wristwatch. She wanted to know how long they would fly on this north-westerly heading. She conjured up a map of the continent in her mind. Although she had no idea of the aircraft's ground speed, the needle on the air-speed indicator quivered at around 475 knots.

After an hour's flight she guessed that they had crossed from Zambia into Angola, and she shivered slightly. Angola was not her number-one choice for a holiday. She had recently been nominated to the African Affairs Committee of the Senate, and she had attended all the special briefings on the subject of Angola. She had also read the confidential reports assembled by military intelligence on that country.

She looked down at the mosaic of savannah and mountains and jungle that passed slowly beneath the Candid and tried to recall every detail that she had read about this troubled land.

Angola had long been the pearl of the Portuguese empire. After South Africa itself, Angola was the richest and most beautiful of all African countries.

This thousand-mile stretch of the West African Atlantic seaboard was rich with marine resources. Vast shoals of pelagic fish swarmed within easy reach of secure natural harbours. Offshore drilling by American companies had recently proved huge reserves of oil and natural gas. Inland lay rich and fertile plains and valleys, marvellous forests of hardwoods, pleasant well-watered highlands from which flowed numerous great rivers. In Africa water was a natural resource almost as precious as oil. Apart from her oil, Angola produced gold and diamonds and iron ore. Her climate was temperate and benign.

Despite all these blessings, Angola had for a decade been racked by a savage and bitter civil war. Her indigenous African peoples had been struggling to throw off the five-hundred-year colonial rule from Lisbon.

The liberation struggle had not been united. Many armies under all the usual flamboyant warlike names had fought not only the Portuguese but each other as well. There was the MPLA, the People's Movement for the Liberation of Angola; the FNLA, the National Front for the Liberation of Angola; UNITA, the National Union for the Total Independence of Angola; and a rash of other private armies and guerrilla movements.

The Portuguese had held on grimly to their colony. Tens of thousands of young Portuguese conscripts had come out to Africa, many of them to bleed and die by bullet and mine and tropical disease far from their native land. Then suddenly had come the left-wing *coup d'état* by the military junta in Mother Portugal, and shortly thereafter the declaration that Portugal was to give Angola its independence and hold popular elections to select a new government and write a constitution.

Now, in the months leading up to the proposed elections, the country was in even greater turmoil than it had been during the civil war, as the various factions jockeyed for power, and the great powers and other African governments played their favourites, while the guerrilla leaders themselves indulged in an orgy of intrigue and torture and intimidation of a population already cowed by years of war. Reading between the lines of the intelligence reports, Isabella sensed that nobody really knew what was happening in Luanda, the capital, let alone in the remote jungles and mountains.

Admiral Rosa Coutinho, the Red Admiral, appointed as the governor-general by the armed-forces movement after the *coup d'état*, seemed to favour Agostinho Neto and his 'purified' MPLA. The purification process consisted of torturing all other factions of the party to death. This was done by gradually tightening a wooden frame around their heads until the skull collapsed.

The American CIA, out of touch as always, appeared to be supporting the FNLA which was the weakest, most tribally based and corrupt of the three, slipping them niggardly amounts of financial aid which the United States Senate would not have approved, had it been aware of them. The Chinese were also betting on the FNLA, as were the North Koreans.

★   ★   ★

The motorcade of black Chaikas crossed the moat bridge and entered the fortress of the Kremlin through the gate below the Borovitskaya Tower.

The two Cuban generals rode in the leading limousine. Senen Casas Requerión was chief of staff of the Cuban army, and with him was his army logistics chief. Colonel-General Ramón Machado was in the second vehicle with President Fidel Castro, acting as host and interpreter for the visiting head of state.

Ramón's promotion had been announced within weeks of his return from Ethiopia where he had masterminded the abdication of the Emperor Haile Selassie, the abolition of the monarchy and the formal declaration by the Ethiopian Derg of a Marxist socialist state.

He was now the second-youngest general in the entire Russian military service, and by far the youngest in the KGB. His immediate senior in the secret service was fifty-three years of age. His predecessor Joe Cicero had only been elevated to general officer rank just before his retirement. The promotion was all the more extraordinary in that Ramón was not a Russian national by birth. His naturalization papers had only been serviced eight years ago.

Ethiopia had been a triumph for him. He had steered the first stage of the revolution through without any visible Russian presence in the country and, more importantly, with the expenditure of a paltry few million roubles.

Following immediately had been his clandestine but equally successful visit to Luanda in Angola where Ramón had met the Red Admiral, Rosa Coutinho. Coutinho was a member of the Portuguese Communist Party. He had been appointed governor-general of Angola by the left-wing military-forces committee which now governed Portugal. He had been charged with organizing the popular elections to select an African government to bring the former Portuguese colony of Angola to independence. However, during his meeting with Ramón he had proven to be a political soulmate.

'We must ensure that under no circumstances popular elections take place,' he had told Ramón. 'If we allow that to happen, then Jonas Savimbi will be the first president of Angola, if only because his Ovimbundu tribe is the largest in the country.'

'We cannot allow it,' Ramón agreed. He did not have to elaborate. Jonas Savimbi was the boldest and most successful of all the Angolan guerrilla leaders. His UNITA army had fought the Portuguese with skill and dogged determination for a decade. He was intelligent, educated and strong-willed. Although he had never declared his political allegiances, he was certainly not a Marxist, probably not even a socialist, and they could not take a chance on him coming to power.

'The only possible solution,' Ramón went on, 'is for you to declare that, owing to the state of chaos in the country, it will be impractical to hold elections. You should then declare that the solution is to recognize the MPLA as the

305

only party capable of assuming the reins of government, and to persuade Lisbon to transfer power to Agostinho Neto and the MPLA as soon as possible.'

Neto was the Soviet choice. He was devious, weak, cruel and malleable. He could be controlled, whereas Savimbi could not.

'I agree,' Coutinho nodded. 'But can I count on full support from Russia and Cuba?'

'If I am able to promise you that support, will you be prepared to hand over to us strategic military bases and airfields to allow us to rush in troops and military supplies?' Ramón countered.

'You have my hand on it.' The Red Admiral stretched across his desk, and Ramón took his hand with a soaring sense of triumph.

He was about to deliver two nations into Soviet sovereignty. Surely no single man had achieved more in Africa.

'I am flying directly from here to Havana,' he assured Coutinho. 'I anticipate that within a matter of days talks between Cuba and Moscow will be under way at the highest possible level. I will have your answer for you by the end of the month.'

Coutinho rose to his feet. 'You are an extraordinary man, Comrade Colonel-General. Seldom have I been privileged to work with one who sees so clearly to the very heart of a problem, and who is prepared to deliver the bold expert cut of a surgeon to excise it.'

Now Ramón sat in the rear seat of the Chaika with President Fidel Castro beside him as they entered the citadel of Soviet socialism. The cavalcade led by the motor-cycle escort moved swiftly up the broad cobbled avenue. They passed the famous armoury, the great treasure-house of imperial Russia which still housed a stunning wealth of ambassadorial gifts and Tsarist regalia, from the crown of Ivan the Terrible to the jewel-encrusted court robes of Catherine the Great.

A queue of foreign tourists at the doors to the museum

watched them pass, their expressions lighting with curiosity as they recognized the great bearded figure of Castro in the second car.

Swiftly they moved on, passing on their left the square around which were clustered the cathedrals of the Archangel, of the Annunciation and of the Assumption. The immense spires and towers and golden domes burnt in the pale spring sunshine. The peach and cherry trees in the gardens were in full blossom. They swung into the square, passed the palace of the Praesidium of the Supreme Soviet and drew up at the front entrance of the Council of Ministers building.

There was an honour guard paraded to welcome them and a dozen political and military dignitaries.

Deputy Minister Aleksei Yudenich stepped forward to embrace Castro and lead him into the Council of Ministers. In the Hall of Mirrors, Castro began to speak from his seat at the head of the long table.

He spoke clearly, pausing at the end of each sentence to allow the Russian translator to catch up with him. Even Ramón, as an old and intimate comrade-in-arms, was fascinated by his grasp of the African situation and his calculated assessment of the risks and options open to them. He had absorbed every word of Ramón's briefing.

'The Western Europeans are divided and spineless. NATO depends militarily on America. They would never be able to muster any organized response to our determined entrance into the Angolan arena. We need not waste serious thought on them.'

'What about America?' Yudenich asked soberly.

'America is still bleeding from the humiliation of Vietnam. Their Senate will never allow American troops to operate in Africa. The Americans have been whipped. They are still snivelling with their tails between their legs. The only threat they pose is that they might choose a surrogate army to fight for them.'

'South Africa,' Yudenich forestalled him.

'Yes, South Africa has the most dangerous army in

Africa. Kissinger may recruit them and send them across the Angolan border.'

'Can we afford to fight the South Africans? Their lines of supply are shorter than ours by ten thousand miles, and their troops are reputed to be the finest bush fighters in Africa. If they are equipped and supplied by America . . .'

'We won't have to fight them,' Castro promised. 'As they cross the border, America and South Africa will be immediately defeated, not by Soviet or Cuban might, but by the practice of white minority government and the policy of apartheid.'

'Explain this to us, Mr President,' Yudenich invited.

'In the West there is such a desire by American liberals and the European anti-apartheid movement to destroy the white régime in South Africa that they will make any sacrifice to that end. They will sacrifice Angola rather than let South Africans defend it. The moment the first South African crosses the border, our war will be won. There will be such an outcry from the American Democratic Party, and from the champions of so-called democracy in Europe, that the South Africans will never get to do any fighting. In the face of hysterical worldwide condemnation they will be forced to retire. Their attempted intervention will settle the matter firmly in our favour. Once the South Africans have tarnished the shield, no Western politician will dare to take it up again. Angola will be ours.'

They were all nodding agreement. All the generals and ministers. Castro had amazed Ramón once again with his powers of rhetoric and persuasion. It was the main reason that Ramón had prevailed upon him to come to Moscow in person. None of Castro's generals or ministers would have been able to swing the issue as he had just done. His shrewd and devious view would appeal irresistibly to the Russian mind.

'He calls me the Golden Fox,' Ramón smiled to himself. 'But he is the king of all the foxes.'

However, Castro was not yet finished. His timing was

consummate. He smiled genially down the long table, stroking the curling bush of his beard. 'Angola will be ours, but that will be only a beginning. After Angola the ultimate prize is South Africa itself.'

They all leant forward eagerly, their eyes shining like a pack of wolves scenting blood.

'Once we have Angola, we will have South Africa surrounded, with bases on her very borders from which our black freedom fighters can strike with impunity. South Africa is the treasury and economic power-house of the whole of Africa. Once we have it, the rest of the continent will fall into our laps.'

He placed his huge hands palm-down on the table-top and leant forward over them.

'I pledge you all the fighting men we need to do the job, a hundred thousand if necessary. If you provide the weapons and equipment and transport, there is a ripe fruit for the plucking. Shall we do it, comrades? Shall we make the bold and courageous stroke together?'

★　　　★　　　★

Only a month later a group of Portuguese military officers, loyal to the Red Admiral Coutinho, handed over the strategic military airbase at Saurimo to Colonel Angel Botello, who was chief of logistics in the Cuban air force. Saurimo was five hundred miles inland from the capital of Luanda, and therefore comparatively secure from surveillance by the CIA and other Western agencies.

The first Ilyushin Candid transport landed at Saurimo twenty-four hours later. On board were a full cargo of military equipment and fifty Cuban 'advisers'. The Russian military observer on the same aircraft was Colonel-General Ramón Machado.

It was an exhausting but exciting period for Ramón. His reputation and his nickname were swiftly spreading the length and breadth of the continent. The Cuban contingent brought the name with them from Havana.

'El Zorro,' they whispered it abroad, 'El Zorro has arrived. Now things will begin to happen.'

Like the fox, his namesake, he was constantly on the move. He seldom slept two consecutive nights in the same bed. Often there was no bed at all but the mud floor of a grass hut, the cramped seat of a light aircraft or the dirty wooden deck of a small launch threading its way through the swamps and sand-bars of a remote African river.

El Jefe had been right as usual. There was no concerted Western response to the Cuban build-up. Admiral Coutinho was able to head off the few timid enquiries, while Western journalists were successfully prevented from collecting hard evidence in the field. The arms and troops were flown in to Saurimo, or shipped to Brazzaville in the Congo and distributed from there by light aircraft and river-launch to the MPLA cadres in their camps deep in the bush.

Angola was only one of many operations that Ramón was running simultaneously. There were Ethiopia and Mozambique to deal with, as well as his network of agents, and the co-ordination of the activities of the South African freedom fighters. Angola was a marvellous new springboard for the liberation movements. Ramón set up training camps for both SWAPO, the South-West African People's Organization, and the ANC, the African National Congress.

The headquarters of the two organizations were sited in separate areas of the country. SWAPO were in the south where they were able to cross the border into South-West African Namibia readily and to operate amongst their own tribes, the Ovahimbo and Ovambo.

However, Ramón maintained a particular interest in the ANC. He never lost sight for a moment of the fact that South Africa was the gateway to the entire continent and the ANC were the freedom fighters of South Africa. Raleigh Tabaka, his old comrade from London, was promoted to ANC chief of logistics in Angola. Between them they chose the site for the main ANC base in northern Angola.

They flew hundreds of hours together in an Antonov

military biplane. They scoured the northern seaside province of Kungo before they found a site suitable for their base.

It was a small fishing village situated on a lagoon and estuary of the Chicamba river. The mouth of the lagoon was open to the Atlantic, and at high tide vessels of two hundred or so tons burden could cross the bar and enter the river. In addition there were extensive fields of peasant cultivation a few miles upstream. Although these had been neglected during the savage decade of civil war, it would require very little effort to open a landing-strip over the level deforested fields. The fishing village had likewise been abandoned during the war and there was no local population which otherwise would have had to be evacuated or eliminated.

However, the main recommendation for the site was its distance from any South African border or base. The South Africans were formidable opponents. Like the Israelis, they would not hesitate to violate any international border in hot pursuit of a guerrilla unit. Chicamba was out of range of the South African Alouette helicopters, and thousands of kilometres of mountain had jungle isolating it from any overland hostile expedition by the Boers. They named the base Tercio.

Raleigh Tabaka took the first cadre of five hundred ANC recruits up to Tercio base in a fishing trawler requisitioned by Admiral Coutinho from the Portuguese canning factory in Luanda.

They began construction work on the airstrip and training camp immediately. When Ramón flew in ten days later the airstrip had been cleared and levelled and was in the process of being surfaced in red clay and gravel that would set like concrete and ensure a good all-weather runway.

On his second inspection, Ramón was so impressed by the remoteness and security of the area that he decided to set up a separate compound near the mouth of the river, overlooking the beach.

He planned this as his own private headquarters. He

always needed a secure base for communications where sensitive KGB training and planning could be undertaken, and where intense interrogation and elimination of captives could be undertaken without risk of discovery or interference.

He ordered Raleigh Tabaka's men to give construction of his own beach compound the utmost priority. On his next visit he found that the fencing and defences had already been laid out and that work on the interrogation-block and the officers' quarters was far advanced.

On his return to Havana, he requisitioned the necessary radio and electronic equipment and had it flown out to Tercio base on the next available transport.

★   ★   ★

On his frequent visits to Havana and Moscow, Ramón kept well abreast of all the dozens of projects he had in progress down the length of the African continent, in particular his own personal case, the operation and control of Red Rose.

Looking back down the years to her recruitment in London and Spain he realized that he had underestimated just how valuable Red Rose would one day become.

Since she had entered the South African Senate she had served on five house bodies. From all of these she had delivered extraordinary intelligence in the form of reports and recommendations on all the various subjects covered by those committees.

Then in February 1975 she was made a member of the Senate Advisory Board on African Affairs. Through her Ramón received the information, only hours old, that President Ford and Henry Kissinger through the CIA had signalled Pretoria that they would not oppose a military adventure by the South African army into southern Angola. He learnt from Red Rose that the CIA had promised South Africa diplomatic support and military equipment to support their thrust towards Luanda.

After alerting his superiors in the Lubyanka, Ramón flew to Havana to consult Castro.

'You were right all the way, El Jefe,' he told him admiringly. 'The Yankees are sending in the Boers to do their dirty work for them.'

'We must let them stick their head into the trap,' Castro smiled. 'I want you to return to Angola immediately. Take my personal orders. Pull back our forces and hold them on a defensive line on the rivers south of the capital. Let them come in before we tweak Uncle Sam's beard and kick the Boers in the *cojones*.'

In October the South African cavalry crossed the Cunene river and made a spectacular dash northwards in their fast Panhard armoured cars. In a matter of days they had swept to within a hundred and fifty miles of the capital. They were superbly trained and well-led young fighting men, and their morale was high, but they lacked bridging equipment to cross the rivers and artillery to engage heavy armour.

When they reached the river, Ramón sent a signal to Havana.

'Now,' said Castro grimly, 'we pull out the rug. Let the armour loose.'

The South Africans were held on the rivers by the Russian T-54 tanks and assault-helicopters. Ramón released the news of the South African presence to the Western media and the diplomatic storm broke just as Castro had predicted.

Nigeria, after South Africa the most powerful nation in Africa, switched its support within days of the South African presence being disclosed to the world by Russian and Cuban intelligence. It abandoned Savimbi and his UNITA movement and formally recognized the Soviet-supported MPLA government. To emphasize its position, Nigeria sent thirty million dollars in aid to Agostinho Neto in Luanda.

In the United States Senate, Dick Clark, the Democratic representative from Iowa, began the process of making certain that the South African expeditionary force in Angola was isolated and deprived of support. He accused the CIA of co-operating illegally with South Africa, and Kissinger and the CIA took evasive action. Members of the joint chiefs threatened to resign unless American support was withdrawn immediately. In December the Clark amendment was rushed through the Senate and all American military aid to Angola was cut off. It had all worked exactly as Castro had planned it.

Another African nation was delivered, trussed and tied, to Soviet sovereignty, and millions of black Angolans were condemned to another decade of brutal civil war.

In Moscow Colonel-General Ramón Machado was awarded the Order of Lenin, first class, and the medal was pinned on his chest by General Secretary Brezhnev personally.

Then Ramón was called urgently to Ethiopia. The creeping revolution there had reached a crucial stage.

★   ★   ★

As the Ilyushin began its descent into Addis Ababa, Ramón sat behind the Russian pilot on the flight-deck so he had an uninterrupted view of the savage mountainous country ahead.

Over the centuries all the trees around the capital had been cut down for firewood, so the hills were bare and desolate. In the misty blue distance rose the peculiar flat-topped mountains known as the Ambas that were so characteristic of this mysterious corner of eastern Africa below the great horn. The sheer sides of the Ambas dropped many thousands of feet into the rocky valleys, in the depths of which great torrents gouged ever deeper into the red earth.

It was an ancient land into which the Egyptian pharaohs had first sent their armies marauding for slaves and ivory and other exotic treasures.

The Ethiopians were a fiercely proud and warlike people,

most of them Christians, but members of the Coptic Church, an ancient branch of the Catholic Church that had its origins in Alexandria in Egypt.

Since 1930 the country had been ruled by the Negus Negusti, the Supreme Emperor, Haile Selassie. He was the last absolute monarch of history who ruled by decree. All his decrees were formally ratified by his Derg, a council made up of nobles and great *rases* and chieftains. So complete was his power that he personally ordered every facet of his country's government from the most momentous decisions of state down to the appointment of middle-ranking provincial civil servants.

Despite these absolute powers and the feudal organization of his government he was a benevolent dictator much loved by the common people for his almost saintly virtues and his total incorruptibility. In stature he was small and delicately boned, with tiny feminine feet and hands and delicate facial features.

In his personal habits he was austere and abstemious. Except on occasions of state, he dressed in unadorned clothing and ate frugally and simply. Unlike other African rulers he accumulated no great personal wealth. His main, perhaps his only, concern was for the welfare of his people.

In the forty-five years since he had been crowned emperor he had steered Ethiopia through rebellion and foreign invasion and turbulent times with a quiet wisdom and tenacity to duty.

Only five years after his coronation, his mountainous kingdom had been invaded by Mussolini's generals and he had been driven into exile in England. His nation had resisted the invader, fighting tanks and modern aircraft and poison gas with muzzle-loading rifles and swords and often with their bare hands.

After the defeat of the axis powers Haile Selassie returned to his Ethiopian throne and ruled in his old benign fashion. However, there were new forces let loose in the world. In his cautious efforts to modernize his country and bring this largely pastoral and agrarian society into the mainstream of the twentieth century, Haile Selassie allowed the virus to enter his little kingdom.

The infection began in the new university that he endowed in Addis Ababa. Long-haired wild-eyed Europeans began to preach to his young students a strange and heady philosophy that all men were equal, and that kings and nobles had no divine rights. As the ageing emperor's physical strength waned, so the very elements seemed to conspire against him. Africa is a land of savage extremes where heat follows icy cold, and drought succeeds flood, and the earth turns bountiful or hostile with neither rhythm nor reason.

A terrible drought fell upon Ethiopia, and with it rode the other ghostly horseman, famine. The crops failed, the rivers and wells dried, and the soil turned to dust and blew away on the desert winds. The flocks and the herds died, and at their mothers' withered dugs the infants were tiny skeletal figures with huge haunted eyes in skull heads too large for their wasted bodies.

The land cried out in agony.

African famine was an old story of no particular interest, and Africa was far away. The world took no notice, until the BBC sent Richard Dimbleby to Ethiopia with a television crew. Dimbleby filmed the dreadful suffering in the villages. He also attended a state banquet in Addis Ababa.

With calculated malevolence he intercut scenes of famine and lingering death with those of feasting nobles dressed in scarlet and gold lace and flowing white robes and the emperor seated at a board that groaned with rich food.

Dimbleby had an enormous following. The world took notice. The young students from Addis Ababa University, trained by their carefully selected mentors, began to march and agitate. The Church and the missionaries preached against total power vested in one man, and dreamt of that elusive Utopia where man would love his fellow-man and the lion would lie down with the lamb.

Many of the members of the Derg saw the opportunity to settle old scores and for personal advancement. In a totally unrelated but significant development, the Arab oil-producers doubled the price of oil and held the world to ransom. In Ethiopia the cost of living soared, placing unbearable hardships on a populace already hard hit by famine. There was runaway inflation. Those who were able hoarded food, and those who could not went on strike or rioted and looted the food-shops.

Many of the young army officers were products of Addis Ababa University, and they led the mutiny of the Army. These rebels formed a revolutionary committee and seized control of the Derg.

They arrested the prime minister and the members of the royal family and isolated the emperor in his palace. They spread rumours that Haile Selassie had stolen huge sums of public money and transferred them to his Swiss bank account. They organized demonstrations of students and malcontents outside the palace. The mob clamoured for his abdication. The priests of the Coptic Church and the Muslim leaders joined in the chorus of accusation and demands for his abdication and the installation of a people's democracy.

The military council now felt strong enough to take the next significant step. Through the Derg they issued a formal declaration deposing the emperor, and sent a deputation of young army officers to arrest him and remove him from the palace.

As they led him down the palace steps the frail old man remarked quietly: 'If what you do is for the good of my people, then I go gladly, and I pray for the success of your revolution.'

To humiliate him they confined him in a sordid little hut on the outskirts of the city, but the common people gathered in their thousands outside the single room to offer their condolences and pledge their loyalty. At the order of the military council the guards drove them away at bayonet point.

The country was ripe, but it was all teetering in the balance when the Ilyushin touched down at Addis Ababa

317

Airport and taxied to the far end of the field where twenty jeeps and troop-trucks of the Ethiopian army were drawn up to welcome it.

Ramón was the first man out of the aircraft as the loading-ramp touched the ground.

'Welcome, Colonel-General.' Colonel Getachew Abebe jumped down from his command-jeep and strode forward to meet him.

They shook hands briefly. 'Your arrival is timely,' Abebe told him, and they both turned and shaded their eyes as they looked into the sun.

The second Ilyushin made its final approach and touched down. As it taxied towards them, a third and then a fourth gigantic aircraft turned across the sun and one after the other landed.

As they pulled up in a staggered row and switched off their engines, the men poured out of the cavernous bellies. They were paratroopers of the crack Che Guevara Regiment.

'What is the latest position?' Ramón demanded brusquely.

'The Derg has voted for Andom,' Abebe told him, and Ramón looked serious. General Aman Andom was the head of the Army. He was a man of high integrity and superior intelligence, popular with both the Army and the civilian populace. His election as the new leader of the nation came as no surprise.

'Where is he now?'

'He is in his palace – about five miles from here.'

'How many men?'

'A bodyguard of fifty or sixty. . . .'

Ramón turned to watch his paratroopers disembarking.

'How many members of the Derg stand for you?'

Abebe reeled off a dozen names, all young left-wing army officers.

'Tafu?' Ramón demanded, and Abebe nodded. Colonel Tafu commanded a squadron of Russian T-53 tanks, the most modern unit in the Army.

'All right,' Ramón said softly. 'We can do it – but we must move swiftly now.'

He gave the order to the commander of the Cuban paratroopers. Carrying their weapons at the trail, the long ranks of camouflage-clad assault-troops trotted forward and began to board the waiting trucks.

Ramón took the seat beside Abebe in the command-jeep, and the long column rolled away towards the city. Parched to talcum by drought and fierce sunlight, the red dust rose in a dense cloud behind the column and rolled away on the wind that came down hot from the deserts to the north.

On the outskirts of the city they met caravans of camels and mules. The men with them watched the column pass without showing any emotion. In these dangerous days since the emperor had been deposed they had become accustomed to the movement of armed men on the roads. They were men from the Danakil desert and the mountains, turbaned Muslims in flowing robes or bearded Copts with bushy hair and broadswords on their belts and round steel shields on their shoulders.

At an order from Colonel Abebe, the jeep swung on to a side-road and skirted the city, speeding down rutted roads between the crowded flat-roofed hovels. Abebe used the radio, speaking swiftly in Amharic and then translating for Ramón.

'I have men watching Andom's palace,' he explained. 'He seems to have called a meeting of all the officers in the Derg who support him. They are assembling now.'

'Good. All the chickens will be in one nest.'

The column turned away from the city and sped through open fields. They were bare and desiccated. The drought had left no blade of grass or green leaf. The chalky rocks that littered the earth were white as skulls.

'There.' Abebe pointed ahead.

The general was a member of the nobility, and his residence stood a few miles outside the city on the first of a series of low hills. The hills were bare except for the grove of Australian eucalyptus trees that surrounded the palace. Even these drooped in the heat and the drought. The palace was surrounded by a thick wall of red terracotta. At a glance Ramón saw that it was a formidable fortification. It would require artillery to breach it.

Abebe had read his thoughts. 'We have surprise on our side,' he pointed out. 'There is a good chance that we will be able to drive in through the gate . . .'

'No,' Ramón contradicted him. 'They will have seen the aircraft arriving. That is probably why Andom has called his council.'

Out on a rocky plain between them and the palace, a staff car was speeding towards the open gate.

'Pull in here,' Ramón ordered, and the column halted in a fold of ground. Ramón stood on the rear seat of the open jeep and focused his binoculars on the gateway in the palace wall. He watched the staff car drive through it, and then the massive wooden gate swung ponderously closed.

'Where is Tafu with his tanks?'

'He is still in barracks, on the other side of the city.'

'How long to get them here?'

'Two hours.'

'Every minute is vital.' Ramón spoke without lowering his binoculars. 'Order Tafu to bring his armour in as quickly as possible – but we cannot wait until he arrives.'

Abebe turned to the radio, and Ramón dropped the binoculars on to his chest and jumped down from the jeep. The commander of the paratroopers and his company leaders gathered around him, and he gave his orders quietly, pointing out the features of the terrain as he spoke.

Abebe hung up the microphone of the radio and came to join them. 'Colonel Tafu has one T-53 in the city, guarding the emperor's palace. He is sending it to us. It will be here in an hour. The rest of the squadron will follow.'

'Very good,' Ramón nodded. 'Now describe the layout of the interior of Andom's palace over there. Where will we find Andom himself?'

They squatted in a circle while Abebe sketched in the dust, and then Ramón gave his final orders.

Once again the column moved forward, but now there was a large white flag on the bonnet of the command-jeep, a bed-sheet that fluttered on its makeshift flagpole. The trucks kept in tight formation. The paratroopers were concealed beneath the hoods of the troop-carriers, and all weapons were kept out of sight.

As they approached the palace a line of heads appeared over the wall above the gate, but the flag of truce had an inhibiting effect and no shot was fired.

The lead jeep drew up in front of the gate, and Ramón assessed its strength. The gate was of weathered teak, almost a foot thick, reinforced with bands of wrought iron. The hinges were rebated into the columns on each side of the gateway. He abandoned any idea of driving a truck through it.

From the top of the wall twenty feet above them the captain of the guard challenged them in Amharic, and Abebe stood up to reply. They haggled for a few minutes, with Abebe repeating that he had an urgent despatch for General Andom and demanding entrance. The guard shouted back his refusal, and the exchange became heated.

As soon as Ramón was certain that all the guard's attention was on the jeep he spoke softly into the two-way radio. The trucks behind the jeep roared forward and then peeled off left and right. They bumped over the rocky ground on each side of the roadway and drew up below the walls. From under the canvas hoods, paratroopers clambered on to the roofs of the vehicles. Ten of them were armed with grappling-hooks which they swung around their heads and then heaved up over the top of the wall. The nylon ropes streamed out behind them and dangled down.

'Open fire!' Ramón snapped into the radio, and a storm of automatic fire swept the top of the wall, kicking lumps of clay and brick from the rim. The ricochets whined away into the branches of the blue gum trees. The heads of guards disappeared instantly, some of them ducking away but at least one of them hit by a bullet. Ramón saw his helmet spin into the air and the top lift off his skull. A pink mist of blood and brain hung in the air for an instant after he was snatched away.

Now the paratroopers were swarming up the wall, three or four of them on each dangling rope at the same time. They were as agile as monkeys, and within seconds thirty of them were over and into the palace grounds. There were bursts of automatic fire and the thump of a single grenade. Seconds later the great wooden gate swung open and Ramón urged the jeep-driver forward.

The bodies of the palace guards lay in the courtyard where they had been shot down. Ramón saw one of his paras huddled beside the gateway clutching his belly with blood oozing through his fingers. The other paras grabbed on to the jeep as it roared forward.

Ramón was standing behind the 50-calibre Browning heavy machine-gun that was mounted above the driver's seat. He fired a long raking burst at the remaining guards as they fled like rabbits into the maze of adobe buildings on the far side of the courtyard.

One of the guards whirled and dropped on his knee. He raised the launcher of the RPG 7 rocket he carried to his shoulder and aimed at the approaching jeep. Ramón swivelled the Browning on to him, but at that moment the front wheels struck one of the corpses and the jeep bounced wildly, throwing his aim high.

The guard fired the rocket and it whooshed across the open courtyard and hit the jeep full in the centre of the radiator. There was a flash and a roar as the rocket exploded. Although the engine block smothered most of the blast, the front suspension collapsed and the vehicle cartwheeled end over end.

They were all thrown clear, but the shattered body of the jeep blocked the entrance and the troop-trucks were backed up beyond the open gateway.

The attack was stalling already, and the defence was

rallying. Automatic fire was stuttering from the windows and doorways of the palace building.

The Cuban paras sprang out of the stationary trucks and rushed forward, but another rocket hissed down the alley facing them. It flashed inches over Ramón's head, blinding him with smoke, and struck the leading truck, ripping the bonnet open and shattering the windscreen. Diesel fuel spilled from the ruptured tank and ignited with a sullen roar. Black smoke billowed over the courtyard.

There was shouting and more firing in front of them. Beside Ramón another para was hit and went sprawling.

Ramón snatched up his machine-pistol and waved the attack forward, just as a heavy machine-gun opened up on them from one of the windows. Ramón rolled under the blast of shot and came up against the mud wall directly below the window. The machine-gun was firing over his head, and the muzzle-blast drove in his eardrums.

Ramón snatched a grenade from his webbing pocket, pulled the pin and went up on one knee to post it through the window. He ducked and covered his ears.

There was a wild shout, and the machine-gun fell silent. Moments later the grenade exhaled in a fiery breath above his head.

'Come on,' Ramón yelled again, and led half a dozen paras through the shattered window. The gun had been knocked off its mounting and the floor was wet and slippery with blood.

It was room-to-room, and hand-to-hand now. The advantage passed to the defenders as they retreated through the maze of rooms and alleys and courtyards, doggedly holding each strongpoint until they were driven from it.

Slowly the attack lost impetus and, although Ramón threatened and swore and tried to inspire them with his example, they bogged down in the twisting alleys and interconnecting passageways and rooms. He realized that Andom was certainly radioing for reinforcements of loyal troops, and that minutes lost now could mean the defeat and failure of the revolution.

He heard Abebe's voice raised angrily, urging his men on in a fog of smoke and dust, and Ramón crawled across to him and seized his shoulder. Face to dusty smoke-grimed face, they shouted at each other to make themselves heard above the cacophony of guns.

'Where is that bloody tank?'

'How long since I called?'

'It's over an hour.' Was it that long? It seemed that minutes had passed since the attack began.

'Get back to the radio,' Ramón yelled. 'Tell them . . .'

At that moment they both heard it, the shrill metallic squeal and the rumble of the tracks.

'Come on!' Ramón lunged to his feet, and they ran together, doubled over, with bullets fluttering in the air around their heads, back through the blood-smeared rooms with walls pocked by bullets and shrapnel.

As they reached the entrance courtyard the tank butted its way in through the blocked gateway. The turret was reversed, the long 55-millimetre gun-barrel pointed backwards. The carcass of the rocket-shattered jeep was forced forward by the mass of armour and it rolled clear of the gateway. The T-53 burst into the courtyard with its diesels bellowing. The turret was open, the commander's helmeted head protruded from the hatch.

Ramón windmilled his right arm in the cavalry signal to advance and pointed into the tangle of alleys and buildings.

The tank pivoted on its churning steel tracks and crashed into the nearest wall. The mud bricks collapsed before it, and the roof tilted and sagged and buried the T-53 beneath it.

The tank shook itself free and roared forward. Ramón and his paras poured into the breach it had opened. Walls toppled and timbers crackled as the steel monster crawled forward, tilting and rocking over piles of rubble and human bodies.

The screams of the defenders rose higher than the uproar, and their firing died away. They came stumbling out of the ruined buildings, throwing down their weapons and raising their arms in surrender.

'Where is Andom?' Ramón's throat was rough and sore with the dust and the shouting. 'We must get him. Don't let him escape.'

The general was amongst the last to surrender. Only when the T-53 flattened the thick mud walls of the main hall did he come out with four of his senior officers. There was a blood-soaked bandage around his forehead and over his left eye. His beard was thick with dust and blood, and one of the scarlet tabs was torn from his collar.

His good eye was fierce. Despite his wound, his voice was firm and his bearing dignified. 'Colonel Abebe,' he challenged. 'This is mutiny and treachery. I am the president of Ethiopia – my appointment was confirmed by the Derg this morning.'

Ramón nodded to his paratroopers. They seized the general's arms and forced him to his knees. Ramón opened the flap of his holster and handed his Tokarev pistol to Abebe.

The colonel placed the muzzle between the captive's eyes and said quietly: 'President Aman Andom, in the name of the people's revolution, I call upon you to resign.' And he blew the top off the general's skull.

The corpse fell face-forward, splattering custard-yellow brains on to Abebe's boots.

Abebe clicked the safety on the Tokarev, reversed it and handed it butt-first to Ramón.

'Thank you, Colonel-General,' he said.

'I am honoured to have been of service.' Ramón bowed formally as he accepted the weapon back.

'How many members of the Derg voted for Andom?' he asked as the column sped back towards Addis Ababa.

'Sixty-three.'

'Then we still have much work to do before the revolution is secure.'

Abebe radioed ahead to Colonel Tafu's squadron of T-53 tanks. They were entering from the eastern side of the city, and he ordered them to surround the building that housed the Derg and to train their guns upon it. Elements of the Army were ordered to seal off all foreign embassies and consulates. No legation staff were allowed to leave the premises, for their own safety.

All foreigners in the country, especially journalists or television personnel, were rounded up and escorted to the airport for immediate evacuation. There were to be no witnesses of what followed.

Small units of Abebe's most loyal troops, backed up by Cuban paratroopers, were rushed to the homes of the members of the military council and the Derg who had declared for Andom. They were stripped of weapons and badges of rank, dragged out and thrown into the waiting trucks and driven back to the Derg, where a revolutionary court awaited them in the main assembly-chamber.

The court consisted of Colonel Abebe and two of his junior officers. 'You are accused of counter-revolutionary criminal acts against the people's democratic government. Have you anything to say before sentence of death is passed upon you?'

They were taken out directly from the trial into the courtyard of the building, placed against the north wall of the chamber and executed by firing squad. The executions were carried out in full view of the revolutionary judges and those prisoners still awaiting trial. The volleys of rifle-fire periodically interrupted the proceedings of the court.

The corpses were tied in bunches by the heels and dragged behind a truck through the streets to the main rubbish-dump outside the city limits.

'The populace must witness the course of revolutionary justice and the price of disobedience,' Ramón explained the necessity of these exhibitions.

The court ruled that the corpses should not be removed from the rubbish-dump, and their families were forbidden to indulge in the ritual of mourning or to exhibit any public signs of grief. The grim work went on until after midnight, and the last batch of criminals was executed in the beams of the headlights of the trucks waiting to drag them to the rubbish-tip.

Although they were both exhausted, neither Ramón nor the future president could afford to sleep until the revolution was secure. Ramón had á bottle of vodka in his pack. He and Abebe shared it as they sat beside the radio and listened to the reports coming in.

One after the other, Abebe's loyal officers with Cuban support took over command of the various units of the Army and seized all the important points in the city and its surroundings.

As the sun rose, they had control of the airport and railway station, the radio and television broadcasting studios, and all the military forts and barracks. Only then could they snatch a few hours' sleep. Guarded by Ramón's paras, they stretched out on mattresses on the chamber floor, but at noon they were in fresh uniforms for the meeting of the purified Derg. There were armed paras at the door of the chamber and T-53 tanks drawn up in the street outside.

As Colonel-General Machado congratulated Abebe, he said quietly: 'If you kill Brutus, then you must kill all the sons of Brutus. In 1510, Niccolò Machiavelli said that, Mr President, and it is still the best-possible advice.'

'So we must begin at once.'

'Yes,' agreed Ramón. 'The Red Terror must be allowed to run its course.'

★　　　★　　　★

'The Red Terror shall flourish.' The hastily printed posters in four languages were pasted on every street-corner, and the hourly radio and television broadcasts proclaimed the new president and exhorted the populace to denounce all traitors and counter-revolutionaries.

There was so much work to do that Abebe divided the city into forty cells and appointed a separate revolutionary

327

court for each cell. The presidents of these courts were loyal junior officers who were given full power to 'undertake revolutionary action'. Each had a team of executioners working under him. They began with the members of the nobility, the *rases* and the chieftains and their families.

'The Red Terror is a proven tool of the revolution,' Ramón Machado explained. 'We know those who will prove awkward later. We know those who will oppose the pure doctrine of Marxism. It is more expedient to eliminate them now, in the first wild flush of victory, rather than undertake the tedious business of dealing with them piece-meal at a later date.' He lifted his cap and raked his fingers through his thick dark curls. He was tired, his marvellous classical features were strained and drawn. Dark smudges underlined his eyes, but there was no uncertainty in those deadly green eyes. Abebe was at once grateful for this strength and awed by this iron resolution.

'We must root out every rotten apple from the barrel. We must eliminate not only the opposition, but also the thought of opposition. We must break the nation's will to resist. They must be cowed and deprived of any sense of self or self-determination. The board must be swept entirely clean. Only then will we be in a position to rebuild the nation in its new and shining image.' The corpses of the nobles and the petty chieftains and their entire families were piled like garbage on the street-corners. The revolutionary patrols drove through the city and picked up at random the children they found playing in the streets.

'Where do you live? Take us to your parents' home.'

The parents were dragged out of their houses and forced to watch as their children were shot in the head at point-blank range. The little corpses were left at the front door, swelling and stinking in the heat. The parents were forbidden to remove them or to mourn them.

'The Red Terror will flourish,' decreed the posters, but in the mountains some of the old warriors and their families resisted the death squads.

The tanks surrounded the villages, and the women and

children and old men were driven into their huts. The huts were set on fire, and the screams mingled with the crackle of the flames. The men were marched to the fields and forced to lie face-down in rows. The tanks drove over them, locking their tracks to pivot on the piles of bodies and grind them into a paste with the drought-stricken earth.

'Now for the priests,' Ramón said.

'The priests were instrumental in the overthrow of the monarchy,' Abebe pointed out.

'Yes, the church and the mosque, the bishops and priests and the imams and the ayatollahs are always useful in the beginning. The revolution can be nurtured in the pulpit, for the priests are by their training unworldly and idealistic creatures who respond to a vision of freedom and equality and brotherly love. They can be easily persuaded, but always remember that they are also in competition with us for the souls of men. When they witness the revolution in action they will challenge us. We cannot brook that competition. The priests must be disciplined and controlled – just as all other men must be.'

They entered the great mosque and arrested the imam's fourteen-year-old daughter. They put out her eyes and cut out her tongue, then they placed two ounces of raw chili pepper in her vagina and took her back to her father's house. They locked her in a room of the house with guards at the door. Her parents were forced to squat outside the door and listen to their daughter's death agonies.

The sons of the abuna, the archbishop of the Coptic Church, were taken to one of the revolutionary courts and were tortured. Their hands and feet were crushed in steel vices and their bodies were burnt with electricity. Their eyes were gouged out and left dangling by the optic nerves on to their cheeks. Their genitalia were cut off and forced into their mouths. Then they were taken home and placed outside the front door. Once again the parents were forbidden to remove their bodies for Christian burial.

The radio and television broadcasts harangued against

the decadence and revisionism of the Church, and the death squads waited at the doors of the mosque when the muezzin began his chant. The faithful stayed at home.

'All the sons of Brutus are dead,' Abebe told Ramón, as they toured the quiescent city.

'Not all of them,' Ramón disagreed, and Abebe turned to stare at him. He knew what Ramón meant.

'It must be done,' Ramón insisted. 'Then there can be no turning back. The ancient bourgeois taboo will be shattered for ever, as it was on the guillotine in the Place de la Concorde and in the Russian cellar when Tsar Nicholas and his family died. Once it is done, there will be no return and the revolution will be secure.'

'Who will do it?' Abebe asked, and Ramón answered without hesitation.

'I will.'

'It would be best that way,' Abebe agreed, and looked away to conceal the relief he felt. 'Do it as soon as possible.'

Ramón drove down through the old quarter of the city. He was alone at the wheel of the open jeep. The streets were deserted, except for the revolutionary patrols. The windows of the houses were shuttered and curtained. No face peered out at him, no children romped in the yards, no voices or sounds of laughter came from behind the closed doors of the mud-brick hovels.

The revolutionary posters were pasted to the cracked and chipped plaster of the walls. 'The Red Terror shall flourish.'

There had been no hygienic services since the Red Terror began. The rubbish clogged the streets, and the sewage-buckets overflowed and puddled in the gutters. The bodies of the victims of the Terror were heaped like cords of firewood at the street-corners. They were so bloated and bullet-riddled that they were no longer recognizable as human. Gas-filled bellies stretched their clothing until it burst at the seams, and their flesh was empurpled and blackened by the sun. The only living things were the crows and kites and vultures that hopped and picked at the piles of the dead, and the fat gorged rats that scuttled away in front of the jeep.

Ramón wrapped his silk scarf across his mouth and nose to protect them from the stench, but apart from that he was unmoved by what he saw around him, as a victorious general is unaffected by the carnage of the battlefield.

The hut was at the end of a noisome alleyway, and there were two guards at the front door. They recognized Ramón as he parked the jeep and picked his way through the accumulated filth. They saluted him respectfully.

'You are relieved of your duties. You may go,' Ramón ordered.

He watched them hurry to the end of the alley before he opened the door and stooped under the lintel.

It was semi-dark in the room, and he removed his sunglasses. The walls were limed but bare except for a silver Coptic cross suspended above the bed. There were rush mats on the stone floor. The room smelt of sickness and old age. An old woman sat on the floor at the foot of the bed. She wailed and pulled the hood of her robe over her head when she saw Ramón.

'Go.' He gestured to the door, and she crawled across the floor, her head still covered, making obeisance and wailing and drooling with terror.

With the heel of his combat boot Ramón pushed the door closed behind her and studied the figure that lay on the bed.

'Negus Negusti, King of Kings,' he said with a dry irony, and the old man stirred and looked up at him.

He was dressed in a spotless white robe, but his head was bare. He was thin, impossibly thin. Ramón knew that he suffered from the ailments of great age, his prostate and digestion were diseased, but his mind was clear. His feet and hands protruding from the folds of the white robe were childlike and emaciated. Each tiny bone showed clearly through the waxen amber skin. His beard and hair were untrimmed and entirely bleached to the lustre of platinum. The flesh had melted from his face, so the nose was thin and aquiline. His lips had shrunk and drawn back. His teeth were yellow and too large for the delicate bones of his cheeks and brow. His eyes were enormous, black as pools of tar, bright as those of a biblical prophet.

'I recognize you,' he said softly.

'We have never met,' Ramón corrected him.

'Still, I know you well. I recognize the smell of you. I know every line of your face and the inflection and timbre of your voice.'

'Who am I, then?' Ramón challenged him softly.

'You are the first of a legion – and your name is Death.'

'You are wise and perceptive, old man,' Ramón told him, and advanced to the bed.

'I forgive you for what you do to me,' said Haile Selassie, Negus Negusti, Emperor of Ethiopia. 'But I cannot forgive you for what you have done to my people.'

'Commend yourself to your God, old man,' said Ramón as he picked up the pillow from the bed. 'This world is no longer for you.'

He pressed the pillow down over the old man's face and leant his weight upon it.

Haile Selassie's struggles were like those of a trapped bird. His thin fingers clutched lightly at Ramón's wrists and plucked softly at his sleeves. He kicked and danced, and the robe rode up above his knees. His legs were thin and dark as sticks of dried tobacco, and the knees were enlarged knots out of all proportion to the skinny shanks.

Gradually his struggles grew weaker, and there was a soft spluttering under his robes as his sphincter relaxed and his bowels voided. Ramón leant on the pillow for five minutes after the old man was completely still. He felt an almost religious ecstasy come over him. Nothing he had done before had ever given him this sense of gratification. It was physical and emotional, it was spiritual and at the same time deeply sexual.

He had killed a king.

He straightened up and removed the pillow. He plumped it up and then lifted the old man's head and set the pillow

332

beneath it. He pulled the hem of the robe down to Haile Selassie's ankles, and folded the little childlike hands upon his breast. Then with thumb and forefinger he drew down his eyelids.

He stood for a long time studying the emperor's death-face. He wanted to fix the image in his mind for ever. He was unaware of the heat and the stench in the closed room. He sensed that this was one of the high points in his life. The frail body epitomized all that he had pledged to destroy in this world.

He wanted the memory of that destruction to be strong and vivid enough to last a lifetime.

★   ★   ★

All possible opposition had been eliminated. The voice of dissent was silenced. The sons of Brutus were all of them dead, and the revolution was secure.

There were many other important issues needing Ramón's attention elsewhere in Africa. With a clear conscience he could hand over his position as security adviser to the People's Democratic Government of Ethiopia. His successor in office was a general in the security police of the German Democratic Republic. He was almost as skilled as Ramón Machado in the enforcement of pragmatic democracy on a recalcitrant population.

Ramón embraced Abebe and boarded one of the Ilyushin transports that now flew regularly in and out of Addis. It was a most convenient port of entry to the entire continent.

They refuelled in Brazzaville and then flew south and west to land on the new airstrip at Tercio base on the Chicamba river just as the sun set into the blue Atlantic Ocean.

Raleigh Tabaka met him. During the drive from the airstrip to Ramón's new headquarters compound in the palm grove above the white coral beach, Raleigh brought him fully up to date with developments during his absence.

Ramón's private quarters were austere. A thatched roof

and large unglazed windows with roll-up blinds of split bamboo; bare uncarpeted floors and chunky but comfortable furniture made by a local carpenter from hand-sawn indigenous timber. Only the electronic communications equipment was modern. He had direct satellite links to Moscow and Luanda and Havana'and Lisbon.

As Ramón entered this simple dwelling he was reminded forcefully of the cottage at Buenaventura in Cuba. He felt immediately at home here, with the trade winds in the palms and the ocean breathing heavily on the white beach below his window.

He was exhausted. This deep bone-weariness had accumulated over the weeks and months. As soon as Raleigh Tabaka left him, he dropped his combat uniform in a heap on the mud floor and crawled under the mosquito-net. The gentle warm gusts of the trades through the open window billowed the mosquito-net and caressed his naked body.

He felt replete. He had performed a difficult but infinitely worthwhile task with skill and success. He knew that he had earned new honours and rewards, but none would be aş satisfying as this deep sense of achievement that buoyed his weary spirit. ´

His creation surpassed that of a Mozart or a Michelangelo. He had used as his raw materials a land and a people, mountains and valleys and lakes and rivers and plains and millions of human beings. He had mixed them on his palette and then, in blood and flames and gunfire, he had fashioned and worked them into a masterpiece. His creation surpassed that of any artist who had lived before him. He knew that there was no God – at least, not as the bishops and imams whom he had so recently disciplined and humiliated imagined God to be. The god that Ramón knew was of this world. He was the twin god of power and political mastery – and Ramón was his prophet. The work had only just begun. First a single nation, he thought, and then another and another, until finally an entire continent. His elation staved off sleep for a few minutes longer, but as he succumbed his mind took another turn.

Maybe it was the hut and the wind and the sound of the sea – whatever the association of ideas, he thought of Nicholas. In the night he dreamt of his son. He saw again his shy reluctant smile, and heard his voice and his laughter in his head, and felt the small warm hand curled in his hand like the timorous body of a tiny creature.

When he awoke the longing was even more intense. While he worked at his desk the image of his son's face receded and he could concentrate on the coded messages from Havana and Moscow that flashed down from the orbiting satellite. However, when he stood up from his desk and looked down through the open window to the beach, he imagined he saw a slim tanned little body splashing in the green surf and heard the sweet treble cries of the child.

Perhaps it was merely a reaction from the slaughter in the streets of Addis Ababa, or the memory of the corpses of the sons of the abuna with their eyeballs hanging on their cheeks and their immature genitals stuffed into their mouths, but over the next few days the desire to see his son became an obsession.

He could not leave Tercio base now, not with so much in play, so many prizes at stake on the great gaming-board of Africa. Instead he sent a satellite message to Havana and within an hour had his reply.

After Ethiopia they would deny him nothing. Nicholas and Adra were on the next transport flight from Cuba. Ramón was waiting at the airstrip when the Ilyushin landed at Tercio base.

He watched his son come down the ramp. He walked ahead of Adra, no longer clinging to her hand like a baby. There was alertness in the way he carried his head, a spring to his step, and a sparkle of curiosity and intelligence in his eyes as he paused at the bottom of the ramp and looked about him keenly.

Ramón felt an extraordinary emotion, an intensification of the longing and pride with which he had anticipated the boy's arrival. No other human being had ever moved him

335

in this way. For long aching moments he watched his son in secret, concealed in the throng of disembarking troops and swarming porters, his eyes hidden behind sunglasses. He was reluctant to give a name to this emotion he felt. He would never have entertained the word 'love'.

Then Nicholas picked him out. He saw the boy's entire attitude change. He started forward at a run, but within a dozen paces he took control of himself. The look of extreme pleasure on his lovely face was swiftly masked. He was expressionless as he walked calmly to the side of the jeep in which Ramón sat and held out his hand.

'Good day, Padre,' he said softly. 'How does it go with you?'

Ramón felt an almost irresistible compulsion to embrace him. He sat very still while he overcame it, then he took Nicholas's hand and returned his formal greeting.

Nicholas rode in the front of the jeep beside his father. Adra sat in the back. They skirted the guerrilla camp on the way from the airstrip to the beach compound, and Nicholas could not contain his curiosity. He asked the first question hesitantly, in a subdued voice.

'Why are all these men here? Are they sons of the revolution like we are, Padre?'

When Ramón replied without any sign of irritability, the next question was bolder. When the reply to that was also friendly, he relaxed further and took a lively interest in everything around them.

The men at the roadside saluted Ramón as the jeep passed. From the corner of his eye he saw Nicholas stiffen in the front seat and return the salute with all the aplomb of a veteran. Ramón had to turn his face away to hide his smile. The men had noticed it also and grinned after the departing vehicle.

When they arrived at the compound, Ramón's orderly had a batch of satellite messages for his attention. However, there was little of importance amongst them, and Ramón dealt with them swiftly. He went to the hut alongside his own that he had allocated for Nicholas and Adra. He heard the boy's excited chatter as he stepped up on to the stoep, but it was cut off abruptly as he appeared in the doorway. Again Nicholas was strange and withdrawn, watching his father warily.

'Did you bring your bathing-suit?' Ramón asked him.

'Yes, Padre.'

'Good. Put it on. We will swim together.'

The water inside the reef was calm and warm.

'Look, Padre. I can swim the crawl now – no more baby paddle,' Nicholas boasted.

With Ramón swimming beside him, he made it out to the reef with only a half-dozen pauses to tread water while he regained his breath. They sat side by side on a coral head, and while they discussed seriously how the reef was formed by millions of tiny living creatures Ramón studied the boy carefully. He was well favoured, tall and strong for his age. His vocabulary had expanded again since they had last been together. At times it was almost like talking to a grown man.

They ate dinner together on the veranda. Ramón discovered how much he had missed Adra's cooking. Every minute Nicholas seemed more relaxed. His appetite was good. He asked for more of the baked mullet. Ramón allowed him half a glass of well-watered wine. Nicholas sipped it like a connoisseur, swelling with pride at being treated as an adult.

When Adra came to fetch him to bed, he slipped off his chair without argument but pulled away from her hand and came around the table to his father.

'I am very happy to be here, Padre,' he said formally, and held out his hand.

As Ramón shook his hand he experienced an actual physical constriction of his chest.

Within a week Nicholas had become a favourite at Tercio camp. Some of the ANC instructors and recruits had their families with them. One of the wives was a trained primary-school teacher from the University of the Western Cape in South Africa. She had set up a school for the children in the camp. Ramón sent Nicholas to take part in the classes. The schoolroom was a thatched building with open sides and rows of benches made of roughly planed native timber.

Almost immediately it was clear that Nicholas was as bright and advanced as children three and four years older than he was. English was the language of instruction, and he made swift progress in it. He had a clear sweet voice and led the singing. He taught them 'Land of the Landless' and the other revolutionary songs which the teacher translated into English. He had brought his soccer ball with him, and this gave him tremendous social prestige amongst his peers. A work detail from the camp under orders from Colonel-General Machado levelled a soccer pitch for the school, laid out the markings in lime and set up goal-posts. Such was Nicholas's prowess on the field that they nicknamed him Pele, and the daily matches became a popular feature of camp life.

As the general's son, Nicholas had special standing and privilege. He had the run of the camp, including the induction classes for new recruits. The instructors allowed him to handle the weapons.

Ramón watched with carefully concealed pride as his son stood up before a class of adult recruits and demonstrated the stripping and reassembling of an AK 47 assault-rifle. Then he took his place on the range and fired a magazine of live ammunition. Twelve of the twenty rounds struck the man-sized target at which he was aiming.

Without Ramón's knowledge, José, the Cuban driver, taught Nicholas to drive the jeep. The first Ramón knew of his son's latest accomplishment was when Nicholas, sitting on a cushion, proudly drove him down to the airstrip to meet the incoming Ilyushin transport flight.

The men along the road cheered them as they passed with cries of 'Viva Pele!'

The camp tailor made Nicholas his own set of camouflage combat fatigues and a soft Cuban-style cap. He wore the cap cocked at an angle over one eye, just as his father did, and imitated Ramón's mannerisms, lifting his cap to rake his fingers through his hair or hooking his thumbs in his belt as he stood at rest. He became Ramón's unofficial driver, and wherever they went huge grins of delight followed the jeep.

On some afternoons Ramón and Nicholas took one of the boats powered by a fifty-horsepower outboard motor and raced out through the pass in the coral reef into the blue Atlantic waters. They anchored the boat over one of the deep reefs and fished with hand-lines. The coral teemed with fish of every possible shape and size and colour. Ramón taught Nicholas how to chop the carcass of a large fish, preserved from their previous expedition, into a fine mince. They mixed this with beach sand to make it sink swiftly and ground-baited the reef below the anchored boat.

Soon they could make out the shadowy shapes of large fish darting and swirling in the blue depths sixty feet below their hull. The scent of the ground bait had goaded them into a feeding frenzy. As they dropped their baited hooks amongst them the thick line was jerked through their fingers and Nicholas squealed with glee.

The reef fish glittered and glowed with peacock blue and iridescent green; with clear daffodil yellow and startling scarlet. They were spotted with jade and sapphire, striped like zebra and splashed with flaming ruby and opal. They were shaped like bullets and butterflies, and winged like exotic birds. They were armed with daggers and barbed spines and rows of porcelain-white fangs. They squeaked and grunted like pigs as they were hauled flapping and squirming over the gunwale of the assault-boat. Some were so large that Ramón had to give Nicholas a hand to drag them from the water. He hated anybody, even his father, to help him. He hated even more to stop fishing at the close of the day.

'One more, Padre – just one more,' he cried eagerly, and in the end Ramón had to take the line out of his hands.

One evening they stayed later than usual. Darkness was

falling as they hauled the anchor and started the outboard. The trade wind had turned chilly, and the wind of their passage blew over them as they bounced over the tops of the swells on their way back to the river mouth. Goose-flesh pimpled Nicholas's arms as he hugged himself. He shivered with cold and exhaustion and the reaction from so much excitement.

Steering the boat with one hand, Ramón put his other arm around Nicholas's shoulders. For a moment the child froze with shock at his unfamiliar touch, and then his body relaxed and he crept closer to his father and cuddled against his chest.

As he steered through the darkness with the small shivering body pressed to his, Ramón was assailed once again by the memory of the abuna of Addis Ababa's sons propped against the front wall of their father's home with empty eye-sockets and each with his tiny dark penis protruding like a finger from between his dead lips. Ramón was not touched by either guilt or regret. It had been necessary, just as once it had been necessary to half-drown the child that now cuddled against his chest. Duty was often hard and cruel, but he had never flinched from its call. Still, he had never felt before the way he did now.

They beached the boat, and handed it over to José, the Cuban driver, to care for. Then they made their way by lantern-light through the palm grove towards the stockade of the compound.

Nicholas stumbled against him in the darkness, and Ramón took his hand to steady him. The child made no effort to pull his hand away.

They walked on without speaking until they reached the gate of the compound, and then Nicholas whispered softly: 'I wish I could stay here at Tercio with you always.'

Ramón pretended he had not heard him, but he found it difficult to draw his next breath.

The signals clerk woke him ten minutes after midnight. It needed only a light tap on the door of the hut for Ramón to come fully awake with the Tokarev pistol in his hand.

'What is it?'

'A Red Rose relay from Moscow,' the clerk answered him. They had strict instructions to call him at any time of day or night for a Red Rose communication.

'I will come immediately.'

The message was in code, and Ramón fetched his copy of the code-pad from the steel safe. They used a 'one-time' pad, a separate code randomly generated by computer for each sheet. He and Red Rose had the only existing copies of the pad, and used a single sheet for each message.

He matched her sheet and began to decode the message.

'Project is code-named Skylight,' the message read. 'First subterranean test of thirty-megaton fission device scheduled October twenty-sixth. Test site located 27°35'S 24°25'E. Full specifications of device on hand.'

Ramón sent his driver to the main ANC camp upriver, and Raleigh Tabaka was in his office within forty minutes.

'We must leave for London immediately,' Ramón told him as Raleigh read the message. 'This is too important to co-ordinate from here. We will orchestrate through the London embassy and the ANC office in the UK.'

Ramón smiled with quiet satisfaction. 'We will have the Boers on the mat in front of the Security Council before the week is out. Once again, they have played right into our hands.'

He woke Nicholas to say goodbye to him.

'When will you come back, Padre?' the child asked bravely, hiding any sign of distress.

'I don't know, Nicky.' Ramón used the diminutive of his name for the first time, and it sat awkwardly on his tongue.

'You will come back, won't you, Padre?'

'Yes, I will come back. I promise you that.'

'And you will let me and Adra stay here at Tercio? You won't send us away?'

'Yes, Nicky. You and Adra will stay here.'

'Thank you. I am glad,' said Nicholas. 'Goodbye, Padre.'

They shook hands solemnly, and then Ramón turned away quickly and ran down the steps to the waiting jeep.

*　　*　　*

Preventing the Skylight test was of secondary importance. It was almost three years since they had first learnt of the South African plans to build a nuclear bomb, and Ramón knew that by now they had a viable weapon. However, a nuclear weapon had very little practical application in the type of bush war that was typically African.

What was of primary importance was to isolate South Africa even further from its last remaining support in the Western world. Already a political pariah, this was an opportunity that he had waited for, to brand her a nuclear rogue into the bargain.

They met in the ambassador's safe room in the cellar of the Soviet embassy. The embassy was set in that intimate diplomatic enclave behind Kensington Palace.

Both General Borodin and Aleksei Yudenich had flown in from Moscow. Their presence gave weight to the deliberations. It underlined both the foreign ministry's and the KGB's renewed interest in the African section, and gave Colonel-General Machado tremendous personal prestige.

The Africans were represented by Raleigh Tabaka and the secretary-general of the ANC. Oliver Tambo, the president of the ANC, was on an unofficial visit to East Germany and could not return to London in time for the meeting.

There was a great deal of urgency, for the South Africans were due to test Skylight within the coming week. Red Rose had reinforced her initial despatch with quite extensive information concerning the enriching of the uranium, the specifications of the actual bomb, its projected delivery in the new G5 artillery round, the position and depth of the test-hole and the ignition system that would be used to detonate the bomb.

'What we have to decide today,' Yudenich opened the discussion, 'is how best to use this information.'

'I think, comrade,' the secretary-general of the ANC cut in eagerly, 'that you should allow us to call a press conference here in London.'

Ramón's lips curled into a small cynical smile. Of course they wanted it. What a blaze of publicity the ANC would bring down upon itself.

'Comrade Secretary-General,' Yudenich smiled broadly, 'I think the announcement would carry a little more weight if it were to be made by the president of the USSR, rather than the president of ANC.' His tone was heavy with sarcasm. Yudenich didn't like blacks.

In private, before this meeting, he had remarked to Ramón that it was a pity that they had been obliged to invite the 'monkeys' rather than deciding the issue between civilized human beings. 'It is difficult to bring one's mind down to their level,' he had chuckled. 'But, then, you have had much experience with them, Comrade. Should I have brought a packet of nuts for them, do you think?'

Ramón sat aloof from the discussion for nearly twenty minutes. The voices of both Yudenich and the secretary-general were becoming louder and more strained. It was Borodin who at last suggested mildly: 'Should we perhaps ask Comrade General Machado's views? His source provided the information – perhaps he has ideas how best to take advantage of it.'

They all looked down the table at him, and Ramón had his reply prepared.

'Comrades, all that you have said has good sense and reason. However, if either the ANC or the president of the USSR breaks the news it will be a one-day sensation. I believe that to extract the most benefit we should draw out the process. We should release a few scraps of information at a time, and allow interest to build up over a protracted period.'

They looked thoughtful, and Ramón went on.

'I also believe that if we break it ourselves, either through Moscow or through the ANC, it will be looked upon as biased or at least highly prejudiced information. I think we should give the news to the most powerful voice in America to spread for us. The voice that governs the United States – and, through it, the Western world.'

Yudenich looked confused. 'Gerald Ford? The President of the United States?'

'No, Comrade Minister. The news media. The true government of America. In their single-minded obsession with the freedom of speech, the Americans have created a dictatorship more powerful than anything we can devise. Let us give this to the American television networks. We make no announcements, we hold no press conferences. We simply give one of them a mere whiff of the scent, show them the tracks of the hare, and let them hunt it down and tear the animal to pieces themselves. You know well how it works; like a pack of hounds their excitement and their blood lust will be more thoroughly aroused if they believe that the prey is theirs alone. They call it "investigative journalism" and give prizes to the ones who do most damage to their government, their allies and to the capitalist system that supports them.'

Yudenich stared at him a little longer before he began to chuckle. 'I hear that in Africa they call you the Fox, Comrade General.'

'The Golden Fox,' Borodin corrected him, and Yudenich burst into full-throated laughter.

'I see you merit your name, Comrade General. Let the Americans and the British do our work for us once again.'

★   ★   ★

The total success of the Skylight operation reaffirmed Red Rose's worth a hundredfold, but brought with it its own problems.

The more valuable Red Rose became, the more skilfully and carefully she must be controlled. Every possible precaution had to be taken to protect and guard her in the field, and to give her incentive to continue. She must be rewarded immediately for Skylight and given access to

344

Nicholas as soon as reasonably possible. However, this again was complicated by Ramón's own changing attitude towards his son.

He was determined that these sickly bourgeois sentiments which recently had intruded on his sense of purpose must never be allowed to interfere with his duty. He knew that, if necessary, given the right circumstances, he must be ready to sacrifice Nicholas, just as he was completely resigned to laying down his own life if duty dictated it.

Until that day, however, Nicholas must never be placed in any position of danger. Especially there must never be the least possibility of Red Rose or any other person laying hands on the boy and removing him from Ramón's custody.

He considered once again arranging the next access at the *hacienda* in Spain. This would mean moving from Tercio; that involved a degree of risk, a very small degree, but a certain risk none the less. It was just possible that Red Rose – say, with the assistance of South African agents – might succeed in spiriting the child to the British embassy in Madrid. He knew that Red Rose possessed a British passport and dual nationality. Spain was no longer secure enough to satisfy Ramón.

Of course, he could arrange the meeting in either Havana or Moscow. This entailed considerable logistical problems in getting Red Rose to those locations. It would also reveal to her beyond any doubt who were her ultimate masters. He wanted to avoid that if at all possible.

The most secure location outside Cuba or Russia was Tercio base on the Chicamba river. It was remote and heavily guarded. There was no foreign embassy within a thousand miles. Nicholas was already installed there. Red Rose could be brought in with very little inconvenience. Once she was at Tercio she would be more completely under his control than in any other place on this earth.

Tercio it would have to be.

*   *   *

Isabella came fully awake with a guilty start. For a moment she did not know where she was or what had woken her. Then she remembered, and realized that it was the change in the sound of the Ilyushin's engines and the canting of the deck beneath her that had woken her. Despite her best intentions, she had fallen asleep in the uncomfortable jump-seat.

She glanced quickly at her wristwatch. Two hours fifty minutes since take-off from Lusaka.

She lifted herself slightly in her seat and checked the instrument-panel over the pilot's shoulder. They were still on the same heading, but they were beginning their descent. The altimeter began to unwind steadily.

She looked ahead through the windscreen of the cockpit. It was late afternoon and hazy, but suddenly the low sun flashed on a large body of water ahead.

Lake? she thought, and searched her memory for one that large. The African lakes all lay along the Great Rift Valley, thousands of miles in the opposite direction. Then suddenly it occurred to her.

'The Atlantic! We have reached the west coast.' She reassembled the map of Africa in her mind. 'Angola or Zaïre, or the Enclave.'

The Candid banked on to an approach heading. The undercarriage whined and vibrated as it was lowered. Ahead she saw white coral beaches, and the shape of the reefs beneath the blue Atlantic waters.

There was a river mouth, with a low surf breaking on the bar and a deeper serpentine channel crawling into the lagoon. The river was broad and brown, but not large enough to be one of the major African drainages, not the Congo nor the Luanda river. She tried to memorize every detail. A few miles above the lagoon the river formed a distinctive ox-bow, a double S. Dead ahead was a long red clay landing-strip, and she made out the thatched roofs of a large settlement in the bend of the river beyond it.

The Candid touched down and taxied to the far end of the strip. As the pilot shut down the engines, a convoy of trucks trundled out to surround it. She saw many armed men in camouflage and combat fatigues.

'Wait,' the pilot told her. 'Men come fetch.'

Two officers entered the flight-deck. One was a major. They were both swarthy and wore moustaches. They were dressed in camouflage with no insignia apart from their badges or rank.

South Americans, she thought. Or Mexicans. And this was confirmed when the major addressed her in Spanish.

'Welcome, señora. You will please come with us.'

'My suitcase.' She indicated her luggage with all the *hauteur* she could muster, and the major snapped an order at his junior. The lieutenant carried her baggage down the ramp and loaded it into a waiting truck.

They drove her in silence for twenty minutes, passing the barbed-wire stockade beyond which stood the thatched buildings she had first seen from the air. There were armed guards at the gate. They followed a single track, and she caught glimpses of the river through the trees. The track became progressively softer and sandier, and she guessed that they were headed towards the river mouth and the sea.

They reached another smaller stockade. The gate was guarded, but they were allowed to pass straight through. The huts were thatched, but seemed smaller and neater than the others she had seen. There were nine of them along the edge of the beach.

As she stepped down from the truck she looked around her. It was a pretty spot, and reminded her of one of the brochures for a Club Méditerranée holiday – sea, sand, palms and thatched huts.

The major escorted her politely into the largest hut, and as soon as Isabella saw the two uniformed females who were waiting to meet her she felt her flesh crawl. She remembered the degrading deep body-search that had been inflicted on her on the previous occasion.

Her fears were without substance. The two young women were almost apologetic as they searched her suitcase

347

and handbag. They patted her down, but did not force her to undress for a body-search.

There was minor consternation when they discovered her camera. It was a small 'Swinger' type Kodak. They discussed it with obvious alarm, and Isabella resigned herself to losing it.

'It is of no value,' she told them in Spanish. 'You may take it if you wish.'

In the end, one of the women took the camera and the two spare rolls of film and disappeared with them through the door at the back of the room.

Ramón was watching through the peep-hole in the wall as the two women signallers conducted the search. He had ordered them to behave with circumspection and not to give unnecessary offence, so he nodded with approval when one of them came through and handed him the camera and film.

He examined them quickly but thoroughly. He exposed a single frame to ensure that the trigger mechanism functioned and that the film wound on properly. Then he nodded and handed the camera back to the woman.

Isabella was surprised and obviously pleased when it was returned to her. Through the peep-hole, Ramón studied her expression with interest. She had grown her hair longer, and her features had matured and become stronger. She was even more poised and self-possessed than she had been when last he had seen her in Spain. She carried authority and success well, and he reminded himself of her considerable achievements and the high place that she had carved for herself in a few short years.

She had obviously kept herself in top physical condition. She was slim and fit-looking. Her legs and arms under the short cotton blouse and Bermuda shorts were tanned and shapely. Her muscle tone was as taut as that of a professional athlete. He considered her objectively and he thought that she was probably one of the three or four physically most attractive women of the hundreds he had known. He was highly pleased with her. She was in large measure responsible for his own career success.

The two women finished the search and repacked and closed Isabella's suitcase. One of them picked it up and asked Isabella to follow her. She took her to the end of the compound to a gate in the screen fence made of dried palm-fronds. Isabella found herself in a small enclosure that contained only two huts.

The woman led her to the nearest of these and ushered her into a single large living-room, with a mosquito-netted bed in a side-alcove. She deposited the suitcase on the bed and left Isabella alone.

Isabella explored quickly. There was a shower-room and earth toilet at the rear. All very bucolic but more than adequate for her needs. It reminded her of one of Sean's hunting camps in the Chizora concession.

She began unpacking her suitcase. There were hanging-space and shelves behind a curtain, but before she could finish the chore a sound carried to her through the open window overlooking the beach.

It was a sound that pierced her soul, the high joyous shout of a child that she would have recognized wherever or whenever she heard it.

She rushed to the window.

Nicholas was on the beach. He wore only bathing-trunks, and at first glance she saw that he had grown inches since their last meeting in Spain.

He had a puppy with him, a black and white spotted mongrel with a thin muzzle and a long whippy tail. Nicholas was holding a stick out of reach as he raced along the water's edge, and the puppy gambolled and leapt beside him trying to reach the stick. Nicholas was shrieking with laughter, and the puppy yapped hysterically.

Nicholas hurled the stick out into the sea and shouted, 'Fetch!' And the puppy plunged in gamely and swam out to the floating stick. It picked it up in its jaws and turned back.

'Good boy! Come on!' Nicholas encouraged him, and as the puppy came ashore it shook a gale of waterdrops over him. Nicholas howled with protest, and seized one end of the stick. Boy and dog began a laughing growling tug-of-war.

Isabella found her vision misting over, and she had to blink rapidly to clear her eyes. She left the hut and went down softly to the high-water mark. Nicholas was so absorbed with his pet that she was able to sit still and observe him for almost ten minutes before he noticed her.

Immediately his manner altered. He pushed the puppy away. 'Down!' he commanded sternly, and it obeyed. 'Sit!' he said. 'Stay!'

He left it at the water's edge and came to Isabella.

'Good day, Mamma.' He held out his hand solemnly. 'How goes it with you today?'

'Did you know I was coming?'

'Yes. I am to be good and kind to you,' he replied frankly. 'But I will not be allowed to go to school while you are here.'

'Do you like school, Nicholas?'

'Yes, Mamma, very much. I can read now. And we are learning in English,' he replied in that language.

'Your English is very good, Nicky. Luckily I have brought you some English books.' She tried to make up for denied pleasure. 'I think you will like them.'

'Thank you.'

She felt rejected, an interloper in his compact little world.

'What is your puppy's name?'

'July Twenty-Six.'

'That is an odd name for a puppy. Why do you call him that?'

He looked astonished at her ignorance. 'July Twenty-Six. It is the date of the beginning of the revolution. Everybody knows that.'

'Of course. How foolish of me.'

He took pity on her. 'I call him just plain Twenty-Six.' He whistled the puppy, and it came bounding up the beach. 'Sit!' he ordered. 'Shake hands.'

The puppy offered her its paw.

'Twenty-Six is very clever. You have trained him well.'

'Yes,' he agreed calmly. 'He is the cleverest dog in the world.'

'My baby,' she lamented silently, 'what are they doing to you? What tricks are they playing on your susceptible young mind that you call your puppy after some violent political event?' She did not know what revolution Nicholas was referring to, but the anguish must have twisted her features, for he asked: 'Are you all right, Mamma?'

'Oh, yes.'

'I will take you to meet Adra,' he invited. As they walked back through the palms she casually tried to take his hand, but he firmly and politely disengaged her fingers.

'I still have the soccer ball you gave me,' he mollified her. She knew she would have to win his confidence and liking all over again, and the knowledge made her eyes sting once more.

'I must take it very easily,' she cautioned herself. 'I mustn't press him too hard.'

She was totally unprepared for the shock of first seeing Nicholas in his combat fatigues. With the cap cocked over one eye and his thumbs hooked in his belt, he swaggered like a legionnaire and strutted for her approval. She covered up her distress and made suitable noises of admiration.

She had brought with her a selection of books that she hoped might appeal to a boy of Nicholas's age. By a fortunate chance one of these was the African classic *Jock of the Bushveld*, a story of a man and his dog.

The illustrations intrigued Nicholas immediately, and he professed to see in Jock a resemblance to his own Twenty-six. They discussed this at great length, and then Nicholas wanted to read the text. It was a simple story, but beautifully written. He read aloud. Despite herself she was impressed by his ability, although once or twice he appealed to her for help with a difficult word or the name of an African animal with which he was unfamiliar.

By the time that Adra came to fetch him to bed, they

had made up most of the lost time and ground, and were once again on the slippery footing of tentative friendship.

'Don't push too hard,' she had to keep warning herself.

As he said goodnight and shook her hand formally, he suddenly blurted out: 'It is a good story. I like Jock the dog, and I am glad you have come to see me again. I don't really mind not going to school.' His outburst had clearly embarrassed him, and he hurried from the room.

Isabella waited until she saw the light go out in his bedroom, then she went to find Adra. She wanted to speak to her alone, and try to make some estimate of just what part she had played in Nicholas's abduction and where her sympathies now lay. She also wanted news of Ramón, and to find out from Adra when she would see him again.

Adra was in the kitchen, washing the dinner-dishes, but as Isabella entered her expression went dead and she withdrew behind an iron-cold reserve. She replied to Isabella in monosyllables and would not meet her eyes. Very shortly Isabella gave up the effort and went back to her own hut.

Despite the fatigue of travel she slept fitfully and woke in the dawn light, eager for her first full day with her son.

They spent the entire day with Twenty-six on the beach. In the bag of gifts that Isabella had brought with her was a tennis ball. This kept boy and dog amused for hours on end.

Then they swam out to the reef. Nicholas showed her how to hook the sea-cats out of their holes in the coral. He was delighted by her horror of the writhing slimy legs of the miniature octopuses and the huge luminous eyes which gave them their name.

'Adra will cook them for dinner,' he promised.

'You love Adra, don't you?' she asked.

'Of course,' he replied. 'Adra is my mother.' He caught himself as he realized his gaffe. 'I mean you are my mamma, but Adra is my real mother.'

The hurt made her want to weep.

On the second morning Nicholas came to her hut and

woke her while it was still dark. 'We are going fishing,' he exulted. 'José is going to take us out in the boat.'

José was one of the camp guards she had noticed on her arrival. He was a dark-skinned young man with crooked teeth and pock-marked face. He was obviously one of Nicholas's favourites. The two of them chatted easily while they readied the boat and the fishing-lines.

'Why do you call him Pele?' she asked José in Spanish, and Nicholas answered for him.

'Because I am the champion soccer-player in the school – not so, José?'

Nicholas showed her how to bait her line, and was patronizingly indulgent of her inability to remove the hook from the mouth of a leaping, quivering fish.

That evening they read another chapter of *Jock* together. When Nicholas was in bed, Isabella tried once again to engage Adra in friendly conversation. She received the same taciturn and hostile response. However, when she gave up and left the kitchen, Adra followed her out into the darkness and gripped her arm. With her lips almost touching Isabella's ear she hissed: 'I cannot talk to you. They are watching us every minute.'

Before Isabella could recover, Adra had disappeared back into the kitchen.

In the morning Nicholas had another surprise for her. He took her down to the beach where José waited for them. At a word from Nicholas he handed over his weapon and stood by grinning with crooked teeth while the boy stripped the AKM. Nicholas's fingers were nimble and fast. He called out the name of each separate part of the weapon as he detached it.

'How long?' he demanded of José as he finished.

'Twenty-five seconds, Pele.' The guard laughed with admiration. 'Very good. We will make you a para, yet.'

'Twenty-five seconds, Mamma,' he repeated to Isabella proudly, and although she was appalled by the demonstration she tried to make her congratulations sound sincere.

353

'Now, José, you must time me again when I reassemble,' Nicholas ordered. 'And you must take my photograph, Mamma.'

The camera was a great attraction, and she obeyed. Then Nicholas posed with the rifle and demanded another photograph. Watching him through the lens, she was reminded strongly of the photographs she had seen of the child warriors trained by the Vietcong. They were children dwarfed by the weapons they carried, little boys and girls with faces like cherubs and big innocent eyes. She had read also of the atrocities committed by these aberrant little monsters. Was Nicholas being turned into one of these? The thought made her physically sick.

'Can I shoot, José?' Nicholas wheedled him, and they argued playfully until at last José allowed himself to be won over.

He threw an empty bottle out into the lagoon, and Nicholas stood at the edge of the water and fired with the selector of the rifle on single shot. The sound of gunfire brought half a dozen paratroopers and the women signallers from the compound. They stood at the high-water mark and cheered him on. On the fifth shot the bottle exploded and there were shouts of 'Viva, Pele!' and 'Courage, Pele!' from the onlookers.

'Take my picture again, Mamma,' Nicholas pleaded, and posed with his admirers on either side of him and the rifle held at high port across his chest.

Adra gave them a picnic lunch of fruit and cold smoked fish to eat on the beach. As they sat together Nicholas remarked suddenly through a mouthful of food: 'José has fought in many battles. He has killed five men with his rifle. One day I will be a true son of the revolution – just as he is.'

That night she lay under her mosquito-net and tried to fight off the dark waves of despair and helplessness that flooded over her.

'They are turning my baby into a monster. How can I stop them? How can I get him away from them?'

354

She did not even know who *they* were, and her sense of helplessness was overwhelming.

'Oh, where is Ramón? If only he would come to me. With his help, I know I can be strong. With him beside me, we can see this dreadful thing through.'

She tried to approach Adra again, but the woman was cold and intractable.

Nicholas was becoming restless. Although he was still polite and friendly, she could tell that he was becoming bored with her company alone. He spoke of school and soccer matches and his friends and what they would do when he was allowed to return to them. She tried desperately to distract him, but there was a limit to the games she could devise, to the fascination of the books and stories she provided for him.

A kind of wild desperation came over her. She dreamt of escaping with him to the safe and sane world of Weltevreden. She imagined him dressed in the uniform of a first-class public school, rather than in military camouflage. She fantasized making some bargain with the mysterious powers that controlled their destinies so completely.

'I would do anything – if only they would give my baby back to me.' Yet, even as she thought it, she knew it was in vain.

Then in the dark and hopeless watches of the night her imagination became morbid. She thought of ending it, ending the torment for both herself and her son.

'It would be the only way to save him, the only way out for both of us.'

She could use José's rifle. She would ask Nicholas to show it to her, and once she had it in her hands . . . She shuddered at the thought and could take it no further.

Colonel-General Ramón Machado recognized the change in her. He had been anticipating it.

For ten days he had been observing her closely. There were cameras and microphones in the huts which Isabella had not discovered. While she and the child had been together on the beach or in the boat they had been filmed with a high-powered telescopic lens. For hours at a time Ramón studied her through binoculars from carefully prepared vantage-points above the beach.

He had watched her first wild elation change slowly to simple single-minded enjoyment of her son, and then slowly sour into despair and corroding discontent as she came to appreciate fully the invidious circumstances in which she was trapped.

He guessed that she had probably reached the stage when she could try something desperate that would destroy all the beneficial results that had been achieved by the visit so far.

He gave Adra new orders.

As she served dinner that evening, Adra abruptly sent Nicholas on an errand that got him out of the hut for a few minutes. Then, as she spooned thick fish soup into Isabella's bowl, she leant so close to her that a loose strand of her hair brushed Isabella's cheek.

'Do not speak or look at me,' she whispered. 'I have a message from the marqués.' Isabella dropped her spoon with a clatter. 'Careful. Give no sign. He says that he will try to come to you, but it is difficult and dangerous. He says that he loves you. He says to be brave.'

All thought of suicide was driven from her mind. Ramón was close. Ramón loved her. She knew deep down in her heart that it would be all right as long as she had the fortitude to brave it through, and Ramón's help.

The knowledge kept her going through the next two days. There was a new sparkle and zest in her that she was able to share with Nicholas. The restlessness and creeping ennui which had begun to affect their relationship evaporated. They were happy again together.

In the nights she lay awake in her hut, no longer devoured by doubt and brooding fears, but waiting for Ramón.

'He will come. I know he will.'

Then one of the women who had met her and searched her luggage on arrival came to her, but with a message.

'There is an aircraft departing at nine o'clock tomorrow. You will leave with it.'

'The child!' she demanded. 'Nicholas – Pele?'

The woman shook her head. 'The child remains. Your visit is terminated. They will fetch you at eight o'clock tomorrow morning. You must be ready. Those are my orders.'

She wanted to take some memento of her son with her. After she had showered and changed for dinner she took a pair of nail-scissors from her toilet-bag and hid them in the pocket of her Bermudas. When Nicholas was seated at the dinner-table she came up behind him and before he could pull away she snipped a thick dark curl from the back of his head.

'Hey,' he protested half-heartedly. 'Why do you do that?'

'I want something to remember you by when I am gone.'

He thought about that for a while and then asked shyly: 'Can I have some of your hair as well – to remember you?'

Without a word she handed him the scissors. He stood in front of her and streamed one of her tresses between his fingers.

'Not too much,' she warned him. He laughed and cut a lock and curled it round his finger.

'Your hair is soft – and pretty,' he whispered. 'Do you really have to go, Mamma?'

'I am afraid so, Nicky.'

'Will you come and visit me again?'

'Yes, I will. I promise you that.'

'I will keep this piece of your hair in my *Jock* book.' He fetched the book and pressed the curl between the pages. 'Every time I read the book I will think of you.'

The moon was almost full. The silver radiance sifted in through the open sides of her hut and cast stark shadows that moved softly across the floor to mark the passage of the hours.

'He *must* come,' she told herself, lying rigid with fearful hope on the hard mattress. 'Please let him come.'

Suddenly she sat bolt upright. She had heard nothing,

seen nothing, but she knew with utter certainty that he was close. She had to force herself not to call his name aloud. She waited with every sense alert, and then suddenly without sound he was there.

He appeared like a wraith in the silver moonlight, and she gagged the cry that rose in her throat. She threw back the mosquito-net and with three quick steps had crossed the hut and was in his arms. Their kiss seemed to last a moment and all of infinity; and then, still without a word, he drew her down the front steps of the hut and into the sanctuary of the palm grove.

'We do not have long,' he warned her softly, and she choked back a sob and clung to him.

'What is happening to us, darling?' she pleaded. 'I don't understand any of it. Why are you doing this to us?'

'For the same reason that you are forced to obey. For Nicholas, and for you.'

'I don't understand. I cannot go on, Ramón. I have reached the end of my strength.'

'Not much longer, my darling. I promise you that. Soon it will be over, and we will be together.'

'You said that last time, darling. I have done all I can. . . .'

'I know, Bella. What you have done has saved us. Both of us, Nicholas and me. Without you we would have long since been destroyed. You have bought time and life for us.'

'They have made me do terrible, terrible things, Ramón. They have made me betray my family and my country.'

'They are pleased with you, Bella. This visit is proof of that. They have given you two weeks with Nicholas. If only you can last a little longer – give them just a little more of what they want.'

'They will never let me go, Ramón. I know that. They will hold me for ever, and bleed the last drop.'

'Bella, darling.' He stroked her body through the thin silk of her nightgown. 'I have a plan. If you can keep them happy just a little longer, next time they will be more

358

lenient. They will trust you a little more. They will start to become careless – and then, I promise, I will bring Nicky to you.'

'Who are they?' she whispered, but he was beginning to make love to her and the question faltered.

'Quiet, my love. Don't ask. It is best you don't know.'

'At first I thought it was the Russians, but the Americans acted on my Skylight message. The Americans used my information on the Angola raid. Is it the American CIA, Ramón?'

'You may be right, my love, but for Nicky's sake don't provoke them.'

'Oh God, Ramón. I am so unhappy. I didn't believe that any civilized people could treat others in this way.'

'Not much longer,' he whispered. 'Be strong. Give them what they want for just a little longer, and then Nicky and I will be with you.'

'Make love to me, Ramón. It's the only thing in the world that can keep me from going mad.'

*   *   *

Nicholas drove her to the airstrip the following morning. He was tremendously proud of his driving skill, and she was effusive in her praise. José and the regular driver were in the back of the jeep, and she overheard a remark that one made to the other that at the time made little sense but stuck in her memory like a burr.

'Pele is the true cub of the fox, El Zorro.'

At the ramp of the Ilyushin they said goodbye to each other.

'You promised to come to see me again, Mamma,' Nicholas reminded her.

'Of course, Nicky. What present should I bring you?'

'My soccer ball is worn and leaking. We have to pump it many times during the match.'

'I will bring you another.'

'Thank you, Mamma.' He offered her his hand, but she

could not restrain herself. She dropped to her knees and hugged him to her breast.

For a shocked moment he stood very still in her arms, and then he tore himself violently from her embrace. His face was scarlet with humiliation. He glared at her, then whirled and ran for the jeep.

She peered down from the small side-window in the flight-deck of the Ilyushin, but Nicholas was gone. She saw the fine pall of dust still hanging over the road to the beach. He left a great emptiness in her soul.

She disembarked from the Ilyushin in Libya where it landed to refuel, and caught a Swissair flight to Zurich. She airmailed postcards to everybody in the family including Nanny, and used her credit cards to establish her presence in Switzerland. She even called on Shasa's bankers in Lausanne to withdraw ten thousand francs and thus allay any suspicions that her father might have about her holiday.

The photographs she had taken of Nicholas were beautiful. She had captured his typical expressions and moods and characteristic poses. Even those of him in his camouflage fatigues handling that dreadful assault-rifle gave her more pleasure than distress.

She was keeping a journal for Nicholas. It was a thick bound book with pockets inside the covers, and it contained every memento of Nicholas that she had accumulated over the years.

There was a copy of his official Spanish birth certificate and adoption papers. She had hired a London firm who specialized in this type of work to trace the Machado family back three centuries. A copy of the family tree and the Machado heraldic arms were in the front pockets of the journal.

There was also the baby bootee that she had retrieved from under his cot in the flat in Málaga. She had pasted in the copies of the reports from his nursery school and the paediatric clinic, together with every photograph they had ever sent her. She wrote her own comments and a descrip-

360

tion of her feelings of love and hope and despair on alternate pages.

When she returned to Weltevreden she added the lock of his hair and the photographs she had taken of him to her hoard, and included a description of their interlude together. She even recorded their conversations and every amusing or poignant comment he had made.

When she felt deeply depressed and unhappy she locked herself in her suite, retrieved the journal from her personal safe and gloated over every item in it.

It gave her the strength to go on.

     ★   ★   ★

The Beechcraft banked into a steep descending turn and the release of gravity made Isabella feel light in the rear seat.

'There,' Garry shouted from the pilot's left front seat. 'See them? At the foot of the hill. Three of them.'

Isabella stared down at the forest-top and the broken ground along the rim of the escarpment. The rock was fractured into battlements and turrets, wild cliffs and tumbled towers like the ruins of some fabulous fairy castle.

The forest filled the valleys and the ravines between the rocky castles with splendid chaos; great tree-trunks towered up a hundred feet or more with widespread branches clothed in autumn livery, gilded with all the amalgams of gold and copper and bronze. Other great trees were already bare of leaf; the bloated baobabs with reptilian bark squatted grotesquely as creatures from the age of the dinosaurs. At the very wing-tip of the Beechcraft a giant African ebony flashed by, its leaves still dark shining green and its top branches studded with ripe yellow fruit.

A flock of green pigeons hurled themselves in wild alarm into the air, and darted by so close that she could see their bright yellow beaks and the beady shine of their eyes. Then abruptly the forest ended and a glade of pale winter grass stretched below them. The Beechcraft roared straight at the tall cliff of rock on the far side.

'There! Can you see them, Bella?' Garry called again.

'Yes! Yes! Aren't they magnificent?' she shouted back.

At the far end of the clearing, three bull elephants ran in single file. Their ears were spread wide as the lateen sail on an Arab dhow. Their backs were humped so that she could see the curved and crested ridge of the spine beneath the grey hide and the gleam of long curved ivory carried high.

As they flashed twenty feet over him, the lead bull turned to confront them. He reached up with a long serpentine trunk as though to pluck them from the sky. Then Garry pulled back on the control column. Gravity sucked at Isabella's bowels, and the aircraft hurtled up to skim the raw blue granite and then bore up high into the cloudless African sky.

'That big one would go all of seventy pounds.' Garry was judging the weight of the bull's tusks as he twisted in the seat, looking back over his shoulder, flying by instinct alone, even in this critical angle of climb.

'Are they in our area, Pater?' he asked, as he rotated the nose down and eased back on throttle and pitch to resume level flight.

'On the edge of it.' Shasa was relaxed in the right-hand seat beside him. He had taught Garry to fly and knew his capabilities. 'That's the National Park over there – you can see the cut-line through the forest that marks the boundary.'

'Those old jumbo are heading straight for it.' Isabella leant on the back of her father's seat, and he turned and grinned at her.

'You bet your sweet life, they are,' he agreed.

'You mean they know which is hunting concession and which is the sanctuary?'

'Like you know the way to your own bathroom. At the very first hint of trouble they head for home and mother.'

'Can you see the camp?' Garry asked.

362

'Just south of that kopje.' Shasa pointed ahead through the windscreen. 'There, now you can see the smoke. The landing-strip runs parallel to that patch of dark Jesse bush.'

Garry eased the power again, sinking back towards the wilderness, winging low over the rough bush strip to check that it was clear.

A small herd of zebra that had been grazing on the grass strip scattered at their approach and plunged away at full gallop. Each of them towed a feather of pale dust behind it.

'Damned donkeys,' Garry muttered. 'Hit one of those and he'll take your wing off.'

Below her Isabella saw an open truck parked near the crude windsock. She looked for her elder brother at the wheel, but it was one of his black drivers. She felt a tingle of disappointment. She hadn't seen Sean in over two years, and she missed him.

Garry turned the twin-engined Beechcraft on to final approach and lined up with the strip. He lowered the undercarriage, and three green lights lit up on the dashboard. His hands were powerful and sure on the controls as he completed his landing checks and brought her in at a steep angle to avoid the tree-tops that crowded the strip.

'He is a marvellous pilot,' Isabella admired his technique. 'Almost as good as Pater.'

Garry had flown them up from Johannesburg in the company jet. They had stayed over in Salisbury at the Monomatapa Hotel. Shasa and Garry had had a meeting with Ian Smith, the Rhodesian prime minister. Then they had flown this last leg in the smaller Beechcraft. The jet needed a thousand metres of metalled runway to make a safe landing, whereas the twin-engined Beechcraft could sneak into the short grass strip at Chizora with a skilful pilot at the controls.

It was a full-flap landing, and Garry set her down firmly, no float or bounce. The machine jolted and pitched to the rough surface. He thrust on maximum safe braking as the wall of trees at the far end of the strip rushed towards

363

them. Then he wheeled her with another burst of engine and taxied in a blown dust-devil to where the truck waited for them.

The camp staff swarmed around the Beechcraft the moment that Garry cut the motors. Shasa opened the hatch and jumped down off the wing to shake their hands and greet each one of them in strict order of seniority. Most of the safari staff had been with the company from the beginning, and so Shasa knew each of them by name.

The pleasure of the camp staff was even greater when Isabella jumped down off the wing, and those marvellous white African smiles stretched to the limit. Although her visits to Chizora were intermittent, she was a firm favourite amongst them. They called her Kwezi, the Morning Star.

'I have fresh tomatoes and lettuce for you, Kwezi,' Lot, the head gardener assured her. The garden at Chizora camp was fertilized with buffalo and elephant dung and yielded fruit and vegetables that would have won prizes at any agricultural show. They all knew Kwezi's weakness for salads.

'I put your tent at the end, Kwezi,' Isaac, the camp butler, told her. 'So you can listen to the birds in the morning. Chef has got your special rooibos tea for you.' The herbal tea from the Cape mountains was another of Isabella's weaknesses.

Garry ran the Beechcraft into its jackal-wire hangar to prevent the lions and hyenas gnawing on the tyres during the night. The staff loaded their baggage on the back of the open truck. Then with Garry at the Toyota's wheel they bumped along the rough track through the combretum forest.

It had been a good rainy season, and game was plentiful. The sandy track was dimpled with their spoor. When they came out into the wide glade in front of the camp, there were herds of zebra and sleek red-brown impala standing out unafraid on the silvery winter-grass pasture. It was one of Sean's strict rules that no shot was ever fired within two miles of the camp. This was no inhibiting restriction, for the Chizora concession spread over ten thousand square kilometres.

The camp overlooked the glade and the muddy waterhole at its centre. Later in the season, when the water dried up, the game would migrate. Then Sean would be obliged to pack up this entire camp and follow them down the escarpment to his other camp-site on the shore of Lake Kariba.

The row of green tents was set back discreetly within the forest, each with its own shower and earthen toilet standing behind it. The dining-tent was surrounded by a thatch-walled boma which was open to the sky. The canvas camp-chairs were set around the camp-fire, great logs of leadwood and mopane which were kept burning day and night. The camp servants all wore crisply starched uniforms, and Isaac, as camp butler, sported a crimson sash over one shoulder.

The portable generator provided lighting and power for the bank of refrigerators and deep-freezers in the mud-walled pantry. From his thatched kitchen the chef conjured up a sequence of gourmet dishes. There were all the refinements of what was known as a 'Hemingway camp'. Chief amongst these were the tubs of ice on the bar table and the regiments of liquor-bottles drawn up in ranks. There were five different brands of premium whisky and three of single malt. A *grand cru* Chablis Vaudésir reposed in a silver ice-bucket. There were also the ingredients for Pimm's No. 1 and Bloody Mary, to cater for those with more mundane tastes. All the glasses were Stuart crystal. The type of clients who could afford the safari fees expected and made damn sure they got these basic necessities of life.

The uniformed attendants had filled the tanks of the individual showers with piping-hot water. While the guests washed off the dust and grime of their travels, they unpacked and laid out their safari clothes in each tent.

Bathed and refreshed, the family gathered at the camp-fire, and Shasa glanced at his wristwatch.

'Bit early for a peg?'

'Nonsense,' said Garry. 'We are on holiday.' He called the barman to take their orders.

Isabella sipped her cold white wine. For the first time in almost two years she felt safe and at peace, and incongruously she thought of Michael. He was the only thing missing. She watched the procession of beautiful wild animals coming down to drink at the waterhole and listened to her father and Garry with only half her attention.

They were discussing Sean's client. He was a German industrialist named Otto Heider.

'He's twenty years older than Sean, but they are soulmates. Both of them are thrusters. God, they take some chances together,' Shasa told them. 'The more hairy and dangerous the action, the more old Otto loves it. He won't hunt with anybody except Sean.'

'I had Special Services run a full report on him,' Garry nodded. Special Services was a closed section of Courtney Enterprises whose director reported directly to Garry. It was his private intelligence system. It dealt with everything from company security to industrial espionage. 'Otto Heider is a player all right. The list of his assets runs to four typed pages, but he is a wild player. I don't think we should get financially involved with him. He takes too many chances. According to my calculations, he is undercapitalized by at least three billion Deutschmarks.'

'I agree,' Shasa inclined his head. 'He's an interesting character, but not for us. Do you know he brings his own blood-bank on safari, just in case he gets stamped on by an elephant or hooked by a buffalo?'

'No, I didn't know that.' Garry sat forward in his camp-chair.

'Fresh sweet blood,' Shasa smiled. 'On the hoof, so to speak. Self-administering transfusions.'

'What does that mean?' Even Isabella was interested.

'He brings two qualified nurses with him. Both blonde, both beautiful and under twenty-five years old, both blood-type AB Positive. If he needs blood, he can tap it

366

straight off one of them and at the same time have expert nursing care.'

Garry let out an admiring snort of laughter. 'And, even if he does not need blood, they are still extremely useful items to have on a safari. The transfusions simply flow in the opposite direction.'

'You are disgusting, Garry,' Isabella smiled.

'Not me! Old Otto is the disgusting one. I think I am changing my opinion of him. We might still do business together. Such forethought is most commendable.'

'Forget it. Otto is flying out first thing in the morning with his two nurses. The client we are really interested in arrives tomorrow afternoon. Sean will drop Otto in Salisbury and bring the other one back—' Shasa broke off and shaded his eyes, staring out across the wide glade in front of the camp.

'I hear Sean's truck. Yes, there he comes.'

The tiny shape of the hunting vehicle darted out of the forest edge a mile away across the open grassland.

'Master Sean is in a real hurry.'

The sound of the truck engine mounted to a roar. A tall column of dust rose into the still evening sky. The animals at the waterhole panicked and galloped for the trees.

As the distance closed rapidly, they could make out the occupants of the open Toyota. The cab and the bodywork had been removed and the windscreen laid flat over the engine bonnet. On a high rear seat were four figures. Sean's two black trackers in khaki fatigues and two white women. These, Isabella presumed, were the German nurses, for they fitted the description, young and blonde and pretty.

In the front passenger-seat was a middle-aged man dressed in custom-tailored safari clothing. He wore gold-rimmed spectacles and a leopard-skin band around his Stetson. He exuded the air of jaunty confidence that marked him as Otto Heider, the client they had been discussing.

Sean was at the wheel of the speeding Toyota, and Isabella could not restrain herself. She jumped up from the camp-chair and ran to the gate of the boma.

Sean wore a bush shirt with two heavy-calibre brass cartridges in the loops on his breast. His shirt-sleeves had been cut away at the shoulders, so that his arms were bare. The muscles were tanned and glowing with abundant health as though they had been oiled. His shoulder-length hair was cut in a Prince Valiant bob. The Comanche-style leather thong around his forehead could not restrain the shimmering jet-black locks that danced and fluttered like a flag around his head as he drove the truck at high speed up to the entrance of the boma.

He hit the brakes so hard that the heavy vehicle spun into a broadside and came to a halt in a billowing cloud of its own dust. Sean leapt out and strode towards them. His khaki shorts were cut away high on the thighs, and his sockless feet were thrust into kudu-skin velskoen.

'Sean!' Isabella let out a happy cry, but he brushed past her with an expression of dark fury on his face. She stared after him in bewilderment.

Sean ignored his father as he had his sister and stopped in front of his younger brother.

'Just what the hell do you think you are playing at?' he asked in a voice that rang with cold fury, and Garry's happy grin faded.

'And I'm glad to see you also.' Garry's tone was mild, but his eyes sparkled with annoyance behind his spectacles.

Sean reached down and seized the front of Garry's shirt. With one clean jerk, he lifted his brother out of the canvas chair. It was a feat of brutal strength, for Garry was a big, solidly built man.

'Let me tell you a little secret,' Sean said. 'I spend four days getting into position for a shot at the only decent bull I've seen all season. At the critical moment you come barging in like von Richthofen and rev the hell out of us!'

'Look, Sean, I didn't. . . .' Garry tried to placate him, but Sean wasn't even listening.

'You goddam pen-pushing office wallah. You soft-arsed tourist playing tough guy. Who the hell are you trying to impress?'

'Sean.' Garry held up both hands, palms open. 'Come on, be reasonable. How was I to know?'

'Reasonable? When you shoot up my concession and chase the hell out of my jumbo. Reasonable? When you screw up my best client and the last shot we will get at a big bull this safari?'

'I said I'm sorry.'

'If you're sorry now, just think how sorry you're going to be five minutes from now,' said Sean. With his left hand still gripping Garry's shirt, he shoved him backwards. Instinctively Garry resisted. Instantly Sean reversed the pressure, and it took Garry by surprise.

Sean did not cock his right hand. He threw the punch only five inches, but the full power of his broad muscled shoulders was behind it and Garry was moving into it. Garry's teeth clicked together in his jaw. As he staggered backwards his spectacles spun from his head. The camp-chair caught him at the back of his knees; he went over backwards, falling heavily and awkwardly.

'Damn it, that felt good,' said Sean, clenching and unclenching his right hand as he moved around the overturned chair to reach him again.

'Sean!' Isabella recovered from her shock. 'Stop it, Sean! Leave him alone!' She ran forward to interpose herself between her brothers, but Shasa caught her arm to restrain her. Although she struggled to be free, he held her easily.

Garry struggled into a sitting position. His expression was dazed. A little trail of blood crept out of one nostril, and he tried to sniff it back. Then he lifted his hand and smeared it across his upper lip. He held the bloodied hand close to his myopic eyes and inspected it with disbelief.

'Come on, Big Shot.' Sean was standing over him. 'Get on your feet. I've been saving up for this.'

'Leave him alone, Sean. Please!' Isabella hated the violence and the blood and this terrifying anger between two people she loved so dearly. 'Stop it! Stop it!'

'Quiet, Bella!' Her father shook her sharply. 'Keep out of this.'

369

Still sitting in the dust, Garry shook himself like a great St Bernard dog.

'Come on, Mr bloody Chairman of the Board,' Sean taunted him. 'Get on your feet, Mr Businessman of the Sodding Year. Let's see your style, Mr Fortune Magazine 500.'

'Leave them, Bella.' Shasa still held her. 'This had to come. It's been brewing for twenty years. Let them work it out.' Suddenly Isabella understood. Sean's choice of jibes was an expression of the envy and resentment that he had accumulated over a lifetime.

Sean was the firstborn, the golden princeling, the pick of the litter. All those honours and titles should have been his. He should have been the prime recipient of his father's favour and approbation, and yet he had lost it all. It had been stolen away from him by the runt.

'Piss-bed,' said Sean. 'Four-eyes.' Those were childhood insults. Isabella had a vivid memory of the lordly superiority of the elder brother. She remembered how in the Cape winters of their childhood, when the snow iay thick on the Hottentots Holland mountains, Sean would turn Garry out of bed in the dawn and send him to sit on the toilet to warm the seat for him. She remembered a hundred other episodes of humiliation and casual bullying by which Sean had reinforced his domination over the weakling.

Garry came to his feet. He had applied twenty years of unremitting labour to building up the sickly body that he had been born with. Now his chest was a barrel of muscle, and the coarse body-hair curled out of the V of his shirt-front. His limbs were almost grotesquely over-developed. However, he stood almost four inches shorter than his elder brother as they confronted each other.

'That,' he said quietly, 'is the last time. It will never happen again. Do you understand?'

'No.' Sean shook his head, his anger contained behind the mocking smile. 'I don't understand, Piss-bed. You are going to have to explain it to me.'

The German client and his two nubile nurses had

climbed down from the Toyota and followed Sean into the boma. Now they were watching with delighted anticipation.

Garry blinked like an owl without his glasses, but his teeth clenched so hard that humps of muscles, like walnuts, bulged on the hinges of his jaw below his ears. Sean leant forward, balanced on the balls of his feet and slapped his cheek lightly, still smiling mockingly, and Garry went for him.

He was fast for such a heavy man, the way a bull buffalo is fast, the way an old mugger crocodile is fast, but Sean was fast as a leopard. He ducked under Garry's rush, and threw a left-hander into his belly just below the sternum of his ribs. It was like throwing a brick at a battle-tank. Garry did not even grunt. He merely hunched his shoulders and came in again.

Sean weaved and danced ahead of him, the insolent grin still on his lips. He was letting Garry come to him, and counter-punching with the rushes. His blows thudded on rubbery muscles as though he were beating a truck tyre with a baseball bat.

The German nurses were squealing with happy horror. The camp servants came running from the kitchen lines. Their heads bobbed up in a row along the low boma wall, wide-eyed with fascination.

'Stop them, Daddy,' Isabella pleaded, but Shasa was assessing his sons with a calculating eye. So far, this was the way he would have expected it to go.

Sean was all flash and style, tossing back his glossy locks after each exchange, taking a moment to glance at his audience, especially the blonde nurses.

Garry, on the other hand, was plugging away solidly, making Sean dance and weave to keep out of range of those massive arms. He was obviously willing to take all the body shots that Sean could throw at him. However, it was surprisingly difficult for Sean to land on Garry's head. He had a trick of hunching those muscled shoulders at the final instant and deflecting Sean's fists.

He was also very quick with his arms, and some of Sean's best punches to the head were caught on Garry's heavy biceps or on his hairy forearms.

At first, Garry's rushes seemed to be without purpose. Then Shasa realized that he was remorselessly driving Sean back into the corner wall of the boma, attempting to pin and grapple him there. Each time, Sean managed to break clear and Garry would begin all over again. He was as patient as a sheep-dog, working him into the position he wanted, grimly accepting the punishment Sean was inflicting. Blood from his nostril was running into his mouth and dripping from his chin into the front of his khaki bush shirt.

By this time Sean's mocking grin was becoming a little strained, and the flow of taunts had long since dried up. His movements were no longer so crisp. On the other hand, Garry moved with the same ponderous rhythm and momentum, pushing Sean back, back, always backwards. Sean's punches were losing their snap, and he threw them less prolifically.

Then Garry blocked him as he tried to pirouette away to the right, at last anticipating his move precisely. Sean back-pedalled quickly to regain poise, and felt the thatch of the wall touch his back. He ducked to go under Garry's outstretched arm, and Garry let his first punch fly.

All the spectators gasped, and one of the nurses squeaked shrilly. Garry's punch was a thunderbolt, with two hundred pounds of muscle and bone and determination driving it. It hissed through the air and, although Sean caught it on his guard, it drove on through. It crashed against the curved dome of his skull, high above the hairline, with a force that made his long shining hair swirl and flicker as though a gust of wind had caught it.

For an instant Sean's eyes rolled fully backwards in their sockets, giving him a blind white stare. His knees buckled and sagged under him. Then he partially recovered, but his face was frosted with pain and his mouth was twisted with panic, as he tried to avoid the next bear-like rush.

Garry charged in, eagerly seizing the moment for which he had worked so doggedly. His arms were spread as though to welcome an old friend or a lover. Suddenly he kicked and spurted like a long-distance runner hearing the bell for the final lap. He had fooled them all, including Sean. They had thought that those ponderous rushes were all the speed he had, but suddenly there was more, much more.

A buffalo bull charges in for the kill in the same fashion, crabbing across the front of his victim, lulling him, making him doubt that he is really the focus of all that mountainous aggression. Then at the last moment he turns in with bewildering speed to hook and gore and trample.

Half-stunned, Sean could not avoid him. Garry's arms snapped around him in a murderous hug, and the momentum of his charge carried them both onwards into the dining-tent. The bar table went over in a shower of ancient spirits, noble wines and precious crystal. They trampled the glittering splinters underfoot, and a heady cloud of fumes enveloped them for a moment before they barged onwards.

The long dining-table, spread with Madeira lace, crashed over. The Rosenthal dinner service burst into ten thousand expensive splinters. As they went out through the back of the tent, they ripped out the guy ropes and the canvas sagged in weary folds. The servants scattered with cries of alarm and excitement and encouragement.

In a ferocious waltz, they whirled each other in erratic circles. Garry's grip was unshakeable. He had double-locked his own wrists behind his brother's back. His arms convulsed, rippling with muscle as they tightened like a python crushing its prey.

One of Sean's arms was trapped in that deadly circle. With the free fist, he beat wildly at Garry's head, but he lacked purchase and the blows had no sting. Although one caught Garry in the mouth and split his lip, it left his big white teeth intact. He merely ducked his head and slitted his eyes and squeezed and squeezed.

With an approving roar from the black audience and feminine squeals from Sean's admirers, they lunged into the far side of the thatched boma wall and it burst open.

The two of them, still locked together, came storming back on to the central stage. One of the nurses was not quick enough to avoid them. She was knocked over in a tangle of long tanned legs, flaring skirts and lacy underwear that might have stopped any lesser show. Nobody even glanced at her.

Garry was trying to swing Sean off his feet, lifting him high with each turn. Although Sean's face was swelling and darkening with blood from the constriction of his chest and breathing, he managed like a cat to come down on his feet after each wild swing until Garry steered him into the middle of the camp-fire. Sean's legs were bare, and the flames licked at them, frizzling the hair off his calves, scorching the thin kudu-skin velskoen.

Sean let out a howl of anguish and bounded high in his brother's arms. He managed to jump clear of the fire, but Garry's grip was inexorable. Grunting with the effort, he forced Sean slowly backwards, bending him like a longbow. Sean's scorched legs buckled, and he sank lower and lower. His knees touched the ground, and Garry bent over him and grunted again as he tightened the circle of his arms another inch.

The air was forced from Sean's lungs in a long hollow groan, and his face suffused with dark blood. Garry grunted again, and his grip tightened another notch, remorseless as a mechanical steel press. Sean's eyes began to bulge from their sockets, and his jaw fell open. His tongue lolled out between his teeth.

'Garry! You are killing him!' Isabella screamed, her concern moving from one brother to the other. Her father held her, and Garry showed no sign of having heard her. He grunted yet again and squeezed.

This time they heard Sean's ribs crack like green twigs. He cried out and went slack as a half-empty bag of wheat

374

in Garry's arms. Garry dropped him and stood back, breathing heavily. His own face was flushed and swollen with the effort.

Sean tried to sit up, but the pain of the cracked ribs lanced him and he moaned again and clutched his chest. Garry smoothed back his hair with both hands, but the unruly crest at the crown of his scalp sprang up again immediately.

'Right,' said Garry calmly. 'From now on you will behave yourself. Do you hear me?'

Sean managed to push himself up on to his knees with one hand, clutching his chest with the other.

'Do you hear me?' Garry asked again, standing over him.

'Screw you,' Sean whispered, and the effort hurt his chest.

Garry leant over and prodded his injured chest with a thick hard thumb.

'Do you hear me?'

'OK, OK,' Sean yelped. 'I hear you.'

'Good,' Garry nodded, and turned to the hovering nurses. 'Fräulein,' he said in passable German, 'I think we have need of your professional services.'

They rushed forward clucking. One on each side of him, they raised Sean to his feet and led him away to his tent.

Shasa released Isabella's arm.

'Well,' he murmured. 'That seems to have sorted that out at last.' And then he glanced at the shambles of the dining-tent.

'I do hope that wasn't the last bottle of Chivas.'

★   ★   ★

Garry sat on the camp-bed, stripped to the waist while Isabella anointed his bruises with arnica salve from the first-aid box. The hectic blotches left by Sean's fists covered his arms and upper body like the dappling of a giraffe's hide. His nose was swollen, and his lip was lumped and crusted with fresh scab.

'I think it's an improvement,' Isabella told him. 'Before your face was only half-nose, now it is all nose.'

Garry chuckled and pinched the end of it gingerly. 'We have taken care of Master Sean. Now it seems as though you are next on the list to be taught a little respect.'

She kissed the top of his head where the tuft stood up from his crown. 'Teddy Bear,' she said. 'You know, Garry, Holly is a lucky girl; you are one hell of a man.' He blushed, he actually blushed, and her love for him was confirmed and strengthened. He was no longer comical, even with the bloated nose and thick upper lip.

*   *   *

Sean groaned again theatrically, and Otto Heider threw back his head and laughed.

'Here!' He poured another three fingers of whisky into the tumbler that stood on the bedside table. 'This is for the pain, like chloroform.'

Sean leant across to take the glass and tossed back the whisky. 'I've been jumped on by buffalo and kicked by jumbo, but this one! Hey, Trudi, take it easy.'

Trudi paused with the surgical tape in her hand, and kissed him full on the lips.

'Be quiet,' she said. 'I am fixing you.' She had a sexy German lisp and soft red lips.

'You are a great little fixer,' he admitted. She tinkled with laughter and resumed work on his injured chest, passing the tape under his armpit to Erica who sat behind Sean on his king-size bed.

'No more *bumsen* for you.' Erica smiled severely. 'Not for many long times.' And passed the tape under his other armpit, back to Trudi.

Otto Heider laughed again. 'Are you going to retire injured and leave me to take care of these two little vixen all on my own?' Otto was amazingly generous to his friends, and Sean was an old friend. Otto shared with his friends. The four of them – Otto, Trudi, Erica and Sean – had

376

done more than merely hunt together. It had been a fun safari. Except for the elephant that Garry had messed up, they had all enjoyed themselves immensely.

'You no good any more. But your brother – he strong like a bull.' Trudi slanted her eyes wickedly. 'He fight good. You think he *bumsen* good?'

Sean stared at her thoughtfully for a moment, and then he began to grin. 'My brother is a prude, a prig. He was almost certainly a virgin when he married that po-faced wench of his. I doubt he would know what to do with a good piece of *bumsen* if you waved it under his nose.'

'We show him what to do with it,' Trudi promised. 'Me and Erica, we show him good.'

'What do you think, Otto?' Sean looked across at his client. 'Can I borrow the ladies tonight? It shouldn't take long? I'll have them back at your tent by midnight.'

Otto shook his head with admiration. 'My friend, you are one funny man. You always make such good jokes. Hey, girls, you like it? What you think? It's a funny joke, hey?'

Sean was laughing with them, holding his injured ribs to cushion them. However, there was a vindictive gleam in his eyes.

Sean understood better than any of them what had happened that day. It had been much more than another brotherly brawl that he had provoked. It had been the ultimate territorial contest of two young bulls in the final battle for dominance and rank. He had lost, and the defeat rankled deeply.

He knew that he could never seriously challenge again. Garry had beaten him in every sphere, from the boardroom to the physical arena. Garry was at last unassailable. All Sean could do now was adulterate his power. He wanted to lay in a little insurance against the stormy days that he was sure lay ahead.

$$\star \qquad \star \qquad \star$$

Garry was having a dream. It was extraordinarily vivid and real. He was being pursued across an open meadow by a horde of dancing wood-nymphs, and his legs were lead beneath him. Each pace was an effort as though he waded through a swamp of hot treacle.

He could see Holly and the children standing at the far side of the meadow. She was holding the baby in her arms, and the other children crowded about her legs, clinging to her skirts. Holly was calling something to him, although he could not hear the words. Tears poured from those lovely bi-coloured eyes of hers.

He tried to reach her, but then he felt the soft warm hands of the nymphs on his body holding him back. He tried to shrug off the hands, but the effort was unconvincing. In despair, he saw Holly and the children turn away from him. She gathered the little ones closer around her, and they faded away into the woods beyond the meadow.

He tried to call to them to wait, but his own thoughts and feelings were confused. The hands on him were exciting. Suddenly his own arousal was overpowering. He no longer wanted to escape. He didn't want the dream to end, for even in his sleep he realized that it was a dream.

He let himself flow with the fantasy, and there were smooth warm bodies pressing close around him. The smell of excited young womanhood was sweet and irresistible in his nostrils. He heard their laughter muffled by his own flesh and the startling sensation of their hot lubricious mouths upon him.

Holly and the children were gone; he had forgotten them, their images were erased by his lust. He felt himself surrendering to it completely.

Then suddenly he was wide awake and he realized that it was not a dream. His bed was filled with squirming bodies. They swarmed over him. He did not know how many hands were stroking and pressing and tugging and caressing him. Silky hair washed over his face like sea-water. Hot wet little tongues licked and probed at him. Long smooth limbs wrapped and enveloped him.

For a moment longer he lay quiescent, and then he let out a cry and sprang upright. The moonlight poured into his tent. The naked feminine bodies glowed like opals as they clung to him.

His elder brother was sitting on the end of his bed. Sean's chest was wrapped in white tape, but there was a boyish grin on his face. 'You have won first prize, Garry old fruit. To the victor the spoils. Enjoy, lad, enjoy!'

'You bastard!' Garry reached for him.

But Sean was gone with an alacrity that discounted the injuries to his chest. The two girls scrambled out of his rumpled bed in a confusion of limbs and bouncing bosoms and bobbing white buttocks.

Garry grabbed them, one under each arm and lifted them as easily as he would a pair of kittens. He carried them out of his tent. They squealed and kicked in the air ineffectually.

He saw his father in the doorway of his tent belting his dressing-gown.

'I say, old chap, what's going on?'

'My darling brother put a bunch of vermin in my bed. Just getting rid of them,' Garry told him politely.

'Pity,' said Shasa. 'Awful waste.' But Garry marched on. Shasa sauntered along behind him, hands in the pockets of his dressing-gown, grinning with amusement.

Isabella was in a short lace nightie, wide-eyed with sleep as she stumbled out of her tent. 'Garry, what on earth have you got there?'

'I should have thought that was fairly obvious.'

'Two, Garry? Isn't that a bit greedy?'

'Ask Sean; it was his idea.'

'What are you going to do with them? May I come along?'

'Delighted. You and Pater can report to Holly for me.'

Garry led the small procession out of the camp, across the glade and down to the edge of the waterhole. It was a cold night; the frost crunched under their feet. The approach to the waterhole had been trampled into a greasy black porridge by the hoofs of the game that drank from it.

'Please, we make little joke,' Trudi trilled from under Garry's arm, wriggling weakly.

'It is joke,' Erica agreed tearfully. 'Please to let go.' She had slipped around and hung head-down in Garry's grip. Her bare bottom flashed in the light of the moon, and she bicycled her legs in the air.

'Me, too,' Garry told them. 'I make little joke. I think my joke better than your little joke.'

His first throw was not his best, a mere twenty feet. But, then, Erica was the plumper and heavier of the two and she classed as a ranging shot. His second throw was much better, all of thirty feet, and Trudi shrieked in flight. The sound was cut off abruptly as she plunged below the icy water.

Both girls came up spluttering and wailing miserably under a coat of glistening black mud.

'Now, that,' said Garry, 'is what I call a real joke.'

*　　　*　　　*

Sean was late for breakfast. He paused in the entrance to the dining-tent, and his eyes narrowed as he glanced around.

The servants had made good most of the damage. The broken furniture had been repaired during the night by the camp handyman. Isaac had put together a scratch dinner service to replace the breakages. Trudi and Erica had washed off most of the mud, but their hair was still drying in coloured plastic curlers. However, none of this held Sean's attention.

He looked to his place at the end of the long table. It was his camp, and that seat was his by tradition and custom. Everybody knew that. His name was printed on the canvas back of the chair.

Garry sat in his top chair. The swelling of his nose had subsided considerably. He had repaired the side-frame of his damaged spectacles. His hair was still wet from the shower. He looked big and cocky and self-satisfied, and he was sitting in Sean's chair.

He looked up at Sean from his hunter's breakfast of impala liver and onions and scrambled eggs. 'Morning, Sean,' he said cheerfully. 'Get me a cup of coffee while you're up.'

There was a sudden silence at the table. Every one of them watched Sean for his reaction. Slowly Sean's scowl faded and he smiled.

'How many sugars?' he asked as he went to the sideboard and took the coffee-pot out of Isaac's hands.

'Two will do.' Garry resumed eating, and an audible ripple of relief ran down the table. Everybody started talking again at the same time.

Sean brought his younger brother the coffee-mug, and Garry nodded. 'Thanks, Sean. Sit down.' He indicated the empty chair beside him. 'We have got a few things to discuss.'

Isabella wanted desperately to listen to that conversation, but the two German girls were giggling and chattering, flirting with Shasa and Otto indiscriminately. She knew that Garry was setting out the programme of meetings that would be taking place in this camp over the next few days. The names of the visitors and every detail about them would be important to her, and to Nicky.

'What about this Italian woman? You've had her as a client before. What's she like?' she heard Garry ask, and Sean shrugged.

'Elsa Pignatelli? Swiss Italian. She shoots well, when you can get her to shoot. Never takes a chance, but when she pulls that trigger something falls down. I've never seen her miss.'

Garry thought about that for a moment, then nodded. 'Anything else?'

'She's bloody-minded. Wants things done her way, and you can't slip anything over on her – eyes in the back of her head. I tried to pad the bill a little. She picked it up right away.'

Garry nodded. 'Doesn't surprise me. She's one of the richest women in Europe. Pharmaceuticals and chemicals.

Heavy engineering, jet engines, armaments. She has run the show since her husband died seven years ago. She has a tough reputation.'

'Last season we took a full-out charge from a wounded jumbo in thick Jesse bush. She stood her ground and put him down with a frontal brain shot at twenty paces. Then she turned on me and chewed me up. Accused me of firing at her elephant. She's tough all right.'

'Anything else? Any weaknesses? Liquor?' Garry asked.

Sean shook his head. 'One glass of champagne every evening. Fresh bottle of Dom Pérignon each time. She drinks one glass and sends the rest away. Fifty dollars a bottle.'

'Anything else?' Garry stared at him through his thick spectacles, and Sean grinned.

'Come on, Garry. She's an old aunty – must be all of fifty.'

'Actually she is forty-two,' Garry contradicted him.

Sean sighed. 'OK, you want to know if we played hide-the-sausage together. Look, I made the offer. Hell, it's expected of me. That's part of the service. She laughed. She said she didn't want to be arrested for child abuse.' He shook his head. Sean didn't like admitting to sexual failures.

'Pity! We have to do business with her,' Garry pointed out. 'I need any leverage I can lay my hands on.'

'I'll bring her in at five this afternoon,' Sean promised. 'Then she's all yours, and the best of British luck to you.'

They all drove out to the airstrip to give Otto and his nurses a send-off. The mood was gay.

Not only had the German girls forgiven Garry for their midnight dunking, but he also seemed to have won their esteem and piqued their interest by his forthright refusal of their offer. They made a huge fuss of him, kissing and hugging him and ruffling his hair until he blushed again.

'Next time, we make good jokes again,' they promised

him. They waved furiously through the side-windows as the Beechcraft roared down the airstrip and flashed into the air. Half a mile out and two hundred feet high, Sean threw the aircraft into a maximum-rate turn and came diving back on them, flashing barely twenty feet over their heads. The girls in the back seat were still waving.

'Cowboy!' gruffed Garry, as he climbed behind the wheel of the Toyota. 'Are you coming, Bella?'

'I'll drive back with Pater,' she called. She knew it would be easier for her to pump her father than her brother. She ran to the second truck and jumped up into the seat beside Shasa.

They were halfway back to the camp before she got her chance.

'So who is Elsa Pignatelli?' she asked sweetly. 'And why haven't I heard of her before?'

Shasa looked startled. 'How did you find out about her?'

'Don't you trust me, Pater? I am your personal assistant, aren't I?' Cunningly she saddled him with guilt, and immediately he began trying to exonerate himself. 'Forgive me, Bella. It's not that I don't trust you. It's all rather hush-hush.'

'She is the main reason for us all being here, isn't that so?'

But Shasa was still being evasive.

'Elsa Pignatelli is an avid huntress, a veritable Diana. She has hunted with Sean for the last three seasons. Her passion is hunting the cats – lion and leopard. You know that Sean has a reputation for bringing in big cats.'

'We haven't come to watch her kill cats,' Isabella pressed him, and Shasa shook his head and relented.

'Amongst the Pignatelli assets are a number of chemical factories – pharmaceuticals, agricultural fertilizers and pesticides, plastics and paints. They hold certain patents that we are interested in.'

'So why didn't Garry fly to Geneva or Rome, or wherever she lives?'

'Lausanne actually.'

383

'So why didn't he go to her, or why didn't she send one of her people to meet him in Johannesburg, instead of this Tarzan setting in the jungle? What precisely is all the mystery?'

Shasa slowed the truck and gave all his attention to negotiating the rocky ford of the river. He did not reply until they climbed the steep opposite bank in four-wheel drive.

'Forgive me for not letting you in on it. I was going to tell you. Our interests are not confined entirely to agricultural pesticides. There would be a lot of unfriendly people out there in the big wide world who would be very interested in any discussions between Pignatelli Industries and the chairman of Armscor.'

'Ah, you are wearing your Armscor hat, so it must be armaments or weapons.'

Speculatively Shasa glanced across at her. She had a brightly coloured scarf bound around her hair like a turban, and the wind had rouged her cheeks. She was very lovely, and Shasa felt a prickle of guilt that he should have mistrusted her. She was part of him; he should trust her as he did his own self.

'You and I have discussed the weapons of last resort,' he murmured.

'Not nuclear weapons?' Isabella said. 'You have the bomb already. All that fuss over Operation Skylight.'

'No, not nuclear weapons,' he sighed. 'Something just as nasty, I'm afraid. You know that I share your distaste for weapons of mass indiscriminate destruction. However, such weapons are not intended ever to be used. Their effectiveness lies in their mere existence.'

'If they exist, then sooner or later some madman is going to use them,' she said flatly, and again Shasa shook his head.

'We've been over this before, my darling. But the bare fact remains that I have been entrusted with the job of providing our nation with all possible means of protecting

384

itself. I have not been given the option of deciding which weapons are morally acceptable.'

'Do we really need some other nastiness?' she insisted.

'There is a groundswell of hatred running against our little country. It is being cunningly orchestrated by a small vicious group of our enemies. They are brainwashing an entire generation of young people around the world to regard us as monsters who must be destroyed at all costs. Very soon these young people will be in positions of authority and command. They are the decision-makers of tomorrow. One day we could see an American naval task-force blockading our coast. We could face a military invasion of, say, Indian troops backed by Australia and Canada and all the members of the Commonwealth.'

'Oh, Papa, that is far-fetched. Isn't it?'

'Still remote,' Shasa agreed. 'But you met influential members of the British Labour Government while we were in London. You spoke to members of the American Democratic Party – Teddy Kennedy for one. Do you remember what he told you?'

'Yes, I remember,' said Isabella, and the memory subdued her.

'We must make absolutely certain that no nation – not even one of the superpowers – can ever with impunity consider armed intervention in our internal affairs.'

'We already have the bomb,' she pointed out.

'Nuclear weapons are expensive, difficult to deliver and impossible to limit or control in their effects. There are other effective deterrents.'

'Elsa Pignatelli is going to provide an alternative? Why should she help us?'

'Signora Pignatelli is a sympathizer. She is a member of the Italian South Africa Society. She knows and understands Africa. She is a huntress and she has other ties with this continent. Her father was on General de Bono's staff when he invaded Abyssinia in 1935. Her husband fought in the Western Desert under Rommel and was captured at Benghazi. He spent three years as a POW in South Africa and developed an affection for the country that lasted his lifetime. He transmitted those feelings to her. She visits Africa regularly, either to hunt or to do business. She understands the problems we face and rejects, as we do, the simplistic solutions which the rest of the world would try to force upon us. This meeting was arranged at her suggestion.'

Isabella wanted to ask questions, but she knew it was wiser to let him come to it in his own time.

She sat silently staring at the rutted track, barely noticing the herd of impala antelope that crossed ahead of the vehicle in a series of lithe bounds. They were lovely but insubstantial as blown smoke through the forest.

'Only four people know about this meeting, Bella. Signora Pignatelli has not trusted her own staff. Apart from Garry and I, only the prime minister is aware of the subject of our meeting.'

Isabella suppressed that sickening sense of treachery that lay at the pit of her stomach. She wanted to warn him not to tell, then she thought of Nicky and she sat quietly.

'Five years ago, NATO had contracted with two chemical companies in Western Europe to develop a nerve gas that could be used under battlefield conditions. Last autumn the contracts were cancelled, mostly due to pressure from the socialist governments of Scandinavia and Holland. However, much work had already been done on the development of these weapons, and one company had produced and tested a gas that met all the original criteria.'

'That company was Pignatelli Chemicals?' Isabella asked. When Shasa nodded, she went on: 'What were the criteria that NATO laid down?'

'The weapon has to be safe to store and transport. Pignatelli developed two separate substances, each on its own absolutely inert and harmless. They can be transported in bulk tankers by road or by rail without any risk whatsoever. But when they combine they form a heavier-than-air gas which is approximately eleven times more toxic than the cyanide gas used in American execution-chambers.'

Shasa pulled off the track and parked the truck on the verge beneath the outspread branches of a flowering kigelia tree, that lovely sausage tree with its gigantic pods the size and shape of polonies.

He lifted Sean's double-barrelled .577 Gibbs rifle off the rack behind the driver's seat and loaded it with two fat brass cartridges from the bandolier.

'Let's go down to the hippo pool,' he suggested, and Isabella followed him down the footpath to the deep green pool of the river. The rifle was insurance, for the hippo has killed more human beings in Africa than all the snakes and lions and buffalo combined.

Yet they did not look dangerous as they wallowed under the bank, only their backs exposed like great black river-boulders. Then the bull opened his jaws in a pink and cavernous gape and showed the curved ivory tusks that could scythe the papyrus reeds or guillotine a full-grown oxen into separate pieces. He turned his piggy eyes upon them and regarded them with a bloodshot malevolence.

They sat side by side on a dead log, and Shasa propped the rifle close at hand. After a moment, the bull hippo closed his jaws and sank back below the surface so that only his eyes and the tip of his small round ears were exposed. Shasa stared back at him as balefully.

'Eleven times more toxic than cyanide gas,' he repeated. 'It is terrifying stuff.'

'Then, why, Pater? It is heinous. Why do it?'

He shrugged. 'To protect ourselves from hatred.' He picked up a pebble from between his feet and lobbed it at the hippo. The pebble splashed twenty feet short, but the bull submerged completely. Shasa went on speaking.

'The gas is code-named Cyndex 25 and it has other desirable properties apart from its ability to deal swift and silent death.'

'How heartening,' Isabella murmured. 'What are they?'

'It is odourless. There is no warning; death comes unannounced. However, it can be given a signature, any signa-

387

ture one chooses – the smell of ripe apples, or jasmine, or even Chanel Number Five if you so wish.'

'That's macabre, Pater. Not your usual style.'

He did not respond to the rebuke. 'It is also highly unstable. Decay time is a mere three hours after mixing. Thereafter, it is absolutely harmless. This is extremely advantageous. You can gas an opposing army, and then move your own troops in to occupy the area three hours later.'

'Charming,' Isabella whispered. 'I have no doubt that the political possibilities have not entirely escaped the prime minister. Say, if a million blacks went on the rampage.'

Shasa sighed. 'It doesn't bear thinking of.'

'But you have thought of it, haven't you, Pater?' He was silent, acquiescing. 'You say that NATO cancelled the contracts. Only Pignatelli Chemicals are manufacturing this Cyndex 25?'

'No. They manufactured and tested the gas. It was the twenty-fifth prototype, hence the numerical designation. But when the NATO contract was cancelled they discontinued production and allowed the original stocks to degenerate.'

Isabella glanced sideways at him. 'Degenerate?'

'As I said before, it is a highly unstable product. It has a very short storage-life – six months. New stocks have to be constantly manufactured to replace those that deteriorate.'

'Lucrative for Capricorn Chemicals,' Isabella pointed out, but Shasa ignored the remark.

'Signora Pignatelli will be able to supply us with blueprints for the plant; it is a complicated manufacturing procedure with very delicate manufacturing tolerances.'

'When will you begin to manufacture?' Isabella asked, and Shasa chuckled.

'Hold your horses, young lady. It isn't even certain that Signora Pignatelli can be persuaded to sell us the blueprints and the formula. That is what we are going to chat about

388

now.' He glanced at his wristwatch. 'Almost lunchtime and we are still half an hour from camp.'

★   ★   ★

Sean called up on the camp radio on the 'unmanned airfield' frequency when he was still forty minutes out. So they were waiting on the airstrip when the Beechcraft slanted in towards the field that evening.

Shading his eyes against the low-lying sun, Shasa made out the head of Sean's passenger through the windscreen as she sat in the right-hand seat. He felt an electric tickle down the back of his neck that was more than simple curiosity. It was extraordinary that he and Elsa Pignatelli had never met, for they came from the same world – that exclusive world of wealth and rank and privilege that knew no national boundaries. They had literally dozens of mutual friends and acquaintances, and he was aware that on several occasions over the years they had been within a few minutes or kilometres of meeting each other. Shasa had been on friendly terms with her husband.

The two men had skied in the same party one afternoon at Klosters and had run the notorious Wang together, that terrible ice wall that hangs above the village. At the time, Bruno Pignatelli had apologized for his wife's absence but explained that she had flown to Rome that weekend to visit her elderly mother. She and Shasa must have passed each other at Zurich airport, travelling in different directions.

On another occasion, during Shasa's tenure at the embassy in London, they were invited separately to a dinner at the Swiss embassy. He learnt afterwards that they would have been table companions, but Elsa Pignatelli had been obliged to cancel for family reasons only days before the engagement.

Since then, Shasa had heard Elsa Pignatelli's name mentioned and discussed in detail at many a society dinner or weekend house-party, often spitefully and vindictively but often again with admiration and open envy. He had seen her photograph in the glossy women's fashion magazines to which Centaine and Isabella subscribed religiously. Courtney Industries had dealt with Pignatelli interests for twenty years to the benefit and satisfaction of both parties. So in the weeks since this meeting had been arranged Shasa had studied all the considerable information about her contained in the file that Special Services had provided.

Sean taxied the Beechcraft to the hard stand of compacted red clay and switched off the engines, and Elsa Pignatelli stepped out on to the wing, then jumped down to earth. She moved with the supple grace of a young gymnast, and yet she was tall and long-limbed. Shasa knew she had modelled for Yves St-Laurent before she married Bruno Pignatelli.

Although he felt that he knew her, Shasa was unprepared for his own reaction to her physical presence. The electric tickle spread from his neck to the back of his arms, and he felt the hair there come erect as she looked around. Her dark gaze swept over Garry and Isabella and the servants and fastened directly on him.

Her hair was very dark, with an almost bluish gloss in the late-afternoon sunlight. It was drawn back severely and secured behind her head in a neat tight coil. This emphasized her fine bone structure, the high, slightly domed forehead and vaulted cheekbones. And yet her features were full and feminine. Her lips looked soft, and her mouth was wide.

'Shasa Courtney,' she said his name as she came towards him with a free hip-swinging model's gait. She smiled, and he saw that her jaw-line was clean. He knew that next year in July she would celebrate her forty-third year. However, her skin was flawless and lovingly cared for under light natural-toned make-up.

'Signora Pignatelli.' He took her hand. It was cool and firm with long narrow bones. Her grip was swift, but strong, the kind of hands that could hold a racket-handle or the reins of a thoroughbred.

He regretted that the contact had been so fleeting, but

390

her eyes were compensation. They were starred with rays of brown and gold that radiated from the central pupil. They were bright intelligent eyes, and the lashes were long and black and curled.

'It is my regret that we have not met sooner,' Shasa said in awkward Italian, and she smiled and answered in faultless English, tinged with only an intriguing hint of an accent.

'Oh, but we have.' Her teeth were startlingly white, but one incisor was just crooked enough to suggest that they were her own and not some orthodontist's artifice.

'Where?' Shasa was surprised.

'Windsor Park. The Guards' Polo Club.' She was amused by his confusion. 'You were playing number two for the Duke of Edinburgh's invitation team.'

'My goodness, that was ten years ago.'

'Eleven,' she said. 'We were never introduced, but we met for approximately three seconds at the buffet after the match. You offered me a smoked-salmon sandwich.'

'You have a marvellous memory,' he admitted defeat. 'Did you accept the sandwich?'

'How ungallant of you not to remember,' she teased, then turned to the others. 'You must be Garrick Courtney?' And Shasa hastened to introduce first Garry and then Isabella.

The servants were loading Signora Pignatelli's luggage into one of the trucks. It was heavy leather luggage with brass-bound corners, and there was plenty of it. Only people who flew in their own jets and were not subjected to the caprice of the commercial airlines' check-in could afford that type and quantity of luggage. There were four long gun-cases amongst it.

'You'll ride with me, signora,' Sean tossed back his hair and called to her as he stepped up into the high driver's seat of his hunting vehicle. She ignored the suggestion and fell in naturally beside Shasa as he crossed to the second truck.

Isabella started to follow them, but Garry caught her hand and steered her towards the seat in Sean's truck which Elsa had refused.

'Come on, Bella. Wise up!' Garry murmured. 'Three's a crowd.'

Isabella started. It hadn't occurred to her – not Pater and the widow! Then she leant briefly against Garry's arm.

'I didn't realize that you included match-making amongst your many talents.'

*　　　*　　　*

At sundowner time, Isaac brought Elsa Pignatelli a seething tulip-shaped glass of Dom Pérignon from a freshly opened bottle, without being ordered to do so. He knew all the foibles of each of their regular clients.

While they sat in the half-circle round the camp-fire, keeping above the drift of blue smoke, Sean called his two trackers to the evening conference. This ritual was mainly for the benefit of the client, for everything of importance had been discussed previously and well out of earshot. However, the average client, and especially the first-timers, were impressed by the flow of Swahili between Sean and his trackers. In addition, being included in the ritual gave them a sense of being part of the hunt, and not merely excess baggage.

The trackers, both of whom had been with Sean since he had been an apprentice in Kenya at the time of the Mau Mau rebellion, were natural actors and hammed it up splendidly. They squatted respectfully on either side of Sean's camp-chair and called him Bwana Mkubwa, or Big Chief. They mimed the animals they were discussing and drew their spoor in the dust between their feet, and rolled their eyes and shook their heads, then hawked and spat in the fire for emphasis.

They were an oddly assorted pair. One was a tall taciturn Samburu with shaven head and classical Nilotic features,

392

Maria Theresa silver dollars set in the enlarged lobes of his ears. The other was a gnome with a puckish face and bright beady eyes.

Matatu was one of the few surviving members of the forest Ndorobo tribe, a people famous for their magical bushcraft, adepts of forest lore who had unfortunately been unable to withstand the impact of progress which had destroyed their forests and contaminated them with all civilization's ailments and diseases, from tuberculosis to alcoholism and venereal disease.

Sean had named him Matatu, or Number Three, because his tribal name was not pronounceable and because he was the third tracker whom Sean had hired. The other two had not lasted longer than a week each. Matatu had been with Sean more than half Sean's lifetime.

Matatu said, 'Ngwi,' and rolled his eyes as he drew the perfect imprint of a leopard's spoor in the dust. Sean questioned him in sonorous Swahili, to which Matatu replied in his piping lyrical voice and at the end spat explosively in the fire. Sean turned to Elsa Pignatelli to translate.

'"A week ago I hanged five leopard baits, two on the river and the others along the rim overlooking the National Park."'

Elsa nodded; she knew the area well from her previous trips.

'"We had one strike a few days ago. An old tabby that came out of the park. She only fed once, and then left it, and we tracked her back into the park. Since then it has been quiet."'

Sean turned back and asked Matatu another question. The little Ndorobo answered at length, obviously enjoying the attention.

'Matatu checked the baits today, while I was fetching you from Salisbury. You are in luck, signora. We have had another strike on one of the river baits. Matatu says it's a good tom. He ate well last night. The impala bait has been hanging for a week, and even with the cool weather it has

393

ripened nicely. If he feeds again tonight, then we'll sit up for him tomorrow evening.'

'Si,' Elsa nodded. 'That's good.'

'So tomorrow morning we can check the bait and shoot a few more impala, just in case we need them. Then after lunch we'll have an hour's lie-down and then we'll go into the hide around three o'clock tomorrow afternoon.'

'You check the bait. You shoot the impala,' Elsa told him. 'Tomorrow morning I have a meeting to attend.' She smiled at Shasa in the chair beside her. 'We have much to discuss.'

★   ★   ★

The discussion took up most of the morning. Garry had made the arrangements with deceptive simplicity. He had sent Isabella off in the Toyota with Sean to check the leopard baits, and had then ordered Isaac and his staff to set up three chairs and a folding table under a msasa tree at the edge of the glade, but well away from the camp itself.

Under the msasa tree, the three of them, Garry, Shasa and Elsa Pignatelli, were as secure from eavesdropping as at any spot on the planet. It was bizarre, Shasa thought, to be discussing such a terrifying subject in such tranquil and beautiful surroundings.

On the other hand, the negotiations did not follow the course that either Shasa or Garry had hoped for. Although Elsa Pignatelli had with her a handsome pigskin attaché case, it remained locked and unopened while they delicately circled around the central issue.

Almost immediately it became obvious that Elsa had not yet made up her mind to proceed with the Cyndex 25 enterprise. On the contrary, she was obviously having serious doubts and misgivings, and would need a great deal of persuasion.

'It is a hideous thing to let loose in the world,' she said at one point. 'My relief when NATO rescinded the original contract and ordered us to allow the existing stocks to

394

degrade and to dismantle the plant was immense. I cannot imagine what possessed me even to consider equipping another plant, especially one over which I would have no direct control.'

All that morning, Shasa and Garry worked to allay her fears. They tried to devise between them some arrangements that would satisfy her demands on control and the ultimate rules of engagement under which Cyndex could ever be used.

'If you were to begin manufacturing, any NATO expert who ever inspected the plant and analysed a sample of the gas would know immediately where the technology was obtained,' she pointed out. 'If that happened and it was traced back to Pignatelli . . .'

She did not finish the sentence, but merely spread those long graceful hands in an expressive Italian gesture. Gradually, as the discussion continued, Elsa moved round in her chair to face Shasa. She began to direct all her remarks and questions to him alone.

It was subtly, almost subconsciously, that she excluded Garry from the exchanges. Beneath his bluff exterior Garry was an intuitive and sensitive negotiator. Before even they realized it, he had detected the currents that ran between these two. He recognized that, belonging to the same generation and the same caste, they shared values and understood a special code that he could not comprehend.

He sensed that Elsa Pignatelli wanted to be reassured not by him, but by the man to whom she was inexorably being drawn. Tactfully he withdrew into silence and watched them fall in love with each other without realizing what was happening to them.

* * *

The hum of the engine of the returning Toyota startled them. Shasa glanced at his watch with disbelief.

'Good gracious, it's lunchtime already, and we have settled nothing.'

'We have two weeks in which to talk,' Elsa pointed out, and rose to her feet. 'We can pick up again from here tomorrow morning.'

As the three of them came back into the boma, Sean was already at the bar table mixing Pimm's No. 1 in a crystal jug. He prided himself on his personal recipe.

'Good news, signora,' he called. 'Can I wheedle you into a festive Pimm's?'

She smiled a refusal. 'I'll have my usual Badoit water with a slice of lemon. Now, tell me the good news.'

'The leopard fed again last night. Judging by the sign, he came in early, half an hour before sunset. So he's starting to get careless and bold, and he's huge. He's got paws on him like snow-shoes.'

'Thank you, Sean. You always find good cats for me, but never so soon. This is the first day of safari.'

'Take a nap after lunch, just to settle your nerves, and we'll go into the hide around three this afternoon.'

Isaac offered Elsa her mineral water on a silver tray, and then distributed the tall glasses of Pimm's to the musical accompaniment of tinkling ice, and Sean gave them a toast.

'To a big old tom leopard death at the base of the tree.' The professional hunter's horror was the cat down from the tree and waiting wounded in the tall grass.

They all drank the toast, and immediately afterwards Shasa and Elsa fell into a quiet but intent conversation that excluded the younger Courtneys. Garry seized on the opportunity to take his elder brother's arm and gently lead him out of earshot.

'How are you feeling, Sean?' he asked.

'Fine. Never better.' Sean was puzzled by this uncustomary brotherly concern.

'You don't look fine to me.' Garry shook his head. 'In fact it is fairly obvious that you are sickening for a go of malaria, and those ribs—'

'What sort of crap is this?' Sean was getting annoyed. 'There's nothing wrong with my ribs that a couple of codeine won't fix.'

'You won't be able to hunt with Signora Pignatelli this evening.'

'The hell I won't. I've set up this cat, and he's a beaut—'

'You will stay in your tent this evening with a bottle of chloroquine tablets beside your bed and, if anybody asks, you have a temperature of a hundred and four in the shade.'

'Listen, Big Shot, you've screwed up my elephant already. You're not going to do the same with my leopard.'

'Pater will hunt with the client,' Garry said firmly. 'You are staying in camp.'

'Pater?' Sean stared at him for a moment before he started to grin. 'The randy old dog! Pater has the hots for the widow, has he?'

'Why do you always make it sound so vulgar?' Garry asked mildly. 'We are trying to do business with Signora Pignatelli, and Pater needs to develop the relationship to a point of mutual trust. That's all there is to it.'

'And when those two geriatric nymphos mess up the leopard, old Sean will be the one who has to go in to clean up.'

'You told me that Signora Pignatelli never misses, and Pater is as good a hunter as you any day. Besides which, you aren't frightened of a wounded leopard, not the fearless Sean Courtney – surely not?'

Sean scowled at the jibe, and then bit back his response. 'I'll go set it up for them,' he agreed, and then smiled. 'To answer your question – no, Garry, I'm not frightened of a wounded leopard, or of anything else. Bear that in mind, old son.'

★　　　★　　　★

Shasa lay stretched out on his camp-bed with a book. The safari camp was one of the few places in his existence where he had the opportunity to read for pleasure rather than for business or political necessity. He was reading Alan Moorehead's *Blue Nile* for the fourth time and savouring

397

every word of it, when Garry popped his head into the tent.

'We have a little problem, Pater. Sean's having a go of malaria.'

Shasa sat up and dropped the book with alarm. 'How bad?' He knew that Sean never took malarial suppressants such as Paludrine or Maloprim. Sean preferred to build up his immunity to the disease and only treated symptoms. Shasa knew also that there had recently appeared along the Zambezi a new strain of 'P Falciparum' that was resistant to the usual drugs, and which had a dangerous tendency to mutate into the cerebral and pernicious form. 'I should go to him.'

'Don't worry. It's responding to chloroquine already, and he's asleep. So you shouldn't disturb him.'

Shasa looked relieved, and Garry went on smoothly: 'But somebody will have to hunt with Signora Pignatelli this evening, and you have more experience than I do.'

★   ★   ★

The hide was in the lower branches of a wild ebony tree, only ten feet above ground-level. Sean had raised it, not to protect the hunter, for a leopard could climb and be in the tree with him before he drew breath, but rather to provide a wider field of view across the narrow stream to the bait-tree.

Sean had chosen the bait-tree with infinite care, and Shasa nodded approval as he surveyed it. Most important, it was above the prevailing easterly evening breeze, so the hunter's scent would be wafted away. Also it was surrounded by dense shoulder-high riverine bush that would give the leopard confidence in his approach.

The main trunk leant out over the riverbed at a slight angle to give the cat an easy climb to the horizontal branch twenty feet above the ground from which the carcass of the impala antelope was suspended by a short length of chain. The foliage of the ebony tree was dense and green.

That would also give the leopard confidence to climb. However, the horizontal branch was open, with a window of blue sky beyond it which would silhouette the leopard as he stretched out and reached down to pull the stinking bait up to him.

The hide was exactly sixty-five yards from the bait-tree. Sean had measured it with a builder's tape, while earlier that afternoon Elsa Pignatelli had sighted and fired her rifle at the marked range behind the main camp. Shasa had set up the target at precisely sixty-five yards, and she had put three shots into the bull's-eye, forming a perfect clover-leaf pattern with the three bullet-holes slightly overlapping each other.

The hide was built of mopane poles and thatch, and was a comfortable little tree-house. Inside were two camp-chairs facing the firing-apertures in the thatch wall. Matatu and the Samburu tracker laid out blankets and sleeping-bags, a tucker-box with snacks and a Thermos filled with hot coffee.

Their vigil could last until the dawn, so they were provided with a powerful flashlight that drew power from a twelve-volt car battery; a hand-held two-way radio to communicate with the trackers; and even a china chamber-pot with a tasteful floral pattern to allow them to last out the night without discomfort.

When Matatu had set up the furnishing of the hide to his satisfaction, he scrambled down the ladder and he and Shasa had a last brief conference beside the Toyota.

'I think that he will come before dark,' Matatu said in Swahili. 'He is a cheeky devil and he gorges like a pig. I think he will be hungry tonight, and he will not be able to withstand his greed.'

'If he does not come, we will wait through until the dawn. Do not return here until I call for you on the radio. Go in peace now, Matatu.'

'Stay in peace, Bwana. Let us pray that the memsahib kills cleanly. I do not want this spotted devil to feast on my liver.'

The trackers waited until the hunters had climbed into the hide and settled down, before they drove the Toyota away. They would park on the crest of the valley two miles distant, and wait for the sound of gunfire or the call on the two-way radio.

Shasa and Elsa sat side-by-side in the two camp-chairs. Their elbows were almost, but not quite touching. The sleeping-bags were spread over the chair-backs, ready to draw over their shoulders when the temperature began to drop. There were rugs over their laps. Both of them wore leather jackets, some protection not only against the cold, but also against sharp curling claws in an emergency.

Elsa had her long rifle-barrel thrust through the firing-aperture, ready to raise the butt to her shoulder with the minimum of movement. It was a 7-millimetre Remington magnum loaded with a 175-grain Nosler bullet that would cover the sixty-five yards to the bait-tree at three thousand feet per second. Shasa had the big eight-bore shotgun as a back-up weapon. Designed for shooting wild geese at long range, it was a devastating weapon for close work.

As the beat of the Toyota engine faded, the silence of the bushveld descended on the river valley. It was a silence that whispered with tiny intimate sounds: the gentle sigh of the breeze in the leaves above their heads, the stir of a bird in the undergrowth along the river, the far-off booming shout of a bull baboon that echoed faintly along the rocky cliffs at the head of the valley and the tiny ticking sounds of the termite legions gnawing away at the dry mopane poles on which they sat.

Both of them had brought books to while away the hours until dusk, but neither of them opened them. They sat very close to each other, and they were vitally aware of each other's proximity. Shasa felt as comfortable and com-panionable in her presence as though they were old and trusted friends. He smiled at the fancy. He turned his head surreptitiously to glance at Elsa, and she had anticipated and was smiling at him already.

She turned the hand that lay on the arm of the chair

between them palm uppermost. He took the hand in his own, and was surprised by the smooth warm feel of her skin and by the sharp emotion her touch evoked. He hadn't felt like that for many a long year. They sat side by side holding hands like a pair of teenagers on their first date, and waited for the leopard to come.

Although all his senses were tuned to the subtle sounds and signs of the wilderness, Shasa's mind was free to wander through the junk-room of memory. He thought about many things in those quiet hours as the sun turned across the blue dome of sky and sank towards the jagged line of hills. He thought about the other women he had known. There had been many of those. He had no way of knowing how many, the passage of time had rendered most of them faceless and nameless. Just a very few would remain with him for ever.

The first had been a sly-faced little harlot. When Centaine had caught them at it, she had scrubbed him in a scalding tub of Lysol and carbolic soap that had taken the skin off his most tender parts. He smiled at that far-off memory.

The other that stood out in his memory was Tara, mother of all his children. They had been antagonists from the very beginning. He had always thought of her as the beloved enemy. Then love had wrested the upper hand, and for a time they had been happy together. Finally they had become enemies again, true enemies. Their enmity had been inflamed rather than mitigated by that brief illusory period of happiness.

After Tara there had been fifty or a hundred others – it did not really matter how many. Not one of them had been able to give him what he sought, nor had they been able to alleviate the loneliness.

Recently, in middle age, he had even fallen into the age-old trap of seeking immortality in those young feminine bodies that were themselves in the flower of their youth. Though the flesh was sweet and firm, he had found no contact of the mind, and could no longer match their energy. Sadly he had left them to their booming mindless music and their frenetic search for they knew not what. He had walked on alone.

He thought of loneliness then, as he did so often these days. Over the years, he had learnt that it was the most corrosive and destructive of all man's ills. Most of his life he had been alone. Although there had been a half-brother, he had never known him as a sibling and Centaine had raised Shasa as an only child.

In all the multitude of humankind that had filled his life, the servants and business associates, the acquaintances and sycophants, even his own children, there had been only one person with whom he had been able to share all the triumphs and disasters of his life, one who had been constant in her encouragement and understanding and love.

However, Centaine was seventy-six years old and ageing fast. He was sick to his soul of the loneliness and afraid of the greater loneliness which he knew lay ahead.

At that moment, the woman who sat beside him tightened her grip on his hand as though she empathized with his despair. When he turned his head and looked into her honey-golden eyes, she was no longer smiling. Her expression was serious, and she held his gaze without shift or embarrassment. The sense of aloneness faded, and he felt calm and at peace as he seldom had in all his fifty-odd years.

Outside their little tree-house, the light mellowed and flared into the soft glow of the African twilight. It was a time of magical stillness, in which the world held its breath and all the forest colours were richer and deeper. The sun sagged like a dying gladiator, and bowed its bloody head below the forest-top. The light went with it, the outlines of the forest trunks and branches faded and softened and receded.

A francolin called in the gloom. Shasa leant forward in his seat and looked through the firing-aperture in the thatch wall. He saw the dark partridge-like bird perched on a dead branch on the far side of the river. Its bare cheeks were bright scarlet, and it cocked its head and looked down from its perch and made that creaking sound like a rusty hinge which was the special warning: 'Beware! I see a killer cat.'

Elsa heard the call and, because she also knew the African wild and understood the meaning of it, she squeezed Shasa's hand briefly and then released it. Slowly she reached forward for the pistol grip of the rifle, and achingly slowly lifted the rifle to her shoulder. The tension in the hide was a palpable charge that held them both in its thrall. The leopard was out there, silent and secretive as a dappled golden shadow.

They were both adepts in the art of the hunter, and neither of them moved except to blink their eyelids and keep their vision clear in the failing light. They drew and released each breath with infinite care, and heard the pulse of their racing hearts beat in their eardrums.

The light was going faster, while the unseen leopard circled the bait-tree. Shasa could imagine him in his mind's eye, each deliberate stealthy pace, the paw raised and held aloft and then laid down again softly, the yellow eyes endlessly turning and darting, the round black-tipped ears flicking to catch the faintest sound of danger.

The outline of the bait-tree receded, the carcass of the impala hanging on its chain was a dark amorphous blob. The open window of sky above the bare branch dulled and bruised to the shade of tarnished lead, and still the leopard prowled and circled in the dark thicket.

Shooting light was almost gone, night came on apace, and then suddenly the leopard was in the tree. There was no sound or warning. The abruptness of it was a little miracle that stopped both their hearts and then sent them racing away at a mad pace.

The leopard stood on the branch. However, he was only a darker shape in the darkness, and even as Elsa laid her cheek to the polished walnut wood of the butt-stock the darkness was complete and the shape of the leopard was swallowed up by the night.

Shasa felt rather than saw Elsa lower the rifle. He stared through the aperture, but there was nothing to see, and he turned his head and laid his lips against Elsa's ear.

'We must wait until morning,' he breathed, and she touched his cheek in agreement.

Out in the darkness they heard the clink of the chain links. Shasa imagined the leopard lying belly down on the branch, reaching down with one front paw to hook the carcass and draw it up, holding it with both front feet, sniffing the putrefying flesh hungrily, thrusting its head into the belly cavity to reach the lungs and liver and heart.

In the silence they heard the tearing sound of fangs in flesh, the grating and splintering of rib bone, the ripping of wet hide, as the leopard began to feed.

The night was long, and Shasa could not sleep. As the hunter, his was the responsibility of monitoring each of the leopard's movements. After the first few hours, Elsa's head sagged against his shoulder. Moving stealthily, he slipped his arm around her, pulled the down-filled sleeping-bag up snugly over her shoulders, and held her close while she slept.

She slept quietly, like a tired child. Her breathing was light and warm against his cheek. Even though his arm went dead and numb, he did not wish to disturb her. He sat happy and virtuous in his discomfort.

The leopard fed at intervals during the night, the chain tinkling and bones grating and cracking. Then there were long periods of silence when Shasa feared it had left, before the sounds began again.

Of course, he could easily have turned the powerful spotlight on the tree and lit the leopard for her. It would have probably sat bemused, blinking those huge yellow eyes into the blinding beam. The idea never even occurred to him, and he would have been bitterly disappointed if Elsa had even contemplated such unfair tactics.

Deep down Shasa disliked the technique of baiting for the great cats. He had personally never killed one of them on a bait. Although in Rhodesia it was perfectly legal,

Shasa's own sporting ethic could never come to terms with luring them into a prepared position to offer a carefully staged broadside shot to a hidden marksman shooting from a dead rest.

Every lion and leopard he had ever taken, he had tracked down on foot, often in the thickest cover, and the animal had been alert and aware of his presence. In consequence he had experienced a hundred failures and not more than a dozen kills in all those years as a hunter. However, each success had been a peak of the hunting experience, a memory to last his lifetime.

He did not despise Elsa or any of the other clients who took their cats over bait. They were not Africans, as he was, and their time in the bushveld was limited to a few short days. They were paying huge sums of money for the privilege, and much of that money was channelled back into the protection and conservation of the species they hunted. Therefore they were entitled to the best-possible chance of success. He did not resent them, but it was not his way.

Sitting beside her in the dark hide, he realized suddenly that his own hunting of the cats was over for ever. Like so many old hunters, he had had his surfeit of blood. He loved the hunting game as much, probably more than he ever had, but it was enough. He had killed his last elephant and lion and leopard. The thought made him glad and at the same time sad, a kind of sweet warm melancholy that mingled well with the new emotion he had conceived for the lovely lady who slept on his shoulder. He thought how he would in future take his pleasure in the hunt through her, the way he was doing now. He dreamt happily of travelling with her to the hunting-fields of the world: Russia for the sheep of Marco Polo, Canada for the polar bear, Brazil for the spotted jaguar, and to Tanzania for the great Cape buffalo with a spread of horn over fifty inches wide. These vicarious pleasures sustained him through the long night.

Then a pair of Heughlin's robins chorused a duet from

the undergrowth along the river, a melodious entreaty that sounded like 'Don't do it! Don't do it!' repeated over and over, at first softly and then rising to an excited crescendo.

At this certain harbinger of the dawn, Shasa glanced upwards and made out the uppermost branches of the ebony tree against the lightening sky. It would be shooting light in fifteen minutes. The dawn comes on swiftly in Africa.

He touched Elsa's cheek to wake her, and immediately she snuggled against him. He realized that she must have been feigning sleep for some time. She had come awake so secretly that he had not realized it. Since then she had been lying against him there savouring their intimate contact, just as he had been doing.

'Is the leopard still there?' she asked, a breath of a whisper very close to his ear.

'Don't know,' he answered as softly. It was almost two hours since he had last heard it feeding. Perhaps it had left already. 'Be ready,' he warned her.

She straightened in her chair and leant forward to where the rifle was propped in the forked rest. Although they were no longer touching, he felt very close to her and his arm tingled with the flow of returning blood which her head on his shoulder had impeded.

The light strengthened. Vaguely he could make out the open window through the foliage of the ebony tree. He blinked his eyes and stared into it. The outline of the branch formed out of the gloom. The branch appeared bare, and he felt the swoop of disappointment for her. The leopard was gone.

He turned his head slowly to tell her so, but he never took his eyes off the branch. He checked the words on his lips and stared harder, feeling the tiny ants of excitement crawl along his nerve ends. The outline of the branch was harder, but it was strangely thickened and misshapen.

Now he could just make out the blob of the dangling impala carcass. Most of it had been devoured. It was a ravaged bundle of bared bones and torn skin, but there was something else hanging from the branch, a long snakelike ribbon. He could not decide what it was, until it curled and swung lazily, and then he realized.

'The tail, the leopard's tail.' Like the hidden creature in the puzzle picture, the whole jumped into focus.

The leopard was still draped on the branch, lying flat, its neck outstretched. Its chin was propped against the rough bark. It was sluggish with the weight of meat in its belly, too lazy to move from its perch. Only its long tail swung below.

He felt Elsa stiffen beside him as she also made out the shape of the leopard. He reached across gently to restrain her. The light was still too poor; they must wait it out. As he touched her arm, he felt the tension in her through his fingertips. She seemed to vibrate like the strings of a violin lightly touched with the bow.

The light bloomed. The shape of the leopard hardened. Its hide turned to buttery gold, studded with black rosettes. Its tail swung gently like a metronome set to its slowest beat. It lifted its head slightly and pricked its ears. The light caught its eyes, a flare of yellow, like a distant flash of sheet lightning. It looked towards them and blinked sleepily in regal indolence, so beautiful that Shasa felt his chest squeezed for breath.

It was time to make the kill. He touched Elsa, a light imperative tap on her upper arm. She settled down behind the telescopic sight of the rifle. Shasa braced himself for the shot and stared at the leopard, willing the bullet into its heart, hoping to see it topple and tumble lifeless from the high branch.

The seconds drew out, each of them a separate age. The shot did not come.

The leopard rose to its full height, standing easily erect on the narrow branch. It stretched, arching its back deeply, digging its extended claws into the bark.

'Now!' Shasa commanded her silently. 'Shoot it now!'

The leopard yawned. Its pink tongue curled out between

the gaping fangs. Its thin black lips drew back into a fierce rictus.

'Now!' With telepathic effort Shasa tried to force her to make the shot. He dared not reinforce the command with a word or touch for fear that he disturb her concentration in the very act of firing.

The leopard straightened and flicked its tail over its back. Then, without further warning, it launched itself into flight and dropped from the branch twenty feet to the soft mulched floor of the forest. It was a leap so controlled and graceful that there was no sound as it landed. The undergrowth swallowed it instantly.

They sat for almost a minute in total silence. At last Elsa set the safety-catch with a click and lowered the unfired rifle and turned her head towards him. In the dawn light, the tears shone like seed pearls on the long curled lashes of her lower lids. 'He was so beautiful,' she whispered. 'I could not kill him, not today, not on this day.'

He understood instantly. This day was their day, their very first day together as lovers. She had declined to desecrate it.

'I dedicate the leopard to you,' she said.

'You do me too much honour,' he replied, and kissed her. Their embrace was strangely innocent, almost child-like, devoid as yet of sexual passion. It was a thing of the spirit rather than of the body. There would be time for that later, all the time in the world, but not today, not on this blessed day.

*   *   *

Sean had made a miraculous recovery from his malaria and was waiting eagerly at the boma gate to welcome the returning hunters. The reputation of a safari company was built upon the quality of trophies it produced for its clients, especially for its important clients.

As the Toyota pulled up he glanced hopefully into the back and his mouth tightened with disappointment. He spoke first to Matatu, and the little Ndorobo tracker shook his head gloomily. 'The devil came late and left early.'

'I'm sorry, signora.' Sean turned to her, and handed her down from the truck.

'That is hunting,' she murmured, and he had never seen her so philosophical before. Usually she was as angry and as impatient with failure as he was.

'Your shower is ready, hot as you like it. Breakfast will be waiting as soon as you have cleaned up.'

The rest of the party were full of condolences when Shasa and Elsa appeared in the dining-tent, both of them showered and dressed in freshly laundered and crisply ironed khaki. Shasa was shaved and redolent of aftershave lotion.

'Bad luck, Pater. So sorry, signora,' they chorused, and were puzzled that the couple looked smug and self-satisfied and fell on their breakfast with as much gusto as if there were a world-record leopard in the skinning-shed.

'We can continue our meeting after breakfast,' Garry suggested over coffee.

'And I'll renew the baits this morning.' Sean came in. 'Matatu says the leopard was never alarmed or spooked. We can try again tonight. This time I'll hunt with you, signora. It takes the touch of the master.'

Instead of accepting the suggestions immediately, Elsa glanced across at Shasa and then lowered her eyes demurely to her coffee-cup.

'Well, actually,' Shasa began, 'to tell the truth, we rather thought, that is, Elsa and I, rather Signora Pignatelli and I. . . .' As Shasa floundered for words, all three of his brood stared at him in astonishment. Was this the master of *savoir-faire*? Was this Mr Cool himself speaking?

'Your father has promised to show me the Victoria Falls,' Elsa came to his rescue, and Shasa looked relieved and rallied gamely.

'We'll take the Beechcraft,' he agreed briskly. 'Signora Pignatelli has never seen the falls. This seems like a good opportunity.'

The other members of the family recovered from their confusion as rapidly as Shasa had. 'That's a lovely idea,' Isabella enthused. 'It's the most awe-inspiring spectacle, signora. You'll adore it.'

'It's only an hour's flight,' Garry nodded. 'You could have lunch at the Vic Falls Hotel and be back here for tea.'

'And you can still be ready to go into the leopard-hide at four this afternoon,' Sean agreed, and waited expectantly for agreement from his client.

Once again, Elsa glanced at Shasa, and he drew a deep breath. 'Actually, we may stay over at the Vic Falls Hotel for a day or two.'

Slowly various degrees of comprehension dawned on the three young faces.

'Quite right. You'll need time,' Isabella recovered first. 'You'll want to walk in the rainforest, perhaps take a raft trip down the gorge below the falls.'

'Bella is right; you'll need three or four days. So many interesting things to do and see.'

'That, Garry old boy, is the understatement of the week,' Sean drawled, and both Garry and Isabella glared at him furiously.

*　　　*　　　*

In the cool clean air, not yet sullied by the smoke of the bush fires of the late winter season, the spray cloud of the Victoria Falls was visible at sixty miles distance. It rose two thousand feet into the sky, a silver mountain as brilliant as an alp of snow.

Shasa shed altitude as they approached. Ahead of them the great Zambezi glinted in the sun, broad and tranquil, studded by its islands on which the forests of graceful ivory nut palms stood giraffe-necked.

Then the main gorge opened beneath them and they peered down in wonder as they watched the great river, well over a mile wide, tumble over the sheer edge of the chasm, and fall three hundred and fifty feet in a welter of

410

foaming waters and blown spray. Along the brink of the chasm, black castles of rock split the flow of the river. Over it all towered the immense spray-cloud which was shot through with rainbows of astonishing colour.

Below the falls the entire flood of the river, a staggering thirty-eight thousand cubic feet a second, was trapped between vertical cliffs of rock and charged, raging at this restraint, into the narrow throat of the gorge.

Shasa banked the aircraft into a tight right-hand turn, pointing one wing into the abyss, so that Elsa could gaze down with her view unobstructed.

With each circuit he allowed the Beechcraft to drop lower until they were in danger of being engulfed by the splendid chaos of rock and water. The silver leaping spray blew over the canopy, blinding them for an instant before they burst once more into the sunlight and the rainbows garlanded the sky around them.

Shasa landed at the small private airfield of Sprayview on the outskirts of the village, and taxied to the hard stand. He switched off the engines, and turned to Elsa. The wonder of it was still in her eyes, and her expression was solemn with an almost religious awe.

'Now you have worshipped in the cathedral of Africa,' Shasa told her softly. 'The one place that truly embodies all of the grandeur and mystery and savagery of this continent.'

*   *   *

They were fortunate enough to find the Livingstone Suite at the hotel vacant.

The building was in the style and dimensions of a bygone era. The walls were thick and the rooms immense, but cool and comfortable.

The suite was decorated with prints of the drawings that the old explorer Thomas Baines had made of the falls only a few years after David Livingstone first discovered them. From the windows of their sitting-room they looked across the gorge and the railway bridge that spanned it. The steelwork of the arched bridge seemed delicate as lace, and the entire structure was light and graceful as the wing of an eagle in flight.

They left the suite and wandered down the pathway to the brink of the gorge and walked hand in hand through the rainforest, where the spray fell in an eternal soaking rain and the vegetation was green and luxuriant. The rock trembled beneath their feet, and the air was filled with the thunder of the falling waters. The spray soaked their clothing and their hair, and ran down their faces, and they laughed together with the joy of it.

They followed the rim of the gorge downstream, out of the spray-cloud. The bright sunshine dried their hair and clothing almost as swiftly as the spray had drenched them. They found a rocky perch on the very edge and sat side-by-side, dangling their legs over the terrifying chasm while the mad waters churned into green whirlpools far below.

'Look!' Shasa cried, and pointed upwards as a small bird of prey stooped out of the sun and fell on whistling knife-blade wings into the flock of black swifts that swirled along the cliff face below them.

'A Taita falcon,' Shasa exulted. 'One of the rarest birds in Africa.'

The falcon struck one of the swifts in flight, killing it instantly in a burst of feathers. Then, binding to its prey, it fell into the void and disappeared from their view in the gloom far below.

That evening they dined on steaks of crocodile-tail that tasted like lobster, but when they went up to the suite they were suddenly both shy and nervous. Shasa drank a Cognac in the sitting-room. When finally he went through into the bedroom, Elsa was already propped up on the pillows. Her hair was down on the shoulders of her lace nightdress, and it was thick and black and glossy.

Shasa was overcome by a sense of panic. He was no longer young and there had been one or two occasions recently with other women which had shaken his confidence.

She smiled and lifted her arms to him in invitation. He need not have worried. She manned him as no other woman ever had. In the morning, when they awoke in each other's arms, the sun was streaming in through the high windows.

She sighed and smiled with a slow and languorous contentment and said: 'My man.' And kissed him.

★   ★   ★

Their illicit honeymoon drew out from one day to the next. They did things together, silly little things for which for many years Shasa had had neither the time nor the inclination.

They slept late each morning and then spent the rest of it loafing in their swimming-costumes beside the pool. They read for hours in companionable silence, stretched out in the sunlight. At intervals, they anointed each other with sun-tan oil, making it a fine excuse to touch and examine each other in leisurely detail.

Elsa was lean and smooth and tanned. The condition and tone of her muscle and skin were the rewards for endless hours of aerobics and callisthenics and beauty care. She was obviously proud of her body. Shasa came to share that pride as he compared her to the other semi-naked bodies sunning themselves under the msasa trees on the green lawns.

Only up very close were the stigmata that life and childbirth had left upon her visible. Shasa found even those small blemishes appealing. They emphasized her maturity and bespoke her experience and understanding of life. She was a woman, ripe and complete.

This was made even more apparent when they talked. They talked for hours at a time. These were lazy contented conversations during which they explored each other's mind in the same way they had explored each other's body in the double bed upstairs in the Livingstone Suite.

She told him about herself with an engaging candour. She described Bruno's slow cruel death as the crab of cancer ate him alive, and her own agony as she watched helplessly. She spoke of the loneliness that followed, seven long years of it. She did not have to tell him that she hoped that was now behind her. She merely reached out and touched his hand and it was understood.

She told him of her children: a son, also named Bruno, and three daughters. Two of the girls were married, the youngest was at university in Milano, and Bruno junior was an MBA from Harvard, now working for Pignatelli Industries in Rome.

'He does not have his father's fire,' she told Shasa frankly. 'I do not think he will ever fill those shoes; they are many sizes too large for him.'

She made Shasa think of his own sons. They spoke of the heartaches and disappointments that their children had brought them and of the rare joys that some had bestowed upon them.

They explored together their love of horses and hunting, of music and art and fine things lovingly crafted, of books and music and theatre. Finally they spoke of power and money, and openly admitted their addictions to all these things.

They held nothing back, and at one point Elsa regarded him solemnly. 'It is too early to be absolutely certain, but I think that you and I will be good together.'

'I believe that also,' he replied as gravely, and it was as though they had made a vow and a commitment.

They danced in the balmy African nights. They laid their cheeks together still hot and brown from the sun, and swayed to the beat of the steel band. After midnight, they at last climbed the broad stairway, hand in hand, to their suite and the wide soft bed.

'Good Lord!' Shasa said with genuine amazement. 'It's Thursday. We have been here four days. The kids will be wondering what on earth has happened to us.' They were at brunch on the open terrace.

'I think they will guess.' Elsa looked up from the mango she was peeling for him and smiled. 'And I don't think that "kids" is the correct description for that rumbustious litter of yours.'

'Van Wyk will be arriving at Chizora tomorrow,' Shasa pointed out.

'I know,' she sighed. 'I hate the thought of ending this, but we must be there to meet him.'

★   ★   ★

Sir Clarence Van Wyk was one of those extraordinary creatures that African evolution sometimes throws up.

He was a pure-bred Afrikaner. His father had been chief justice of South Africa when it was part of the British Empire, and he had received his hereditary title when it was still permissible for a South African to accept that honour.

Sir Clarence was a product of Eton and Sandhurst. He had been an officer in a famous Guards regiment, and was heir to the considerable family estates in the Cape of Good Hope. He was also the minister in Ian Smith's government specifically charged with funding the debilitating guerrilla warfare in which Rhodesia was engaged, and in evading the comprehensive mandatory sanctions that the British Labour Government, the United States and the United Nations had placed upon these perpetrators of unilateral independence.

Garry and Shasa had arranged this meeting during their stop-over in Salisbury on the way to Chizora. Sir Clarence was an avid big-game hunter, and they had promised him a bit of sport in the intervals between their deliberations.

Sir Clarence arrived at Chizora in a Rhodesian air-force helicopter. He had with him two of his aides and a pair of bodyguards, all of whom threatened to put a strain on the safari camp. The staff and facilities were geared to entertaining a much smaller number of guests. However, Sean had been given plenty of notice, and additional equipment, staff and stores had been sent down from Salisbury by truck.

The conference-table under the msasa tree was extended and additional chairs set out for Sir Clarence and his team. Isabella joined them as her father's personal assistant. From the beginning Sir Clarence made no attempt to conceal his interest in her.

At six foot five inches, Sir Clarence towered above even Shasa or Sean. He was a most impressive figure of a man whose plummy upper-class English accent and classical features belied his Afrikaner origins. He had a brilliant financial and political brain and a reputation as a lady's man.

Under the msasa tree, they negotiated the marketing and transportation of a nation's wealth and produce, and the commissions and handling fees due to each of them.

Rhodesia was a primary producer, which simplified these deliberations considerably. Her small-scale mines that worked narrow quartz reefs nevertheless turned out a considerable gold production. This did not concern them here, for gold was anonymous. There was no 'Made in Rhodesia' stamp upon it, and its high value-to-bulk ratio made it readily transportable and disposable.

It was different with the other primary products of the country: tobacco and rare metals, chiefly chrome. These had to be transported in bulk, their country of origin had to be concealed and then they must be disseminated to the markets of the world.

From Rhodesia, the railways ran southwards to the harbours of Durban and Cape Town in the Republic of South Africa. That was the natural route for these treasures to go. For years now, ever since the Smith Government's declaration of independence, Garry Courtney and Courtney Enterprises had played a leading rôle in helping Rhodesia evade the sanctions campaign against it.

Now there was to be an ambitious new strategy. After carefully studying the Pignatelli group of industries, Garry and Sir Clarence were offering Elsa Pignatelli the lucrative opportunity of taking part in these anti-sanctions activities.

Pignatelli Industries owned the second-largest tobacco

company in Europe, after the British American Tobacco Company. In addition, they had a controlling interest in Winnipeg Mining in Canada, and operated a stainless-steel mill and vanadium refinery in southern Italy near Taranto.

All this dovetailed neatly with Rhodesia's need to find a market for her products, but there was hard bargaining ahead.

Although it was conducted in a superficially civilized and friendly atmosphere, these were all shrewd and merciless financial predators locked in a contest of minds and wills. Isabella watched them with awe. Her brother used his bluff, almost bumbling manner, his myopic ingenuous gaze and hearty laugh to conceal the steely calculating mind.

Elsa Pignatelli, poised and beautiful, shamelessly exploited her looks and her charms and used the feminine rapier against their masculine cutlasses. She matched and met them with ease.

Sir Clarence was suave and his manners courtly. He held the line like the Guardsman he was and made them pay dearly for every inch he was forced to yield. Then he counter-attacked with consummate timing.

Shasa sat aloof at his end of the table, leaving most of the bargaining to Garry. However, when he spoke, his comments were pithy and apposite, and very often served to break a log-jam in the negotiations and to propose the equitable compromise.

The sums of money they were discussing were of numbing magnitude. While Isabella recorded the minutes of this conference, she amused herself by calculating two and a half per cent of three billion dollars. That would be the Courtney Enterprises share of the loot in the coming twelve months alone, all of it earned without any additional capital investment on their part. When she had the total worked out, she looked at her brother with renewed respect.

At noon the conference adjourned for an elaborate lunch. In the air-force Alouette helicopter Sir Clarence had brought with him a selected baron of the finest Rhodesian beef. Sean and his chef had passed the morning in barbecueing it to golden-brown perfection over a fire of mopane coals. They cleared their palates with a glass of Dom Pérignon while they watched Sean carve pink slices from the joint and the juices spurted and sizzled from around the blade.

During the luncheon, Sir Clarence demonstrated as great a skill and finesse as he had at the conference-table in his attempts to cut Isabella out of the herd and put his brand upon her.

Isabella was flattered by his attentions and more than a little tempted. He was a superior man, a dominant herd bull. Power is a wonderful aphrodisiac for any woman. In addition, he had thick wavy dark hair with just a touch of grey at the temples. She liked his eyes. He was so tall, and he amused her with his urbane wit.

She found herself smiling at his sallies, and once she glanced down at his feet. They must be size fourteen in those gleaming hand-made chukka boots, and she smiled again thoughtfully. Perhaps that was a fallacy, but nevertheless the possibility was intriguing.

She could almost hear Nanny's rebuke ring in her ears. 'All the Courtneys got hot blood. You must be careful, missy, and remember you are a lady.'

She knew he was married, but it seemed a long time since she had taken comfort from a man's body, and he was so big and powerful. Perhaps, if Sir Clarence continued to demonstrate the requisite amount of class and stamina – then perhaps, just perhaps he stood a chance.

After lunch they returned to the conference-table. It seemed to Isabella that their minds had been stimulated rather than dulled by the Dom Pérignon.

At four o'clock Garry glanced at his watch. 'If we aren't to miss the evening flight, then I suggest we adjourn until tomorrow morning.'

They drove down to the pools in both trucks to shoot the evening flight of ring-necked doves coming in to drink.

Sir Clarence had contrived, without making it too obvious, to seat himself beside Isabella in the leading truck.

However, at the last moment just as they were about to pull away, she jumped down and ran back to sit beside Garry in the second truck. She didn't want to make it too easy for Sir C. She sensed that he enjoyed the chase as much as the kill. Garry was in an ebullient mood. As he drove he slipped one arm around her shoulders and squeezed her.

'God, I love it,' he exulted. 'I love Harold Wilson and James Callaghan and all those sanctimonious little bleeding hearts in the General Assembly of the United Nations. I love being a sanctions-buster. It's exciting and romantic. It makes me feel like Al Capone or Captain Blood. Yo ho ho, and a bottle of rum. It gives me a fine feeling of patriotism and the opportunity to make a telling political statement, while at the same time I can pocket seventy-five million pounds in lovely hard cash that the taxman will never see. It's beautiful. I love all sanctioneers and prohibitionists.'

'You are incorrigible.' She laughed at him. 'Isn't there any limit to your appetite for riches?'

At that he sobered and removed his arm from her shoulders. 'You think I'm avaricious?' he asked. 'It's not so, Bella. The truth is that I am a player in the great game. I don't play for the monetary prize, I play for the thrill of winning. I was a loser for too much of my life. Now I must be a winner.'

'Is that all there is to it?' She was also serious now. 'You are playing with the wealth and well-being of millions of little people to gratify your ego.'

'When I win, then those little people win. The sanctioneers seek to inflict starvation and misery upon millions of ordinary people in order to enforce their particular political vision. That, in my view, is a crime against humanity. When I frustrate their efforts, I strike a powerful blow for the little people.'

'Oh, Garry, you aren't a white knight. Don't pretend to be one – please!'

'Oh, yes, I am,' he contradicted her. 'I am one of the white knights of the capitalist system. Don't you see that?

419

The only way out of our dilemma in southern Africa is through the education and upliftment of the people, particularly the blacks, and by the creation of wealth. We must steer for a society based not on class or caste or race or creed, but on merit. A society in which every person can pull his full weight and be rewarded in proportion to that effort – that is the capitalistic way.'

'Garry, I have never heard you speak like that before, like a liberal.'

'Not a liberal, a capitalist. Apartheid is a primitive feudal system. As a capitalist, I abhor it as much or more than any of the sanctioneers. Capitalism destroyed the ancient feudalism of medieval Europe. Capitalism cannot co-exist with a system that reserves power and privilege to a hereditary minority, a system which suppresses the free-market principles of labour and goods. Capitalism will destroy apartheid if it is allowed to do so. The sanctioneers would deny and inhibit that process. By their well-intentioned but misguided actions they bolster apartheid and they play into the hands of its perpetrators.'

She stared at him. 'I've never thought about it that way before.'

'Poverty leads to repression. It is easy to oppress the poor. It is almost impossible to oppress an educated and prosperous people for ever.'

'So you will point the way to freedom through the economic rather than the political kingdom.'

'Precisely,' Garry nodded and then he boomed out that big laugh. 'And I'll set a fine capitalistic example by making myself seventy-five million pounds a year in the process.'

He braked the truck and turned off the track, following the leading Toyota with Sean at the wheel down to the pools in the mopane forest.

These were shallow depressions, known in Africa as pans, filled with a muddy grey water. They were warmed by the sun and heavily laced with the pungent urine of the elephant herds that regularly bathed and drank in them. Despite the temperature and flavour of the water the flocks of doves preferred them to the clear running water of the river only two miles distant.

The birds came in the hour before sunset in flocks that filled the air like blue-grey smoke. In their tens of thousands they winged in along established flight-lanes.

Sean set up his guns on these lanes, five or six hundred metres from the water. He did not wish to prevent the birds from drinking by placing the guns over the pans. Instead he forced them to run the gauntlet to reach the water. As a matter of honour, each gun was expected to observe strictly the daily bag-limit of fifty birds, and to attempt only the difficult challenging shots at high, swiftly flying doves.

The guns were placed in pairs. Not merely for company, but also to check each other and see fair play, and to provide an appreciative audience for those finely taken doubles or that beautifully led shot at a blue streak passing a hundred feet overhead at seventy miles an hour.

Quite naturally, Elsa paired with Shasa, and their cries of 'Bello! Molto bello!' and 'Jolly good shot! Well done!' rang through the mopane as they encouraged each other.

Garry and Sean made a pair on the west side of the pans. Deliberately they placed themselves behind a tall stand of timber so that the doves were forced high and hurtled into their view over the tree-tops without warning, presenting a shot so fleeting as to call for lightning reflexes and instinctive calculation of lead.

Once Sean missed his bird, shooting two or three feet behind it. Garry swivelled with the long Purdy mounting to his shoulder and brought the escaping dove tumbling down on a trail of loose feathers. Then he looked across at his older brother with his spectacles glinting gleefully and boomed with laughter. Sean tossed back his hair and tried to ignore him, but his face darkened with fury.

Isabella was left with Sir Clarence at the south end of a grassy glen out of sight of the rest of the party. She was shooting the gold-engraved 20-gauge Holland & Holland that her father had given her. However, she had not fired it for almost a year, and her lack of practice showed up in her shooting.

She clean missed the first three birds in succession and then pricked one. She said: 'Damn! Double damn!' She hated to wound them.

Sir Clarence took an accomplished double, then set his shotgun against the trunk of a mopane tree and crossed to where she stood.

'I say, do you mind if I give you a few tips?' he asked.

When she smiled at him over her shoulder he came up behind her. 'You are allowing your right hand to overpower the gun.' He folded her in his arms and took her hands in his huge fists. 'Remember, your left hand must always dominate. The right hand is there only to pull the trigger.'

He mounted the gun to her shoulder for her and squeezed her left hand on to the forestock for emphasis.

'Head up,' he said. 'Both eyes open. Watch the bird, not the gun.'

He smelt masculine. The perfume of his aftershave lotion did not entirely conceal the odour of fresh male sweat. His arms around her felt very agreeable.

'Oh,' she said. 'You mean like this?' And she pushed backwards gently with her hard round buttocks as she aimed over the barrels.

'Precisely.' There was a catch in his voice. 'You have got it exactly right.'

'Goodness gracious me!' She used one of Nana's cherished expressions to herself. 'He is size fourteen all over.' She had to work hard to prevent herself giggling like a schoolgirl.

Sir Clarence was warming rapidly to his self-appointed task as tutor, and Isabella told herself firmly: 'That's enough already. We don't want to spoil him.' And gently freed herself from his embrace.

'Let me try it,' she said, and shot the next dove so cleanly that it did not even flutter a wing.

'You are a natural,' he murmured, and she turned her head away to conceal her smile at the *double entendre*.

'I understand from your brother that you are also a first-class horsewoman,' he pursued relentlessly, not waiting for her reply. 'I have recently purchased a magnificent Arab stallion. I doubt there is another like him in Africa. I'd love to show him to you.'

'Oh?' she asked with feigned lack of interest, concentrating on loading the shotgun. 'Where is he?'

'On my ranch at Rusape. We could have the Alouette drop us off there on the way back to Salisbury tomorrow afternoon.'

'I might enjoy that,' she agreed. 'I'd like to meet your wife. I've heard that she is a delightful lady.'

He fielded it without a blink. 'Alas, my wife is in Europe at the moment. She'll be away for another month at the least. You'd have to put up with me alone.' He gave the last sentence another subtle emphasis, and this time she could not prevent herself smiling.

'I'll have to think about that, Sir Clarence,' she said. 'I imagine that you are rather a large handful to put up with.' And this time his grave expression cracked and he smiled back at her.

'Nothing that you couldn't handle, my dear.'

She wondered what the reward from her mysterious masters would be if she could present them with not only the anti-sanctions strategy but also the complete Rhodesian order of battle. 'All in the line of duty,' she assured herself.

'Full bag!' Shasa called across to Elsa. He broke open his shotgun and placed it across the crook of his arm. He called to the two black children: 'Pakamisa! Pick them up!'

They scampered away to pick up the last two doves. Shasa and Elsa sauntered back to where the trucks were parked beyond the pan. The sun was almost on the tree-tops, and the thin stratum of cloud above it was gilded to brightest gold – the colour of a wedding ring, Shasa decided for no apparent reason.

'All right,' Elsa said suddenly, as though she had reached a difficult decision.

'Forgive me' – he was puzzled – 'what is all right?'

'I trust you,' she said. 'There will be conditions attached, but I will give you the blueprint for the plant and the formula for Cyndex 25.'

He drew a slow breath. 'I will try to be worthy of your trust.'

That evening, as they sat at the camp-fire withdrawn from the rest of the party, she set down the conditions.

'You will give me your personal guarantee that Cyndex will never be used except on the express authority of the prime minister or his successors in office.'

Shasa glanced across the flames to make certain that they were not overheard. 'I swear that to you. I will obtain the prime minister's written agreement.'

'Now, as to the rules of engagement, Cyndex will never be used on any section of the South African people,' Elsa went on carefully. 'It will never be used in internal political or civil conflict. It will never be used to quell an uprising of the populace or in a future civil war.'

'I agree.'

'It may be used only to repel a military invasion by troops of a foreign power. Then only when the use of conventional arms fails.'

'I agree.'

'There is one other condition – a little more personal.'

'Name it.'

'You will come to Lausanne personally to arrange the details.'

'That will be my particular pleasure.'

It was the last morning of safari. The guests had packed and were ready to leave Chizora. Their luggage was stacked outside each tent, ready for the camp staff to collect.

The business was done, and the contracts signed. Elsa Pignatelli had agreed to assist with the marketing of Rhodesian tobacco and chrome – for a princely fee – while Garry Courtney had undertaken to provide shipping and false documentation for these materials from South African ports. His rewards for these services would include extension of the Chizora hunting concessions as well as his monetary commissions.

The entire party was due to be ferried back to Salisbury in the Rhodesian air-force helicopter. The helicopter had already been in radio contact with the camp when it was airborne and only a hundred nautical miles out. They had expected it to land in the glade in front of the camp thirty minutes ago. It was overdue, and they were worried.

In small groups they stood around the camp-fire in the boma sipping a final Pimm's No. 1. Instinctively they kept glancing to the sky and listening for the sound of the Alouette's rotors.

Sean and Bella were together. 'When are you coming to Cape Town?' she asked her eldest brother.

'I'll try to get down at the end of the season, if you promise to line up some crumpet for me.'

'Whenever did you need help?' she asked, and Sean grinned and kissed her.

'I'm not as bad as Pater,' he protested. 'Look at the old dog. He's off to Europe with the widow, I hear.'

They both looked across at Elsa and Shasa.

'It's puke-making at their age,' Sean teased, and Isabella came loyally to her father's defence.

'Daddy is one of the most attractive—'

'Cool it, Bella.' He squeezed her arm. 'Worry about Sir C. You'll be lucky to escape with your virtue. They don't call him Cantering Clarence for nothing.'

As if in response to his name, Sir Clarence drifted across to Isabella and quietly spirited her aside.

'We'll drop the others off at Salisbury,' he murmured, leaning over her solicitously. 'Then the helicopter can take the two of us on to my ranch. We don't have to make a fuss about our little excursion, do we?'

'Of course not,' Isabella agreed sweetly. 'We don't want my papa – or Lady Van Wyk – spoiling our innocent interlude of horse appreciation.'

'Exactly,' he agreed. 'Some things are best . . .' He

broke off as the radio in Sean's tent crackled urgently and then burst into life.

Sean bounded from the boma and disappeared into his tent. More than any of them, he had been worried by the overdue helicopter. They heard him acknowledging his call-sign from the approaching helicopter.

'Tugboat, this is Big Foot. Go ahead.'

'Big Foot. We have a change of plan. Please inform the minister that this flight is being diverted to hot-pursuit operations. We will pick you up with your recce team in sixteen minutes. I have ten Scouts on board. Alternative arrangements will be made for ministerial transport as soon as possible. Over.'

'Roger, Tugboat. We will be ready for pick-up. Standing by.'

'War is such a damned nuisance,' Sir Clarence sighed. They had overheard every word of the radio exchange. 'We will have to sit around here until they can send another chopper to fetch us.'

'What has happened?' Isabella demanded.

'Terrorist action,' Sir Clarence explained. 'Probably an attack on a white farm somewhere. Our helicopter is being diverted. The pursuit takes precedence over all other traffic. Can't let these murderous swine get away with it – have to keep the morale of the farmers up.'

He didn't mention how desperately short of military helicopters the Rhodesian air force was, but shrugged instead.

'It does look as though the Fates are conspiring against us.'

'Perhaps we'll just have to postpone our little arrangements—' She broke off as Sean came out of the tent shrugging on his light pursuit-harness, with its canvas pockets for ammunition and grenades and water-bottles. His FN rifle was slung over one shoulder, and he was bellowing.

'Matatu, come on, you skinny little bugger. We've got real work to do now. Hot pursuit.'

The diminutive Ndorobo tracker appeared like a grinning black jack-in-the-box.

'Hai, Bwana,' he piped in Swahili. 'We will roast some ZANLA testicles on the camp-fire tonight.'

'You bloodthirsty little devil. You love it, don't you,' Sean grinned with his own fierce joy, and then turned to the others clustered in the centre of the boma.

'Sorry, folks. Have to leave you to make your own way back to Salisbury. Matatu and I have a date.' He singled out Garry in the group. 'Why don't you ferry them up to Salisbury in the Beechcraft? With all that luggage it will take you a couple of trips, but it's better than sitting around waiting for the chopper to be free.'

He broke off and cocked his head to listen. 'Here she comes now.'

He moved quickly amongst them, shaking hands in brief farewell.

'Will we see you again next season, signora? Next time, I promise you a big leopard . . .'

'Sorry to bump you off the flight, Sir Clarence.'

'Cheerio, Dad. Keep out of mischief . . .' This with a wink and a glance at Elsa Pignatelli.

''Bye, little sister.' He kissed Isabella, and she clung to him for a moment.

'Be careful, Sean. Please don't let anything happen to you.'

He hugged her and laughed at the absurdity of that idea. 'You are in more danger of receiving incoming fire from Sir C,' he chuckled.

He looked up at the sky, and the helicopter was a black insect shape above the trees.

He crossed to shake his younger brother's hand. 'Damn it, Garry. Who wants your job – when I can be doing this?'

While they waited for the helicopter to settle Sean stood in the gateway of the boma with Matatu.

Isabella felt her throat close up and tears prickle her eyes. They made such an incongruous pair, the tall heroic figure of her brother with flowing locks and tanned muscular limbs and the wizened black gnome at his side. As she watched, Sean dropped one hand on the little man's shoulder in an affectionate embrace, an affirmation of the trust bred between them in a hundred desperate adventures and the mark of the special bond between these two warrior hunters.

Then they were racing forward into the blown dust-cloud of the hovering helicopter, ducking low under the spinning blur of the rotors, and scrambling into the open hatchway.

Immediately the machine rose and went boring away into the south-east, keeping low over the tree-tops, not wasting a moment in the climb for altitude.

★   ★   ★

The ten Scouts were seated along the benches in the main cabin of the helicopter, each of them heavily pregnant with their body harnesses and packs, draped with belts of ammunition and grenades and water-bottles, their bare arms and legs blackened. Only their teeth sparkled in faces that were either smeared with camouflage cream or were naturally dark. At least half the Ballantyne Scouts were loyal Matabele.

It was well known that blacks and whites fighting together as comrades tended to bring out the best qualities in each other as warriors. The Ballantyne Scouts were the crack unit of Rhodesia's fighting forces, although the Selous Scouts and the Special Air Services and the Rhodesian Regiment would split your crust if they heard you say it.

As Sean clambered into the cabin, he recognized every man of them, and greeted them by name. They returned the greeting with a laconic economy of words that belied their awe and respect. Sean and Matatu were already a living legend in the Scouts. The two of them had trained most of these tough young veterans in the subtle skills of bushcraft.

Roland Ballantyne, the founder and commanding colonel

of the Scouts, had tried every ruse to inveigle Sean in as his second-in-command – so far without success. In the meantime he called upon Sean and Matatu whenever there was a heavy contact in the offing.

Sean dropped on to the seat beside him now. He snapped on his seat-belt. While he began rubbing camouflage cream into his face he shouted above the clatter of the rotors: 'Greetings, Skipper. What's the rumble?'

'Bunch of terrs hit a tobacco farm outside Karoi yesterday evening. They ambushed the farmer at the homestead gate. Shot him down as his wife came out on the veranda to welcome him. She held them off alone all night in the farmhouse – even under rocket-fire. Gutsy bird. Some time after midnight they pulled out and gapped it.'

'How many?'

'Twenty plus.'

'Which way?'

'North into the valley.'

'Contact?'

'Not yet,' Roland shook his head. Even under the camo cream he was lantern-jawed and impressive. He was probably five years older than Sean. Like Sean he had built a hell of a reputation in the few short years since the bush war began.

'Local unit is following up but making heavy weather, losing ground every hour. The gooks are running hard.'

'They'll bombshell and try to lose themselves amongst the local black population in the Tribal Trust area,' Sean predicted as he bound a grubby scrap of camouflage-net over his shining shoulder-length locks. 'Get us to the follow-up unit, Skipper.'

'We'll be in radio contact any minute—' Roland broke off as the flight engineer beckoned him to the radio handset. 'Come on.' He unbuckled his safety-belt and led the way down the vibrating, bucking aisle between the benches. Sean followed him. He stood beside Roland, bracing himself against the bulkhead and craning his head to listen to the tinny disembodied voice in the microphone. 'Bushbuck. This is Striker One,' Roland spoke into the mouth-piece. 'Do you have contact?'

'Striker One. This is Bushbuck. Negative. I say again negative on contact.'

'Are you on the spoor, Bushbuck?'

'Affirmative, but chase has bombshelled.' That meant that the terrorist gang had split up to hinder the pursuit.

'Roger, Bushbuck. As soon as you hear our engines give us yellow smoke.'

'Confirm yellow smoke, Striker One.'

Forty-five minutes later, the helicopter pilot picked out the smoke-signal, a canary-yellow feather drifting over the dark green roof of the forest. The helicopter dropped towards it, and hovered above the grass-tops in an open glade between the trees standing in the tree-line. They saw the police unit who had pushed the pursuit thus far. It was obvious at a glance that these were not élite bush fighters, but garrison troops from Karoi. They were townies and reserves doing their monthly call-up duties and not enjoying the chase one little bit.

Sean and Matatu exited together, jumping the six feet to earth and landing like a pair of cats, in balance with hot guns. They spread out swiftly and took cover while the helicopter soared and hovered two hundred feet above them.

It took them fifteen seconds to make certain that the police had the drop area secure, then Sean ran across to the leader of the pursuit unit.

'OK, Sergeant,' he snapped crisply. 'Hit your bottle. Drink, man, drink.'

The sergeant was red-faced, burnt by the sun, and overweight. Even in the valley heat, he had stopped sweating. It had dried on his shirt in irregular white rings of salt. He didn't know enough to keep himself from dehydrating. Another hour and he would be a casualty.

'Water is finished.' The sergeant's voice was hoarse. Sean tossed him a precious water-bottle, and while the man drank asked; 'What's the line of spoor?'

The sergeant pointed to the earth ahead of him, but already Matatu had picked up the sign left by the fleeing gang. He scampered along it, cocking his head to study the fine details which were invisible to any but the truly talented eye. He followed it for a mere fifty paces and then doubled back to where Sean waited.

'Five of them,' he chirped. 'One wounded in the left leg . . .'

'The farmer's widow must have given them a good run.'

'. . . but the spoor is cold. We must play the spring hare.'

Sean nodded. The 'spring hare' was a technique that he and Matatu had worked out between them. It could only be effective with a tracker of Matatu's calibre. They had to be able to guess where the chase was heading. They had to have a good idea of the line and rate of march before they could leap-frog – or spring-hare – down the line.

Here there was no doubt. The band of terrorists must keep northwards towards the Zambezi and the Tribal Trust lands where they could expect to find food and shelter and some rudimentary medical treatment for their wounded. There were many sympathizers amongst the black Shona and Batonka tribesmen who lived along the valley rim. Those who would not co-operate willingly would be forced to do so at the muzzle of an AK 47 assault-rifle.

All right, so they would keep on northwards. However, the wilderness ahead was vast. There was hard going and broken terrain, rocky valleys and jumbled granite kopjes. If the fleeing band turned only a few degrees off the obvious line of march, they could disappear without trace.

Sean ran out into the open glade and signalled the circling Alouette, holding his arms in a crucifix. The helicopter responded instantly.

'OK, Sergeant,' Sean called. 'Keep after them. We'll go ahead and try to cut the spoor. Maintain radio contact – and remember to drink.'

'Right on, sir!' the sergeant grinned. The brief meeting

had given him and his men fresh heart. They all knew who Sean was. He and Matatu were legend.

'Give them hell, sir!' he yelled up at Sean, and Sean waved from the open hatch of the Alouette as they soared away.

Sean swallowed half a dozen codeine tablets for his ribs, which were beginning to ache, and washed them down with a swig from his spare water-bottle. He and Matatu crouched together in the opening of the hatchway, peering down at the canopy of the forest five hundred feet below. Only at moments like these, when the hunt was running hot and hard, could Matatu subdue his terror of flying.

Now he leant so far out of the hatch that Sean had an arm around his waist to hold him from the drop. Matatu was positively shivering in his grip, the way a good gun-dog shivers with the scent of the bird in his nostrils.

Suddenly he pointed, and Sean yelled to the flight engineer: 'Turn ten degrees left.'

Over the intercom the engineer relayed the change of course to the pilot in the high cockpit.

Sean could see no possible reason for Matatu's turn to the west. Below them the forest was amorphous and featureless. The rocky kopjes that broke the leafy monotony were miles apart, random and indistinguishable one from the other.

Two minutes later Matatu pointed again, and Sean interpreted for him: 'Turn back five degrees right.'

The Alouette banked obediently. Matatu was performing his special magic. He was actually tracking the fugitives from five hundred feet above the canopy of trees, not by sight or sign, but by a weird intuitive sense that Sean would not have credited if he had not seen it happen on a hundred other chases over the years.

Matatu quivered in Sean's grip and turned his face up at his master. He was grinning wickedly, his lips trembling with excitement. The blast of the slipstream had filled his eyes with tears, and they streamed down his cheeks.

'Down!' he yelped, and pointed again.

'Down!' Sean yelled at the flight engineer. As the helicopter dropped, Sean looked across at Roland Ballantyne.

'Hot guns!' he warned, and Roland signalled his men. They straightened up on the hard benches and leant forward like hunting dogs on the leash. As one man they raised their weapons, muzzles high, and with a metallic clatter that carried above the roar of the turbo engines they locked and loaded.

The helicopter checked and hovered six feet above the baked dry earth. Sean and Matatu jumped together, and cleared the drop zone.

As soon as they were clear they went down into cover, facing outward. Sean's FN was at his shoulder as he scanned the bush around him. The Scouts came boiling out of the hatchway, and scattered to adopt a defensive perimeter. The helicopter climbed away empty.

The second they were in position Roland Ballantyne signalled across to Sean with clenched fist 'Go!'

Well separated, Sean and Matatu went forward. The Scouts spread out and covered them, eyes glinting and restless trigger-fingers cocked. Matatu had brought them down in a bottle-neck where a series of steep rocky ridges formed a funnel. The apex of the V was cut through by a dry riverbed. Storm water over the millennium had sculpted a natural staircase that climbed the ridge, and the elephant herds that used this natural pass had worn the contours and levelled the gradients.

Would the fleeing band have traded time for stealth? Would they have chosen the elephant highway, rather than toil up the jagged rocky ridge at another, less obvious point?

Matatu flicked his fingers underhand, signalling Sean to cast the eastern approach to the pass. Sean was as good a tracker as any white man alive. To save precious time Matatu would trust him with such a simple cast as this.

Sean moved across the sun, placing it between him and the ground he was searching. It was the old tracker's trick to highlight the spoor. He concentrated all his attention on the earth, trusting the hovering Scouts to cover his back. They were all good men; he had trained them himself.

He felt the little electric thrill of it as he picked it up. It was close in against the cliff-face. One of the round water-worn river-boulders had been displaced. It was sitting a quarter of an inch askew in the natural dish of earth that had held it. He touched it with a fingertip just to check. He would not call Matatu and risk his scorn until he was certain.

'Little bugger will mock me for a week if I make a bum call.'

The boulder was the size of his head and it moved slightly under his finger. Yes, it had been recently dislodged. Sean whistled, and Matatu appeared at his side like the genie of the lamp. Sean did not have to point it out. Matatu saw it instantly and nodded his approbation.

The file of fugitives was anti-tracking skilfully. They had moved up the water-course in Indian file, keeping in close under the precipitous rocky side. They had used the river-boulders as stepping-stones to hide their tracks, but this one had been slightly dislodged by the weight of the men passing over it.

Matatu darted forward. A hundred or so paces further on he found the spot where the wounded terrorist's foot had slipped off one of the stepping-stones and touched the soft white sand. The foot had left a brush-mark. Only the highly trained eye would have noticed the faint shade of colour difference between the surface grains and the freshly exposed grains of sand from below.

Matatu knelt over it and studied the faint scuff-mark, then he blew gently on the surrounding sand to gauge its friability. He rocked back on his heels while he pondered the factors that had effected the colour difference in the grains – the moisture content of the sand, the angle of the sun, the strength of the breeze and, most important, the time elapsed since the sand had been disturbed.

'Two hours,' he said with utter finality, and Sean accepted it without question.

'Two hours behind them,' Sean reported to Roland Ballantyne.

'How does he do it?' Roland shook his head in wonder. 'He brought us straight here, and now he gives us the exact time. He's gained us eight hours in fifteen minutes. How does he do it, Sean?'

'Beats me,' Sean admitted. 'He's just a chocolate-coated miracle.'

'Can he spring-hare us again?' Roland demanded. He spoke no Swahili; Sean had to translate.

'Spring-hare, Matatu?'

'Ndio, Bwana,' Matatu nodded happily, and preened under the patent admiration of the colonel.

'Leave four men to follow up on the ground,' Sean advised. 'Tell them to follow the water-course and there's a good chance they will pick up the spoor at the top.'

Roland gave the orders, and the four Scouts moved away up the funnel in good order. Sean called down the helicopter, and they scrambled aboard.

They flew on into the north. However, they had not been airborne for more than ten minutes before Matatu wriggled in Sean's grip and yelped: 'Turn! Turn back!'

Under Sean's direction the helicopter made a wide circle, and Matatu was leaning halfway out of the hatch. His head swung quickly from side to side as he peered downwards, and for the first time he seemed uncertain.

'Down,' he cried suddenly, and pointed to a long streak of darker-green vegetation that filled a shallow kidney-shaped depression in the terrain ahead of them.

The Alouette descended gently, warily. Matatu pointed out a landing-zone at the far side of the depression.

The scrub below them was dense and thorny, and the ground was studded with ant-heaps. These were bare towers of concrete, hard red clay each as high as a man's shoulder, like headstones in a cemetery; they would make the landing difficult and dangerous.

Little bugger is taking us into the worst-possible LZ,

Sean thought bitterly. Why does he have to choose this particular spot?

The helicopter checked in mid-air, and Sean turned his head and yelled at Roland: 'Hot guns, man!' And then followed Matatu. They landed side by side and scurried forward, dropping into cover behind one of the ant-heaps.

He did not turn his head to watch the other Scouts come out of the hatch. He was watching the tangled thorn scrub out ahead, sweeping his flanks with a darting penetrating scrutiny, holding the FN levelled and his thumb on the safety. Although it was a million-to-one chance that there was a terrorist within five miles of the LZ, still the landing drill was second nature to all of them.

'No gooks here,' Sean assured himself. And then incredibly, stunningly they were under fire.

From the thorn scrub on their left flank AK fire raked them. The sharp distinctive rattle of the fusillades swept over them. Dust and chips of red clay flew from the side of the ant-heap only inches in front of his face. Sean reacted instantly. He rolled and re-aligned, and as he brought the FN to bear he glimpsed from the corner of his eye a grisly little cameo of death.

One of the Scouts, the last man out of the hatch, was hit. As his feet touched the ground, a burst of AK fire caught him across the belly. It doubled him over and drove him backwards three sharp paces. The bullets exiting from his back pulled his body out of shape. They sucked half his guts out of him, and blew them in a misty pink streak through the stark sunlit air. Then he was down and gone into the scrub.

As Sean returned fire the realization flashed in upon him: Matatu has dropped us into direct contact. He punctuated his thoughts with short measured bursts of the FN. The little bugger has been too bloody good this time. He has dropped us right on their heads.

At the same time he was assessing the contact. Obviously the gang had been taken as unaware as they were. They

436

had not been able to prepare any kind of defence, nor had the time to set up an ambush. Probably they had heard the roar of the approaching helicopter and then only seconds later the Scouts had begun dropping amongst them.

Surprise, Sean thought, and shot at the muzzle-flashes of an AK that were fluttering the leaves of a thorn bush only thirty paces ahead.

From experience he had learnt that the Shona guerrillas facing him were first-class soldiers, doughty and brave and dedicated. They had two weaknesses, however. First, their fire-control was poor; they believed that sheer weight of fire made up for inaccuracy. Their other weakness was the inability to react swiftly to surprise. Sean knew that for another minute or so the terrorists in the scrub in front of him would be disorganized and flustered.

Hit them now, he thought, and snatched a phosphorus grenade from his webbing. As he pulled the pin from the grenade he opened his mouth to yell at Roland Ballantyne: 'Come on, Roland. Sweep line! Charge the sods before they settle down.'

Roland beat him to it. The same thoughts must have raced through his mind. 'Take them, boys! Sweep line – on the charge!'

Sean leapt to his feet and in the same movement hurled the grenade in a high arcing trajectory. It fell thirty yards ahead of him, and the thorn scrub erupted in a blinding white cloud of phosphorus smoke. Flaming fragments, burning with a dazzling white radiance, showered over the area.

Sean raced forward, conscious of the small dark shape that ran at his heels. Matatu was his shadow. Other grenades were exploding across the front, and the thorn scrub was thrashed by the blasts and lashed by the sheets of automatic fire that the Scouts threw down as they charged.

The gang broke before them. One of them ducked out of the bush ten paces ahead of Sean, a teenager in tattered blue jeans and a soft camouflage-cap. Burning globules of phosphorus had adhered to his upper body. They sizzled

437

and flared, leaving smoking black spots on his arms and torso. The smoke smelt like barbecueing meat.

Sean shot him, but the burst was low. It broke his left hip, and the boy dropped. The AK rifle flew from his grip, and he rolled on to his back and held his hands in front of his face.

'No, Mambo!' he screamed in English. 'Don't kill me! I am a Christian – for the love of God, spare me!'

'Matatu,' Sean snapped without checking or looking round. 'Kufa!'

He jumped over the maimed guerrilla. The magazine of his FN was half-empty. He could not afford to waste a single round, and Matatu had his skinning-knife. He spent hours each day honing the blade. If he had been a section leader, Sean might have saved him for interrogation; but Matatu could cut this one's throat. Cannon-fodder like him was of no use to them, and medical attention was expensive.

The Scouts swept the bush, and it was over in less than two minutes. It was no contest. It was like pitting Pekinese puppies against a pack of wild dogs. The Scouts charged through and then whirled and came back.

'Secure the area,' Roland Ballantyne ordered. He was standing less than twenty yards from Sean. He held the muzzle of his rifle pointed at the sky, and the heated metal distorted the air around it in a watery mirage. 'Well done, Sean. That little black devil of yours is a charm.' He glanced across at Matatu.

Matatu was straightening up from the corpse of the hip-shot terrorist. He had slit his throat with a single stroke, across the side of the throat and up under the ear to catch the carotid artery.

He was wiping the blade of his skinning-knife on his thigh as he scurried back to his rightful place at Sean's side, but he grinned an acknowledgement at Roland Ballantyne. Both of them were distracted, still heady with the euphoria of violence and blood.

The corpse of one of the other guerrillas lay in the scrub between them. The flesh and clothing still smouldered with burnt-out phosphorus, and the man's clothing was splattered with bright blood from his gunshot wounds. Roland Ballantyne walked past him with barely a glance. It was impossible that the terrorist could have survived such terrible injuries.

The terrorist rolled over abruptly. He had been concealing a Tokarev pistol under his shattered chest. With his last flutter of life he lifted the Tokarev and he was close enough to touch Roland with the muzzle.

'Roland!' Sean screamed a warning, and although Roland reacted instantly it was too late. The shot would take him in the spine from a range of three feet.

Sean did not have time to raise the FN to his shoulder. He fired from the hip, pointing and aiming instinctively. The bullet caught the terrorist in the face. His head burst like an over-ripe water-melon hit with a pick-handle, and he flopped over on his back. The Tokarev slipped unfired from his nerveless fingers.

Roland Ballantyne straightened up slowly, and for a long moment he stared down at the corpse. The man's legs were kicking and trembling convulsively. Roland contemplated his own mortality and saw the agony of his own death reflected in the man's bulging eyeballs.

He tore his gaze away and looked across at Sean.

'I owe you one,' he said curtly. 'You can collect any time.' And he turned away to shout orders at his Scouts to gather the kill. There were green plastic body-bags in the hovering Alouette.

*   *   *

Le Morne Brabant was a jagged mountain of black volcanic lava that seemed to tower over them threateningly, even though they were almost four miles out on the oceanic stream.

These sapphire currents that eddied around the toe of the island of Mauritius created an enrichment of marine life that big-game anglers around the world recognized as a 'hot spot'. There were other famous grounds such as those off the ribbons of the Great Barrier Reef, at Cabo San Lucas on the Californian peninsula or in the lee of the island of Nova Scotia. At all these points the concentrations of vast shoals of bait-fish attracted the ocean predators – the giant marlin and the tuna species. The sports anglers of the world came to pit their skill and their strength against these sleek monsters.

Shasa Courtney always insisted on chartering the same boat and the same island crew. Each boat sets up its own individual vibration in the water, a combination of engine and propeller and hull configuration which is as unique to that boat as a fingerprint is to the man. That vibration either attracts or repels fish.

Le Bonheur was a lucky boat. She pulled fish, and her skipper had eyes like a gannet. He could spot the flash of a single sea-bird diving on a school of bait-fish on the horizon, or at a mile's distance pick out the sickle-shaped dorsal fin of a cruising marlin and estimate the fish's weight to within ten kilos.

Today, however, they were desperate for a bait. They had been out for almost two hours without putting a bait on the outriggers.

Everywhere they looked there were shoals of bait-fish. The Indian Ocean seemed to swarm with their multitudes. They darkened the surface of the water like patches of cloud shadow, and dense flocks of sea-birds circled over them, screaming and diving in avaricious hysteria. Every few minutes a volley of leaping bonito would burst through the surface and arc in glittering silver parabolas through the brilliant tropical sunshine.

They were being panicked and driven up by the great pelagic fish that circled in the depths below the shoals. It was one of those crazy days that occur all too seldom in a fisherman's life when there are simply too many fish. The ravenous predators were harrying the shoals so viciously that they were unable to feed. All their energy was diverted to avoiding the voracious charging monsters that tore through the shoals. They ignored the small finger-length feather lures with which the crew of *Le Bonheur* were trying to tempt them.

Standing on the flying bridge fifteen feet above the deck, Shasa could see deep into the limpid blue waters. He could clearly make out the hordes of bonito, like fat cigars as long as his forearm, dodging and ducking through *Le Bonheur*'s wake. They almost touched the feather jigs as they darted past them.

'We need one – just one bait,' Shasa groaned. 'On a day like this it's an iron-clad guarantee of a marlin.'

Elsa Pignatelli leant over the bridge rail beside him. She wore only a tiny flaming scarlet bikini and she was tanned and smooth as a loaf of honey bread crisp from the oven.

'Look!' she cried, and Shasa whirled just in time to see a marlin come out of the water alongside *Le Bonheur*. It was driven high into the air by the speed and power of its own charge as it split a shoal of bonito. Its eyes were the size of tennis balls, and its spike was the length and thickness of a baseball bat. The water streamed from its flanks in silver cascades, and it wagged its great head in the air. In the excitement of the feeding frenzy, it had changed colour, like a chameleon, and burnt with bands of electric blue and lilac that turned the tropical blue of the sky pale in contrast.

'A grander!' Shasa shouted the colloquial name for a fish that would push the scale beyond the mystic thousand-pound mark.

The marlin fell back and hit the water flat on its side with a report like a shot of cannon.

'A bait!' cried Shasa, clutching his brow like a Shakespearian tragedian. 'My kingdom for a bait.'

The other half-dozen boats of the Black River fleet that they could see scattered to the horizon were suffering the same agonies. They could hear the frustrated lamentations of their skippers on the ship's radio. Nobody had bait, while out there the marlin were waiting to commit suicide.

'What can *I* do?' Elsa demanded. 'Do you want me to

propound a little of my witchcraft and weave a spell for you?'

'I don't know if that would be strictly ethical,' Shasa grinned back at her. 'But I'm willing to try anything. Weave away, my lovely witch!'

She opened her purse and found her lipstick. 'Tom Thumb, Thomas à Becket, Rumpelstiltskin!' she intoned solemnly, and drew a scarlet hieroglyph on his naked chest which had a distinctly phallic outline. 'I diddle you! I fiddle you! I doddle you! I doodle you!'

'Oh yes. I love it,' Shasa laughed out loud. 'I could get seriously hooked on your type of magic.'

'You have to believe in it,' she warned him, 'or else it just won't work.'

'I believe,' said Shasa fervently. 'Oh, how I believe in doodling you!'

Down on the deck below them one of the crew squealed suddenly, and they heard the tinny whirr of the ratchet on one of the small bait-rods.

Shasa's laughter was cut off abruptly. For an instant he stared at her with awe. 'Damn me! You really are a witch,' he muttered, and he dived for the ladder and slid down to the deck.

The deck-hand brought the skipjack bonito over the side and cradled him lovingly in his arms. The fish quivered and struggled, but he cushioned its fat round body against his chest. It was a pretty metallic blue and silver, with a pointed snout and sharp-bladed tail-fins. Its lower body was laced with lateral lines of black. Shasa saw with relief that it was lightly hooked in the hinge of the jaw. There was no damage to its gills.

He slipped the small hook from its jaw and ordered the deckie: 'Turn him!' The deckie inverted the bonito, and immediately its struggles ceased. Holding it upside down was a trick that disorientated and quietened it.

Shasa had his bait instruments laid out like those of a surgeon. He selected the long crochet-hook and worked it carefully into the front of the bonito's eye-socket. The blunt steel tip pushed the eyeball aside and did not damage it in the least. He steered the needle into the natural canal through the bone of the fish's skull. The tip emerged from the same spot in the opposite eye-socket. The fish showed no sign of distress and lay quietly in the deckie's arms.

Shasa hooked a loop of 120-lb Dacron line over the steel crochet-hook and gently drew the line back through the wound. He dropped the crochet-hook and snatched up the huge 12/0 marlin-hook. With a series of quick deft turns he had attached the hook firmly between the bonito's eyes. The fish was still alive and virtually unharmed. Its eyesight was unimpaired.

Shasa stood back and nodded to the deckie. He knelt on the gunwale and lowered the bonito over the side, solicitous as a nursemaid. As soon as it was released, the fish darted away, drawing the heavy steel trace and the attached Dacron line behind it. It disappeared almost instantly into the blue depths.

Shasa stood beside the fighting-chair. The stubby rod was set in the gimbal. The Fin-Nor Tycoon reel was made of gold-anodized marine-grade aluminium alloy. Still it weighed over five kilos and held over a kilometre of the braided Dacron line. The line hissed softly as it streamed off the reel. Shasa adjusted the tension on it with a light touch of his fingertips.

He had marked the line with wraps of silk thread at intervals of fifty yards. He let out a measured hundred yards before he tightened the drag lever of the reel.

The deckie was already lowering the halyard of one of the twenty-foot outriggers that protruded like whippy steel antennae from each side of the hull. The purpose of the outrigger was to hold the lines separated and to allow the slack bight of line to drop back when the marlin struck.

'No,' Shasa stopped him. 'I will hold it myself.'

This was a more precise method of determining the depth of the bait and amount of drop-back. However, it required patience and experience and fortitude to hand-

443

hold the line rather than merely to loll in the chair and leave it in the clip of the outrigger.

Carefully Shasa stripped a hundred feet of line off the big Fin Nor and coiled it on the deck. Then he perched on the stern of *Le Bonheur* and called to the skipper: 'Allez!'

The skipper engaged the gear lever, and the propeller began to turn lazily. The diesel engine was ticking over at idling revs and *Le Bonheur* began to inch forward against the scend of the swells.

Slowly she built up to a leisurely walking speed. The tension on the line in Shasa's hand increased. He could feel the weight of the bonito on the other end. The fish began to follow the boat like a dog on a leash. Shasa judged the depth of the bait by the angle at which the line entered the water. He could tell the condition and liveliness of the bonito by the faint vibration of its tail and the intermittent tugs and jerks it gave as it attempted to turn or dive.

Within minutes Shasa's arm was numb and cramping, but he ignored the discomfort and called up to Elsa on the bridge: 'How about a little more of your "fiddle me diddle me" magic?'

'It only works once.' She shook her head. 'From here on you are on your own.'

At slow speed *Le Bonheur* rolled sluggishly over the swells, and at Shasa's order began a wide and gentle turn up into the north.

Halfway through the turn, the line went slack in Shasa's hand and he stood up quickly from his seat on the gunwale.

'What is it?' Elsa called down eagerly.

'Probably nothing,' he grunted, but all his concentration was on the feel of the line.

It came taut again, but now the bonito's movements were altered. He could feel its frantic struggles transmitted through his fingertips. It ducked and dived and tried to turn, but the gentle progress of *Le Bonheur* drew it forward remorselessly.

'Attention!' Shasa alerted the crew.

'What's happening?' Elsa asked again.

444

'Something is frightening the bonito,' he answered. 'It's seen something down there.'

He could imagine the terror of the small fish as the gigantic shadow circled it stealthily in the blue underworld of the ocean. The marlin would be wary. The bonito was behaving unnaturally. It should have darted away instantly. The marlin stalked it gingerly, but soon its appetite would exceed its caution. Shasa waited a minute and another minute, crouched over the transom, rigid with excitement.

Suddenly the line was plucked from his fingers, but for an instant he felt the mighty weight and majesty of the marlin as it struck the bonito with the broad blunt edge of its spike.

'Strike!' Shasa howled, holding both arms above his head. 'Stop engines!'

Obediently the skipper slipped the gear lever into neutral, and *Le Bonheur* wallowed, dead in the water. Shasa picked up the line again and held it with the lightest pressure of his fingertips. It was slack; no sign of life. The bonito had been killed instantly by that massive blow.

Vividly he imagined what was happening in those mysterious blue depths. The marlin had killed and now it circled again. It might lose interest, or become alarmed by the unnatural movement of the carcass. It was essential that no movement or drift on the line scared it off.

The seconds dripped like treacle, slow and sticky.

'He is making another circle,' Shasa tried to encourage himself. Still nothing happened.

'Il est parti,' the skipper announced lugubriously. 'Il a refusé.'

'I'll kick your pessimistic butt if you wish it on me,' Shasa told him furiously. 'He hasn't bloody well *parti*-ed. He's coming around for another circle.'

The line twitched in his fingers, and Shasa let out a shout of relief.

'Le voilà! There he is!'

Elsa clapped her hands. 'Eat, fish. Smell that lovely sweet flesh. Eat it,' she implored.

445

The line jiggled and tugged softly, and Shasa let a few inches slide through his fingers. He could imagine the marlin picking up the carcass in its horny beak and turning it head-first to swallow it down.

'Don't let him feel the hook,' Shasa whispered a prayer. The loop of line should allow the point of the hook to lie flat against the bonito's head as it slid down the marlin's gaping maw. If, however, the loop had twisted or hung up – Shasa did not want to think about that.

There was another long pause, and then the line came taut again and began to move off with sedate but purposeful momentum.

'He's swallowed it,' Shasa exulted, and let the line flow through his fingers; coil after coil unwound from the deck and slipped away over the transom.

Shasa leapt to the swivel chair and swung himself into the seat. He clipped the harness to the rings on top of the glittering Fin-Nor reel. The harness formed a hammock-like sling around his lower back and buttocks and was attached directly to the reel.

Only the ignorant, or the deliberately misinformed, believed that the angler was buckled into the chair like a fighter pilot and that this gave him some sort of unsporting advantage. The only thing that kept him in the chair was his own strength and balance. If he made a mistake, the fish, weighing over a thousand pounds, as fast and powerful as a marine diesel engine, could pluck him and the rod effortlessly over the side and give him a very swift trip down to the five-hundred-fathom mark.

As Shasa settled behind the rod and engaged the brake, the line came up short against the spool and the rod-tip bowed over, as though it was kow-towing to the fish's brute strength.

Shasa thrust his feet against the footboard and took the strain with his legs.

'Allez!' he yelled at Martin the skipper. 'Go!'

The diesel bellowed as Martin opened the throttle wide and a dense cloud of oily black diesel smoke belched from the exhausts. *Le Bonheur* leapt forward and crashed her shoulder into the swell.

No man had the strength to drive the point of the huge Mustad hook into the iron-hard mouth of the marlin. Shasa was using the power and speed of the boat to set the hook, to bury the barb deep in the horny beak. The spool of the reel hummed against its own massive brake-pads, and the line streamed away in a white blur.

'Arrêtez-vous!' Shasa judged that the hook was in. 'Stop!' he cried, and Martin closed the throttle.

They stopped and hung in the water. The rod was arched over as though the line were attached to the bottom of the ocean, but the reel was still, held by the brake.

Then the fish shook his head, and the power of it crashed the butt of the rod back and forth in its gimbal as though it were a twig in a high wind.

'Here he goes!' Shasa howled. The fish had been taken aback by the unexpected drag of the line, but even *Le Bonheur* had been unable to move his massive body against the drag of the water.

Now at last he realized that something was seriously wrong, and he made his first mad run. Once again the line poured off the reel in a molten blur, and Shasa was lifted high off the seat like a jockey pushing for the post. So great was the friction in the massive Fin-Nor reel that it began to smoke. The grease on the bearings melted and boiled. It bubbled and spurted from the casing in steaming jets.

Leaning back with the full weight of his body, Shasa kept both hands well clear of the humming reel. The Dacron line was as dangerous as the blade of a butcher's bandsaw. It would take off a finger effortlessly or slash skin and flesh and muscle to the bone.

The fish ran as though there was no restraint upon him. The line on the spool melted away, three hundred yards were gone, then four, and in seconds half a kilometre of line had gone over the side.

'He's a goddam Chinaman and he's going home to daddy,' Shasa yelled. 'He's never going to stop!'

Abruptly the ocean parted in a maelstrom of white water, and the fish came out. Such was his girth and mass that he gave the illusion of moving in slow motion. He rose into the air, and the water poured from his body as though from the hull of a surfacing submarine. He came all the way out and, though he was five hundred yards from *Le Bonheur*, he seemed to blot out half the sky.

'Qu'il est grand!' shrieked Martin. 'Je n'ai jamais vu un autre comme ça!' And Shasa knew it was true – he had never seen a fish to match this one, not by half. He seemed to light the heavens with a reflected blue radiance, a flash of distant lightning.

Then, like a steeplechaser taking a fence, the fish reached the zenith of its leap and curved back to the surface of the ocean. It opened in a shockwave to his bulk, and then he was gone, leaving them all shaken by the memory of his majesty.

The line was blurring from the reel. Though Shasa had the brake dangerously heavy, pushing the drag up near the 120-pound breaking-strain, it still streamed away as though there were no check upon it.

'Tournez-vous! Turn!' There was an edge of panic in Shasa's voice, as he yelled at the skipper; 'Turn and chase him!'

With full rudder and opposite engine-thrust Martin spun the boat on its heel and they roared away in pursuit of the fish. *Le Bonheur* was rushing into wind and current, and the swells battered her. She dug her nose into them and burst them open in white spray. Then as she leapt over the crests she was almost airborne, and came pounding down into the troughs on her belly.

In the chair Shasa was thrown around mercilessly. He hung on to the arms of the chair, and rode the swells with his legs, his backside not touching the seat. The rod was bent like a longbow at full stretch. Even though *Le Bonheur* was running at full throttle, he was still losing line. The marlin was outrunning them by ten knots. The line on the reel wasted away, and Shasa watched helplessly as the spool seemed to shrink.

'Shasa!' Elsa shrieked from the bridge. 'He has turned!' She was so excited that she spoke in Italian. Shasa had by now enough practice with the language to understand her warning.

'Stop! Arrêtez!' he howled at the skipper.

For no apparent reason the marlin had suddenly turned completely about and was charging back towards the boat.

This was not yet apparent from the direction that the line was running into the water. The marlin had thrown a half-mile loop in the line, which was potentially catastrophic. The side-drag of the loop in the water could snap the heavy line like cotton when the marlin came up tight on it. Elsa had spotted the turn in the very nick of time.

Shasa had to pick up that loop before the marlin passed under the boat. He pumped with his legs in a powerful mechanical rhythm, coming up to gain a foot of line, sinking down to give himself slack to take it on to the reel with two quick turns of the handle. Up and down he bobbed, grunting for air with each cycle, legs and arms working together, and the wet line coming on to the spool under such tension that a fine haze of droplets sprayed from the braid. The line was cutting sideways through the water, slicing a tiny feather from the surface. The loop was shrinking. The fish passed under the boat. The line began to straighten.

Shasa pumped with a frantic rhythm, getting those last few turns of line on to the reel.

'Turn now!' he gasped. Sweat was pouring down his naked chest. It mingled with the lipstick design that Elsa had drawn and ran down to stain the waistband of his shorts. 'Turn quickly! Quickly!'

The fish was tearing away in the opposite direction, and the skipper got *Le Bonheur* around just as the line came up tight again. The full weight of the fish came down on the rod-tip, and it whipped over like a willow tree struck by a gale of wind. Shasa was levered up out of the chair to the full stretch of his legs, and the strain on the line was ounces short of snapping it.

He thumbed off the brake, releasing the tension, and the line crackled off the spool at fifty miles an hour. With despair he watched as those precious feet of line which he had won back with so much effort blurred effortlessly over the side.

'Chase him!' he blurted, and *Le Bonheur* pounded after the fish.

It was exquisite teamwork now. No single man could subdue a fish like this alone and unaided. The handling of the boat was critical, each turn and run and back-up had to be quick and precise.

Precious seconds before it was apparent to the men on the deck below, Elsa called out to warn of each new wild evolution of the great fish. For an hour those irresistible rushes never ceased. Every second of that time the thin strand of Dacron was under immense pressure, and Shasa stood in the chair and used his weight against it, pumping the rod and churning the reel. He took turn after agonizing turn on to the spool and then watched it dissipate again as the fish made another charge.

One of the deck-hands spilled sea-water from a bucket over his shoulders to cool him. The salt burnt the abrasions around his waist where the nylon straps of the harness had rubbed through his skin. The blood seeped from the injuries and stained his shorts watery pink. Every time the fish ran, the harness cut in a little deeper.

The second hour was bad. The fish showed no sign of weakening. Shasa was streaming with sweat, his hair was sodden as if he stood under a shower. The galls of the harness around his middle were bleeding freely. The working of the boat hammered his thighs against the arms of the chair, and he was bruising extensively. Elsa came down from the bridge and tried to pack a cushion between the harness and his torn flesh. She gave him a handful of salt tablets and made him drink two cans of Coke, holding them to his mouth while he gulped them down.

'Tell me something,' he grinned crookedly at her with agony in his single eye. 'What the hell am I doing this for?'

'Because you are a crazy macho man. And there are some things a man must do.' She towelled the sweat off his face and kissed him with a fierce protective pride.

Some time during the third hour Shasa got his second wind. Twenty years ago it would have come sooner and lasted longer. The second wind was an extraordinary sensation. The pain of the galling harness receded, the cramps in his arms and legs smoothed away, he felt light-headed and invincible. His legs stopped juddering under him, and he planted his feet more firmly on the footboard.

'All right, fish,' he said softly. 'You have had your innings. Now it's my turn.' He leant back with all his weight against the rod, and felt the fish give.

It was only a tiny check on the rod. A shudder of movement, but down there in the blue depths the great fish had stumbled slightly.

'Yes, fish,' Shasa whispered, as his spirits soared, 'it's hurting you, too, now, isn't it?' He pumped with legs that were once more strong beneath him and laid four tight white coils of line on the reel – and he knew that they would stay there this time. The fish was coming at last.

By the end of the fourth hour the fish had no more wild dashing runs to make. He was fighting deep and dogged, making slow, almost sedate circles three hundred feet below the drifting boat. He was working on his side, offering as much resistance as possible to the pressure of rod and line. He was almost four feet deep across the shoulder and he weighed nearly three-quarters of a ton. The great half-moon of his tail swept back and forth to a stately beat, and his enormous eyes glowed like opals in the semi-dark. Waves of lilac and azure flame rippled across his body like the aurora of the Arctic skies. Around he went, and around again in steady sweeping circles.

Shasa Courtney was crouched in the fighting-chair, bowed over the rod like a hunchback. All the euphoria of the second wind had evaporated. He bent and straightened

451

his legs with the deliberate agony of an arthritic, and every muscle and nerve screamed a protest at the movement.

Fish and man had established a dreadful pattern in this final phase of the struggle. The fish went out on the far lap of its circle, and the man hung on grimly, his sinews strained to the same pitch as the Dacron line. Then the fish swung through the circle and came back in under the boat; for a few moments the tension on the line abated and the arc in the rod straightened.

Shasa took two quick turns of line and then hung on again as the fish swung on to the outward leg. With each circle he recovered a few feet of line, but he paid the full price for it in sweat and pain. Shasa knew he was coming to the end of his endurance. He thought about the risk of doing permanent damage to his body. He could feel his heart pulsing like a swollen fragile sac in his chest, and his spine was shot through with fire. Soon something must snap or burst inside him, but he pulled with all his remaining strength and felt the fish give again.

'Please,' he whispered to it. 'You are killing us both. Just give up now, please.'

He gathered himself and pulled again – and the fish broke. It rolled like a waterlogged tree-trunk and succumbed to the pressure of the rod. It came up, sluggish and heavy, and thrust its head through the surface so close to the stern of the boat that it seemed to Shasa that he could reach out and touch one of its great glowing eyes with the tip of the rod.

It stood on its tail and pointed its nose spike to the sky and shook its head the way a spaniel coming ashore shakes the water from its ears. The heavy steel trace whipped and whistled around its head, and the rod was battered and slammed from side to side. The butt clattered and banged in the gimbal, and the line flashed and looped and traced sweeping designs in the air.

Still the fish stood in the water and opened wide its mighty triangular beak and kept shaking its head, and Shasa was helpless in the face of such power. He could not control it. The rod was jerked back and forth in his grip, and he watched the steel trace flog like the lash of a bullwhip.

With a sense of despair he saw the long shank of the hook twist and flick in the hinge of the open jaw. The gyrations of the fish were working it loose from the bone.

'Stop it!' he gasped at the fish, and tried to haul it over on its side. He felt the hook come loose and slip and skid across the bone, before it caught again. The fish gaped at him, and he saw the hook still holding lightly on the very lip of the iron black beak. One more shake of the head and the hook would be catapulted away on the swinging steel trace.

Shasa rose up in the chair and gathered the last of his strength. He hauled the marlin backwards, and it toppled and crashed back into the sea in a smother of foam.

'The trace,' he croaked at the deckie. 'Get the trace.' A direct pull on the steel wire trace would bring the fish under control.

During all four hours of the struggle, no person other than the angler had been permitted to touch the rod or the line to assist in the capture. Those were the rules of the sporting ethic laid down by the International Game Fishing Association.

Now with the fish played out and lying beaten on the surface the crew were permitted to handle the thirty-foot steel trace, which was attached to the end of the line, and to hold the fish with it while the flying gaff was driven into its flesh.

'Trace!' Shasa pleaded, as the deckie with heavy leather gloves reached out over the stern and tried to get a hand to the top swivel of the trace. It was just beyond his fingertips.

The marlin wallowed on the surface, rolling and pitching like a dead log in the swells.

'One more time.' Shasa rose up and braced himself behind the rod. He pulled with a steady even pressure. The hook was holding only by its needle point, the barb was not buried – the slightest twist or jerk could free it.

The second deck-hand stood ready with the flying gaff, a massive stainless-steel hook on the end of a detachable pole. Once that hook was plunged into the marlin's shoulder, the struggle would be over.

The top swivel of the trace was six inches from the fingertips of the gloved hand, and the marlin fanned its tail, a last exhausted effort. The tip of the rod gave a little nod, almost as though approving the gallant spirit of the fish – and the hook came free.

The rod snapped straight and the hook flicked through the air and clattered against *Le Bonheur*'s gunwale. Shasa fell back with a crash into the chair. Only forty feet away the marlin lay on the surface with its back and the tall dorsal fin exposed. It was free but too spent to swim away; its tail made only convulsive spasmodic movements.

They all stared at it, until Martin the skipper recovered his wits. He slipped *Le Bonheur* into reverse and backed her up on the wallowing monster.

'On l'aura! We will have him!' he yelled at the gaff man, as the marlin bumped against the stern. The deck-hand sprang to the transom and raised the gleaming hook high to drive the point into the fish's unprotected hump.

Shasa tumbled from the chair, his legs buckling weakly under him. Only just in time, he managed to seize the deckie's shoulder and arrest the blow before it was struck.

'No,' he croaked. 'No.' He wrested the gaff from the man's hand and flung it on the deck. The crew stared at him in astonishment and chagrin. They had worked almost as hard as Shasa had done for this fish.

It did not matter. He would explain to them later that it was unethical to free-gaff a fish. The moment the marlin threw the hook, the contest was over. The fish had won. To kill him now would be a deadly offence to all the ethics of sportsmanship.

Shasa's legs could no longer support his weight. He collapsed across the transom. The fish still lay on the surface beneath the stern. He reached down and touched

454

the colossal dorsal fin. The edge was sharp as a broadsword.

'Well done, fish,' Shasa whispered, and his eyes stung with the salt of his own sweat and with other things. 'It was a hell of a fight. Good for you, fish.'

He stroked the fin as though it were the body of a lovely woman. His touch seemed to galvanize the marlin. The strokes of his tail became stronger and more regular. His gill plates opened and closed like a bellows as he breathed and he moved away slowly.

They followed him for almost half a mile as he swam upon the surface with his fin standing in the blue like a tall tower. Shasa and Elsa stood hand-in-hand at the rail in silence and watched the strength and vigour return to the great fish.

Faster beat his tail, and he steadied in the water and pressed against the swells with all his former majesty. Gradually the tall fin sank below the surface, and they saw the long dark shape of his body recede into the depths. There was one last flash of light like the reflection from a mirror deep in the blue water and then the fish was gone.

On the long run back to port, Shasa and Elsa sat very close together. They watched the lovely emerald gem of the island grow before them, and once or twice they smiled at each other in quiet and perfect accord.

When *Le Bonheur* ran into the Black River harbour and came into the dock, the other boats of the fleet were already tied up alongside. On the scaffold in front of the clubhouse hung the carcasses of two dead marlin. Neither of them was half the size of the fish that Shasa had lost. A small admiring crowd was gathered around them. The successful anglers were posing with their rods. Their names and the marlin's weights were chalked on the glory-board. The Indian photographer from Port Louis was crouched over his tripod recording their moment of triumph.

'Don't you wish that your fish was hanging there?' Elsa asked softly, as they paused to watch the scene.

'How beautiful a marlin is when he is alive,' Shasa

murmured. 'And how ugly he is when he is dead.' He shook his head. 'My fish deserves better than that.'

'And so do you,' she said, and led him to the bar in the clubhouse. He moved stiffly, like a very old man, but his bruises gave him a strange masochistic pride.

Elsa ordered him a Green Island rum and lime.

'That should give you strength to get you home, old man,' she teased him lovingly.

Home was Maison des Alizés, the House of the Trade Winds. It was a rambling old plantation-house, built a hundred years ago by one of the French sugar barons. Shasa's architects had renovated it and restored it in authentic detail.

It sat like a glistening wedding-cake in twenty acres of its own gardens. The old French baron had begun a collection of tropical plants, and Shasa had added to these over the years. The pride of the collection was the Royal Victoria waterlilies whose leaves floated on the gleaming fish-ponds. The leaves were four feet across and curled at the edges like enormous platters, and the blooms were the size of a man's head.

Maison des Alizés was situated below the massif of Le Morne Brabant, only twenty minutes' drive from the clubhouse at Black River harbour. This was the main reason that Shasa had purchased it. He referred to it as his fishing shack.

As they drove up under the spreading canopy of the ficus trees, Shasa remarked: 'Well, it looks as though the rest of the party has arrived safely.'

Half a dozen cars were parked along the curve of the driveway, in front of the main portals of the house. Elsa's pilot had ferried the two engineers from Zurich in her personal jet. They were the technical directors of Pignatelli Chemicals who had developed the process and designed the plant for manufacturing Cyndex 25. Shasa had met Werner Stolz, the German director, during the delicate preliminary discussions in Europe. These had gone smoothly, under Elsa's skilful direction.

456

The technical directors and engineers of Capricorn Chemical Industries had come in from Johannesburg to attend this conference. Capricorn Chemical Industries was a fully owned subsidiary of Courtney Industrial Holdings. Under Garry's chairmanship, Capricorn was the largest manufacturer of agricultural fertilizers and pesticides on the African continent.

The company had its main plant near the town of Germiston in the industrial triangle of the Transvaal. The existing plant already incorporated a high-security section which manufactured highly toxic pesticides. There was adequate space available to double this facility. The Cyndex plant could be set up without any fuss or undue public speculation.

The technical representatives of Pignatelli and Capricorn had come together here to discuss the blueprints and the specifications for the new plant. For obvious reasons, it would have been unwise to conduct this meeting on the site in South Africa. In fact Elsa had insisted that none of her staff should ever visit the plant or have any connection with the enterprise that could be traced back to Pignatelli.

Mauritius had offered a perfect venue for this meeting. Shasa had owned Maison des Alizés for over ten years. He and his family and their guests were frequent visitors. Their presence here was unremarkable, and Shasa was on excellent terms with the Mauritian government and most of the influential figures on the island. The Mauritians treated the family as honoured and privileged guests.

Before his illness Bruno Pignatelli had also been a keen big-game angler who visited Mauritius regularly. So Elsa was also well known and respected on the island. Nobody was going to pry into her affairs or make awkward enquiries about her reasons for being at Maison des Alizés with a team of her engineers and consultants.

Shasa and Elsa were still keeping up appearances and exercising elaborate decorum, even to the extent of occupying separate, but interconnecting, suites on the top floor of Maison des Alizés. The family thought this little charade

457

was hilarious. They were all waiting for the two of them in the gazebo on the lawn above the fish-pools when they came down for evening cocktails.

Elsa had bathed Shasa and anointed his bruises and scrapes, so he looked very dapper and refreshed, and limped only slightly as they strolled down the front steps together. He was dressed in a cream tropical silk suit with a crisp new eye-patch, and she wore a full-length gauzy chiffon with a frangipani spray in her hair.

'Look at the little devils. Do you really believe that they are just jolly good pals?' Garry demanded with a twinkle in his eye, and Isabella and Holly had to cling to each other for support. Even Centaine covered her smile with the Japanese fan and turned away to speak to one of the engineers.

Isabella had every reason to be at Maison des Alizés even though the Senate was in session. She was on the board of directors of Capricorn Chemicals. Since the trip to Chizora Concession when she had first learnt of the Cyndex project, Isabella had shown a sudden interest in CCI. She had succeeded in having herself appointed to the Senate standing committee on agriculture, and after that it had required only a few subtle hints for Garry to offer her a seat on the CCI board. She had rapidly become an active and valuable addition to the management team of Capricorn and had never missed a meeting of the board. She had taken a particular interest in the Cyndex project, and Garry had naturally included her in this gathering.

Garry had also seized the opportunity of bringing Holly and the children along for an unscheduled holiday. Although he would be heavily occupied with the technical discussions, he hoped to be able to spend some time each day with his family. Holly had been complaining recently that they saw so little of him, and the children were growing up so quickly that he was missing a big slice of their childhood. These days Centaine Courtney-Malcomess never missed a chance to be with her great-grandchildren, and she had insisted on boarding the Lear when it took off from Lanseria private airport outside Johannesburg.

Indeed, so large had been the family contingent and the weight of their luggage that the other Capricorn directors had been obliged to catch the next commercial flight.

Maison des Alizés was bursting at the seams, every bed was occupied and they had set up two extra cots in the nursery for the babies. Centaine had borrowed extra trained staff from La Pirogue, the five-star beach resort just down the coast at Flic and Flac to deal with the invasion. Then she had sent the Lear back to Johannesburg to bring in supplies of such essentials as Imperial caviare and vintage Krug and fresh fruit and baby-foods that were unobtainable on the island.

The Krug was flowing freely now as Shasa and Elsa joined the party under the frivolous fretwork roof of the gazebo. There was an exuberant orgy of kisses and handshakes and back-slapping and happy cries of greeting.

Elsa had been presented to Centaine only briefly the previous evening when the old lady arrived at Maison des Alizés. Even though Centaine had been tired by the long jet flight, they had warmed to each other immediately. Centaine had squinted at her in that particular way she had when she was concentrating deeply. Then her eyes had straightened and she had smiled and held out her hand.

'Shasa has told me many good things about you, but I suspect that's not half of it,' she said in Italian, and Elsa had smiled with pleasure at the compliment and at Centaine's command of her language.

'I did not know you spoke Italian, Signora Courtney-Malcomess.'

'There is still much we have to learn about each other,' Centaine nodded.

'I look forward to that,' Elsa replied. They had recognized kindred spirits and now, under the gazebo, Elsa moved naturally to Centaine's side and kissed her cheek.

Well, Centaine thought complacently as she took Elsa's arm, Shasa took long enough to find this one, but she was well worth waiting for.

Garry's children were chasing each other around the gazebo, and their shrieks and howls detracted a little from the sophisticated ambience of the gathering.

'I must admit,' Shasa remarked as he regarded his grandchildren balefully, 'that I'm becoming more like Henry the Eighth every day – I prefer small children in the abstract.'

'As I recall, at that age you were every bit as bad,' Centaine rallied immediately to the defence of her brood of great-grandchildren, but at that moment a particularly piercing squeal made Shasa wince.

'For that one alone you would have boiled me in oil. Mater, you are in danger of becoming a doting great-granny.'

'They'll soon have enough of it,' Centaine smiled down on them fondly.

'Not before I do, I assure you,' he muttered, and went off to where Bella was chatting to the Pignatelli engineers.

Isabella had set out to be charming to the German director, and by this time he was throwing off sparks. For Isabella there was a bizarre sense of unreality about the scene. She felt like an actress in a Franco Zeffirelli movie. The gleaming ivory house, the weird shapes of the trees and tropical plants, the gigantic fronds of the Royal Victoria waterlilies floating on the ponds and the shoals of multi-coloured ornamental carp sailing beneath them, all contributed to a fantastic dreamlike setting. The laughter and the disjointed enigmatic conversations in different languages and the cries of the children were all so inconsequential when set against the true reason for this gathering.

There was Nana holding court like a dowager empress, and Holly and Elsa Pignatelli wearing precious chiffons and silks that cost a working man's wages for a year. While somewhere far away her little Nicholas dressed in combat camouflage and played with the ghastly weapons of war, with soldiers and terrorists for companions.

Here she flirted with this balding middle-aged man who looked like a grocer or a barman, but who was in reality the purveyor of death in one of its least attractive guises.

Here she smiled at her big teddy bear of a brother and linked arms with her beloved father while she conspired to betray them both, and her country to boot. Here was the shell, the beautiful, groomed, intelligent, successful young woman, fully in control of her destiny and the world around her. While within was the terrified confused creature, suffering and bereaved, the pawn of powerful shadowy forces in a game that she did not understand.

'One day at a time,' she warned herself. 'One step at a time.' And the next step was the Cyndex 25 project.

Perhaps this would be the ultimate endeavour that Ramón had promised her. Once she had given them the Cyndex project, perhaps they would be able to escape from the web – she, Ramón and Nicholas. Perhaps then the nightmare would end.

★   ★   ★

The conference began the following morning in the dining-room of Maison des Alizés. They sat beneath the revolving punkah fans at the long walnut table which extended to seat thirty persons and they talked about death. They discussed the mechanics and the chemical structure of death. They argued the packaging and the quality control and the cost-efficiency of death, as though talking about manufacturing potato crisps or face cream.

Isabella steeled herself to show no reaction to the things she heard discussed at the long table. She had learnt never to underestimate the powers of observation of her brother Garry. Behind the horn-rimmed spectacles and bluff genial façade he missed very little. She knew that he would pick up any sign of horror or revulsion that she showed. That would probably be the end of her involvement in the project.

The Pignatelli technicians had prepared a dossier. The copies were contained in untitled but handsome pigskin folders which were placed on the dining-room table in front of each of them. The dossier was exhaustive and covered every aspect of the problem of manufacturing, storing and deploying the nerve gas.

Werner Stolz, the technical director, took them through the dossier a paragraph at a time. As horror unfolded on horror, read out in Werner's clipped sibilant German accent, Isabella found that she had to exercise all her self-control to keep her expression neutral and businesslike.

'Cyndex 25 is a volatile gas consisting of an organophosphorus compound of the Alkylphosphonic Fluoridic Acid Group. Gases of this composition are known as G agents and include Sarin and Soman.

'However, Cyndex 25 has desirable features that differ distinctly from these older types of nerve gas. . . .' As he enumerated these features Isabella was appalled by his choice of the adjective 'desirable', but she nodded thoughtfully and kept her eyes on the dossier.

'Cyndex 25 has a unique and highly aggressive combination of properties. These are high toxicity, rapid action, percutaneous effectiveness as well as absorption through the lungs and mucous membrane of the human body. Other advantages are high cost-effective ratios. By reason of its dual chemical structure, it is safe to manufacture, store and handle. Once the two agents which make up Cyndex 25 are mixed, the gas becomes highly unstable and has an extremely short effective lifespan. Thus it is more readily controlled in the field. After the elimination of the threatened population, the treated terrain can be more swiftly taken under friendly control.'

He beamed down the table at them benignly. 'I would like now to discuss each of these properties in greater detail. Let us take the question of toxicity. Cyndex in either vapour or aerosol form absorbed through the lungs has an LD^{50} dosage' – he smiled apologetically – 'which means that it will kill fifty per cent of the threatened population of moderately active adult men in two minutes, and a hundred per cent of the population in ten minutes. This is not significantly more rapid than Sarin, but it is in its percutaneous effect that Cyndex comes into its own. It is absorbed much more rapidly through the skin, the eyes, the nose, the throat and the digestive system than Sarin. One microlitre of Cyndex – and I remind you that is a millionth part of a litre – applied to naked skin will incapacitate a man in two minutes and kill in fifteen minutes. This is approximately four times more potent than Sarin. Although atrophine injected intravenously within thirty seconds may inhibit the process and reduce some of the symptoms, it will not arrest spontaneous collapse of the respiratory system and subsequent death by suffocation. I will come later to the specific symptoms of exposure to the agent, but let us now discuss the cost of manufacture. Please turn to page twelve of the dossier.'

They obeyed like schoolchildren, and Werner Stolz went on: 'You will see from the bottom line of our estimate that at this point in time the plant will cost in the region of twenty million US dollars and the direct cost of manufacture will amount to twenty dollars per kilo.'

Isabella wondered, even in the stress of listening to these horrific details, why the use of newspeak clichés such as 'bottom line' and 'this point in time' annoyed her so. I wish he would speak plain English, she thought, as if that would somehow make the facts more palatable. Werner was still speaking.

'Translated into comparative terms that means that the entire plant would cost the same as a single Harrier jet fighter from British Aerospace and the cost of manufacture of a stock of Cyndex sufficient to ensure the defence of the country for twelve months would be equivalent to the purchase of fifty Sidewinder air-to-air missiles . . .'

'That's an offer we just can't refuse,' Garry chuckled, and Isabella felt a stab of hatred for him that shocked her with its intensity.

How can he joke about something like this? She dared not look up at him. He might have read her thoughts. Werner nodded and smiled agreement with Garry.

'Of course, Cyndex needs no special vehicle for dissemination. Ordinary crop-sprayer aircraft such as those in day-to-day use in agricultural situations can be readily adapted for the purpose. The gas may also be delivered by artillery projectile. The new G5 long-range howitzer being developed at present by Armscor would be ideal.'

At noon they broke for a swim in the pool and a buffet lunch on the terrace. The discussion dwelt largely on Elsa and Shasa's recent visit to the Salzburg Festival where Herbert von Karajan had directed the Berlin Philharmonic Orchestra. They went back into the dining-room to listen to a description of the symptoms of Cyndex 25 poisoning.

'Although it has never been tested on human subjects, we have determined that the symptoms of a moderate exposure to Cyndex aerosol will not differ greatly from other G agent nerve gases,' Werner told them. 'These would commence with a sensation of tightness in the chest and difficulty in breathing, followed by copious running of the nose and a burning, stinging pain in the eyes and a dimming of vision.'

Isabella felt her own eyes begin to sting in sympathy, and she dabbed at them surreptitiously.

'As these symptoms become progressively more intense, there will be heavy salivation and frothing at the mouth, sweating and trembling, nausea and belching, sensations of heartburn and stomach cramps which will lead swiftly to projectile vomiting and explosive diarrhoea. These will be followed by involuntary urination and bleeding from the mucous membrane of the eyes, nose, mouth and genitalia. Trembling, twitching and giddiness and muscle cramps will lead to paralysis and convulsions.

'However, the immediate cause of death will be total collapse of the respiratory system. Cyndex owes its superior toxicity to the ease with which it penetrates the blood–brain barrier in the central nervous system.'

They were silent and subdued for a full minute after Werner finished, and then Garry asked softly: 'If Cyndex has never been used on human subjects, how do you anticipate these symptoms?'

'Initially by extrapolation with the effects of other G

464

agent nerve gases, Sarin in particular.' Werner Stolz paused, for the first time showing some sign of embarrassment. 'Thereafter the gas was tested on primate subjects.' He cleared his throat. 'Chimpanzees were used in laboratory tests.'

With an effort Isabella prevented herself making some gesture of disgust and outrage. However, her horror became almost uncontrollable as the director went on remorselessly: 'We found, however, that chimpanzees are extremely expensive laboratory animals. You are fortunate in that you have access to an almost unlimited supply of cheap and entirely satisfactory laboratory animals in the shape of *Papio ursinus*, the chacma baboon, which is indigenous to South Africa and still occurs there in large numbers.'

'We aren't going to test on live animals?' Isabella's voice was shrill even in her own ears, and immediately she regretted the outburst and tried to recover her poise. 'I mean, is it really necessary?'

They were all staring at her now, and she flushed with anger at her own lack of self-control. It was Garry who broke the silence.

He spoke lightly, but there was a steely glint behind the lenses of his spectacles. 'The baboon is not my favourite animal. I have seen them kill the newborn lambs at Camdeboo to eat the milk curds in their stomachs. Nana will tell you about their depredations on her roses and vegetable garden. I am sure we all share your distaste and your reluctance to see unnecessary suffering inflicted on any living thing.' He paused. 'However, in this instance we are considering the defence of the country, the safety of our nation – and the expenditure of many millions of Courtney money.'

He looked across at Shasa, who nodded agreement.

'The short answer is, I am afraid, yes. We must test. Better that some animals should die than our own people. It is not a pretty thought, but it is essential. I'm sorry, Bella. If it offends you, then you don't have to have anything further to do with the project. You can resign your seat on the Capricorn board and we'll say no more about it. We will all understand and respect your feelings.'

'No.' She shook her head. 'I understand the necessity. I'm sorry I raised the subject.' She realized how close she had come to letting Nicholas and Ramón down. Their safety and freedom were worth any price she might be forced to pay. She forced herself to smile and speak lightly: 'You don't get rid of me that easily. I'll keep my seat, thank you very much.'

Garry studied her face for a second longer, then he nodded. 'Good. I'm glad we have settled that.' And he turned his full attention back to Werner Stolz.

Isabella composed her expression into one of polite attention and clasped her hands in her lap. 'This is one project that Red Rose will have no qualms about reporting,' she promised herself.

*　　　*　　　*

Isabella sent the Red Rose despatch three days after she arrived back in Cape Town.

Over the years a routine had developed between her and the forces that controlled her. When she had information she sent a Red Rose telegram to the address in London and usually within twenty-four hours she received instructions for a dead drop. These always took the same form. She was given the time and location at which to park her Porsche. The location was always a public carpark. Sometimes the Parade at the old fort, or a drive-in cinema, or one of the large supermarkets in the suburbs.

She wrote out her message on sheets of the one-time pad and left them in an envelope under the driver's seat with the door unlocked. When she returned to the Porsche half an hour or so later the envelope was missing. When they had a message or instructions for her the same method was employed, except only that when she returned to the

Porsche there was an envelope containing typed instructions under the driver's seat.

At the end of the conference at Maison des Alizés Garry had personally collected all the leather-covered dossiers and seen to the shredding of the contents. He was very concerned that no detail of the Cyndex project fall into unauthorized hands. Isabella had made a few careful notes during the discussions, but he had relieved her of these also.

'Don't you trust me, Teddy Bear?' She had made a joke of it, and though he chuckled he had been adamant.

'I don't even trust myself.' And he had held out his hand for her notepad. 'You want to remember any details, you come and ask me, Bella, but you don't write down anything – I mean *anything*.'

She knew better than to make an issue of it.

Even though she had no notes to refer to, the Red Rose report that she sent was shaky only in the area of the chemical composition of Cyndex 25. She knew that it was an organophosphate of the G group of nerve gases but could not recall the exact atomic structure of the constituent parts or the sequence of manufacture. However, she gave them the proposed location of the plant and the tentative timetable for construction. The forecast was that the plant would be in production within seven months.

At this stage the only ingredient that needed to be imported was a phosphate precursor – again she was uncertain of the exact chemical structure of this agent. However, she was able to report that the reason that this catalyst could not be manufactured in South Africa – at least, for the time being – was that the correct grade of stainless steel for the redoubt in which it was mixed was not obtainable locally. However, the state-owned steel works of ISCOR would work on the production of this grade of steel and it was anticipated that they would be able to supply within eighteen months. After that time Cyndex would be a hundred per cent locally manufactured. In the meantime the precursor would be supplied through a Pignatelli front

467

company in Taipei who were already holding stocks sufficient for the first year of operation of the Capricorn plant.

Apart from the problem with the supply of chemical-grade stainless steel, the other difficulty that the conference had foreseen was the availability of skilled technicians to operate the plant. Pignatelli Chemicals had declined to provide any personnel. It was anticipated that these would be recruited in Britain or in Israel. The conference had placed emphasis on the security clearance of any foreign technicians who were thus engaged.

The rest of Isabella's report covered the transportation, storage and dissemination of the gas in battlefield situations. Both Puma helicopters and Impala jet fighters of the South African air force could be adapted to serve as delivery vehicles. In addition, work would begin immediately on the design and testing of a shell for the G5 howitzer which would be designated '155 mm CW (Chemical Warfare) ERFB Cargo'. This shell would deliver eleven kilos of Cyndex 25 to a maximum range of thirty-five kilometres. The rotation of the shell in flight would centrifugally open valves in the cargo-head and mix the two constituent ingredients of the gas prior to impact in the target area.

She was fully aware of the value of this information and so she was emboldened to add a final line to the twenty-six pages of her report.

'Red Rose requests access as soon as possible.'

She waited anxiously for a reaction to her request after she had delivered it. There was none.

As time passed with no reply she understood that she was being punished for her impertinence, and at first she was defiant. Then as the weeks became months she started to become truly worried. At the end of the second month she sent an abject apology to the London accommodation address.

'Red Rose regrets importunate request for access. No insubordination was contemplated. Awaiting further orders.'

It was another month before those orders came. She was

instructed to use any means necessary to ensure that she was a member of the team from Capricorn Chemicals that would travel to London and Israel to interview and recruit personnel for the operation of the Cyndex plant.

Isabella had difficulty imagining how she could justify any claim to be a member of the recruiting team. What possible reason could she give Garry that would not immediately arouse his suspicions as to her motives? She agonized over this for weeks before the next board meeting of CCI, and then at the meeting itself it all fell into place with an ease that amazed her.

The subject of recruitment came up at the meeting, even though it was not on the agenda, and Isabella saw her opportunity and gave her views on the subject in an impromptu but articulate and well-reasoned address.

When she finished, she saw that she had impressed Garry, and he remarked in not entirely jocular fashion: 'Perhaps we should send you to do the job, Dr Courtney.'

She shrugged, not to appear over-eager. 'Why not? I could fit in a little shopping – I need a few new frocks.'

'Typical woman,' Garry sighed, but six weeks later she found herself back in the Cadogan Square flat. The personnel manager of CCI was ensconced in the Berkeley Hotel, only a short walk from Cadogan Square. The two of them conducted the preliminary interviews in the dining-room of the flat.

The night she arrived in London, there was an anonymous phone caller. She did not recognize the voice. The message was simple.

'Red Rose. Tomorrow you will interview Benjamin Afrika. Make certain that he is selected.'

She couldn't place the name, so she looked up the application in her file. To her surprise she found that Benjamin Afrika had been born in Cape Town. This, however, seemed to be his strongest claim to the job on offer. Despite the fact that his academic qualifications were good, he was really too young – only twenty-four years of age. He had four A-levels and a BSc in chemical engineering from Leeds University with two years' experience as a scientific assistant with Imperial Chemical Industries at one of their factories near Liverpool. At the salary they were offering she could have found a hundred applicants with similar or better qualifications in South Africa.

She could not squeeze him into any of the vacant senior posts. There were, however, two more junior positions to fill.

Benjamin Afrika was the third interviewee on the morning's list. He walked into the Cadogan Square dining-room at eleven o'clock in the morning, and Isabella felt herself go icy cold with panic.

Benjamin Afrika was a coloured man, but this was not what caused her consternation. Benjamin Afrika was her half-brother, the man whom she knew as Ben Gama, bastard son of her mother and the notorious terrorist and black revolutionary Moses Gama.

So great was the shock of seeing him that she was unable to utter a word. A host of turbulent thoughts tumbled in confusion through her mind as she stared at Benjamin. She thought how his name, and the name of Tara Courtney, their mother, was never mentioned at Weltevreden – even after all these years the scandal and tragedy surrounding them cast a dark shadow over the family. How would it be possible for her to secure employment for Benjamin in one of the Courtney companies? Nana would have a hernia, and Pater would throw a blue fit. Then there was Garry . . .

Fortunately for Isabella, the CCI personnel manager was also evincing symptoms of acute distress, but the source of his concern was much more straightforward than Isabella's. It was merely the colour of Benjamin's skin. In the long pregnant pause that followed Benjamin's entry, Isabella was able to take control of herself again and bring some order to her jumbled emotions. Benjamin had shown no sign of recognition, and she took her lead from him.

Abruptly the CCI manager leapt to his feet. To compensate for his initial reaction he now became over-effusive and ducked round the desk to seize Benjamin's hand.

'I'm David Meekin, head of personnel at CCI. I'm delighted to meet you, young man,' he babbled enthusiastically, and pulled out a chair for Benjamin. 'We have been studying your credentials and your CV. Very impressive – I mean truly impressive.'

He seated Benjamin and offered him a cigarette. 'This is Dr Courtney who is a director of CCI,' Meekin introduced them.

Benjamin half-rose from his seat and made a small bow. 'How do you do, ma'am.'

Isabella did not trust herself to speak. She nodded and then gave all her attention to Benjamin's letter of application while Meekin began the interview.

He asked the usual questions about the work that Benjamin had done at ICI, and his reasons for wanting this job, but clearly Meekin's heart was not in the task. He wanted to get it over with. Meanwhile, Isabella was working out her own plans. If she had not recognized Ben's name, Afrika, then it was highly unlikely that anyone else at home would do so, either. Apart from Michael, no other member of the family, as far as she knew, had ever met Ben. There was no reason why they ever should. He would be a junior employee in one of a hundred factories in a town over a thousand miles from Weltevreden. Michael, of course, could be relied on to support her and Ben completely.

David Meekin had no more questions to ask, and he glanced at Isabella enquiringly.

'I see you were born in Cape Town, Mr Afrika,' she spoke for the first time. 'Do you still have South African citizenship? You haven't taken naturalized British citizenship?'

'No, Dr Courtney,' Ben shook his head. 'I am still a South African. I have a passport issued by South Africa House here in London.'

'Good. Can you tell us something about your family? Do they still live in Cape Town?'

'Both my father and my mother were schoolteachers.

They were killed in a motor accident in Cape Town in 1969.'

'I'm sorry.' She glanced down at her file. It was possible that Tara, their mother, had tried to conceal the facts of Ben's birth by contriving a false birth certificate. She could check that easily enough. She looked up again.

'I hope you will forgive my next question, Mr Afrika. It may sound impertinent. However, Capricorn Chemicals is a defence contractor to Armscor, and all its employees are vetted by the South African security police. It would be best if you tell us now if you are, or have ever been, a member of any political organization.'

Ben smiled softly. He really was a good-looking young man. By some fortunate chance he seemed to have inherited the best features from both sides of his racial ancestry.

'You want to know if I am a member of the ANC?' he asked, and Isabella's mouth tightened with annoyance.

'Or any other radical political organization,' she said curtly.

'I am not a political creature, Dr Courtney. I am a scientist and an engineer. I am a member of the Society of Engineers, but of no other body.' So he was not interested in politics?

She remembered the bitter political argument they had become embroiled in at their last meeting – when was that? Almost eight years ago, she realized with surprise. Of course, the Red Rose instructions that she had received gave the lie to his protestations. None the less, she had to cover herself.

'Again you must pardon the personal nature of my questions, but your frank replies now may save us all a great deal of embarrassment later. You must be aware of the racial situation in South Africa. As a coloured person you will not be allowed to vote, and furthermore you will be subject to a body of legislation and a policy known as apartheid, which, to say the least, restricts many of the freedoms which you will have taken as your natural right here in England.'

'Yes, I know all about apartheid,' Ben agreed.

'Then, why would you want to give up what you have here and return to a country where you will be treated as a second-class citizen, and where your prospects of advancement will be limited by your skin tone?'

'I am an African, Dr Courtney. I want to go home. I think I can be of service to my country and my people. I believe I can make a good life for myself in the land of my birth.'

They stared at each other for long seconds, and then Isabella said softly, 'I can find no fault with those sentiments, Mr Afrika. Thank you for coming to talk to us. We have your address and telephone number. We will contact you one way or the other, just as soon as we are able to do so.'

When Ben had left neither she nor Meekin spoke for a while. Isabella stood up and moved to the window. Looking down into the square she saw Ben leave the front door of the building. As he buttoned his overcoat he glanced up and saw her in the second-floor window. He lifted one hand in farewell and then set off towards Pont Street and turned the corner.

'Well,' said David Meekin beside her, 'we can cross that one off the list.'

'For what reason?' Isabella asked, and Meekin was flustered. He had expected her to agree immediately.

'His qualifications. His experience . . .'

'The colour of his skin?' Isabella suggested.

'That, too,' Meekin nodded. 'He would be in a position at Capricorn where he might have to give orders to white employees. He might actually have white females under him. It would cause ill-feelings.'

'There are at least a dozen black and coloured managers in other Courtney companies,' Isabella pointed out.

'Yes, I know,' Meekin acceded hurriedly, 'but they have coloureds and blacks under them, not whites.'

'My father and my brother are both very eager to advance

473

blacks and coloureds to managerial positions. My brother in particular feels that bringing all sections of our community to prosperity and responsibility is the only recipe for long-term peace and harmony in our country.'

'I would agree with that one hundred per cent.'

'I found Mr Afrika a most personable young man. I agree that he is a little young and lacking in experience for either of the senior posts, however—'

Meekin changed tack, like the corporate survivor he was. 'I'd like to suggest that we short-list Afrika for the post of technical assistant to the director.'

'I agree with your suggestion wholeheartedly.' Isabella smiled her sweetest, most winning smile. Her estimate had been correct. David Meekin's most firmly held principles were subject to negotiation.

They finished the interview with the last candidate at four o'clock that afternoon and, as soon as Meekin had left Cadogan Square to return to the Berkeley Hotel, Isabella telephoned her mother.

'The Lord Kitchener Hotel, good afternoon.' She recognized her mother's voice.

'Hallo, Tara. It's Isabella.' And then for emphasis, 'Isabella Courtney, your daughter.'

'Bella, my baby. It's been ever so long. Let's see now – eight years at least. I thought you'd forgotten your old mamma.' She always made Isabella feel guilty, and she made a lame excuse.

'I'm sorry, Tara. The pace of life – I don't seem to have time for anything . . .'

'Yes, Mickey tells me that you have been ever so successful and clever. He says that you are Dr Courtney now, and a Senator,' Tara gushed on. 'Mind you, Bella, how you can bring yourself to have anything to do with that bunch of racist bigots that call themselves the National Party? In any civilized society, John Vorster would have been sent to the gallows years ago.'

'Tara, is Ben there?' Isabella cut her off.

'I thought it was too good to be true that my own

daughter wanted to talk to me.' Tara's tone was martyred and long-suffering. 'I'll call Ben.'

'Hello, Bella.' He came on the phone almost immediately.

'We must talk,' she told him.

'Where?' he asked, and she thought swiftly.

'Hatchards.'

'The bookshop in Piccadilly? OK. When?'

'Tomorrow, ten in the morning.'

Ben was in the African Fiction section, thumbing through a Nadine Gordimer novel. She stood beside him and picked a book at random from the shelves.

'Ben, I don't know what this is about.'

'I'm applying for a job, Bella. It's as simple as that.' He smiled easily.

'I don't want to know, either,' she went on quickly. 'Just tell me – do you really have valid papers in the name of Afrika?'

'Tara registered my birth in the name of a coloured couple, friends of hers. She was never married to my father – and of course their relationship was illegal. She could have been imprisoned for being in love with Moses Gama and giving birth to me.' His tone was easy; there was even a light smile on his lips. She looked for some sign of bitterness or anger, but found none. 'Officially my name is Benjamin Afrika. I have a birth certificate and South African passport in that name.'

'I have to warn you, Ben. There is terrible bitterness and hatred in the Courtney side of the family. Your father was convicted of murdering Nana's second husband, I mean Centaine Courtney-Malcomess's husband.'

'Yes, I know.'

'You and I will never be able to acknowledge each other in South Africa.'

'I understand.'

'If Nana, if my grandmother or my father ever found out about you – well, I just don't know what the consequences would be.'

475

'They won't find out about it from me.'

'If it was up to me, I would not . . .' She broke off, and lowered her voice. 'Ben, be careful. We have never had a chance to become close; a chasm divides us. Nevertheless, you are my brother. I don't want anything to happen to you.'

'Thank you, Bella.' He was still smiling softly, and she knew that she could never penetrate the curtain.

She went on quietly, 'I will warn Michael that you are coming home. Please believe me that I will help you in any way that I can. If you need me, let Michael know. It would be best if we do not contact each other once you arrive in the country.'

Impulsively she dropped the book she was holding and embraced him.

'Oh, Ben, Ben! What a terrible world we live in. We are brother and sister, and yet . . . It's cruel and inhuman – I hate it.'

'Perhaps we can help to change the world.' He returned her embrace quickly and then they drew apart.

'There are many things that I can never tell you, Ben. Forces beyond our control. If we try to oppose them, we will be crushed. They are too powerful for us.'

'Still, some of us must try.'

'Oh God, Ben. You terrify me when you speak like that.'

'Goodbye, Bella,' he said sadly. 'I think we might have been good for each other – if only things had been ordained differently.' He placed the Gordimer novel back on the shelf and without looking back walked out into Piccadilly.

* * *

Over the years it had become traditional that whenever Isabella was in Johannesburg she stayed with Garry and Holly.

Before she gave up her career to become a full-time wife and mother, Holly had been one of the leading architects in the country. Her designs had won international awards.

476

When they came to build their own home, Garry, who was never one to stint, had given her an open budget and egged her on to design her final masterpiece. She had managed to combine opulence and space with such good taste and invention that their home was Isabella's favourite retreat. She preferred it even to Weltevreden.

As always the family breakfasted on the man-made island in the centre of the miniature lake. On a morning such as this, when the highveld sunshine decked the world in splendour, the roof of the pagoda had been rolled back by its electrically powered machinery and was open to the sky. The flocks of pink flamingo on the lakeshore were free-ranging birds, persuaded to interrupt their continental migrations by this jewel-like stretch of open water.

The older children were in school uniform ready to leave for their daily penance. Isabella was feeding the latest addition to Garry's family, her year-old god-daughter – an exercise which they both enjoyed immensely. It aroused all Isabella's frustrated maternal instincts.

Garry, in his shirt-sleeves and broad, brightly coloured braces at the head of the breakfast-table, had just lit his first cigar of the day.

'Who was the one that accused me of being squeamish?' Isabella demanded of him as she shovelled a teaspoonful of egg into her god-daughter's mouth and then scraped up the overspill as it trickled down her chin.

'It's not a case of squeamishness at all,' Garry protested too loudly. 'I've got five meetings this morning, and Holly's charity ball this evening. Give me a break, Bella.'

'You could have cancelled any one of those meetings,' Isabella pointed out. 'Or all of them.'

'Look, Mavourneen, there'll be so many politicians and generals crowding the place that there is nothing I could add to the proceedings.'

'Don't come over all Irish with me, begorrah. You are funking it, Teddy Bear, and we both know it.'

Garry let out one of his evasive guffaws, and turned to

477

Holly. 'What time do we have to be there this evening, lover?' But Holly was on Isabella's side.

'Why are you making Bella go through with this awful business?' she demanded.

'I am doing no such thing,' Garry was unconvincingly indignant. 'It's her decision entirely.' He glanced at his wristwatch, and then growled with theatrical menace at his children.

'You monsters are going to be late for school. Get out of it!' They showed not the least sign of terror as they lined up to kiss him goodbye, and then clattered off over the bridge like a squadron of cavalry.

'Me, too.' Bella wiped her god-daughter's face and stood up, but Garry stopped her.

'Look, Bella, I apologize. I know I hinted that you couldn't take it. You are as tough as any man I know. You don't have to prove it.'

'So you admit you are chickening out, then?' she asked.

'All right,' he capitulated. 'Hell, I don't want to watch it. You don't have to, either.'

'I am a director of Capricorn,' she said, and gathered up her handbag and briefcase. 'I'll see you at eight.'

As she climbed into the Porsche she felt a twinge of guilt. The true reason for her determination to witness the Cyndex 25 tests was not one of duty, not even to demonstrate her toughness. The last Red Rose communiqué she had received had promised her access to Nicky as soon as she reported that the tests had been successfully carried out.

The drive down to Germiston took her a little over an hour on the new highway. Holly had designed the Capricorn Chemicals plant, and her taste and touch were distinctive. It did not look like a factory. There were lawns and trees, and a cunning exploitation of the terrain so that the least pleasing features of the industrial buildings were disguised or concealed. Those buildings that she had been able to clothe in glass and natural stone were given prominence. The various units were scattered over many hundreds of acres.

The prancing goat figure of the Capricorn logo surmounted the main entrance-gateway. Isabella pressed her electronic key-card into the lock and the gates trundled open. The uniformed guards saluted her as she drove through.

All the visitors' slots in the carpark behind the main administration block were filled. Most of the visiting vehicles were black limousines sporting ministerial number-plates or military pennants on the bonnet.

She rode up in the lift, and as she stepped into the director's suite she surveyed the room swiftly. It was a small, almost intimate gathering. Not more than twenty persons were present, and she was the only woman. The politicals and the civil servants were in regulation dark suits, and the military were in uniform. There were all branches of the service represented, including the security police, and they were all of staff or general rank.

She knew more than half those present, including the cabinet minister and the two deputy ministers. A refreshment-table had been laid out, including alcohol, but nobody was drinking anything stronger than coffee. The conversations were exclusively in Afrikaans, and she was struck once again by the major difference between the two white races. The English section was preoccupied with luxury and material possessions, with finance and commerce. The Afrikaner lived in the halls of political and military power. Here were gathered some of the most powerful men in the land. Though paupers compared to the Courtneys, their political influence dominated the entire society. Compared to them the Courtneys were of little account. Within the citadel of power the military men, rather like their Russian equivalents, formed a caste of their own before whose strength even the state president bowed his head.

Within seconds she had singled out the most influential men in the room and made her way towards them, exchanging greetings and hand-shakes and smiles with the others as she passed. In this patriarchal society she had carved an unusual niche for herself. They accepted her as almost an equal.

'I'm a sort of honorary male,' she smiled to herself, and shook hands with the minister of defence, then turned to his deputy with a controlled and friendly smile.

'Good morning, General De La Rey,' she greeted him in fluent colloquial Afrikaans. Lothar De La Rey had been the first grand passion of her life. They had lived together for six months, before he had dropped her and gone off to marry a good Afrikaner girl of the Dutch Reformed faith. If he had not, he would not now be a deputy minister, and a man who it was whispered had no ceiling on his political future.

'Good morning, Dr Courtney.' He was as polite, but he could not keep his eyes on her face. They slid over her body in swift appreciation.

Go ahead, lover boy, she thought, knowing that she had never looked better in her life. Eat your heart out – then go home to your fat little farm-girl.

Despite her lingering resentment she had to admit to herself that he also was looking good. So many Afrikaners put on weight once their Rugby-playing days were over. Lothar was as lean and hard and clean-cut as he had been ten years before. He was probably just about ripe for a little fling, she thought, and he would certainly have some interesting pillow-talk.

I'd love to have my revenge on you, she thought. She had once contemplated suicide for him. It would give her pleasure to place him on the list of Red Rose's informers. Then quite suddenly she thought of Ramón, her Ramón, and her physical interest in Lothar subsided.

Only in the line of duty, she decided – and at that moment the Capricorn general manager caught her eye.

She made a short welcoming address to the company and apologized for the absence of the chairman. Then she

480

invited them through into the projection room for the presentation.

The video film that Capricorn had prepared was of high professional quality. It included computer-generated simulations and artist's impressions of the deployment and dissemination of Cyndex 25 under combat and battlefield conditions. As the video ran, Isabella glanced round the semi-darkened room. She could see that all the military men were passionately excited by this new weapon. They watched the screen with a deadly concentration and when the tape came to an end they broke into animated discussion amongst themselves.

When Paul Searle, the Israeli technical director whom Isabella had recruited in Tel Aviv, stood up and called for comment, they bombarded him with searching questions. Isabella noticed that up to this time there had been no sign of Ben. His brown face had been discreetly kept in a back room somewhere. Inevitably one of the generals asked the question that Isabella had been dreading. He put it bluntly.

'Has this gas ever been used on a human population? If so, can you give us details?'

'Perhaps the general can provide us with a few surplus Cuban POWs from Angola?' the director asked, and they laughed delightedly at the graveyard humour.

'Seriously, General, the answer to your question is no. However, it has been tested extensively overseas under laboratory conditions with excellent results. In fact we have arranged for you to witness our own first test today.'

The pesticide and poisons division of Capricorn Chemicals was situated half a mile from the administrative block. The party drove down in a convoy with the minister's black Cadillac in the lead. Isabella sat beside him in the back seat and pointed out features of the Capricorn plant.

'This section here is the uranium enrichment plant. You see how we have made it appear to be merely an extension of the main bulk phosphate refinery . . .'

The minister of defence had the reputation of possessing a fiery temper. However, she had always got on well with him, and respected him for his dedication and political acumen. They chatted in friendly fashion during the short drive until they drew up at the front gate of the pesticide and agricultural poisons plant. This was a separate compound within the main complex.

It was surrounded by a twelve-foot diamond-mesh fence. There were prominent warning notices placed at intervals along the fence. These featured red skull-and-crossbones designs with warnings in three languages: 'Danger! Gevaar! Ingozi!'

The guards at the main gate had Rottweiler guard-dogs on leads. The plant was screened by a grove of trees. The building was long and low, the walls were of natural stone and all the external windows were smoked one-way glass. There was a further security check at the entrance, and even the minister was asked to pass through the electronic scanner.

The Israeli director led them down a series of carpeted corridors, each separated by steel fire- and gas-proof doors, until finally they entered the new Cyndex extension. The building was still so new that it smelt of raw concrete. They assembled in a small entrance-lobby. The gas-doors closed behind them, and the director addressed them.

'Strict safety procedures are in force in this section of the building. You will notice the air-conditioning.' He gestured at the panels in the walls. 'The quality of air in the building is strictly monitored at all times. In the highly unlikely event of a leak developing, the air can be pumped out and changed within ten seconds.' For a few minutes more he elaborated on the building's safety features. 'However, for your further safety, before entering the main plant you will be required to don protective suits.'

There were separate changing-rooms for the sexes. In the women's room a coloured female attendant assisted Isabella to strip to her underwear, and then she hung her suit in one of the lockers for her. She helped Isabella into the one-piece white protective overall that had been laid out for her. There were white plastic boots and gloves, and she showed Isabella how to place the helmet over her head and switch on the compressed-air supply. There was a clear plastic visor, and the air-cylinder was contained in a neat back-pack that formed part of the helmet attachment. There were built-in headphones that permitted normal conversation.

Isabella returned to the lobby and rejoined the rest of the party.

'If we are all ready, my lady and gentlemen?' The director turned to the door in the far wall. It slid open, and they trooped through. There were four technicians to welcome them. Isabella noticed that, while the visitors wore white suits, the four technicians were in chrome yellow and the director's suit was tomato red for easy identification.

One of the yellow-suited technicians ushered them down yet another short corridor. As they went, he fell in beside Isabella.

'Good morning, Dr Courtney,' he said softly, and with a small shock she recognized his voice and she looked into his visor.

'Hello, Mr Afrika,' she murmured. 'How are you enjoying your job with Capricorn?' It was the first time she had seen him since London.

'It is very interesting, thank you.' That was all that passed between them before they entered the test-room, but Lothar De La Rey had been watching her. As they seated themselves in the row of padded leather armchairs Lothar took the seat beside Isabella and asked: 'Wie is die kaffir? Who is the nigger?'

'His name is Afrika. He has a degree in chemical engineering.'

'How do you know him?' Lothar insisted.

'I was on the selection committee who recruited him.'

'He has security clearance, of course?'

'Of course. He was cleared by your own department,' she added artlessly. He nodded, and they turned their attention back to the director.

'These are the test-cubicles.' At the end of the room

483

were four windows that looked in upon separate chambers; each was the size of a telephone booth – or a toilet cabinet was a better description, Isabella decided.

'The windows are of double armoured glass,' the director pointed out. 'And you will notice the monitors above each.' He pointed to the electronic panels on which vital life functions were displayed in green LED printout.

Behind the windows, strapped to bare white plastic chairs were four small humanoid figures. For a moment Isabella thought they were children – and then the director explained.

'The test subjects are baboons of the genus *Papio ursinus*. They may seem unfamiliar to you, because they have been shaved to resemble human subjects more closely. You will notice that Number One is almost completely unprotected.'

The naked shaven body strapped to the chair in the first cubicle was pathetically vulnerable-looking. The infant's disposable nappy which was its only garment added to the poignancy.

'Number Two is wearing clothing that resembles normal military uniform.'

This baboon was dressed in a miniature suit of combat fatigues, but the arms and head were unprotected.

'Number Three is fully covered except for eyes, mouth and nose.' The animal wore gloves and a soft plastic hood which left only its face bare.

'Number Four is equipped with a fully protective suit, similar to those which have been issued to you. These will be worn by friendly forces when handling or disseminating Cyndex 25.' He paused. 'I may add that subjects One, Two and Three have been sedated. There will be physical symptoms apparent upon application of the test agent, but these are reflexive reactions of the central nervous system and should not be construed as indicating the degree of suffering that the animal is undergoing.'

Isabella felt her stomach muscles tightening, and despite the filtered air she was breathing her chest felt tight and constricted.

'Cyndex 25 is colourless and odourless. However, for safety reasons we have added the scent of almonds to our gas. There will be no aerosol mist or any other indication of its application, except via the monitoring equipment. The readout will show parts of Cyndex 25 in one hundred thousand parts of air.' He paused and cleared his throat. 'Now, gentlemen – and my lady – if you are ready, we will proceed with the demonstration.'

The minister nodded his helmeted head, and the director gave a terse order into the microphone on his desk. Isabella imagined Ben or one of the other technicians adjusting the controls in the back room.

For a few seconds nothing happened. The breathing and the heartbeats of the four baboons continued sedately tracing regular luminous green patterns on the screens.

Then the panel registering the concentration of Cyndex 25 in the inflowing air flickered and moved up from zero to 5 – five parts of nerve gas in one hundred thousand parts of air.

Within seconds the displays began to alter – all except that above the fully suited baboon. The heartbeats accelerated swiftly, the breathing became rapid and deep. The changes were most violent on the display panel above the naked ape.

Isabella stared at it in horror. She saw its eyelids flicker, and tears began to run down the shaven face. It mouthed the air, its tongue lolling and rolling between its lips. Strings of silver saliva drooled down on to its chest.

'Fifteen seconds,' intoned the director. 'Subject Number One is now incapacitated. Number Four is unaffected, Two and Three are registering medium to acute symptoms.'

The naked baboon began to writhe and struggle against the retaining straps. Isabella tasted the bitter bile rising in the back of her throat and swallowed it down.

Suddenly the baboon opened its mouth wide and shrieked. The thin agonized cry carried to them even through the double-glazed windows. It ripped along Isabella's nerve-endings. She clenched her fists and felt

485

cold sickly sweat break out beneath the clinging white suit. Beside her she felt Lothar De La Rey stir, and all around her the other men made small instinctive gestures of revulsion and discomfort. They were soldiers and policemen hardened to atrocity and suffering, yet they shuffled their feet, clenched gloved hands or made ducking, twisting movements of their heads.

All three of the exposed animals were twitching and kicking, rolling their heads, arching their spines in spasmodic convulsions. The mucous linings of their tongues and of their open screaming mouths turned a bright boiled scarlet, their fluttering streaming eyeballs glazed over with a network of bloodshot veins. They began to vomit. The nappy that the first baboon wore was soiled by a spreading stain of urine and faeces.

Isabella fought down the waves of nausea that rose to engulf her. She wanted to scream, to run, to hide from the horror of it.

'One minute five seconds. Number One all vital life-signs terminated.' The pathetic childlike corpse hung against the straps. Its shaven nakedness was aberrant and obscene.

'Two minutes fifteen seconds. Number Two terminated.'

'Three minutes eight seconds. Number Three terminated.'

'You will notice that Number Four is totally unaffected. The suit has afforded complete protection.'

Isabella rose to her feet. 'Excuse me,' she blurted. She had been determined to outlast any of the men in the room. Her vow was forgotten now. She fled down the corridor and burst into the women's changing-room.

She ripped the helmet from her head and dropped on her knees and clutched the cold porcelain of the toilet-bowl with both hands. She choked and sobbed, and her horror and pity and guilt shot up her throat in a thick bitter acid stream and spewed into the bowl.

★   ★   ★

After what she had just experienced Isabella could not bring herself to return to the blissful domestic environment of Garry and Holly's home.

She left the Capricorn plant without seeing the minister or Lothar or any of the other officials. She drove without attention to her surroundings. She drove fast, too fast, pushing the Porsche up near its top speed. She was trying to expurgate her shame in the elemental and purifying sensation of speed. The attempt was not successful. After an hour she turned back towards Johannesburg and slowed the Porsche to a more moderate pace.

The fuel-tank was almost empty, and she pulled into the next service station that she reached. While the attendant refuelled her tank she realized that she had lost track of her whereabouts. This was not her home town. She knew only that she was somewhere in the network of roads and the maze of residential suburbs that surround the huge industrial and mining complex of the city of Johannesburg.

She asked the attendant which was the quickest route from here back to Sandton. As soon as he explained where she was, she realized that fate or her own subconscious had guided her. She was only two or three miles from Michael's home. A few years previously, Michael had bought himself a smallholding of fifty acres on which stood a dilapidated farmhouse. It was close enough to the offices of the *Golden City Mail* for him to commute to work. Michael had set about renovating the house on a do-it-yourself basis. He planted a hundred or so fruit trees, much to the delight of the birds and locusts and aphids, and he kept a flock of chickens that wandered into the kitchen and defecated on the sink and down the refrigerator door.

'Well, it's their home, too,' Michael had explained to her when she remonstrated. 'A turd or two never hurt anybody.' Although Michael's original intention had been to convert the birds into an endless series of *poulet rôti* and *coq au vin,* he had so far not been able to bring himself to chop off a single head. Some of the birds had already died of old age.

'Michael!' Isabella felt her spirits lighten and she checked her wristwatch. It was after six. He should be home by now. 'Michael is exactly the person I need right now.'

As she drove along the winding track through the scraggly blue-gum plantation that marked the boundary of Michael's estate, she saw his Volkswagen Kombi parked in front of the house. Michael's old Valiant had finally passed away. She smiled as she remembered Michael's description of how an electrical short-circuit had self-ignited in rush-hour traffic and the ancient vehicle had given itself a Viking's funeral and created a five-mile traffic-jam as its own cortège of mourners. She noted that the Kombi, acquired secondhand, seemed not to be in much better shape.

One half of the tin roof of Michael's home was painted in fresh sparkling apple green, the other half was in genuine red rust. He had lost heart in the middle of the renovations.

Michael had also cleared a landing-strip down one boundary of his property and had registered it as a private airfield with the directorate of civil aviation. He kept his old Cessna Centurion aircraft in a hangar at the far end of his fruit orchard. The building was constructed with secondhand corrugated-iron sheets that Michael had purchased cheaply from a scrapyard. The resulting edifice was very much in keeping with Michael's usual style.

She found him in the hangar working in the interior of the blue and white aircraft. She tugged at the leg of his overalls, and he crawled out backwards and registered surprise and pleasure. They hadn't seen each other for almost a year.

After he had kissed her, he fetched a bottle of wine from the rusty old refrigerator in the corner and filled two tumblers. Only then did Isabella notice that he seemed nervous and distracted. He kept glancing at his watch and going to the door of the hangar. She was hurt and disappointed.

'You are expecting somebody,' she said. 'I'm sorry,

Mickey. I should have phoned you beforehand. I hope I haven't put you out.'

'No, of course not. Not at all,' he assured her, but stood up with alacrity and obvious relief. 'But . . . well, to tell the truth . . .' his voice trailed off, and once again he glanced over her head towards the door.

One of his lovers, she thought bitterly. He's worried that I will meet his latest fancy boy. She resented him not being available when she needed him so badly, and cut short their farewells.

She watched him in the rearview mirror as she drove back through the trees. He looked lonely and vulnerable, and her anger at him evaporated.

Poor dear Mickey, she thought. You are as lost and unhappy as I am.

She checked the Porsche at the gate to the property, and then pulled out and turned eastward on to the main tarmac highway heading back towards Sandton. There was another vehicle approaching. It was a nondescript grey van. As it drew level, she casually glanced sideways at the driver and immediately straightened up in the seat. The driver was her brother Ben. He had not noticed her and was in conversation with the black man who sat in the passenger-seat beside him. The passenger was much darker-skinned than Ben, a full-blooded Zulu or Xhosa, with striking features and a smouldering expression. It was not the kind of face that one would readily forget.

She slowed the Porsche and watched the departing vehicle in her rearview mirror. Suddenly the rear brake-lights of the van glowed red, and then the turning-indicator began to flick on and off. The van turned into the track leading to Michael's house and disappeared amongst the blue gums.

'Mystery solved,' Isabella muttered, and accelerated the Porsche. 'Although I don't understand why Michael didn't want me to see Ben. He knows that I arranged the job at Capricorn for him.' She considered it for a moment longer. 'It must be the man with Ben. That's a face to remember. I wonder who he is?'

It was almost eight and the sun had already set when she pulled into the garage under Garry's house in Sandton.

'Damn it,' Garry greeted her as she entered the living-room. 'Where the hell have you been? Do you know what the time is?' Both Garry and Holly were in evening dress. It was not often she saw Garry angry.

'Oh my God! The ball! I'm sorry.'

Then Garry saw her face, and immediately his anger smoothed away. 'Poor Bella. You look as though you have had a lousy day. We'll wait while you change.'

'No, no,' she protested. 'Go ahead. I'll follow you.'

For Isabella the evening was a disaster. The partner who Holly had arranged for her was a university professor and a total bore. Because she was a senator he wanted to discuss politics all evening.

'Don't you think I get enough of that?' she asked tartly, and he sulked at the rebuke. She left early. The rest of the night was troubled and nightmare-ridden. She dreamt of the shaven ape dressed in military battledress and strapped into the white chair.

Somewhere in her dreams the tortured creature changed identity and became her own little Nicky in his suit of camouflage. She woke in a cold trembling welter of sweat and horror.

She could not risk sleep again, nor the fantasies that sleep might bring. She sat in a chair and read until dawn defined the outline of the windows. She ran a bath, but before she could step into it there was a knock at the door of her suite. When she opened it, Garry stood on the threshold in a silk dressing-gown. His hair was in disarray and his eyes were bleary and swollen with sleep.

'I have just had a call from Pater at Weltevreden,' he told her.

'At this hour? Is everything all right? Is it Nana?'

'No. He told me to tell you that both of them are well.'

'Then, what did he want?'

'He wants you and me to fly down to Weltevreden immediately.'

'Both of us?'

'Yes. You and me. Immediately.'

'What on earth for?'

'He wouldn't say. Just that it's a matter of life and death.'

She stared at Garry. 'What can it be?'

'How soon can you be ready to leave – half an hour?'

'Yes, of course.'

'I'll ring Lanseria Airport and tell them to have the Lear ready and the pilots standing by.' He checked his watch. 'We can be in Cape Town before ten o'clock.'

When they landed at Cape Town's D. F. Malan Airport, Klonkie the chauffeur was waiting for them. He drove them directly to Weltevreden.

Shasa and Centaine were waiting for them in the gun-room. By family tradition the gun-room was where the most dire and unpleasant subjects were addressed and thrashed out, both figuratively and literally. For it was here, across the big leather armchair, that Shasa had administered corporal punishment to his three sons. A summons to the gun-room was never taken lightly, and Isabella felt a prickle of apprehension as she and Garry entered.

Nana and Shasa stood shoulder-to-shoulder behind the old desk, and their expressions were so bleak that Isabella stopped dead in her tracks and Garry bumped into her from behind. She hardly felt it.

'What is it?' she asked fearfully, and then she realized that Nanny was also in the room, standing in front of the stone fireplace. The old coloured woman had been weeping. Her face was swollen with grief, and her eyes were bloodshot. She clutched a sodden handkerchief in one hand.

'Oh, Miss Bella,' she sobbed. 'I'm so sorry, child. I had to do it – for your sake. . . .'

'What on earth are you talking about, Nanny?' Isabella started towards her, to comfort her – and then she stopped again.

A dreadful sense of disaster overwhelmed her as she realized what lay on the desk in front of Nana and Shasa.

'What have you done, Nanny?' she whispered, chilled and stricken with despair. 'You've destroyed us.'

On the desk was her leatherbound journal. Nanny had been into her safe.

'You have destroyed me and my baby. Oh, Nanny, how could you do this to us?'

The journal was open at the page which contained the lock of Nicky's hair. On the desk-top beside it lay his knitted baby bootee and the copy of his birth certificate.

'Oh, you stupid prying old woman.' Isabella's anger boiled over. 'You'll never know what harm you have done. You've killed my Nicky. I'll never forgive you for this, never.'

Nanny wailed with despair, then covered her mouth with her wet handkerchief and fled from the room.

'She did it because she loves you, Bella,' Shasa told her sternly. 'She did what you should have done eight years ago.'

'It was none of her business. It's nothing to do with any of you. You don't understand. If you meddle with this, you will put Nicky and Ramón in terrible danger.'

She ran to the desk and snatched up the journal and clutched it to her chest. 'This is mine. You have no right to interfere.'

'What is happening here?' Garry stepped up beside Isabella. 'Come on, Bella. If you are in trouble, then it concerns all of us. We are a family. We stand together.'

'Yes, Bella, Garry is right. We stand together.'

'If only you had come to us right away—' Centaine broke off, and sat down behind the desk. 'Recriminations will not help us now. We have to work this thing out – all of us together. Sit down, Bella. We can guess most of it. You must tell us the rest of it. Tell us about Nicky and Ramón, all of it.'

Isabella swayed on her feet, confused and torn by the torment of her emotions. Garry wrapped a thick muscular arm around her shoulders to steady her.

'It's OK, Bella. We are all here behind you now. Who is Nicky? Who is Ramón?'

'Nicky is my son. Ramón is his father,' she said softly, and buried her face against the great comforting barrel of his chest.

They let her cry for a while, and then Centaine lifted the telephone. 'I'll call Doc Saunders. He can give her a shot to calm her.'

Isabella spun towards her. 'No, Nana. I don't need anything. I'll be all right. Just give me a minute.'

Centaine set the telephone back on its cradle, and Garry led Isabella to the buttoned-leather sofa and sat beside her. Shasa came to sit on her other side, and they held her between them.

'All right,' Centaine said at last. 'That's enough. You can weep later. Now we've got work to do.'

Isabella straightened up, and Shasa handed her the handkerchief from his breast pocket.

'Tell us how it happened,' Centaine ordered.

Isabella took a deep breath. 'I met Ramón at the Rolling Stones concert in Hyde Park when Daddy and I were living in London,' she whispered. Her voice strengthened as she went on. She spoke for almost half an hour. She told them why she and Ramón had been unable to marry and how they had gone to Spain for Nicky's birth.

'I was going to bring him here to Weltevreden. Ramón and I planned to be married here just as soon as he was free.'

She told them how Ramón and Nicky had been abducted. She told them of the water torture of the infant she had been forced to witness and the nightmare of her existence since then.

'What did they want from you, these mysterious people? What price did you have to pay for Ramón and Nicky's safety? What did you have to give them in exchange for

493

the chance to visit Nicky?' Shasa demanded harshly.

Centaine thumped her cane on the wooden floor. 'That is not important at the moment. We'll deal with that later.'

'No,' Isabella shook her head. 'I don't mind answering. They wanted nothing from me. I think that they were forcing Ramón to perform some service for them. They rewarded him by allowing me to visit the two of them, Ramón and Nicholas.'

'You are lying, Bella,' Shasa accused her harshly. 'Ramón Machado is using you. You are being forced to work for him and his masters.'

'No.' She was appalled that he had seen through her lies so easily. 'Ramón is as helpless as I am. We are being threatened and blackmailed—'

'Stop it, Bella,' Shasa cut her short. 'You are the one being forced to pay the price. Nicholas is the hostage. Ramón is the evil puppet-master who pulls the strings.'

She cried out with anguish: 'No! You are wrong! Ramón is—'

'I'll tell you who Ramón de Santiago y Machado is. Yes, you provided us with his family-tree and his full names and date of birth,' Shasa pointed out, and Isabella clutched the journal protectively. 'You know that I have friends in Israel. One of them is the director of Mossad. I telephoned him. He ran Ramón's name through their computer. They link into the CIA computer. Our own security forces also have an open file on Ramón de Santiago y Machado. In the three days since Nanny brought your journal to us, I have been able to discover quite a few interesting facts about your Ramón.' He jumped up from the sofa and crossed to his desk. He pulled open one of the drawers and returned with a thick file which he slammed down on the coffee-table in front of her. Press cuttings and photographs and documents and reams of computer sheets spilled out from between the bulging covers.

'This came in last night in the Israeli diplomatic bag from Tel Aviv. I didn't call you until I had studied it. It makes interesting reading.' Shasa picked out a photograph from the pile. 'Fidel Castro's victorious entry into Havana in January 1959. Those are Che Guevara and Ramón together in the second jeep.' He flipped over another glossy black-and-white print. 'The Congo, 1965. Patrice Lumumba Brigade. Ramón is the second white man from the left. The corpses are executed Simba rebels.' He picked out another. 'Ramón with his cousin Fidel Castro after the Bay of Pigs. Apparently, Ramón was instrumental in gathering the advance intelligence of the landing.' He scuffled through the pack of photographs. 'This one is fairly recent. Colonel-General Ramón de Santiago y Machado, head of the African section of the fourth directorate of the KGB, receiving the award of the Order of Lenin from General Secretary Brezhnev. Very handsome in his uniform, isn't he, Bella? Look at all those medals.'

She cringed away from the photograph as though her father held a black mamba.

Garry leant across and took the photograph out of Shasa's hand. 'Is this Ramón?' he demanded of her, holding it before her face. She dropped her eyes but would not answer.

'Come on, Bella. You must tell us. Is this your Ramón?'

Still she refused to reply. Shasa had to shock her into acceptance. 'It is all an elaborate deception. He probably singled you out as his victim. He almost certainly arranged the abduction and the water torture of your son. He has been toying with you ever since then. Did you know that his nickname is El Zorro Dorado? It seems that Castro himself selected the name, the Golden Fox.'

Isabella's head jerked up. She remembered the remark made by José, the paratrooper, that had puzzled her at the time. 'Pele is the cub of the fox, El Zorro.' Somehow that was the last tiny detail that forced her to face the truth.

'El Zorro – yes.' Her expression hardened. The first gleam of burning hatred showed in her eyes. She looked instinctively towards her grandmother.

'What are we going to do, Nana?' she asked.

'Well, the first thing we are going to do is rescue Nicholas,' she said briskly.

'You don't know what you are saying, Nana,' Garry objected. His expression was stunned.

'I always know what I'm saying,' Centaine Courtney-Malcomess told him firmly. 'I'm putting you in charge, Garry. This takes precedence over everything else. You can have whatever you need. I don't mind what it costs. Just get me that child. That's all that counts. Do I make myself clear, young man?'

Garry's bemused expression cleared slowly. He began to grin.

'Yes, Nana, you make yourself abundantly clear.'

* * *

Garry converted the gun-room at Weltevreden into his operations-room.

He could have chosen any of a dozen better-equipped facilities in one of the Courtney conference-centres or boardrooms. Somehow none of these had the secure family atmosphere of this room, which had for so long been the centre of their lives. None of the others queried his choice.

'This is restricted to the family. We bring in nobody from outside until it is absolutely necessary,' he warned them.

He set up two large boards on easels, one each side of the desk. On one he hung a large-scale map of Africa, south of the Sahara. The second board he left blank for the time being, except for a photograph which he pinned at the top.

It was one that Isabella had taken of Nicholas on the beach. He was in bathing-trunks, his hair tousled by sea-salt and wind as he was laughing into the camera.

'That's to remind me what this is all about,' Garry told them. 'I want to imprint that face on my mind. As Nana has said – from now on that is all that counts. That face. That child.'

He scowled at it. 'All right, young Nicky, where are you?'

He turned to Isabella, who was seated at the desk, and placed the heavy volume of *Jane's All the World's Aircraft* in front of her.

'OK, Bella. Let's presume that it was a Russian military freighter that flew you from Lusaka to this base where you met Nicky. Let's find what type it was.' He opened the book in front of her and began turning the pages.

'That's it,' she said, and stabbed at one of the illustrations.

'Are you certain?' he demanded, and leant over her shoulder.

'Ilyushin Il 76. NATO reporting name Candid,' he read aloud. '*Jane's* lists its estimated cruise speed as 750 to 800 kilometres an hour.'

He jotted it down on his navigation-pad. 'OK, you say the course was 300 degrees magnetic and the flying time was two hours fifty-six minutes. We know it was on the Atlantic coast – let's mark that up on the chart.'

He went to the map and set to work with the dividers and protractor.

'Garry' – Isabella was worried – 'just because Nicky was there last year does not mean that he will still be there, does it?'

'Of course not,' he agreed without looking round from the chart. 'However, from what you tell us, Nicky seemed to be settled at that camp. He was in school and had been there long enough to make friends and build a reputation as a soccer-player – Pele?' He turned and beamed at her through his spectacles like a friendly goldfish. 'We know from both Israeli and South African intelligence reports that your friend El Zorro is still operating in Angola. He was spotted in Luanda by a CIA agent as recently as fourteen days ago. And we have to start planning somewhere. Until we find out for sure that Nicky is not there, we'll presume he is.'

He stepped back from the map. 'There we go,' he

muttered. 'It looks like somewhere north of Luanda and south of the Zaire border. There are five, no, six river-mouths in that general area within a hundred miles of each other. Cross-winds could have made a ten-degree deviation in the Candid's course either way.'

He came back to the desk and picked up the large sheet of art paper on which Isabella had sketched from memory a map of the airstrip and river-mouth. He studied it dubiously, and then shook his head. 'It could be any one of the six rivers shown on the map.' He peered closely at the map. 'They are the Tabi, the Ambriz, the Catacanha, the Chicamba, the Mabubas and the Quicabo – do any of those names ring a bell, Bella?'

She shook her head. 'Nicky called the base Tercio.'

'That is probably a code-name,' said Garry, and pinned her sketch-map beside Nicky's photograph on the second board. 'Any comments so far?' He looked across at Centaine and Shasa. 'What about it, Pater?'

'It's a thousand kilometres from the Namibian border, which is our nearest friendly territory. We can forget about any overland attempt to reach Nicky.'

'Helicopters?' Centaine asked. Both men shook their heads simultaneously.

'Out of range, without refuelling,' Garry said, and Shasa agreed.

'We'd be flying over a battle zone. According to our latest intelligence the Cubans have a solid radar chain covering the Namibian border and at least a squadron of MiG-23 fighters based just north of the border at Lubango.'

'What about using the Lear?' Centaine insisted, and both men laughed.

'We can't outrun a MiG, Nana,' said Garry. 'And they've got more guns than we have.'

'Yes, but you can circle around them, fly 'way out over the Atlantic and come back in behind them. I know fighters can't fly very far, and the Lear can go to Mauritius.'

They stopped laughing and looked at each other. 'You

think she got rich by being stupid?' Garry asked, and then addressed her directly.

'Supposing we could get there in the Lear, then what? We can't land or take off – the Lear needs a thousand-metre runway. From what Bella tells us, it's a short strip and a guerrilla training base with South American or, more likely, Cuban paratroopers guarding it. They aren't going to hand Nicky over to us, not without an argument.'

'Yes. I expect we'll have to fight,' Centaine nodded. 'So now it's time to send for Sean.'

'Sean?' Shasa blinked. 'Of course!'

'Nana, I love you,' said Isabella, and picked up the telephone. 'International, I want to put an urgent call through to Ballantyne Barracks at Bulawayo in Rhodesia.'

The call took almost two hours to come through, by which time Garry had telephoned the airport and spoken to his pilots. The Lear was already on its way to Bulawayo when Sean finally came on the line.

Garry said, 'Let me talk to him,' and took the telephone out of Isabella's hand. They argued for less than a minute, and then Garry snarled: 'Don't give me that crap, Sean. The Lear will be at Bulawayo airport within the next hour to pick you up. I want your hairy arse on board, but pronto. I'll phone General Walls or Ian Smith if necessary. We need you here. The family needs you.'

He hung up and looked at Centaine. 'Sorry, Nana.'

'I have heard the expression before,' she murmured. 'And sometimes a little strong language works wonders.'

★   ★   ★

Major Sean Courtney of the Ballantyne Scouts stood before the makeshift situation-board in the Weltevreden gun-room and studied the photograph of his nephew. His promotion to major and second-in-command of the Scouts was only three months old. Roland Ballantyne had finally manoeuvred him into a full-time billet with the regiment.

'You can see he's Bella's boy. Takes after her. Ugly little

499

brat.' Sean grinned at her. 'No wonder she's been keeping him up her sleeve.'

She stuck out her tongue at him. He was good for her; he gave her hope again. He was so hard and competent and tough-looking, he brimmed with such sublime confidence in his own strength and immortality that she had to believe in it, too.

'When will they let you see Nicky again?' he asked, and she thought for a second. She could not tell him about the promise to give her access as soon as the Cyndex 25 tests were completed. That would mean admitting to all of them that she was a traitress.

'I think it will be soon. I haven't seen Nicky for almost a year. It must be soon. Days rather than weeks from now.'

'You won't go,' Garry cut in. 'We aren't going to give you into their clutches again.'

'Oh, shut up, Garry,' Sean snapped. 'Of course she has to go. How the hell will we know where they are holding Nicky, if she doesn't?'

'I thought . . .' Garry began, his face flushing with anger.

'OK, matey. Let's make a bargain here. I run the actual operation – you are responsible for all the logistics and back-up. How about it?'

'Good!' Centaine cut in. 'That's the way we'll do it. Go on, Sean. Tell us how you'll carry out the rescue.'

'OK. In broad outline, this is it. We will work out the details later. First of all we have to accept that it's a fully offensive operation. We are sure as hell going to run into heavy opposition. They are going to try to kill us – we've got to kill them first. We are not going to mess around. If we want Nicky, we have to fight for him. However, if things go wrong, we might have to face a political and legal storm both here and abroad. We might be deemed guilty of anything from terrorism to murder. Are we prepared to accept that?'

He looked around the circle of attentive faces. They all nodded without hesitation.

'Good. That's settled. Now for practicalities. We assume Nicky is being held in northern Angola at this coastal base. Bella goes in as she did last time. Once she is in position with Nicky she calls us in.'

'How?' Garry demanded.

'That's your problem. You have Courtney Communications at your beck and call. Get them to come up with some kind of miniature radio or even a transponder. As soon as she is in position, Bella will activate it and give us a fix.'

'OK,' Garry agreed. 'We have those electronic position-markers that we use for flagging aerial geological surveys. We should be able to adapt one of those. How will Bella smuggle it in?'

'Again, that's your problem,' Sean told him brusquely. 'Let's get on with it. So Bella is in the target area. She gives us a fix. We go in—'

'How?' Garry asked again.

'There is only one way – from the sea.' Sean swept his hand across the map of the southern Atlantic and down to the nose of the African continent.

'We've got the trawling and canning factory at Walvis Bay. One of those new long-range trawlers of yours, Garry, the ones you send down to Veema Seamount. They'll do nearly thirty knots, and have a range of four thousand miles.'

'Damn it, yes!' Garry beamed. '*Lancer* has just finished a major refit in Cape Town docks. She is at sea at this very moment, on her way back to Walvis Bay. I'll tell them to hold her there, fully refuelled and ready for sea. Van Der Berg, the skipper, is a first-class seaman.'

'Tell them to unload the nets and all the other heavy items we won't need,' Sean added.

'Right. I'll also arrange extra war and all-risks cover on the insurance policy. I know the way you bang up equipment.' Garry was becoming indignant. 'Hell, you went through four Landcruisers last year.'

'That's enough squabbling.' Centaine brought them

firmly back on track. 'Tell us, Sean. Are you going to sail *Lancer* into this river?'

'No, Nana. We'll use landing-craft to run into the beach, inflatables with outboard motors. Do you know anybody at Simonstown naval base?'

'I know the minister of defence,' Bella cut in. 'And Admiral Keyter.'

'Beauty!' Sean nodded. 'If you get the boats, see if you can also get permission for a dozen or so boat-handlers to volunteer for a little extra-curricular fun and games. Those naval commandos are hot babies, and they will fall over themselves for a chance at a good barney. Play up the fact that it's an ANC training base that we are going to hose down and that we'll be doing them a good turn.'

'I also know the minister. I will go with Bella to see him,' Centaine agreed. 'I guarantee you all the special equipment you need. Just give me a list, Sean.'

'I'll have it ready by tomorrow morning.'

'What about weapons – and men?'

'Scouts,' Sean told them. 'They don't come any better. I trained them myself. I'll need about twenty men. I know exactly who I want. I'll talk to Roland Ballantyne right away. Things are pretty quiet up there in Rhodesia at the moment, the rainy season. He'll let me have them. I might have to break one of his legs, but he'll let me have them. They'll need a couple of days of boat training, but they'll be ready to go by the end of next week.' He looked across at Isabella. 'It all depends on you now, Bella. You are our hunting dog. Lead us to them, lass.'

★   ★   ★

Eleven days after she sent the Red Rose coded confirmation that Capricorn Chemicals had successfully tested Cyndex 25, Isabella received permission and instructions for a visit to Nicholas. She was instructed to take the South African Airways flight to London that refuelled in Kinshasa on the

Congo river and to disembark at this stop-over instead of continuing on to London.

She would be met at Kinshasa airport.

'It's looking good.' Sean was jubilant as he placed his finger on the map. 'Here's Kinshasa. It's within three or four hundred kilometres of the expected target area. They are going to pick you up on the doorstep, not the round-about route via Nairobi and Lusaka that they sent you on last time.' He looked across at Isabella. 'So they want you to take next Friday's flight? If it works out, that means you will probably be in position on Saturday, or Sunday at the very latest. We will sail from Walvis Bay in *Lancer* just as soon as I can get up there. The boys have finished their training, and all the equipment is on board *Lancer*. They have been sitting around doing nothing for almost a week – they'll be glad to be on their way.'

He studied the map and then punched his calculator. 'We can be in position one hundred nautical miles off the mouth of the Congo river by Monday the twelfth. How does that suit you, Garry?'

Garry stood up and went to the map. 'I'll be waiting with the Lear at Windhoek Airport – here. I will make my first fly-over on the night of Monday the twelfth. I'll have to head out to sea at least five hundred miles before I can turn back. That's the estimated range of the Cuban radar net in southern Angola. Five hundred miles is well beyond the operational range of the MiG squadron at Lubango.' He touched the Cuban base on the map. 'All right, then I'll hit the coast at the mouth of the Congo here and fly south down the coast until I pick up the signal of Bella's transponder.'

'Hold on, Garry,' Shasa intervened. 'How's that working out?'

'The boys at Courtney Communications have done a damn fine job in the short time they had available.' He opened his brief-case. 'This is it!'

'A bicycle pump?' Shasa asked.

'Apparently Nicky is a soccer star. He asked Bella to

503

bring him a new ball, and he complained that they had to keep pumping his old ball. The pump is a natural accessory to go with the ball. It should arouse no suspicion. This one is in perfect working order.' He demonstrated a few strokes of the pump, and the air hissed out in a satisfactory manner.

'The transponder is fitted into the handle of the pump. It has a thirty-day battery life. It is activated simply by twisting the handle like this.' He showed them. 'There is one drawback. We have had to make the transponder small enough to fit into the handle, and in the process we have been forced to reduce the power of the signal. It has a range of less than twelve kilometres, even with the very sensitive antenna that we have fitted into the Lear. I'll have to fly in that close before I pick up the signal.'

'What about Cuban fighters in the north?' Shasa asked anxiously.

'According to South African intelligence, the nearest squadron is based at Saurimo. I will make one quick run down the coast. As soon as I pick up Bella's signal, I'll head back out to sea. I've worked it out on paper; even if Cuban radar picks me up as I enter Angolan airspace and they immediately scramble a flight of MiGs from Saurimo, I should be able to turn out and run for it before they can catch me.'

'What about SAMs?' Shasa persisted.

'Intelligence reports the Cuban SAM regiments are all in the south.'

'And if Intelligence is wrong?'

'Come on, Pater! Sean's running a hell of a lot more risk than I am.'

'This kind of thing is Sean's job, and he has not got a wife and a flock of kids.'

'Do we want to get Nicky out – or what?' Garry turned his back on his father, ending the exchange. 'All right, where was I? Yes, I pick up Bella's signal. I turn out to sea and make radio contact with *Lancer* as she lies off the Congo mouth. I give them the fix on the base, and then I just come on home.'

'I rather think,' Shasa drawled nonchalantly, 'that I'll go along with you for the ride, Garry!'

'Come on, Pater, you're Battle of Britain vintage. Act your age.'

'I taught you to fly, my boy, and I can still fly circles around you any day of the week.'

Garry glanced across at Nana for support. Her expression was stony. He threw his hands in the air and began to grin.

'Welcome aboard, Skipper,' he acquiesced.

*   *   *

'Goodbye, Nana.' Isabella hugged the old lady with a sudden despairing strength. 'Pray for us.'

'You just bring my great-grandson here to me, missy. He and I have got a lot of catching up to do.'

Isabella turned to her father. 'I love you, Daddy.'

'Not as much as I love you.'

'I have been so stupid. I should have trusted you. I should have come to you right in the beginning.' She gulped. 'I've done terrible things, Daddy. Things I haven't told you about yet. I wonder if you'll ever be able to forgive me.'

'You are my girl.' His voice was husky. 'My very special, my only girl. Come back safely – and bring your baby with you.'

She kissed him and held him hard. Then she whirled and almost ran through the international departures gate of Jan Smuts Airport.

Centaine and Shasa stood staring after her long after she had disappeared. Overhead the airport loudspeaker system was already calling her flight.

'This is the final call for all passengers travelling on the South African Airways SA 516 to Kinshasa and London.'

Centaine turned away and took Shasa's arm. She limped heavily on her stick. Her leg always seemed to get worse when she was worried or under unusual strain.

The chauffeur had the car parked at the main entrance,

although one of the traffic constables was trying to move him on. Shasa settled Centaine in the back seat and then went round to the other door and climbed in beside her.

'There is something we haven't talked about yet.' Centaine took his hand.

'Yes,' Shasa agreed. 'I know what you are going to ask. What have they extorted from Bella? What price have they made her pay?'

'She's been working for them for years, ever since the birth of the child. That is obvious now.'

'I don't want to think about it,' Shasa sighed. 'But I know we'll have to face it, sooner or later. This bastard who has tied her up is a general in the KGB – so we know who Bella's masters are.'

'Shasa.' Centaine hesitated, and then her voice firmed. 'You recall the Skylight scandal?'

'I'll never forget it.'

'There was a leak – a traitor,' Centaine pressed on doggedly.

'Bella knew nothing about Skylight. I was very careful to keep her out of it,' Shasa said hotly.

'Do you remember the Israeli nuclear scientist who came down to Dragon's Fountain? What was his name – Aaron somebody? Bella had a little fling with him. You told me that her name was in the security register at Pelindaba. She spent the night with him.'

'Mother, you aren't suggesting . . . ?' Shasa broke off. 'My God, do you realize what information she has had access to over the years? As a senator, and as my assistant, most of the sensitive Armscor projects have passed over her desk!'

'The Cyndex project at Capricorn,' Centaine nodded. 'She was at the tests only a few weeks back. Why is she being allowed to see Nicholas now? Has she given them some special piece of information, do you think?'

They were silent for a long time, and then Shasa asked softly: 'Where does loyalty to the family and to one of our children end – and loyalty and patriotic duty to our country begin?'

'I think that you and I will have to face that question very soon,' she sighed. 'But let's see this other business through first.'

★   ★   ★

Lancer was tied up at the hospital jetty alongside the Courtney canning factory in Walvis Bay. She was a 250-foot stern trawler but she had the sleek lines of a modern cruise liner. She had been built to work in any fishery in any ocean, to get there fast, stay at sea for months at a time and then to get back to port just as fast.

Sean stood on the jetty and looked her over. He did not like her bright yellow paintwork; it was much too visible. On the other hand, her stern chute would make for easy launching and recovery of the landing-boats. Anyway, it was much too late to do anything about the paintwork now, he decided.

Half the Scouts were lining the rail of the trawler, and as soon as they recognized him they launched into a chorus of 'Why Was He Born So Beautiful?'.

Sean gave them the finger. 'No goddam respect,' he lamented, and ran up the gangway. They were delighted to see him and crowded around him to shake his hand. Much of their enthusiasm was a symptom of boredom; for these highly trained fighting men a week of inactivity had been almost insupportable.

They were all dressed like trawlermen in worn and faded jeans, tattered woollen jerseys and an assortment of caps and balaclava helmets.

Sergeant-Major Esau Gondele was a full-blooded Matabele, an old comrade in a dozen desperate contacts and battles. He saluted Sean and then grinned as Sean punched his arm.

'You're out of uniform, Esau. Take it easy, brother.'

Twelve of the twenty Scouts that Sean had chosen were

Matabele, the others were young white Rhodesians – nearly all of them the sons of ranchers and game wardens and miners who had been brought up in the bush.

In the Scouts there was no awareness of colour. As Esau Gondele once remarked to Sean: 'The best cure for racism is have somebody shoot at you. Man, it does not matter then what colour the arse is that comes to save yours – black or white, you're ready to give it a big fat kiss.'

Sean had worried about the naval commandos from Simonstown who were handling the inflatables. They were all tough young Afrikaners. They might have trouble fitting into this multi-racial team.

'How are you getting on with the rock spiders?' Sean asked Esau Gondele, using the pejorative slang for an Afrikaner.

'Some of them are my best friends already, but still I wouldn't want one of them to marry my sister,' he chuckled. 'No, seriously, Sean, they're all right. They know their job. I told them they don't have to call me Baasie, and they saw the joke.'

'OK, Sergeant-Major. We are leaving port at nightfall. It's unlikely that there'll be anybody here taking an interest in us. But we'll take no chances. You and I are going to check equipment before we sail, and then we'll brief the boys as soon as we cast off.'

The crew accommodation was cramped and spartan. The Scouts and the six commandos crowded into the mess, perched on the table and the bunks. Within minutes the air was fogged with cigarette smoke and *Lancer* pitched and rolled heavily to the thrust of the cold green Benguela current.

All the Scouts that Sean had chosen were proven sailors who had done boat patrols on the choppy waters of Lake Kariba. *Mal de mer* was the reason that he had not sent for Matatu. The little Ndorobo would have been puking his heart out by now. It felt strange going into an operation without Matatu at his side, like going on a journey without a St Christopher. Matatu was his good-luck charm. He put that thought out of his mind, and looked round the crowded mess.

'Can you all see?' Sean had tacked the maps up on the bulkhead. There was a chorus of assent.

'We are heading up here.' He prodded the map. 'And the mission is to pick up two prisoners, a woman and a child.'

There were groans and raspberries of mock disappointment, and Sean grinned.

'It's OK, don't panic. There'll be plenty of gooks. It's hot guns all the way, gentlemen, and open season.'

The groans turned to ironic cheers, and Sean waited for them to settle down.

'This is a sketch-map of the target area. As you can see, it's pretty rough, but it gives you some idea of what to expect. I expect to find the prisoners being held in this compound here, near the beach. Probably in this hut. I will lead the rescue party. We will go in with three of the boats.'

He noticed Esau Gondele squatting on one of the bunks with a South African naval commando squashed up on each side of him. The three of them were sharing a cigarette, passing the butt from hand to hand as they listened to his briefing. 'What price apartheid now?' Sean smiled to himself, and went on.

'If there is going to be any serious trouble, it's going to come down this road alongside the river from the terrorist camp near the airstrip, here and here. Sergeant-Major Gondele will lead the support unit up the river in the other three boats and set up a road-block to prevent any gooks coming through. You will have to hold there for thirty minutes after you hear the first shot fired. That will give us time to spring the prisoners. Then you pull out and get back down-river and hotfoot out to sea to RZ with *Lancer*. It's simple, and it must be quick. We aren't going to hang around a second longer than necessary, but if you can sort out a few of the uglies while you are about it nobody is going to complain. OK, now we'll go over it again in detail and tomorrow we'll practise launching the boats and recovering them again in rough water. We'll do that every day, plus weapons drill and equipment checks – you aren't going to have much time to write home before we hit the beach on the night of Tuesday the thirteenth. Keep that date open. Write it down.'

★   ★   ★

The commercial flight landed at Kinshasa in the middle of a tropical downpour. Rainwater cascaded down the windows as the aircraft taxied to its berth, and Isabella was soaked in the few seconds that it took to leave the aircraft and board the airport bus.

As she had been promised, there was someone to meet her as she came through the Customs and Immigration barrier. He was a good-looking young pilot in plain khaki flying-overalls without any insignia or rank. When he greeted her in Spanish she was able to detect the Cuban accent, now that she knew to listen for it.

He insisted on carrying her suitcase and the box of gifts for Nicky and flirted with her brazenly in the ramshackle taxi that drove them from the main airport building down to the private and charter section of the airfield.

By the time they got there, the rain had stopped. Although heavy cloud still covered the sky, it was stiflingly hot and humid. He loaded her luggage into the back compartment of a small single-engine aircraft. She did not recognize the type. It carried no insignia other than an enigmatic number, and was painted an overall drab sandy colour.

'Are we going to fly in this weather?' she asked him. 'Isn't it dangerous?'

'Ah, señora, if you die you will die in my arms – what a glorious passing!'

As soon as they were airborne he placed his hand on her thigh, the better to point out the passing scenery.

'Keep your hands on the wheel. Keep your eyes on the

road.' She lifted his hand and gave it back to him. He flashed his teeth and his eyes and laughed as though he had made a conquest.

She could not remain angry for long. Every minute they kept on this heading confirmed the fact that she was being taken to the base where last she had seen Nicky. Two hours later she made out the grey expanse of the Atlantic beneath the lowering cloud-banks ahead.

The pilot turned south along the coast, and then she sat up straight in the seat and her spirits took wing. She recognized the oxbows in the river and the open mouth to the sea. The pilot pulled on flap and lined up for a landing on the red clay strip.

Nicky, she thought. Soon now, my baby. Soon we'll be free again.

As they taxied in, she saw him. He was standing on the front seat of the jeep. He had shot up at least another two inches, and his legs seemed too gawky and coltish for his body. His hair was longer than she remembered and curled out from under his camo-cap, but his eyes were the same. That marvellous clear green that sparkled even at this distance. As soon as he recognized her behind the windscreen, he waved both hands over his head, and his teeth flashed in the darkly tanned and beautiful face.

In the jeep with him were the driver and José, the Cuban paratrooper. They were grinning as widely as Nicky as she climbed out of the front seat of the aircraft.

Nicky jumped out of the jeep and ran to meet her. For a heady moment she thought he might rush into her arms, then he got control of himself and offered her his hand.

'Welcome, Mamma.' She thought the strength of her love might choke her. 'It is good to see you again.'

'Hello, Nicky.' Her voice was husky. 'You have grown so much I hardly recognized you. You are becoming a man now.'

It was the right thing to say. He hooked his thumbs into his belt and called imperiously to José and the driver: 'Come and take my mother's luggage.'

'Right away, General Pele.' José gave him a mock salute, and then to Isabella: 'Greetings, señora. We have been looking forward to your visit.'

I'm everybody's favourite aunt now, Isabella thought cynically.

From her box of goodies she gave José and the driver each a two-hundred pack of Marlboro cigarettes, and her popularity was enhanced a hundredfold. In Angola, Western cigarettes were hard currency.

As Nicholas drove them down to the beach he chattered happily, and though she showed flattering interest in everything he had done and achieved since their last meeting she was checking her surroundings with a much more businesslike eye than she had previously. She realized that she had made serious errors in the sketch-map that she had drawn for Sean. The training base had been enlarged since her last visit. There must now be several thousand soldiers here, and she saw some kind of artillery parked under camouflage-nets. They looked like long-barrelled anti-aircraft guns. Further on she noticed parked trucks with dish-shaped radar antennae pointed skyward, and she thought of her father and Garry bringing the Lear in overhead. There was no way to warn them of these changes.

When they reached the beach compound, Isabella checked the distance registered on the speedometer. It was only 3.6 kilometres from the airstrip to the beach – much closer than she had estimated. She wondered just how this might endanger the rescue operation. Reinforcements could be rushed in more swiftly than Sean had allowed for.

José carried her luggage into the guard-house. Waiting for her were the same two women who had met her before. However, their attitude was friendlier and more informal.

'I have brought you a gift,' Isabella greeted them, and gave them each a bottle of perfume which she had chosen for size rather than for subtle aroma. They were delighted and sprayed themselves so liberally that the air in the room was difficult to breathe. It was some minutes before they could get around to searching Isabella's luggage.

This time the camera was passed without comment, though they lingered longingly over her cosmetics. Isabella invited them to try a little of her lipstick, and they accepted with alacrity, and admired the results in the mirror of Isabella's compact. The atmosphere was more that of a gathering of old friends than of a security screening.

By the time they came to examine the box of gifts for Nicholas their hearts were obviously no longer in the task. One of them picked out the deflated soccer ball. 'Ah, Pele will like this,' she cried, and then Isabella's nerves prickled with tension as she handled the pump.

'For the ball,' she explained.

'Sí. I know, to pump air.' The woman gave it a few desultory strokes and then dropped the pump back into the box.

'I am sorry to have inconvenienced you, señora. We only do our duty.'

'Of course. I understand,' Isabella agreed.

'You will stay with us two weeks. That is good. Pele has been very excited that you are coming. He is a good boy. Everybody likes him very much. Everybody is very proud of him.'

She helped Isabella to carry her cases across to the same hut that they had given her on her last visit.

Nicholas was sitting on her bed, already in his swimming-trunks.

'Come, Mamma, we will go for a swim now. I will race you out to the reef.'

He swam like an otter, and she was hard-pressed to keep up with him.

That evening when just the two of them were alone in her hut, she gave him his gifts from the box. Although the soccer ball was the greatest hit, he also enjoyed her choice of books and clothes. She had brought a selection of colourful surfer's baggies and T-shirts which delighted him. There was also a Sony cassette-player and a box of music cassettes. His favourites were Creedence Clearwater Revival and the Beatles.

'Can you rock 'n' roll?' she asked. 'I'll show you.' And she put a Johnny Halliday tape on the player.

They gyrated around the hut in their bathing-suits, shrieking with laughter, until Adra called them for dinner. Adra was as taciturn and withdrawn as ever, and Isabella ignored her and concentrated all her attention on Nicholas. She had stored up a selection of elephant jokes for him.

'How do you know that the elephant has been in the refrigerator? You see his footprints in the butter.' He loved that one. In return he told her a joke that he had heard from José the paratrooper. It left her gasping for air.

'Do you know what that means?' she asked in nervous trepidation.

'Of course,' he told her. 'One of the big girls at school showed me.' And Isabella thought it prudent not to pursue the subject.

After they had seen him to bed, Adra walked with her to the hut and Isabella whispered: 'Where is Ramón, the Marqués? Is he here?'

Adra looked around carefully before replying. 'No. He will come soon. I think tomorrow or the next day. He says he will come to you. He says to tell you he loves you.'

Alone in her hut, Isabella found that she was trembling at the prospect of meeting Ramón again, now that she knew him for what he was. She doubted whether she would be able to act naturally towards him. The thought of making love to him terrified her. Surely he would sense the change in her feelings towards him. He might take Nicholas away, or have her imprisoned.

'Please, God, let Sean reach me before Ramón does. Keep him away until Sean comes.' She lay awake that night, cold with dread that Ramón would suddenly appear out of the darkness and she must take him into her bed.

As before, she and Nicholas spent the next two days swimming and fishing and playing with Twenty-Six on the beach. The puppy had grown into a lanky, long-tailed, cross-eyed dog with floppy ears that Nicholas adored. It

514

shared his bed with him; Isabella did not have the authority to forbid it, even though Nicholas's long legs were speckled with flea-bites.

On the Monday night, while she watched Nicholas prepare for bed, she reached up casually and took down the bicycle pump from the shelf above his bed on which the new soccer ball held pride of place. She twisted the handle and heard the faint internal click as the transponder switched on. She replaced the pump on the shelf just as Nicholas came back from the bathroom smelling of the peppermint toothpaste she had brought from Cape Town for him.

As she leant over the bed to tuck in the mosquito-net he reached up unexpectedly and threw both arms around her neck. 'I love you, Mamma,' he whispered shyly, and she kissed him.

His mouth was soft and moist and warm and tasted of toothpaste, and she thought her heart would burst with love of him. Quickly embarrassed by his own display, Nicholas rolled over, pulled the sheet up to his chin, closed his eyes tightly and made ostentatious snoring sounds.

'Sleep well, Nicky. I love you, too – with all my heart,' she whispered.

As she walked back to her own hut, thunder growled and lightning flickered across the night sky. As she looked up, a heavy drop of warm rain struck her on the centre of her forehead.

★   ★   ★

It was very quiet in the cockpit of the Lear. They were at forty thousand feet, almost service ceiling, as high as they could get for maximum endurance and speed.

'Enemy coast ahead,' Shasa said softly, and Garry chuckled.

'Come on, Pater. People only say things like that in World War Two movies.'

They were high above the cloud mass in a world of

enchanted silver moonlight. The cloud below them shone with the peculiar brilliance of an alpine snowfield.

'One hundred nautical miles to run to the mouth of the Congo river.' Shasa checked their position on the screen of the satellite nav system. 'We should be almost exactly overhead *Lancer*'s station.'

'Better give them a call,' Garry suggested, and Shasa switched radio frequencies.

'Hello, Donald Duck. This is the Magic Dragon. Do you read?'

'Hello, Dragon. This is the Duck. Reading you ten and ten,' the reply was immediate, and Shasa smiled with relief as he recognized his eldest son's voice. 'Sean must have had his thumb on the button,' he murmured and keyed his microphone. 'Stand by, Duck. We are heading for Disneyland.'

'Have a nice trip. Duck is standing by.'

Shasa swivelled in the co-pilot's seat and looked back into the Lear's passenger-cabin. The two technicians from Courtney Communications were crouched over their equipment. It had taken them ten days to install all the special electronics. Much of it was state-of-the-art equipment which was still under test with Armscor and had not yet been issued to the air force. It was not built into the Lear's body, but strapped and screwed to the cabin floor. Their intent faces were painted a witch's green by the glow from the display panel, and the enormous headphones distorted the shape of their heads.

Shasa switched to the intercom. 'How you doing, Len?'

The head engineer glanced up at him. 'No radar lash. We are receiving normal radio traffic from Luanda, Kinshasa and Brazzaville. No signal from the target.'

'Carry on.' Shasa turned. He knew that the new frequency-search equipment was skipping through the bands. It should pick up any military traffic from Luanda or Saurimo military bases. The antenna mounted under the Lear's belly would warn them if they were detected by hostile radar. Len, the radio engineer, had been chosen for his command of Spanish. He would be able to monitor any Cuban radio traffic.

'OK, Garry.' Shasa touched his arm. 'We are overhead the Congo mouth. Your new heading is 175.'

'New heading 175.' Garry stood the Lear on one wing-tip as they turned east of south to run parallel with the coast-line.

By some freak of wind and weather, a deep hole opened in the cloud mass beneath them. The moon was directly overhead and only two days from its full. Its light beamed down into the chasm, and forty thousand feet below they saw the platinum gleam of water and the dark shape of the African coast.

'Ambriz river-mouth in four minutes,' Shasa warned.

'We have initiated search for target signal,' Len confirmed in his headphones.

'Overhead Ambriz,' Shasa intoned.

'No target signal received.'

'Catacanha river-mouth in six minutes,' Shasa said.

He hadn't really expected the Ambriz to yield results. It was the outer limit of their search-cone. He looked ahead and grimaced. Directly in their track a gigantic mountain of menacing black cloud rose hammer-headed into the stratosphere. He estimated its height at sixty or seventy thousand feet, 'way above the Lear's ceiling.

'How do you like that Charlie Bravo?' he asked, and Garry shook his head and looked down at the screen of the weather radar set. The enormous tropical thunderstorm showed up as a lurid and ferocious crimson cancer on the screen.

'Ninety-six miles ahead, and it's a real Lulu. Looks like it's sitting right over one of our target river-mouths, the Chicamba.'

'If it is, it will wipe out any signal from Bella's transponder.' Shasa was looking worried.

'We wouldn't be able to fly through that anyway,' Garry growled.

517

'Overhead the Catacanha, Len. Are you picking up anything from our target?'

'Negative, Mr Courtney.' And then his voice changed. 'Hold on! Oh shit! Somebody is hitting us with radar lash.'

'Garry' – Shasa reached across to shake his shoulder – 'they've picked us up on radar.'

'Switch to the international frequency,' Garry said, 'and listen.'

They sat frozen in their seats listening to the static of that great turbulent storm ahead.

Suddenly the carrier band hissed and a voice cut in clearly. 'Unidentified aircraft. This is Luanda control. You are in restricted airspace. Identify yourself immediately. I say again, you are in restricted airspace.'

'Luanda control, this is British Airways Flight BA 051. We have an engine malfunction. Request a position fix.' Shasa began a garbled delaying argument with Luanda. Every second he could gain was crucial. He asked them for a clearance to land at Luanda, and pretended not to be receiving or understanding their refusals and urgent orders to vacate national airspace.

'They haven't fallen for it, Mr Courtney,' Len warned him as he swept the military frequencies. 'They have scrambled a flight of MiGs from Saurimo airfield. They are vectoring them in on us.'

'How long before we cross the Chicamba river-mouth?' Garry demanded.

'Fourteen minutes,' Shasa snapped back.

'Well, Lordy, Lordy!' Garry grinned. 'We are on a head-on course with those MiGs. They are coming in at Mach 2. This is going to be fun.'

They sped southwards into the silver moonlight.

'Mr Courtney, we have more radar lash. I think the MiGs have got us on their attack radar.'

'Thank you, Len. Chicamba river in one minute thirty seconds.'

'Mr Courtney.' There was a strident tone to Len's voice. 'The MiG leader is reporting target acquisition. They are on to us, sir. The attack radar lash is increasing. The MiG leader is requesting weapons-free.'

'I thought you said they couldn't intercept us,' Shasa asked Garry mildly. 'I thought we were out of their operational range.'

'Hell, Dad, anyone can make a mistake.'

'Mr Courtney!' Len's voice was a shriek. 'I have the target signal, weak and intermittent. About six kilometres. Dead ahead!'

'Are you sure, Len?'

'It's our transponder for sure!'

'The Chicamba river-mouth. Bella is at the Chicamba!' Shasa shouted. 'Let's get the hell out of here.'

'Mr Courtney, the MiGs are weapons-free and attacking. Radar lash is very strong and increasing.'

'Hold on,' Garry called. 'Grab your hats.'

He rolled the Lear wing-over into a dive.

'What the hell are you doing?' Shasa shouted as he was pressed back into the co-pilot's seat by the G force. 'Turn and get out to sea.'

'They'd nail us before we'd gone a mile.' Garry held the Lear in the dive.

'Christ, Garry, you'll tear the wings off us.'

The airspeed indicator revolved swiftly up towards the 'never exceed' barrier.

'Take your choice, Pater. We tear the wings off her – or the MiGs shoot the arse off us.'

'Mr Courtney, the MiG leader reports missile-lock.' Len was stuttering with terror.

'What are you going to do, Garry?' Shasa grabbed Garry's arm.

'I'm going in there.' Garry pointed at the soaring moon-washed mountain of the thunderstorm. It was a sheer precipice of turbulent cloud that obscured the heavens ahead of them. The cloud-banks boiled and seethed with the great winds and air-currents within. Lightning flashed and glowed deep in the belly of the storm.

'You are crazy,' Shasa whispered.

519

'No MiG will follow us in,' Garry said. 'No missile will hold its lock with all that energy and electrical discharge burning around us.'

'Mr Courtney, MiG leader has fired a missile – and another. Two missiles running . . .'

'Pray for us sinners,' Garry said, and held the Lear down in its death-dive; the airspeed needle went through the 'never exceed' barrier.

'I think this is it.' Shasa's voice was matter-of-fact, and as he said it something struck the Lear a crashing blow. She flipped over on to her back, the ball of the flight director spun like a top in its cage, and then they were into the storm.

All visibility was wiped out instantly and thick grey cloud like wet cottonwool engulfed them. They were thrown on to their safety-harnesses as the storm attacked the Lear. It was a ravening beast that clawed and lashed them.

The Lear tumbled and swirled like a dead leaf in a whirlwind. The instruments on the control-panel spun and toppled, the altimeter yo-yo'd as they dropped into the void and then hit a vicious updraught that hurled them up two thousand feet and twisted them wing over wing.

Suddenly the cloud was lit by internal lightning. It dazzled them, and rumbled through their heads, drowning out the agonized shriek of the Lear's jets. Blue fire danced on the metal skin of the aircraft as though she were aflame. They hit the bottom of another hole with a force that plunged them against the padding of their seats and buckled their spines. Then they were hurled aloft only to plunge once again. All around them the bodywork of the Lear creaked and groaned as the storm tried to rip her apart.

Garry was helpless. He knew better than to fight the wheel and rudders and increase the brutal stress on her control-surfaces. The Lear was fighting for her life. He whispered encouragement to her and held the control-wheel with a light and loving touch, trying to ease her nose up out of the graveyard spiral.

'Courage, darling,' he whispered. 'Come on, baby. You can do it.'

Shasa was clinging to the arm-rests of his seat and staring at the altimeter. They were down to fifteen thousand feet and still dropping. None of the other instruments was making any sense. They jerked and wavered and kicked.

He concentrated on the altimeter. It unwound jerkily. Ten thousand, seven, four thousand. The strength of the storm increased; their heads were whipped back and forth, threatening to snap their spines. The shoulder-straps cut painfully into their flesh.

Something broke in the fuselage with a tearing crash. Shasa ignored it and tried to focus on the altimeter. His vision was starred and disorientated by the Lear's vicious plunges.

Two thousand feet, one thousand – zero. They should have hit the ground, but the tremendous changes of barometric pressure within the swirling body of the storm had thrown out the reading.

Suddenly the Lear steadied, the turbulence abated. Garry pressed on rudder and stick, and she responded. The flight director stabilized and rotated towards the vertical as the Lear rolled back on to even keel and they burst out of the cloud.

The change was stunning. The noise of the storm gave way to the low hum of the jets. Moonlight flooded into the cockpit, and Shasa gasped with shock.

They were almost upon the surface of the sea, skimming over it like a flying fish rather than a bird. A drop of another hundred feet would have plunged them beneath the green Atlantic rollers.

'Cutting it a little fine, son.' Shasa's voice was hoarse, and he tried to grin, but his eye-patch had been shaken loose and hung down under his ear. He adjusted it with fingers that trembled.

'Come on, Navigator,' Garry chuckled unconvincingly. 'Give me a course to fly.'

'New course is 260 degrees. How is she handling?'

'Like a breeze.' Garry turned gently on to the new heading. The Lear came round serenely and sped out into the Atlantic leaving the dark continental mass astern.

'Len.' Shasa turned in the seat and looked back into the cabin. The technicians' faces were pale and washed lightly with the sweat of terror. 'What do you make of the MiGs?'

Len stared at him like an owl as he tried to adjust to the shock of still being alive.

'Pull yourself together, man,' Shasa snapped at him, and Len stooped quickly to his control-panel.

'Yes, we still have contact. MiG leader is reporting target destroyed. He is short of fuel and returning to base.'

'Farewell, Fidel. Thank the Lord that you are a lousy shot,' Garry murmured, and kept the Lear low down in the surface clutter where the shore radar would have difficulty picking them up. 'Where is *Lancer*?'

'Should be dead ahead.' Shasa thumbed the microphone.

'Donald Duck, this is the Magic Dragon.'

'Go ahead, Dragon.'

'It's the Chicamba. I repeat the Chicamba. Do you copy that? Over.'

'Roger. Chicamba. I say again Chicamba. Did you have any trouble? We heard pom-pom jet traffic south-east of here. Over.'

'Nothing to it. It was a Sunday-school picnic. Now it's your turn to visit Disneyland. Over.'

'We are on our way, Dragon.'

'Break a leg, Duck. Over and out.'

It was half-past five on Tuesday morning when Garry put the Lear down on the tarmac at Windhoek Airport. They climbed down stiffly and stood in a group at the foot of the steps, overcome by a sense of anticlimax. Then Garry walked to the nearest engine which was softly crackling and pinking as it cooled.

'Pater,' he called. 'Come and have a look at this.'

Shasa stared at the alien object that had buried itself in the metal fuselage below the pod of the Garrett turbo-fan engine. It was painted a harsh industrial yellow, a long finned arrow-like tube, that protruded six feet from the torn metal skin of the Lear.

'What the hell is that?' Shasa asked.

'That, Mr Courtney,' said Len, who had come up behind him, 'that is a Soviet ATOLL air-to-air missile that failed to explode.'

'Well, Garry,' Shasa murmured, 'Fidel wasn't such a lousy shot after all.'

'Bless Russian workmanship,' Garry said. 'Perhaps it's a little early, Dad, but could you stand a glass of champagne?'

'What a splendid idea,' said Shasa.

*   *   *

'The Chicamba river.' Shoulder to shoulder, Sean and Esau Gondele leant over the chart-table. 'There she is.'

Sean laid his finger on the tiny insignificant nick in the outline of the continent. 'Just south of Catacanha.' He looked up at the trawler skipper. Van Der Berg was built like a Sumo wrestler, squat and heavy, with a leathery skin burnt and desiccated by sun and wind.

'What do you know about it, Van?' he asked.

'Never been in that close,' Van shrugged. 'Just another piss-willy little river. But I'll get you as close as you want to go.'

'A mile off the reef will do very nicely.'

'You've got it,' Van promised. 'When?'

'I want you to keep below the horizon all of tomorrow, then at nightfall you can take us in at 0200 hours.'

For the Scouts, the witching hour was always two hours after midnight. It was then that the enemy would be at his lowest ebb, both physically and mentally.

At one o'clock in the morning Sean held his final briefing in the crew mess of Lancer. He checked each man separately. They were all dressed in navy-blue fisherman's jerseys and jeans, and black canvas rubber-soled combat-boots. On their heads were knitted black woollen caps, and

523

all their faces and hands were black, either naturally or with camo-cream.

The only uniform items they wore were their webbing, all of it supplied by the South African defence force from Cuban equipment captured in the south of Angola. Their weapons were Soviet AKM assault-rifles, Tokarev pistols and Bulgarian M75 anti-personnel grenades. Three men in Esau Gondele's section would carry RPG 7 anti-rank rocket-launchers. Part of the agreement with the South Africans for their co-operation was that nothing would ever be traced back to them.

One at a time, they stepped up to the table and handed over all their personal items, signet rings and dog-tags and pay-books, wallets and wristwatches, and any other form of identification. Esau Gondele sealed them in separate envelopes and issued each of them with an identical black waterproof digital wristwatch to replace their own.

While this was happening the trawler captain called on the intercom from the bridge: 'We are seven nautical miles off the river-mouth. Bottom is shoaling nice and gently. I'll have you in position a few minutes before time.'

'Good on you,' Sean told him, and then turned back to the ring of black faces. 'Very well, gentlemen, you know what we are after. Just a few airy thoughts to occupy those busy little minds of yours – if you are going to cull anybody, just make sure that you don't take out the woman or the child. She's my sister.' He let that sink in for a moment. 'Thought number two. The sketch-maps I have shown you are more fantasy than fact. Don't rely on them. Thought number three. Don't get left behind on the beach when we pull out. Chicamba is no place to spend a holiday. The food and the accommodation are rotten.' He picked up his rifle from the bunk. 'So, my children, let's go and do it.'

Lancer groped towards the shore with radar and depth-sounder. All her running lights were extinguished. Her engines were ticking over, so she barely maintained steerage. In the darkness ahead Sean could make out the inter-mittent luminous flare of the surf breaking on the outer reef. There were no lights ashore. The land itself had been absorbed by the night. The cloud overhead was unbroken. No glimmer of star or moon came through.

Van Der Berg straightened up from the radar-hood. 'One mile off,' he said quietly. 'Water is six fathoms and shoaling.' He glanced across at the dark figure of his coloured helmsman. 'Stop engines.'

The tremble of the engines through the deck beneath their feet ceased, and *Lancer* wallowed like a log.

'Thanks, Van,' Sean said. 'I'll bring you back a nice present.' He ran lightly down the companionway to the main deck.

They were waiting in the stern, each team standing by its own black rubber landing-boat. Sean smelt the musky odour in the air and grimaced. He didn't like it, but the use of 'boom' before a contact had become a tradition in the Scouts.

'It's an old African custom,' he consoled himself. 'The mad Mahdi's fuzzy-wuzzies smoked it before they revved old Kitchener at Khartoum.'

'Sergeant-Major, the smoking-light is out,' he grated, and he heard them shuffle in the darkness as they rubbed out their cannabis cigarettes on the deck. Sean realized that the smoke dulled the edge of their fear and bolstered that reckless bravado that was also part of the Scouts tradition, but he had never used it. He relished the sensation of fear; it throbbed in his blood and beat in his brain. He was never more alive than at a time like this, going into battle and mortal danger. He would not wish to shade that pure clean flame of fear.

One at a time the flexible rubber hulls, laden with men and equipment, slid down the stern chute of the trawler and splashed softly on to the water. The boatmen started the Toyota outboards and they burbled gently in the night. Even on a still and windless night like this, the sound would not carry a hundred yards.

They formed up into a long black snake, a boat's length between them. Sean was in the leading inflatable with three of his best men. The boatman shone a hooded pen light over the stern to keep the boats that followed on station. They moved off quietly towards the land.

Sean was standing in the stern. On a lanyard around his neck was a small luminous compass, but he relied mainly on the nightscope to bring them into the shore. It was a Zeiss image-enhancer. It looked like a large pair of plastic-coated binoculars.

Ahead of him the breaking surf flared green fire in the lens, and he made out clearly the dark spot in the line that marked the river-mouth. He touched the boatman's shoulder to redirect him. The next wave lifted and shoved them as it slid by under the hull, and they heard its hoarse susurration on either hand as they ran through the pass into the calmer waters of the lagoon.

Through the Zeiss lens he saw the shaggy tops of the palms silhouetted against the cloud-banks and the open throat of the river ahead. He flicked the pen light, and Esau Gondele's boat moved up alongside.

'There she is.' He leant over to whisper to the big Matabele and pointed out the river-mouth.

'I see it.' Esau had his own nightscope held to his eyes.

'Tear their nuts out!' The pod of three attack-boats moved off together, and Sean watched them disappear into the river and merge with the loom of the land.

He whispered to the boatman and they turned parallel with the beach. As they ran down the lagoon, Sean scanned the shore through the Zeiss lens. Half a mile from the mouth he made out in the gloom of the palm grove the square outline of a hut and then beyond it a second. 'It fits with Bella's description,' he decided.

They ran towards the beach. Now he saw the gleam of metal above the nearest hut. It was the tall Christmas-tree antenna and dish of a satellite communications centre.

'That's it.'

Sand grated softly beneath the keel of the inflatable and they leapt over the side into blood-warm water that reached to their knees. Sean led them ashore. The beach sand was so white that he could see the little ghost crabs scuttling away ahead of them. The men raced to the edge of the palm grove and dropped into cover below the high-water ridge.

Sean took a few moments to check his bearings. According to Isabella's description of her first visit, the communications centre was where they had received and searched her. She told him there were two or three female radio operators running the centre. In addition she had counted approximately twenty para guards who were billeted in the barracks beyond the wire.

The gate to the compound was always locked at sunset. She had warned him of that. There was always a sentry posted there. He patrolled the wire, and they changed the guard every four hours.

'Here he comes now,' Sean murmured as he saw the dark shape of the sentry moving along the barbed-wire fence. He lowered the nightscope, and whispered to the Scout who lay beside him: 'Twenty paces ahead, Porky. He's moving left to right.'

'Got him.' Porky Soaves was a Portuguese Rhodesian whose speciality was the slingshot. He could hit a dove on the wing at fifty metres. At ten metres he could drive a steel ball-bearing clean through the bone of a man's skull.

He slid forward like a night adder, and as the Cuban sentry came level he rose on one knee and drew like a longbow man. The double surgical-rubber strands of the slingshot snapped, and the sentry collapsed without a sound into the fluffy white sand.

'Go!' said Sean softly, and the second Scout ran forward with the heavy wire-cutters. The strands of barbed wire made little musical pinging sounds as they parted. Sean ran to the opening.

As each of the Scouts slipped through the hole in the wire, he slapped their shoulders and pointed them to their targets. He sent two of them to the main gate to take the sentries there, two to shut down the communications centre and the rest of them to hose down the barracks at the rear of the compound and to cull the garrison guards.

If the arrangements were the same as last time, the first hut on the right of the radio room should be Isabella's. Nicky would be in the second one with his Cuban nursemaid. Isabella called her Adra. From Sean's estimate of the situation, the nursemaid was one of the uglies. She would have to go. He would cull her at the first opportunity.

Sean ran towards the line of huts, but before he reached them a woman started to scream in the communications hut. The sharp hysterical bursts of sound raked Sean's nerve-endings. The screams were cut off by a short burst of automatic fire.

Here we go! Sean thought, and the night erupted with gunfire and flame and the mortal thrill of combat.

*   *   *

Isabella slept fitfully and woke a little before midnight to the sound of thunder and of jet engines passing at altitude overhead. She threw aside the mosquito-net and ran out into the night.

The wind generated by a mighty thunderstorm that was moving up from the south flapped the skirts of her nightdress around her bare legs and rattled the palm fronds.

The sound of jet engines rose and fell as wind and cloud blanketed it. It seemed to her that there was more than one aircraft up there above the cloud. She hoped that one of them was the Lear with her father and Garry aboard.

'Have you picked up the signal?' she wondered, as she strained her eyes into the black heavens. 'Can you hear me, Daddy? Do you know I'm here?'

She saw nothing, not even the shine of a single star, and the sound of engines overhead faded and left only the soughing of the wind and the rumble and crash as the thunderstorm fired its opening broadsides.

The rain began to fall again, and she ran back into the hut. She dried her hair and her bare feet and stood at the window looking down towards the beach.

'Please God. Let them know we are here. Help Sean to find us.'

At breakfast, Nicholas said to her: 'I haven't had a chance to try out my new soccer ball.'

'But we've played with it every day, Nicky.'

'Yes, but . . . I mean with good players.' And then, realizing what he had said: 'You are a good player – for a girl. I think you would make an excellent goalkeeper – with some more practice. But, Mamma, I would like some of my friends from school.'

'I don't know.' Isabella looked at Adra. 'Are your friends allowed here?'

Adra did not look round from the wood-stove. 'Ask José,' she said. 'Perhaps it will be allowed.'

That afternoon José and Nicholas arrived at the compound with a jeep-load of small black boys. The soccer match on the beach was noisy and passionately contested. On three occasions Isabella and José had to untangle a knot of punching and kicking bodies. After each battle, play was resumed as though nothing had happened.

Isabella was selected as goalkeeper for the Sons of the Revolution. But after she had let through five goals Nicholas, the team captain, came to her tactfully. 'I think you are tired, Mamma, and would like to rest now.' And she was sent to the sidelines.

The Sons of the Revolution beat the Angolan Tigers twenty-six goals to five, and Isabella felt very guilty about those five. After the final whistle Isabella produced a two-kilo bag of toffees and chocolates from her gift-box, and her lack of athletic prowess was immediately forgiven by her captain and both teams.

At dinner Nicholas chatted easily, and Isabella tried to act as naturally, but her eyes kept straying to the window of the hut and the beach. If Sean were coming, he would come tonight. She noticed Adra watching her thoughtfully.

She made another effort to follow Nicky's conversation, but she was thinking about Adra now.

Could they take her with them? she pondered. Would she want to come? Adra was such a reticent and secretive person that she could never even guess at her true feelings, except her love for Nicky – that was all that was certain.

Could she trust her enough to warn her of the rescue? she wondered. Should she give Adra the choice of coming away or remaining? In fairness, could she take Nicky from her after all these years of devotion to him? Surely it would break her heart, and yet could she trust her enough to tell her? Could she risk their freedom, hers and Nicky's, and could she risk the lives of her brother and all those other gallant young men who were attempting to rescue them? More than once during the meal she was on the point of speaking to Adra, but each time she shied away from it at the last moment.

When she tucked Nicky into bed he lifted his face to her and she kissed him quite naturally. He held her tightly for a moment.

'Do you have to go away again, Mamma?' he asked.

'Would you come with me, if you could?' she countered.

'And leave Padre and Adra?' He lapsed into silence. It was the first time he had ever spoken to her of Ramón, and it troubled her deeply. Was it respect or fear she had detected in his voice? She could not be certain.

On an impulse she began: 'Nicky, tonight – if anything happens, don't be afraid.'

'What will happen?' He sat up with interest.

'I don't know. Probably nothing.' He looked disappointed and dropped back on the pillow.

'Good night, Nicky,' she whispered.

Adra was waiting for her in the darkness between the huts. It was the opportunity Isabella had waited for.

'Adra,' she whispered. 'I have to talk to you. Tonight . . .' she broke off.

'Tonight?' Adra prompted her, and when still she hesitated Adra went on: 'Yes, tonight he will come. He says to expect him. He could not come before, but tonight he will come to you.'

Isabella felt panic rise to wash reason away. 'Oh God – are you sure?' Then she caught herself. 'That is wonderful. I have waited so long.'

All thoughts of warning Adra of the rescue attempt were wiped from her mind. How could she face Ramón – now that she realized what a cruel and evil monster he truly was? How could she let him touch her without trembling?

'I must go now,' Adra whispered, and slipped away into the darkness, leaving her alone with her terror. She had planned to wear jeans and a jersey beneath her nightdress ready to leave when Sean came, but she dared not do that now.

She lay so long alone in the darkness beneath the mosquito-net that at last she began to hope that Sean would come to her before Ramón did, or at least that dawn would save her.

Then suddenly she knew that he was in the hut with her. She smelt him before she heard him. The faint but distinctive odour of his body that had always aroused her so readily. Her nostrils and every nerve in her body jumped tight. Her breathing seized up in her throat.

She heard the whisper of his feet across the floor of the hut, and then his touch upon the bed.

'Ramón.' Her breath escaped on an explosive gust.

'Yes, it is me.' His voice struck her like a blow in the face.

She felt him lift the mosquito-net and she lay rigid. His finger-tips brushed her face, and she thought she might scream aloud. She did not know how to act, what to say to him. 'He will know.' She realized that she was panicking. She dare not move or speak.

'Bella?' he said, and she heard the first suspicion in his tone. In sudden inspiration she reached up and seized him.

'Don't talk,' she whispered fiercely. 'I cannot wait another moment – don't say anything. Take me now, Ramón.'

She knew she was not acting out of character. Often in that distant happy past she had been like this – urgent, wild with desire, brooking not an instant's delay.

She sat up and began to tear at his clothing. I have to keep him from talking, from asking any questions, she thought desperately. I have to quieten and reassure him that nothing has changed.

With terror in her heart and the smell of him filling her head she let his hands lift her nightdress and then the hard smooth naked length of him slide into the bed beside her.

'Bella,' he whispered harshly. 'I have wanted you too much for too long.' And his mouth covered hers. It felt as though he were sucking out her very being from between her lips, the way he might suck the juice and flesh from a ripe orange.

With shame at the perversity and treachery of her own body she felt herself overwhelmed by raw sexual passion. She was making love to a sleek and beautiful animal, something inhuman and cruel and infinitely dangerous. Fear mingled with lust to spur and goad her. She felt like that doomed creature in the bull-ring of Granada whose tragic struggle and lingering death had moved her so when long ago she and her love had been fresh and young.

At last when they were spent together, he lay on top of her as though he were dead. She could not move; her guilt and his weight threatened to suffocate her. She hated herself almost as much as she hated him.

'It was never like that before,' he whispered. 'You never did that to me before.'

She could not trust herself to reply. She could not know what might come out once she began to speak. She realized that she was on the verge of a terrible destructive madness – and yet when he lay beside her and he stroked her and gently touched the most intimate parts of her body her thighs fell apart and she felt her flesh melt and her bones soften.

He began to speak softly. He told her how he loved her.

He spoke about the future, when the three of them would be safe and happy in some secure and secret place. His lies were beautiful; they conjured up wonderful pictures in her mind. Although she knew that they were false, she wanted desperately to believe them.

When at last he fell asleep with his face pressed between her naked breasts, she stroked the crisp springing curls of his head with a terrible regret and a longing for things which she knew did not exist. So deep was her distress that it had driven from her consciousness all other thoughts, until abruptly and shockingly the night was ripped through by the screams of a woman and the sound of gunfire.

She felt Ramón come awake and at the same instant spring from the bed, naked and lithe as a jungle cat. She heard the metallic snicker of a firearm as he snatched the pistol from the holster that lay on the floor beside the bed. The night was lit by flame and explosion. She saw Ramón silhouetted against the light from the window. He held the pistol at the level of his eyes, pointed at the roof, ready for instant use.

Then she heard Sean's beloved voice, shouting for her in the darkness beyond the window: 'Bella, where are you?'

She saw Ramón's dark shape dart to the window, and the pistol glinted in the light of an exploding grenade as he levelled it.

'Look out, Sean!' she screamed. 'Man with a gun!'

Ramón fired twice, changing position between each shot. There was no answering fire from beyond the window. She realized that Sean dare not fire for fear of hitting her or Nicky.

She rolled from the bed and dropped to the floor on hands and knees. Frantically she crawled towards the door. She wanted to get to Nicky, she had to get to Nicky.

Halfway across the hut she felt Ramón's muscular bare arm whipped around her neck from behind, and he forced her to her feet. With the last of her breath, she screamed: 'Sean! He has got me!'

'Bitch,' Ramón hissed in her ear. 'Treacherous bitch.'

And then he raised his voice. 'I'll kill her!' he shouted. 'I'll blow her head off.'

Then he dragged her to the door and forced her down the steps. 'Move, bitch,' he grated. 'Keep moving. I know who Sean is. He won't fire – not with you as a shield. Move!'

The pressure on her throat was choking her. She could not resist it. He ran with her towards Nicky's hut. The communications hut was in flames. From its thatched roof flame and sparks towered into the night sky. It was as bright as a stage. The serpentine shadows of the palm trunk writhed upon the pale sandy earth.

They burst into Nicky's hut. Adra and the child were crouched in the centre of the floor. Adra was covering Nicky with her body.

'Padre!' Nicky shrieked.

'Come with Adra,' Ramón snapped at him. 'Keep close to her. Follow me.'

In a tight group they left the hut and moved towards the carpark. Ramón held Isabella from behind; with his free hand he pressed the pistol to her head.

'I'll blow her head off,' he called into the dancing shadows. 'Keep your distance.'

'Please, Padre, do not hurt Mamma,' Nicky wailed.

'Keep quiet, boy!' Ramón snarled at him; and then, raising his voice again: 'Call your dogs off, Sean. Unless you want your sister and her son to die.'

After a moment, Sean's voice bellowed out of the shadows: 'Hold your fire, Scouts! Back off, Scouts!'

Ramón kept them moving towards one of the jeeps. Isabella was choking for breath, the muzzle of the pistol was pressed so hard into her ear that the tender skin tore and a drop of blood ran down her neck.

'Please, you're hurting me,' Isabella gasped.

'Don't hurt Mamma,' Nicholas cried, and twisted out of Adra's grip. He ran to Isabella's side, and for a moment Adra was isolated, offering a clear shot.

In the darkness beyond the firelight a yellow flower of

gun-flame bloomed, and a single bullet whiplashed across twenty yards of open ground.

The side of Adra's head dissolved in a liquid red smear. She was snatched over backwards to hit the earth with her arms flung wide open.

'Adra!' Nicky screamed, but before he could run to her Ramón grabbed him around the waist.

'No, leave Adra,' he snapped. 'Stay close to me now, Nicky.'

The three of them were in the centre of a brightly lit stage. There was no other living soul in view. The corpse of one of the Cuban woman signallers lay curled against the wall of the burning building, and two dead paratroopers lay at the gate to the compound.

Ramón called out an order in Spanish to any of his paratroopers that might still be alive, but he knew it was a vain effort. He knew the quality of the attackers. He had recognized the name of her brother the instant Isabella called it out. Sean's shouted order addressed to the Scouts had confirmed it. He guessed that his men were all of them dead. They had probably died in that first storm of gunfire.

These were the notorious Ballantyne Scouts, he was certain of that, but how they had got here eluded him. He knew only that Isabella had somehow managed to call them in. They were out there in the shadows, and they would strike the same way they had killed Adra, swiftly and with deadly accuracy, if he gave them the faintest chance.

The only advantage he had on his side now was time. He knew that Raleigh Tabaka would have heard the gunfire and would be leading a relief column of his guerrillas down from the airfield. They would be here in minutes. He backed towards the nearest of the three parked jeeps in the motor pool.

Sean watched them over the sights of the AKM. He lay at the base of one of the palms, the outline of his head broken by a pile of dead fronds. At this range of forty yards the assault-rifle with the rate-of-fire selector on single shot was only accurate enough to put a bullet into a two-inch circle. He had aimed for the bridge of Adra's nose and hit her in the left eye. The bullet had sheared off the side of her skull.

That kind of accuracy was not sufficient to risk a shot at Ramón Machado. The man was good. He was using his two hostages for maximum cover, ducking and weaving like a boxer so that Sean could never hold a steady bead on his head.

To Sean, his sister's naked body was disconcerting and shocking in the yellow firelight. Her breasts were very pale and tender-looking; the stark black triangle stood out clearly at the base of her belly. He knew that his Scouts were watching her.

Even in the stress of battle, the way that Ramón Machado held her against his own naked body infuriated Sean and threatened to impair his judgement. He was tempted to risk a shot. His finger on the trigger lacked only an ounce of pressure, but Ramón ducked his head behind Isabella's shoulder as they reached the jeep.

Ramón slid into the driver's seat and dragged Isabella and the child in with him. The engine started with a bellow, and sand spun from beneath the rear wheels as Ramón accelerated towards the gate.

Sean fired a burst, low at the nearest back wheel, and saw a bullet strike sparks from the spinning steel hub. Then the jeep crashed into the barrier gate and ripped out one of the poles. The gate crumpled before its rush, and the vehicle bounced through the wreckage and roared down the track dragging a tangle of wire and fence-poles behind it like a sleigh.

Sean leapt to his feet and raced to the second jeep. Four of his Scouts were pelting for the same vehicle and they piled into the back of it as Sean started the engine. He spun it in a wide circle and then gunned it through the ruined gate. They jolted over the mangled frame and then roared in pursuit of Ramón and his hostages.

If Isabella's sketch-map was accurate, this track would

take them down along the river towards the airstrip, and Esau Gondele's road-block.

Esau would hose anything that came down the track, from either direction. An RPG 7 rocket would turn Isabella and her son to mincemeat.

Sean thrust the palm of his hand down on the horn-ring and blew a long wailing blast. He hoped that Esau Gondele might understand the warning and hold his fire, but he knew it was a forlorn hope. Smoked up with boom, the Scouts would be hot and quick on the trigger.

He had to overtake them. He shoved the pedal flat and roared into the standing wall of white dust left by the vehicle ahead of him on the narrow track. The track turned abruptly right, and for a second he lost it and slewed over the verge. The jeep canted over on its outside wheels and they crashed and tore through the light brush before he got her back on to the track.

The angle of the breeze altered as they turned, and the dust was blown aside. Only fifty yards ahead he saw the tail-lights of the escaping vehicle, and he hit it with the full beam of his headlights.

In the front seat Ramón Machado was driving with one hand. His other arm was locked around Isabella's shoulders, holding her in an awkward cramped position. Her head was twisted around on the long column of her neck. Her hair fluttered and rippled in the wind, and her eyes were dark and wide with terror in the pale oval of her face. She was shouting something at him, but the words were whipped away by the wind.

Nicky was clutching the back of Isabella's seat. He was dressed in a white T-shirt and shorts. He was also looking back at the pursuing jeep, and even in these desperate moments Sean was struck by the resemblance of the child to the mother. His fury at the man who threatened them smoked in his brain, and armed him with reckless courage.

Then he realized that the other jeep was down on one side. The burst of fire he had given it had ripped the nearside rear tyre. Long tattered shreds of black rubber peeled from the spinning rim. The tangle of fencing wire and the crumpled pipe-frame of the gate dragged behind the damaged vehicle like a drogue, tearing up a spray of sand and dust from the track and slowing it down.

He was gaining on them rapidly. The track had turned away from the beach and was running alongside the steep bank of the river. The mangrove trees loomed in the headlights of the two racing vehicles, and between their trunks the dark water glinted sullenly.

Ramón glanced back over his shoulder and realized that the other jeep was only three feet from his tail-gate. He ducked his head and released his grip on Bella. He snatched the pistol from his lap and twisted around to aim at Sean's face. The range was under twelve feet, but both jeeps were pounding and swerving over the rough track. The bullet struck the side-post of the windscreen and ricocheted away into the darkness.

One of the Scouts thrust his rifle forward to return fire, but Sean struck the barrel upwards.

'Hold your fire,' he shouted, and drove into the back of the other jeep with a ringing clash of metal.

The impact snapped their heads backwards, and Nicky was thrown over the rear seat with his legs kicking in the air as he struggled to regain his balance.

'Jump,' Sean howled at Isabella, but before she could react Ramón grabbed her again and pulled her close.

Once again Sean butted his jeep into the back of the other vehicle. It crushed in the tail-gate and slewed it half off the track.

Ramón was struggling one-handed to hold it on the road. The back end was swinging wildly. Dust boiled out from the rear wheels in a cloud, half-blinding Sean. Isabella was screaming, and Nicky scrambled up and crouched on the rear seat. His face was white and terrified.

Another bend in the track flung the leading vehicle up on to the verge. While Ramón tried desperately to control it, Sean saw his chance and gunned his own jeep up alongside it. For a second they were racing side-by-side like a team in harness.

Ramón Machado and Sean Courtney looked into each other's eyes at a distance of six feet, and hatred flashed between them like a discharge of static electricity. It was a primeval emotion, a deep atavistic understanding as two dominant males met and recognized that one must kill the other.

Sean spun the wheel hard left and swerved into him, forcing his far wheels off the track. The bole of a palm tree wiped off the paintwork and smeared the metal down the length of the vehicle. Ramón swerved back and hit Sean as hard.

Then Ramón released his grip on Isabella and once again snatched the pistol from his naked lap and thrust it into Sean's face, reaching out between the speeding jeeps. Ramón's face was a dark mask of fury and hatred.

Isabella threw herself sideways and grabbed the steering-wheel. As Ramón fired she wrenched it over with all her strength. The bullet flew away into the night, and the jeep whipped into a murderous skid and plunged over the riverbank.

In the instant before it disappeared Sean saw both Isabella and Ramón hurled head first against the windscreen, and from the back seat Nicky's small form was catapulted high into the darkness. Then he was past, braking hard, wrestling with the wheel as the jeep slewed into a broadside skid. The moment he had her under control, Sean snapped the gear lever into reverse and roared backwards to the point where the other vehicle had disappeared.

Dust still hung in the air, and the earth at the crest of the bank was torn by the spinning tyres. Sean leapt from the driver's seat and ran to the top of the bank. The jeep was in the river below him. The headlights were still burning beneath the surface, like two drowned moons. She had capsized, and her rear wheels were spinning in a froth of white foam. Nicky's small crumpled body lay on the bank at the water's edge.

Sean launched himself down the bank. Sliding and slipping, he kept his footing like a cat and used his momentum to carry him out in a long clean racing dive. He hit the water flat like an Olympic racer.

He drove himself down deep. The headlights burnt through the murk, and his underwater vision was blurred and distorted. He reached the carcass of the submerged jeep and pulled himself down under it. The air in the rear fuel-tank was holding it just clear of the muddy bottom, and he wriggled into the opening.

Something pale loomed in front of him, and he reached out and touched a naked body. Quickly he ran his hands over it and touched large smooth breasts. He reached up and seized a handful of the long floating hair and dragged Isabella out from under the wreck.

He surfaced with her in his arms and found with relief that she was choking and gasping and struggling weakly. He dragged her to the bank. One of the Scouts had shown enough presence of mind to drive the jeep to the lip of the bank so that the beam of the headlights shone down and gave them light.

Isabella crawled naked and running with water to where Nicky lay and drew him into her lap. He began to struggle and kick.

'My father,' he wailed. '*Mi padre!*'

Knee-deep in the mud, Sean peered down into the water. Water had flooded the engine of the jeep and stalled it, but the lights still burnt in the depths.

Swiftly he weighed the need for haste against his desire to find Ramón Machado. He knew that reinforcements must even now be on the way from the guerrilla camp. They had only minutes in hand. He was about to turn away and go to help Isabella, to get her and the child up the bank, when he saw a flash of movement in the water. A shadow passed as though a shark had swum between him and the submerged headlights.

Bastard! he thought, and shouted to his men on the bank above him: 'Bring me my rifle.'

540

One of them came sliding down the bank. Before he could reach Sean and hand him the AKM, there was a swirl in the muddy water. It was far out in the river at the edge of the light, and Ramón's head burst through.

'Get him!' roared Sean. 'Nail the bastard!'

Ramón's hair was slicked down over his eyes, and water streamed down his face as he gasped wildly for air. One of the Scouts on the bank fired a short burst, and the bullets flickered a spray of water from the surface around Ramón's head. Ramón drew another breath, and ducked under. For a moment his bare feet showed above the surface, kicking in the air, and then he was gone.

'Bastard! Bastard!' Sean swore, and snatched his own AKM from the hands of his Scout as the man reached him. He fired a long angry frustrated burst into the river, and the bullets chopped up a patch of dancing froth on the spot where Ramón had disappeared.

Then he checked his fury and waited for Ramón's head to show again, but the tide was ripping downstream carrying everything with it. Out there were dark and twisted mangroves behind which Ramón could shelter, and beyond the beams of the headlights the waters were dark and obscure.

After another minute he knew he had lost him. He had to let him go. He crushed down his frustration and his hatred and turned back to Isabella. She was wet and smeared with mud. The edge of the windscreen had opened a cut in her hairline, and a trickle of blood diluted by river-water was spreading down her face.

Sean shrugged out of his sodden jersey and helped her into it.

As she thrust her arms through the sleeves she gasped: 'What happened to Ramón?'

'The bastard gapped it.' Sean hauled her to her feet. 'Time is wasting. We're out of here.'

Nicky broke from his mother's grip and darted to the edge of the water.

'My father – I will not leave my father.'

Sean grabbed him by one arm. 'Come on, Nicky.' Nicholas whirled and sank his small white teeth into Sean's wrist.

'You little swine.' Sean clouted him open-handed across the side of his head, almost knocking him off his feet. 'No more of your little dago tricks, matey.'

He picked him up, kicking and fighting, and slung him over his shoulder.

'I will not go. I want to stay with *mi padre*.'

Sean grabbed Isabella's hand and, carrying Nicky easily, he pulled her up the bank. There were other figures around the jeep, and for a moment Sean did not recognize them. He dropped Isabella's hand and lifted the AKM by the pistol grip.

'Hold it, Sean,' Esau Gondele cautioned him as he ran forward.

'Where did you spring from?'

'You almost ran into our ambush,' Esau told him. 'You were just one second away from getting an RPG rocket up your backside. We are back there.' He pointed up the track.

'Where are your boats?'

'Two hundred yards up-river.'

'Pull your men out – we'll hitch a ride back with you.' He broke off and cocked his head.

'Douse those lights,' Esau Gondele snapped at one of his men. He leant into the parked jeep and hit the switch. The headlights faded.

In the darkness they stood listening.

'Trucks coming fast from the direction of the airstrip.' They all heard them clearly in the stillness.

'More gooks,' Esau agreed.

'Take us to the boats,' Sean ordered. '*Tout de suite* – and the tooter the sweeter.'

They ran in a group, keeping to the track. A hundred yards along, Esau Gondele whistled, the sharp double flute of a night-flying dikkop, one of the Scouts' recognition-signals. The whistle was repeated from the darkness just ahead, and Sean stumbled over the dead palm trunks that they had dragged across the track as a road-block.

'Come on,' Esau Gondele called them off the track. 'The boats are this way.'

As he spoke they saw the moving headlights through the trees ahead. A convoy of vehicles was speeding down the track towards them from the direction of the airstrip.

Nicholas was still kicking and struggling in Sean's grip, and Isabella was trying desperately to reassure him.

'It will be all right, Nicky darling. These people are our friends. They are taking us home to a safe place.'

'This is my home – I want my father. They killed Adra. I hate them! I hate you! I hate them!' he screamed in Spanish.

Sean shook him violently. 'One more peep out of you, my old China, and I'll knock your cocky little head right off your shoulders.'

'This way.' Esau Gondele led them at a run away from the road-block. Within fifty yards they reached the riverbank where the boats were moored.

Sean glanced back and saw the convoy of trucks come rumbling around a bend in the road. The beams of their headlights swept overhead, but they were hidden from them by the angle of the riverbank. In the lights Sean saw that the back of each truck was crowded with armed men.

Sean lifted Isabella into the nearest inflatable boat, and she tripped on the wet folds of the jersey that hung around her legs and sprawled in the bilges.

'Clumsy bint,' he grunted, and threw Nicky into the boat after her. It was a mistake.

Nicky rebounded like a rubber ball, and as Sean tried to grab him he ducked under his arm and shot up the bank.

'You little devil.' Sean whirled and went after him.

'My baby,' Isabella cried, and jumped out of the boat. She sloshed through the mud and raced up the bank in pursuit of the two of them.

'Come back, Nicky – oh, please, come back.'

He was running towards the approaching convoy. Like

a hare he ducked and dodged through the brush ahead of Sean. He was twenty feet short of the track when Sean dived and caught him by the ankle. Seconds later Isabella tripped over them and sprawled full-length on the soft sandy earth.

The headlights of the convoy swept over them, but the three of them were lying behind a clump of low bush, concealed from the men in the cab of the leading truck. Nicky screamed again and tried to crawl away, but Sean pinned him and covered his mouth with the palm of one hand.

The trucks bore down upon them and then braked as they saw the palm trunks that blocked the road. The leading truck in the convoy drew up only twenty feet from where they lay in darkness.

Still smothering Nicky under him, Sean reached out and pushed Isabella's face down to the earth. A white face shines like a mirror.

From the cab of the truck a man jumped down and ran forward to inspect the road-block, then he turned and shouted an order. A dozen guerrillas in combat camouflage swarmed from the back of the truck and seized the tree trunks.

As they lifted and dragged them clear, the headlights lit the face of the officer who commanded them. Isabella lifted her head and saw his features clearly. She recognized him immediately. It was not a face ever to forget. The last time she had seen this man he had been a passenger in the van driven by her half-brother, Ben Afrika. The two of them had been on their way to a rendezvous with Michael Courtney. He was probably the finest-looking black man she had ever seen, tall, regal and fierce as a hawk.

He turned his head and, for a moment, seemed to stare directly at her. Then he turned again to watch his men roll the logs aside. The moment the road was clear he strode to the cab of the truck and vaulted into it. He slammed the door, and the truck roared forward.

The troop convoy followed it. As the last pair of headlights swept past them, Sean tucked Nicky under his arm, pulled Isabella to her feet and hurried her back towards the riverbank.

Sean kept a firm grip on the scruff of Nicholas's neck in the leading boat as the flotilla ran back down-river. The glow from the burning huts lit the underbelly of the clouds, and even above the sound of the outboard motors they heard the shouts and the sound of automatic gunfire.

'What are they shooting at?' Isabella asked, as she huddled against Sean for warmth.

'Probably at shadows – or at each other,' he chuckled softly. 'Nothing quite like a nervous gook with a rifle in his hand for burning up ammo.'

The outgoing tide sped them through the mouth into the lagoon. Through his nightscope Esau Gondele picked up the wake of the other flotilla of inflatables heading back from the beach. They came together as they reached the pass in the reef and in line ahead headed out into the open sea.

Lancer in her bright yellow paint showed up through the lens of the nightscope at half a mile distance.

As soon as they had recovered the last inflatable through the stern chute of the trawler, she opened up her engines and ran for the open Atlantic.

Sean turned to Esau Gondele. 'What was the butcher bill, Sergeant-Major Gondele?'

'We lost one man, Major Courtney,' he replied as formally. 'Jeremiah Masoga. We brought him back with us.' The Scouts always retrieved their dead.

Sean felt that familiar sickening pang; another good man gone. Jeremiah was only nineteen years old. Sean had already decided to give him his second stripe. He wished now that he had done it before this. You can never make amends to the dead.

'Three wounded; nothing bad enough to make them miss the party tonight.'

'Put Jeremiah in the refrigerated hold,' Sean ordered.

'We'll ship him home as soon as we reach Cape Town. He'll get a regimental burial with full honours.'

When they were still two hundred nautical miles from Table Bay, Centaine Courtney sent out a Courtney helicopter to pick up Sean and Isabella and Nicky. The old lady could not wait any longer to meet her great-grandson.

*   *   *

Ramón clung to the roots of one of the mangrove trees to steady himself against the drag of the outgoing tide as it funnelled through the river-mouth. The razor-edged shells of the fresh-water mussels that covered the stem cut into his hand, but he hardly felt the pain. He was staring out across the river.

The reflection from the flames of the burning compound flecked the surface of the water with sovereigns of gold.

The boats passed within fifty feet of where he crouched chin-deep in the mud and slime of the mangroves. Their motors buzzed softly in the stillness of the night. Their outlines were indistinct, three dark hippo shapes that passed swiftly on the tide heading for the mouth and the open sea – but he imagined that one of the figures in the leading boat was smaller than the others and wore a pale T-shirt.

It was only then, in the moment of losing him, that he realized that he was, after all, just another father. For the first time in his life he acknowledged his love and dependence upon that love. He loved his son and he was losing him. He groaned in anguish.

Then rage boiled up in him and burnt away all other feeling. It was a consuming anger against all those who had inflicted this loss upon him. He stared into the empty darkness that had swallowed his son, and the fire of vengeance burnt through every fibre of his being. He wanted to shout this fury after them. He wanted to rail against the woman, he wanted to curse and scream out his frustration, but he caught himself. That was not his way. He must be cold and sharp as steel now. He must think clearly and with icy purpose.

The first thought that came into his mind was that he had lost his hold on Red Rose. She was no longer of any value to him or the cause. Now she was the sacrifice. He knew how to destroy her and all those around her. The hilt of the weapon was in his head; it only remained to unsheathe it.

He pushed off from the mangrove and let the tide sweep him into the curve of the river, swimming across it with an easy breast-stroke. The bottom shelved gently under him, and he touched sand and waded ashore.

Raleigh Tabaka was waiting for him beside the burnt-out ruins of the communications centre. Ramón dressed hastily in borrowed trousers and jacket; his hair was still damp and matted with river-mud.

Smoke from the smouldering buildings hazed the first grey light of dawn. Raleigh Tabaka's men were recovering the corpses and laying them out in a long row under the palms. In *rigor mortis* they were locked into the attitudes in which they had met their deaths. It was a grotesque charade show.

José, the paratrooper, had one arm thrown over his face as though protecting his eyes. His chest was mangled by grenade shrapnel. Adra's arms were extended as though she hung on a crucifix, and half her head was missing. Ramón glanced at her without particular interest, as he might at a worn-out article of clothing which no longer had any utility for him.

'How many?' he asked Raleigh Tabaka.

'Twenty-six,' he replied. 'All of them. There were no survivors. Whoever it was, they did a thorough job. Who were they? Do you have any idea?'

'Yes,' Ramón nodded, 'I have a very good idea.' And before Raleigh could speak again Ramón told him: 'I am taking over the Cyndex project – personally.'

547

'Comrade-General' – Raleigh frowned with affront – 'that has been my operation from the very beginning. I have controlled the two brothers.'

'Yes,' Ramón agreed implacably. 'You have done very well. You will receive all the recognition that you deserve. But I am taking over the direction of the project. I will leave for the south as soon as an aircraft is available. You will accompany me.'

★　　　★　　　★

'It doesn't end here, Bella,' Shasa said gravely. 'We cannot just pretend that nothing else happened. I did not want to complicate the rescue attempt by considering the full murky depths of this whole dreadful business. However, now Nicholas is safe here at Weltevreden we are forced to do so. Many people, including the members of your family, risked their lives for you and Nicholas. One gallant young man, a stranger, a trooper of Sean's regiment, died to save you. Now you owe us the truth.'

They were assembled in the gun-room once again, and Isabella was on trial before the family.

Her grandmother sat in the chair to one side of the fireplace. She sat very straight. Her hand on the ivory head of her cane was blue-veined beneath the thin parchment of skin. Her hair, once a thick unmanageable bush, was now the purest silver cap washed with a hint of blue. Her expression was severe.

'We want to hear it all, Isabella. You will not leave this room until you have told every detail.'

'Nana, I am so ashamed. I had no choice.'

'I did not ask for excuses and self-abasement, missy. I want the truth.'

'You must understand, Bella. We know that you have done terrible damage to the national interest, to the family, to yourself. Now it is our duty to contain and control that damage.' Shasa stood in front of the fireplace with his hands clasped under the tails of his blazer. His tone had

548

moderated. 'We want to help you, but we must know the truth before we can do so.'

Isabella looked up at him with a hunted expression. 'Can I talk to you and Nana alone?' She glanced at her brothers. Garry lolled in the armchair under the window with thumbs hooked in his gaudy braces. He rolled an unlit cigar from one side of his mouth to the other. Sean sat on the window-sill, his legs thrust straight out in front of him. His bare arms, tanned and sleek with muscle, were crossed over his chest.

'No,' said Centaine firmly. 'The boys have risked their lives for you and Nicky. If you have stored up more trouble for yourself and the family, they are the ones who will be called upon to bail you out. No, you don't get out of it that easily. They deserve to hear everything you have to tell us. Don't leave anything out – do you hear me?'

Slowly Isabella lowered her face into her hands. 'They gave me the code-name Red Rose.'

'Speak up, girl. Don't mumble.' Centaine banged her cane on the floor between her feet, and Isabella started and looked up.

'I did everything they told me to,' she said, looking the old lady in the face. 'When Nicky was still an infant, just over a month old, they made a film and showed it to me. They almost drowned my baby. They held him by the feet and ducked him . . . ' She broke off, and then drew a deep breath to steady herself. 'They warned me that in the next film they would cut off parts of his body and then send them to me – his fingers, his toes, his arms and legs and then . . .' She choked on the word. 'And then his head.'

They were all silent and appalled until Centaine spoke. 'Go on.'

'They told me I must work for Daddy. I must inveigle myself into his Armscor work.' Shasa winced, and Isabella twisted her fingers together. 'I'm sorry, Daddy. They told me that I must enter politics, stand for Parliament, use the family connection.'

'I should have suspected your sudden political aspirations,' Centaine said bitterly.

'I'm sorry, Nana.'

'Don't keep saying you're sorry,' Centaine snapped. 'It does not contribute anything worthwhile and it is damnably irritating. Just get on with it, child.'

'For a while they asked nothing of me – for almost two years. Then the orders started to come. The first was the Siemens radar chain.'

Shasa grunted and was about to speak, then he checked himself and reached for the handkerchief in the breast pocket of his blazer.

'Then they wanted more and more.'

'The Skylight project?' Shasa asked, and when she nodded he glanced at Centaine.

'You were right, Mater.' He looked back at his daughter. 'You will have to write it all down. Everything you ever gave them. I want a list – dates, documents, meetings, everything. We must know everything that is compromised.'

'Daddy . . .' Isabella began, and then for a moment she could not go on.

'Spit it out, missy,' Centaine ordered.

'Cyndex 25,' Isabella said.

'Oh God – no!' Shasa breathed.

'That was why they gave me access to Nicky this last time – the Cyndex specifications and Ben.'

'Ben?' Garry straightened up in his chair. 'Who is Ben?'

'Ben Gama,' Centaine said harshly. 'Tara's little black bastard, the son of Moses Gama. The man that killed my Biaine, the man that disgraced this family.' She looked at Isabella for confirmation.

'Yes, Nana. My half-brother, Ben.' She looked at her brothers. 'Your half-brother, too, only he doesn't call himself Ben Gama now, he calls himself Benjamin Afrika.'

'Why do I know that name?' Garry asked.

'Because he works for you,' Isabella said. 'They made me arrange a job for him. I recruited him for Capricorn

550

when I was in London. He works for Capricorn Chemicals as a laboratory technician, in the poisons division.'

'In the Cyndex plant?' Shasa asked with disbelief. 'You didn't get him in there?'

'Yes, Pater, I did.' She was about to apologize again but then looked at her grandmother's face.

Garry leapt out of his chair and strode to the desk. He seized the telephone and spoke to the operator on the Weltevreden exchange.

'Get me a call to Capricorn Chemicals – you've got the number, haven't you? I want to speak to the managing director immediately – it's urgent, very urgent. Call me back here the moment you have him on the line.'

He replaced the telephone. 'We'll have to have him, Ben, we'll have to have him taken in for questioning right away. If they placed him in the plant, it was for some good or, rather, for some nefarious reason.'

'He is one of them,' Centaine burst out. None of them had ever heard such bitterness in her tone or seen such hatred on her face. They all stared at her in horror. 'He is one of the revolutionaries, the destroyers. With that black Satan as his father and Tara to poison his mind over all the years, he must be one of them. God grant that we can prevent whatever terrible thing they are planning.'

They were all of them subdued by the horror of their imaginings.

The telephone split the silence, and Garry snatched up the receiver. 'I have the managing director of Capricorn on the line.'

'Good. Put him on. Hallo, Paul. Thank God, I got you. Hold on one second.' He pressed the 'conference' key on the telephone so that they could all hear the conversation.

'Listen, Paul. You have an employee in the poisons division. In the new pesticide plant. Benjamin Afrika.'

'Yes, Mr Courtney. I don't know him personally, but the name is vaguely familiar. Hold on, let me get the computer print on him. Yes, here we go. Benjamin Afrika. He joined us in April.'

'OK, Paul. I want him arrested and held by the company security guards. He is to be held completely incommunicado, do you understand that? No phone calls. No lawyers. No press. Nothing.'

'Can we do that, Mr Courtney?'

'I can do anything I want to, Paul. Bear that in mind. Give the order for his arrest now. I'll hold on while you do it.'

'It will take two seconds,' the managing director agreed. They heard his voice in the background as he spoke to security over the internal circuit.

'All right, Mr Courtney. They are on their way to get Afrika.'

'Now, listen, Paul. What is the position with the Cyndex manufacturing programme? Have you started to ship to the Army yet?'

'Not yet, Mr Courtney. The first shipment is due to go out next Tuesday. The ordnance are sending their own trucks.'

'OK, Paul. What stocks are you holding at the moment?'

'Let me check the computer.' Paul's voice was starting to betray his agitation. 'At the moment in the five-kilo artillery canisters we have 635 each of Formula A and B, in the fifty-kilo aerial cylinders we have twenty-six of each of both formulas. They will go to the Air Force at the end of next week—'

Garry cut him off. 'Paul, I want a physical count of every canister and cylinder. I want some of your senior men in the storage area right away to check the serial numbers of each piece against the plant manifest – and I want it done within the next hour.'

'Is something wrong, Mr Courtney?'

'I'll tell you that when you have the results of your stock-take for me. I'll be waiting at this number. Come back to me as soon as you can – or come back a damned sight sooner than that.'

As he hung up Sean demanded: 'How soon can you get us to Capricorn?'

'The Lear is out of action. DCA want a full overhaul of the airframe and a new airworthiness certificate after that missile strike.'

'How soon, Garry?' Sean insisted, and Garry thought for a second.

'The Queen Air is so slow, but it will be quicker than waiting for the scheduled flight to Johannesburg. At least we will be able to fly directly to the airstrip at the Capricorn plant. If we leave in the next hour, we could be there early this afternoon.'

'Shouldn't we notify the police?' Shasa asked, and Centaine banged her stick imperiously.

'No police. Not yet – not ever, if we can help it. Grab Tara's black bastard and beat the truth out of him if we have to, but we must try to keep this in the family.' She broke off as the telephone rang.

Garry picked it up and listened for a few seconds. Then he said: 'I see. Thank you, Paul. I'm flying up right away. I should be at the Capricorn strip by one this afternoon.' He hung up and looked around their anxious faces. 'The little brown bird has flown. Benjamin Afrika hasn't showed up at the plant for the last four days. Nobody has heard from him. Nobody knows where he is.'

'What about the stocks of Cyndex?' Shasa demanded.

'They are checking them. They'll have the results when we land at Capricorn,' Garry told him. 'Pater and Nana must stay here at Weltevreden to liaise at this end. If you need to get a message to us while we are in the air, you can telephone Information at Jan Smuts Airport control and get them to relay.' He looked across at his brother.

'Sean will come with me. I might need some muscle.'

Sean sauntered across to his father and held out his hand. 'Keys of the gun-safe, please, Pater.'

Shasa handed them over, and Sean turned the lock on the heavy steel door and swung it open. He stepped into the safe and studied the rack of revolvers and pistols for a moment before he selected a .357 magnum Smith & Wesson revolver. He took down a packet of ammunition from the

553

shelf above it and thrust the revolver into the belt of his jeans.

'I'd better take one as well.' Garry went to the safe.

'Garry,' Isabella called after him, 'I'm coming with you and Sean.'

'Forget it, Mavourneen.' Garry didn't even look round at her as he selected a Heckler & Koch 9-millimetre parabellum from the rack. 'There is nothing further that you can contribute.'

'Yes, there is. You don't know what Ben looks like. I can recognize him – and there is something else I haven't told you yet.'

'What is it?'

'I'll tell you when we are in the air.'

*   *   *

Garry levelled the twin-engine Beechcraft Queen Air on her northerly heading and turned in his seat to beckon to Isabella where she sat in the main passenger-cabin.

She unfastened her seat-belt and went up to the cockpit, and leant over the back of Garry's seat.

'OK, Bella. Let's hear it. What else can you tell us?'

She looked across at Sean in the co-pilot's seat.

'Do you remember the night at the Chicamba river when Nicky tried to escape and you and I ran back to catch him?'

Sean nodded and she went on: 'You remember the guerrilla officer in the first truck, the one who supervised the clearing of the road-block? Well, I got a really good look at him and I knew I had seen him before. I was absolutely certain of it, but it didn't make any sense, not until now.'

'When and where had you seen him?'

'He was with Ben – and they were going into Michael's farm at Firgrove.'

'Michael?' Garry cut in. 'Our Michael?'

'Yes,' she confirmed. 'Michael Courtney.'

'You think Michael is mixed up in this?'

554

'Well, don't you think so? Otherwise what would he be doing with that ANC terrorist commander – and Ben?'

They were all silent thinking about it for a while, then Isabella went on: 'Garry, you obviously suspect that Ben has stolen a cylinder or two of Cyndex. If he's mixed up with terrorists, how do you think they would use it? Spray it from an aircraft perhaps?'

'Yes, that is the most likely way.'

'Michael has a plane at Firgrove.'

'Oh shit,' Garry whispered. 'Please don't let it be true. Not Mickey – please, not Mickey.'

'Michael has been publishing that commie rag of his for years,' Sean pointed out grimly. 'And he's got very chummy with a lot of the uglies in the process.'

Nobody answered him. Garry said: 'Bella, get us each a Coke, please.'

She went back to the refrigerator in the bar and brought two cans. They drank, and Sean lowered the can and belched softly. 'The Rand Easter Show opened this morning,' he said, and Garry looked at him.

'What the hell has that got to do with it?'

'Nothing.' Sean grinned at him wickedly. 'The Rand Easter Show – the biggest, glitziest show in the country. Half a million people all in one place. All of industry showing its products, the farmers, the businessmen – every goddam tinker, tailor and Indian chief will be there. The grand opening this evening at eight o'clock, the fireworks display, and the military tattoo and the stock-car racing and the show jumping. The prime minister making a speech, and all the big shots in their dark suits and carnation button-holes. Hell, of course, it means nothing.'

'Don't fool around, Sean,' Garry grated at him.

'You're absolutely right, Garry.' Sean kept on grinning. 'I mean, at heart the ANC are really decent civilized fellows. Just because they let off a few car bombs, and put burning motor-car tyres around people's necks, doesn't mean they don't have beautiful souls. Hell, don't let's judge them too harshly. A Russian limpet mine in a crowded supermarket is one thing, but they'd never dream of spraying the Rand Easter Show with Cyndex 25 would they?'

'No.' Garry shook his head. 'I mean, Ben and Mickey are our own brothers. They wouldn't – no . . .' His voice trailed off, and then he said angrily: 'Damn it, if only we had the Lear, we'd be there by now.'

The radio squawked, and Garry adjusted his headphones.

'Charlie Sierra X-Ray, this is Jan Smuts Information. I have a relay for you from Capricorn. Are you ready to copy?'

'Go ahead, Information.'

'Message reads: All stocks and serial numbers tally. Message ends.'

'Thank God,' Garry breathed.

'Tell them to check what's inside the cylinders,' Sean suggested mildly, and Garry's expression altered.

'Information, please relay to Capricorn. Message reads: Take samples from all containers. Message ends.'

Garry removed his headphones. 'I want so badly for it not to be true,' he said. 'But you're right, Sean. They aren't idiots. It would be simple enough to stamp a couple of empty cylinders with false numbers and substitute them in the stock-room.'

'How much longer?'

Garry checked his navigation. 'Another hour – thank the Lord for this tail-wind.'

Sean looked round at his sister. 'Do me a big favour, sweetheart. Next time you fancy a little bit of nooky, pick somebody a mite tamer – like Jack the Ripper.'

The Capricorn airstrip was marked by the gigantic figure of the goat laid out artistically in white quartz. It stood out clearly on the brown veld from a distance of five miles. Garry touched down smoothly and taxied to the hangar building where four vehicles and a group of Capricorn employees headed by Paul, the managing director, were waiting to receive them.

As Garry and Sean jumped down from the Queen Air

556

and turned to give Isabella a hand, Paul rushed forward.

'Mr Courtney, you were right. Two of the small canisters contain only carbon dioxide gas. Somebody has switched them. There are ten kilos of Cyndex 25 out there somewhere!'

They stared at him in total horror. Ten kilos could wipe out an army.

'It's time to call in the police. They've got to pick up Ben Afrika. Do we have his address?' Sean asked.

'I have already sent somebody to his home,' Paul cut in. 'He isn't there. His landlady says she hasn't seen him for the last few days. He hasn't eaten or slept there.'

'Firgrove,' Isabella said softly.

'Right,' Garry snapped. 'Sean, you'd better get out there right away. Take Bella with you to show you the way and to identify Ben if you run into him. I'll run things from this end. I'll be in the boardroom. Call me as soon as you get to Firgrove. I'll get police back-up for you and raise hell all round. We've got to get hold of those missing canisters.'

Sean turned to Paul. 'I need a car – a fast one.'

'Take mine.' He pointed to a new BMW parked next to the hangar. 'The tank is full. Here are the keys.'

'Come on, Bella. Let's go.' They ran to the BMW.

'Don't get stopped by the traffic cops, Fangio,' Bella warned him, as he pushed the BMW hard along the highway. 'We should have sent the cops out to Firgrove before we left Cape Town. God, it's three o'clock already.'

'We couldn't do anything until we were sure that someone had ripped off a couple of Cyndex tanks,' Sean pointed out.

He leant across and switched on the car radio. Bella glanced at him enquiringly.

'Three o'clock news,' he explained and turned to Radio Highveld. It was the third item on the newscast.

'Since this morning record crowds have been passing through the gates of the Rand Easter Show. Today is the opening day. A spokesman for the show committee stated that by noon today more than two hundred thousand visitors had already entered the grounds.'

Sean switched off the set and then slammed his clenched fist against the dashboard of the BMW.

'Michael!' he shouted. 'It's always the bleeding hearts that are capable of the wildest excesses. How many innocents have been tortured and murdered in the name of God, peace and the fellowship of men?' He hit the dashboard again, and Bella reached across to touch his arm.

'Slow down, Sean. You take the next exit right.' Bella hung on to the door-handle as he swung the BMW into the bend.

'How much further?'

'Only a couple of miles.'

Sean pulled back the tail of his coat and drew the Smith & Wesson from his belt. With his thumb he spun the chambers.

'What are you going to do with that?' Bella asked nervously. 'Ben and Mickey—'

'Ben and Mickey have got nice friends,' he said, and slipped the revolver into his belt.

'There it is.' Bella leant forward in the seat and pointed ahead. 'That's the gate to Mickey's place.'

Sean slowed the BMW and turned off on to the dirt track. He drove sedately through the blue-gum plantation until they glimpsed the buildings ahead. Then he stopped and reversed the BMW across the track.

'Why are you doing that?' Bella asked.

'I'm going in on foot,' Sean told her. 'No point in announcing my arrival.'

'But why are you parking across the road?'

'To stop anybody trying to leave in a hurry.' He pulled the keys from the ignition and jumped out. 'You wait here. No, not in the car. Hide in the trees over there, and don't even stick your head up until I call you out, do you hear?'

'Yes, Sean.'

'And don't slam the door,' he told her as she slipped out

of the passenger-seat. 'Now, give it to me. Where does Mickey keep his plane?'

'Behind the house at the end of the orchard.' She pointed. 'You can't see it from here but you won't miss it. It's a big corrugated-tin shed, all rusty and ramshackle.'

'Sounds like our Mickey,' Sean muttered. 'Now, remember what I told you. Stay out of the way.' He began to run.

He stayed off the track and kept the trees of the orchard and the chicken-shed between him and the buildings. It was only a few hundred yards to the veranda of the main house. There were chickens clucking and scratching around his feet as he crouched behind the wall and quickly surveyed the building. The front door and all the windows were wide open, but there was no sign of the occupants.

Sean vaulted easily over the wall and slipped through the front door. The sitting-room and kitchen were empty, although dirty dishes and glasses were piled in the sink. There were three bedrooms, and all of them had been recently occupied. The beds were unmade, and there was discarded clothing on the floor and men's toilet items in the bathrooms and on the dressing-tables.

Sean picked up a shirt and turned the collar. A name-tag embroidered in red thread was stitched into the inside of it: 'B. Afrika.'

He dropped the shirt and ran back silently to the kitchen door. It stood open on to the orchard of scraggly insect-ravaged fruit trees. Beyond them rose the corrugated-iron roof of a large shed, and from a stubby roof-mast a sad-looking wind-sock drooped like a used condom.

Sean darted into the orchard and dodged between the fruit trees until he reached the wall of the shed. He flattened himself against it and laid his ear to the thin corrugated galvanized sheet. Through it he heard the murmur of men's voices, too indistinct to understand the words. He checked the revolver in his belt, making certain the butt was at hand for a quick draw, and he eased himself along the back wall of the shed towards the small green wooden door.

Before he reached it, the door swung open and two men stepped out into the sunlight.

*   *   *

Ben Afrika was good with his hands and prided himself on the quality of his workmanship. He knelt on the pilot's seat of the Cessna Centurion aircraft and tightened the final bolts that held the twin cylinders to the deck in front of the right-hand passenger-seat.

He had drilled the bolt-holes with care so as not to damage any of the control cables which ran under the floorboards. Of course, he could have let the cylinders lie loose on the cabin floor, but that would have offended his engineering sense. There was always a danger of air turbulence in flight that might damage the valve or the tubing. He had positioned the steel bottles so that, while in flight, either the pilot or his passenger could reach the valve-handle readily.

The bottle that contained element A was painted in a black-and-white chequered pattern with three red rings around the middle. Element B was in a crimson bottle with a single black ring. Each bottle was stamped with its unique serial number.

It had taken all Ben's skill to forge two ordinary medical oxygen-bottles to exactly the same exterior appearance. He had engraved the serial numbers by hand. The bottles were small enough to be smuggled in and out of the Capricorn plant in pockets specially sewn into his overcoat. It had called for ingenuity and immaculate timing to get them through the security check at the main gate of the plant.

The bottles were joined by a stainless-steel T-piece that screwed into the special left-hand thread in the necks. Ben had turned the fittings on the small secondhand lathe in the rear of the hangar. To operate them, first the taps on each bottle were screwed open, and after that a half-turn on the swinging valve-handle of the T-piece allowed the twin elements to mingle and become active. From there the nerve gas flowed under pressure into the flexible armoured hose. The hose led back between the front seats into the rear luggage-compartment.

Ben had drilled a three-centimetre hole clean through both the floorboards of the compartment and the outer metal skin of the Centurion. The end of the gas-hose passed out of this hole and protruded ten centimetres below the fuselage. He had fixed the hose in place, and sealed the narrow gap where it passed through the fuselage with Pratleys putty that dried as hard as iron.

The gas would spray from below the aircraft well behind the line of the front seats, and would be carried back in the slipstream without any danger of reaching the occupants of the Centurion. However, as an added protection they would wear safety-suits and breathe bottled oxygen during the release of the gas.

The suits hung on the hangar wall, ready to be donned in minutes. They were commercially marketed full-length protection-suits approved by the Fire Department for use by proto rescue teams in the gold mines.

For a second time Ben put a spanner on each of the hose connections and the joints of the T-piece to satisfy himself that there were no leaks. At last he grunted with satisfaction and backed out of the open cabin-door. He wiped his hands on a piece of cotton waste and went across to the workbench against the nearest wall.

The other two men were leaning over the bench studying the map. Ben came up behind Michael Courtney and draped his arm affectionately over his brother's shoulders.

'All set, Mickey,' he said in his incongruous south London accent.

Then he gave his full attention to Ramón Machado. Ben hero-worshipped this man. When he was alone with Michael he often discussed him with the awe of an acolyte discussing the omnipotence of the Pope. Michael, on the other hand, realized the hideous nature of their mission, and it had taken many months of soul-searching for him to convince himself that this was something that had to be done if the struggle was to succeed.

Ramón seemed to sense his lingering reluctance and turned to him now. 'Michael, I want you to ring Met and get a final weather forecast for this evening.'

Michael picked up the telephone from the bench in front of him and dialled the number of the weather information services at Jan Smuts Airport and listened to the pre-recorded announcement.

'Wind is still 290 degrees at five knots,' he repeated. 'No change since this morning. Weather is settled. Barometric pressure steady.'

'Very well.' Ramón picked up his red marker-pencil and circled the position of the showgrounds on the large-scale aeronautical map. Then he marked in the wind direction.

'OK. This will be your line of approach, about a mile up-wind of the target. Try to maintain a thousand feet above ground-level. Open the gas-valve as you pass the water-towers. They are very prominently lit with navigational warning lights.'

'Yes,' Michael said. 'I flew over the area yesterday. The stadium will be floodlit, and there will be a laser show – I can't possibly miss it.'

'Well done, Comrade.' Ramón gave him one of his rare irresistible smiles. 'Your preparations have been excellent.'

Michael looked down, and Ben interjected: 'I heard on the one o'clock news that by noon more than two hundred thousand visitors had already passed through the showground turnstiles. It will be more like half a million by the time Vorster starts his official opening speech. What a blow we'll strike for freedom today.'

'Vorster's speech is scheduled to start at seven p.m.' Ramón picked up one of the advertizing brochures issued by the show committee. He studied the opening programme. 'But it might be a few minutes late. We must allow for that. He will probably talk for between forty minutes and an hour. The military tattoo begins at eight p.m. When will you take off?'

'If we take off from here at 1845 hours,' Michael worked it out, 'it's about forty-eight minutes' flying. I timed it yesterday. That will get me over the target at thirty-three minutes past seven.'

'That would be about right,' Ramón agreed. 'Vorster should still be speaking. You will make two passes across the range. A thousand feet above ground-level, one mile up-wind. After the second pass you turn west and head directly for the Botswana border. What is your estimated flying time to the rendezvous with Raleigh Tabaka?'

'Three hours fifteen minutes,' Michael replied. 'That gets me there approximately eleven o'clock tonight. By that time any residual gas will have degraded.'

'Raleigh Tabaka will light the airstrip with flares. As soon as you land remove all the gas equipment and set fire to the plane. From there it's up to Raleigh to get you out to Zambia and Tercio base.'

Ramón studied their faces. 'That's it, then. I know that we've gone over it a dozen times, but are there any questions?'

The brothers shook their heads, and Ramón smiled wryly. Despite the difference in the colour of their skins and the texture of their hair, there was a strong resemblance.

The revolution could never go forward without this kind of obedience and unquestioning faith, Ramón thought, and he felt an unaccustomed envy of such uncomplicated trust. Let them believe that this single act would change the world and herald the perfect dawn of universal socialism and brotherly love. Ramón knew that nothing was so simple.

He envied them their faith, but he wondered if they truly had the stomach to live through the stark reality of the slaughter of half a million lambs, and the Red Terror which must follow the successful onslaught of the revolution. Sublime belief in the ultimate rightness of their action might permit them to turn the valve on a pair of innocent-looking steel bottles, but could they endure the

563

reality of half a million corpses twisted and contorted in piles of hideous death? he wondered.

Only the steel men survived. These two were not of that temper. The Red Terror would claim them as it did all weaklings. After tonight their usefulness would be reduced. They would be expendable.

He touched Michael's shoulder gently. He knew that Michael liked to be touched by another man. He let the touch become a caress.

'You have done wonderfully well. Now you must eat and rest. I will leave you before you take off this evening. I salute you both.'

They walked in a group to the door in the rear of the shed, but before they reached it Michael stopped.

'I want to look at Ben's installation of the bottles, and go over my own checks,' he said diffidently. 'I want to be absolutely certain.'

'You are right to want everything perfect, Comrade,' Ramón agreed. 'We'll have something for you to eat when you come up to the house.'

They watched him climb into the cockpit of the Centurion, and begin checking the instruments before they walked together to the door.

Ramón threw open the small back door in the rear wall of the hangar, and as he and Ben stepped through into the sunlight together Sean Courtney was crouched against the side-wall on their left-hand side, staring at them.

Only six feet separated Ramón and Sean, and their mutual recognition was instantaneous. Sean reached under his coat and plucked out the big magnum revolver. The double-action pull on the trigger delayed the shot a fleeting part of a second, and Ramón seized Ben Afrika's arm and pulled him forward between them. With a muzzle-flash that was bright even in the sunlight, Sean's shot crashed into Ben's body.

The hollow-point bullet struck him on the tip of the left elbow and mushroomed instantly. It ploughed through his arm and into his flank. The entry-wound into his body was the size of an egg-cup. The bullet struck his last rib and began to break up. Fragments were deflected into his lung; others tore through his entrails. A splinter of the copper jacket cut between the vertebrae of the spine and half-severed his spinal cord.

Ben was flung sideways by the impact and he slid down the wall, leaving a bright smear of his blood across the rusty corrugated iron. Ramón Machado ducked back into the hangar before Sean could bring the revolver down from the head-high recoil. He kicked the door closed behind him and snatched the Tokarev automatic from his shoulder holster.

He snapped two quick shots through the thin wall, aiming for where he judged Sean was standing. Sean had anticipated this, and had dropped flat and flipped over twice. He estimated Ramón's stance from the sound of the shots and the angle of the bullets cutting through the corrugated-iron wall. He fired double-handed, and the heavy bullet punched a hole through the wall and missed Ramón's head by a foot.

Ramón ducked behind a drum of Avgas and shouted across the hangar at Michael as he sat at the controls of the aircraft.

'Start up!'

Michael had been frozen with shock in the pilot seat of the Centurion, but at Ramón's order he recovered and flipped on both master switches and both magnetos and turned the key. The Centurion's engine fired and caught. He pushed the throttle open, and she roared eagerly and strained against the wheel-brakes.

'Get her rolling,' Ramón shouted, and fired two more shots through the wall at random.

The Centurion moved forward towards the open hangar-door, gathering speed swiftly, and Ramón raced after her, ducked under the wing and jerked open the passenger-door.

'Where is Ben?' Michael shouted at him as he scrambled into the seat.

'Ben is finished,' Ramón shouted back. 'Keep going.'

'What do you mean, *finished*?' Michael twisted in the seat and closed the throttle. 'We can't leave him.'

'Ben is dead, man.' Ramón caught his hand on the throttle. 'Ben has been shot. He's finished. We have to get out of here.'

'Ben—'

'Keep her going.'

Michael pushed the throttle open once again and swung the Centurion on to the runway. His face was twisted with grief.

'Ben,' he whispered, and let the speed build up until the Centurion was taxi-ing tail-up along the strip. They reached the end, and he used brake and engine to swing her around, facing back down the runway into the wind.

'The engine is cold,' he said. 'She hasn't had a chance to warm up.'

'We've got to chance it,' Ramón told him. 'The police are going to be swarming in. They're on to us; somehow they've tumbled to it.'

'Ben?'

'Forget about Ben,' Ramón snapped. 'Get us into the air.'

'Where are we going – Botswana?' Michael still hesitated.

'Yes,' Ramón told him. 'But first we are going to finish this operation. Head for the showgrounds.'

'But . . . but you say the police are on to us,' Michael protested.

'How can they stop us now? It will take an hour to get an air-force Impala into the air – go, man, go!'

Michael pushed the pitch fully fine and opened the throttle wide. The Centurion bounded down the strip.

As the speed built up they saw a figure run out from behind the hangar. Michael recognized his brother.

'Sean!' he exclaimed.

'Keep going,' Ramón told him.

Sean dropped on one knee at the verge of the runway, and as the Centurion raced towards him he thrust out both

566

arms towards it in the classic double-handled grip and fired three deliberate shots. Each time the heavy recoil threw the muzzle of the revolver towards the sky.

The last shot struck the windscreen, and they both ducked instinctively. It left a silver cobweb in the Perspex pane, and then Michael rotated the Centurion's nose and they skimmed over the boundary fence and bore up into the clear blue highveld sky.

At two hundred feet the cold motor stuttered and coughed, then it caught again and ran smoothly.

'Head for the showgrounds,' Ramón repeated. 'We won't get Vorster, but it's still a good target. There are two hundred thousand of them.'

Michael levelled out at a thousand feet and turned on to his track.

★   ★   ★

As the Centurion soared overhead, Sean emptied the revolver, blazing up at its belly. He saw no sign of his bullets striking, and the landing-wheels of the Centurion retracted as she rose unharmed into the sky.

Sean jumped to his feet and sprinted into the hangar. He saw the telephone on the workbench.

'Thank God!' He ran to the bench and snatched it up.

As he dialled the Capricorn number, he noticed the open map under his hands and the Rand Easter Show brochure. The red-marked notations on the map ringed the location of the showgrounds, and a broad arrow indicated the wind direction and speed.

The operator on the switchboard answered on the third ring. 'Capricorn Chemical Industries, good day. How may I help you?'

'Get me Mr Garry Courtney in the boardroom. I'm his brother. This is an emergency.'

'He is expecting your call. You are going straight through.'

As he waited Sean glanced quickly around the hangar.

He saw the safety-suits hanging on the wall beside the door.

'Is that you, Sean?' Garry's voice was strained.

'Yes, it's me. I'm at Firgrove. It's as bad as we feared. Michael and Ben and the Fox. The target is the show-grounds.'

'Did you stop them, Sean?'

'No. Michael and the Fox are airborne. They took off two minutes ago. They are almost certainly heading for the showgrounds.'

'Are you sure, Sean?'

'Of course I'm bloody sure. I'm in Mickey's hangar and I'm looking at a map right now. The showgrounds are marked and the wind speed and direction. There are two smoke-proof suits hanging on the wall – they didn't have a chance to get into them.'

'I'll warn the police, the Air Force.'

'Don't be a prick, Garry. It will take an order from the chief of the defence force and the minister before they'll send up a fighter or a helicopter gunship. That could take a month of Sundays. By then two hundred thousand people will be dead.'

'What must we do, Sean?' At last the administrator deferred to the man of action.

'Take the Queen Air,' Sean told him. 'She's faster and bigger and more powerful than the little Centurion. You have to intercept them and force them down before they reach the show.'

'Describe Mickey's Centurion,' Garry ordered crisply.

'Blue on top. White belly. Her markings are ZS – RRW, Romeo Romeo Whisky. You know the location of Firgrove and their course to reach the show.'

'I'm on my way,' said Garry, and the connection clicked and went dead.

Sean picked up the Smith & Wesson from the bench-top where he had dropped it, and spilled the empty cases from the chambers. From his pocket he pulled the box of ammunition and reloaded swiftly. He ran back to the door and with the revolver held ready he stood clear and kicked it open. Immediately he dropped into a gunfighter's crouch and aimed through the doorway.

Ben had dragged his paralysed legs only a few yards before he collapsed. He lay in a huddle at the foot of one of the peach trees. He was bleeding copiously; bright arterial blood had soaked his shirt and the tops of his trousers. His left arm hung by a tatter of mangled flesh. The shattered bone was spiked through the meat like a skewer.

Sean straightened up and safed the Smith & Wesson. He walked through the door and stood looking down at Ben.

Ben was still alive. He rolled over painfully to look up at Sean. His eyes were brown as burnt sugar and filled with a dreadful anguish.

'They got away, didn't they?' he whispered. 'They will succeed. You cannot stop us. The future belongs to us.'

Isabella came running through the trees. She saw Sean and swerved towards him.

'I told you to keep out of the way,' he growled at her. 'Why can't you ever do as you're told?'

She saw Ben lying at his feet and stopped short.

'It's Ben. Oh God, what have you done to him?'

She started forward again and dropped to her knees beside the prostrate body.

Carefully she lifted Ben's head into her lap, but the movement tore something in his injured lung and he began to cough. A mouthful of blood spilled between his open lips and poured down his chin.

'Oh God, Sean. You've killed him!' Isabella sobbed.

'I hope so,' Sean said softly. 'With all my heart, I hope so.'

'Sean, he's your brother.'

'No,' said Sean. 'He's not my brother. He's just a lump of shit.'

★ ★ ★

As Garry Courtney started the engines of the Queen Air, he was calculating furiously.

Capricorn was almost sixty miles closer to the showgrounds than Firgrove, and in addition the Queen Air was seventy or eighty knots faster than the Centurion at the cruise. It was seven minutes since Sean had called him, nine minutes since Mickey had taken off.

It was all running very close. He dared not try to guess where to intercept the Centurion and try to cut its track. There was only one sure course open to him. He had to fly directly to the showgrounds, then turn and head back on the reciprocal of Michael's heading. He had to risk everything on a head-on interception.

As he opened the throttles and ran the Queen Air out on to the runway, he found with mild surprise that he still had a half-smoked cigar between his teeth. In the panic of getting to the aircraft he had forgotten all about it. As he lifted the big twin-engined machine into the air, he drew deeply on the cigar. It was the very best Havana, and he smiled at the irony. The fragrant smoke calmed his nerves a little.

'I'm not as good at this as Sean is.' He spoke to himself. 'Give me a hectic day on the Stock Exchange or a nice bloody takeover deal any day.' He pushed the Queen Air right over the manual, squeezing an extra fifteen knots out of her.

He picked out the showgrounds from almost seven miles out. A pod of giant balloons floated above it like colourful whales. The vast carparks were a-glitter with reflected sunlight from thousands of vehicles.

He turned back on to a direct heading for Firgrove and leant forward in his seat, peering ahead through the windscreen and puffing on the fat cigar. He was still running calculations of speed and time and distance through his head.

'If I'm going to meet them, it should be five or six minutes—' He broke off as a beam of sunlight reflected from something ahead and below caught his eye. He pushed his horn-rimmed spectacles up on his nose, once again hating his weak myopic eyes and peered fretfully down, trying to find it again.

He had left the built-up residential areas behind, and was flying over the open countryside, studded with small villages and criss-crossed with roads. The patterns of ploughed lands and plantations of trees disturbed his eye, and threw up a hundred decoys and optical tricks to confuse him. He searched frantically, sweeping the open sky briefly and then concentrating on the earth below. He expected the Centurion to be well under him.

He saw the shadow first. It flitted and jumped like a grasshopper across the fields. A moment later he saw the tiny blue aircraft. It was a thousand feet below him and two miles directly ahead. He pushed the nose of the Queen Air down into a dangerous altitude and dived to intercept.

The two aircraft were converging at almost five hundred knots, and before Garry could get the Queen Air down to the same altitude as the Centurion it had passed like a blue flash below him.

Garry hauled up one wing into a maximum-rate turn and came round behind the Centurion. He used the Queen Air's superior speed and the dive to overhaul the smaller aircraft.

*   *   *

'We'll be there in about ten minutes,' Michael warned Ramón. 'You'd better get ready.'

Ramón leant forward and reached down to the gaudily painted cylinders bolted to the floorboards between his feet. Carefully he opened the tap on the neck of each of the bottles. He felt the rush of internal pressure checked immediately by the gate of the main valve in the connecting T-piece.

Now it needed only to thumb the valve-lever across, half a turn in an anticlockwise direction, to send the mixed and activated gas hissing into the long hose and spraying out through the nozzle under the Centurion's belly.

Ramón straightened up and glanced across at Michael in the pilot's seat beside him.

'All set—' he began, and then broke off and stared with astonishment through the side-window beside Michael's head.

An enormous silver fuselage filled the entire frame of the window. Another aircraft was flying wing-tip to wing-tip with them, and the pilot peered across at them. He was a large baby-faced man with dark horn-rimmed glasses and the stub of a cigar clamped in one corner of his mouth.

'Garry!' shouted Michael in consternation. Garry lifted his right hand and stabbed downwards with his thumb, an unmistakable gesture.

Instinctively Michael flung the Centurion into a tight descending turn, and dropped away towards the earth like a stone. He levelled out just above the tree-tops.

He glanced in his rearview mirror and saw the Queen Air's round silver nose a hundred yards from his tail and closing rapidly. He hauled the Centurion up and around hard, but the moment he levelled out the silver machine loomed up beside him. Garry had always been a far better pilot than he was, and the Queen Air had the wings to outfly him.

'I can't get away from him.'

'Fly straight for the target,' Ramón ordered brusquely. 'There is nothing he can do.'

Michael had hoped that Ramón would abandon the operation now, but reluctantly he turned back on to his original track. He was down to two hundred feet above the tops of the tallest trees. Garry followed him round and came up alongside him. Their wing-tips were only a yard apart.

Once again Garry signalled him to land. Instead, Michael snatched up the microphone of his radio, knowing that Garry would be tuned to 118,7 megahertz.

'I'm sorry, Garry,' he cried. 'I have to do it. I'm sorry.'

Garry's voice boomed through the radio speaker into the cabin. 'Land immediately, Mickey. It's not too late. We can still get you out of this. Don't be a fool, man.'

Michael shook his head vehemently and pointed ahead.

Garry's expression hardened. He dropped back, and before Michael could react he slid in sideways and thrust the Queen Air's wing-tip under the Centurion's tail. Then he came back hard on the control-wheel and flicked the smaller plane's tail up, so she tumbled forward into an almost vertical dive.

The Centurion was too low and the dive too steep for Michael to recover before he hit the top branches of a tall blue-gum tree.

Michael threw up his hands as he saw it coming, but a dry branch as thick as a man's arm stabbed through the windscreen that had been weakened by Sean's bullet. The point of the branch caught Michael at the base of his throat. It found the notch between his collar-bones and went through with the ease of a hypodermic needle, transfixing his upper torso and coming out between his shoulder-blades.

The momentum of the falling aircraft snapped the branch off, and the jagged butt protruded from his throat like an ugly twisted lance.

The Centurion drove on, crashing and crackling through the tree-tops. First one wing then the other were ripped away, braking the aircraft's speed, until it fell clear of the trees and the wingless fuselage hit the ground, and bounced and skidded to rest at the edge of a field of standing maize stalks.

Ramón Machado dragged himself upright in the seat, amazed that he was still alive. He looked across at Michael. Michael's mouth was wide open in a silent shriek; the jagged branch stuck out of his throat, and a fountain of his blood spurted over the remains of the shattered windscreen.

Ramón released the catch of his seat-belt and tried to lift himself out of his seat. He found himself anchored, and he looked down. His left leg was broken. It was twisted like a piece of boiled spaghetti between the seat and the gas-cylinders. The leg of his trousers was ripped up to the knee, and the stainless-steel valve-handle was buried deeply in the flesh of his calf.

As he stared at it, he became aware of the faint hiss of escaping gas. His leg had twisted the valve-handle into the open position. Cyndex 25 was spurting into the hose and spraying from the nozzle under the fuselage.

Ramón grabbed at the door-handle and threw all his weight upon it. It was jammed solid. He placed both hands under the knee of his injured leg and hauled upon it, trying to pull it free. The leg elongated, and he heard the ends of shattered bone-shards grate together deep in his flesh, but it was held inexorably as in a bear-trap by the stainless-steel valve-handle.

Suddenly he smelt the odour of almonds; his nostrils began to burn and sting. Silver mucus flooded from both nostrils and drooled over his lips and down his chin. In their sockets his eyes turned to coals of fire and his vision dimmed.

In the darkness the agony assailed him. It surpassed any conception that he had ever had of pain. He began to scream. He screamed and screamed sitting in a puddle of his own urine and faeces until at last his lungs collapsed and he could scream no more.

★   ★   ★

Centaine Courtney-Malcomess sat on a fallen log at the edge of the forest and watched the puppy and the child at play.

The puppy was the pick of Dandy Lass of Weltevreden's last litter before Centaine had been forced to have the gallant old bitch put down. The puppy had inherited all her mother's best points. She would be a champion also, Centaine was convinced of it.

Nicky was working her with an old silk stocking stuffed with guinea-fowl feathers. He learnt as quickly as the puppy. He seemed to have a way with dogs and horses.

It's in his blood, Centaine thought complacently. He's a true Courtney, despite the name and the fancy Spanish title.

She went on to think of her other Courtneys.

Tomorrow Shasa and Elsa Pignatelli were marrying in the little slave church that Centaine had so lovingly restored. It would be one of the biggest weddings to be held in the Cape of Good Hope for at least a decade. Guests were coming from England and Europe and Israel and America.

There would have been a time not so many years ago when Centaine would have wanted to make all the plans and supervise all the preparations for the wedding herself. Now she was content to leave it all to Bella and Elsa Pignatelli.

'Let them get on with it,' she told herself firmly. 'I've got my hands full with my roses and my dogs and Nicky.'

She thought about Bella. Bella was contrite and chastened, but Centaine was not satisfied that it was enough. She had debated long and hard with herself and with Shasa before at last agreeing to cover for the girl and shield her from the full consequences of her treason and the righteous fury of the law.

Still, she has a penance to perform. Grimly Centaine justified her leniency. Isabella will dedicate the rest of her life to making amends. She owes a lifetime of service to every member of this family and to all the people of this wonderful land of ours whom she betrayed. I'll see to it that she pays all her debts in full, she thought purposefully, and then turned to watch the puppy find the feather-bag that Nicky had hidden in the reeds down by the stream, the puppy's long silky tail waving like a triumphant banner as she came to deliver it to her young master.

At last the boy and the dog came to sit at her feet together, and Nicky put one tanned bare arm around the puppy's neck and hugged her.

'Have you decided on a name for her yet?' Centaine asked. It had taken her almost two years to break down the child's resistance to her, but she felt that now she had at last won him over from his memories of Adra and his previous life.

'Yes, Nana. I want to call her Twenty-Six.' Nicky's English had improved vastly since she had enrolled him at Western Province Junior School.

'That's an unusual name. Why did you choose it?'

'I had another dog once – he was called Twenty-Six.' And yet Nicky's memories of that other time had almost faded.

'Well, that is an excellent reason – and it's a fine name. Dandy Twenty-Six of Weltevreden.'

'Yes! Yes!' Nicky hugged the puppy's neck. 'Dandy Twenty-Six.'

Centaine looked down on him fondly. He was still a mixed-up and confused little boy, but he was a thorough-bred with the blood of champions in his veins.

Give us time, she thought. Just give me a little more time with him.

'Shall I tell you a story, Nicholas?' she asked. She had the most wonderful family stories, of elephant hunts and lions, of wars with Boers and Zulus and Germans, of lost diamond mines and of fighter planes and a thousand other things to thrill the soul of a small boy.

So now she told him a story of shipwreck and of a castaway on a burning shore. She told him of a journey through a cruel desert with little yellow pixies as companions – and he walked every step of the enchanted way beside them.

At last she looked at her wristwatch and said: 'That's enough for today, young master Nicholas. Your mother will be wondering whatever has become of us.'

Nicholas sprang up to help her to her feet, and the two of them walked down the hill towards the big house with the puppy gambolling around them.

They walked quite slowly, because Nana had a sore leg, and Nicky took her hand to help her over the rough places.